MW00680768

# An Anthropologist Under the Bed

Review Copy
Not For Sale

© 1999 Author Niehoff. All rights reserved.
ISBN 0-9643072-5-1
Library of Congress Catalog Card No: 98-94187

Book design and typography, Cover design:
Mary Ellen Alton, MEA Design Group
Editing: Julie Porter

Printed in the United States of America

1st Printing

Niehoff, Arthur H., 1921-
    An anthropologist under the bed : the human way of sex / Author Niehoff –
1st ed.
        p.  cm.
    ISBN: 0-9643072-5-1

    1. Reincarnation–Fiction.  2. Sex customs–Fiction.
    3. Mate selection–Fiction.  4. Marriage customs and rites–Fiction.
    5. Anthropologists–Fiction.  I. Title
PS3564.I3456A68 1999                    813.54
                        QBI98-1508

# An Anthropologist Under the Bed

Author Niehoff

THE HOMINID PRESS - BONSALL, CALIFORNIA

Also by Author Niehoff

*On Becoming Human*

*Takeover: How Euroman Changed the World*

*On Being a Conceptual Animal*

# DEDICATION

In the front of most books there is a dedication, usually to a family member, a spouse most often, less often to children. The idea almost always is that the person(s) so indicated have encouraged or helped the author complete the task of producing a book. I have done the same in earlier books I have had published.

But this time I will break the pattern by making a negative dedication, designating someone who unwittingly drove me to write the book. I did it not because of her encouragement, but because she created very unpleasant conditions. And since the only version of our breakup has been through the courts, I have vowed that if I ever published this work, I would offer my version.

The divorce was a dreadful event, probably the worst I have suffered. And lest readers think I am making all this up, I will describe two fantasies that are still in my memory now, fifteen years later. Both involved hand grenades. In one, I would creep up at night to the bedroom window and toss the grenade through the window where she was sleeping. In another, I would fasten a grenade on the steering column of her car so that when she pressed the starter, it would explode.

How did such an unpleasant event, the divorce, come about? The following is my reconstruction: I was served divorce papers one morning after she had run out of the house the previous evening, following an argument. It was a shocking surprise to me since we had had arguments before. We had always made up afterwards. She claimed in the divorce papers that I had struck her with some groceries and that when she had first returned, I had threatened her with a "pointed object." It was a screwdriver, which I had in my hand from fixing a lighting fixture when I answered the door. Anyway, the assistant minister testified that because he had a Master's degree in psychology he could recognize a violence-prone man when he saw one. My remembrance is that, because she insisted she be given the groceries which I had just brought home, I tossed the bag in her direction and it broke, spilling items on the floor. In any event, she asked the judge to eject me from the house, which he did at the preliminary judgment. My lawyer, which I arranged for as soon as I could, informed me that judges practically always eject married men from their houses when wives accuse them of violence. On these preliminaries the authorities hardly look at evidence.

Anyway, when we got to the regular hearing, I was permitted to testify. The judge decided that because I had no record for violence or any other criminal acts, toward her or anyone else, he couldn't justifiably eject me from my own house. So, apart from setting up spousal support and other expenses for her, he divided the house. She would get two-thirds and I one-third. Furthermore, she was enjoined to have a solid partition built in the hallway separating the two sections. And that is where I stayed for the next several months—until I could take it no longer and moved away.

Except for a telephone call she made many years later, she refused to talk to me or answer any letters. Needless to say, I was depressed. Then after I got physically settled in my new quarters, I reassessed my future. I would have to fight out the divorce while trying to manage my finances and teaching career, as well as hold on to my calm.

I couldn't sleep well at night, so I adjusted by working at my typewriter. In short order I finished the book I was working on. But since my divorce case seemed nowhere near settlement, I decided to do another. What better than a fictional account of an adversarial divorce? So for many months I pounded away on that one.

The divorce was still not settled, so I decided on another, which became *An Anthropologist Under the Bed*. I must have finished it in Costa Rica where I went to regain my calm, or in my apartment in Alhambra, California, where I went after that.

I kept writing—both essays and books, and ultimately went into independent publishing. And since I was doing none such before the separation, I feel strongly that her influence, unintentional as it was, was the primary driving force. And so I dedicate this work to CAROL, without whose influence it would never have been written.

# FOREWORD

As we move toward the millennium, with technology becoming our master, not our servant, the search for "answers" to life's mysteries is moving away increasingly from a study of "the others" toward a focus on the experience of the individual. At the same time, Eastern religion teaches us that all living beings are interconnected. The deepest layers of personal experience unify us all, but with one powerful exception. And that is gender. Men's and women's experience of life seem to be profoundly different.

Beginning with the 1960s and through the '90s we learned that powerful truth in many ways. The experience of men and women in bed, "fucking" (he) or "making love" (she), provides the clearest laboratory to view, describe, study, and understand that difference between men and women.

Feminism, and its literature, opened up men's eyes to the reality that men did not know or understand women at all. Before feminism, so long as women accommodated men, as they traditionally had, men could feel secure in the belief that men and women made a natural, loving coupling. He was convinced that the "healthy" man could love a woman, support a family, be loved and appreciated by her, and live happily ever after. The shock of awakening from that illusion regularly rumbles through the lives of the broken men who believed that mythology.

Feminism exposed the hidden rage and reality of women's experience of relationships with men. Miscommunication and anger are noted in the unending stream of articles, books, and discussions on harassment, sexuality, spousal violence, divorce, and custody battles. There are millions of "singles" longing for love from the other gender, yet overwhelmed by the sense of impossibility of creating a connection that feels good and can be trusted.

While the feminist pioneers, in the process of stripping us down to expose the deeper realities, have produced an extensive literature, the personal literature of men is relatively sparse. Understanding the experience and reality of men in relationship to women requires a focus on men's sexuality, particularly on their obsessive preoccupation with it, because sex is the way most men express their personal selves and try to get their intimate needs met.

The anthropology of men as a gender in relationship to women is in large part the exploration of the male sexual impulse. Men who are willing and able to articulate their experience, and to "idea flip" (a Niehoff phrase), make a contribution to that understanding. When a book on the subject is written with breadth of perspective and a keen sense of personal detail that naturally provides it with humor, we are enlightened, educated, and amused. That is what *An Anthropologist Under the Bed* succeeds in doing.

Looking at the sexual experience from the vantage point of a "Transitionee," in a place where people go after they die and await their next "assignment," Niehoff takes us on a journey through the life and sexual experience of a variety of living beings, from his own father, his first wife's mother, a Hindu colleague from his fieldwork days, a Latina woman, a chimp, and a cockroach, among others. And finally to the most thorough and detailed story of his own sexuality.

And as he does this, Niehoff describes and tries to understand why and how a man and woman choose each other, have sex/make love, and in his case, when it all crashes, ask "why" again and pick up the pieces. When an anthropologist can write, describe, explore and entertain us in a style as humorous and compelling as Roth, Miller, or Bukowski, and provide insights and on-target descriptions of the male–female sexual dance, we have a gift of a wonder book.

While Arthur Niehoff has written an anthropology of sex, he has also written a description from the male perspective of the experience of relating sexually to a woman. I learned and laughed (what a dynamite combination) from this anthropological ride by an academician who can write, teach, and entertain with the best of them.

Herbert Goldberg
Psychology Professor, Clinician, and Author:
*The Hazards of Being Male*
*What Men Really Want*

# CHAPTER 1

When Martin Neumann opened his eyes, he saw a long dark tunnel with the sides and floor covered by some kind of sound proofing material. Indirect light marked the way, but far off at the end there seemed to be a single bulb. He tried to concentrate, to understand where he was, but no useful thought emerged. There seemed to be little else to do but go on. At the end of the tunnel, Martin saw an elevator. A couple of people were waiting, a well-dressed older male and a younger woman who smelled strongly of perfume. Martin looked back down the corridor and saw several other figures approaching slowly.

He stood in puzzlement. Where was he and what was he doing? It was an unusual feeling because he had practically always been aware of what was going on. Even when he had had the strokes, he had lost consciousness for only a short time. And each time he recovered, he had known immediately where he was.

The single amber light that had been flashing above the elevator door went out and a green light came on. The door opened. Martin got on with the others, by that time five or six. There was no console for the different floors. Muzak played. Martin could clearly feel the movement as the elevator rose.

Entering what looked like a waiting room, Martin saw chairs and couches all around, not opulent but comfortable. Lamps and small stacks of magazines were arranged on end tables. There were six doors in the opposite wall. A well-dressed middle-aged woman sat at a receptionist's desk in the middle of the room. Periodically, she would answer the phone and ever so often call out to someone. Martin noticed that she spoke fluent Spanish and, it seemed, Chinese. At least when she spoke to one Asian man, Martin thought it sounded tonal. That was odd. The woman certainly looked like she was of Northern European ancestry. It would be most unlikely in an office in southern California that they would have a receptionist who spoke both Spanish and Chinese.

As he looked around, he noticed that the others seemed to be quite varied. There were men and women and apparently many ethnic types; furthermore, there didn't seem to be any particular indication of class. Working class people as well as professionals were there together. The only special characteristic that he could pick out was that most seemed to be older than average. Probably a medical office.

He didn't have long to wait before the receptionist called, "Martin Neumann, Room Four, please."

"Thanks," he said, getting up, while wondering where she got his name. He was sure he had not given it to her. But in any event it seemed proper to proceed. He opened the door to Room Four, which was another office. The door swung shut noiselessly behind him. There was nothing unusual about the office: a desk with chairs at both sides, and across the room a coffee table with low chairs. The man at the desk was heavy though not fat. He seemed to be in his early sixties, comfortably though not modishly dressed. He was smoking a pipe and looking at a paper on his desk. He was vaguely familiar. Looking up, he smiled at Martin. "Have a seat." He motioned to one of the chairs next to the desk.

Martin walked over and sat down. The man offered his hand, saying, "I'm Harold Oldenberg, glad to see you."

"How do you do? I'm Martin Neumann."

"Yes, I know."

Martin studied the round-faced man in puzzlement.

Then as if he were reading Martin's mind, the man said, "I suspect you may be a little uneasy."

"Yes, that's true, though I think that is putting it mildly. I don't know where I am and what I'm doing. In fact, I don't know why I'm here."

The man puffed on his pipe which smelled good. Pipe smoke still evoked pleasant memories, even after all the years since Martin had given up smoking.

The man said, "You need not worry. It's normal at this stage to be a little uneasy."

"I'm really puzzled," Martin said, "What do you mean, at this stage? At this stage of what? That's the problem. Here I am in this strange office and I don't even know what kind of office it is or why I'm here. Is this a medical office? Are you a doctor? Or a psychiatrist? Or what? That's what bothers me. I don't know why I'm here. I'm not sick, am I?"

The man chuckled and leaned back. "That's a lot of questions. And as an educated man, you know that I can't answer all of them at the same time. So I'll just begin with the first. It's central anyway and will probably answer most of the others. First I'll tell you what the stage is and what the function of this office is. Like everything else in the world you grew up in, it has a label. Well, the label is Transition, this is the stage of Transition, and this office is in the Department of Transition."

Martin stared at the man. "Transition of what, from what to what?"

The man smiled again. It's a transition in existence, from one life to another."

Martin looked at the guy incredulously. It didn't make sense. They weren't communicating. And yet the man seemed to be the embodiment of reasonableness. Martin said, "Would you mind going over that again? I just don't get it. I understand all the words, but together they don't make sense."

"Certainly. The office you are now in is a part of the Department of Transition, where there is a transition from one life to another. And that's what you and I have to arrange."

The man just sat there, watching Martin calmly. Martin suddenly realized why Oldenberg had such a calming effect. He strongly resembled Martin's old anthropology professor, Conrad Marcus, the man who had gentled him through his Ph.D. and could always offer a bit of unprepossessing counsel. Martin figured this resemblance of Oldenberg to his old benefactor helped make it possible to accept this preposterous news.

The heavy-set man continued, "I know it is difficult to get the idea across at first, at least to people like yourself who have always demanded evidence for your beliefs."

Then a sort of awareness began to come over Martin. It wasn't exactly like a light bulb, but more the simple idea that what this fellow was saying explained several occurrences better: the awakening from some state that had not been sleep, walking down the long, black, velvety corridor, the mixed though older group of people in the waiting room, the multi-lingual secretary. The situation was still nonsensical, but less so. At least it seemed worth some discussion. Martin said, "Well, if you're saying it's a transition from one life to another, that implies that one such has ended, or is ending, and another has begun, or is beginning. Is that correct?"

Oldenberg smiled, evidently at Martin's perception. "That's the idea."

Martin stopped then and thought long. "Do you mean to say that I and the others who are passing through this office are in the process of going from one life to another?"

"That is correct."

Martin was suddenly amazed that he did not feel very different, not even depressed. After all, it was rather astonishing information. And he was even more amazed that he was beginning to accept what this genial fellow was telling him. He said, "Why, if that is true, I've either just died or I'm about to. And look, here I sit with a fully functioning body, talking to you as if you were a clinician. Are you sure you're not a psychologist or shrink, or something like that, and that this isn't an elaborate hoax?" Then he added, "Or is this some kind of experiment? I've heard of those experiments they did to get people to admit to totally false images. I mean, I'm really here, aren't I? You can't say that I, the person Martin Neumann, am not sitting here in this chair, can you? And if so, I couldn't be dead, could I? And what about all those other people out there? They looked real enough to me."

Oldenberg's pipe had gone out. He tamped the burnt tobacco with a little metal tool and then struck a wood match to relight it. The flame darted into the mixture and then leapt back each time the man exhaled. "Let me try to explain," he said. "All this won't be unfamiliar to you since you have dipped into metaphysics and Oriental beliefs to a certain extent. I know it's a bit of a shock, not exactly what you expected, but it's not all bad when you consider the alternatives. In the first place, you're not dead in the Western sense, although in that sense you did die. You must remember the multiple strokes you had. And you know you were already an old man. What was it, eighty-three years? Well, according to the actuarial statistics, that's a long life for a man. And you must remember that you added on twenty-four years since the first stroke. That's not bad for an Earthling, I can assure you."

Martin stared at the man with a mixture of amazement and the beginning of comprehension. He started to say, "I just . . ."

For the first time, Oldenberg interrupted, though ever so gently. He held his pipe out to indicate that he wanted to continue. "I think if you'll just let me go on for a minute, I can lay it out pretty well. Then if you have any questions, I'll be glad to try to answer them."

That made sense, Martin thought. As it was, he was getting the story piecemeal. He might as well get it all at once. "Okay," he said.

"Well, to put it very simply, you did die from a stroke. But unlike the idea most prevalent in the West, that did not end your existence as a being. Now, I suspect, knowing something of your background, that you have little belief in a life after death. Being the empiricist you are, and also being locked into linear thinking, you probably thought that the

end of an existence was the end of that individuality, that death termi-
nated the being. But I suspect that since you have been interested in
Oriental, and particularly Hindu, thought for some time, you might
still have some slight belief in other kinds of time, in particular cyclical
time. Without going into the details of metaphysical explanation, I can
tell you that in the System we usually operate on the basis of cyclical
time. That is, occurrences take place in cycles, they don't just start, go
through a middle stage, and then end. And so with beings, they go
through cycles. I'm sure you know something about that. The Hindus
called it 'the wheel of karma.' And anyway, without going into excessive
detail, it is the system of reincarnation, of the soul passing from one
body to another. And that's where you're at. You're ready to go into
your next existence."

Martin wasn't exactly floored, but he did have to admit that was the
most profound statement about the state of his being that he had ever
heard. All he could think of to say was, "Wow!"

"Just take your time and think it over for a minute," Oldenberg said.
"Or better yet, how would you like to have a cup of coffee or tea, or a
glass of wine? We could have it over there." He motioned toward the
coffee table.

"Okay," Martin said as the other man rose to his feet. "I'll have a
glass of wine. Do you have rosé?"

"I'm sure there's some in the cabinet."

They both moved to the coffee table. Martin sat down. Oldenberg
got two glasses of wine. He put them on the table and sat down also.
Then he knocked his pipe out and began to refill it.

Martin said, "I'm afraid this opens up so many possibilities, I just don't
know where to begin."

"Well, you know you don't have to understand everything at once.
You will undoubtedly be passing through the offices of other Transition Masters as the cycle progresses. And you will pick up some information each time."

Martin thought out the next question very carefully. This fellow, Oldenberg, he decided, was very good at answers to what seemed like impossible questions. Martin finally said, "The one thing, which may seem
rather mundane to you but which bothers me a great deal, is the nature of this place, and you particularly. Why is it that, with something so
profoundly different as this occurring, everything seems so ordinary?
You must realize that for all practical purposes, except for a few irregularities such as the variety of people and the fact that the receptionist

seems to be a polyglot, this place could easily pass for a large medical or psychiatric office. I mean, for a person with a title like 'Transition Master,' you have to admit that you're a pretty ordinary-seeming professional man. I think I told you already that you remind me of my old professor, Conrad Marcus."

When Oldenberg picked up his wine glass, he jiggled it and spilled a little on the table. He reached over for a Kleenex. "True, all true. But that can be explained fairly easily. As you are undoubtedly aware, the idea of a transition from one life to another is not always easy to accept; particularly for Westerners because of their notion of linear time with a beginning, middle, and end. The idea that what you thought was the end is only the beginning of the next phase takes a little getting used to. Even for people like yourself who have a theoretical grasp of the process. So we try to keep things as customary as possible. For instance, it is no accident that I appear to be like your old professor. My image was modified for that reason. As a matter of fact, the outward appearance of all Transitioners has been so modified."

The Transition Master waved his hand as if to stop the next query, saying, "But please don't ask me to tell you how images are modified in the System. It would take us too far astray. Just remember that even your own people, especially those in your entertainment industry, are quite capable of modifying appearances with considerable success. And also, before you ask about it, the fact that you still have substance—and for all intents and purposes the same as the incarnation you had in southern California when you died—is also unimportant. We are at a place in the System where images can be modified fairly easily. And so far as the Transition Process is concerned, it doesn't matter anyway. The only thing of significance is the essence of you, what I believe your religious practitioners call 'the soul.' And believe me, your essence is there, sitting on that chair in some kind of body."

Martin finished his glass of wine.

"Would you like a refill?"

"Sure, it's not bad. Tastes like California jug wine. Had it at many a student party."

"I think it is. We usually try to use local products. That also tends to make people more comfortable while still keeping costs down. You'd be surprised at the cost accounting that goes on here in the System."

Martin sat for a long time considering that one. Whatever else, the whole affair was interesting. And he knew he could almost be hooked because of that alone.

He supposed that he had not had any greater fear of death than most Westerners, either religious or freethinking. But he had to admit that he had been intent on avoiding the state of what he had thought of as nonbeing as long as possible. And though in his lifetime he had toyed with other ideas, he had to be honest and admit that he had retained pretty much to the end the idea that death would be all she wrote. Perhaps the idea of reincarnation, most of which he had gotten while studying Hindu and Buddhist culture, had been the most interesting. But again, he had been such a thorough empiricist that he had never really believed it. It had remained merely an attractive idea. And now to realize that he was a participant in the process was downright exciting. The bizarre thought occurred that it was almost worth dying for. And he had to admit that, despite how hard he had tried to hang onto the last life, it hadn't been all that great.

Martin chuckled at himself when he thought of the phrase he had just mentally used, "his last life." He was already accepting the state of his being as outlined by Oldenberg. He grinned when he spoke again. "Well, it is interesting, I must say that."

The plump man smiled in return. "That's a good attitude, though I'm not surprised. I rather expected you'd come to that decision fairly quickly. That's one good thing about you empiricists, you are usually willing to change your opinion in the face of new evidence." He paused, then continued, "I suggest that we go on to the matter at hand. Though, if you wish, I might take one other question. I'm sure you have many, but as I said before, you will get to them through successive meetings."

"Okay, there is one, though I think by now I can almost answer it myself. And that is about the System that you refer to. What exactly is that?"

"That's a common question," Oldenberg answered. "And I think it can be taken care of rather quickly. This is part of the Supreme Bureaucracy, the organization that controls the universe. I can't give you all the details without a chart. But I can explain it in a simplified way that I think will be enough for our purposes. Since you are a professor of social science, you understand the need for organization. Animals that live in groups must have rules of order. Ultimately we, the sociocultural animals, get bureaucracies. The universe is no different. There is the supreme corporation, Universe Limited, and within it many subdivisions. They are the Systems. And I'm sure you can imagine that in such a vast entity as the universe, there are quite a variety of such. Well, I won't bother you with the details of their characteristics. But the one we are concerned with is called the Sentience System. It includes all units that have life; the beings that have the capacity to reproduce themselves. And, as you may be aware, there are quite a number of such possible places in the various corners of the Milky Way and other galaxies. But the one with which we are concerned is only on Earth, and it is a sub-sub-division called the System of Animatism. It takes in all living forms. But those involved in the Transition Process are what you Westerners have labeled animals. The plants, also a part of the Sentience System, are taken care of in a different Process. And to cap it all off, humans, or *Homo sapiens,* as your people have so grandly named themselves, are currently the most visible type in the System of Animatism. Okay?"

"Wow." Martin sat silently for a moment, wondering whether he was partially stunned or exhilarated by the vastness of conceptualization. Then he said, "Yes, it all makes sense, though it is a little mind blowing for someone like myself who just yesterday was walking around in his avocado grove, admiring the southern California sunset. But one very small question and then I'm ready to go on. From what you say, all animals are included in the System. Is that correct?"

"Yes, it's very similar to the original Hindu concept. Theoretically, a being can be reincarnated into any animal form. And if you're wondering why there weren't any nonhumans in the Transition office, it's just that they are taken care of elsewhere. There are many places for transitions, and, as you can well imagine, the facilities must necessarily be different for so many greatly varying forms."

"Okay," Martin said. "I'm ready. What do we do now?"

"Well, all we have to do is decide what your next incarnation will be. And I think we can do that shortly." He looked at his watch. "I'm sorry, but I do have another appointment in about twenty minutes. We usually schedule one transition for an hour. And incidentally, in case you are wondering, we do use linear time also. Scheduling is one of those uses, of course."

"So how do we decide?"

"Primarily it is a matter of how well you fulfilled your role in your previous life. As you probably remember, in the traditional Hindu system one moves up and down the scale according to how well one lived in the previous life."

"Yes, I remember. I suppose I personally did so-so, although I don't exactly see how it works with us in modern America. I can see how the idea of traditional roles worked in traditional India, where most people followed the life roles of their parents. But we are an achievement-oriented society, and we keep changing all the time, and rather fast at that. After all, I came from a working class background and ended up as a Ph.D. in anthropology."

"That's true, and we could get into a lengthy discussion about that also, but I don't think it will be necessary. You did have some kind of social rank during most of your adult life; upper middle class, I believe the sociologists called it." He paused, and then said, "In case you are interested how I know your social position, I did scan your Life Tape before we met."

Martin did not know exactly what that was, but by then he had been introduced to so many new ideas that he just let it slide. Also he realized that time was slipping away. There could be endless discussions on almost every point. And evidently they really did have to get on with it. Furthermore, he had to admit that he was getting very interested in the idea of another incarnation. Why, one could almost do a kind of research through it. One would literally be living a different life.

Then another fascinating idea occurred to him. This was the answer to one of the most basic problems he and all other life scientists had always faced—establishing empathy. A person was always locked into his or her own perceptions by her or his unique personality. You could never really get into another person's skin to see how he or she viewed the world. But with this process you would literally get into others' skins. You would know how someone else felt and perceived the world, as well as what they did. Why, he could be a woman, or a person from another culture or generation. It was truly mind-boggling.

Oldenberg spoke to him then, seeming to notice that his mind had wandered off. "Is there something special you are thinking about?"

Martin paused to organize his thoughts, then answered, "As you know, I was a cultural anthropologist in my last life. And though I did a number of studies of other cultures, I always had the nagging feeling that my perceptions were superficial. I just never felt confident that I could see the world as the people I was studying saw it. You are probably aware that this is an old problem with humans, not to mention other forms of life. How much did Skinner ever know about what the pigeons were thinking when they went around in figure eights? All he could do was describe what the pigeons were doing. And even outside of science, I've always been bothered by the fact that I never really knew what others were thinking or feeling. For instance, I never did find out why my last wife divorced me. Conditions actually seemed to be getting better between us until the day of the incident that provoked her to seek the divorce. And California divorce law being what it has come to be, I couldn't even get a verbal reason for the divorce. The only reason now permitted for dissolution of marriage in California is 'irreconcilable differences.' And that in essence is saying nothing except that, whatever the reasons are, they will not be stated."

Oldenberg was tapping his pipe again. And although he was not at all obvious about it, he seemed to Martin to be getting a little impatient. And he had a right. This was from his point of view another tangent. But Martin was so enthused by where his mind had taken him that he couldn't stop. All he could do was try to cut it short. He said, "I know I'm using some of your time again, and I'll do my best to be brief as possible. But unless it's against all rules, please let me finish this thought. You have no idea how exciting this is to me."

"Okay, we don't like to quash enthusiasm here in the Transition Division, but I do hope you'll try to keep it short."

"Well, what I'm thinking is that if one goes through these successive transitions, one really goes from one personality type to another, whether because of culture, sex, or just individual temperament. It would be perfect empathizing. You would really see through the other person's eyes, since for that time you would be that person. It would be a marvelous method for research or just general understanding. A fiction writer might give one of his arms to be able to see through the eyes of others." Martin corrected himself, saying, "Maybe 'leg' would be better, so he could keep his arms for writing."

"Yes, all that is true, I'm sure," Oldenberg said. "And I can see how it would interest you with your social science background. But our primary concern here is to get individuals through their transitions. As you know, final salvation is not possible in the Hindu system until the wheel of karma is broken and further incarnations do not occur. So I must insist that we go on with your case."

The man was obviously stiffening and Martin could see why. But he just could not drop his current bent. He said, "Okay, I understand. But if you don't mind, if I wouldn't be fouling up the Process too much, couldn't I have lives that would make some sense in terms of learning something? I mean with some special theme? I could still fulfill the other requirements, like moving up or down the scale in accordance to how well I lived the role of my traditional life. Do you see what I mean?"

"Oh yes, very well. And I must say I find it kind of interesting too. After all, even if we Transition Masters are not social scientists, we do have to go through a process of evaluation. And I'm sure you will agree that scientific research of the kind your people do does include evaluation." Oldenberg rubbed the balding spot on the back of his head and said, "There are some problems but maybe we can work them out. What particular theme did you have in mind?"

Martin sat back, pleased that everything was turning out so well. It was unbelievable, the amount of change that had taken place in his life since the day before. And the coming prospect was actually exciting. In no time at all he would be entering someone else's skin. And he knew with hardly any thought what he wanted to concentrate on. He wanted to experience pairing behavior from all points of view. He said, "Okay, I'll make it very short because I know my time is about up. As I'm sure you know, or have records of, I have had a number of relationships with women in my lifetime. And even so, I spent the last twenty years mostly alone. I frankly never did figure out how such pairings worked, or at least not fast enough. It's really been a puzzle to me, despite the fact that I was a social scientist. I don't know why that should bother me since I know that in my world a high percentage of psychiatrists were crazy, lawyers were crooked, and doctors were drug addicts or alcoholics. But it does.

"So, I guess what I'd like to have would be a variety of lives with different pairings or mating relationships. You know, male and female. Homosexual pairing has never interested me much. Also I guess it's not been central, since it doesn't contribute to reproduction. Could I do that?"

"I guess so," Oldenberg said doubtfully, "though there are a lot of problems if you try to do it directly. But I do understand your interest, even without being an Earthling. The main problem, as I see it, is that of transition. For you to know these other lives, it would be better if you merely viewed them rather than depending on them for transition.

"Anyway, we do have a slot in the System that might help. On occasion we call on Systems Research to study a Universal Process. Researchers then write up a report, which is passed upward. Whether such reports are read is quite another matter. But I probably don't have to tell you anything about bureaucracies and their use—or lack of use—of research results.

"What we would do here is give you a Transition Abeyance. The closest to that in your Earthling concepts would be Limbo, which I believe is a transition status your Christian metaphysicians worked out. You would then take on the duties of a System Research Scientist, and in that sense you would be in the role of a Transitioner, though admittedly a minor one.

"Then, once your report was finished, we would administratively change you back to Transition Track, and you would go on with your future lives. You might even use some of the insights you got through your little study to continue on the Track. I think this would be fairly interesting for you, and I must say it would give me a break in my regular Transition duties. We could discuss some of your findings.

"You could of course utilize the facilities that exist in Systems Research, which would be of considerable help; things such as the Life Tapes and the Perception Viewers.

"So far as the topic is concerned, that's fine. As you know, heterosexual mating has been going on ever since bisexuality evolved. It's been fundamental for these millions of years for the redistribution of genes in each generation, and as far as it goes, I suppose it could be considered to have been fairly successful."

Oldenberg paused for a few seconds, then said, "Though I believe there have been some problems in the process. Perhaps your little project would give some indication as to which direction the mating pattern is going in the future. Anyway, it would be interesting. And as you know, the likelihood of the report being read by any of the brass would be slight indeed.

"All I have to do is make a couple of telephone calls and get administrative approval from Central and you can get started. If you'll just wait a minute, I'll take care of that and get you a guide to show you your office and the facilities." No electronic device was visible, though it was apparent that the Transitioner's voice was being sent somewhere.

"Fine, fine. No rush." Martin crossed his legs and watched Oldenberg speak into the phone. Martin could hardly contain himself, the anticipation was so great. The way things had worked out in that office, he thought, were next to incredible. But of course he realized he was still thinking in terms of life systems—no, that wasn't the proper term— human systems. But the Universal System was something else.

The Transition Master leaned back and said, "Okay, it's all set up. You will continue for an indefinite time as Temporary Systems Research Scientist assigned to the Transition Office of the Subsystem of Sentience in the Sub-subsystem of Animatism. Your project will be named Heterop, short for heterosexual pairing, and I will be your monitor."

"Great—I'm very pleased. You have no idea how interesting this will be to me. You know, frankly, I hardly had any belief in the afterlife. So you can imagine how exciting this is by comparison."

"We're always pleased when our Transitioners are satisfied." He reached for his pipe, saying, "I'll just put a call in to your guide. I think Genevieve is up. You'll find her very pleasant." He began to fill the pipe. "By the way, while we're waiting, I'd like to ask one thing: Do you have any idea what particular type of couple you'd like to start on for your project?"

"Well, I think I'm still locked into linear thinking. I know it may be inappropriate now, but the only models I can think of are ones that existed in my life before. I keep thinking I'd really like to know how some of my ancestors handled this problem."

"Oh, that doesn't pose any difficulty," Oldenberg said as he struck a match to relight his pipe. "You will find there are discs of all the individuals who ever lived. I'm not exactly sure why we keep them all, but on occasion System Researchers come around to study some esoteric topic. And then too, you know how bureaucracies are: they just don't know how to get rid of records. I understand the government bureaucracies in your former country kept great storehouses full of records that hardly anyone ever used. But they wouldn't dispose of them. Genevieve will show you the files of our records."

"Then I guess the person I'd like to start on would be my father. I've always wondered how he managed his pairing life. You know things were quite a bit different then."

"Very well. I'm sure Genevieve will get you started, as well as show you your living quarters and the other facilities. And I shall look forward to some of your reactions after you have gone over the man's life. Bruno—wasn't that his name?"

"Yes, Bruno Neumann."

Martin stood behind the white-coated young lady named Genevieve. She seemed to be an amiable person and quite knowledgeable as well. As they had walked down the corridors of the Research Division, she had apprised him of the various departments and activities. She had first taken him to his quarters, which seemed comfortable, though not luxurious, then to the cafeteria and recreation center. He was particularly pleased to find they had a well-stocked library and a listening room for music. The records would help him to while away his evenings. But the big thing was the Life Disc stacks and Viewer. She introduced Martin to the gray-haired head librarian, Mrs. Morrison, and explained what he would be doing. The librarian promised to give him all the help he needed. It seemed they had a floppy disc inscribed with the life of every person who had ever lived. It seemed incredible that such a wealth of information was available, and Martin had wild fantasies of all the people whose lives he would like to see: Darwin, Copernicus, Galileo, Gutenberg, Da Vinci, Alexander the Great, Gautama, Jesus, Akhenaton, Sequoyah. But then too, he might look at some from remote times and places, a man of Cro-Magnon, a Neanderthaloid, *Homo erectus, Australopithecus.* He would be able to settle for all time how his primitive forebears got up from their shambling four-footed gait to become tool- and weapon-wielding bipeds.

But he quickly snapped himself from that reverie. He might watch some of those discs just for entertainment during his spare time. But he had to face the fact that he was on a project. And this was evidently work time. The guilts of a lifetime had not left him even though he was no longer alive, he was amused to realize.

Mrs. Morrison said, smiling, "Would you like to try one now, Dr. Neumann? I'm sure Genevieve will show you to a viewing room and how the Viewers work."

"Yes, I guess I'd better get started."

"So, do you want me to give you a random disc? Or is there a special one that would interest you?"

"I may as well begin on my project. Could I get the one I'm starting on?"

"Certainly. Just fill out a call slip with the name, life span, and place." She gave him a pink slip with blank spaces. He took it over to a writing shelf and entered the name, "Bruno Neumann."

Life span; he couldn't give that exactly. He puzzled while studying the slip. Genevieve looked over his shoulder, "Any trouble?"

"I've always been terrible at remembering birthdays and important dates, including my own. I'm sure I can't remember my father's birth date or the date of his death."

Genevieve said, "That's just for identification purposes. Many people can't remember the exact dates of life spans other than their own. Just try to figure it out approximately. Do you know about what year he died?"

"Yes, it was the year I was on my way to India for my first real overseas field trip. Let's see, that would be 1953."

"Okay, you have one date. Now do you know approximately how old he was?"

"He was fairly young. He died of strokes and high blood pressure in his mid-sixties, I would think sixty-five or sixty-six."

"Okay, there you are, subtract sixty-five from fifty-three which would give you minus twelve or the year 1888. His life span would be 1888 to 1953, give or take a year, okay? And the place would be no problem, would it?"

"No, it would almost all be in Indiana, though at two different places. Is the state enough, do you think?"

"Oh yes, I'm sure Mrs. Morrison can get it with that amount of information. You should hear how little some researchers give her, and she still gets almost all of them. She's really quite good, I can assure you."

In no time at all she brought out the disc, which, in his earth mind mode, still seemed too small to contain the details of an entire life. He had an eerie feeling as they walked down the hall toward one of the viewing rooms. He was holding an electronic replication of the entire life of one of the persons most significant to his own being. The person on that disc had supplied half the genetic material, plus nobody knew how much conditioning, to the man he, Martin Neumann, came to be. It was almost like holding a spirit.

But then they were at the viewing rooms. He could see several, each with a closed door. An amber light glowed over some. Genevieve said, "Those are occupied. Whenever you come, just take one where no light is on."

They entered an empty room that contained a control table and two chairs. On the facing wall there was a screen about four feet square. "I'll show you how to install the disc the first time, then you can do it alone. It's not difficult."

She stuck the disc into a slot. "Okay, now I'll show you the controls."

She flicked the power switch to "ON". A picture came into focus of a globular body pulsating slowly. It was surrounded by much smaller, tadpole-like creatures, which kept whipping their tails, moving erratically toward the globe. Finally one managed to penetrate the larger body and was engulfed.

"My gosh, what was that? I thought this was the disc of the life of Bruno Neumann."

"Oh, it's not very important, but the discs all start at the beginning, linear time in this instance," she smiled conspiratorially. "And that is simply the spermatozoa entering the egg that will turn out to be the person you are interested in. You don't have to watch all of a disc. In fact, very few researchers or Transition Masters do. There are many things, probably most, that will not be all that pertinent for your research, and you can pass them by. That's what this control is for. It will speed up the picture to where it will be a blur, where separate images are not distinguish-

able. Down to a complete stop if you happen to want to see a scene without motion, to study it minutely. She demonstrated.

He said, "That's really neat. You Transitioners have really developed
an elaborate technology."

"Oh these ideas are not so new. The movie industry on your planet
has been using editorial machines not too different from these for some
time. Actually, the only really new thing that you will be using are the
discs, the reduction of a total life into a single package, plus the storage
and retrieval facilities."

"Okay, but I must say I'm impressed. However, I'll take your word for
it. Anything else I should know?"

"Oh yes, you have controls for all the senses, primarily vision and
hearing, but odor and touch also." She indicated those. "You just switch
on the button marked "Audit" when you want to hear the sounds and
particularly the speech. Otherwise your picture will be silent. The same
goes for odor and touch." She demonstrated, "Okay?"

"It sounds fine."

"I would suggest you try it for a while, and if you need more help,
just ring this buzzer. It would probably be worthwhile to just practice
for an hour or so." She paused. "Oh yes, you can reverse the images
with this button, in case you want to see a scene over again, or go back
to any you saw earlier."

She left. Martin turned to the screen. At first he watched many early
scenes in entirety, the development of the fetus, the birth, his father as
an infant, and the early stages of growth. But he soon became highly
selective, speeding up most scenes to a quick scan but slowing down on
a few that seemed to be particularly important.

# CHAPTER 2

The boy standing in front of the barn was wearing overalls, a long-sleeved denim shirt, and a straw hat. Bruno Neumann was waiting for Mr. Gunzberg to bring the cow. He glanced at the bull on the other side of the fence. A rope was attached to a post on one end and to a ring in the animal's nose on the other. Bruno studied the bull's large nuts. They hung down in a velvety sac. Bruno felt his own through the pocket of his overalls. They were so small by comparison. The bull stared at him with red-rimmed eyes, careful not to turn his head too far. That would make the ring hurt.

Some chickens were scratching in a manure pile just outside the stables. Bruno watched the rooster. It sidled up to one hen and did a stiff-legged dance. The hen ignored the larger bird. The rooster picked at something in the manure, making a rapid clicking sound. Another hen came to see what the rooster had found. The rooster raised his head and stared at the hen for a moment. Then he ran four long steps to grab the hen by the top of her head with his beak. The hen squatted, half spreading her wings. The rooster jumped on the hen's flattened back. Bruno saw the rooster twist his tail under the hen's tail, thrusting forward. In a few seconds the rooster jumped off, shook his wings and crowed. The hen shook her body, raising a cloud of dust.

The chickens were always doing that, Bruno thought, more than any other animals on the farm. The others, like the cows and pigs, only did it once in a while, when they came in heat.

He heard his father speak to Mr. Gunzberg. Then to him: "Open the gate, Bruno."

As the boy was opening it, he noticed the bull shuffling and stretching the rope to its limit, his head half-turned toward the cow.

Hans said to Mr. Gunzberg, "Hold on to the cow so it doesn't try to

run. There should be plenty of room if we just get the cow next to the
fence."

Hans pulled out a pitchfork from the straw stack and took a position
alongside the bull. The animal was breathing heavily, and Bruno could
see his glistening pecker starting to come out. The bull turned his head
and moved a step toward Hans, whoe raised the pitchfork and prodded
the animal in the nose, bringing out a small trickle of blood. "You got
to watch that dang bull when you bring a cow in heat. He usually ain't a
bad bull, but I seen him go after a man when a cow was brought up."

Bruno knew his father could handle that bull or just about any other
animal. Once he had seen Hans get so mad at a horse that he had picked
up a heavy board and smashed it over the animal's head. The horse
had caved to its knees, but luckily didn't die. Hans had walked around
and kicked it with his wooden shoes until it stood up again, shaking its
head dizzily.

Mr. Gunzberg pulled the cow up to the fence and backed her toward
the bull. The cow kept looking around, rolling her eyes. Finally she was
close enough. The bull reared up on his hind legs and tried to straddle
the cow. How big the bull was when he was standing up like that, Bruno
thought. The bull's pecker was straight out, and it must have been a
foot long. The cow kept moving around and the bull kept slipping. The
bull's legs slid off.

Mr. Gunzberg said, "The dang cow just won't stand still."

"You got to hold it tight, Georg," Hans said. "It may take a minute.
That dang bull ain't got the range yet."

The bull's sides were heaving. He rested awhile, then tried again.
The cow didn't move so much, but still the bull didn't get it in. Hans
said, "That dang bull ought to be doing better than that. The next time
we're going to have to help him. Here Bruno, you take the rope and if
the bull comes at me, you give it a hard yank."

Bruno took the rope and when the bull got astraddle again, Hans
stepped in and took the bull's big pecker with his gnarled hand and
shoved it toward the cow's hole. The bull looked sideways but did not
stop pushing. The pecker went in after many pushes. The cow stood
still. Hans stepped back, wiped his hand on his overalls, and reached
over to get his straw hat. Bruno watched the hard pushing and bulging
eyes of the bull. The cow just stood still, holding all that weight.

"I think that'll take care of it," Hans said. "Looks to me like you got a
good calf started."

Bruno walked into the kitchen. His sister Mary was helping his mother at the stove while Hermione was putting the knives and forks on the table. Bill was sitting on the floor next to the wood-box, playing with chips, and Leo lay quietly in the cradle. Hans was sitting on the carved wood chair, smoking his corncob. The kitchen was full of the smell of food: fried ham and potatoes, sliced cucumbers and tomatoes, bread and butter. Henrietta had made fresh bread that day, enough to feed the family for a week.

Bruno sat on the bench next to the flat iron cooking stove. He watched Henrietta as she moved rapidly back and forth in front of the stove. She was shorter than most women but very quick. Bruno could not imagine her not working. Her long dress brushed against the bottom of the stove and the wood-box as she moved pans, skillets, and bowls about. She stopped in the middle of her work and pushed strands of black hair back from her face. "Did you help your father up at the barn, Bruno?"

"Yah, they bred a cow."

"That's good to help your father."

Bruno had a lot of trouble making up his mind to speak. He wanted to tell Henrietta all about it but wasn't sure she would let him. He still remembered the time when she was washing him in the wooden tub and his own pecker had come up. He had said, "Oh look, Mom, it's just like the animals."

But she had slapped it and said, "That's not what boys do, Bruno."

And his pecker had gone down fast.

But still he had asked, "What do boys do, Mom?"

She had said, "You're not old enough to know about that yet, Bruno. Let's just get you washed."

He had thought he would ask Hans, so the next day he had said, "Pa, why do peckers come up?"

And Hans had answered. "What, on animals or people?"

And he had said, "Either, they seem the same to me."

But Hans had looked at him, a little angrily, Bruno thought, and said, "Animals and people ain't the same, boy. That's why we go to church and animals don't. But anyway, peckers come up for making young ones. But that's enough now. You just get on up to the chicken house and get the eggs."

As Bruno sat there, at the side of the stove, he wondered why grown-ups didn't like to talk about peckers, of people that is. Hans and the other men didn't mind talking about animals. Bruno remembered how Hans and Mr. Gunzberg had laughed about the size of the bull's pecker before it had gone into the hole and how limp and small it was afterward. That was another thing, he thought; the hole on the cows and pigs, it didn't even have a special name. It wasn't just a hole though, it had sort of rounded ridges or flaps on the sides, but even so, they didn't call it anything special. Only the bull's thing had a special name. And it was the same as the name of his own, even if Hans said animals and people were completely different. Bruno watched Hermione and wondered whether she had a hole with ridges like the cow.

He spoke to Henrietta again. "I held the bull while Pa helped it do the breeding."

Henrietta didn't answer, continuing to slice the bread. However, Mary asked. "How'd you help, Bruno?"

He felt a little uneasy, knowing this was not the kind of talk he had ever heard when men and women were together.

He said, "Oh, I just did what Pa asked me to."

Mary stopped working and stood facing Bruno. "I mean, what did you do exactly?"

"Oh, it wasn't nothing. I just held the rope and opened and closed the gate, and things like that."

"I mean what was Pa doing? What is breeding anyway?" Bruno knew Mary was almost two years younger than him, just ten. And besides girls probably didn't know as much as boys, particularly about breeding. He answered, "Well, he was just helping the bull out. He . . ."

Bruno was already aware that Henrietta was looking at him with a funny face, wiping her hands on her apron, when Hans spoke, "Now Bruno, that's enough. You know better than to start talking about things like that when your Ma and the girls are here."

Hans was just a little angry. But Bruno knew how fast he could get real mad and before you knew it, his big, calloused hand would hit you on the side of the head.

"Yah, Pa." Bruno clenched his hands to be ready to throw them over his ears if Hans started to come toward him.

Henrietta became calm again. "I think we can go to the table now. Dinner's ready."

She gave baby Leo a piece of bread to chew and kicked one of the dogs which had gotten up and sniffed toward the table. The dog went back behind the stove. She put Bill in the rough unpainted high chair that all the kids had used. Hans sat down at the head of the table and Bruno sat next to him. Then Henrietta, Mary, and Hermione sat down for prayer. Afterward, Henrietta and Mary would get back up to bring the bowls and platters of food. Hans put down his pipe. "You can say the prayers, Bruno."

That had been his job for three years. Once in a while Mary had to do it and probably the other kids when they got old enough. But being the oldest, Bruno started out on most things. Bruno put his hands together and bowed his head.

"Bless us, our Lord, for these Thy gifts . . ." he began.

* * * * *

The children grew, the parents got older. The boy, Bruno, being the oldest, took over more and more jobs alongside his father.

* * * * *

The hill country of southern Indiana was a patchwork of woods and fields. Though men were working here and there, there was a beehive of activity on one farm. At the barn, a threshing machine powered by a steam engine was in operation. That had to be before 1946, because by then the combine had replaced the older machinery everywhere.

The steam engine was a squat cylinder, enlarged at one end so that wood could be thrown into the burner. A stack belched smoke. A large power wheel turned on one side, keeping the belt going. Men with loaded wagons were forking sheaves of ripe grain onto a moving conveyor belt. Down below, men were filling gunny sacks with wheat grain that was pouring from a tube. On the other side of the machine, a long tube kept spewing out the wheat stems. There was already a good-sized straw stack.

The line of wagons moved up. The two men on the nearest side started forking sheaves onto the belt. They were dressed like all the other men, in overalls, full-sleeved denim shirts, straw hats, and work shoes. A streak of sweat ran down the middle of each man's back and the rims of their hats were wet from sweat. Every so often each would lift his hat and wipe his forehead and neck with a large red kerchief.

Apart from their height, the two were about the same build, thin and muscular. One was about six feet tall, the other two or three inches less. The shorter was Bruno Neumann in the full strength of early manhood. He was a good-looking fellow with an open, agreeable expression, apparent even when he was working. There were crinkles in the corners of his eyes, even though he must have been in his early twenties. Like the other farmers, he had never worn sunglasses. His skin was smooth and slightly dark. He must have shaved recently.

The other man was Bruno's younger brother, Bill.

They finished unloading the wagon, and Bruno, standing upright, took the reins while Bill sat on the wagon bed, his legs dangling. Bruno drove the horses under a big sycamore, where he and Bill loosened their harness. They watered the horses in a nearby trough and forked them some hay. The men then went to the pump and sloshed water on their faces. They wiped themselves with a communal towel.

Bruno said, grinning, "That was a good morning's work. Looks like we might finish today."

"Yah, I think so. There's just the one field down on the lower forty. Where do we go tomorrow?"

"I think we got the day off. The next place is the Meiers' and it takes a day for the steam roller to get over there and set up."

Bill took out a sack of Bull Durham to make a cigarette, while Bruno took a wad of tobacco from his bag of Mail Pouch. Their faces relaxed as they smoked and chewed. Bill said, "I think Lorena is waiting for you. I saw her once when we came in to unload. She waved."

Bruno grinned. He liked Lorena Kreuger. He had taken her to a barn dance a couple of times where they had kissed out back. But then her brother had come along. She had large tits even though she wasn't very fat. He had been able to feel them through his shirt. Bruno thought Lorena was a good girl though and a hard worker. Henrietta had even joked with him once or twice about him marrying her. Bruno said to Bill, "Maybe she'll bring one of her apple pies. I could eat half a one now."

Bill knocked the ash off his cigarette. "She probably will. She knows how much you like them. Let's go over to the food table. I'm hungry too."

As they were walking over, Bruno asked, "How about Wilma? Will she be here today?"

"I don't think so. Her family lives too far away."

There were half a dozen men standing in front of the boards that were serving as tables. They were overloaded with food. First was the meat section with fried ham, sausage, chicken, and even one dish of beef, plus dishes of gravy. Beyond were the vegetables, mashed and boiled potatoes, corn on the cob, cooked green beans with chunks of bacon, sliced tomatoes and cucumbers, and cole slaw. Then came the pies, rhubarb, raspberry, peach and apple. There were also a couple of cakes. Many flies hovered over that section and were waved away regularly by one of the Ottmeier girls. After that were plates of homemade bread, butter, preserves, small pickles, pickled beets, pickle-lily, lemonade, and iced tea. The women stood on the other side of the board table, helping the men by spooning out portions or filling the bowls when they got low. Lorena was behind the meat section. She had on a long flowered dress, cut low, just showing the top of her tits. Her hair was in a roll on the back of her head like most of the other women. She leaned over when Bruno and Bill came to fill their plates. She smiled, "Hi Bruno, are you hungry?"

He grinned back, crinkling his eyes, "Sure am. Could eat a horse."

"I brought the beef," she said. "I saved it for threshing." She hesitated, then said, "I knew you liked it."

He smiled back, and it was clear why a young girl on the lookout for a husband would be attracted to Bruno Neumann. He was a good-looking young fellow, but also he had such a gentle face. His brown eyes were particularly kindly. "I'll take some of your beef then," he said.

She reached over and put an extra large piece on his plate.

"Also that's my gravy. That's good on the potatoes."

"I'll come back for that."

As he moved on, she said, "You should take some of my apple pie too, Bruno."

"I don't think I have room for it."

"You can come back and get a clean plate. I'll save you a piece."

The two men sat on a rough bench under the tree, eating as only working men can, with complete concentration. Other men were scattered around, sitting on makeshift seats, all eating.

When they had finished eating, Bill said, "She really likes you, Bruno. I think she wants to marry you."

"Well, you know I can't marry nobody now. It looks like I'll be going off in another month or so."

It was still hard to believe, becoming a soldier in the American Expeditionary Force and going off to France to fight the Bosch, the Huns, as they called them in the papers. It would be really strange to meet some, maybe as prisoners, and talk to them in their own language. It had bothered some of the fellows, but Father Bertrand had gone through that in several sermons. It didn't make any difference that almost everyone's ancestors in that parish had come from Germany and almost all the older people spoke German; they were all Americans, Father Bertrand had said. And the Bosch under the Kaiser had committed atrocities. That was killing children and raping Belgian women. Bruno had heard they were going to stop teaching any classes in German in the church school.

Bill said, "Do you want to go?"

"Sure, it's my patriotic duty. And I guess I can kill some Bosch as well as the next one." The Kaiser's soldiers were probably as bad as they said in the papers, Bruno thought, but it didn't give him a good feeling. He had studied in German at the Wertzberg Grammar School and he still spoke it with Hans and Henrietta. Bill and the younger ones were not learning to speak it.

Bruno stood up, grinning, "I'm going for my apple pie."

Lorena was alone at her end of the table. "Did you like my beef, Bruno?"

"Sure, it was real good. We don't ever have beef in the spring and summer. Ma says it's too hard to can. Besides, we don't kill a steer every year. Mostly we just have pork and chicken."

Bruno knew the Kreugers were better off than his family. They had 150 acres of land and almost half of it was in fields. The Neumann place had only sixty acres, much of it still in woods. If he would marry the Kreuger girl, he could probably work on her father's place, at least until he got enough to get a place of his own. They didn't have any boys. But then what was he thinking of; he had to go off to fight the war.

She said, "Are you ready for the apple pie? I saved a big piece for you." She moved to that end of the table and lifted a cloth. The pie was underneath, protected from the flies.

"That really looks good," Bruno said, reaching over. "Do you have another piece, for my brother?"

She pursed her lips in a mock frown. "Oh Bruno, that's the last. But there's rhubarb left. It's very good. Do you think he'd like that?"

"I think so. Anyway, I'll take him a piece."

As he was about to turn back, she said, "Bruno, I don't have anyone to take me home tonight. Do you think you could give me a ride?"

Bruno stopped. It was almost four miles, and over those dirt roads and with tired horses it would take almost two hours. They would probably work late to finish up, and it would be dark before they got to her house. Bill was going off to visit Wilma afterward, so Bruno would be alone. He said, "Do you think your folks would mind?"

"No, I told them I might come home with you, and my mother said it was alright."

Bruno put the removable seat on the wagon after he was finished with the last load. It was just getting cool as he drove the horses to the eating area. Lorena had two baskets covered with cloth, full of leftovers and dirty dishes from the day's spread.

"Whoa!" Bruno called out in his deep voice, pulling back on the reins. Pet and Duke stopped short. She put the baskets on the wagon bed behind the seat. Bruno reached down and took her hand to pull her up. He was surprised by her lightness, despite the fullness of her body. When she swung her leg up, he could see the white cotton stocking almost up to her knee. She settled down next to him and he slapped the horses' withers. "Giddyup!" The wagon creaked into motion.

It was fine to ride over the hills and down the hollows at that time of day, just before sundown. Locusts were zee-zeeing yet with the last heat of the day, and a whippoorwill could be heard in the distance. The sky was still mostly clear, though there were some clouds on the horizon beginning to change color.

Bruno felt tired but comfortable since the day was about over. He would sleep well, and the next day would be easy since he wouldn't have to go threshing. Maybe he would go up to the woods and split logs for the winter woodpile or maybe fix fences. That old rail fence always needed fixing. Every time a cow leaned against it, one of the logs fell off.

He felt Lorena's body rubbing against his as the wagon jolted over ruts and rocks. He looked at her and smiled. She smiled back and said, "You know, Bruno, my folks wouldn't let me do this with just anyone, to come home alone in the dark."

"I guess that's right. Most of the girls go with their brothers or sisters, or at least in groups. Why do you think it's alright with your folks for you to come with me?"

"My folks like you, Bruno, 'specially my mother. She thinks you're a good man and a hard worker." She paused a moment, then said, "I like you too, you know."

Bruno blushed, visible even on his sun-darkened face. He took off his hat and wiped his forehead with his kerchief. The white area from the hat line to the beginning of his hair, which was always protected from sunlight, was deep red. He said, "I like you too, Lorena."

He kept his eyes straight ahead, clicking to the horses periodically.

About halfway home they came to a ford across Salt Creek. Bruno stopped the horses in the middle and let the reins go slack. "The horses need to drink," he said. "They got to drink often on a hot day like this."

It was very peaceful, the water gurgling through the wagon wheels, a soft breeze coming up the creek. In the distance the quivering call of a screech owl, marking the beginning of night. Bruno took off his hat and put it on the seat. Lorena turned around and got something from the basket. She turned to him and said shyly, "Do you want a drink of whiskey?"

He had taken drinks at barn dances and a few times when he was with other men, even a couple of times when there were girls in the group. But Hans and Henrietta didn't drink and didn't approve of it so he never felt good about it. Besides, he didn't really like the way it burned. This was the first time any girl had offered him any. He looked at the bottle.

She said quickly. "My brother just gave it to me to take home. But he wouldn't mind if we took some."

She was a good girl, Bruno thought. Also, he wanted to put his arm around her. And then he thought that it would be alright because he was going away soon and they probably drank whiskey in the Expeditionary Force. "Alright," he said.

She unscrewed the top and handed him the bottle. He put it to his mouth and swallowed a little. It burned like fire, just like before, but he didn't cough. His eyes watered a little.

"I'll take a little too," she giggled.

They both had another. "How do you feel?" she asked.

"I'm alright. It's just hot. But it makes you feel warm inside."

The horses finished drinking and stood quietly in the middle of the stream, their only movement an occasional switching of their tails to brush off flies. "I guess we ought to be moving along," he said. Then he noticed she had her arm around his waist. He made a sudden decision and put his around hers. She laid her other hand across his, saying, "Why don't we drive over to the side there? I see a little place off the road."

"But Lorena, it's getting dark. We ought to be getting you back."

"Oh, that's alright. We'll just tell my folks that one of the wheels came off and you had to fix it. She leaned toward him then and kissed him on the edge of his mouth. It was a short kiss but he liked it. He looked at her. She said, "Did you like that?"

"Yah." He squeezed her waist and slapped the reins. "Click, click, Giddyup."

The horses pulled out and he turned them toward the little side road. It was darker there than on the main road. When he stopped, she offered him the bottle. "Why don't we have another drink?"

When he swallowed that time, the burning was almost pleasant. His body felt very warm and comfortable. She took another drink and then capped the bottle. Bruno turned and kissed her full on the mouth. She returned his kiss. He felt a little dizzy. She took his hand from around her waist and put it on one of her tits, outside the dress. He could feel the nipple through the cotton cloth.

They kissed and hugged for a long time. His pecker became hard. He was also aware that it was getting darker, and he was worried that some other wagon or buggy would come by, maybe even a car. It was almost too late though.

Then he realized she had unbuttoned her dress and slipped one of her tits out. He put his hand on it and pressed. She moved her legs closer. She was breathing heavily when she said, "We could get down and lie in the grass over there."

He had seen the grassy spot when they first came, though it had become so dark he could still only barely make it out. His pecker was pushing hard against his overalls. He had found out, shortly after Hans had told him that people weren't like animals, that with peckers they were. At least men got hard peckers just like bulls. He knew then what he wanted, too: he wanted to go into her hole, just like the bull.

But that was a sin, as Father Bertrand kept preaching in his sermons. Even thinking about it was a venial sin that you had to confess.

Bruno pulled away suddenly. Lorena said, "What's wrong? Did I do something?"

"We shouldn't be doing this," he said. "It's a sin. I think you should cover yourself up."

She pushed her tit back into her dress and buttoned up. "I don't think it's so bad, Bruno. Men and women are supposed to do this."

"Only if they're married. Otherwise, it's adultery." Bruno couldn't help thinking he might have been wrong about Lorena. She might not be such a good girl after all.

She said, "Not what we were doing."

"But that's what leads up to it. Anyway, I figure we ought to be heading for home."

Bruno's nuts ached as he took up the reins and started the horses up.

\* \* \* \* \*

Young men left factory and farm and put on heavy woolen clothing and hats with flat brims to go off to train how to kill other men. Among them, Bruno traveled by train and in the depths of a great ship, meeting more different kinds of people than he had ever imagined. One military camp after another, and then he was carrying the disassembled parts of a machine gun from one muck trench to another. Day followed day, then weeks, then months, and almost a year of slogging through mud, creeping forward, scuttling back, and jumping for cover whenever a new barrage opened up. But most of the time he waited in the muck.

\* \* \* \* \*

The two men in uniform were walking along a creek bordered by poplars. Most of the fields were in pasture. A little group of cows were grazing off to the right.

Bruno Neumann said, "They look like pretty good animals, like they'd give a lot of milk."

McGahey said, "I wouldn't know. I never saw any cows before coming in the army. Which is not surprising because they don't have any in Chicago except at the stockyards. And I never did go out in the country. You're one of the first country guys I ever knew."

They came to a small bridge and sat down on a concrete abutment. Bruno saw small fish swimming in the fast-moving water. He felt at peace, saying, "Well it looks like it's about over, don't it? The Bosch have had about enough. I guess we Yanks showed them."

Bruno still felt a little strange talking about Germans like that, especially since he had learned that the prisoners were not much different from the boys at home. He had never seen or heard any that seemed like they could commit atrocities. But it was a war and they had started it. And it had been hard riding the boxcars, standing in wet trenches night after night waiting for another bombardment, then going over the top with machine gun belts or the gun itself. At least he had never had to fire the gun. But then the Bosch had gotten him in that one bombardment. Bruno put his hand on his chin to feel the scar where the shrapnel had hit.

McGahey said, "At least we finally got a leave. Maybe the armistice will come before we have to go back."

"Yah, maybe. I was getting tired of it. Every day more talk about an armistice, then the next morning another bombardment. At least we're winning."

"What will you do after the war?" McGahey asked.

"I'll go back to the home place. But maybe I won't stay. I been thinking of going up to the northern part of the state. They got some big farms there and I heard they can always use more hands." Bruno thought about it for a minute. "Or I might even go to the city. There's plenty of jobs there now."

"You ought to come to Chicago. I could show you a lot of girls."

"No, if I go, it will probably be Indian City. I might take my brother Bill along. He's never been any farther than Greentown. I don't think he'd want to go that far."

"Well, if you change your mind, you know you got a place to go in Chicago, to Phil McGahey's place, where all the girls are. 'Course they're mostly Irish. I don't know if you like Irish girls, you being a German."

Bruno didn't answer. He had an idea that he ought to marry a Catholic girl. As far as he knew, though, most of the Irish were Catholic too.

McGahey said, "Look, what's coming down the road?"

Bruno had seen the figure earlier and noticed even at a distance that she had on a long skirt. He figured she was one of the local farm women. The two men were well back from the lines. There hadn't been any fighting in that area, and the farm people were going about their regular work. The camp he and McGahey had walked from was for recuperation from front line duty. Men who had been on the front lines a long time or who were suffering from shell shock were sent to Camp Briggs for as long as they could be spared from their outfits. But since the war was almost over, there were many doughboys in France, and replacements were not hard to get.

When the woman got nearer, Bruno could see that she was young, dressed in the clothes of an ordinary French farm woman. Her dress wasn't too different from the dresses of the women at home. She had a full body and strong legs. Her tits seemed medium sized, though the dress was full enough that Bruno couldn't be sure.

She glanced at them when she got near. McGahey called out, *"Bonjour mademoiselle."*

He had learned more French words than most of the men, though all had memorized a few. Bruno had tried German on a few, but if they understood, they wouldn't let on.

The girl answered, *"Bonjour."*

McGahey stepped to her side and began walking with her. Bruno put himself next to McGahey. Bruno's buddy then began to use all the French words he knew, probably about ten. Bruno knew more but he kept quiet. McGahey looked at Bruno a couple of times, grinned, and nodded his head. The girl also looked around McGahey toward Bruno. He smiled at her.

McGahey had long used up the few French words he knew and began using simple English words and pointing. "Me Phil. Him Bruno."

The girl smiled, then pointed at herself, saying, *"Moi Yvette."*

McGahey turned to Bruno, "She says her name is Yvette."

"Yah, I heard."

They had come to a place where the main road turned away from the creek. A path continued parallel to the stream. Thick grass grew on its banks.

McGahey was pointing in that direction, saying, "We go there, *allez.*"

"*Non, Non,*" the girl said and stopped.

McGahey put his hand on her arm, "*Allez* there, no?"

"*Non, Non,*" she repeated. And then she said something long, while pointing at Bruno.

"I wish I could figure out what she is saying," McGahey said, "though I think she wants you, Bruno. And you know I think she might do it. We couldn't both have her. So why don't you take her?"

Bruno looked at the girl, who was smiling at him. Her skin was very light, and wisps of hair peeked out from under her head scarf. How could he do anything with her? He didn't even know her, much less not being married to her. Bruno knew that many of the men, probably most, lay with French girls, usually paying them with food or chocolate, but he hadn't. He had his faith, and one day he would get a wife, farm, and family. But he also knew that he would like to lay with a woman. He said, "I can't Phil. Where I come from we were taught different. We're not supposed to lay with a woman until we're married. And then it's supposed to be for having children."

McGahey put his hand on his friend's shoulder. "Oh, I know, Bruno. That's nothing new to me. You don't think Irish Catholics don't get the same line. But things are changing. And besides, this is war and you're a hero. Also she's not even an American. Go on." He gave Bruno a little shove.

The girl smiled at Bruno and said, "*Venez.*"

Bruno didn't know what that meant, which wasn't surprising, given the little French he knew. But he turned in her direction.

McGahey said, "I'm leaving, Bruno. Good luck." He bent over and whispered in his friend's ear, "Don't forget the main words, "*Couchez avec moi?*" And he turned to walk down the road.

She spoke again at length and started down the path along the creek. Bruno followed, his excitement about equal to his feeling of guilt. He watched her feet. She was wearing rough leather shoes, nailed to wooden soles. She sat in the grass and held her hand up to him. He put his hand in hers and sat down beside her. She talked, naming things, he thought, because she kept pointing. *Arbre, vache, encloture, moi, Yvette, Française, Bruno, Americain.*"

Bruno repeated the words after her while looking into her eyes, which were very blue. She smiled frequently. Bruno smiled back. He felt very weak. They kept talking. Finally she said, *"Moi Paris maison, vous Chateaudun, soldats maison."*

Chateaudun was the recuperation camp where he was billeted. He nodded, *"Oui, oui."*

She wrote what he figured was her name and address on a piece of paper and gave it to him. Then she said, *"Votre nom?"* and something he couldn't understand.

He looked at her and said, *"Oui, oui."* He didn't really know what she wanted but he always said *oui* when he wasn't sure.

She said, *"Moi Yvette Desplaines, vous Bruno qui?"* She gave him a piece of paper and crayon.

He thought he understood. She wanted his name and maybe his address. He didn't feel good about giving it to her. He didn't know her and wouldn't see her again. He felt very strange just being there. But she was very insistent. She pointed to the paper several times and said, *"Votre nom, votre nom."*

Finally he put it down, "Bruno Neumann, Corporal, Camp Briggs, Chateaudun, France."

She put the paper in a pocket of her dress. Then she leaned over and put her hands on his shoulders. He looked at the clear blue eyes in the pink face and felt very warm. Then almost without deciding to do it, he put his cheek against hers. He had thought at first he was going to kiss her but just before he got to her lips, he decided against it. He didn't know exactly why, but he thought she might be a loose woman and she might have laid with a lot of soldiers. Why she might even have laid with some Bosch for money.

She let her hands fall to around his back and squeezed. When they came apart, they sat looking at one another for a long time. And again, almost without his deciding, he said the words, *"Couchez avec moi?"*

All he could think of when he said them was that the devil was prompting him. But the excitement of her body so close kept that idea from staying too long. She lay back and Bruno rolled toward her. From then on, his thoughts were not clear because of his excitement. He only knew that he started to get on top of her but she said, *"Attendez, attendez,"* while pulling up her dress and taking off some kind of bloomers.

Then he did get on top and put his hands on the ground to hold himself up. He felt her open her legs and reach down to unbutton his pants. His pecker was as hard as a board. She helped him put it in and he began to pump. He was surprised how well he could do it without ever having been told how, or practicing.

She put her face up toward his, saying, *"Embrassez-moi, embrassez-moi."*

By the way she offered her lips he was sure she wanted him to kiss her. He started but pulled away. He just couldn't go that far. He pumped harder, and her body began to twist. She was holding herself from the ground to get the maximum from his thrusts. He could feel himself going very deep into the warm, wet hole. What he thought of more than anything else was that it was almost exactly the same as the bull and cow. He pumped still harder. She closed her eyes and began to moan. Then he was pushing so hard he couldn't have stopped if he had wanted to. He pushed harder. The explosion was like one of the flares going off over no-man's-land. Her moan changed to a low cry, "Eeaah!"

He fell on top of her and closed his eyes. Then he was aware that all motion had stopped. He felt drained. After a bit he opened his eyes. Hers were still closed, her head lying slightly to the side. She looked completely peaceful. Bruno shook her gently. Her body was limp. He pulled out and got on his knees. Her thing was not very pretty, all wet with a milky liquid. He put his pecker in his pants and buttoned up. Some of the liquid on his pants was beginning to dry. He reached down and pulled down her skirt. Reaching over, he shook her again gently, asking, "Are you alright?" His voice sounded so loud.

Still she did not move. He could see her breathing though and was thankful for that. But what was wrong? Had he hurt her? None of the animals ever did anything like that. Was this his punishment? What if someone came along? How could he explain?

He stood up and looked down at her. She still did not move. All of a sudden he decided, grabbing his cap, turning, and breaking into a run down the path. He never turned to look around, running as fast as he could until he was across the bridge, beyond the poplars, and around a bend in the road. He was short of breath when he slowed to a fast walk, continuing toward the camp without pause.

Bruno took the letter from his pocket and looked at the envelope. It read: *Corporal Bruno Neumann, Camp Briggs, Chateaudun, France.* There wasn't a return address, but the stamp was French and the postmark said, "Pigalle, Paris." He studied the letter. The date was there as well as his name, "Cher Bruno." But except for a few words, he could not read the rest.

He put it back into his pocket and walked to Jeffrey Fortier's bunk.

Jeffrey was the only one in the barracks who really knew French. His family had brought him to Louisville from Quebec. Jeffrey was lying on his bunk, smoking a cigarette. He said, "Get some mail, Bruno?"

"Yah, I got a letter from my folks and another one."

"Things okay with your folks?"

"Yah, my Pa is getting on but he's keeping the farm going. Also two of my brothers are there. And my mother is well." He hesitated then brought out the letter. "But what I wanted to talk to you about is another letter I got. In French. I wondered if you'd tell me what it says. I know German but not much French."

Fortier swung his legs down. "Sure. From a girl?"

"Yah, how'd you know?"

"I didn't. But there's not many guys who get letters in French from anyone but girls. I've translated several."

Bruno felt a little relieved. At least Jeffrey wouldn't be easily surprised. Bruno handed the letter to the other soldier. Fortier glanced at it quickly then came back to the beginning. He said, "She says, 'Dear Bruno, I hope you remember me. My name is Yvette Desplaines. We met near the village of Lepont. You had come there from the American camp at Chateaudun. I was returning from a visit to my aunt.'"

Bruno felt very uncomfortable and kept looking at Fortier to see whether he would grin. Bruno almost wished he had not asked his friend to read the letter. But Jeffrey just kept going as if it were nothing special.

"'I liked to meet you and I hope you liked to meet me,' she says. 'And maybe you can come to Paris to see me. I can show you a lot of places. And if you want a nice souvenir, I have a German pistol for you.'"

Jeffrey finished, saying, "Then she gives some directions for how to get to her house and her address. Then she says, 'You can write me when you are coming. Send it to this address.'"

He handed the letter back to Bruno, saying, "So you got a girlfriend in Paris, eh, Bruno? Ooh, la, la. Looks like she really goes for you."

Bruno was sure his face was red, and he wanted to get away. It had been so hard to explain what had happened to McGahey. And to have another of his buddies know made him feel very uncomfortable. He said, "Thanks Jeffrey," and started to turn away.

But Fortier said, "So, when you going to Paris, Bruno? I think you can get a leave this weekend. There's plenty of trucks now. According to this letter, she'd be very pleased to see you."

"I can't go now," Bruno said and turned away quickly, not wanting to continue.

As he walked away, he knew he would never go. What he had done was wrong. It was a mortal sin, and it would probably take him a long time to get it off his soul. It was good that he had started to do penance already. When he put his hands together under the blanket at night it was the first thing he prayed for. But he had to get to a confession as soon as he could. He just hadn't made up his mind whether to do it with one of the army chaplains or wait until he got back to Wertzberg and Father Bertrand.

\* \* \* \* \*

As Bruno approached the outskirts of Wertzberg in the buggy, a car appeared from around the bend. It rocked and jolted but kept coming steadily. He watched it carefully, trying to figure out whether it was a Model T or one of the others. There seemed to be many new kinds since he had come back from France, but there seemed to be two Model Ts for every other car.

The horses were getting used to them. Bruno didn't even have to pull off the road, though he did pull to one side. The car came abreast and the man inside waved. It was Mr. Hoehn, one of the biggest landowners in the parish. The car went on.

Bruno had mixed feelings as he drove down the main street. This was his first trip to the little town since he had come back. In one way he was pleased. At times he had thought he wouldn't make it. Life in the trenches had been hard. Now everyone treated him and the others who had returned like heroes. But he didn't feel as comfortable as before. Maybe, he thought, it was like the man said, "How you going to keep them down on the farm once they've seen Paree?"

He missed his buddies. And he'd seen many things while he was gone that he would like to get. Maybe someday he'd even be able to get a Model T. Living in that log building covered with clapboard that Hans had built didn't seem so good any more.

He took the two bags of wheat to the miller first. Mannhart was there with one of his assistants. Both were dusty with flour. Bruno tied Duke to the post and reached for a bag. Before he could lift it, Mannhart proclaimed loudly, "Here's Bruno Neumann, one of our heroes." He put his hand out and Bruno took it. "Hi, Mr. Mannhart."

"We heard you was back. We looked for you in church last Sunday but didn't see you. But your sister, Anna, was there and she said you was home. How's it feel to be back in the country again? Though I guess you saw some of their farms too, eh?"

"Yah, we saw some. It's not too much different. Except they don't have many machines over there. The women still wash clothes by beating them on rocks."

"But you must have been in the big cities too. How was gay Paree? They say that all you doughboys was welcome there."

The thought of the French girl flickered through Bruno's mind and increased his unease. That was why he was in Wertzberg, to go to confession at last after holding off for several months. It had worried him. What if something had happened and he would have had a mortal sin on his soul? Maybe after confession he would begin to feel better. He said, "Paree is alright. But the French aren't very clean and they eat funny things. Did you know they eat snails and frogs?"

"Yah, we heard some of those things. I guess you doughboys saw a lot of strange sights." He reached over for Bruno's bag of wheat. "I guess Henrietta wants some flour. With all those big kids there, she must have a lot of baking to do."

"There's lots of hungry mouths," Bruno said.

He stayed outside until the miller had ground the flour. From his back pocket he produced a packet of Mail Pouch, wadding up three fingers full into his mouth. As he chewed, the sweet, sharp taste of the tobacco made his saliva run. He spit once.

What should he do, get the groceries first or go on to the church right away? Confessions would start soon, but they lasted only two hours. If the line was long, he might not get in. That would mean another week because it was too far from the farm to come in again before the next Saturday. He decided he would go to Confession first. Then he'd be able to go to Communion the next day, the first time since before he had lain with the French girl. He could get the groceries afterward.

"Here's one bag," Mr. Mannhart said. "I'll get the other and you can go on. I guess you got a lot of things to do and people to see. I know one girl who would like to see you—Lorena Kreuger."

Bruno remembered that he had answered one of her letters while in France, but only one. He said to Mr. Mannhart, "Yah, maybe I'll stop by their farm on the way home."

"Here's the other." Mannhart dropped the second bag on top of the first. A little puff of flour dust flew out. Bruno said, "Hans said he'll take care of it next time he sees you. But here's some eggs Henrietta sent." He gave the miller the eggs, which were in one of the new containers with a separate section for each egg.

"That's alright," Mannhart said. "Anytime you need some work, come back. After all, you're one of our returned doughboys and it wouldn't be right not to help you fellas."

Bruno got back on the buggy and headed for St. Ignatius. It was a plain, small place compared with the gigantic cathedrals of France. It was built entirely of wood, with a spire on one end and a cross on top. There were colored windows on both ends, but they had only a few colors compared with the big windows in the French cathedrals. Bruno wished he could have seen some of the cities of Germany too, but he never had the chance. They had been the enemy.

It was cool and dark inside. Two older women were kneeling in one of the back pews. Six or seven people stood in line back from the Confessional box, all with folded hands and eyes cast downward. Bruno blessed himself at the holy water font, dipping his fingers in the water and crossing himself on the forehead. He walked to one of the pews, genuflected, and went in to kneel. Putting his head down, he closed his eyes to prepare for the Confession. He had done it so many times he didn't need to check the list any more. He could remember the main sins: taking the name of the Lord in vain, missing Sabbath or holy days, failing to honor father or mother, lying or stealing, and having evil thoughts about those things. But this would be different from all the rest. He had committed fornication; and he had not just thought about it, he had done it.

In the quiet coolness of St. Ignatius, that occurrence seemed so distant that he almost felt it had been a dream. But inside he knew he had really done it, that he had been in France and he had lain with that woman. He got up and walked to the end of the Confessional line. The man ahead turned and recognized him, nodded, then turned back. Bruno kept his hands together and waited.

Then it was his turn. He walked to the cubicle and knelt. Behind the lattice partition he could see the priest's head. The image wasn't clear enough to be sure it was Father Bertrand though Bruno knew that unless he was sick, the senior priest always heard Saturday's Confessions. When the priest spoke, Bruno knew it was Father Bertrand. He said the Confessional prayer, then, "Yes, my son?"

Bruno also did his prayer, the one he had been saying ever since he was a small boy. "Bless me Father, for I have sinned . . ." And then he told the regular ones, how many times he had lied, how often he had been disobedient, and the other venial sins. And he paused.

After a bit Father Bertrand said, "And is that all, my son?"

Bruno began. "No, Father. I've come for a very special sin, a mortal sin. I haven't been to Confession or Communion since I was in France."

There was no sound except the regular breathing of the priest. Bruno continued. "I committed the sin of fornication, Father."

When Bruno paused again, Father Bertrand said, "Can you tell me about it, my son?"

Bruno explained then what had happened in the field and finished by saying, "I know it was wrong, Father. I knew it even then. But it seemed I just couldn't help it. It seemed like the temptation was too strong."

The priest said, "Have you ever done this before?"

"No, Father."

"And you're not married, are you, my son?"

"No, Father."

"You are right to wish forgiveness, my son. Fornication is a sin and needs penance. It's not as bad as adultery, but it's still wrong. However, you were tempted by evil. And you were far away from home, living a strange life. Young men who go far away and mix with strange companions are doubly tempted. So it wasn't as bad as it would have been here at home, even if it was wrong. So you will still have a penance.

"But more than that, you should think about getting married soon. As long as you are not married, you will have the temptations of fornication and adultery. And you know the church teaches you that the purpose of laying with a woman is to have children. That is a sacred responsibility. But to lay with a woman just for pleasure is a sin."

"Yes, Father."

"Do you have any plans for getting married?"

"No, Father. I just got back from the army two weeks ago."

"Alright. I'll give you your penance, which will be fifty Our Fathers and fifty Hail Marys and three Novenas. You can do those after Mass so you won't have to make a special trip to town.

"But you will have to be very careful now, my son. Because the temptation will be greater. And you should think about getting married as soon as you can so you can start bringing up a Catholic family."

"Yes, Father. Is that all?"

"Yes, my son." And he gave the closing blessing.

\* \* \* \* \*

Like many of the young men, Bruno left the country. After working in the cornfields of northern Indiana for a couple of years, he went to Indian City, where the money was.

He took what jobs he could get with a grade school education, living in boarding houses, along with the other young fellows from the country. And he married a country girl who had come to the city to work as a maid. His children came in due time, and Bruno supported them as a good Catholic father should.

* * * * *

Bruno was sitting at the kitchen table with a cup of coffee. Esther was working in front of the stove, frying bacon and boiling potatoes. She was getting heavier. She had been such a slim young woman when he met her, but as the children came along, Rosalie, Martin, Catherine, and Flora, Esther had put on weight. She wasn't really fat, but you couldn't call her thin either. But she was a hardworking woman, had been from the day he had married her. It stood to reason though, since she had also been raised on a farm.

She stopped for a minute and faced him, brushing some of the hair back from the front of her face. He had always liked her brown hair. She said, "How was work today?"

"It was alright. The customers really seem to like that new soft white bread. The women say the kids and husbands like it in their lunches."

How surprised they had been when he brought the new bread home the first time and squeezed it completely flat. It sprang right back up. It was helping sales, though nobody could buy very much then, right in the middle of the Depression.

"What made you come home late?"

"I met one of my old buddies from the war. We talked over old times. He's a hardware salesman now. Covers the southern part of the state, doing very good even in these times."

She took the potatoes off the stove and poured the water into the sink. She pulverized them with the hand masher. Her arms were quite strong even though they were getting just a little heavy. She said, "I'll make the gravy and we'll be ready. Rosalie can set the table."

"What else are we having?"

"There's cabbage slaw in the ice box, and I baked an apple pie."

He had told her very soon after they were married how much he liked apple pie, and she had fixed it as often as she could. "You want me to call Rosalie?" he said.

"No, wait a minute. I want to talk to you about Martin, and I don't want any of the other kids listening."

"What's the matter? Has Martin been doing something wrong?"

"Well, it's not exactly wrong, but I asked Father Flanagan about it, and he said we should watch the boy. And I think you ought to talk to him."

"What is it? What has he done?"

"Well, you know I told you about the public library. Martin goes over to use it so much now. He gets so many books he can hardly carry them home. And some of them are pretty strange. I think many are on the League of Decency list. I think he's got one about evolution—you know, the atheistic idea of men coming from monkeys. I don't know for sure, though, because he hides them."

Bruno frowned. "We'll see about that. I know Martin is a headstrong boy, but this is going to be a Catholic home, and no one is going to bring books here that the church is against."

I just think you ought to talk to him, Bruno. You know you have to bend the tree when it's young. He's only thirteen years old."

Bruno paused for a minute. The family was growing up. How long since he had been through the Great War and left the country. Since then he had come to the city, gotten married, and had four children. And Martin, the second, was getting big enough to go hunting. When Bruno wrote Bill about the Thanksgiving hunt, he would tell him that he would be bringing Martin along and ask them to have a .22 rifle for the boy.

Bruno said, "Should I call Rosalie to set the table now?"

"Yes, it's time. I'll fix the gravy."

They sat at the table the usual way, Bruno on one end, Esther at the other, two kids on each side. Martin sat next to Bruno. Rosalie and Esther got all the food on the table, then sat down. Bruno said, "You say the blessing, Martin."

The boy looked up. "I don't feel like it. Let Rosalie do it."

Bruno said, "Rosalie is helping fix the table. You do it." He didn't know what made the boy like that. Bruno would never have thought of contradicting Hans. He remembered that if he had, Hans's hard hand would be against the side of his head in a minute, making his ears ring. He had learned that it didn't even help to duck when Hans tried to hit you.

Martin said, "I don't like to say it, Pop. I don't know what it all means."

Bruno was getting mad. He could feel the blood racing in his head. He said, "You don't need to understand it all. That's the prayer for this house and as a Catholic boy, you'll say it, and when I tell you to. And I'm not telling you again."

Martin didn't answer right away. The room had become quiet. Bruno had to fight himself not to hit the boy. Esther said, "Now come on, Martin, do as your father tells you. You're holding up the meal."

Martin said, "Oh, alright. But I still don't understand it." He began, "Bless us, Our Lord, for these thy gifts..."

Esther passed the bacon and potatoes to Bruno. He helped himself and passed them to Martin. The other food started the rounds. When the meat plate got to Flora, she said loudly, "There's just one piece of bacon left and Martin has two pieces. I don't think that's fair."

Martin said, "I'm bigger than you and I'm a boy."

Bruno said, "Now you children quit that arguing. Martin, why don't you give her half of one of your pieces?"

The boy said, "I don't think it's fair because I'm bigger." But he cut one piece in two and forked one half to her plate.

She made a face.

Esther said, "I've got more than I need. Here, Martin, you take a piece." Then she said, "Now you kids just get on with your supper and quit fighting."

Everyone ate. Bruno took seconds of most things, washing the food down with coffee. When everyone was finished with the main course, Esther took the pie around, giving each a piece. It was as good as any Bruno could remember from the farm days, spiced with cinnamon. Esther cooked well. All the kids ate theirs, too.

Esther said, "Do you want another piece, Bruno? I have another in the oven, keeping it warm."

"Think I will," he said. "That was good apple pie. And as the man said, 'There ain't no pie but apple pie.'"

Catherine said, "Me too."

"If you kids want some more, you can have half a piece," Esther said while she was putting Bruno's on his dessert plate.

While eating his last, Bruno turned to Martin. "Your mother tells me you're reading a lot of books now."

"Um hmm."

"She also tells me that some are pretty peculiar, not the kind of books that people bring into a Catholic home." Martin didn't answer.

"Like she says that you got one on evolution, about monkeys changing into people. That right?"

Martin didn't look at his father directly, and mumbled, "I don't know."

Bruno was getting angry again. He just couldn't figure out what it was about the boy that got him that way so fast. He said, "What do you mean, you don't know? You either got the book or you ain't. I want you to tell me if you got it."

Martin quit eating and pushed himself back from the table. He said, "I guess so."

"Why do you read books like that? I can tell you that when I was a boy, we didn't bring books like that home."

Martin just sat there. He was getting more and more stubborn,, Bruno thought. The kids these days just didn't realize how much freedom they had. And they got harder to handle all the time. Bruno said, "Well, what you got to say for yourself?"

Finally Martin answered, "I don't know what Mom means. I just have a book about animals." Then he added, "She didn't even see it."

Esther said, "Why don't you get the book and show it to your father?"

Martin looked down and said with a slight whine, "I don't know why; I didn't do nothing. What's wrong with a book about animals?"

Bruno put his hand down hard on the table, not a blow exactly, but hard. "I'm just tired of this. I don't know why we can't have a meal in peace sometime. Always arguing about one thing or another. I don't want any books in this house that are against Catholic teaching. And Martin, if your mother says it's against the church, I want you to get rid of it. And I don't want any others like that brought in here again."

Bruno stood up and pushed the back door open. He walked through the grape arbor to the back where the chicken coop and vegetable garden were located. From inside the shed door he got the package of Mail Pouch from the top of the door beam. He wadded the twisted brown strips into a quid and put them into his mouth. As he chewed, the juice started to build up.

Esther had never liked his tobacco chewing. The farm men where she had grown up had done it too, but her father had not. And she always said it was so messy, especially in the city. In a way she was right. There just weren't the places to spit there were on the farm. Why, apart from the courthouse and a few other buildings, you couldn't find spittoons anywhere anymore. And Esther had never let one in their house.

She really didn't know how good it had been to have a quid in your mouth when you were out in a dusty field, hoeing corn all day. But of course she was right in saying that he wasn't working in the fields any more. Being a delivery man, he worked on paved streets all day, and he sure didn't have to work so hard as in the old days.

Bruno had a full mouth of juice by then, so he pursed his lips and squirted out a stream. It hit the bottom of a fence post, almost splattering a fly. Esther just didn't know how good the sweet, sharp taste of chewing tobacco was.

When he was finished, he spit the wad into a clump of weeds and headed toward the house. He stopped in front of the door, took out a stick of gum, unwrapped it, and put it into his mouth. At least with that he could go on chewing, but the taste sure wasn't the same.

* * * * *

Bruno sat in the easy chair, reading the sports page. It looked like the Cincinnati Reds really had a chance for the World Series, though the Brooklyn Dodgers were going to give them a hard time. He put the paper into his lap for a minute, thinking it was too bad Indian City didn't have a National League team. Then he could take Martin and maybe get him interested. That was one of the troubles with the boy, he never followed the sports. Always busy with those strange books. Anyway, Bruno figured he could take Martin over to Lincoln Park Sunday and they could watch the local game together. The boy didn't seem to mind that.

Esther sat in the other chair, darning socks. She always kept busy. Bruno watched how fast her fingers moved, pushing the needle in, then drawing the thread out. When she came to the end, she pulled the thread all the way out, tied it quickly and bit it off, starting right away on the next hole.

Bruno thought of her body then, the large tits, sagging a little since the four births. Her waist wasn't as narrow as it used to be either, and her legs were heavier too. But still it felt good to push into her until his juice came squirting out. He said, "I'm about ready to go to bed, Esther. How about you?"

She didn't look up right away. Then she said, "I'm not quite ready yet. I have all this mending to do. Why don't you just go on."

He wondered whether she really knew he wanted her to go with him, that he would like to lay with her. So he said, "I'd like you to go with me, Esther."

She kept mending, her eyes on her work. In a low voice she said, "I've got all this mending. The kids hardly have any socks to go to school with. You go ahead. I'll be there a little later." She added, "As soon as I'm finished with this."

He put the paper down alongside the chair. "Alright, I'll wait for you."

He walked up the stairs and into the bedroom to undress, leaving his B.V.D.s on. The room was clean and everything in place. Esther was a good housekeeper. After washing and shaving in the bathroom, he returned to the bedroom and climbed in bed without turning off the light.

He said his nightly prayers in bed, a habit he had kept from his army days. Sometimes he and Esther did them together and sometimes with the kids. But usually he did them by himself.

He lay in the smoothness of the bedclothes, thinking of Esther's warm body. His pecker started to harden. He put his hand on it and that made him think of the times long ago when Hans and the other farmers had taken the bulls' and stallions' peckers in their hands to help them. But that thought still bothered him. Despite all his praying and going to church, he still found it difficult to keep from thinking of animals and people as the same in many ways.

Bruno wondered why his thoughts wandered off in wrong directions so often. He went to church regularly, said all his prayers, and did all the things he had been taught when he was a child and still the temptations came often. Like even then wanting to lay with Esther. He knew he wanted it for the pleasure, not to make more children. He wanted to feel the hard squirt of juice into her body just for the feeling. And not only was he not trying to have more children, he had let Esther get that rubber thing from the doctor to prevent more. They had argued a lot about that and said many prayers, but Esther just wouldn't give up. She had told him that she wouldn't let him lay with her any more unless she could get the rubber thing. He knew where she kept it, on top of the medicine cabinet where the kids couldn't get to it. She called it a diaphragm. The church was against that, he knew for sure. They were both sinning. But still he didn't seem to be able to resist the temptation.

Bruno sat up. He couldn't sleep, his mind was so full of thoughts about women's bodies, laying together, temptation, and sin. And his pecker was still hard. He got out of bed and walked to the head of the stairs. He could see the dim light from where Esther must still be sitting. There was no sound from there nor from anywhere else in the house.

The kids were all in their rooms. Bruno called in a lowered voice, "Esther, do you want to come to bed now?"

No sound. He went down a few steps to where he could see her sitting. She was looking at him. He said, "Didn't you hear me?"

"Yes."

"Why didn't you answer?"

"I was going to. I was just trying to get the piece finished that I was working on."

"Won't you come to bed now?"

She looked very serious when she spoke, "Not tonight, Bruno, I don't feel very good. I think I'm getting the flu."

He stood there a moment, knowing that that was just an excuse. She was feeling sick much more lately. Ever since the last child was born, she had tried to get out of coming to bed with him more and more.

But maybe she was sick this time. She did look kind of peaked. Bruno said, "You ought to take something for it."

"I will."

He said, "Goodnight," and turned to go back to bed.

He got under the covers and rolled and tossed for a while, but went to sleep before she came.

\* \* \* \* \*

The Depression waned and another war came, again against the Germans. The war ended and the Germans lost again. Fortunately, nothing happened to Martin. The children grew up and went off to begin their own lives. Bruno worked at various delivery jobs, and Esther maintained the house for the two of them.

\* \* \* \* \*

Bruno had finished the deliveries and was eating his dinner before going off for the collections. He had the truck parked under a large elm toward the end of the route. It was quiet and cool there, only an occasional car or pedestrian passing. He reached back, got a quart of milk and took the top off. The company let him drink as much as he wanted so long as he saved the caps and left a little in the bottom of each bottle. He didn't know why they had rules like that, but he was just a delivery man. Anyway, the company provided everyone with good equipment. He had been the last to change from a horse and wagon to a truck five years before. You had to look hard to find a horse on the streets any more. Even down in the country they didn't have many any more. The whole country was changing to machines. That was what made progress. Why, even in the war they had just fought, everything had been machines. 'Course there had been machines in the Great War too, but nothing like the airplanes and ships and all the rest that Martin and the other servicemen had had to learn to use. But as they said, progress had to come.

Bruno opened his milk bottle and took a long swallow. Then he opened his lunch bucket. It had two meat sandwiches, a banana, and a piece of cake. He took out one of the sandwiches, unwrapped it and opened the two pieces of white bread. It was meat loaf, left over from the other night. Esther always was good at using leftovers. That had been a big help during the Depression, though it wasn't so necessary any more. He took a big bite.

A woman walked down the street, holding a dog on a leash. When she got near, Bruno recognized her as Mrs. Compton, one of his customers. She smiled as she passed. "Having your lunch, Mr. Neumann? I guess you get hungry after all those deliveries."

"Yah, Mrs. Compton, this is one of the best parts of the work."

"Hope you enjoy it." She continued on.

When he had eaten the two sandwiches, he had almost finished the bottle of milk. Should he have another? It wouldn't cost anything just so long as he saved a part of it. A pretty good company, he thought. The bread company had not allowed anything like that. You were responsible for every loaf you took out, and the checking had been very careful. He decided and took another bottle to have with the cake. It was chocolate, one of his favorites. Since the Depression had ended, Esther's cooking had become better and better. Bruno patted his stomach. He had started a little pot a few years back. He knew it was Esther's rich cooking.

Bruno finished off his dinner and put the wax papers back into his lunch bucket. Then he lit his pipe. He had started that when he had given up chewing tobacco completely. Esther had found him chewing a couple of times in the back yard and convinced him to quit altogether. In a way, it was better, he thought. He still had chewing gum. He took a couple of deep draws and checked his customers' book, putting a marker in the Masterson page. He started the motor.

Mrs. Masterson answered the door quickly and, after getting her purse, paid in full. He really didn't have much trouble on that route, not like over near the tracks where all the Kentuckians lived. Here the customers were mostly honest and reliable people. Mrs. Masterson ordered an extra bottle of chocolate daily in future deliveries.

Bruno went to the next, Mrs. Eva Golden. She was a widow who had lost her husband during the war. She told Bruno that he had been an officer in the navy and his ship had been sunk by a submarine. Bruno knocked on the door. No one came right away. He knocked again. A dog barked, and footsteps approached the door. It opened and the woman stood there, a German shepherd at her side. It barked once but didn't act very mean. She said, "Now King, that's enough. Stop that barking. It's the nice milk man."

The dog began wagging its tail. She said, "King isn't really a mean dog, but I keep him here because I'm all alone and he barks. It makes me feel better."

"I can see that it ain't a mean dog," Bruno said. She was wearing a long house dress that opened at the bottom when she walked. He could see one of her legs through the open flap. He quickly turned to his collection book. "Let's see, Mrs. Golden, your bill for this month is eight dollars and sixty cents."

She said, "I'll have to go get my purse. Why don't you come in and wait? It's windy out here." She held the door open, and Bruno could just barely see the beginning of her tits at the top of her dress.

"Alright," he said and entered the house. The dog sniffed his legs and wagged its tail. Then it flopped onto the floor. Mrs. Golden retrieved her purse in the rear of the house.

"Why don't you sit down?" she said. "You can do it easier that way. Maybe you'd like a cup of coffee."

The coffee sounded good after his lunch. Since he had started with the milk company, he had stopped bringing coffee in his lunch bucket, drinking milk instead. "Alright," he said. "That sounds good." He sat down on the couch and started to write out a receipt. She set her purse down and left the room again.

She brought the coffee on a little tray, along with cups, spoons, and cream and sugar containers. On another dish she had a couple of pieces of strudel. "I thought you might like something sweet with your coffee," she said.

As she walked toward him, her dress opened at each step, and he could see her legs almost up to the knees. They weren't as heavy as Esther's had become. She sat down on the couch and poured the coffee.

Bruno had thought she would sit on one of the easy chairs across the room. Her nearness made him a little nervous. He didn't look at her because he knew that if he did, he would be tempted to look at the front of her housecoat. He kept his eyes down while he drank his coffee.

"Don't you want to try a piece of the strudel?" she asked.

"I guess I'm pretty full, Mrs. Golden. I just finished eating."

"For a hardworking man like you, I would think you'd need to eat a lot. I'll bet your wife feeds you good, doesn't she?"

"She cooks good."

"I'm pretty good too," she said. "Though of course I don't have a man to cook for now. But Harry used to always say he liked my cooking. I made the strudel. Why don't you try a piece?"

Bruno looked at her then and, just as he had feared, his eyes went to the top of her housecoat. He was almost certain that it was more open than before, that another button was undone. He could see the beginning roundness of her tits. They didn't seem to sag. When he lifted his eyes, hers met his and she smiled. He blushed because he knew she had seen him look. He reached immediately for a piece of the strudel, saying, "I'll try it. It sure looks good."

After that, Bruno was very careful to keep his eyes away from her. He ate the cake fast, washing it down with coffee. Then he took up his account book and said, "I guess I'd better make the collection and be on my way. I have a lot of customers to see this morning."

She didn't reach for her purse, instead saying, "I bet you're not in that much of a hurry. You look to me like a man who can get his work done quickly. And here I am all alone. When you leave, I won't have anything to do but clean the house."

Bruno started to get nervous again. He said, "I know, Mrs. Golden, but I do have to be on my way."

"Alright." She reached for her purse and got out the money. When she handed it to him, she let her hand stay for a second on his. He looked up and she was looking at him, smiling. He pulled his hand away, not so fast to hurt her feelings, but fast enough that he could get away quickly. He put the money in his collection purse even without putting the bills in their proper order, then stood up. "I've got to be on my way," he said. "I think it's getting late."

He felt sure she knew how nervous he was, but he couldn't help it. The temptation was too much. It made him think of that time more than thirty years before when he had lay with the French girl, the only time he had fornicated. He could never forget it, though by this time he figured he had gotten it off his soul through penance. But Mrs. Golden was taking him down the same path. He couldn't trust himself to stay any longer. He was still too weak, he knew, even after all those years and all the prayers.

She said, "You don't really need to hurry on my account, Mr. Neumann, but I guess you know your business. You just remember you are welcome any morning." She added in a low voice, "I like you, Bruno."

As he was hurrying down the sidewalk, he felt a great weight lifting from his shoulders. He had lived through the temptation without falling. But he also knew that he would have to get her transferred to another carrier. It was a good thing she lived just on the end of the route; he could probably get Jimmy Hendrickson to take her.

\* \* \* \* \*

Times got better. Bruno and Esther learned to live alone. Not much occurred except that Bruno worked, changing jobs again when he got older, while Esther continued to keep house. Then he could no longer work.

\* \* \* \* \*

Bruno lay back on his pillow, looking at the picture of Jesus on the far wall. He thought he should tell Esther when they were alone to arrange to have one of the priests over for his Confession and Communion. He had had too many blackouts by then to count on having much time left. Dr. Jones was a good doctor, but how could he help if it was really Bruno's time? At least, Bruno thought, he had better medical help than Hans had when he suffered his strokes.

Bruno heard the girls talking to Esther downstairs. Probably she was giving them coffee. Then their voices became louder. They were coming upstairs. Rosalie and Catherine entered the sick room. Esther had put him there when they brought him back from the hospital the last time, she staying in their old bedroom. The doctor thought it would be best for him to be in bed alone while he was sick. Before the last strokes, Bruno had still liked to be in bed with Esther, even though she had become quite heavy. And she didn't mind as long as they didn't lay together.

Both girls gave him a kiss on the cheek. "Ugh," Catherine said. "You're so scratchy. You need a shave, Dad."

He waved his hand weakly. "That's how it goes when you get old and sick."

"Dad, you're not so old. You're only fifty-nine. Old age doesn't start until you're in your sixties or seventies. And everyone gets sick. You have to think positive. You're going to get well. Why, all of us have to go to Florida again, to catch some of those big ones. Mom's ahead of you on size, you know."

Bruno realized then that he had not been thinking of doing any fishing or anything else in the future since the last strokes. It almost seemed to him that he was preparing to die. But there was no reason to make the kids feel sad. He said, "Yah, I guess so. But what's the reason for shaving?"

"It'll make you feel better. And then you'll look better. Besides, do you want all your women scratching themselves when they give you a kiss?"

Rosalie spoke, "I'll shave you, Dad, while I'm here today. I do it all the time for patients in the hospital. I'm pretty good at it."

"Alright," he said. "You girls win."

"How are you feeling?" Catherine asked.

"Oh, I'm alright so long as I stay on the medicine, I guess."

"You got to do that," Rosalie said. "That's very important. I talked to Dr. Jones yesterday and he said he had seen complete recoveries of people who had much worse strokes than you did."

Bruno was used to them by this time. They would say anything to make him feel better. They were good girls, but he didn't believe them. These things were what healthy people always said to sick ones. He said, "How are the kids? I miss seeing them. You know how a grandpa is, he wants to see his grandchildren all the time."

"Oh, they're okay." Rosalie said. "I just didn't bring them with me because the doctor said you needed all the quiet you could get."

"The same with me, Dad," Catherine said. "You know how my brood is. They'd be into some kind of trouble before you knew it. Clark and Gary wanted to come, but I told them they'd have to wait until you were feeling better."

"Why don't you girls sit down?" Esther said. "I've got to get Bruno's medicine. Just make yourself comfortable."

"Okay, Mom," Rosalie said. "And while you're at it, could you bring Dad's shaving stuff? I've got to leave in no more than an hour. I'm on the afternoon shift this week."

"Me too," Catherine said. "I've got to be back when the kids come home from school."

When Esther was gone, Catherine turned to Bruno. "Are you feeling weak or depressed, Dad?"

He looked at her, "I'm alright I guess, considering. I do feel very weak. And I can't do much now. It doesn't make a person feel good."

"You got to be very positive about it, Dad. You have to be convinced you're going to get well. You know, mind over matter."

He didn't answer. He didn't want to hurt Catherine's feelings, and she was trying to help, but he didn't want to lie either, especially then. But he really didn't think he was going to get well. The last series of strokes had been just too much. And whatever the medical people did, his blood pressure never really came down. He just smiled.

Rosalie spoke, "Mom just told us the good news about Martin." Bruno smiled openly about that. It was the best thing that had happened. He said, "Yah, he's coming day after tomorrow, and bringing his little boy along. I'm glad Mom called him."

Catherine said, "I'm glad too. I just never could understand how you and Mom could do that. Almost three years, and he tried, you know, and you and Mom just sent the letters back. Why, he's your only son. And you always knew how headstrong he was."

"I guess it wasn't so good what we did. We both always liked Martin. But he got on the wrong track somewhere, and there didn't seem like there was anything else we could do. I guess it was all that college education he got that made him so atheistic. I still don't know what that 'anthropology' is except that it's about how people are descended from monkeys. I guess we could have put up with a lot of that, but when he refused to have his son baptized, me and Esther decided we had to do something. We talked it over with the priest, you know. And he said it was alright to stop answering his letters or visiting him."

Catherine said indignantly, "I just can't believe some of these priests. Those old parish priests, like Father Flanagan, sure don't know anything about psychology. To tell you not to write your own son. I just don't know. Sometimes I think that even if some of the beliefs are right, those old-fashioned priests are enough to drive you out of the church."

Bruno smiled again. "Well anyway, that's patched up. And I'll be very glad to see him after all this time. I hear tell he's a big professor now. I guess I'm not too surprised when I remember all those books he used to read when he was little." He grinned at the thought. "He never did learn mathematics good like I always told him to. But I guess he can get along without it in his work."

After the girls had gone home, including Flora who had come later, Bruno lay quietly. They were good daughters, he thought. They had been restless when they were young, but all had finally settled down and married Catholic boys and began to raise their own families.

Things had changed so much since he had left the farm, but some things seemed to be like in the old days. People still married and raised families. All but Martin. He had always been different. They had tried to teach him but he just would not give in. Oh well, he was still a good boy and beginning his own family even if his wife wasn't Catholic. Maybe someday he would come back to the church. At least they would get to see him again. Bruno was very pleased at that thought.

Esther walked into the room. "Are you about ready to have the light out? Or would you like me to fix you a hot chocolate before you go to sleep?"

"I guess you can turn it off. I don't feel like looking at the paper any more."

"Okay. You know you need all the rest you can get." She flicked the wall switch and the overhead light went off. She stopped in the doorway, her heavy body framed by the hall light. She gazed long at him then said, "Sure there's nothing else I can get you?"

"No Esther, I'm fine."

She turned and went back downstairs.

# CHAPTER 3

Oldenberg was on the phone when Martin entered the office. Without putting his hand over the mouthpiece, he said, "Just sit down, I'll be right with you."

Martin sat in the chair next to the desk. Though Oldenberg's mouth was moving, there was no audible sound. Probably another of the futuristic electronic gadgets which seemed to be so commonplace there, Martin thought.

The plump man smiled a couple of times, then seemed to laugh, although that too was inaudible. Finally, he placed the phone back on the cradle. "One of my colleagues," he said. "He has a particularly difficult type, a very orthodox person who keeps insisting that the situation be cut and dried. This Transitionee is sure he deserves to go directly to heaven, and my colleague is telling him it's not that simple."

Oldenberg paused. "You'd be surprised at the arguments some people put up. They have been so deeply conditioned by their various cult leaders that they find it impossible to make the slightest modification of their ideas of the afterworld. Of course, we manage to bring them around after awhile. But my colleague, Steward, is new as a Transition Master and doesn't know many gambits yet. He'll be okay, but in the meantime I give him helpful hints when he's in difficulty."

Martin said, "This operation is certainly very interesting. I just can't get out of my mind the facility of using your Life Tape system. It makes me want to see all kinds of lives."

Oldenberg leaned back in his chair. "I take it then that your viewing came off satisfactorily. Genevieve work out alright?"

"Oh yes, everything was fine. I stuck to the one tape, my father. There were a few parts about which I knew something, but most I had not shared, of course."

"No problem with the mechanics?"

"No, I experimented with the scanner for a couple of hours, then could handle it with no difficulty. I found the speed control a most useful device to pass up most of the detailed events. I'm afraid I only looked at seven or eight scenes at normal life speed with all sensory input controls on. The others I let flicker by rapidly."

"I suspected you'd pick up that habit quickly. After all, even though time here is practically limitless, one still gets bored, and the real fact is that many parts of most lives are repetitious. It's almost inevitable that a viewer will pick out a few scenes for concentration."

Oldenberg reached for a bowl of candy and pushed it toward Martin. "Have a mint," he said.

Martin took one, unwrapped it, and popped it into his mouth.

Oldenberg said, "Well, did you find out anything interesting?"

"I guess the main thing I noticed was that my father was a pretty sexual man, what has come to be known by the most recent generation of our people as 'horny'. But he kept it under pretty strict control. So far as I could make out, he only slipped once. Even so, he carried a lot of guilt feelings throughout his life. Because of his religious beliefs and early training, he was a very moral guy. In those days they were taught that the only reason for sex relations was to have babies. To sleep together just for pleasure was considered immoral. Of course, things were changing even then, and it didn't exactly work like that, but the religious teachings did load a guy up with guilt feelings."

Oldenberg tapped the desk with a pencil, his eyes twinkling. "Well, Martin, what do you think about that idea? What do you think sexual relations should be for?"

"I confess that I operated through most of my life with the idea that sex should provide pleasure, like eating or evacuating. After all, the sensation is usually pleasant, at least for the male, isn't that so?"

"Yes, I think that's approximately correct," Oldenberg answered.

Martin continued, "I always thought the pleasure principle was built into the sex drive as a biological imperative, without which insemination would rarely take place."

"Yes, I would agree with that too, that if animals, including your own species, had not had the drive to inseminate one another, they would of course have died out. But even so, you must recognize that the pleasure principle need exist in only one sex."

"I do, I do. And I had never realized it so clearly as I did on Bruno's life tape in the scene when he witnessed the copulation of chickens.

There is little doubt that the insemination takes place through a relationship that in human terms can only be called rape. The rooster forces himself on the hen."

Oldenberg chuckled like a beneficent professor. Then he said, "Of course, nowadays the technology of your own species has come to the point where you really don't need bodily insemination any more. Artificial insemination is being used more and more by animal breeders, and though I know there is a lot of hullabaloo among your theologians, legalists, and academics about the morality of the issue, I suspect it will only be a matter of time before artificial insemination will be the norm among humans also. After all, from the point of view of breeding, it is considerably more efficient."

Martin supported his head in his hands, in a thinking posture. "Yes, I would have to agree that for reproduction the sex drive is hardly important any more, at least among *Homo* and the creatures he breeds. But I really didn't think much about the biological aspects of the sex drive before, at least not so far as my own actions were concerned. I'm sure it must be in my records somewhere, but you may be aware of it anyway, Mr. Oldenberg, that I produced only one child, and during the last thirty years of my life, my tubes had been cut surgically to prevent insemination. I was obviously primarily concerned with pleasure so far as the sex act was concerned."

"Ah yes," Oldenberg said, rubbing his pencil against his cheek. "You people in the technologically advanced nations have cut back more and more on your family size and resorted more and more to either chemical or surgical inhibitors to insemination. But you see, it wasn't quite the same in the old days. You came from a family of four children, which was already a reduction in size from the previous generation. I believe your mother was using one of those crude mechanical devices that women resorted to before the pill came along. But not your grandmother, remember. She had either eleven or twelve children, I believe. And that means it was unlikely that she took any measures to prevent births. I could look it up on her Life Tape, but I don't think it really matters that much."

"True, true. The thing that bothers me though, is that if the sex drive evolved solely for reproduction, how come there is so much disappointment and frustration involved with it? After all, even though Bruno would have worked to support all the children he would get, the poor guy was largely disappointed sexually throughout his life, even with his wife. And from others he was cut off by his moral code. It almost seems that the system has evolved to produce frustration, and perhaps even unhappiness."

Oldenberg heaved a large sigh. "Well, we are going to be discussing this whole issue of happiness further, I'm sure. But I think that for the time being it is well for you to remember that existence is the prime consideration in the Sentience System, not whether creatures get great joy out of life. As you may imagine, emotional states such as joy or happiness as ends in themselves are creations of your mentalists. I believe the people among you who make their living just by thinking, philosophers I think you call them, have had a big hand in it."

"Admittedly, we in the Sentience System recognize that attitudes exist among living creatures, but we consider them as instrumental only. Creatures are happy or unhappy only because the particular feeling helps perpetuate that form of life. Thus, one of the predators such as the lion is hungry when it has not eaten for several days. Its hungriness, which is undoubtedly more frequent than fullness, is a kind of unhappiness. And to get rid of its unhappiness, the animal goes out to hunt. Killing and eating the flesh of another animal makes it happy for a brief time, but from the point of view of the System, it simply enables the animal to continue and perhaps to breed. Thus, with the sexual urge, creatures become dissatisfied when they don't couple, which drives them to couple, and in the old days this resulted in reproduction. The pleasure or happiness, as you wish to call it, was only a means of achieving an end in the System."

Oldenberg paused but then capped his mini-lecture, saying, "I must say that this idea is by no means something that exists only among us Systemicists. You have had speculators and theorists among your own people who have figured it out more or less. Probably the best known was your Charles Darwin."

"Yes, I recognize much of what you say from my own studies. The ironic part of it all is that I never really applied a lot of what I learned academically to my own personal life. And I guess I continued almost to the very end thinking that pleasure and happiness were ends in themselves."

"Don't feel bad. You are in good company. You humans seem to be able, far more than most creatures, to maintain multiple ways of considering the same information. Consistency has never been a strong point among members of your species."

Martin sighed. "Ah yes, we even developed a name for it—compartmentalization."

Oldenberg started scribbling absently on a pad. He said, "I have a committee meeting in a few minutes but we still have a little time. Is there anything else you wanted to comment on?"

"There are a couple of other things and then I'll be on my way also. One is that I noticed that despite the frustration from lack of sexual fulfillment, my father actually seemed to have had a fairly satisfactory family life. I was a pain in the neck to him and to my mother, but generally he seemed to enjoy most of his relationships, both in his family of orientation and in that of his procreation. And above all else, I noticed that he never really had long periods of aloneness. The only real such time was his army years, though even there he cultivated a lot of buddies. Otherwise he seemed to be with people who loved him to the very end. Perhaps this strikes me so forcefully because I have been aware of the long periods of solitude in my own life. I had a feeling that his life was the way it was supposed to be somehow, despite the frustrations. After all, we as a species are supposed to live in groups, not alone, are we not?"

Oldenberg said, "There's no doubt about that. In his time, the family was still functioning well. And though we in the System are hardly concerned with the amount of satisfaction that individual creatures get from their lives, most of us agree that satisfied animals tend to perpetuate themselves better than dissatisfied ones. And, for better or worse, the social system called the family seems to have provided a maximum degree of satisfaction. One of the things that you may have noticed is that divorce was not a consideration then, no matter how much frustration occurred."

"Yes, I don't think it was ever discussed or considered as a possibility. But of course Bruno's religion forbade it."

Oldenberg laughed gently. "That's true so far as a particularistic explanation is concerned. But the real fact is that until recent times, no matter what religion, divorce was not common among most people. It has only become so common with the emphasis on individualism and the growth of urbanization. As you know, when such happens, people don't really want large families any more; and when they don't, they don't really care strongly if they stay married or not."

Evidently Martin's face lit up then because Oldenberg smiled and asked, "What did you just think of?"

"I just had an idea in this regard. From my own family experience, I could come up with an interesting generalization. The degree of viability of the family is directionally proportionate to the number of children and the degree of use of birth control. Also, whether the family lived in the city or country seemed to have been important. Thus, my grandparents who lived in the country had twelve children, and all evidence is that they practiced no birth control. My parents, who were raised in the country but moved to the city in their lifetime, had four children, and then my mother began using birth control. I, on the other hand, was born in the city, used birth control from the beginning, yet had one child, but then in my middle years had an operation that prevented any future impregnations. Martin laughed softly. "I suppose many of the next generation will have no children and will have an operation even before their first sex act. Does that sound reasonable?"

Oldenberg smiled in agreement just as a good professor should, Martin thought, giving encouragement to his student researcher for the slightest originality. Probably Oldenberg was perfectly aware of those correlations. Anyway, Oldenberg said, "Well, certainly the fact that people have smaller families is correlated with the use of birth control. Also that people in your technologically advanced societies are going that way has been documented by legions of your social statisticians, sociologists I think you call them. And, as you know, several of the most highly industrialized societies have come to a no-growth rate, which of course means that quite a few people are having no children. Of course, a society that doesn't reproduce itself at all is going to die out. I believe there have been a few such among your people. One which I recall is the Shakers. I remember quite a number of Shaker Transitionees in the eighteenth century who were all recruits to the cult. But when they stopped taking in new blood from outside and continued to forbid sexual reproduction, the numbers dwindled fast. I believe there are six to ten adherents still surviving.

"But apart from such deviant groups, heterosexual coupling has continued enough for societies to at least reproduce themselves. And I guess until artificial insemination is accepted generally by your species, the sex drive will remain as the basic force for reproduction."

"Okay," Martin said. "I think that's all I need to talk about now. Seeing my father's life has opened a number of new vistas to me. But the one thing I wondered about throughout was how the woman's side was working. In that era it was thought that the woman's needs were frequently sacrificed for the benefit of the male. At least that is the basic idea of the women's liberation groups that have become so vociferous since the 1980s. Of course, this idea too is tied up with the concept of individual happiness, which you indicated was not of paramount importance in the operation of the Sentience System. But I suppose, apart from what light viewing my mother's mating pattern might throw on my ideas, I do have a personal interest. I know more about her than most other females, but also I was largely conditioned by her. And the attraction of seeing life through the eyes of someone of the opposite sex is great indeed. I'm sure you can imagine that, knowing my social science background. Anyway, do you think it would be okay to view Esther's life?"

Oldenberg grinned again. He obviously found much of this interesting. "Of course, you must realize that doing such a thing will violate one of your most deeply entrenched human prohibitions, the incest taboo. You won't be involved directly, of course, but as I understand it, you humans have evolved the idea that even indirect participation is improper, that is, watching the acts."

That stopped Martin for a minute, but not for long. After all, even when he had been alive, he had never been thoroughly committed to human systems, probably a consequence of his inclination toward the biological sciences. Certainly the idea of incest had not been a powerful emotional no-no, even though he had never been involved in any act with a female relative. But even so, the drive to see what happened to his mother was too much to resist. He said, "I don't think it will bother me. After all, you know we anthropologists have long been known as peepers, in sexual activities as well as others. I still recall from my student days the definition of a Navaho family—that's a good-sized Indian group we have in the southwestern United States. It was said to have been made up of a husband, wife, and children, and an anthropologist under the bed."

Oldenberg chuckled.

Martin continued. "In any event, the incest taboo couldn't be operative here, could it? After all, this is the afterworld, or better put probably, the otherworld. And we are all dead, or nonexistent somehow, my mother as well as me. Surely, it won't matter now, will it?"

"No, I didn't say it would. I merely mentioned that fact because it seemed interesting. No, I think it will be perfectly feasible for you to view your mother's life next."

With that, Oldenberg stood up. "I'm going to have to leave you now. If you need help, I can buzz Genevieve. Okay?"

"Sure, that's fine. I can find my way back, no sweat. Shall I check back after I've viewed her life?"

"By all means. I'll be interested in your reaction."

They left together.

# ESTHER

Myriads of long-tailed tadpoles whipped themselves through fluid toward a pulsating globule. One managed to enter and was quickly engulfed. The fetus that would be the woman who would be the mother of Martin, Esther Schleimer, began to grow. Birth, infancy, and young childhood flickered by. Esther grew bigger, first living in the country, then moving to a small town, soon joined by her sister, Marie, going to school, helping her mother at home, and playing on the street by her father's brickyard.

\* \* \* \* \*

Esther sat on a pile of bricks, looking worried. Marie skipped by with a jump rope. "Come on, let's go play."

Esther didn't answer.

Marie said, "What's the matter, cat got your tongue?"

"Oh, be quiet. You just go on."

Instead Marie stopped to gaze at her sister. "Esther, why are you acting so funny? I didn't do nothing. Are you sick or something?"

How could Esther tell her younger sister; how could she tell anyone since she didn't even know what it was herself?

This was the third day, and the pain and blood were worse. Marie couldn't help. Maybe no one could, except God, or maybe the Virgin Mary.

Marie was still standing there, looking at her. "Come on, we got time before Pa comes home for dinner. Why don't you get up?"

How could she tell her sister that she might start dripping blood again, that the pad she had put there might slip again or get soaked and begin running through? Oh, Jesus, Mary, if it would only go away. If not, there didn't seem to be any way out but to tell her mother. But then what? If she was dying, she really didn't want to know it. And if it was something bad, her mother might punish her. Her mother might even tell Pa. She could just see the angry expression on his face as he came toward her with the switch. Finally, she said, "I'm alright, Marie. You just go on and play. I don't feel like it."

But Marie was stubborn. She just stood there and said, "No, I'm not going without you. I think something's wrong. And I want you to tell me or I'm going back to tell Ma. I'm your sister, ain't I?"

Then Esther couldn't hold back any more. She started weeping. Marie put her arm around her sister's neck. "Tell me what it is, Esther. Maybe it's not so bad as you think."

She blurted out, "I'm bleeding."

Silence, then, "What do you mean? I don't see nothing."

"I'm bleeding from my bottom. It's the second time and it hurts and I just don't know what to do."

"Oh my gosh. You ought to go tell Ma. Probably you should go to a doctor. I'll go back with you."

"I'm afraid to. You know how Ma and Pa are if it's anything about the bottom. I'm afraid she'll think I did something and she'll tell Pa and he'll take the switch to me."

Marie tried to wipe the tears from her sister's face with the hem of her skirt. "Oh dear, oh dear. But we've got to do something. You might really be sick."

Esther sniffled. Marie said suddenly, "I know, we'll go over and talk to Mrs. Bergmann. She told us to come over any time we needed to ask anything. And she doesn't seem so nervous about talking about bottom things. We won't even have to tell Ma. It wouldn't be a bad thing to talk to her, would it?"

"I don't think so. It's just that Ma and Pa don't like her very much. They say she and her husband don't go to church very often. And I never seen them there."

"Well, we just won't have to tell Ma we went there."

Esther tried to adjust her bloomers, concerned about the pad inside. Marie wiped Esther's face again and took her hand. They walked up the street to the Bergmann house.

"Let's go around the back," Esther said. "I don't want anyone to see us."

"I don't care."

Marie knocked on the door. A youngish-looking woman answered. Her skirt only came halfway down from her knees. To Esther she was the prettiest woman in that part of town. The woman said, "Oh, Esther and Marie, my two favorite girls. How are you?"

Marie answered, "Oh, we're fine, Mrs. Bergmann, thank you. How are you?"

"I'm fine. But Esther looks so serious. Are you alright too, Esther?"

"Yes ma'am." She tried to smile. "Could we come inside a minute?"

"Why sure, girls." She opened the door and stood to one side.

They stopped just inside the door. Esther wouldn't dare go inside someone's house without being asked.

As if reading Esther's mind, the woman said, "Why don't you come into the parlor and I'll get you both a glass of lemonade and some cookies?" She walked ahead and showed them where they could sit, her skirt swishing.

When she had gone into the kitchen, Esther whispered to Marie, "Oh, I wish we didn't come. I feel so scared. What if she tells Ma?"

"Don't worry so much. I don't think she'd do anything like that. And you have to do something, Esther."

Mrs. Bergmann brought back lemonade and cookies on a tray. She gave each of the girls a glass and passed the plate of cookies. Sitting down, she said, "That should make you feel better. You look so worried, Esther."

"Thank you ma'am." Esther took one and began to nibble on it.

All three sat for a while, sipping from their glasses and munching the cookies. Finally, Mrs. Bergmann broke the silence. "You girls are so serious today. Why aren't you out playing? You're not like this usually. Did you come over to tell me something?"

Esther kept her eyes focussed on the glass in her hand. Marie looked toward Mrs. Bergmann. "We did. We're kind of scared, Mrs. Bergmann. Something happened, something bad. And we're scared to tell our Ma."

Esther was so nervous she was twisting the end of her belt. She also kept shifting around, worrying that blood would ooze out on her dress or on the chair.

Mrs. Bergmann said, "It's alright to tell me if you want."

Marie answered again. "Probably Esther should tell, but I think she's afraid because it happened to her." She paused, but when no one said anything, continued. "So I'll tell, even if it's about her. We decided to come together, so I think it's alright."

Then she gushed it out. "Esther's got something wrong with her bottom. She's bleeding and her stomach hurts and she doesn't know what to do. We thought you might know if it was some kind of sickness or something."

Esther felt so ashamed she could crawl. The only thing that kept her there was her fear that there was something bad wrong. Mrs. Bergmann answered right away. "Esther, how old are you?"

"Thirteen, ma'am."

"Have you had this bleeding before?"

"Yes ma'am, one time. It was several weeks ago though, and I ain't had nothing since."

The woman came over to sit alongside the girl, putting her arm on her shoulder. "I guess nobody ever told you about periods, did they?

Your mother or anyone else?" She sighed. "Oh my, oh my, when will it all end? You poor dear, no wonder you're so frightened. No one ever told you anything. Well, you don't have to worry, you're not sick, I mean not in the way you think. You're just starting your monthly periods. All girls begin that about when they get to your age."

Esther looked at her then. "You mean I'm not going to die, or anything?"

"No, not from that. You don't even need to go to a doctor."

"But I'm bleeding, more this time than the last. Won't that hurt me?"

"No, it won't. It's not fun, but it won't hurt you in the long run. In fact, it's a part of making babies." But then she hesitated. "I guess you don't know anything about that either, do you?"

Marie, who had been listening attentively, commented, "I know where babies come from. My friend, Margie, told me. They grow inside your stomach and they come out your belly button."

Mrs. Bergmann smiled. "Well, that's not exactly right. They do grow inside the woman, but they don't come out through the navel. They come from the same place where Esther's bleeding now."

"Will I bleed like that too?" Marie asked.

"Yes, you'll start in two or three years."

Mrs. Bergmann patted Esther on the shoulder. "What did you do about soaking up the blood, Esther? If no one told you anything, what did you use?"

Esther looked down again, still twisting the end of her belt. She answered without raising her eyes. "I didn't want Ma to find out, so I was careful. But I got some old towels from where she wouldn't notice. I folded them and put them inside my bloomers."

"Oh, you poor dear. There's some regular pads you can buy. They're called sanitary pads. There's also a little belt that holds them up. I think you're going to have to talk to your mother about that. Then she can buy you some."

"We don't have much money. Pa is sick a lot and can't make enough bricks. And he has to buy medicine. Besides, I'm afraid to tell Ma about it."

Mrs. Bergmann said, "But it's alright, Esther. You didn't do anything wrong. This happens to all women. But if it still bothers you, I can come down and talk to your mother."

Esther spoke quickly then, "Oh no, I don't think you should do that. She wouldn't like you to tell her, I think."

Then Marie blurted out, "We didn't tell her we were coming here.

My Ma and Pa think you and your husband are not real good because you don't go to church all the time."

The woman stood back then. "Ah yes, I understand. Your mother and father are very religious, aren't they?"

"Yes, we're good Catholics," Marie said. "We even have one sister, Harriet, who's studying to be a nun."

"Okay, I won't tell them. But one of you is going to have to, and soon. The periods will be coming every month." She reached for the glasses. "Do either of you want some more lemonade?"

"No ma'am," Esther said and stood up. Marie did the same and said, "I think we'll go now, if we can be excused."

When they were in front of the house, Marie said, "Aren't you glad we went there? Now you know you're not going to die."

"She was nice," Esther answered. "Don't you think it's funny that someone who doesn't go to church can be so nice?"

"I guess so." Marie started to pull her jump rope out of her dress pocket where she had coiled it before they went into the house. "Do you want to go play now?"

"No, I don't feel like it. Also, I think it's time to get home to help Ma with dinner. Pa will be home soon."

"Well, I'm going down to play for awhile. I'll go on the next street though so Pa don't see me on his way home."

"All right, but don't stay too long. You know how mad Pa gets if we're not both there on time."

Esther turned and started walking toward their house, her face still worried. It would be so difficult to tell her mother. There was no thought of telling her father. She was sure she couldn't do it when she first got home. Her mother would be working too hard getting dinner ready. Then when her father got home, she wouldn't do it for fear of getting him mad. Perhaps after dinner, she thought, when she was in the kitchen washing the dishes while Marie and her mother were putting things away. She decided to say a couple of Hail Marys before she got home.

\* \* \* \* \*

Esther finished grammar school. Not too long afterward, she started working cleaning other peoples' houses. Then she got a job in the shirt factory, which paid more.

\* \* \* \* \*

She was a pretty girl in her late teens, her figure good, thin at the waist but full at the bust. Her hips were just a little heavy. She had attractive brown hair, a little longer than most girls her age.

She bent over the machine, rapidly sewing the sleeves to the body of each shirt, throwing each into the basket for the following seamstress and then beginning on the next. It was tiresome, monotonous work. She did the same thing day after day for ten hours. But at least it paid more than housework. And what else could you do in Leschamps? There weren't any other factories. Pa had been getting worse and worse, and there just wasn't enough to keep the house going. Her mother even took in washing to keep them going.

All of a sudden she felt the closeness of another person. She turned her head, and just next to her was Fletcher, the foreman. His face was just behind and to one side of hers and his arm was behind her back, the hand on the work area of the sewing machine. He was so close she jerked. A strong odor of cigarette smoke came from him. He grinned, "How's it going, Esther? Keeping up to rate?"

They worked on a piece rate, and she got paid for the number she got sewn. If there were too few, she would lose her job.

"Sure, Mr. Fletcher. I been sewing a long time, I can keep up."

He reached down and picked up one of the shirt pieces, saying, "This looks like it'll pass. You do pretty well, Esther. Doesn't look like you'll have to find another job right away."

She kept moving the seams under the punching needle, keeping her eyes down. She had to be careful with him, she knew; he was always after the sewing girls.

He stood up and took out a pack of cigarettes. He was one of the first men she knew who smoked ready-mades all the time. "I'd offer you one, Esther, but I know you don't smoke. You don't have any bad habits, do you?"

"No, I just do my work and go home."

"Don't you ever go out? I know some good places to go. And I could take you in my new Ford. How'd you like that?"

"I don't think so. I'm pretty busy at home and work, Mr. Fletcher. My Pa isn't very well, and I have to help my Ma."

"Well, you're not going to waste all those good looks just taking care of your folks, are you? You must have some time to go out." He put his hand on her shoulder.

She stiffened, wondering whether she should excuse herself to go to the toilet. She shouldn't make him mad, but she knew she couldn't go out with him. Her parents would never let that happen. He wasn't even

Catholic. She said, "No, Mr. Fletcher, thanks, but I don't have any extra time."

He didn't move his hand. Esther knew she was blushing from nervousness. She started to go crooked on the seam. Finally she stopped and lifted the pressure plate.

He said, "What's the matter, Esther, having a little trouble on the seam?"

She pulled the shirt back and began to take out the seam she had just sewn. "Mr. Fletcher, I can't work well with you standing so close. It makes me nervous. I'll have to do this over."

Then he did take his hand off her shoulder and moved back a step. "Sorry, Esther, but you don't need to be nervous because of me. I just want to be friendly. I don't know why some of you girls are so standoffish. Probably your religion. You're Catholic, aren't you?"

"Yes."

He dropped his cigarette on the floor and ground it out with his shoe, saying, "Well, I just don't know what it is about you Catholic girls not wanting to be friendly. You miss out on a lot of fun that way. Also you know there's promotions to be had in the factory. We'll need a new quality checker soon. How'd you like that?"

She didn't answer. She had heard that he made promises like that to a lot of girls, but they had to go out with him before they could get any advancement. And even then, they didn't always. Anyway, he wasn't the kind of man her folks would want her to marry, if for no other reason than that he wasn't their religion. Besides, he probably wasn't a good man.

\* \* \* \* \*

Pa was sitting on a rocking chair on the front porch when she came home. She stopped for a minute. "How you feeling, Pa?"

"Passable. The hip aches from the dampness." He pushed the rocker a little harder.

"I'm sorry, Pa. Did you take your medicine?"

"That don't do much good. My bad leg is a punishment for my sins, and medicine don't help much."

"Yes, Pa. Can I get you anything from inside?"

"No, I'm alright. You just go in and help your Ma."

She wondered where Marie was and why she wasn't helping. After all, she, Esther, had been working since seven o'clock. But she never argued with Pa, so she went on in.

Walking toward her room, she thought of Pa. She felt sorry for him. His leg certainly gave him a lot of pain, and it had been that way so long. A log had fallen on it just after he got married, they had told her, and it got smashed so bad it never healed right. And it had made him grouchy. She could still remember the switchings he used to give her on the legs when he got mad. Now she had to work so hard at the shirt factory and hand over all of her salary besides.

In the room she shared with Marie, she reached under her mattress for the letter. It was getting dog-eared on the flaps and fingerprinted on the page. She took it out of the envelope and sat on the bed to read it again. She figured she had read it already nine or ten times. It said:

Dear Esther:

I got your leter a week ago and I been wanting to right you but I been so busy. Their's so much to do in the city that you don't have much time. You just wouldn't know the diference between Leschamps and Indian City. You can go out evry night if you want, and even have men to pay for you to shows or other entertain-ments. I know many men that would like to meat you. So why don't you come? What can you do there in Leschamps? There's nothing to do. Also everybody knows you their and is reddy to talk about you whatever you do.

You ask about work. There are lots of jobs in diferent kinds of factories but you can find work in other places too, like in restau-rants and stores. And there are many rich people who want girls from the country to work as maids. That's what I do and my Missus is always telling me I should ask my friends from Leschamps to come up here, that she knows a lot of people who would give them jobs. I think that's the best kind of work. You have your own room and you get plenty of food and the work ain't hard, and the pay is enough too. Besides, there's lots of things the rich people throw away that you can use. I get almost all my clothes from the Missus and her daughters. I just take them in on the sewing machine and they fit good. The sewing machine is new.

And their's so many things to do in the city, Esther. You just can't guess how much. So I think you should come soon. I'll meet you at the Interurban Station. Just write me when you'll come.

Yours truly,
Mildred Hartsock

Esther was reading it over the second time, trying to decide what to do, when she heard Marie coming. The younger girl flounced into the room and threw her books on her bed. "Where you been?" Esther asked. "You been out of school a long time. Why wasn't you here to help Ma?"

Marie snickered, "Ma didn't ask me to be home. I guess she figured you could do it a lot better than me."

Esther looked at her younger sister angrily. "I don't know why you're like that, Marie. Here I am coming home after working ten hours and you ain't done nothing but go to school and you want me to do the work in the kitchen too. And besides, I give all my money to Pa. Where do you think you get your money for books and tablets and pencils? Why, if it wasn't for you, I could maybe have gone to high school."

Marie lay back on her bed. Esther could see the roundness of her breasts. They were almost as big as her own. Marie said, "Oh, quit pitying yourself. I'll be going to work too in a couple of years, and then you can keep some of your money."

That was true. Marie would graduate from grammar school the next year, and a year later she would be sixteen, old enough to begin in the shirt factory.

Marie said, "What's that letter?" She spoke in a singsong. "I know you read it every day and I also know where you hide it."

Esther decided almost at once. She said, "It's from Mildred Hartsock. Do you remember her? She was in my grade."

"Sure, I know her. She was the fast girl."

"I don't know why you say that. Just because she went out with several boys. But I think she's alright."

"She went to Indian City, didn't she?"

"Yeah, that's where this letter's from. She lives and works there, for some rich people. They're so rich they give all their clothes to her after they've worn them a couple of times. She doesn't even have to buy any."

Marie sat up, showing interest. She said, "You think that's really true?"

"You don't think she'd tell a lie, do you?" Esther felt a little guilty about how she had exaggerated but told herself it was only a white lie. It didn't hurt nobody.

Marie became thoughtful. "I guess there are some real rich people there. Wouldn't you like to go there too? I know I would."

Esther couldn't hold back any longer. "That's what I'm going to do. That's why I wrote her. I'm going to tell Ma tonight."

Marie's eyes widened. "You are? Are you really? What will Ma say? She won't want you to go up there where there are all those men from everywhere. Most are not even Catholics. I've heard that girls have to be real careful there. Don't it scare you?"

Although it did, Esther was not about to admit it. After all, she had never been anywhere but in the country and the little town of Leschamps. She hadn't even been as far as Wrightsville, eighty miles away. She said, "I don't want to stay here all my life. There's no future working in the shirt factory."

Marie swung her legs down from the edge of the bed. "But what about Pa? What's he going to say? I don't think he'll let you. And besides, who's going to help him with money?"

"I don't know exactly how, but I know I'm going to do it somehow. I'm going to tell Ma tonight and maybe she'll help me tell Pa."

Marie got up then. "It sounds so exciting. I'd like to do that too. Do you think when I get bigger, I could come there too?"

All of a sudden Esther felt important. She was really going to do it, she was going to the big city. No more small towns or country for her. And who knew what wonderful things might happen to her there? She said, "I'm going down right now to help Ma and talk to her before Pa comes."

Marie came over and put her arm around her big sister's waist. "Do you think I could see the letter sometime?"

"Maybe."

* * * * *

Esther Schleimer matured into an attractive, full-bodied woman. She went to the city and worked as a house maid, sending money home to her parents in Leschamps. However, she was careful with her money and from the beginning put some into a savings account. After a few years, she helped her sister get a job with another wealthy family.

Esther did not go out as much as she had thought she would, though sometimes she and one of her friends went out with men together. Esther learned to let them kiss her, but that was all she would allow. The only other experience with men she had was with the grown son in the house where she worked. He tried to kiss her at first, but she never let him, and he finally stopped trying. Other than that, she went to church regularly, visited friends, and read books and magazines, even occasionally some that were on the forbidden list.

Then she met Bruno Neumann at a church social, a good-looking young man with kindly brown eyes.

* * * * *

Esther, in the back of the church with Marie, was dressed in a white bridal gown, one that Mrs. Peters had paid for when Esther gave notice. Bruno didn't want her to work after they got married.

Marie said, "You look so nice. The dress is beautiful. Do you feel excited?"

"I guess so," Esther answered. She felt nervous but happy. This was what a good Catholic girl had to do if she didn't go to the convent to become the bride of Christ. And she never thought about that. One in the family was enough anyway, though Harriet had seemed to want to get married at first too. But when young Kurt Schmidt, whom she had been seeing for three years, left without any explanation, she decided to go to the convent.

Esther felt good about Bruno. He was a good, hard-working man who had never tried to do anything with her other than get a goodnight kiss. He was a steady worker in a Turkish bath. She thought he was a smart person because he had learned to do that since coming to the city. And he was very steady about his religion, going to Mass every Sunday and regularly to confession and communion.

"And just think, you'll be going all the way to Cincinnati for a week, and staying in a big hotel. It sounds wonderful." Marie reached up to straighten Esther's veil and to tuck in a clump of hair that had come out of the band. Esther's hair was short in the new bob style.

A couple of Marie's friends came in and admired Esther. Then Ma arrived. She was wearing better clothes than Esther could remember, though she still had the long dress of the old fashion. She looked very serious as she studied her daughter from different angles. "That's a nice dress, Esther. It must have cost a lot."

"I guess so, but I don't know how much. I told you Mrs. Peters bought it for me."

"In a way it's a kind of waste. A person only gets to wear it once. Of course, if you could pass it on to your daughter, it wouldn't be so bad. But the styles change so much that the daughter doesn't want what her mother wore."

It was just like her mother, Esther thought, to be considering the cost of everything, even if it was for one of the most important days in a girl's life. But Esther knew how her mother had scrimped and saved all those years. So she tried to make her feel better. "It doesn't matter to Mrs. Peters, Ma. She has so much money she can buy any dress she wants, for herself, anyone in the family, or anyone else. Why, do you know, they have two cars."

Esther's mother looked a little more serious, even a little sad. She said, "I guess it's nice to have so much money. I know it would have helped a lot to have had more for your Pa's sickness."

"How is Pa after the long trip?"

"Oh, he's passable, I guess. His leg isn't giving him any more trouble than usual. He can manage to take you to the front of the church. But be sure and walk slow."

"Oh, I will, Ma. I know how it hurts him." She paused then said, "I still think it would have been alright to have his brother give me away. Then Pa wouldn't have had to come here for the wedding. Me and Bruno could have visited him afterward, either on our way to Cincinnati or coming back."

Her mother shook her head in that determined way of hers. "I told you, Esther, he wouldn't think of not doing it, unless he couldn't even get up. We're a Catholic family, and we raised you girls to be good Catholics. And getting married is one of the holy sacraments. It's a father's duty to be there, that's the way your Pa feels."

Esther was sorry to have gotten into that discussion. Though her mother was right, it made her feel bad then. She just didn't want to hear any more about it. She put her hand down on her lower stomach because the ache was getting worse.

Marie said, "What's wrong, Esther, do you feel bad?"

"I think I have to go to the bathroom. Do I have time?"

Marie looked at her new watch, the one she had bought after saving for many months. "I think so, if you hurry. It's just across the hall. I'll look out to see if the coast is clear."

Esther's dress swished as she went into the bathroom. She dreaded looking but if it was true, she would have to do something. She locked the door, checked to see that there was no window, then pulled her dress up and her bloomers down. She stared in disbelief for a minute when she saw the dark stain. How could it happen, on this of all days? Her periods had become pretty regular, though she usually did get cramps before. But it was almost a week early. Of course, this had happened a couple of times before, but she just had not imagined it would happen now, on the day of the wedding.

She folded some toilet paper and put it on the inside of her bloomers. Maybe the full flow wouldn't start right away. Then she went to the sink and washed her hands. She looked at her face in the mirror, wondering what Bruno would think. He was a kind man though, and probably wouldn't blame her. But no matter what he thought, they were supposed to lay together after becoming married, and this would only put it off. She patted some loose hair back in place and went back to the other room. Marie said, "Are you alright? You look so pale. Nothing happened, did it?"

"Where's Ma?"

"She went to see if Pa was ready, down at the end of the hall. You know, she's very nervous."

Esther sighed in relief. "Oh, I'm so glad she's not here. I couldn't talk about it in front of her."

"What's wrong ?"

"Oh Marie, I'm starting my period. And I don't even have a sanitary napkin."

The younger woman brought her hand to her mouth. "What a time to have it. Is it the right time?"

"No, it's early, but it's all the excitement. Do you have one?"

"No, but there's a drug store just across the street. I can get Millie to run over and get you some. Do you think you'll be alright until after the ceremony?"

"I guess. What else can I do but go on now?"

Marie looked at her watch again. "Yes, it should start in about five minutes. I think Pa is waiting on a chair at the end of the hall."

"I'll be alright."

The woman who helped in special church services came to the door then. "It's time, girls. Are you ready?"

"Um hmm," Marie answered. "Just let me put some rouge on Esther." She opened her compact and rubbed the cloth pad on the chalky pink stuff, dabbing it on Esther's cheeks.

"Just hurry. The priest is ready to come out now."

"Alright," Marie said and opened the door for her sister.

Pa got up with obvious pain when Esther approached him and held her arm out. He was dressed in a black suit with a white shirt and high, stiff collar, the kind that young men no longer wore. He took her arm seriously, without a smile. But then, she recalled as they began walking slowly, he rarely ever smiled. He was a stern but good man. She tried to set her pace to his limp, while concentrating on whether any blood was flowing. But she knew that even if there was any, she would be unlikely to know it until everyone else had, and even so, what could she do? She couldn't very easily turn and leave the church. She turned her mind to the organ music, the slow walk, and Pa's tight grip on her arm.

They made their way slowly up the aisle to where Bruno and his brother Bill were standing, both with dark blue suits and flowers in their buttonholes. Esther was only vaguely aware of the peoples' faces turned toward her and Pa. Then they were standing in front of the priest, reciting the words. The last thing she remembered before she pulled up her dress to kneel was what looked like a red spot on the floor. She recognized with relief that it was only a piece of lint, probably from one of the priest's robes. With relief, she knelt next to Bruno, who, though very serious also, glanced at her and grinned ever so little.

* * * * *

Esther and Bruno lived together in a rented house for a while, but then, with their accumulated savings, moved into one of their own. A child was born, then another and another. They were pretty children, but they made a lot of work for Esther. Her days were mostly the same: up early, fix breakfast for Bruno, then take care of children, feeding, cleaning, diapering, cleaning up the kitchen, washing clothes, cleaning the house, sewing or patching clothes, fixing food and feeding the children again, reading in snatches, more cleaning and sewing and baking, fixing dinner for Bruno, eating, feeding children, cleaning up the kitchen, sewing or patching clothing, reading a little, listening to the radio, putting the children to bed, then to bed herself, laying with Bruno every third or fourth night, and sleep.

Sunday was different because of church and Bruno being home all day. They took the first child along to church, with two she went less, and finally with three, they went to different Masses, Bruno staying with the children while she went. After church she would fix a big meal of roast beef, meat loaf, or baked ham with pie or cake. Sometimes, one of Bruno's brothers or sisters came for Sunday dinner, or else Marie with her new husband, dapper John. He was the best-looking man in either family, always in spats, and usually wearing a straw hat. In summer he always wore white or brown and white shoes. Sunday night, if relatives were there, they would usually play euchre or pinochle.

And the kids grew.

Then Esther's Ma and Pa sold their place in Leschamps and came to live with them in Indian City.

* * * * *

Esther walked out to the front porch where Pa and Ma were sitting on the swing, watching the cars and passersby. They just sat there all the time, doing nothing day in and day out. Sometimes Ma would come in the kitchen to help, but she criticized Esther so much that she was happier when her mother stayed out. "We're about ready to eat," Esther said. "Do you want to get ready?"

Pa asked, "What're we having tonight?"

"Liver and onions and mashed potatoes," she answered, wondering what complaint would follow. Sure enough, one did. "I think you have that too much, Daughter. I don't think it's good for you all the time. And I don't think it goes good with my medicine."

All of a sudden, Esther felt tired. Since the folks had come, she had tried to do everything she could to make them feel at home but it was always criticisms, one after another. And it was the same with Bruno. He also had done all he could, getting special medicines for both of them, taking them to the doctor, and listening to Pa criticize everything. They had even sold their house and moved into the bigger one Pa had bought, just to take care of the old folks. And never a word of appreciation. Of course, she knew that good children had a duty to take care of their aging parents, but at least the old folks could offer a word of appreciation once in a while. But she still tried to answer Pa without getting into an argument. "I don't think we have liver so often, Pa. And it's one of the cheapest meats. Besides, we have a big family to feed. And the nutrition book says it's full of iron and everybody needs that."

Pa pulled on his long, yellowing mustache, the one he had grown as a young man to cover his harelip. In her memory it had first been brown, then gray, and finally yellow. He said, "I don't care about what no book says. We didn't need to read about things before eating them in the old days. Besides, I don't know why you have to get cheap meats all the time. What ever happened to all the money I gave you and Bruno?"

"We used that, Pa. You don't know how fast money goes here in the city. It's not like Leschamps. Everything's so expensive. Just last week liver went from 12¢ a pound to 15¢, but even so, it was cheaper than ham or pork chops, which were 21¢ and 23¢ a pound."

"I just don't know where all the money goes," Pa whined. "And the medicine costs so much too. Didn't that last prescription cost $3.48?"

"I think so, Pa, but you have to ask Bruno for sure."

She heard the kids arguing from the back of the house, Martin and Rosalie, it sounded like. It was probably about who was going to set the table. In the background she heard little Flora beginning to cry from her crib. Esther said, "I'm going to have to go back now. I have to change the baby, and the kids are arguing. And Bruno will be home soon."

Ma said, "Do you want me to help?"

"No, I can do it. You just take care of Pa."

Before she got away, Pa had one more comment: "You should make those kids mind better, Daughter. They're always making noise and arguing. I know in the old days kids wouldn't be given that much freedom. You and your sisters were never allowed to act like that."

"Yes, Pa." She hurried toward the back of the house.

At last it was quiet. Ma and Pa and the baby asleep in their own rooms, and the three older children in their own beds also. Bruno was listening to the Major Bowes Amateur Hour. "He always seems to know what to say," Bruno said, "no matter who comes on his show."

"Yes," she said absently, just barely aware of the radio voices. Bruno continued, "I guess with the salary he gets that he ought to be able to talk good. I heard a man say he gets two thousand dollars a week. That's a lot of *gelt*."

"Um hmm." She was still thinking about the visit to the doctor's office. She had known from the beginning that it was wrong to stop lives that way. But what else could she have done? The births had been getting harder and harder, but the last had been scary. The pains had been so hard until they gave her the spinal that she thought she was going to die.

Afterward she had felt so tired she hardly even wanted to see the baby. It was good she didn't have to nurse like the farm women had to do in the old days. But when the doctor told her she shouldn't have any more, she had two feelings, one of relief and the other about the wrongness of it. Because who had the right to say whether a baby should be born or not? Certainly not a doctor. No one but God, she knew.

"All these radio performers get a lot of money," Bruno said, "even more than baseball players, a man told me the other day."

Esther heard the words but she kept to her own thoughts. What had finally convinced her was that the nurse was a Catholic and she had said it was alright. Esther knew she should have asked the priest, but she didn't. She was afraid he might say no.

"When I used to work at the Turkish Bath, we used to get entertainers," Bruno said. "They were always telling funny stories. There was this one dancer, his name was MacDonald, who used to do a little jig right there in the Turkish Bath."

And then she thought she would die of embarrassment, getting a device from the doctor. If the nurse hadn't stayed in the room she couldn't have gone through with it. And even then it wasn't easy, especially how to put it in. It was a good thing the doctor had the nurse show her how to do that. Esther knew she never would have been able to push that rubber thing in with a man watching.

Bruno switched off the radio. "How's your Pa?"' he asked. "Is he getting any better?"

"No, I don't think he's really going to get well again. He doesn't do anything, just sits all day while Ma takes care of him. 'Course I'm sure his leg is giving him a lot of trouble, and now with the diabetes too."

"How's your Ma; she seems kind of peaked too."

"She's not well either. You know they had a hard life. They never had much money and had to work hard. And they never did go to doctors if they could help it. Pa was always worried about spending too much money."

"Yah, that's the way it was in the old days, especially out in the country. Nobody had much money. That's why everybody came to the city. The old folks in Wertzberg are not much better off. But they just won't leave. It's a good thing Herman and Tillie want to stay down there. They can take care of them."

Bruno stood up. "Well, that's the way it is when you get old. You can't take care of yourself good any more. That's when it's a good thing to have children. Just think how hard it would be for your Ma and Pa if they were alone in Leschamps. He's not been able to work for years now, and he's just barely able to get around."

"Yes, having someone to help you is good then. But that's your duty too."

Bruno yawned. "I'm ready to hit the hay, Esther. How about you?"

"Yes, I'm very tired. There's so many people to cook for and take care of now, the four kids, Ma and Pa, and you and me. It seems I never have any time to myself any more.

"Okay, let's go hit the hay then." Bruno started for the bedroom.

"I'll be there in a minute. I want to check on the kids first, to see if they've said their prayers and turned out the lights."

When Esther came into the bedroom, she checked to see if the baby was asleep. Bruno was sitting on the edge of the bed in his undershorts and shirt. He had given up B.V.D.s the year before. She sat on the other side of the bed to take off her stockings, shoes, and dress. She reached for her nightdress. "Will you turn out the light, Bruno?"

He hesitated as if to say something but then reached over and switched it off. She stood up to take off her slip and brassiere and pulled the long nightdress over her head, leaving her bloomers on.

She knelt down to say her prayers.

When she got in bed, Bruno rolled over and kissed her. His face was smooth from shaving. He wasn't on top of her but she could feel his member fully hard. She kissed him back lightly to let him know that she would do her duty as a wife but not hard enough to encourage him. It was four days since they had lain together, but she was so tired she wished he would forget it. However, he got more active and soon was reaching down to pull up her nightdress.

"Bruno," she said, "wait a minute, I have something I want to tell you."

He pulled his hand away.

"Will you turn on the light?" she said. They had a small bed light on the night table where they kept the prayer book. He pulled the light switch and sat up.

She said, "I'm tired, Bruno. But we can lay together if you want. I know it's been several days. But before, I have to tell you something."

He looked at her in puzzlement. She had not noticed before how moist Bruno's brown eyes were. Anyway, she got up too and propped herself against the pillow. "It's about laying together." Then without pause she blurted out, "I got a birth control device."

He looked at her seemingly without understanding. Finally, he said, "A what?"

"They call it a diaphragm. The wife has to put it in before laying with her husband."

Then it seemed he was beginning to understand. He said, "You mean one of those things that prevents having babies?"

She nodded. Feeling guilty, she spoke quickly to explain what it was. "It's made out of rubber. It keeps the man's part from getting to the woman's part."

"But Esther," he said at last, "that's a sin. You know good Catholics are not supposed to stop babies artificially. Why, Father Flanagan was just preaching about that a couple of weeks ago." He looked at her, seemingly in disbelief.

She glanced down and, taking one end of the bedcover in her hand, began twisting it. "The doctor said it wouldn't be good for me to have any more babies. You know I told you how hard it was the last time."

His eyes softened a little when he said, "I know, Esther. But I don't think we're allowed to take that in our own hands. You know what the priest said, that it was taking someone else's life just as much as a murderer would."

"I know, Bruno. I feel as bad as you do but I'd be scared to have another baby. I might die." And then she added, "And you know, we have four healthy kids now. I think God would be satisfied with that."

He shook his head as if somehow he was misunderstanding what was happening. "But Esther, I don't think we have a right to decide. Did you ask the priest?"

"No, but the nurse was a Catholic and she said it was alright."

"But she can't decide something like that."

It seemed that the talk would go on for hours. And though Esther knew Bruno was right, she was also sure she wasn't going to have more children. Though she didn't really feel like it, she decided the best way to end it was to let Bruno lay with her. She said, "It won't bother us laying together, Bruno. You won't even feel it, the nurse said." She put her hand on his and could see his eyes soften immediately.

He put his arm around her shoulder, saying, "Well, I don't think it's right, and I think you ought to ask the priest, but there may be some excuse if your health is at stake."

She squeezed his hand. "I will, Bruno. I'll go in the next couple of days. And I'll go in now and put it in. You won't even be able to tell."

He hesitated so she got up quickly. "I'll be right back." She went into the bathroom and reached for the little rubber disc on top of the medicine cabinet where the kids couldn't reach it.

\* \* \* \* \*

The Depression waned. Bruno changed jobs. Both Ma and Pa died, as did Bruno's father. The children grew. Rosalie got to be fifteen years old, Martin fourteen. Esther's hair was beginning to turn gray though Bruno's was still dark. Esther became a little heavier.

\* \* \* \* \*

She sat in the front seat next to Bruno, the kids in back. They had just bought the Model A a few months before, their second car. It had a lot more room than the old Model T. And it seemed to run better. Esther just couldn't get used to the speed on the highway, though she felt comfortable with Bruno driving. She thought she really should learn so she could get the kids to the doctor if necessary but she didn't really want to. It would make her nervous.

The kids were arguing. Catherine said, "Mom, I don't have any room. Rosalie keeps pushing me."

Rosalie answered, "Oh, I'm not. She's just fibbing."

Catherine said, "She doesn't want me to get her dress messed up. She's just trying to save it so the boys can see her. I know."

Rosalie, "Oh, keep quiet. What do you know? I didn't even want to come along. I knew how crowded it would be in the back seat."

Bruno spoke then, "Now you kids keep quiet. I'm tired of all that arguing. You'd think you been going all day instead of just a little more than an hour. Besides, we'll be there in a little bit. We just passed the old Mueller place. That means it's only five more miles. And let's see, at forty-five miles an hour, that's just a little over six minutes."

Bruno just loved to do arithmetic problems, Esther thought, whether in his head or on paper, and he was good at them too.

The kids began twisting around and pushing one another again. Esther turned around and raised her hand, saying, "Now that's enough. You heard your father. If you don't quit, I'm going to give you a slap."

"Aw Mom," Catherine said in a whiny voice. Esther couldn't hold herself back any more, saying sharply, "There, you've got one," and giving Catherine a slap on the cheek. Catherine just looked at her sulkily.

Then they were driving down the main street of Wertzberg, which was paved to the edge of town. There were many cars, mostly older ones. A couple of buggies were there, the horses tied to the only hitching post left. A few old people still used horses and buggies. Esther felt proud of their new car as Bruno drove the length of the street, waving at people as he passed. Esther knew he had many friends in the Wertzberg parish. He parked on the grass just beyond the open space they used for picnics and reunions. This was the annual church reunion. They made a few hundred dollars each year, but even more importantly, it was a time for all the people who had left to come back for a day and meet old friends.

They got out of the car. Martin said, "I want to go down to the games."

"There's Eunice Meier," Rosalie said. "Can I go over to see her?"

"Me too, I want to go with Rosalie," Catherine said.

"Oh, you're too little. We don't want you with us." Rosalie said as she waved at her cousin.

"You kids can go ahead and play," Bruno said. "But be back at the eating tables in an hour. I'm going to get the tickets. Your mother and I will meet you there."

"Okay, Pop." They ran off.

Esther watched them go. They were good-looking children, enough to be proud of, Rosalie and Catherine with their brown hair and eyes, Martin and Flora blond with blue eyes. There were no better-looking kids among Bruno's relatives. 'Course, being from the city, Esther thought, they were also dressed better than country people.

Because none of the other kids wanted Flora along, she went with her parents, holding Esther's hand. As they moved toward the crowd under the big sycamore, Bruno waved. Several people waved in return. Esther could see Bruno's brothers, Bill and Helmut, and their wives off to one side. She walked alongside Bruno to the shady area. He strolled over to the group of men, and she turned off to join the women's group. Mary and Hermione were there, each with some of their own children along. Both were plump women, like most others Esther's age and older. Mary held out her hand. "Hi Esther, down in the country for the day?"

Esther took the other woman's hand, noticing how rough it felt. Country women worked very hard, she thought. She answered, "Yes, you know that Bruno wouldn't miss the annual church reunion if he could help it. And especially now with the new Ford, it's so easy to come. Bruno had been wanting to try it out on the highway. It's really nice but almost scary, it goes so fast. There's lot more room for the kids too than we had in the old Model T."

Hermione said, "We saw you coming down the street. And everybody said, 'I bet that's Bruno and his new Model A.'"

Esther couldn't help feeling proud. Even though a lot of people seemed to be getting cars then, not everyone, particularly the country people, could afford a new one. Bruno had been a dependable, hard-working man, though she had helped save the money, she thought. Even so, they had to get the car on time payments. They had talked a lot about that but had finally decided to go ahead, especially since the payments were only $30 per month. Everyone seemed to be doing that.

Esther said, "How's Henrietta?"

Hermione answered, "Oh, she's fine. She's back working in the church kitchen. You know her, she's been in the kitchen so long, you just can't keep her out of it. Some women get tired of cooking, but not Henrietta."

"How old is she now, almost eighty, ain't it?"

"Yah, she's seventy-eight, but it don't slow her down none."

"Who's she living with now?"

"With us," Mary said. "She's been with us for three months now and will probably stay another three months. Then I think she's going to stay with Wilma and Bill for awhile."

The group met at the eating tables, the kids having lost all their freshness. Martin was particularly dirty. Esther demanded, "Did you wash your-self?"

"Um hmm. At the pump."

"You don't look very clean. What you been doing?"

"I was down by the creek with Bobby Meier."

"I don't know why you did that, at a church reunion. You're supposed to stay clean sometimes."

"Aw Mom, it's no fun otherwise. Kids don't just want to stand around and talk."

Bruno looked at the boy, then said, "Why don't you wash again. You look like you still need it."

Martin looked sulky but didn't say anything more, getting up to head toward the pump.

Shortly after he returned, the women began carrying the food in bowls and platters: ham, chicken, beef, veal, gravy, corn on the cob, mashed potatoes, potato salad, buttered green beans, succotash, breaded toma-toes, sliced tomatoes, sliced cucumbers, pickled beets, pickles, pickle-lily, homemade bread, butter, jam, and for dessert several kinds of fruit pies, angel food cake, devils food cake, pound cake, canned peaches, and Jello.

When Bruno got to dessert, he leaned back, saying, "Out here in the country is the only place a person can get food like this any more. The city may be alright for some things, but it takes the country for real food."

Esther said, "I know I shouldn't, but I think I'll try a piece of that devils food, it looks so good."

\* \* \* \* \*

The next war came. Martin and Rosalie went off, he as a flyer, she as a nurse. The others grew up too. Rosalie and Martin never returned home, marrying and starting families of their own. Soon the others were mar-ried too and off on their own. Esther and Bruno moved to a smaller house, a double so there would be rent from one side. Bruno lost his job with the milk company since people didn't want it delivered any more. They bought all their groceries, including milk, from super-markets. Bruno worked as a janitor, and then in a brush factory. Esther kept house and got a little heavier despite going on frequent diets.

\* \* \* \* \*

Esther finished cleaning up the dishes and walked into the living room.

Bruno was sitting deep in the easy chair, watching television. He was scrunched down so far that Esther could just barely see him. She sat opposite and took some sewing from the basket she usually kept there.

Instead of starting to sew, however, Esther studied Bruno. It seemed all of a sudden that he was much smaller than she remembered. His face was deeply lined and his jaws sunk a little. That was from the false teeth he had had for several years. He hardly seemed to be aware of the program, his eyelids drooping and once in a while his head nodding. He was tired most of the time these days.

She said, "How was work today?"

His mouth was still a little open when he turned toward her. He looked vacantly for a moment, like a person just waking up. Then he smiled, his eyes crinkling at the corners. Bruno had always smiled a lot, she thought, no matter what happened. He said, "It was about the same, maybe a little dirtier. The men in the bristle department worked overtime."

"You look so tired."

"Well, I had to stay a little late to clean up after them. And my back gives me a lot of trouble these days. I probably need to see a chiropractor."

"You need to take care of yourself, Bruno. You know you only got one body."

He turned back toward the TV again. She pulled out one of Bruno's blue work shirts that had a rip in the back. Deftly she pulled the sides together and bound them with fast in-and-out motions of the needle. She was used to patching and could do it mostly without thinking. However, this particular evening she felt restless. She said, "You haven't had any more dizzy spells, have you?"

He kept his gaze on the picture tube awhile but finally turned in her direction, a little more awake than before.

"Just once, but it was very slight."

"I think you ought to see the doctor about them."

"Well, one of these days. But it ain't nothing serious. Just the high blood pressure, and you know all us Neumanns have had that." He reached over and turned off the set. "Did you hear from the girls today?"

"Rosalie called. She's having some trouble with her Tony. He won't ever give her any money. He does all the shopping and she has to get by the best she can."

"I'm not too surprised. Tony provides for her and the kids but he's like most Italians. He wants to be boss of everything. But Rosalie should have known that when she married him."

Things were different today, Esther thought. In the old days a wife wouldn't complain if her husband was a good provider and wasn't mean to her. But now they expected a lot more. She thought back and could hardly remember her mother complaining even when she had to take in wash to keep the family going.

"Are they coming over for dinner, Sunday?" Bruno asked.

"Yes, Rosalie is bringing the dessert."

"Are the others coming too?"

Flora and her family will be here for dinner but Catherine can't make it. She'll be coming over later for coffee and dessert though."

"Sounds like a regular family reunion," Bruno said, grinning. "It'll be bedlam with all those kids in the house."

He lapsed into silence for a bit, then, "The only one missing will be Martin. And I sure would like to see his little Pete."

She picked up another piece and began sewing with determination.

Bruno said, "I still don't know if we did the right thing. After all, he is our own son."

Esther stuck the needle into her finger. She pulled it back quickly and put the finger into her mouth to suck the blood. She should have been using the thimble, she knew. Then she pulled the finger out of her mouth and said, "You know we talked about it several times and even discussed it with Father Flanagan. You can't let a Catholic boy not even baptize his own son. And we did tell him we weren't going to write or see him any more if he didn't do that. And he just went his own way anyway." She sighed, "Oh, that Martin was always so stubborn."

Esther was sorry that Bruno had brought the subject up because she knew she would be thinking about Martin for a long time afterward.

Bruno said, "I know, but I'd still like to see him and the boy."

He leaned back in the chair and said nothing more. Soon he was nodding again. His head would drop in successively longer falls until it woke him up. He would look up with a vacant stare until he recognized where he was, then grin and settle back again. Once he jerked awake and said, "I guess I should turn on the set."

But he didn't and was soon dozing again. Finally, awaking again, he said, "I guess it's time to hit the hay." And he got up.

"Yes, you look like you need to get some sleep. Do you want anything?"

"No, I can sleep like a baby now. That's one thing old Bruno Neumann don't need no help with."

"Goodnight." He turned and went toward the steps.

Esther watched him go up the stairs slowly, holding the banister carefully at each step. He was slightly bent, she noticed, having become an old man. But then he turned the corner and was out of sight. She felt more relaxed than at any time during the day. Ever since the kids had left, she hadn't been so tired. There wasn't so much to do, only taking care of the house and cooking and cleaning for Bruno. But more than that was the comfort of not having to go to bed with him much any more. Usually he was too tired, and unless she got into bed with him before he went to sleep, he didn't seem to care. And that certainly wasn't often. Still, every few weeks she did, just to let him know they were still man and wife. But it got to be less and less. And it was funny, she thought, since she had long gone through her time of life change and didn't even need to use the diaphragm any more. Ah well, she thought, it was time to be giving that up. She reached over to get the book she had gotten from the library, *Patterns of Culture* by Ruth Benedict. The librarian had told her that it was a famous book on anthropology, which was Martin's field. She heard the toilet gurgle once when Bruno flushed it, but then the house became quiet. She opened the book

\* \* \* \* \*

Like his father, Bruno died of a stroke. Esther stayed in the house for many years, cleaning and cooking for herself and sometimes for the children when they came to visit. Esther visited her sisters and traveled with her own children on occasion. She also went on several guided tours sponsored by the church. The children's children grew up, and some of them came to stay with her for weeks or months when they had problems at home. She went to church on her own as long as she could, but then it became difficult to walk so far and she went by taxi or had one of the kids take her. But it became harder and harder to live alone, especially in the winter and when her diabetes got worse.

\* \* \* \* \*

Esther sat in a wheelchair on one side of the Possum Run Rest Home dining room. It was not very noisy, mostly just the tinkle of knives, forks, and spoons on plates and against cups. She could see others at the tables nearby, about half sitting in wheelchairs, the others in regular chairs. Her tablemate, Mrs. Gossen, kept saying over and over, "I told them not to bring me peas. I don't like peas. They're too hard to eat."

Esther looked at her own plate. It had peas also, besides mashed potatoes covered with gravy and some kind of meatloaf. She took her fork and poked at the peas.

Mrs. Gossen said, "See what I said. They just keep rolling around when you try to pick them up."

Esther then began poking the meatloaf, though without making any effort to cut it up. One of the attendants came over, a fat girl in white by the name of Clara. Most of the girls there were fat. The old people were too, she thought. Esther looked at her own flabby forearm. She used to go on diets, she remembered. But she had worked then too, cleaning the house and tending her garden. In the rest home she just sat or lay in bed. She didn't eat much, she thought, but she didn't do nothing either.

The fat girl said, "Now, Mrs. Neumann, we don't seem to be eating very well, do we? And we're not going to get well that way, are we? We've got to get our strength up so we can walk again, now don't we?"

Esther just kept poking at the meatloaf. She thought how many meatloaves she had made in her lifetime. And they had been pretty good. She had been a pretty good meatloaf maker. She wasn't bad at making gravy either. At least Bruno and the kids had liked it. When she took meatloaf and gravy to a church supper, it was unusual to bring any back.

The voice of the fat girl kept getting louder. At last Esther could make out the words. "Now, Mrs. Neumann, are you listening to me? 'Cause if you don't listen to me, I'm going to have to tell Dr. Carson. And he won't be happy if he knows you don't listen."

Esther looked at the round, pudgy face. The mouth was moving constantly, making funny shapes. There was noise coming from it, but it wasn't interesting. Esther just nodded her head.

Then she heard almost all the fat girl said: "Okay, that's better. Now, I want you to eat some of your dinner. I'm going to cut up your meatloaf and stay here until you eat it, or at least most of it."

Esther stared at the girl apathetically, wondering why she didn't feel like answering her. Esther knew she could talk; it just didn't seem worthwhile. The gray meat fell apart when the girl pulled at it with the fork. Esther's wouldn't have done that. The meatloaf mixture had needed more eggs as binding, she thought, and she could have told the cook. But they didn't want her in the kitchen. They didn't want her anywhere but in her room or the dining room or the hall, practicing with her wheelchair. Ever since the girls had taken her out of her house, it had been that way. And they didn't really want to hear anything from her either.

The voice intruded again. "Now there it is, Mrs. Neumann, cut up and ready to eat. Here take the fork and start eating."

Esther took the fork and studied it. It didn't look much different from all the forks she had seen in her lifetime; but still it was more interesting than the food.

"Now, just get started. Don't sit there daydreaming. You got to eat for your strength, and your visitors will be here soon too. Don't you want to meet them in your room?"

Esther decided to say something. "Who?"

The girl said, "It's your two nice daughters, I think. And they might bring you a surprise. Wouldn't that be nice? Now you start eating."

Esther put the first piece of meat into her mouth. It tasted gray too, but still she chewed it slowly. She didn't have enough teeth to chew very fast.

The girl said, "Now, that's nice. And I want you to keep eating while I go over there and help Mrs. Gossen."

Esther kept chewing and mushing her food and got most of it down. Only the Jello and bread were left. She tried a piece of the bread because it looked soft and white like the bread Bruno used to deliver. But it was getting dried out from being unwrapped so long. She wouldn't have let that happen to bread that she served. After one bite she put it down.

The girl came back from one of the other tables. "Now that looks better. Don't you want to eat your Jello?"

"Don't want no more Jello," Esther said, a little surprised by how much she had just said.

"Would you like something else? Some ice cream, maybe?"

"No." Esther put her hands together to show that she wouldn't eat any more.

"Okay, I guess that's alright. Maybe you can have something later. Are you ready to go back to your room now? I think your daughters will be here soon."

"Yes," Esther nodded.

The girl rolled her chair backward, swivelled it, and pushed her past the other tables and down the corridor. They passed Mr. Henry, who was pushing himself in his wheelchair. He said, "Hi Esther, why don't you roll yourself? Otherwise your muscles will get soft."

For a moment Esther felt a little angry. That Mr. Henry was always telling her and everyone else what to do. But just as quickly her feelings became quiet again. She just shook her head as they passed.

Soon Esther was lying on the bed with the television on. A program master was talking to different people, first on the stage and later in the audience. Esther turned the remote control volume switch. It came on very loud. Mrs. Harrison pulled her curtain back. "That's too loud. I'm reading."

Esther turned the volume down, down, down, until she couldn't hear the voices any more. She didn't care anyway. She stared at the man moving down the aisles with the microphone and wondered vaguely what he could be talking about so constantly when she had so much trouble thinking of anything she wanted to say to anyone. She turned it off and put the remote switch panel on the bedside table. She lifted a piece of the coverlet and twisted it between her fingers.

The voices of the girls in the corridor were coming toward her room. Catherine's was higher and she sounded a little excited. The two came into the room. "Hi Mom." Catherine gave her a peck on the cheek. "How are you?"

Her voice was loud as if she thought Esther couldn't hear very well.

"I'm alright."

Rosalie fixed her pillow. "Are they treating you okay?"

"I guess so. But we're old people." It seemed that she ought to explain herself further but it didn't seem worth the trouble.

"Now Mom, you shouldn't say things like that. You're just as old as you feel. You're just sick. But you got to keep trying to get well. The nurse says you won't hardly even try to wheel yourself. And you know you got to try."

The two sat down. Rosalie handed her a paper bag. "Look, I brought you something. A surprise."

Esther put her hand inside and brought out a funny looking candy or fruit bar. She turned it over slowly.

"Do you know what it is? It's good and it's good for you."

Esther continued to study it.

"It's called a granola bar. It's a kind of health food. The kids eat them. Gregory bought these for you."

"He's a nice boy," Esther said. She could still remember when he had stayed with her for a couple of months because he couldn't get along with his father. He was always very neat.

"Why don't you eat one now?" Rosalie said. "The nurse says you don't eat very much. This would be good for you." Esther just kept holding the bar listlessly. "Here, let me unwrap it for you."

Catherine looked at her in her serious way and said, "Mom, all the papers for the house were signed this week. The money was put in a trust fund in my name."

Esther just stared at her.

Catherine added, "We thought you ought to know, Mom, even though the power of attorney is in my hands."

Esther didn't like Catherine. She said, "You sold my house without asking me and you kept all the money?"

Catherine sighed. "I explained all that to you, Mom. We had to sell it because you couldn't take care of it any more. And the reason it's in my name is so you can collect Medicare in the rest home. If it was in your name, they'd want you to pay."

Esther said, "I don't believe that."

Rosalie, "Mom, you shouldn't be like that. Catherine has been working a lot on this, dealing with lawyers and banks and real estate people. And she's done it all for your sake."

Esther became silent, twisting the coverlet again.

Rosalie, "You're lucky, Mom, to have a daughter who would work so hard for you."

More silence, then Esther: "I wish Bruno was here. He wouldn't have let anyone take my money."

# CHAPTER 4

**M**artin was in the waiting room when Oldenberg arrived. The plump man said, "I just need to make a couple of quick telephone calls and then we can go over your findings. You can come and wait inside, though. I'll have Miss Grady bring us some coffee, okay? We have top-grade Costa Rican or Nilgiri. Would either of those please you?"

"I'd love to have a cup of Nilgiri. I still remember with pleasure that fine, aromatic coffee I used to get at the India Coffee House."

"Okay, come on in."

Martin sat in the same chair as before while Oldenberg put his calls through. Again Martin was impressed that he couldn't hear a sound when Oldenberg's lips moved. The coffee arrived on a small tray with two cups and saucers, sugar, and cream in pitchers. One and a half teaspoons and a little cream. Martin took a sip. The flavor was as good as he remembered.

Oldenberg finished his phoning and rolled his chair to the side of the desk to join Martin. "Not bad, eh? It really is one of the richest coffees, though evidently few of your people know about it."

"That's true. But then, I suppose it's just as well, so little seems to be produced. May I?" Martin asked, indicating the ceramic coffee container from which he had removed the cozy.

"Please. I'll light up my pipe, then we can get into the business at hand—your new discoveries, which I presume were interesting."

Martin watched the Transition Master strike three large matches before he got one lit. As the plump man sucked in the smoke, Martin, remembering his own pipe-smoking days, anticipated the sharp, aromatic taste. Soon, Oldenberg was puffing away, a satisfied expression on his face. He leaned back. "So, what extraordinary insights did you get from seeing your mother's life?"

Martin felt he could read a little humor in the man's tone, if not condescension. The man was acting very much like a graduate student adviser. Such people undoubtedly heard similar reports over and over, each time from students who thought they had found something original. But then Martin pulled himself up—this wasn't a university, and he wasn't a graduate student talking to his chief adviser. Martin was in the afterworld, however different it was from what he had imagined. From an earthling's point of view, Martin was a dead man even if he was still preoccupied with the affairs of life.

Oldenberg cut into his reverie. "I seem to have lost you, Martin. Is there something special on your mind?"

Martin shook his head to stop the drifting. "Oh no, nothing new. I still have difficulty comprehending where I am, what state I'm in, and what I'm currently doing, that's all."

"That's normal. Nothing to worry about. After all, the Transition Process is pretty far from what they taught you. I hope you don't get too preoccupied thinking about it. Believe me, after awhile you'll stop."

Martin sighed. "I'm sure you're right. And I think I'm okay now. I'm coming back to thinking about my mother, Esther."

"As I recall, you were particularly interested in knowing whether the female of your species perceived her mating life differently from how the male did. So, did you find anything significant in that regard?"

"One of the big problems seems to be how much of a person's behavior is a consequence of their personal experiences, what we called their *nurture,* and how much is a consequence of their biological makeup, what we called their *nature.*"

"No doubt about it." Oldenberg swiveled his chair around to stare pensively out the window. "It is indeed difficult to separate the consequences of experience from those of biological inheritance. Was there something particular in your mother's life that made you think about that?"

"I just can't know for sure, but it seems to me that certain incidents might have left indelible marks on her personality. For instance, she seemed to have entered into nubility in a particularly difficult way. Her first menstruations were very traumatic for her. And the problem was made so much more serious by the fact that she could hardly talk about it in her family. They were very strict. Now that's a kind of thing a man never has to go through, and it must indeed be difficult."

"What do you mean, menstruation or talking about it? Because if you mean talking about it, you have to remember that it was no more possible for your father to talk about his genital affairs. Admittedly, he didn't menstruate, but you said he had strong sexual feelings and there was hardly anyone he could discuss them with. As I recall, you said the only person he felt free to tell about his one extramarital affair was his priest."

Martin scratched the back of his head. "Yes, I know. It was typical of those times. You just didn't talk about sex. Sometimes I wonder how they got any information across, how people ever learned enough to inseminate each other."

Oldenberg chuckled. "Now come on, you're not giving biological drives enough credit. With that line of reasoning, you'd have to deduce that all the other animals would fail to inseminate one another. After all, they don't talk about sex or anything else. I mean they do not have true language that would permit them to discuss any complex activity. And we know that they reproduce. No, I'm afraid that you are still confusing reproduction and sex as a way of providing personal satisfaction. The real fact is that reproduction can go on quite well with very little sex and with only a minimum of satisfaction to the individual. Some satisfaction may be needed, admittedly, but not much."

Martin picked up a pencil and began tapping it on the table. "Yes, I agree. I must admit it is probably my biggest block, to get to the stage of considering sex as a means of reproduction rather than something to provide pleasure. But I'll keep it in mind, and perhaps when this is over, I will have shifted in my ideas."

"But anyway, to get back to Esther. I take it you felt she got less out of the sexual relationship than Bruno. Is that so?"

"Yes, I think that was the case. I wouldn't say that she didn't like sex, but she could do with a lot less than he could. And despite all, I think she really liked the man, perhaps loved him, though at that time they didn't bandy the term *love* about as they did later on."

"No, it seems to me that came when people really came to emphasize the pleasurable aspect of sex and pairing. After all, you must realize that your parents were still in the period when sex was considered a means of reproduction. They were deliberately creating a family as a duty." He paused, then continued, "But to get back to the original point, I take it that you feel your mother suffered a lot in her introduction to sex and that affected her attitude the rest of her life. Is that the idea?"

Martin thought about it for a while, beginning to doodle on the note pad he had brought along. Then he answered, "I'm not absolutely sure. I suppose Bruno had a lot of problems in those early years too, and as you say, he didn't have anyone to talk with, any more than Esther did."

"I suspect that as you go farther on this little study, you will come to realize that much of the so-called trauma you got from your sexual experiences is a consequence of the extraordinary importance you gave it in your lives. As you know, when your people got fully into the era of individualism, you developed large professions primarily concerned with solving sexual problems or their aftermaths. I think your Sigmund Freud and the field of psychoanalysis are the best known. If I am correct, those practitioners try to explain most life problems as a consequence of some kind of sexual trauma."

"I can see that," Martin replied, "and perhaps people in other times and places didn't take it so seriously. Probably my parents were transitional in this kind of behavior as they were in many others. After all, they were that generation that came from a country background but adapted to a new way of life in the city. Even the idea of limiting their family size was a new one, although admittedly not easy for either to accept. But my mother did manage to begin using a contraceptive."

"Yes, there was a lot of change in their lives. But you'll have to admit that your parents maintained quite a few traditional attitudes as well. They remained a strong reproductive unit, raising four children."

"No doubt that there were continuities from their farm backgrounds that probably contributed to the strength of the family unit. One was the dominance of the male, a real peasant trait. Nevertheless, it probably helped in keeping the family together, a woman accepting the word of her father when she was young and then that of her husband. I'm sure it wasn't always pleasant, but I think it gave a lot of stability to the family. Although even that was changing. Esther was starting to assert herself in differences with Bruno. In the old days she would probably not have insisted on the right to use a contraceptive against the teachings of the church."

"Yes, that's probably true."

That insight did not grab the attention of the Transitioner. He said, "Anything else?"

Martin flipped his pad to study notes he had jotted down while watching his mother's Life Tape. He stopped at one. "Well, Esther was like Bruno in that she accepted mating as an exclusive lifetime affair—she just didn't think of messing around, much less separation. That too was a traditional attitude. And I now think that in the long run it provided a relatively satisfactory life for her. At least she spent more than thirty years living in a close social unit, with three generations, in fact." He paused then. "But I suppose she lived too long because the last years of her life were not so great; she lived alone, at home first, and then in a retirement home."

Oldenberg rocked his chair up and down slowly. "Of course you know your species evolved a life span that does not make much sense biologically. To be perfectly blunt, people in your favored cultures live too long. As you probably know, all of the individuals of other species die soon after their reproductive years. And that makes a lot of sense biologically. Moreover, even in your own species this was the case until quite recently. The tribespeople of the world and even the peasants up until the nineteenth century had average life spans of forty years or less. But then you Westerners came up with many medicinal discoveries, and this, associated with your cult of individualistic rights, resulted in keeping hundreds of millions of people alive who in the old days would have been long dead."

"How true," Martin said. "Moreover, this occurred in the same period when family values were declining. I couldn't help noting that though Esther kept her parents in her own home in their old age, despite the grouchiness of the old man, she was put into an impersonal institution the moment she couldn't take care of herself. None of her children wanted her in their house."

Oldenberg had ever so light a smile on his face. "Yes, I'm afraid your people reached another quandary in that contradiction. While they emphasized individual rights and developed ever more elaborate methods of keeping people alive, they got less and less capable of maintaining a comfortable life-style for the survivors. But of course, as I mentioned before, your species has never been known for its consistency."

"One of the things I noted in the nursing home, which I know is reflected in the social statistics, was that the great majority of survivors were female. Just like Esther, many outlived their husbands."

"True, women just don't kill themselves off so fast. And that is an even greater biological anomaly. While the male can inseminate a female well up into his sixties or seventies, the female is usually biologically unproductive before she is fifty." He chuckled. "I must say you hominoids have made few attempts to adapt to your biological heritage."

Martin slumped in his chair, listening. He just could not get the various pictures of Esther in her old age out of his mind. Was that where it all led? Was there no other way to end up?

Oldenberg interrupted his thoughts. "You seem to be sunk into some deep introspection."

"Yes, going back over the older generation's private lives is a little heavy, even in the state I'm in now. You must have noticed such a reaction in other Transitionees."

"Well, Martin, you must know that most Transitionees are here only a short time, usually one hour, and then they are off to their next life. You are a special case, you know. Others don't spend time in the Life Library, viewing the lives of their parents or others." Oldenberg waved his pipe toward Martin. "However, it seems to me that you got some interesting leads from viewing your parents' lives. All in all, they seem to have led fairly complete lives even though they were hardly satisfactory by current standards. But they did not worry about deep passion, love, as so variously described by your writers and film producers. Even so, they must have gotten some emotional and even sexual pleasure from being together. And they did stay together as long as both were alive. They didn't jump into affairs or seek divorce on impulse. The fact that your mother had to live alone for almost twenty years was a consequence of other changes that occurred in their lifetimes. How could dear old Esther have realized, even while she was taking care of her obstreperous old father, that she was the last of her kind? That her children and so many others of the next generations would hardly consider taking their parents into their homes? Perhaps the last most important bond, security in old age, was being abandoned by the family. It may have been a great institution for a long time, but its day seems to be largely over."

It was a great summing up, Martin thought. Too bad he had never had a professor like that in his college days. Then perhaps he wouldn't have had to live through all the changes in his lifetime, and after, understanding them only after the fact, if at all. But then again he was lucky, he thought. How many guys had the chance of continuing their studies after they died?

Oldenberg broke in. "So where to now, Martin? Do you have any ideas as to what kind of life you want to do next?"

Martin pulled himself up, coming back to the otherworldly present. "I'm not really finished with that generation. It puzzled me so much in life and helps me to understand so much more of what happened to me, you know. And, as you may remember, one of the end products of this study for me personally is to help decide where I'll go in my next life." Martin quickly added, "Of course, I do fully intend to write the report."

The plump man was jotting down something on his pad. "So do you have any particular person in mind?

"As a matter of fact, I do. He was the father of one of my wives. I met him several times, but I was told much more about him. His life was puzzling to me then, but now when I think back on it, it seems to fit into the puzzle. Could I take a look at the life of Josh Bingham?"

"That seems reasonable. But is there anything more that you think you can get out of it that you didn't from the life of Bruno?"

"In many respects their lives were the same. Although there were some differences in their ages, they shared many customs and beliefs of the past generation. But one main difference was that Josh was a professional, an educated man, well established financially and socially, not a farmer who had become a worker in the city. He also was from a different part of the country, where quite a few customs were different. I guess, though, that it was mainly a difference of class. I wonder whether that affected his attitudes and behavior?"

"Perhaps. I would think anything that changes one's social position ought to affect behavior. Though there are probably some cross-cutting patterns that can affect many classes. Anyway, your choice seems reasonable enough."

Martin quickly added, "And perhaps a strong personal need for me is to try to figure out his daughter, so different from him in respect to mating. I married her, you know, and so far as their mating practices were concerned, there seemed to be no commonality except they both believed in marriage. However, even there, the conception of the two was quite different. In other respects she took a lot from him, but not in how she paired with men."

"Alright Martin, as they say among your Christians, you have my blessing."

# JOSH

Joshua Bingham grew up in the southern town of Emmetsville. It was a well-to-do, established neighborhood, the houses of brick, and the sidewalks well shaded. His house was of medium size for the neighborhood. They had had a car ever since Josh could remember.

The boy grew tall quite early. His brothers and father were also tall. It ran in the family. When he became old enough, Josh attended the local school, also of brick. It was near enough to walk. His father would take him and his brothers in the Essex when the weather was very bad, though that wasn't too often; it only snowed once or twice a year. Except for two or three Asians, the children in his school were all white.

Very early Josh began going to the Methodist Church with his parents and brothers. From then on he never missed a Sunday except when he was sick, which was very rare. He also early began taking part in family prayer meetings and took his turn saying grace before meals.

In his spare time, Josh played with the neighborhood boys or rode his bicycle with one of his brothers or friends to fish in the local ponds or streams. The town was small enough that they could get to a number of fishing holes in a half hour or less. They caught bream, crappie, or channel cats.

Then when he was fourteen, just beginning his first year of high school, he began helping his father in the drug store.

* * * * *

Josh was walking down Ash Street with George Hurley, carrying his books in a briefcase. George had a strap around his books. The air was becoming a little cooler as the shadows began to lengthen. The zee-zee of the locusts was background noise that Josh hardly heard. It was just a part of summer evenings that he had heard ever since he could remember. It was pleasant walking slowly along the shady sidewalk toward the drugstore.

George spoke: "How do you think you'll like the new Latin teacher?"

Josh answered in a very slow drawl. Being Southerners, both boys lengthened their vowels but Josh's were drawn out the longest and spoken the slowest. "He seems alright. What do you think?"

"I guess he's okay. He didn't give so much homework. Anyway, I'm glad to have that instead of German. Why did you pick Latin, Josh?"

The tall, red-haired boy thought about it for a while, then answered, "Well, my daddy wanted me to. He says it's good to know if you go into medicine or the sciences, or even law. Most of the prescriptions in the drugstore are in Latin."

"Yeah, I guess that's right, and I guess your daddy wants you to go to college, doesn't he?"

"Yeah." Josh couldn't remember an age when it wasn't assumed that he would go to college, his brothers too. His daddy talked about medicine and law most, but even dentistry or engineering might be alright. Josh wanted to tell someone about his other idea but was a little reluctant. Not many boys talked about that. But he really liked George Hurley, so he said, "'Course there's another field you can use Latin in." Pause. "I'm considering that."

George picked up a stick and trailed it along an iron picket fence. He said, "What?"

Pause, then: "Theological school. I've been thinking I'd like to go there."

George lifted the stick off the fence and looked at Josh. "Really? You'd like to go there? I never did think of that. But maybe it's alright. At least it's not like being Catholic so you couldn't even get married."

"Anyway, I haven't told my daddy yet. And I don't know for sure. I was just thinking about it."

A group of three girls were on the other side of the street, going in the same direction. They came abreast of the two boys, who quickly saw that they were the focus of the girls' attention. Two of the girls laughed and giggled and pointed toward them, and the third, a girl with long black hair, didn't say anything. She looked embarrassed. The talkative ones pushed her forward a couple of times and pointedly giggled toward the boys.

"What's that Irene Stiles and Mavis Herschell doing?" George said. "They're acting goofier than usual."

"I don't know, but I think they're trying to send some message about Elvira. They keep pointing to her and laughing."

"Yeah, because she's so shy. She's very pretty, though, don't you think?"

Josh had noticed Elvira Potter very early in their home class. She had a nice face and body. Her breasts were growing already. He had even spoken to her a couple of times very briefly, but she had just blushed without answering him. He said, "Yes, she's nice."

"I got an idea," George said. "When we get to the corner, why don't we cross over and talk to them? We could tease them. You're not late for the drugstore yet, are you?"

"No, I don't have to be there until 4:30. That's when Daddy has his busy time. But what will we do with the girls? They're acting awfully silly."

"I don't know, but it might be fun. You know Irene Stiles is having a scavenger hunt next week and I'm going. Are you?"

"I didn't get an invitation. I heard about it but just the girls were invited, and each had to invite some boy. That's the way they do at scavenger hunts, I guess. My brother, Theo, has been to some and he told me."

"That's right. Helen Broderick invited me." They had reached the corner then, at the same time as the group of girls, who were giggling more than ever. The dark-haired girl, Elvira, was obviously blushing.

"Come on," George said. "Let's cross over."

"Oh alright." Josh followed his friend.

They crossed and the light changed again for "Go" up Ash Street. The girls laughed and started across. "Come on," Irene Stiles said. "Don't stay in the middle of the street, silly. You can get killed that way."

"Come on," George said to Josh, but loud enough for the girls to hear. "Though I don't know exactly why. These girls are so silly you can hardly talk to them. Besides, I don't think they'd care if we'd both get killed, do you, Josh?"

Josh was getting uncomfortable. He really didn't like to tease, and being so close to the girls made him feel funny, sort of embarrassed. He said, "I don't think they want us here, George. Why don't we let them go on alone?"

"No, come on," George said. "That's just the way girls talk to boys, Josh. Ain't it, girls?"

"Don't be silly, George Hurley," Mavis Herschell said. "Just 'cause you're in high school don't make you any genius."

The boys were keeping just behind the jostling girls, two of which kept turning around, talking and giggling, Elvira Potter keeping a little ahead, with her eyes forward.

"I guess I'm smart enough. I noticed the algebra teacher asks me for answers pretty often."

"Oh, that don't mean much. Everyone knows boys are better than girls in math, but I bet you don't know many big words. I bet you don't know what 'superciliousness' means or 'disestablishmentarianism.'"

Josh just kept quiet, looking uncomfortable.

The other girl, Irene Stiles, said to her friend, "Come on, Mavis, don't argue with him. Remember what we want to do."

"Okay, you go ahead and tell him."

Irene turned to the other boy. "You don't have a girl to take to the scavenger hunt, do you, Josh?"

He glanced at a dog that was sniffing another, noticing from the corner of his eye that Elvira was looking away also. "No."

"Well, you'd like to go, wouldn't you? It's at my house."

Josh knew he would and had felt a little bad that he hadn't been asked.

She said, "Well, Elvira here doesn't have anyone to go with her yet and she told us she'd like to ask you. But she was too bashful to do it alone. Wouldn't you like to go with Elvira?"

Josh answered in one of his slowest drawls. "Well, I don't know."

"Sure Josh, come on. We can go together."

"Look, we'll ask Elvira," Mavis Herschell said. "You want Josh to take you, don't you Elvira?"

She nodded, her cheeks blushing.

The two boys hurried down the last block before getting to Bingham's Drugstore. The girls had turned off two blocks back. George said, "I'm glad you're going, Josh. You'll like it. You know they give you a list of crazy things to get and the one who gets most wins the prize. They'll probably have kissing games afterward too."

Josh didn't answer. The other boy said, "You don't need to be bashful, Josh. Girls won't hurt you. You just have to kid them around. They like that."

Josh wondered why he always felt so uncomfortable when he was around girls. He knew he liked them, but they sort of scared him too. It took too much nerve to ask them to do something with you. It was much easier to go fishing.

George Hurley put his arm on Josh's shoulder. "Don't get nervous about it, pal. We'll be together all the time. If you need any help, I'll be there."

He was a good buddy, Josh thought. And he seemed to be so easy with girls.

They reached the drugstore. George stopped outside. "How long you got to work, Josh?"

"I stay until Daddy closes, 6:30. There's usually a lot of people comes in then."

"Do you have any free time before you quit?"

"Sometimes. It depends on how many people come in. I just help out when Daddy and Theo are too busy. Daddy does the prescriptions, and Theo usually handles the other sales. When he gets too busy, I help with the lotions and shampoos and other nonprescription items."

George said, "The reason I was asking is because there's something I'd like to see, and maybe get one. Think you'd have time to show me?"

"Maybe, it's hard to know. What is it?"

George hesitated before asking, "Do you sell condoms in your store? That's what I'd like to look at. But I don't think I want to ask your father."

Josh knew they did. He had seen Theo take them out from the shelf below the cash register. A man would walk up to the counter and wait until no other customers were around and then ask in a low voice for a packet of Hercules or Rams. Theo would put the container in a bag so you couldn't see what was inside. Josh had studied the packets when no one was there, wondering what a rubber looked like. But he had said nothing about it to Theo or his daddy.

Josh said to George, "Why don't you ask Theo? He sells them."

George answered. "I'd feel funny. He's your big brother. Why can't you show me one when no one's there?"

"What do you want to do with it? You know men buy them to use with women."

"Aw, I don't know. But they say a guy should take a packet along when he goes on a date. You never know what'll happen. And I heard that Helen Broderick has put out already."

Josh couldn't quite believe what George was saying even though his friend was a year older. It didn't sound right though. Anyway, he said, "I guess I can show them to you if my brother's gone and no one else is around. Though it would be harder to sell you a packet. They cost three for a dollar, I think. But Theo usually rings up the cash register."

"Well, let's just go in and see. I can wait around a while if there's people. Let's just try, okay?"

They walked into the store. Josh could see his daddy in the back behind the prescription counter, mixing something. Theo was near the cash register. An older man was waiting in the prescription section, and a young woman was near the cash register. The two boys went behind the counter down from Theo. Josh put his briefcase on an empty space under the counter. He pointed to a chair, "You can sit there for a minute. I'll go see if my brother needs any help."

As he walked up to the cash register, he checked the shelf below. The condoms were there. Theo was putting something in a bag for the woman. He looked sideways and said, "There's nothing to do right now. But just wait. I need to go to the bathroom."

Josh leaned back and studied the aspirins and nose drops and other patent medicines that were on top of the counter near the cash register. The woman paid for her purchase and left, and the man came up with his prescription. Theo took the bill offered and rang up the charge. The man gave him the money and Theo returned the change. "I'm going back now. Probably there won't be anyone, but if it's a simple item, you can handle it. If not, call Daddy."

Josh looked back and could see his daddy checking over some other prescription slips. "Okay. How long will you be?"

"Maybe ten minutes. I want to get a smoke." He turned toward the back of the store.

Josh looked up again and saw his daddy was still occupied. He turned toward George Hurley and made a cupping gesture to tell him to come. George stood up and hurried to Josh's side. "What luck," he said. "Where'd your brother go?"

"Oh, he just went to the bathroom for a smoke. He'll be back in about ten minutes."

George quickly glanced back at Josh's father. "Your daddy's busy too. That's plenty of time. Let's see them."

Josh was having second thoughts about the whole affair. What if someone came in or Theo came back too soon and caught them? Besides it wasn't right to do something in secret, maybe even a little sinful. He said, "I don't know if I should, George. My daddy never told me I could handle these before. I think it would be better if you waited and asked Theo."

George said, "Why, that's them over there, isn't it? I don't see how it could hurt for us to just look at them. Come on, Josh, there's nothing bad about it. Your father sells them."

Josh hesitated just a little longer, then said, "Okay, but you got to hurry. Which one you want to see?"

George studied the open cartons. "What's reservoir tips?" he asked.

"I don't know for sure but I think it's a little sac on the end. You know, for the male liquid. They call it semen."

"How'd you find that out?"

"Oh, I read it in a medical book. My daddy has several medical books at home. Theo does too. He's going to medical school next year, you know."

"Okay, let me see the one called Man. Also one of the Rams."

Josh reached over and got out two packets which he handed to George who studied them carefully, turning them over and reading all the fine print. "Look," he said. "They both say 'For Prevention of Disease Only.' I thought men used them because they didn't want to make babies. I've heard that some girls who put out won't let you unless you wear one."

Josh was becoming more and more uncomfortable. "I don't know about that. But I think you ought to hurry, George. What if Theo comes back early? What do you want to do? You want one?"

George kept turning the packets over and over. "I just don't know. Could you sell me just one, I mean, could you open the packet?"

"No, I couldn't do that. I don't think Theo ever does," Josh said nervously, looking toward the back. "But you got to make up your mind."

"I got the money alright, from my allowance. But I can't decide which one. You got any ideas which is best?"

"I don't know. I told you I never did talk to Theo or my daddy about them. I don't think they'd want to talk about them." Suddenly Josh felt that someone was looking at them and he raised his eyes. His daddy was looking in their direction. But just as their eyes met, his father turned his glance down and began on another prescription. Josh reached over for the packets. "You have to decide right now, George, or I'm going to put them back. Theo will be coming any minute now."

"Okay, I'll take the Rams. That's a dollar, ain't it?"

"Yeah, give me the money." Josh hurriedly took the bill and put it into the register, closing the cash drawer as quietly as he could. In fact, he had to do it twice because the first time he did it so gently the drawer came out again.

"Here, take them," he said, handing the packet to his friend. George quickly pushed them into his pocket. Almost at the same time a woman walked through the door, and shortly after Josh could hear Theo returning. He said to George, indicating the end of the corridor, "Why don't you go back there to wait? I'll be there as soon as Theo gets back."

George said, "I'm not going to stay long. I got to get home. I'll just get my books and see you tomorrow."

"Okay." As George walked away, Josh looked up quickly and sure enough his daddy was watching again.

Josh was in his room, studying algebra. His daddy came in and Josh turned to face him. "How's school, Josh?"

"It's pretty good. I think I'll like Latin."

"Think you'll have time to help in the drugstore after school?"

"Sure Daddy. I can even do some of my homework when I'm there."

"I'm glad to hear that. We can use you, son, though we don't want to take you away from your studies. They're the most important thing for you now. But a couple of hours would be a big help."

Josh nodded. "I like to help you and Theo, Daddy."

His father was smoking a cigarette and looked around for an ashtray. He found none and finally walked to the window and tapped the ash off outside. He returned, hesitated, but then spoke. "There's another thing I wanted to talk to you about. It's that boy you go around with now, the one who was in the drugstore today, George Hurley. Well, I don't want to tell you what to do, Josh, or who to see. But I think I should give you advice when I think it's needed."

A heavy weight dropped in Josh's stomach. He had been worrying ever since they had left the drugstore that something like this would happen. He had kept very quiet all evening, going to his room as soon as he got home, coming down for dinner, eating quietly, and returning as soon as he was excused to continue his studies. But he hadn't been able to get it off his mind.

"Well, you know Josh, we Binghams believe in breeding, that who your family is makes a lot of difference. And we believe that our family has good lines." He hesitated, but began again. "However, even with good blood lines, it's important who you go around with. And if you get in with the wrong kind of people, things can go bad anyway. Now, why I'm bringing this up is because that fellow, George Hurley, has a pretty mixed-up past. We don't really know the family background because his mother came to this town by herself; so no one knows anything about her husband. Most people believe she is divorced. She could be a widow, but if she is, we think she'd tell someone."

Josh was beginning to feel bad. He liked George Hurley, but his daddy was the most important person in his life. He let his head hang, listening.

"And it's pretty well known that she brings men to her house. She's not what you would consider a moral woman." Another pause while his daddy put out the cigarette on the metal flange of the window sill. "And I'm afraid that kind of example has affected the boy. He seems to be a little too grown up. It's said he already goes with girls who don't have the best reputations." His daddy quickly added, "It's not the boy's fault, but others have to be careful with him. You know, Josh, I'm telling you all this for your own good."

"Yes Daddy, I know. But I don't do anything with George. We just walk to school together sometimes." Suddenly Josh remembered that he had agreed to go to the scavenger hunt with George. He was deceiving his daddy for the second time that day. He felt worse than ever.

His daddy went on, to the topic Josh feared most. "I know how you must feel about this because he's your buddy. But believe me, Josh, there are some things I know better than you. And I don't want to accuse you, or him, of anything, but I know you boys were doing something with the prophylactics this evening."

That was a word that men sometimes used instead of condoms. It was also written on the packets. Josh had looked it up in a medical dictionary and knew it meant an antiseptic of some kind, though he couldn't exactly figure out how. He felt all of a sudden like telling his father everything. He began, "Oh, Daddy, we didn't do anything very bad but . . . "

His daddy put his hand on the boy's shoulder and said, "You don't need to tell me about it, Josh. I'm just concerned about your future. And I think you'll be a lot better off if you don't see too much of that boy in the future. There's lots of other good boys in your school."

Josh felt miserable. He was at least glad that his daddy had not asked what they did with the condoms. His father finally said, "And so far as the prophylactics are concerned, Josh, I think you're still too young to be interested in them. Your work now is to get a good education. There'll be plenty of time to get involved with girls. Besides you know we are a Christian family and we believe that sexual acts should be between husband and wife only. That's all I'm going to say now. When you get a little older, we can talk about this more."

Josh just sat there in pain and embarrassment, thankful only that his daddy had not talked about the drugstore incident any further. But the thought that kept returning was, "Why did his daddy sell the condoms if he didn't approve of them?"

\* \* \* \* \*

The boy grew tall, even compared with the other boys in that privileged neighborhood. He was even a little taller than his brother, Theo, though by the way Kermit, his younger brother, was growing, it seemed that he might be even taller. Josh's light skin was liberally covered with freckles, seeming appropriate for his bushy red hair.

Apart from helping in the drugstore, fishing occasionally, and yard work, Josh's time was mostly spent with his books. He graduated with honors from high school and was accepted in Prince University Medical School immediately after receiving his B.S. in biology, *summa cum laude*. Josh's application was approved almost as a matter of course. Since Prince University was in Emmetsville, Josh was able to stay home during his entire education, replacing one set of books with another in his upstairs room.

\* \* \* \* \*

Josh strode down the hospital corridor in his smock, his stethoscope sticking out of his pocket. It was busy as usual with visitors, nurses, aides of various kinds, and patients in wheelchairs or walking slowly, usually with no apparent goal. Josh had been on that floor for three years, so he knew many people. He nodded or spoke to others in white smocks or uniforms as he passed.

Turning the corner into the admittance area, he thought how tired he was. He had been on night duty for two weeks, which left him hardly any extra time. During most of the day he was going over his books. But at least he was coming near the end. Next he would have his residency and then he could begin his own practice. And there was Alma.

He entered the large room, which contained a central desk and separate cubicles on the sides. This was where incoming patients had to fill the several forms required by the hospital, particularly concerning their financial background. Without good credit references or insurance, they could be turned away. Then they would have to go to City Hospital. But it didn't happen often because most of the people who came had already been referred by doctors who had practicing rights in the hospital, and most of them had no charity patients. They had referred such people to City Hospital in the first place. Even so, it sometimes happened. And it was Alma's job to get them transferred without a lot of bad feeling. She handled that well.

Josh saw her talking to a man and his wife. She was speaking very seriously, tossing her head in the attractive way she had. Josh admired her brown, wavy hair and even features. She wore glasses, but they seemed appropriate. Her skin was light and smooth. She was only wearing lipstick and dressed simply but attractively in a white blouse and navy blue skirt. Looking up, she saw him. When she smiled, her face was very pretty. She opened the fingers of one hand twice, her lips moving at the same time to indicate ten minutes.

Josh grinned back and moved his hands back and forth to indicate that she didn't need to hurry. He nodded at the receptionist at the center desk and sat down where he could watch Alma.

He had dated off and on during his college years, but only occasionally, being too busy with his studies to do more than that. He had first seen Alma in an English literature class in the last of his undergraduate years. The class was interesting even though he had known by then that he would go into medical school. But still he had needed to keep up his grade point average, so he had kept at Chaucer and Shakespeare and Dickens. He had stayed in the back of the classroom though, and she was in the front row. The professor called on her more often than anyone else. Whenever Josh's attention wandered away from the lecture or discussion, he would catch himself watching her. She would be looking at the professor, jotting down notes, or checking something in her text. He thought she had looked at him a couple of times, but couldn't be sure.

Then one day when he was hurrying across the campus to the literature class, he heard footsteps approaching from behind. She came abreast of him and said in a most open but pleasant manner, "Hi, know me? I'm in your English Lit class." And she held up the text to prove it.

He grinned, blushing a little perhaps, but saying, "Yes, I know. I've seen you there."

"I'm Alma Wicks. What's your name?"

"Josh Bingham." Then he had said, too formally he thought immediately after, "I'm pleased to meet you."

"Oh, I'm glad. But you sound so serious for a big tall redhead." She laughed.

They crossed the campus to class together, she doing almost all the talking, he responding simply, sometimes blushing.

They met sometimes after that, going to or from class. She talked most while he listened. Then he graduated and they didn't see one another for a long time. It wasn't until four years later that he met her again. He was an intern by then and walking through that same office when he noticed her typing. He stopped to wait until she got to the end of a sentence and looked up. Instant recognition, even if it had been the first time she had seen him in a medical smock. Her face lit up. She said, "English Literature 408. Mr. Red Bingham."

"Hello," he said. "You work here?" The question was obvious, he realized, even as he said it. But he could rarely think of smart things to say.

"It's not exactly literature," she said. "But it does help keep a person going. I'm trying to finish up my teaching credential. But look at you, a real doctor now. That's what you said you were going to be, isn't it? And I'll bet you're very good at it too, though sometimes your patients probably have trouble understanding what you want, you speak in such a low voice."

He grinned because she had kidded him before about how low he always spoke.

And that was how it had begun again. After that, Josh would stop in and see her after rounds or whenever he had some free time. After some months, he started to take her out on weekends. They went to restaurants and movies and concerts, and afterward when he took her home in his daddy's car, she would kiss him goodnight.

She finished with the couple she had been talking to and walked over to where Josh was sitting. "So, the great Dr. Bingham is here," she teased. "Saved a lot of lives today, doctor?" she said.

He grinned in acknowledgment though he couldn't think of anything quick to say in reply.

"You look tired, Josh. You've been working too hard."

"It's my turn on night duty. And there's so few older doctors around if you get a difficult case."

"Are you free now? I can get away for a half hour. We could go to the cafeteria for coffee and a sweet or even outside if you'd like. We could go over to Burns. Doesn't that sound good?"

He got up. "Let's go over to Burns. I want to tell you something."

"Just let me tell Carol I'll be gone for half an hour so she can have my next appointment wait if I'm a little late."

Josh waited patiently and when they got to the door, opened it for her. They walked slowly toward the coffee shop, his smock flapping, she walking near him.

"It'll be good when you don't have to do such long hours any more, Josh. I think it's too hard on you."

"Well, it won't be too long now. You know, I have only three months of the internship left."

A group of nurses and a couple of interns came by, returning from the place Josh and Alma were headed for. They greeted one another.

"We'll be finished at the same time," she said. "I'll get my credential then."

"You've had to put in a lot of hours too," he said. "Working and studying at the same time."

She laughed. "That's the way it is if you're not rich, if your daddy doesn't own a drugstore."

He knew she would have finished well before if she had not had to work so long. But her mother was a widow who just barely managed to get by. At least he knew they came from a good family, from old Maryland stock.

The two of them arrived at the coffee house and selected a rear booth. Several people from the hospital nodded or spoke as they passed. One fellow with black hair, heavy glasses, and dozens of pencils sticking out of his pockets said, "Hey Josh, come here a minute?"

Josh said to Alma, "Why don't you order for me too? I'll just have coffee and a piece of lemon meringue pie."

"Sure, Josh. But don't be too long. I only have half an hour."

"I won't. But it's probably something about one of the patients. Hal is working in the lab now." He stepped over to his colleague's table. "What's up?"

"Just a minute of your time, Josh. I know you and Alma have to get back. But I wanted to ask you something since you and me registered the same time and have the same classification. Have you heard anything from the draft board?"

"No, did you?"

"Unh unh, but several guys did. They got new classifications and some think they're going to be drafted even before they finish their residency. I'm worried about it."

Josh thought Hal could have waited to ask him that, rather than stopping him when he was using what little free time he had. Not that Hal knew what he was going to ask Alma, what he had been building himself up to for two days. But also Josh knew what a worrier Hal was. And a guy had to help his buddy when he could. He said very slowly, in his deep voice, a way of speaking he had already noticed was reassuring to patients, "I wouldn't worry about it, Hal. They're going to need a lot of doctors for certain, but I don't think they'll cut off their residency. They'll probably need doctors with a lot of experience, just to supervise medical corpsmen."

Hal looked relieved. "I just don't want to become a corpsman myself. And now that I got accepted, I want to get my residency done."

Josh glanced back at the booth where Alma was sitting. A girl had brought the coffee and pie. He said to Hal, "I have to go now, Hal. I have to be back on duty in twenty minutes and I need to talk to Alma a minute. Why don't you see me after my rounds? You know where I'm at, Room 488."

"Okay Josh. Sorry if I spoiled anything."

"No, that's alright, but you know how it is when you're on call." He walked back to the booth and sat across from Alma.

"Hal looks worried. A bad case?"

"No, it's nothing like that. Hal's just worried about the draft."

"Are you?"

Josh put sugar and cream in his coffee. "No. We'll all get commissions and it may not even last long enough for us to see active service. But I feel sure they'll let us finish our residencies."

He took a piece of the pie and chewed it slowly. Then he put his fork down. "That's what I wanted to talk to you about, Alma. I got my acceptance a couple of days ago to Brown General Hospital in Damascus."

Her eyes sparkled, and she touched his hand lightly. "Oh, why didn't you tell me? That's great news."

He ate more pie.

She said, "Oh, Josh, you're acting so funny. You ought to be celebrating." She paused. "Though I didn't have any doubt about it."

"Oh, it's nothing special. Almost everybody who gets their internship gets to go on. It's just what hospital you go to." He could hardly tell her that he had been planning this conversation for two days, repeating many times the exact phrases he would say. But it didn't come out as he had expected.

She said exuberantly, as if to make up for his low key, "Oh, Josh, did you know you're almost a real doctor now?"

He grinned, but then instead of continuing on the pie, he put down his fork. "You know Alma, Damascus is across the state, about two hundred miles away. I'll probably be very busy there. I wouldn't have much time to come back to visit. So what I was thinking is, why don't we get married as soon as I'm finished here?" He stopped then because even though they had understood for some time that they were going to get married, he had never actually asked her.

"Josh, is this a proposal?" She put her hand on his.

He knew he was blushing, but what could he do? Even Alma, whom he had known for almost four years, made him embarrassed. He said, "I thought it was sort of understood. But I guess I never did ask specifically, did I?"

She laughed again, "No, you didn't, Josh Bingham, but I really thought you would. I've noticed that you haven't been dating other girls very much."

She was joking again because he hadn't dated any others since he started seeing her. Anyway, the fat was in the fire, as his Grandfather Moses used to say, and it was kind of a relief. At least he didn't have to make any more plans. He waited quietly.

She laughed again. "What are you waiting for, Josh?"

He knew his blush was getting deeper. He didn't stammer when he answered though, just spoke lower. Whenever he felt unsure of himself, he spoke lower. His words came out like cold molasses. "I'm waiting for your answer, Alma."

She squeezed his hand and for a moment he was afraid she would lean across the table and kiss him but she just said, "Of course, Dr. Bingham. I thought you always knew I would."

\* \* \* \* \*

They married with the blessings of his family and her mother. Many of his relatives, along with her few, came to the wedding. The years of Josh's residency and wartime service passed and they returned to Emmetsville, where Josh began his long career as a pediatrician. Alma had worked as a teacher during the war years but did not begin again when they returned to Emmetsville. Instead, she became a full-time housekeeper, spending much of her time taking care of the three children as they came along in those first years of marriage. She cooked rich food and Josh put on a few pounds.

* * * * *

He very carefully put the bandage back over the boy's eye. "That looks good," he said. "It will be healed in no time. And then you can go back to play with your friends again, Herbert. I'll bet you miss them."

The boy did not respond, staring at the ceiling with the unbandaged eye.

"How are you feeling otherwise?" Josh asked.

"Alright," the boy said in a voice that was just barely audible.

The woman across the bed, his mother, spoke. "I think he's depressed, Dr. Bingham. He doesn't want to talk about it."

Josh smiled. "That's not unusual, Mrs. Madden. It's quite a shock for a boy his age to have something like that happen."

The woman started twirling her hands. "I just felt something would happen. I didn't even want him to play with firecrackers, but Mr. Madden said that was normal for a boy. But I was really scared of that little cannon. I just knew it was something like that when they called me."

Josh wished she would stop. It was apparent that the boy was feeling low, maybe even depressed, but this didn't help. It probably made him feel worse. Josh said, "It's alright, Mrs. Madden. Herbert has healed very well, and there are ways for fixing it up. He can get a glass eye identical to the other one. And there won't be any scars on his face."

Josh tried to turn back to the boy because the faster he got out of his depression, the better. It wasn't easy, Josh already knew, for a young fellow to accept a permanent loss of an eye or a limb, but it occurred. For a moment Josh wondered how his young Norman would accept such a loss, but he came back quickly to the matter at hand, the Madden boy. "I know, Herbert, that you are feeling a little sad. That's natural for a boy your age. But accidents are a part of life, and we have to adjust to them."

The boy remained immobile, continuing to stare at the ceiling with his remaining eye. "You'll be able to do almost all the things you did before, and your new eye will hardly be noticeable." There was no use telling the boy that though the facsimile would be very close to the real eye, it wouldn't move in synchrony with the real one. There had not yet been found any way to attach the muscles to glass. Josh put his hand on the boy's shoulder. "Now doesn't that make you feel better?" He said, "I'll bet you thought you would have to wear a black patch."

The boy moved, turning his head ever so slightly toward Josh, but still remained silent.

Josh heard footsteps coming from behind and quickly noticed the odor of perfume. One of the nurses had entered the room. The scent stirred him, but he kept his attention focused on the boy. "It's alright, Herbert, if you don't want to talk about it right now. But you shouldn't think about it too much." Then, with inspiration, "I know, what you need is something good to eat." Josh turned to face the nurse. "I'll bet we can get Nurse Jane to have some ice cream sent up for you special. Wouldn't that be a good treat?"

The boy, who was slightly plump, turned his head toward Josh, saying, "I guess so."

"It'll be no trouble, Doctor," the nurse said.

Josh started to turn away but stopped and said, "And Herbert, I want you to tell the nurse to call me any time you feel like talking. I might be busy but I'll come as soon as I can. She can call me on the intercom."

The boy finally looked at Josh and nodded. Josh turned to leave. The boy's mother said, "Thanks doctor."

The nurse walked alongside Josh as he headed down the corridor. "That was very good with the boy, Dr. Bingham," she said. "If anything ever happens to my boy, I surely want you to be his doctor."

Josh blushed, saying, "It's just something you have to do."

\* \* \* \* \*

It was a substantial brick house on a three-quarter-acre yard, covered with well-tended grass and overshadowed by several eastern hardwoods. There were flower beds along the sidewalks and near the house and in the back a small vegetable garden. Off in one corner was a pile of mulched leaves and grass stems.

Josh was kneeling in the grass next to the border strip along the sidewalk. He was dressed in baggy khakis that he got from war surplus. He could no longer fit into the ones from his service years. He had just finished digging up the strip to plant tulips and daffodils for spring. Eight-year-old Constance was helping, putting the bulbs in at six-inch intervals while he covered them. She was dressed in a corduroy dress and penny loafers.

"Why do you plant them now, Daddy, when they don't come up before spring?"

It was a clear cool autumn day. The leaves on most of the trees were beginning to turn color. Josh answered, "Well, they go through a period of dormancy in the ground. It's like sleeping. The bulbs put out roots and gather their strength so they can push the flowers out in the spring."

"But you don't do that to all the flowers. You don't plant roses in the fall."

She was a talkative little thing, he thought, something she got from her mother for sure. Patiently, "Plants are different. Some have to be planted as seeds and others as bulbs. And some, like roses, are planted as small bushes. Plants are like animals, Constance, there are many different kinds and they grow differently."

She reached the end of the row and got up on her knees. "There, we did it, Daddy, three whole rows." She looked back down the newly planted strip, saying, "Oh, this is fun, Daddy. There'll be so many flowers in the spring." She stopped to think for a minute, then said, "But they have such funny names. Daffodils sound like daffy and tulips sounds like two lips. Why do flowers have such funny names, Daddy?"

"I don't know, Constance. That's just the names they have. If you want, we can look them up in the dictionary when we go in. It tells you where words came from."

"That'd be fun. I'd like to do that."

Josh looked up then at the house and yard. It was probably an average one in Glenarm Acres, one of the better suburbs. But even though his practice was getting better all the time, he wouldn't have been able to swing it without a loan from his father.

He heard the other girls playing on the sidewalk a little way down from the street. He turned to see Harriet and her friend, Julie, both on minibikes and calling to one another as they coursed the sidewalk. "Where's Norman?" he asked Constance.

"I think he's in the playroom, probably with his erector set."

Josh had a feeling of fulfillment, surrounded by his own growing children in a comfortable house and neighborhood. Two squirrels racing along the top of a hickory branch caught his eye. He watched them race around the tree trunk then returned his gaze to little Constance brushing the dirt off her knees. Josh thought he was a man of nurturance, he made things grow. It was a good feeling. He came back to the then and now, saying, "I think it's time to go in soon. Your mama probably has supper ready."

"Should I call Harriet?"

"Why don't you go down and tell her? I don't think it sounds nice for little girls to yell up and down the street. I'll gather up the tools and take them into the garage."

"Okay, Daddy." Constance skipped down the walk toward her sister while Josh gathered the planting implements. He took them into the garage, carefully placing them on their proper hooks or shelves. He stopped at his workbench and picked up the fly he had been working on. It was a tiny red tuft attached to a small hook with two translucent plastic wings sticking out of each side. He tested the tuft and wings to see whether the glue was fully set. Satisfied, he took a small cardboard and pulled off eighteen inches or so of black thread. Carefully, he knotted it at one end, then began to wrap it round and round just below the eye where the leader would be attached. When it was fully wrapped, he took the brush from the glue pot and dabbed it on the wrapped thread. When it dried, it would be rock hard. He put the hook end of the fly into the tiny vise, more to keep from losing it than to keep it tight while setting. He leaned back then to imagine the fat bream or bass that would appear from under lily pads and burst from the water with gaping jaws, to get caught on his handiwork.

His reveries were broken by the sound of the girls' voices. He could hear Harriet sniffling in between cries at Constance. The two came around the corner, Harriet pushing her bike. As soon as she saw Josh, she dropped the bike and ran to him, crying loudly, "Daddy, Daddy, Constance knocked me off the bike and hurt me."

One of Harriet's arms was lightly skinned. "Here, let me look at it." He squatted and took the girl's arm in his hand. Taking his handkerchief out, he brushed the dirt off and turned the arm gently. "Well, it's okay, I think. Doesn't look like anything that a little soap and water wouldn't take care of."

"But Daddy, she was so mean to me," Harriet sniffled. "Aren't you going to punish her?"

Constance said, "Daddy, I didn't do anything. She said she wasn't ready to come home yet so I just held her bicycle and it tipped over."

Josh had just taken off the support side wheel the day before. He had thought it was too early for a child of six but Harriet had made such a fuss because her friend Julie had just had hers taken off. Harriet spoke again without ceasing to sniffle. She had become good at that.

She sniffed, "Daddy, she did push me. She wanted to do something mean just because I wouldn't do what she wanted right away."

Constance broke in, "Daddy, that's a fib. I didn't."

Josh reached down and picked Harriet up. He was surprised at her weight already. Constance put her hand on his pant leg. He said, "Now girls, there's no need for quarreling. No one got hurt. We should all be thankful for that. And I'm sure it was an accident. Constance will try harder for it not to happen again, I'm sure. So why don't we just forget it and go upstairs for supper? I bet Mama has something good, like pecan or peach pie. And maybe we can have some ice cream with it."

Harriet slowed in her sniffling but before stopping completely, reiterated, "Well I think Constance ought to be punished because she's mean to me."

Josh patted her brown curls. "Alright now. Let's just forget about it and go upstairs for dinner."

Constance said grace when they were all seated at the dining room table. As soon as she was finished, Cora, the maid, brought in the platters and bowls of food: shepherd's pie, string beans, candied sweet potatoes, sliced tomatoes, and gravy. She set them in front of Alma, who proceeded to fill a plate for Josh first, then one for each of the children, passing them down to each person in turn. Harriet said, "I don't want any vegetables, Mama. Just give me shepherd's pie and sweet potatoes. And don't we get any cornbread?"

"You have to eat some of everything," Alma said. "Vegetables are good for you."

"But sweet potatoes are vegetables."

"But they're starchy," Alma said.

"I know, but ain't they vegetables?"

"Don't say 'ain't'. And you can't just eat starchy things. Now you just go ahead and eat some of everything. You don't have to eat it all, but you have to eat some. And yes, we are having cornbread. Cora hasn't had time to bring it out yet."

Just then the black woman brought a flat baking pan of golden cornbread, cut into rectangles. "Oh, give me some," Constance said, her eyes sparkling in anticipation.

The black woman, who was wearing a gray uniform with a white apron, looked at Alma, who said, "You can go ahead and serve the children a piece first, Cora."

"Yes, ma'am," she said in the long-voweled speech of the deep south.

She had come to Emmetsville from Mississippi three years before.

Cora returned to the kitchen.

Soon all the family members were eating, and conversation lagged. Alma broke the silence. "Josh, Cora's leaving next month. She's going to work in the furniture factory. I just hate the thought of breaking in another girl. And you know it's so hard to get a good one. If they're not lazy, they steal. I just know we should have raised her wages."

"Well, you know she is getting pretty good pay," he said. "Eighteen dollars a week, plus board. That's almost as much as the nurse's aides get."

"I know, but she can get more at the furniture factory. I just don't know why we couldn't have raised her salary to twenty-four dollars." Alma had set her knife and fork down and was staring at Josh.

He looked at her and thought that she was still a pretty woman, with very curly brown hair. And though she disliked wearing them, her glasses were not unbecoming. She didn't have the thin figure of her college days, but you couldn't call her fat either. One unusual thing happened when she had put on weight. Unlike most other women who got heavier, instead of her breasts getting larger, they just seemed to have disappeared, submerged in the extra flesh. She was a dedicated mother though, he thought. And she cooked well, especially pies and cakes. Josh said, "I don't know, Alma. That seems like a pretty good salary for a maid. And we do have to watch our money some. You know we want to get you a new station wagon this year. And they're going up all the time."

The telephone in the small alcove rang. Alma said, "That's probably for you, Josh. There's already been a couple of calls this afternoon. I asked them if it was an emergency and when they said it wasn't, I didn't call you. Though I don't know why they call you on your afternoon off. I told you I don't think you should give your home number to all your patients."

He started to get up. "Did you get their names and numbers?"

"Of course. Don't you think I know how to do anything? You must remember, Josh, I got paid for arranging things for people for years."

"I didn't mean anything, Hon. I just wanted to be sure," he added, "so I could call them back."

He walked to the phone. "Hello," in his deep, low voice.

"Dr. Bingham?"

"Ye-es. Who is this, please?"

"It's Mrs. Manning. I'm calling about my Jamie. He went out swimming this afternoon and came home all wet and tonight he has a fever."

Josh could imagine Mrs. Manning's agitated face. The boy was her only son and since her husband had left her, he was the most important thing in her life. Every little change in his health had her on the phone. Josh said patiently, "Are there any other symptoms?"

After Josh finished with Mrs. Manning, he stood at the phone for a moment considering the possibility of returning the other calls. He had seen the names and numbers while waiting for Mrs. Manning to explain everything about her boy's condition. Alma's voice intruded, "Josh, aren't you coming back to the table?"

He turned then. "Sure Alma, I'm coming."

When he sat down again, Harriet and Constance were bickering, while Norman was playing with what was left on his plate. Alma said, "I told Cora to bring the dessert because the children were getting anxious and I didn't know when you were coming back."

"Alright." Josh took a drink of water from the cut crystal glass, a wedding present from his brother, Theo. The kitchen door opened and Cora brought in a pineapple upside-down cake, the fruit pieces and sides encrusted delectably with golden carameled sugar.

"That looks very good," he said. "Did you make it, Alma?" She began cutting wedges and putting them on dessert plates, saying, "Of course. You should know by now that I usually make the main dishes, but always the desserts, no matter how busy I am. And I can tell you that with hauling the girls around, watching Norman, doing the shopping, and paying the bills, and all the other things, it's not easy. But I wouldn't neglect the family whatever happened."

Josh quietly began to eat a little more of what was left on his plate. It was cold by then though, and the shepherd's pie in particular didn't taste so good. He pushed his plate forward a little. Alma said, "Are you finished with that? If you are, I'll have Cora take your plate to the kitchen."

"I think I've had enough, though I want a piece of that delicious-looking cake." He thought he might even have two pieces.

The children were busy eating theirs, hardly looking around. Alma cut a larger piece and put it on a plate for Josh. She took his main plate and put it on the small separate table she used for that purpose. She handed him his cake.

He found it to be just as good as it looked, the sweet, fruity glaze having just the right crunchiness. Before he could compliment Alma, she began. "Josh, I just don't think it's right for you to let all your patients call every night, even on your afternoon off. It ruins every meal. Other doctors don't do it unless there's an emergency. You have to think about your family sometime."

Josh kept eating, though he said between bites, "I know, Alma. I'll try to explain to my patients better and not have them call me unless it's urgent." Pause, then, "But some of the parents just have to talk to someone."

She looked exasperated. "Oh Josh, you're incorrigible. You're just a softy. Besides, you're supposed to cure people's illnesses, not listen to all their worries. You're a medical doctor."

Josh thought that was the idea he had had when he went to medical school but it hadn't turned out that way. As many people, particularly parents, had to tell you their troubles as needed medicine. They believed you were doing something for them if you listened patiently. It was an irony though, he thought, that this worked with almost everyone except Alma. No amount of listening seemed to pacify her. Even so, she was his wife.

Alma said, "I just hope you do something about it, Josh, though I just know you won't."

Josh had finished his cake. Alma said, "Do you want another piece?"

He smiled. "Sure, Hon. It was delicious."

She took his plate and put another large piece on it. Before beginning to eat it, he said, "Alma, I've been thinking about Cora and I think I can work it out so we can raise her wages." That might make them a little tight in the budget, but if he had to he could easily get a small loan, his practice was getting so good. Why, if he could just collect all his back medical bills, it would be more than enough.

Alma said, "I thought that with how well your practice was getting, you could at least do that. But you know I'm no expert in money matters."

\* \* \* \* \*

The years passed uneventfully except for the growth of the children and the aging of Josh and Alma. Her hair started to turn gray, though it remained full. Josh's red hair remained unchanged. Both he and Alma filled out a little more, though neither came to be fat. She went on diets periodically, though with little long-term effect. His practice continued to grow so rich he joined a corporation of doctors. He also began to lecture at the university. There was always enough money, though little extra.

* * * * *

Josh was going over the charts in the ward office on the third floor. He was vaguely aware of bodies moving about him but kept his attention focused on the charts in front of him, visualizing each sick little person. Then he became aware of a slight swishing sound and a scent. He looked up. Nurse Clinton was standing in the doorway. She smiled when their eyes met. "Is there a doctor in the house?" she said teasingly.

"Hello," he said. "I'm just going over the charts before the interns come."

Four interns were due in fifteen minutes to accompany him on his late morning rounds. He had developed the habit of going over the charts beforehand. That way he would have more definite ideas of what to suggest when the students gave him their ideas. He was aware of the nearness of the woman, as well as her scent. It was a little strong for a hospital, but acceptable. But then, perhaps he was over-conscious of a little perfume since Alma hardly ever used any. The nurse said, "Sounds like a good idea, though if what I've seen is typical of you, Doctor, it's hardly necessary. But now I can understand why the interns come up here too."

"What do you mean?"

"I guess I'm telling tales, but usually the interns come in before you do and go over the charts too."

Josh chuckled. "I didn't know that."

"You know, Dr. Bingham, you've got quite a reputation around here." She leaned over to put the medicine list on a hook, so close she brushed Josh's shoulder with her breast. He leaned back so quickly that his movement was conspicuous.

She grinned at him, "What's the matter, doctor, did I bump you?"

He knew he was blushing when he answered. "No, I just wanted to get out of your way."

"Or maybe you thought I was fragile or something, aye? That a little bump might hurt me."

He was getting nervous and he knew he was probably blushing. Teasing made him very uncomfortable. He just said, "Oh no, I wasn't thinking anything."

She opened the chest and began assembling the medicine for the other end of the hall, saying over her shoulder, "Will you need me for rounds?"

"No, I can't think of anything special this morning. Thanks, Miss Clinton. He knew she was divorced, but she was so young he felt uncomfortable calling her Mrs.

She set the medicine tray down and came back out, placing herself in front of him. He couldn't help being aware of the shapeliness of her body, particularly her legs. When he looked up, she had that teasing look again as she said, "For anything else?"

For a moment Josh couldn't figure out what she meant. He said very slowly. "I don't understand."

"I mean do you want me for anything else?"

He still couldn't fathom her meaning well. Was the young lady offering to help him on some other task or did the question have other implications? He had recognized that teasing way for several weeks and it had made him increasingly uncomfortable. He had tried to make his visits to her ward as brief as possible. He had thought it must have been just the difference in their ages. She must have been fifteen years younger. He said, "No, Miss Clinton, I'm fine." Thinking she would go about her business.

Instead she remained standing in front of him. He kept his eyes on his charts as long as he comfortably could but finally had to look up. She was looking straight at him, the grin still on her face. Her blond hair was coiled in a knot on the back of her head, her nurse's cap pinned to it rakishly. For a fleeting moment he thought of that long hair being uncoiled and falling over her shoulders. Momentarily he had a fantasy of running his fingers through it. But then he shuddered inwardly and deliberately changed images. He evoked the mind picture of Constance, now a tall girl in high school, and Harriet just finishing grade school, and Norman, a gangly boy of ten.

The nurse said, "Dr. Bingham, you're daydreaming." She laughed.

"I guess so," he said and began to turn back to his work, wondering why he could never think of any clever things to say to persons like her.

She said, "You know, doctor, you work too hard, every day, and even on Saturday." She added, "And sometimes you even come on Sunday, they tell me." She laughed. "You know, all work and no play, and all that."

He had heard nurses tease doctors many times, but he had noticed that they were usually with men who teased back. He couldn't understand why anyone would do it to him. He always kept to his work. Still uncomfortable, though getting a little displeased also, he answered. "I have my own kinds of recreation, Miss Clinton."

She apparently detected his disturbed tone when she said, "I didn't mean anything by that, Dr. Bingham. I was just talking, you know, to help pass the time faster." Then she went back to her desk and began going through papers.

He felt a little bad that he might have hurt her feelings. That kind of teasing talk went on all the time, and she probably did it naturally. He looked at her in profile and couldn't help admiring the evenness of her features. He said, "I didn't mean anything critical, Miss Clinton."

She looked up and smiled again. He could see thoughts fleeting through her mind expressed on her face. Finally she said, "I was just going to ask you to join us after work at Harry's Bar. Several of the nurses and doctors go there for a drink or so to relax. I thought you might like it too."

He was momentarily dumbfounded. He had heard some of the others talk about that, but most were single. There were a few married doctors, but it was hardly the kind of group a family man would become a part of. Things could happen that were hardly moral. He said then, very slowly and seriously, "Miss Clinton, you know I'm married and have a family. And that's not the kind of group I go out with. Besides, I only take an occasional drink."

She stood up abruptly, a slight look of anger on her face. "I didn't mean anything, Dr. Bingham. It's just a little social group. Married people can go also. But I don't want to make an issue out of it."

One of the nurse's aides came then and Nurse Clinton turned to her. "Annie, the new beds came in last night and they're a little more complicated. I set one up in Room 408. You get Matilda and meet me there and I'll show you how they work."

She walked off down the hall with the aide, and he rapidly finished the last chart.

\* \* \* \* \*

Josh was sitting in the living room, smoking a late pipeful. He knocked out the ashes and put the briar down. The flames in the fireplace were low, so he got up and put another log on. For several minutes he sat watching the flame as it began to grow, curling around the split oak on both sides. Little explosions of sparks occurred periodically. He looked at his watch, 10:15.

Constance came in, holding one of her books. She had become a tall girl with tightly curled red hair. Her breasts were developing. Her hips too were getting larger, partly, Josh figured, because of her emerging womanliness, partly because, like her mother, whatever extra weight she put on went to her hips. She said, "Hi Daddy, what are you doing?"

He waved toward the side table. "Oh, I've just been reading some journals."

"You have so many, don't you? Being a doctor sure is hard work, isn't it?"

"There's a lot to read, Pumpkin. That's why I'm glad you are becoming a good reader."

She sat down on the deep pile rug between him and the fireplace. The flames highlighted her red hair. She said, "I don't know what I'm going to be when I grow up. Maybe I'll be a doctor too, or maybe I'll be a literature teacher. I love poetry, Daddy. Browning is my favorite. Who do you like best?"

He thought for a moment. "I guess Longfellow or Emerson."

"Oh, I like Longfellow too, particularly 'Evangeline.' I think it's so sad what happened to her."

Josh put his hand on her frizzy hair and pleasured in the feel of the wiry ringlets. "What do you do to fix your hair, Hon?"

She shook her head. "Oh, Daddy, it's so bad. The other girls all have long straight or wavy hair. And mine is so frizzy, it's like a colored person's except for the color. You know Cora's is kind of like mine except it's black. And she even gets hers straightened."

"But you do something to yours, too, don't you? Doesn't your mama help you?"

"Sure, I set it two or three times a week. The other girls set theirs to wave it but I set mine to straighten it out. And I go to the beauty parlor once a week. Mama lets me do that. But nothing lasts long. About one day after a setting at home it's as kinky as before. And after going to the beauty parlor, it's only good about two days." She put her hands up and grabbed both sides of the wiry shock, crying, "All the other girls have such nice hair. Even Harriet does. And I have this. Daddy, why would God give me such kinky, red hair? Doesn't he know how important hair is for a girl?"

Josh patted her hand, saying, "Now, now, Pumpkin, it's not that bad. I know it's a little different, but it's really a very nice color. And think how hard some girls have to work to get theirs curly."

She answered, "But mine's not curly, it's kinky. And that's different." She shook her head again. "I just hate it, Daddy."

"Oh, now I wouldn't say that, Hon. It's just different, that's all. And think of the good things, think about how thick it is. Why, I'll bet a lot of girls with thin hair would love to have yours. And think of the other good things, like how healthy and smart you are. You know, you shouldn't blame God for the little things you don't like. We don't know why he made things the way he did. God works in mysterious ways, you know. You'll understand better when you grow up."

Josh decided to light up again. He reached for his pouch and filled his pipe to the brim. Pressing the tobacco down, he looked around for his lighter. Constance shot to her feet. "I see it, Daddy, it's on the floor. You must have dropped it. I'll get it." She slid over and reached under the chair where he was sitting, pulling out the cylindrical pipe lighter. She got on her knees, "Can I light it, Daddy?"

He smiled. "Sure, Hon. That would be very nice."

She snapped the starter press, and a small jet of flame darted out. Holding it over his pipe, she held it steadily until he began puffing smoke.

He took it out of his mouth after a full draw, blowing the smoke out slowly and with pleasure.

She leaned back. "Oh Daddy, I like it so much when you smoke your pipe. It smells so good. And you look so happy." She thought for a moment, then, "I wish I was a boy because then I'd smoke a pipe too. Daddy, can I smoke a pipe when I get bigger?"

She was leaning against his leg. He let his hand rest on her head. "Well, Pumpkin," he said in his drawlingest voice. "You know there are some things men can do and others that women can. Like you know that ministers and doctors are men most of the time, and women are nurses or secretaries. And you know that men are soldiers while women are very good at keeping house and taking care of children. So, there's lots of little customs that men have while women have others. Women fix their hair and make themselves pretty, while men smoke pipes and watch sports."

Constance picked up a stick and began striking the frame of the fire grate, saying, "Well, I don't think it's fair. I don't know why a girl can't do what a man can. Men get all the fun of smoking, so why can't women?"

Josh sighed and patted her head again. "That's just the way it is. I don't know all the reasons why people can do what they can or cannot do."

Constance pulled her knees under her. Her plaid skirt came just to the edge of her knees. "Anyway," she said, "there's still a lot of things we can do. I'm glad I can go fishing even if I am a girl. I really like that, Daddy."

"I'm glad of that, Pumpkin. It's a very healthful way of spending your leisure time. It doesn't hurt anyone, and you get out in the good clean air. And sometimes you even get some fish." He chuckled. "That bass you caught on Fishers Lake wasn't bad. It weighed 2½ pounds, you know. And I was proud of the way you played it."

"Oh, it was fun, Daddy. I just can't wait every week for the day to go fishing. Are we going this Saturday?"

Josh grinned with pleasure as he too anticipated cruising along the shore in the aluminum boat, casting flies to the edge of the reeds and lily pads, expecting each time a voracious bluegill or largemouth bass to burst out. And with his own children it was so much better. He said, "I think so, Constance. Unless there's some kind of emergency at the hospital. But you can probably count on it. We'll go just after lunch."

"Oh goody. Where will we go?"

"Well, we could go to the TVA dam for channel cats. They bite good in the fall. But you know, we'd have to do bait fishing for them. Otherwise, if you want to go fly fishing, we could try Black Lake. I heard from one of the other doctors that the smallmouths were biting good there."

"Oh, I want to go fly fishing, Daddy. I like that best. Can we do that?"

"No reason why not, so long as the weather's good." Constance put down the stick she had been playing with and turned to face Josh directly, looking at him in her super-serious way. "Daddy, there's another thing. Could you show me how to make flies? I want to learn, and you know how to do it so good."

He grinned. "Sure, Hon, it's not hard."

Josh puffed on his pipe again, creating a cloud of smoke. He looked at his watch, 10:47, late for a schoolgirl, he thought. "Don't you think it's about time for you to be getting to bed, Hon?"

The frizzy-haired girl didn't answer immediately, instead pushing with her stick against a small beetle that had crawled out from under the bark of the heating log and was sluggishly trying to get across the tiled area in front of the fireplace. It had evidently been partially numbed by heat or smoke. Constance put her stick in front of it and the beetle first tried to climb it, but after falling back several times, decided to try to go around. Each time it got around the stick and began crawling away again, she would move the stick in front of it and it would repeat the process. It seemed her mind was elsewhere.

Josh watched her for a bit, then said, "You ought to throw the beetle in the fire, Hon. Your mama wouldn't want it in the house."

"Okay, Daddy." She picked up a loose piece of bark and scooped up the insect, to drop it onto the burning logs. The tiny creature curled and twisted into a charred ember almost instantaneously. In no more than a couple of minutes all traces had disappeared as if the creature had never existed.

Constance still gave no indication of leaving, again playing with the stick. Josh said very softly, "Hon, I honestly think it is time for you to go to bed. You know you have to get up early for school. And now during your growing years, sleep's very important."

She stood up slowly and tossed the stick into the fire. It burst into flame. She turned toward him. "Okay, Daddy. I don't feel sleepy, but I guess it is time."

She bent over and gave Josh a kiss on the cheek. He patted her arm. When she stood up, she said, "Can I read a little before I go to sleep, some poetry maybe?"

Josh looked at his watch again, three before eleven. "It's very late, Hon. I think you ought to get to sleep as soon as you can. I think you should just read your prayer book for five or ten minutes and then turn out the light."

She looked resigned, then, "Oh, alright. That's another bad thing about being a kid; you have to go to bed so early."

He chuckled. "Yes, I know, but as I said before, you must remember the good things. And Hon, you'll be grown up before you know it."

She picked up her book from the coffee table and started across the room. Josh watched her slightly uneven sway. She had the same kind of poor set to her hips as her mother. He thought perhaps they should take her to see another orthopedic specialist. They might be able to do something about it yet. Otherwise, it could get arthritic early. Then he thought about her teeth. They really did need braces. It wasn't that her teeth were terribly out of place, but a little correction then would carry her through the rest of her life. And good teeth were so important to a young woman. Josh sighed inwardly, thinking that at least they had done the surgery to remove the birthmark when she was quite young.

Constance stopped in the middle of the room and turned around, hesitating at first.

Josh said, "Did you want to say something, Hon?"

"Yes, but I don't want you to be mad, Daddy. And maybe it's something you wouldn't want me to ask."

"Well, Pumpkin, you can try. It's probably not so serious as you think."

She said, "It's about you and Mama, Daddy." She hesitated again.

"Ye-es." Very slowly.

"It's that you stay down here every night by yourself and Mama goes to bed early. I thought husbands and wives were supposed to go to bed together. Isn't that so?"

Josh felt he was reddening, surprised that it was happening in front of his daughter. But he answered calmly without too much hesitation. "Your mama gets very tired, Hon. You know she has a lot of work to do, taking care of us all."

"But you work hard too, Daddy. It seems to me that you work as much as Mama. And she has Cora to help."

"But you know she thinks there are some things a mother ought to do, like cooking. And I have a lot of help at the hospital also."

Constance hesitated again but then came out without further encouragement. She was becoming more outspoken, much more than the other children. "Another thing is your beds. I thought married people were supposed to sleep together. And you have separate beds."

Josh was becoming uncomfortable. He still remembered clearly what had happened. They had slept together in the same bed for the first four or five years of marriage, and most nights they went to bed at the same time. But after the birth of Harriet, Alma wanted a separate bed. She said she couldn't sleep because of his snoring. And she stayed up later with him too, knitting or reading, while Josh read his journals or worked on some project for the house. But she started to go to bed earlier by herself more often, usually complaining that she was tired or had a headache. So, they had come to an arrangement of separate beds, she retiring early while he stayed downstairs until one or two a.m. before going to his own bed. On rare occasions he got into bed with her, but more often than not she didn't want to make love then either. So he did it less and less.

Josh looked up at Constance. "Well, Pumpkin, married people do both. Some sleep together, and others have separate beds. People are different. And your mother gets very tired at night, so we decided it would be best to have separate beds." He broke the train then though, and said in a little stronger tone, as strong as he ever used, "But I think that's enough for now. It's getting late, and this is a complex subject. I think you should be getting off to bed. You'll understand about these kinds of things better when you're grown up." Josh felt a little uneasy that he was not explaining any better, but he was getting too uncomfortable.

Constance looked at him for a moment, then tossed her head. "Okay, Daddy, I'm going. But when I get married, I'm going to sleep with my husband, in the same bed."

Josh looked at her a little sadly. "I think that's very good, Hon. But now off you go. We can talk about this again some other time."

His firstborn turned and walked away.

Josh heard her footsteps recede up the stairway and finally fade out. Quietness settled. Very faintly he heard the deep throaty call of a hoot owl, perched in the deodar across the road, he figured. He reached over for the television guide and was pleased to find a John Wayne film. His favorite actor. He turned on the set. Settling down into the easy chair, he relit his pipe.

* * * * *

Josh worked hard and soon became known as one of the best pediatricians in the state. He was offered an adjunct professorship at the university, which he took, and where he afterwards gave lectures twice a week. More money came in, but more was spent also, so there was little accumulation. Life at home remained much the same. Alma managed the housework and did the errands. There was less to do for the children as they grew up. Her health was good enough, though her eyesight became quite poor. Without her glasses, she could just barely distinguish objects. At her request, Josh moved into a separate room. That way, when he came up late at night, he didn't disturb her at all. The children continued to grow well and to do well in school. Constance was in her last year at Meredith Manor, already accepted at Holman University in Oklahoma. Josh hadn't wanted her to go so far, but she was more and more headstrong. And it was a good Protestant school, though he would have preferred it not to be Baptist. But at least it was almost all white, as Meredith was. Josh and Alma had early decided to send her to Meredith, which was a private school where there were no colored people. He didn't have anything against the desegregation that had come, but the public high schools had gone way down scholastically since all the poorer-class colored from the rural areas had come. It was more expensive to send the children to private school, but you could be sure they were getting a good education that way.

* * * * *

Josh looked out over the backs of the parishioners in the Emerson Methodist Church and felt comfortable. They were singing Psalm 82, "The Guiding Light," which he could follow with hardly a thought. After all, he had been coming for almost fifty years, and even in the Presbyterian Church where he had gone before marrying Alma, that had been a favorite. He gazed at the well-dressed men, almost all in good, conservative suits, shirts, and ties, like him. The women wore brighter dresses, and many had hats on. There were no shabby people visible. It was a well-to-do congregation.

Josh's eyes stopped at the cluster that was his family: Alma, head straight ahead, singing loudly and off key. Constance was next to her, most conspicuous by her bright red hair, in small waves for the special service. She must have set it the night before, or perhaps she had gone to the beauty parlor. She would have done her best for Christmas. Harriet was on the other side of Alma, not so tall and with hair not so conspicuous. She had her psalm book open and was reading the words of the song. Next to her was Norman, almost as tall as Constance already. He was going to be the biggest in the family, Josh thought, just like Grandpa Harry. Just then the boy turned his head and caught Josh's eye. The boy grinned. Josh raised his hand ever so slightly. The boy turned back to the singing.

The vocal ended and Pastor Sanders read a passage from one of St. Paul's letters to the Corinthians. It was just as familiar as the psalm. That was as it should be, Josh thought, since he had been reading the Bible faithfully every night since he was eight. He probably knew it as well as most young ministers.

The pastor finished the commentary on the reading, made the usual parish announcements, and finished with a special call for generosity. "Dear brothers and sisters in Christ, we are indeed happy to be gathered here today, the most important in the year, the birthday of Christ. It is a time above all others, when we rejoice in our Christian heritage and togetherness. And it is as it should be, a day of rejoicing with our near and dear. We show our love to the other members of our families and friends by giving gifts. These are marks of our love for one another, as well as rejoicing that we are Christians. And we dine well this day in the bosom of our families, another of the celebrations of our joyousness. And all that is as it should be.

"But as you know, there is another side to Christianity, a very important one. Christianity is a faith that takes in all people everywhere. There are no chosen people. All believers are chosen. The true Christian has concern for all. Moreover, we know that many people in the world lack the very basics we take for granted, much less the luxuries that so many of us are so fortunate to have. They call those countries underdeveloped. We are concerned about the people who live there, so many of whom lack the bare essentials of food, clothing, and medicine. And though we think of them often, at no time do our thoughts turn to them more fully than at Christmas.

"And today, as announced earlier, we have a special collection, one that has become traditional throughout the Protestant Council, the Underdeveloped World Fund. As most of you know, this money is put into a central depository and then distributed to the neediest countries. It will buy food for the hungry, clothing for the needy, and medicine for the sick, channeled through Protestant mission houses."

He paused, then added. "I urge you to give generously. Then you will be participating in the true spirit of Christmas when you leave the church to go to your family celebrations." The pastor returned to the altar bench and sat down.

Gerald Blackburn, who was across the aisle, nodded to Josh, and the two turned to walk back to the little cubicle where wicker collection baskets were stored. Each man got one. They started at the front and began passing in the baskets, aisle after aisle, moving toward the rear. Some people smiled at Josh as he stood at the end of their aisle, waiting for the basket to come back. He would nod slightly.

When the basket got to his family group, Alma put in the envelope Josh had given her that morning. It had $25, $10 more than the year before. But that was alright, he thought, they could afford it; and Josh had always believed that giving to the needy was part of the Christian spirit. The children also put in dollar bills; Josh couldn't tell exactly how much, but it seemed that Constance put in three while the others put in two each. They didn't have to do that; he hadn't even suggested it. And it was money from their allowances, money they would do without the next week or so. They were growing up to be good Christians, Josh thought, and the idea gave him pleasure.

Gerald Blackburn put the collection away in the cloth bag left for that purpose. The collectors stood at the back of the church for the rest of the service. Josh thought about his contribution. He had been a lay assistant for five years by then. It hadn't been hard, just helping at one Sunday service and sometimes at one service on Saturday or during the week, besides meeting with the other assistants and the pastor once every three to four weeks to discuss parish problems. And that was little enough when you considered all the benefits that came from the church. Josh still felt a twinge of guilt that he had not gone to theological school. At least this was one way he could give to the cause. Furthermore, he thought, raising a Christian family was not insignificant. He looked again at his tall, healthy children clustered around Alma.

The new Buick station wagon rode well with a full load. Josh didn't like it as much as the jeepster he used for fishing, but you had to admit that it rode smoother and was roomy. Alma was in front, two covered dishes on the seat between them. The children were in the back with plenty of space. Behind them were a couple more dishes of food, plus presents for all the relatives. This year the annual Christmas dinner was at his brother Kermit's house. The brothers, with their wives and children, would be there as well as Josh's father, who would be brought from the nursing home by Theo. Each group would bring presents and food. The turkey was always provided by the house where the gathering was being held. It would be a full house, even fuller now that the children were getting big. But the whole family got together only once in a while these days. Later other relatives would stop by for a drink or dessert.

Josh steered the car easily, thinking there had been a good family Christmas already. After church there had been hot Duncan Hines sweet rolls and chocolate, then everyone had gone to the tree to distribute the presents. There had been so much, and at least everyone got something they could use: Alma a new sewing machine and several new garments, Constance a set of luggage to go off to college with, Harriet a new coat and some other clothes, and Norman a new fly rod. And even though he had been getting them for 10 to 18 years by this time, Josh figured he could still use more pipes, and the smoking jacket would come in handy on late winter evenings.

"Josh, be careful, you almost hit that dog!" Alma's voice broke into his thoughts.

They had been no nearer than thirty feet from the dog, which Josh had seen the moment it started across the street. It was her eyes probably, he thought. He said, "I saw the dog, Alma. I was ready to stop."

"Josh, you make me nervous with the chances you take. It doesn't matter when we get there exactly. You know the party will be going on all afternoon and well into the night. And if I know some of your cousins, Will Corwin in particular, there will be plenty of drinking. But we can take our time."

Constance broke in. "Mama, there was plenty of time. I don't think Daddy came near hitting the dog. It's probably just that you don't see so good any more."

That did it for Alma. She said in her iciest tone, "I'll just appreciate it, Miss, if you'll stay out of this. I can certainly deal with my own husband without your help."

"Well, you don't have to get so mad, I was just trying to help."

"You know, Josh," Alma said to him as if Constance weren't there, "Now that your daughter is going off to college, she's taken on all kind of airs. She hasn't even been there yet and listen to her. You'd think no one else ever went to college."

Constance leaned back against the seat, momentarily seeming to sulk. But she suddenly spoke again, "Mama, I wish you wouldn't talk to Daddy as if I'm not here."

"Just listen to that," Alma said. "A mother spends the best years she has raising her children, cooking, cleaning up after them, fixing their clothes, teaching them manners, and what do they do when they get big? They start telling you what you can and can't say. It's disgraceful, that's what it is."

Josh wished the two of them wouldn't get started that way, especially on Christmas. He knew that Alma and Constance could go on bickering like that for a long time. And it had been getting worse the last few years. He couldn't understand why, when they seemed alike in so many ways. Fortunately, he thought, they would spread out as soon as they got to Kermit's house. "I wish you wouldn't do that now," Josh said in low key to both of them. "Christmas is a day for good spirits." Then quickly, to change the subject, he said, "Alma, Theo is bringing Daddy, isn't he?"

"Yes, I talked to Winnie after church. They were going to do the same as us, distribute the presents in the immediate family after church, and then go by the nursing home to pick him up on the way to Kermit's. She said he's pretty good, though he's getting thinner all the time. He doesn't eat right. Also his mind wanders sometimes. He mixes things up. Often he thinks he's a boy again."

Josh thought about his daddy's situation still with mixed feelings. The man had been seventy-nine when they had put him in the home, but he had managed in the drug store until he was seventy-four. When his wife had died, he just no longer seemed to be able to keep going right. He started coming late to work and began to drink. And that was something for him, since he had drunk very little during his lifetime. But the worst part was that he quit eating right. He didn't know how to cook, but even more important, he didn't seem to care. Josh and his brothers had talked it over and figured he would be best off in a home. Josh had thought it would have been better for the old man to stay with one of them, but the other two or their wives didn't want him. And certainly Alma had not. They had enough problems, she had said, and she didn't want to pick up after a drunken old man. And so Josh's daddy had been put into the Magnolia Rest Home. But Josh still didn't feel right about it. He said to Alma, "Daddy should be pleased to see all the clan gathered together again. He always liked that."

"But one thing you ought to watch, Josh. See to it that he doesn't take a drink. You know how he is once he gets started. At least in the nursing home they have him off it. And as a doctor, you know it isn't good for a man his age."

Josh still had difficulty accepting medical advice from Alma, who had no medical training, but he said nothing. It would only make her angry, he knew.

When they arrived at the house, there were already several other cars, and you could see people moving about inside with drinks or edibles in their hands. Alma brought the candied sweet potatoes in their baking dish, and Josh carried the succotash. The children brought the presents and the other two dishes of food. Shortly after Josh knocked on the doorway, it was opened and Kermit answered, his wife behind him. "Ah Josh, old man, thought you'd never get here. And Alma and all those big kids. Come in, come in. It's cold out there."

They all trooped in and spread out quickly, Alma and Harriet taking the food to the kitchen while Norman and Constance took the presents to the table set aside for that purpose. It was already stacked high. Josh stayed just inside the door for a moment and surveyed the scene. It was a large room with a fireplace at one end, a fire burning. His daddy sat on a rocker just to one side of the fireplace, a glass of what appeared to be eggnog in his hand. Other upholstered chairs and couches were placed along the walls and in the lower seating area to one side. Up above were the Christmas tree and three tables, one for the presents, one for drinks, and one for snacks. Beyond was a long table with place settings for about twenty people. A dozen or so people were standing about the snack and drink tables while others were on various sofas or chairs, all talking, eating or drinking. Two or three waved at Josh.

Josh's pensive observation was broken by his brother. "Come on, Josh, bring your coat in here and I'll take you over for some eggnog. You look like you need a little Christmas cheer."

\* \* \* \* \*

Constance never returned home, finishing college with a degree in literature and then getting married. Josh never met her husband, a man who had not finished high school and who evidently had no family. According to her, his father had abandoned them when Roald had been quite young. In any event, Josh had not been consulted about any part of it. Constance had gone to work as an accountant after a specialized course. Harriet too got married but to an engineer from an old family in Winston-Salem. She began to put on weight not long after her wedding and had become quite plump. Both Constance and Harriet had children not long after getting married. Only Norman was still home, enrolled as a premedical student at Prince University.

Little changed in Emmetsville. Josh continued working in the Hospital and lecturing at the university while Alma kept house. It became neater than ever. Since the girls were gone, there was little to get out of place. And Norman was very neat. They got some new furniture, a color TV, and Alma had most of the house redecorated. Josh got a new four-wheel-drive vehicle and went fishing whenever he could, either with Norman or by himself. Otherwise, he puttered around the yard in his spare time.

\* \* \* \* \*

The spread of Los Angeles from the air was hard to believe after Emmetsville. As far as you could see there were strings of lights, usually at right angles though in some places curved, evidently following the outlines of hills and valleys. There were super-bright moving ribbons of light at intervals between rows of lights of ordinary brightness. Those must be the freeways, Josh thought, looking out of the window as the plane continued to descend. His ears popped several times.

It had been a pleasant flight and certainly different from what he was used to. He knew New York and Miami but since the days of his World War II service, he had not been west of the Mississippi. He really did not enjoy traveling very much. And if Constance had not become so independent, he would hardly have had to do it at this stage of his life. He sighed inwardly. What else could he do though, she was his daughter.

When the light came on, Josh checked his seat belt in preparation for the landing.

Constance was waiting for him alone. Other than looking a little agitated, he thought she looked pretty good. She put her arms around him and gave him a tight squeeze. "Oh Daddy, I'm so glad to see you. I've been counting on your coming so much."

Josh noticed that she had lost most of her southern accent. Not too surprising, he thought, after being in the west for almost twelve years. Josh returned her embrace, though not so hard. He wasn't used to putting his arms around grown women, including his daughters or his wife, these days. "Glad to be here, Pumpkin. You know I'm always ready to help if you need me."

He thought, still with some bitterness, that she had not asked for any advice when she decided to get married but that when things didn't work out so well, she called on him. And who was this man she married, Roald Larson, a man with no education or family background at all. Josh had never wished to write or talk to the man on the telephone. And now Constance was about to divorce him. How conditions had changed, Josh thought, from when he had gotten married.

He said, "Where's Larry?"

"He's with a sitter; we'll see him as soon as we get back."

The last of the passengers were filing out of the waiting room. Josh said, "Are you ready to go? I've got one bag to pick up."

"Sure, it's this way." She took him by the arm, and they headed toward the escalator. "It's a good walk," she said.

As they threaded their way past other passengers, Josh said, "How's Larry taking it? It must be hard on an eight-year-old."

"Oh, he's alright; he's a self-reliant boy. You know I told you that Roald always let him do anything he wanted. That was one of the problems. It's very hard to tell Larry anything. He just does whatever he wants, without telling you if he thinks you'll try to stop him. I blame Roald for that."

How ironic, Josh thought, that Constance would criticize her son for being independent when from sixteen on she had been so headstrong that he and Alma couldn't tell her anything. And she too would do things in secret if she thought he or Alma would try to stop her. After all, she had been seeing boys for almost two years before they found out about it, and then she was only sixteen years old.

"Does he miss his father?" Josh asked.

"I guess so, but he doesn't talk about it."

At the baggage claim area, they located their carousel. "There's a bench. Let's sit down. It'll be a little while," Constance said.

They sat down and Josh studied the crowd. It was indeed different from a group in a waiting area of an eastern airport, most informally dressed and with much brighter clothing. Most men wore open-necked sports shirts or turtleneck sweaters. They also had much longer hair than Easterners. A few, like Josh, wore suits and ties. Many women wore tight, revealing clothes and spike heels. In the east, a lot of them would be thought of as loose women, if not prostitutes. Probably the show business influence, Josh thought.

He turned back toward Constance. "And how's Roald now?" She looked a little angered, and Josh noticed how far out her frizzy hair was sticking. "I guess he's alright. I don't really know. He's in the Hellman Psychiatric Institute. That's a good one."

"I thought you told me he had gotten out."

"Well he did, and I still don't know how. But he can be very convincing when he wants to. And that was the bad period. He came back to the house to see Larry while I was gone, and even after I had him evicted."

Josh still couldn't understand very clearly why she had had her husband evicted in the first place since he had never seemed to have done anything violent or dangerous. But for that matter, Josh didn't clearly understand why she had decided to divorce him except that seemed to be what people did in California a few years after getting married. They fell in love as in the movies and all was sublime for a while, but then for a wide variety of reasons, they divorced, which was not so often depicted in the movies. They didn't seem to consider family responsibilities very much.

The bags started spewing out onto the conveyor belt and down to the now turning carousel. Travelers lined up two or three deep to watch for their own. "Shall we go over there and watch?" Josh asked.

"Oh, no rush. I think we can see it from here."

"How did they get him back in then?" Josh asked.

"Who? Where?"

"Roald, into the psychiatric institute."

"Oh, I got an anti-harassment order out, and my lawyer called his place of employment, and I guess they told him he'd have to get more treatment or he would lose his job."

It was still difficult for Josh to understand the extent of legal maneuvering that Constance and other Californians seemed to be involved in. Everything seemed to be ultimately settled in court.

"There's my bag," he said, and they both stood up. They walked out into the balmy night. Josh heard a rattling sound and looked up to see the woody leaves of palm trees clacking against one another. It was a different world, he thought, lotus-land they called it, a place of palm trees and balmy weather and movies and drugs and love and divorce.

Constance handled her Oldsmobile very well, Josh thought, wheeling down the freeway with great ease. She changed lanes frequently as they sped southward.

"How's Harriet?" she asked without turning her eyes from the traffic.

"She's alright, I guess. Her husband provides for her quite well, though he's gone most of the time. They have a very nice house, and the children are healthy. She complains a lot, and the last time she visited us, she was quite heavy."

"She's always been like that," Constance laughed. "Whenever she had some problem, couldn't get a date or pass one of her exams, she would fix herself an ice cream sundae. It's the best indication of how unhappy she is."

Josh took out his pipe. "'Okay if I smoke in the car?"

"Sure, Daddy, you know I like the smell of your pipe."

As he started to fill it, she asked, "And Norm?"

"He's fine, getting through medical school with honors and has a regular girl now. You might remember her, Kathy Hobbs. They were in the same high school class. She's a nice girl."

"Not really, Daddy. It's been a long time."

They turned off the freeway and onto a main street. She said, "This is Hermosa Avenue. It goes pretty close to our house."

Service stations and fast food restaurants were still brightly lit. There were few people walking. This was the city the automobile made, he thought, not Detroit.

Constance said, "And Mama, how is she?"

"She's about the same. Her eyes are a little poorer, but otherwise she's alright."

"She on a diet?"

That irritated Josh a little. He knew Alma was a little overweight. But for that matter, he was a little heavy too. But what business was it of Constance's? He said, "I don't know."

Constance looked at him with a pixieish expression, hesitated, then said, "I don't suppose you go into her room these days, do you?"

The anger rose, but at the same time he wasn't too surprised. Constance, of all his children, would be able to say something like that. Even so, he quickly decided he wouldn't make an issue of it. He was there to help, not to get involved in one of the arguments that had come so easily these last few years. He said with as much coldness as he was capable of, "I don't know what you mean, Pumpkin."

She continued to grin, "I think you do, Daddy. But I don't want to make you feel bad."

They rode in silence for a bit, Josh wishing the moment would pass but fearing that Constance would continue in the same vein, as she did so often. Once she got started on something, she just couldn't drop it easily. She had never learned to quit when a topic got into touchy territory. And so it happened. She spoke without turning away from her driving, a slight smile on her face. "You know, Daddy, you could learn about the California way while you're here, how to divorce when your spouse doesn't meet your needs. Everyone does it here."

Josh couldn't believe that remark; it was too flip. No one but Constance could have made it to him, but even for her it was too much. She was his daughter and daughters didn't talk to their fathers like that. But he figured maybe he still didn't understand fully what her meaning was. He said, "I don't know why you say that to me, Daughter. Why would I want to learn about divorce?"

Josh could hardly believe the determination and even righteousness on her face when she answered. "You know, I told you before that I didn't think married people should stay together just for convenience. They should help fulfill each other's needs, and if they don't, they ought to separate. And you know what I think about you and Mama. She hasn't fulfilled your needs for a long time. Why, a lot of women would be interested in a very successful doctor like you who is still good-looking and healthy. For an older man, you still have a lot of sex appeal."

That almost floored Josh. He clamped down on his pipe for as long as he could because he hated scenes, and this certainly wasn't the time and place for one. But he had to answer. No matter how hard it was for him, he couldn't let this pass. When he did answer, he had himself under full control, and he spoke in his lowest, most measured tone. He knew his face was flushed from his anger. He said, "Constance, I'm sorry you brought this up, and especially now. I think it's in poor taste, I suppose what they call the new morality. But I'm going to answer you anyway. And then I hope not to hear anything like that from you again. First, you do not seem to understand the sacred nature of marriage and the family. Although you go to church regularly and seem to be a good believer, you do not seem to understand that part of the teachings. Marriage is a sacred event, which I think you would know. Moreover, it is considered to be a lifetime union."

Her face had lost the slight trace of mockery, and Josh could see a flush on her cheeks also, a bit of the Bingham inheritance, he thought. He continued, reemphasizing his point. "One gets married for life according to the church. And everything is not always wonderful, and some needs might not be met. But unless there's some very bad defect on the part of one person, one stays married. Now you know I was never perfectly happy about your marriage to Roald. And I was especially not happy that you chose not to marry in the church. But even so, it doesn't make me happy that you are divorcing him."

By then Constance had recovered from Josh's remarks, saying, "But, Daddy, Roald has been acting funny. He thinks everyone is out to get him. And he wouldn't ever listen to me. And he has that weird religion, Rosicrucianism. I don't think he would ever have gone for psychiatric help if I hadn't made him."

Josh waved his pipe. "I know you told me those things on the telephone, but I never heard about them before, during the years you were satisfied with your marriage."

She said, "But the psychiatrist says he's paranoid."

He looked at her then, wondering if they were really father and daughter. He didn't seem to think like her. He said, "Now Daughter, I've heard quite a few psychiatric diagnoses in the hospital. And I don't put so much credence to them. You get two psychiatrists and you usually get two opinions."

She started in again but for one of the first times he could remember, he cut her off. He said, "Anyway, what really upset me was what you said about me and your mama. You don't have any right to judge her, but more important than that, and this is the last I'm going to discuss it, your mama and I were married for a lifetime, and that's the way it's going to be. That's what a proper Christian marriage is."

That time Constance did not respond, and they drove in silence the rest of the way, Josh feeling very bad, but satisfied that he had said it. They turned off the main avenue and onto three or four residential streets, stopping in front of a modest wood frame house. Josh noticed a cluster of banana stalks and some brilliantly flowered bushes in one corner of the yard. He said, "Looks very tropical."

She didn't answer, leading him up the sidewalk. She took him to the spare room. The house was very still; obviously there was no one there. He followed her out and began walking about, looking around. She spoke, "I guess you're tired, huh, Daddy?"

"A little, but I'm alright. I'd like to see the boy."

"That's no problem. He's just across the street with Mrs. Jones. Her husband doesn't make very much where he works and she's always anxious to make a little extra money. And Larry likes her. She lets him do anything he wants. I'll just run over and get him."

"One thing though, before you go, which I think is better to discuss before the boy comes."

She paused in front of the door. "Yes?"

"What I want to know is what you want me to do while I'm here. I don't quite know since Roald is in the hospital anyway."

"When I called you I didn't know about that, that he'd go back. He was out then and I was afraid."

"Why, did he do anything?"

"Not exactly, but he used to come to the house while I was at work, and Larry would let him in. Larry didn't tell me at first. I guess he was afraid I'd tell him not to. Anyway, later I found out he was telling Larry how mean I'd been to him, and how he was going to make me pay. And then finally he brought this whip, a regular coiled up whip, and he put it on my bed and told Larry that was what he ought to use on me."

Then, as if to make it clear she was not making this up, she said, "I saved it. I'll show it to you later. That scared me, so I had all the locks changed on the house and gave Larry strict orders not to let his daddy in. Also, that's when my lawyer called Roald's plant, and they told him to go back to the hospital. You know, that's what an anti-harassment order does. They almost always issue those when they have a divorce in California because husbands frequently harass their wives."

Josh could hardly believe the ins and outs of the affair. Although he knew what the word *harass* meant, he had rarely heard it used. It was worse than what he had heard the soap operas were like. How his daughter got involved in something like that, he just could not understand. And he, Josh, would actually be taking a part. He said, "So what do you want me to do in particular?"

"Oh Daddy, there's nothing exactly you have to do now. I have a lawyer and the minister helps me and there's always my therapist. But I just wanted you to be with me now. It's been pretty difficult lately. You know things are not quite the same here as in Emmetsville."

"I can see that." Josh sat down and reached for a mint in a small bowl on the end table. Then he said, "Why don't you go on and get the boy. I want to see my grandson."

\* \* \* \* \*

Josh and Alma stayed on in the same house after Norm got married and set up his own household. Norm finished his residency in pediatrics and joined Josh's medical group when he returned. Josh slowly transferred his own patients to Norm, young Dr. Bingham. Harriet moved around with her engineer husband, taking care of the children and eating to keep her mind off her troubles. A few years after her divorce,

Constance got married again, only to divorce a second time after four years. Alma's eyes got worse and worse until she could only read large print for a few minutes at a time with a large magnifying glass. When Josh retired from the practice, he spent a lot of time reading to her.

* * * * *

Josh sat in a rocker in front of the picture window in the late afternoon, watching the action at the bird feeder. A gray squirrel was trying to get up the post and would go through elaborate contortions to get around the metal deflector to the platform above where the seeds were. But so far it hadn't made it. It would first put its front paws on the outer edge of the metal flange and give a hard push with its hind feet, trying to increase its grasp. But then its front paws would lose their grip and it would drop. Several times a blue jay darted at the struggling creature. After each failure, it would hop around the pole several times, eyeing the platform, studying the problem, but invariably would go back up the pole and try the same maneuver, only to fall again.

Interesting creatures, Josh thought vaguely, though he also knew there were too many since he had stopped working in the yard. They dug up his bulbs and were forever scampering across the roof, trying to get into the attic. He had put the air rifle away some four or five years before, and the squirrels and rabbits had multiplied rapidly.

Norm was sitting on the couch, smoking a cigarette. "How are you feeling, Daddy? You seem a little depressed."

"I'm alright," Josh said in his still deep soft drawl.

He was just tired most of the time, he thought. Nothing was of much interest. That was why he had been watching the squirrel. And he had even been surprised that the furry creature's actions had interested him so much.

"You know there's nothing seriously wrong with you. Do you sleep alright?"

"Yes, I don't have any complaints."

Norm stubbed out his cigarette. Josh thought momentarily of the pipe he had given up about three years before. They had convinced him to stop smoking and drinking after he had that mild coronary. Losing the occasional mixed drink had been no problem, but he still frequently missed his pipe. Norm said, "You know, Daddy, I don't think you're active enough. It's not good for you to just stay by yourself in the house all day. You know you used to go fishing and work in the yard so much, besides working at the office and hospital all the time. Now, you're just mostly sitting."

It was true, he thought, but that didn't help. He could hardly get interested in even those things he could still do. And especially since Alma had passed away. It had been only three months, but it seemed a lot longer.

Norm continued. "I know how much you miss Mama, like we all do. But you know, Daddy, she had a good life and she went to her just reward. And she'd want you to take care of yourself even after she was gone."

She had tried to the very end, Josh thought, to struggle against her failing eyesight. And she had never gone totally blind. But that fall down the stairs and the broken hip had taken a lot out of her. She had never again tried to move without someone's help. They had certainly made her comfortable, but she had lost her will by then.

At least her death had been pretty good, he thought. They had said their prayers together that night after a visit by Norm and Harriet. Matilda, the nurse who stayed during the day, had given her some sleeping medicine. Josh remembered he had sat by the bed for more than an hour while she slept, he mostly thinking of former fishing trips. Alma had slept peacefully, and he finally left the room. When they found her in the morning, she was in almost the exact same position and with the same facial expression.

Josh became aware of Norm's voice again. "Daddy, it seems to me that it would be better if you were with other people more. You know it was alright when you and Mama were here together. But you don't have enough company now."

Josh knew where Norm was heading; he was going to suggest a retirement home again. But the idea of meeting others and making friends again was just too tiring. He said, "I have Matilda here during the day, and there are visitors."

"Well, you know I don't want to press it, but I think you should seriously consider a home. You might like it."

Josh pulled the blanket up farther on his knees and without turning toward Norm, said, "No Norm. This is my house, and this is where I'll stay. I thank you for your consideration, but I know what I want to do."

Josh wasn't sure what time it was when he woke up, probably ten or eleven o'clock. A tree branch rubbed against the side of the house once in a while. Otherwise there was no sound. He pulled the blanket off and began the process of getting up. It wasn't so easy now that he had gotten much heavier and the arthritis had become painful in his hips. He levered himself up with his hands on the arms of the rocker. For a moment he thought of getting a glass of milk, but the idea wasn't very appealing. He headed for the bedroom instead.

He put his clothes carefully on the tallboy Alma had gotten for him some forty years before and put his shoes in the closet rack. She had certainly been a neat woman, he thought. Then he put on his pajamas and knelt down at the side of the bed with his prayer book. Without opening it immediately, he spoke directly to his God in a low voice, "Dear God, tonight I lay myself down to sleep with a weary heart. I am an old man who has tried to do his duty throughout a lifetime, but now I am tired. My wife, Alma, has departed, and without her my life is not complete. Things were not always perfect between us, but we helped each other as much as we could during our lifetime together. But with her gone, I no longer feel at peace. I feel sure she has joined you in the afterworld, and since I miss her so much, I would just as well join her too. I know we are supposed to accept our life as it is given, to accept your will, but I hope mine is about over."

Josh opened the book to prayer no. 185 and began to read slowly. Then he pulled the covers back and climbed underneath. Turning off the bed lamp, he lay on his back with his eyes wide open and tried to imagine life everlasting.

# CHAPTER 5

Martin waited in front of one of the chairs until Oldenberg arrived. Although he knew it didn't make any sense, he still felt the other man was his professor. And although there were many differences, he felt like he had so many years before when Conrad Marcus had taken him to the Harvard Club dining room in New York for the first time. He still felt he should show deference to the Transitioner despite his easy ways.

"Just go ahead and sit down," the plump man said.

"I'll wait until you're seated."

Oldenberg pulled a chair out and sat down. It was upholstered on the arms, back and seat. Martin followed suit, finding his chair quite comfortable. Except for the much greater range of physical types, the diners surrounding them could easily have fit into the Harvard Club group. "I still can't quite get used to the idea that executives and office people here appear generally so similar to those on Earth—I mean, on the living Earth," he corrected himself.

"Yes, I know," Oldenberg replied. "But as I explained to you earlier, our Department of Illusions is quite advanced. They can make things appear to be almost whatever is desirable."

Martin sighed. "Well, I am steadily getting used to more and more things, and I imagine I'll get used to this also. Incidentally, I do appreciate your inviting me here."

It was the Transitioners' dining room and the first time Martin had come there. Otherwise, he had been eating in the main cafeteria along with the secretaries, service people, and a few other researchers.

"It's my pleasure," Oldenberg replied. "After all, it seems clear now that you will be around for a little while. You may as well take advantage of some of the better accommodations." He picked up the large clear plastic pad that had a row of punch buttons on the bottom with numbers on them. Martin picked his up too. The face was blank, and he couldn't make out its function. Oldenberg offered then, chuckling, "I imagine this puzzles you, eh Mr. Neumann? Well, it's really very simple; it's a menu. The buttons are just for punching in the language, you know, simultaneous translation, plus some variation in food, you know, cross-ethnic, cross-System, nutritional, and such. There are some exotics from some of the other world systems where certain Transitioners come from, you know, like edible clay dishes from the Blue World or unicellular soups from the Water Planets. But there's a fairly broad menu from Earth too. Most of the Transitioners are pretty adaptable and adjust to local diets after a short sojourn. If you'd like the earth menu, just punch the combination 3-8-1. I think I'll do the same. I usually try their daily special. Since it changes regularly, it is one way to become familiar with a variety of earth dishes.

Martin punched the numbers, and the menu appeared in softly lit letters. The special was beef stroganoff. Quickly scanning the page, he was pleased to find a vegetarian plate, a salad with a large number of ingredients, plus garlic bread and split pea soup. The waiter arrived very shortly and took the order. Oldenberg ordered a bottle of Chablis for the two of them. Then he settled back and opened: "Well, Martin, how did it go on the last one? A Mr. Joshua Bingham, I believe."

"Fine, fine, very interesting. I'm afraid I spent more time on him than I should have. You know this is a real trip for a basic voyeur. We anthropologists have long been suspected of being frustrated peepers. We justified our curiosity in our work by calling it field work. Joshua was the father of my second wife, though he was only slightly older than me. My wife, Constance, was some twenty years younger than me."

"And as I remember, you were interested in finding out whether a difference in social position would make any difference in marital or sexual adjustment, is that right?"

Martin picked up a spoon from the cutlery lying very neatly alongside his plate and played with it, rubbing his finger across the design. "Yes, Josh was a professional man, a well-known doctor in a southern town. He would be upper middle class, I suppose, in contrast to my father, who was working class. And even besides being a doctor, Josh was a fairly well-educated man. He actually read outside his profession."

The waiter appeared with the bottle of wine, already opened and in a plastic container, packed in ice. With a flourish, the man took the bottle out and wiped it with a cloth he had draped over his forearm.

Then he poured Oldenberg's glass about one third full. To complete the ritual, the Transitioner whirled it in a circular motion, then sipped it. He nodded his head in approval, and the waiter poured both glasses full, twisting the bottle at the end of each pour to flip off the last drop. The man could have done well in a classy French restaurant, Martin thought. Nothing low class about the Transitioners' dining room.

"So, what did you find out?" Oldenberg asked. "Did this man, Josh, work out a mating life any better than your own father, Bruno? I mean, did his more favored social position seem to make a difference?"

Martin sipped his wine and found it very palatable. He liked wines slightly more sweet, but he could make it, he assured himself, with Chablis the rest of his life if nothing else were available. "Surprisingly, their mating lives were very similar," he said. "Despite the difference in education and background from Bruno, Josh, who was a Southerner, seemed to have had almost the same moral standard. He was married only once, and he never messed around outside his marriage. Furthermore, he raised a family of God-fearing children, just like Bruno tried to do. Bruno even had one brief affair, you may remember, something Josh assiduously avoided. It wasn't that he didn't have any chances, because he was a good-looking, successful man. But he just was trained not to do that. They really took the anti-adultery rules seriously in that generation."

Oldenberg sipped from his wine glass also, then took a piece of hard crusted French bread from the cloth-covered basket and proceeded to butter it. He was probably a good eater, Martin figured.

The Transitioner said, "You know, I've only been on Earth assignment for about two years, and the whole time in an office in your country. I've been in two other centers and it seemed to me that the social parallels were considerable. People from one part of the country seemed to act very similar to people from another part. And even when there have been differences in social status, there seemed to be a common core of behavior. Now, admittedly, when you get someone of a very different ethnic background, they would have different behavior. But this man, Josh, was a white Protestant, wasn't he, while your father was a white Catholic? And whatever the members of those cults may think of the differences, from a cross-cultural point of view, they are not very great. Certainly the code of morality seems to be much the same."

The waiter brought the soup. Martin dipped his spoon into the bowl with pleasurable anticipation. It tasted good except that it lacked salt. He reached for the container and sprinkled the white grains in liberally, remembering with pleasure the first time he used the salt in the

Transition cafeteria. Since he was in the afterworld, he was already dead and didn't have to worry about high blood pressure any more. That had been a relief after avoiding the stuff for twenty or more years. After a few spoonfuls, he said to Oldenberg, "I suppose you're right, though somehow I had the idea that social position would make more of a difference."

"I'm sure it does in some respects, but you must know that you Americans have been a very moralistic people from the beginning, from your Pilgrim ancestors, and that has crosscut a lot of other distinctions." He paused then. "And since you have been so interested in the question of life satisfaction, how did you find that with this man, Josh? Did he seem to be more or less satisfied than your father, that is, insofar as his mating life went?"

Martin put his hand under his jaw, and resting his head there lightly, spoke directly to the plump man. "Well, it's funny how similar it seemed to that of Bruno. He too appeared to be a man with considerable sexual needs, which were hardly shared by his wife. In their early years they seemed to provide each other mutual satisfaction, and enough to produce several children, including my future wife. But this faded rapidly as the children grew up, and Josh simply shifted his interests to his work, fishing, puttering in the yard, and his children. You might say that he really didn't have a mating life to speak of after the first ten years."

"And yet I take it, he continued to fulfill his family responsibilities, is that right?"

Out of the corner of his eye, Martin saw the waiter bring a tray and set it on a folding table. He waited. Martin finished his soup, then leaned back while the waiter took up the soup bowls and arranged the other dishes in front of them. Martin continued, "Yes, he did, and in fact he seemed to shift his affection toward the children. Which if you knew his wife, Alma, wasn't too hard to understand. Despite the fact that she was educated too and from a better class, she could be a real nag. But Josh never revolted. He was indeed a patient man."

Martin took a bite of garlic bread. It was generously flavored and he savored it. Chewing thoughtfully, he added, "You know, though, that I'm beginning to feel that the particular temperaments of the people in that generation and before were not really so important. They simply planned from the beginning to stay married and they stuck to it. If they didn't get everything they wanted in their relationship, they stayed married anyway. They really thought the family had some social importance, so different from my own generation when divorce became endemic. But by my time people were getting married primarily to fulfill each other's personal emotional needs. And when their expectations fell short of reality, which was practically inevitable in some fifty percent of the cases, they got divorced."

Oldenberg appeared to be enjoying his stroganoff. He stopped chewing for a moment, however, saying, "Yes, there does seem to have been a considerable change that took place in social mores between those generations. But of course Earthlings generally, with their development of culture, seem to have been speeding up their rate of change in all kinds of ways, and geometrically. You know they lived as primitive hunters and gatherers with a simple division of labor and with male dominance for at least five million years. But then when they began living in settled communities and relying on domestic plants and animals some ten thousand years ago, they began changing rapidly, and the rate of change has been constantly speeding up. It's hardly any wonder that things in your generation were a lot different from those in the previous one."

Martin was amazed at Oldenberg's grasp of basic anthropological ideas but then realized that, despite the ordinary appearance of the man, he really knew little about him. In any event, it was pleasurable to be able to talk to someone with whom he shared so many ideas. In a raised tone of voice that indicated his excitement, one of his oft-criticized characteristics on Earth, he went on: "I was particularly interested to see the conflict emerge between Josh and his older daughter, Constance. As you may remember, she is the one who became my wife. Anyway, Josh put a lot of effort into raising his children and seemed to have done fairly well. At least the thing he was most concerned with, his religious beliefs, were transferred to all three. And that included Constance. But one part of his beliefs, that about marriage, just did not stick. And I suppose that was a consequence of the changes that were going on all around. In any event, Constance became a modern in that regard. I suspect I'll be telling you more about her later since she became so deeply involved in my own life, but for the time being it is sufficient to note that Constance took off on the divorce way. And though she and her father were very close in many ways, they just did not see eye to eye with respect to marriage. Josh believed marriage was for a lifetime, and Constance believed it should continue so long as both spouses fulfilled each other emotionally, a very modern idea."

Martin stopped then and gazed at the elaborate chandelier, thinking about the dismal end of his marriage with Constance. He was surprised that he could have carried that feeling all the way into the afterworld, but there it was.

Oldenberg spoke. "It seems apparent that you are still caught up by your feeling for that woman, that you never really got her out of your mind."

Martin jerked himself back to reality. "Yes, I think that's true. It isn't so much that I missed her so terribly or was so disappointed after the break came, but that things were never really resolved. We parted in total misunderstanding and there was never any means after that to communicate again in a reasonable way. I think in a sense it is a product of the system that developed in my lifetime, and particularly in California, for separating marital partners. It seems that all one did when one began a standard divorce there was to talk in frustration to lawyers who had no basic interest in the feelings of the people involved. They would say all a nasty divorce was about was property. But of course it was far more than that. It was about love and hate and loss and revenge and anger and frustration and other powerful emotions."

Martin stopped. He was drifting back and this wasn't the right time. He was long gone from the breakup, a life and more away. And he was currently concerned with Josh, not his daughter. He said, "I'm sorry, it was foolish of me to drift back to those old feelings. Let us continue with the discussion of Josh's affairs."

"Very well. Is there anything more you wish to say about what you observed that might contribute to your understanding?"

"Not much. All things considered, Josh seemed to have had a pretty good marital life, though the sexual part certainly wasn't much. But he was surrounded by relatives and people who liked him almost all his life. He certainly did not have to deal with the problem that became so widespread in my lifetime, loneliness. Even with his wife, there seemed to be considerable satisfaction in that regard. And she was hardly someone who was easy to get along with. But at least she stayed with Josh all his life and contributed in ways she could, cooking, keeping the house neat, and running errands as long as she could. I found it quite touching that, only a few months after she died, Josh too willingly gave up his will to live. He was so used to her, with all her carping, that he couldn't live without her. In retrospect, I see far more to lifetime marriage than I did when I was alive, when so many of us substituted the idea of deep emotional feeling, love, as the rationale for staying together."

Martin paused again for a moment, reliving some of the scenes he went through in his lifetime. But then he turned to his food and proceeded to finish the salad and bread.

Oldenberg had finished his, so he spoke. "One thing you didn't mention, Martin, in your concern with life satisfaction, is that Josh brought to maturity a respectable number of his own species, three, as your own father did with four. He fulfilled his role as a male member of his species, which as I mentioned before is the primary rating criteria from the point of view of the System. And he even got certain satisfactions in the process, as you admit, even though he hardly lived out a wild love affair."

"Yes, it's true. I would be the last to deny that. As I watched Josh defending himself to his daughter, I think my sympathies were almost totally with him, though in life I'm afraid I agreed mostly with her. But I must say she was a lady with a very good line." Martin sighed. "As they say, live and learn." He laughed. A little ruefully he realized, "even after you die."

The waiter appeared again to clean off the dishes. He passed the menu pads to the two men. "Would you like some dessert, Martin?" Oldenberg asked. "They make quite good ones."

"I suppose one punches the numbers again, eh?"

"Yes. And I particularly recommend the baked Alaska."

Martin could hardly remember how long it had been since he had tried that flash-baked ice cream dish. He could dimly remember having made one or so sometime in his early married years. There wasn't anything so fantastic about it except the idea of baked ice cream. But he was full and it had been so long since he had stopped eating sweets that he automatically refused. "No thanks, I'll just have coffee."

Oldenberg turned to the waiter. "I'll have the baked Alaska." When the man had left, Oldenberg turned to Martin again. "Well, where to on Project Heterop? Have you had about enough with that generation? You know as well as I that there are a wide variety of other ways for mating in other cultures and species. I should think that with your cross-cultural interests, you would be particularly interested in how they do it in other cultures."

"That is true in a way. But you know I got into this to a considerable extent because of my personal interests. You may remember that I told you in the beginning that I had been really baffled in my efforts to understand how the mating system worked during my own lifetime. And it bothered me since I was paid as a social scientist most of my working life. I guess once I lucked onto the opportunity to learn how some of those lives that I had known partially while I was alive had actually been lived, I just couldn't pass it up. It's a personal hang-up, I admit. But you know many of us believe that the initial motivation for a lot of research stems from our personal interests. We study questions that have puzzled us in our own lives. I once worked for a geneticist who studied birth abnormalities in mice. His son had a genetic birth defect that restricted him to the wheelchair throughout his life. You have perhaps heard of other medical men who have concentrated their lives on research problems concerning ailments that some of their family members had contracted. So too, many individuals from ethnic minorities, persons who have suffered discrimination themselves, have turned their attention to the study of ethnic relations. And I suppose it was the same with me when I got the second chance to study what had been to me a baffling human relationship, the mating drive. And I guess the most intriguing lives, at least in the beginning, were those with whom I had had some connection in life. I'm sure that's why I started on my own parents and then went to one of my former wife's parents."

The waiter brought the baked Alaska and coffee for both. "That looks very good," Martin said. "I'm sorry in a way that I'm not hungry any more."

"We can still order you one."

"No, I'm alright with the coffee."

Before he began on the dessert, Oldenberg said, "I still think you should at least get some cross-cultural data. And for that you will of course need to look at the lives of some people in other cultures." He paused then. "I don't really want to dictate how you do your study, but I think an outsider's view should help you."

For a moment Martin had begun to bridle, thinking that despite his monitor's much broader background, and his seemingly gentle demeanor, the man was still going to take the role of an authoritarian graduate student adviser and try to push him to fulfill his own, the adviser's, needs. But the softened explanation made Martin relax again. He said, "Well Prof—I mean, Transitioner Oldenberg, I couldn't agree with you more. And I do certainly want to get away from Euro-American culture." Pause. "For that matter, the idea of seeing the lives of non-humans in this respect has occurred to me. During my last years of teaching, we had a controversial new field, called sociobiology, which attempted to explain a much greater part of human behavior as simply a product of our biological heritage." Pause again. "But could I try just one more?"

"One more what?"

"One more person's life from my parents' generation and culture."

Oldenberg picked up his spoon to get started on the dessert, which was beginning to melt. "Sure, if you think it's important. You know there is no immediate need to conclude the study. But I would like to have an idea what person and for what particular reason." Whereupon he began to cut into the toasted meringue crust with his spoon.

Martin said, "One thing that really intrigues me still, despite what you have told me as to the primary function of the mating drive being whether it can really help in giving life satisfaction. I know that if a couple live together at least until they have brought their children to maturity, from the point of view of the System, they have fulfilled their sexual roles. But I just can't get it out of my mind that there ought to be more to it than that. I'm afraid that is another of my hang-ups, derived from the ideas of romantic love that I absorbed in my own growing up. Mating and pairing ought to contribute to an individual's happiness."

Oldenberg's eyes crinkled. "I can guess what you're about to suggest, what kind of life you'd like to see."

"What ?"

"You want to know whether, of people who stayed together for a lifetime, there were none who were really happy in the emotional and sexual aspects of their relationship. As to what particular person, I can hardly guess."

Martin grinned. He was impressed by Oldenberg's perception, even though he knew the man was almost astral. He said, "That's exactly it. Here I've seen three people, two men and one woman, and they stayed with their spouses all their lives, raising their families, and they even got certain satisfactions, but they were hardly soul mates, in either feelings or sex. I'm wondering whether those things were even possible, at least for a lifetime."

"Let me say that the idea of romantic love lasting a lifetime does not have a long history in your species. As you probably know, it is historically traced back to the early Middle Ages, when the upper classes didn't have enough to do to amuse themselves because the peasants were doing all the work. So they developed the art of dalliance in which men and women played games of emotion with one another. Even so, it was an activity for the privileged classes only. So far as we know, the alliances of the ordinary people, the peasants and artisans, were based on much more mundane considerations. Whether people loved each other was a secondary consideration. What was really important was whether the man could provide economic support and protection, and whether the woman could cook, keep a house going, and raise children. This only changed when your people became urbanized and concerned so much with individual needs. Then almost everybody, with the assistance of the mass media, particularly your dream factory, Hollywood, became concerned with love. But of course by that time the need for a family system had greatly declined." Pause. "But even so, there shouldn't have been any reason why affection with emotional and sexual satisfaction, couldn't have occurred on occasion in earlier times. My feeling is that it wasn't very common, but I would guess it occurred sometimes."

"That's it. What I want to do is to see a life in that same generation where there might really have been lifetime love. And I would agree that from my observations there weren't many. But I think I know one that might have been so. I want to see what the ingredients of such a relationship would actually have been, that rare phenomenon, the happy marriage." Momentary pause. "Furthermore, I think I even know one in that generation, at least from what I heard and briefly saw. But I'd like to see the details. That will even me up also, in that generation, with two men and two women. And that appeals to my sense of balance. How does that sound?"

Oldenberg, finished with his ice cream dish, sipped his coffee. He said, "I don't have any basic objection, though I think that after this you should go a little farther afield, you know, to other times and places." Pause. "And who is the person in particular? You say you have someone in mind that you knew."

"It's the mother of my first wife, Amelia. Her name was Emma Fields."

"Alright. But I think you might keep this one a little briefer." He thumbed through the copy of the account Martin had just finished on Josh Bingham. "Your stories are getting fairly long. And as you know, whatever little chance a research report, even a preliminary one, has of being read, the longer it is, the less likely."

"I'll try," Martin said, and they both stood up to leave.

# EMMA

The birth was normal. The girl was born at home in a small town in Kentucky, the local doctor on call. She was of medium size and quickly contented. At home she was easy to care for, being readily accepted by her brothers and sisters. When she played on the street, she was almost always watched over by one of her older sisters. She grew to be a very pretty little girl with wavy dark brown hair that her mother cut in a bob, the style at the time. They moved to a town in Arkansas called Maxwell when she was five years old. She finished primary school there and then started high school. The family wasn't rich, but they weren't much poorer than the other families in town. They didn't have a car, but one could get almost everywhere in that town by walking. It was also small enough that everybody knew everybody else, either directly or by reference. The main recreation was talking. Every evening when it cooled off, people sat on their porches, talking to family members or neighbors.

* * * * *

Emma was sitting on the aisle in the third row of the history room. It was her second year, and she was used to the idea of going to different rooms by that time. Also she liked Miss Greene, the history and civics teacher. The room was fairly quiet except for the occasional rustle of paper as a student thumbed through his or her notebook. Miss Greene looked toward the class and said, "Today children, we are going to discuss the division of our government. Our forefathers established a system of checks and balances in which one part would be balanced against the others. And there were three main divisions. Do you want to tell me what they are?" She looked expectantly at the students. They squirmed and shuffled their feet collectively. She waited a moment, then checked her grade book. Looking up, she said, "Harry Burns."

In the back of the room, a scrawny boy with freckles and red hair squirmed in his seat. His face began to turn red. Finally he said, "Ma'am, I think it's the president and . . ."

Miss Greene said, "Someone else."

Again, squirming and silence. Three girls and one boy put up their hands. One of the girls was Emma. The teacher said, "No, I know you students. You always study your lessons. We need to get the others involved." She looked at her grade book again. "Mr. Rob Fields. You should know this." She indicated a good-looking, medium-tall boy with dark hair, sitting on the opposite side of the aisle from Emma. He looked directly without squirming or fidgeting. After thinking for a moment, he said, "The legislative, and . . ."

Miss Greene waited a bit, then answered, "That's right, but I thought a smart boy like you would know all of it."

He smiled and said, "I couldn't study last night, ma'am. I had to work late in the store taking inventory."

The room settled into quietness again. The teacher said, "Well thank you for that. And there's only one more government division. I'm sure many of you know that. But we've got to get on to other things. So I'll call on someone I think knows it." She surveyed the room quickly then, "Emma Parker, I saw your hand up. And I bet you'd like to help a good-looking young fellow like Rob Fields, wouldn't you?"

Emma directed a quick glance at the boy, then, turning back to the teacher, said, "Yes ma'am, it's the judicial."

"That's right, that's the three, the executive, legislative, and judicial. Now, let's go on to discuss the functions of each, what they do in government."

A sense of relief flooded the room as the squirming stopped. Rob Fields looked toward Emma, and their eyes made contact. They held it a little longer than normal, then turned back to their books.

When Emma left the school building, she saw him sitting alone on the bench across the sidewalk, directly on her way home. He was watching her. From behind, her friend, Anne Foster asked, "You want to come to my house for a while?"

"No, I should go home. My ma is expecting me to help in the kitchen."

"Okay, maybe some other night. We could play games awhile."

"We'll see. I'll see you tomorrow."

She kept her eyes down as she approached Rob, though sneaking glances at him. He was very good looking, she thought, one of the best in class. His hair was straight and black and his skin a little dark. He was lean and muscular. She knew he was on the basketball team. She also knew he didn't go with anyone steady, though she had heard other girls talk about him several times.

When she got abreast of him, he stood up and spoke. "Hi, Emma. Thanks for helping me in civics."

She looked up then as if she had just noticed him, though she was fairly certain he knew she had seen him. She was impressed that he could speak out so openly with no hesitation or embarrassment. He had none of the silliness of most of the boys. She said, "Oh, it wasn't anything. Besides, I wanted to help Miss Greene. I like her a lot."

She had slowed but not stopped. He came alongside. "Can I walk with you a-ways?"

She blushed a little, but in pleasure rather than embarrassment. "I guess so." She added, "I'm going home."

"That's okay, I'm going that way too for a few blocks." He set his pace to match hers, and they walked together in the shade of the overhanging trees. In silence a short while, then he: "You seem to know your lessons all the time. You must study a lot."

"Just a couple of hours at night. Most of the lessons are not real hard."

"I guess so. Probably I don't study enough. I'm usually pretty tired when I come home."

"You work every night, don't you?" she asked. She knew he was a helper in the IGA Store. She had seen him there several times when her mother had sent her to get some groceries. In fact, she had gone there a couple of times when she didn't have to.

"Yeah, I have to help at home. My pa isn't well. He doesn't work all the time."

"That's too bad. I hope he gets better soon."

"I don't know. He has bad kidneys, and I think that's hard to cure."

Emma had heard that Rob's father drank a lot and that was what had made his kidneys bad. She had heard her own father speak about the evils of drink and that people oughtn't do it. She had never been around anyone who drank.

It was too bad though that Rob had to work because of his father's illness. 'Course, other boys worked too, carrying papers and cutting lawns and helping their fathers, but most didn't work as much as Rob.

He said, "You know, Emma, I think you're nice. I like to talk to you."

She blushed, but she answered with pleasure, "Thanks, I like to talk to you too."

He said, "I was wondering if maybe we might study together sometimes. I get off at the store by eight. We close at six but it takes about two hours to get ready for the next morning. I could be at your house by quarter past eight. Is that very late for you?"

She smiled openly, "I usually start studying right after supper, that's about six, but I don't have to go to bed until about eleven. I could change it a little." Pause. "Or I could study some before, then I'd know most of the things when you came."

He smiled too, and his dark brown eyes sparkled. She liked him even better then.

They reached Main Street. Almost all the stores were there, and at the end was Marston's Hotel, the only one in town. It was a place where most of the customers were salesmen who stopped overnight. In the other direction you could see Curley's Restaurant and Hill's Drug Store. Just one block beyond was the IGA. He said, "I guess I'll have to turn off here. You go the other way, don't you?"

"Yes, I have to help my ma at home."

They stood for a moment on the corner, looking at one another. She said, "I really enjoyed walking with you, Rob." Pause. "And I'd like to study with you when you can make it."

He answered. "Okay, maybe tomorrow night." Pause. "Also sometime, if you'd like, maybe you'd come to Hill's Drug Store for a soda with me."

"I think so. I'll have to ask my ma first, but I think she'll let me."

Unwillingness to break off, but he did it. "I have to go now. I'll see you in school tomorrow."

"Bye-bye." She turned quickly toward home and walked more joyously than she could remember for a long time.

\* \* \* \* \*

Emma saw Rob through their high school years. At first he went with other girls occasionally but then quit to go only with her. He worked evenings and on weekends until school was finished, then got a fulltime job at Bee's Hardware Store. Emma went to work as a waitress in Curley's Restaurant when she finished school.

\* \* \* \* \*

The two of them were walking on the dusty road. They had waited until they got out of town before holding hands. It was a pleasant walk to Sycamore Gullies. There were few cars or occasional buggies. They had done it several times before, usually on Sunday when he was free.

"Did you tell your ma where we were going?" he asked.

"No, but she didn't ask me. She probably knows. I think it's alright with her. She likes you, Rob."

He pulled his hand loose from hers and put his arm around her waist. "So you think she and your pa will approve our getting married."

She smiled at him. "I think she already knows. And since she hasn't said anything, I think she approves." They had just gotten engaged a week before and were dying to tell people. But they were waiting to find out whether Rob would get a raise so they could know when to set the wedding.

They turned down a bend in the road and heard a dog barking loudly. A rabbit scurried through the logs of a rail fence and came running straight at them. The dog came following it shortly, a long-legged animal that appeared to be mostly collie. It scrambled over the fence, jumping and clambering up one side and falling and running down the other. It picked itself up quickly and raced straight down the road after the rabbit.

"Oh, the dog is going to catch the rabbit," she cried. "Please help it."

He jumped and waved his arms, yelling at the same time, "Stop, stop!"

The rabbit stopped in surprise, but with the reflexes of a survivor, instantaneously went into motion again, changing direction. It scurried back up the clay wall, sliding back a couple of times, but flailing its legs with renewed energy each time until it tumbled over the top. Clumps of clay rolled back. The rabbit scurried under the lowest rail, and they could hear the weeds breaking as it passed. The dog also skidded to a stop. It stood there looking perplexed, a little cloud of dust settling around it.

"Oh Rob, the rabbit escaped. You did it!" Emma threw her arms around him and squeezed. She turned toward the dog then. "Come here, doggie. It's alright." The dog stayed where it was, its tail drooping.

She said, "I think it's the Potter's dog. His name is Pal." Back to the dog: "Here Pal, here Pal."

The dog wagged its tail and stepped tentatively toward them. They both petted it when it got near. She said, "That's alright, Pal. You didn't want to do anything bad. That's what doggies do, they chase rabbits. We just didn't want anything happen to that rabbit."

They continued on down the road then, the dog turning back in the direction the rabbit had gone, sniffing as it went. Emma held Rob's hand tighter, "Oh Rob, I'm so glad you saved the rabbit." She squeezed. "You know, I feel so good and safe when I'm with you."

They passed cows and horses and mules in pastures and fields of corn and cotton. There were birds, field sparrows, sometimes warblers or bluebirds, and in the distance, crows. They saw farmers in fields a couple of times, and cars passed twice. But generally they were alone. In Maxwell, you didn't have to go far in any direction to get into the country.

It got warmer as morning latened. The palms of their clasped hands became moist with perspiration.

The road dipped to lower ground where many sycamores grew. It was parklike off to the right, mostly in shade, the ground covered with long grass. A few cows stood lazily at the other end of the field. A barbed wire fence ran along the edge of the road. A gray lizard scurried around one of the posts and raised its head over the top to stare at them. Emma could see its blue throat. "Oh, look at the lizard," she said.

They both stopped and watched the bobbing head of the little reptile with its unblinking eyes. She said, "It's so peaceful here. I always feel that I'm a thousand miles away from anybody when I come here.

How does it make you feel?"

He pulled his hand away and put it on her waist.

"I feel real good too, Em."

"You know, there's so many girls I went to school with that want to go away to Memphis or St. Louis. They say there's nothing to do here. But I don't feel like that. I really like it here, don't you?"

"Sure Em. It's a good place to live."

She put her arm around his waist. "Let's go over there in the grass, away from the road. Over there where it's real thick." She pointed at the spot.

"Okay." He stepped to the fence and put one foot up. "Let me go over first. Then I can help you."

She nodded, and he stepped up to swing his leg over, clearing the top strand. He stepped down on the other side, and she put her foot up, pulling up her skirt so she would swing clear. When she was at the top, he reached across and took her arm. She let him take some of her weight as she swung her leg across, aware of the leg exposed a little above the knee. She could feel the strength of his grip, so when she stepped down to the next strand and felt his other arm under her back, she released her foot and handhold. He was holding her then, one arm under her back, the other under her knees, she with her arms around his neck. Instead of putting her down, he carried her to the grassy place. She could feel his strength and let her body relax, gazing into his face only a few inches away.

He lowered her gently and got on his hands and knees over her, gazing into her eyes as fixedly as she did into his. Then he lowered himself and kissed her, first long, then deep. It was the first time he put his tongue into her mouth. She responded. He put one arm under her head, lifting it so he could kiss deeper. Soon she felt his other hand moving down to her breast. She put her hand up and pushed it aside gently. His hand continued down, however, until it was fumbling under the bottom of her skirt.

Her body became stiff, partly automatically, partly because she didn't feel right about that. She put her hand on his and pushed it away. He jerked up. "What's the matter, Em?"

She lowered her eyes. "Rob, I don't want to go any farther. Not till we're married."

"But we're already engaged, aren't we?"

Since he had pulled his hand away and was again holding himself up on his hands and knees, she put her hand on the back of his head.

"Sure, honey, but I think it's better to wait until we're married before—we sleep together." She stroked the back of his neck at the hairline.

He looked long at her as though wondering what to do next but then let himself down, turning to one side. He lay beside her then, his arm across her stomach. "I think it would be alright, Em, but I don't want to make you feel bad. I can wait."

She knew then how important Rob was to her.

\* \* \* \* \*

Emma and Rob got married and went to live in a small wooden house three blocks from Main Street. She quit working, and in a little more than a year the first child, Eloise, was born. Rob stayed at Bee's Hardware Store and got to know where every size nut, bolt, nail, and screw were located, as well as whom he could sell to on credit and whom he had to be careful with. In about a year and a half, Wilbert was born.

\* \* \* \* \*

Her sister, Gertrude, had come to Emma's for coffee. They were sitting at the dining table, a cup in front of each, a peach upside-down cake cut in pieces before them. Baby Wilbert was playing with blocks on the rug. The sounds of children's voices came from the sidewalk. Eloise and her friends.

"Can I get you another cup of coffee?" Emma asked.

"Sure, Sis, you know me, I can drink the stuff all day."

Emma brought the blue enameled pot from the kitchen and filled both cups. Gertrude stirred sugar into hers, but Emma took hers with nothing added.

Gertrude said, "Little Wilbert looks very healthy. He's getting bigger every day. How old is he now?"

"Year and a half. And how's Wally?"

"He's okay. He's with his grandmother now. She likes it when I leave him with her. And Wally likes her, she spoils him so much."

Both sipped their coffee. Emma said, "Won't you have another piece of cake? It'll get stale if it isn't eaten right away."

Gertrude patted her hip. "Oh, Sis, I'd like to, it's so good. But everything I eat goes right here. And Bert has been making comments lately. So I'm trying to lose a little weight."

Baby Wilbert started to cry. Emma looked over and saw him with his finger in the hot air duct. He was pulling as hard as he could, and the harder he pulled, the more he cried. She stood up and walked to him.

His finger was in one of the rectangular holes. Once inside, he had turned the finger and was trying to pull it out at right angles from the way it had gone in. "Don't cry, baby," she said in a calming voice, "Mama will help."

She took the little hand and gently turned the finger. It came out instantly and the baby stopped crying just as fast.

She picked the infant up and carried him back to the table. Settling into her chair, the baby in her lap, she asked her sister, "I don't think a little piece of that cake will hurt him, do you?"

"No, at a year and a half he can start eating all kinds of things. And that'll take his mind off the hurt."

Emma broke a small piece from the slice on her plate and gave it to the child, who almost immediately popped it into its mouth.

"How are things at home?" Emma asked. And with only a short pause, "I mean with Bert."

They were all worried about Gertrude's husband because he was drinking beer lately, hiding it somewhere in the barn and having a bottle when he went to feed the pigs or milk the cows. But Gertrude didn't answer directly. She said, "What do you mean?"

Emma didn't want to intrude, though she was worried. She was so happy that Rob never drank at all. But she had to answer, so she said, "I mean about his drinking beer."

Gertrude colored very quickly, but Emma couldn't be sure whether that meant Gertrude was embarrassed or angry. But she wanted to help her sister, not make her feel bad, so she quickly added. "I don't want you to worry, Gert. Maybe he'll stop. It's one of those times when it would be good to know how to say some prayers if it would only do some good."

Her sister had calmed, the color of her skin becoming normal again. She gazed down at the cake, crumbling the edge with her fork. "I keep hoping, Sis, and I've told him many times how bad it is, but I know he still keeps some hidden in the barn. You know he's a good, hardworking man and he's never mean, but you'd be surprised how stubborn he is. You couldn't tell by looking at him."

The baby was dropping crumbs and drool on Emma's apron. She wiped it with a cloth she kept in her pocket. Then she reached her hand across and patted Gertrude's. "Just be patient, Gert. And maybe he'll change." Pause. "Maybe I could get Rob to talk to him sometime when he comes over or when Rob goes over there. You know Rob never drinks at all, and I'm so thankful for that."

The baby was finished with the morsel of cake and was reaching for more. Emma held him back while getting him another piece. He stuffed that in his mouth even more quickly. Emma wiped his face and hands with the cloth and put him back on the floor.

She was surprised when Gertrude said, "But there's other things about Rob that you can't be so thankful about."

It came out of the blue and caught Emma at a loss for a moment. Although Gertrude had a sharper tongue than her other sister, she wasn't really mean. Emma said, "What does Rob do? He works hard and brings his money home and plays with the children."

She was too embarrassed to say that he slept with her often too, even though a little less often than when they were first married.

"I know, I know, on the surface it looks like Rob is an ideal husband and father. But you know as well as I do that he is a very good-looking man and was always very popular in high school. Well, some people say he is seeing Maxine Wilson again, you know, the blonde girl he used to go with before going with you. You know her husband left her."

Emma knew that she was blushing, even though she couldn't believe what was being said, not of her Rob. Why, he came home right away after work every night, and he was home every Sunday. She said, "I don't understand. Rob doesn't stay out. How could he even have time to see someone else?"

"They say he sees her on his lunch hour. You know she doesn't live far away."

Emma thought and thought, as though somehow she could make the idea go away. But she knew her sister wouldn't make up something like that. It was one of those impossible situations when it was too painful to believe either side. So she said, "Thanks, Sis, but I just can't talk about this any more."

Rob came home at six thirty, his regular time, carrying the bag of groceries she had asked him to bring. He walked into the kitchen where Emma was finishing the dinner preparation, setting the groceries on the table. "Hi, Hon," he said and gave her a squeeze around the waist.

"Hi, Rob. Have a good day?"

"Nothing unusual. Business about normal. The only thing different was that we got two wagon-loads of Germans from Hanover. You know, the ones who won't use autos and the men won't shave and the women wear bonnets and long skirts. They came for hardware because there was a big fire in the hardware store in their community. Usually they trade among themselves."

The German Catholic community of Hanover had been there, twenty miles from Maxwell, almost a hundred years. They usually kept to themselves.

Rob sat down on the kitchen chair and lit up a cigarette. Emma watched the cloud of smoke that soon formed above his head. That was the only bad habit that she had known he had; he smoked so much. It made him cough when he got up in the morning. And he smoked ready-made cigarettes all the time, twenty cents a pack. That made a considerable dent in the weekly budget. The only time his breath didn't smell like tobacco was just after he brushed his teeth in the morning. But she hadn't said anything. It didn't seem right considering he had been a model husband in all other ways. But now she didn't know. Even so, she said nothing about his smoking. She put down the spatula she was using for the eggs and went to the next room for an ash tray. "How long will it be, Hon?" he asked.

"Just a few minutes. Then you can call Eloise. Wilbert should still be sleeping."

She didn't want to, but the idea had been nagging her ever since Gertrude had brought it up. Even so, she couldn't ask him directly; it would seem so accusing. So she said only, "You didn't go out today, did you?"

He stubbed out the cigarette. "What do you mean? I had my lunch."

She fixed his lunch every day, and he carried it in a paper bag. She felt badly because it sounded like she was questioning him, but at that moment she couldn't stop. "I just meant, did you go for a walk or meet any people or anything?"

Then he looked at her differently, and she felt she had gone too far. He said, "I really don't know what you're driving at, Hon, but you sound like you want to know something in particular. Is there something special?"

For a moment she thought she would ask him directly, but then she knew she had never done anything like that before. The thought of it sounding like she was accusing him was too unpleasant. She couldn't so she said, "No, nothing Rob, nothing. Would you call Eloise?"

He stood up and gave her a hug across the shoulders and then left to fetch his daughter.

\* \* \* \* \*

Life was uneventful for Rob and Emma and the children from then on. There were two more, Bertram and Amelia, the last many years later. The children grew up and went to school in that quiet town. One after another they married and got jobs to begin families of their own. Rob and Emma visited relatives or friends on Sundays and holidays and went to Memphis or St Louis a few times. Rob continued at the hardware store, even through the Depression, and though there was never very much, they finally got enough together to buy a wood frame house for $3,000. Rob's hair turned gray, though Emma's remained dark through their married years.

\* \* \* \* \*

Emma was sitting quietly in the front of the funeral home, Amelia by her side. The sickening aroma of too many cut flowers filled the air. Emma wasn't weeping any longer, simply staring straight ahead. Neighbors came in to look in the casket, then near where Emma was sitting. "We wish to offer our full condolences, we know how much you miss him. But we want to let you know that he was very beloved in this town. He was a very good, honest family man."

Or, "Mr. Fields was a highly respected and loved member of this community. We know he will have gone to his just reward."

Or, "Our sincere condolences now at your time of great bereavement."

Emma would nod at first, but she finally stopped. Amelia, her tall, slender last-born would then thank them and explain, "She's still in a partial state of shock. But I'm sure she thanks you for your kindness."

Amelia had come for the funeral from Rockville State College where she had started in library science two years before. She was a calm, intelligent-looking girl with much self-possession. Everyone said she looked much like her father.

Emma had turned inward after the night of his passing and hardly heard the voices around her. She kept going over and over the way it had happened, and she couldn't stop even though by then it seemed that no new thought could come. It was like a record that would go to the end and then start back again at the beginning, not a broken record that kept repeating itself over and over.

He had waited too long. Day in and day out, week after week, month after month, year after year, so often a cigarette in his mouth. It had cost a lot of money through those years of the Depression when there wasn't much. But he had worked steadily and never wasted money otherwise, on drinking or running around, or even on clothes. They had raised the family on what he had brought home. Who could deny him the one great pleasure throughout the day, his Lucky Strikes or Camels? And who could have known what was going on inside him all that time, when he seemed so healthy? He practically never missed work. However, she had worried about his cough for years, and when it got worse, she had finally told him he ought to see a doctor. But he was the seventh son of a seventh son and he believed he had curative powers himself. In fact, many other people did too and they would frequently come to see him in the evening about their arthritis or stomach disorders and he would tell them what drugs to buy or what herbs to collect. Naturally, he had thought he could cure himself.

So he had used his own cough syrup. He even cut down on his smoking, but when the cough got better he went back to more than a pack a day again.

Amelia's voice broke into her sad reverie. "Mom, are you alright? You look so far away." Her daughter squeezed her arm lightly.

Emma didn't answer, merely turning her gaze toward the tall girl and smiling.

The girl repeated, "Mom, you look so far away. Are you feeling good enough to go to the cemetery?"

Emma forced herself back into her daughter's world. "I'm alright, just tired."

"It's okay, Mom. It won't be too long, and I'll be with you the whole time."

Emma had finally gotten him to let a doctor come, after he had been ill for two weeks with a bronchial infection. Doctor Jameson had told him to cut down on his smoking but didn't tell him to quit, probably because he smoked himself. Rob had recovered but after that the cough never went away any more, and sometime at night or in the morning, he would wheeze.

Emma had talked to the children about it, but except for Amelia, they all smoked too and didn't think it was anything serious.

Eloise arrived, along with her husband and children. She gave Emma a kiss on the cheek. "How are you feeling, Mom? You look pale."

Emma smiled but when Amelia squeezed her arm, she spoke, "I'm alright, just tired."

Eloise patted Emma on the back. "It'll be over soon."

The twins, Paul and Pete, came up and gave Emma a kiss. "Hi Grandma." Then Paul said, "If we can help in any way, tell us, Grandma."

She smiled at them and reached her hand out as if to touch one but failed to reach either and brought the hand back. It was as though she had tried to reestablish contact with the ongoing world but failed.

Then had come the diagnosis of cancer. He had tried more of his own treatments, but when the second X-rays came in, showing he had even more than the first time, he had quit that. It was steadily downhill after that. There were the X-ray treatments, then the morphine, and he had lost his appetite and began to get thinner and thinner. And despite the morphine, the pain got worse and he coughed blood. He had quit looking at her or the children for a week or so before he passed away, turning inward toward some other place.

She had wished she could pray then, that her parents would have given her some belief, but she had none. And it didn't seem right to pray, particularly since he never had.

Wilbert and Bertram were there then, their wives and children in the background. They came up and each gave her a peck on the cheek. They both had a tobacco odor on their breath. Wilbert asked, "Are you feeling alright, Mom?"

Emma smiled but when Amelia squeezed her arm, she said, "Okay."

"You can come home with us after the funeral," he said. "All the children will be there. Marilyn has fixed a good meal, grits, and poke selet and ham hocks."

Emma smiled.

Rob had finally quit coughing late one night, and it had bothered her at first. She had crept into his room (they had taken separate rooms during the last siege) several times and was reassured by his breathing, even though she could hear the wheeze. Then she had fallen to sleep in the other room because she was so tired. And he had passed away. In the morning he was still and white, his eyes looking off to one side as they had during the last couple of weeks. Her last thought was that she might have done more to get him to cut back on his smoking. But he was such a good man that you didn't want to cut into his few pleasures.

"Mom, come on, we're going now. Everyone's waiting." It was Amelia again, lifting Emma's arm.

"Where's Rob?" she said without getting up.

"They've already taken the casket out. It's in the first car. We'll follow next."

Amelia looked so serious. Emma hoped she wouldn't cry, and she didn't. She smiled at her daughter and stood up slowly. "I hope it's a nice place—one Rob would like."

\* \* \* \* \*

Emma stayed in that same house twenty-three years more, cleaning the house and cooking the little food she ate. The boys came every few days to help her fix broken things. But even so, the house became more and more decrepit. There were holes in the floor in the kitchen and living room, where countless footsteps had worn through. And the old shed collapsed and the outdoor toilet, one of the few left in town, was in pretty bad condition. And Amelia too finally married, bringing her husband, a young man from Ohio, home to visit. Emma was happy that he was a Catholic. She thought maybe Amelia might become one too.

* * * * *

Emma sat on the swing on the front porch in the late evening. It would grow dark soon, and she would go inside to watch wrestling. She didn't know why she found it so interesting to see those big men throw each other around and twist and pound one another on the head and body, but she did. She thought how she hadn't watched them before, not when Rob was still there, but then she realized that Rob had died before TV had come. Even so, she wondered whether Rob might have liked to watch. He probably would have kept her company even if he didn't like it; that was the way he was.

She pushed against the post with her foot every few swings because her legs wouldn't reach the floor. When Wilbert had put the swing up, he didn't take into account how short she was. It was hot, and she fanned herself periodically with a Japanese folding fan.

A lizard raced across the floor of the porch and stopped at the edge to stare at her. There were so many lizards in Maxwell, she thought, and they stopped to stare at her so often. This one stayed motionless for a long time and finally scurried out of sight.

It was getting dark. The locusts were zizzing at their loudest. The sound came from all directions. She knew they were everywhere this time of the year. Wilbert and Bertram used to catch them when they were little and tie threads around them, letting them fly about on ten- to fifteen-foot tethers.

A man turned the corner carrying a bag of groceries, and Emma started for a moment. The man looked like Rob coming home from work. But the thought didn't last long. She had had it too often already during the more than twenty years since he was gone. It had been frequent at first but, as the years passed, less. The man crossed the street and walked by her house. It was Mr. Silver, who just lived three doors away. He said, "Hi, Mrs. Fields. How are you feeling?"

"Tolerable."

It became darker, and she thought of getting up to turn on the light. Some of the children would be coming and they always complained when the lights were off. But she dallied. It was more pleasant swinging back and forth in the darkness as it was getting cooler. Besides, she knew her joints would ache if she got up. She thought momentarily that it would be good then to have some of Rob's salve. She didn't really think it helped much but a lot of people did think so, and it would make her think of Rob.

A car swung around the corner up the street and approached the house. It stopped in front and Wilbert got out of the driver's door, Marilyn from the passenger's side. They came to the porch. "Mom, are you there?"

"On the swing."

"Why don't you turn on the lights?" They came up the steps. "A person wouldn't know anyone was here."

"I was going to, but it was so peaceful and quiet, swinging here and listening to the locusts, that I didn't want to get up."

"You know we worry about you sometimes, Mom. And when the lights aren't on, we think maybe something happened. The electricity don't cost that much."

Wilbert sat down and produced a pack of cigarettes. "You want one, Marilyn?"

"No, I don't feel like it now."

Wilbert lit up, and Emma could see the crags of his lean face. He blew out smoke and coughed once.

"How you feeling, Will?"

"Fine, Mom. How about you?"

"Tolerable."

"What'd you eat today?"

"Some white meat and turnip greens and bread."

"You just eat once?"

"Don't have much appetite."

"You got to eat more than that, Mom. You'll get weak. You look kind of poorly, don't she, Marilyn?"

"Looks like she could eat more."

"You have any other complaints?" the son asked.

"Just an old lady aching in my bones."

"You want me to have Doc Ames over again to see if he can do something?"

"No need. Can't do much now, Will. Just old age." She pushed against the post with her foot and the swing started moving again.

Wilbert stood up. "Whew it's hot. Mom, you got anything cold in the fridge?"

"Some Dr. Pepper and Dee Gee Cola."

"You want one?"

"No, not thirsty."

"How about you, Marilyn?"

"Sure, bring me one."

His footsteps creaked across the worn floorboards. Nearing the kitchen, the footsteps broke their pattern. A scraping sound, followed by the sound of his body hitting something, then a low, angry voice. Silence, then the light was switched on. Light flowed out to the porch. Marilyn called, "What's wrong? You alright, Will?"

"Sure, be out in just a minute."

Will came back with the two cans of soda, giving one to Marilyn. He flipped the top of his and took a long swig then sat back down, though more carefully. "I fell in there. My toe got caught in one of the holes." He turned toward Emma, "You know, Mom, this house is dangerous. I don't see how you keep from falling all the time, and especially when you don't keep the lights on."

Emma continued to fan herself. "It's alright. I know where the holes are."

"But you could hurt yourself, Mom."

She didn't answer, so he spoke to Marilyn: "Don't you think it's dangerous?"

"I don't like to go in the house because I don't know where the holes are."

"You know, Mom, we could get the floors fixed but then there's the walls—the wallpaper's coming off and there's holes in the plaster, and that shed in back is ready to collapse. The house ain't worth it, Mom. Anybody who'd buy this lot would tear it down."

Emma had already been through this several times, and she knew where it would lead. The children would do whatever they could to get her out. They were good children, and they truly wanted to help, but they just didn't know how important the house was.

Wilbert continued, "I was talking to Eloise about it again today, and she agrees too that you ought to move, Mom. She said for right now you could come stay with her. You know she has that back room. And after a while you could come over and stay with us for awhile, couldn't she, Marilyn? Then you'd see a lot of the twins. They could help take care of you."

"No need," Emma said with as much forcefulness as she ever had. "Alright here. Know where the holes are."

"Mom, you're so stubborn."

Wilbert was a good boy but he didn't know about the house. If it were taken away, or if she was moved away from it, there would be hardly anything left of Rob. She had this secret fear that she might even forget him. And in a way, she felt she wouldn't exist then either, because she couldn't imagine herself existing without Rob. Wilbert and the others didn't know how hard it had been to keep memories of Rob alive all those years, but without the house it would have been almost impossible. She stopped swinging and said, "Thanks Wilbert, and tell Eloise thanks too, but I have to stay in my own house."

He sighed. "Maybe we can fix some of the worst holes. I'll talk to Bertie about it. The whole floor really needs to be torn out and a new one put in. But that wouldn't make any sense in such an old house."

"It's alright."

"I noticed another thing, Mom. You always seem to have some food out, some fried white meat or a piece of bread or cheese. I don't think you should do that. It's not sanitary."

"I just leave a little. It's for the mice. There's a family of them. They even know me, and if I'm very quiet, they'll come out and nibble on the food while I'm there."

"Gosh, Mom, you shouldn't do that. That's what I mean. Mice carry diseases; you oughtn't to feed them. Whatever happened to that cat I brought you? That's what you need to catch them, a cat."

Nothing particular had happened to the cat except that when it got big it had started wandering a lot, and it caught birds and even a couple of mice. Emma just didn't feed it regularly and it kept wandering more and more and finally it didn't return. But she had felt better then, because it seemed to her that the birds and mice belonged to the house as much as or more than the cat did. Emma said, "It just didn't come back."

"I could get you another one if I thought you'd take care of it. But I don't think you like cats, Mom. Maybe what you need is some traps or poison, 'cause you got to get rid of those mice."

That was alright, she thought, because they wouldn't know she wasn't using them and they'd feel better. She said, "Traps are alright."

A long pause. The calls of whippoorwills from opposite directions, calling one another. Then Wilbert spoke, "I want you to think about staying with us, Mom. Will you do that?"

"Alright."

She walked across the yard from the outhouse carefully, though it wasn't difficult. She knew every inch of the way, and there was a well-worn path. It was the last trip for the night, and she walked a little faster because the wrestling matches would be on in a few minutes. And her favorite, Fantastic Freddie, would be in the final, fighting Indian Joe.

Emma was especially careful on the stairs into the kitchen because the second step was loose and there was a nailhead sticking up in the last one. But she knew just where to put her feet and did not slip. The screen door was a little ajar, but she knew how to close it. It wasn't too important anyway, because mosquitoes could come through the holes in the floor.

She got a Dr. Pepper from the fridge and put a small piece of cheese on the window sill next to the table. The mice could get there easily, and they liked that place because it was in shadow.

She turned all the lights off in the kitchen and living room except one small wall lamp. For a moment she felt guilty about what Wilbert had told her. But Wilbert and Marilyn left some time ago. The television set was on a little table against the wall. She sat in the wood kitchen chair across from it and set her Dr. Pepper down on a little side table. The easy chair and couch they had bought when Rob was still alive were in the room also, but they were very old, worn at the corners, with holes in a couple of the armrests. She had put doilies on the holes. Emma didn't like to sit in them much because they were hard to get up from. The straight-backed chair was easier.

She took a sip of her Dr. Pepper and swallowed slowly, staring at the blank television screen. She shuffled into the kitchen, where she took out her dentures and dropped them into a glass of water. She smacked her lips and gums a couple of times, savoring the relaxation. Then she returned to her seat in front of the set and turned it on.

The announcer walked around the ring, holding a microphone in one hand and waving his other in grand flourishes. Dressed in a formal evening suit, he was almost the same as a circus manager. He intoned nonstop in singsong, "Tonight we are particularly favored by the presence of that well-known champion, Mighty Mouse, who as you know has had twenty-eight victories in a row, defeating such great fighters as Jack the Giantkiller, Horrible Harry, and the Lone Ranger. And though he weighs in at a mere 194 pounds, he more than makes up for his diminutiveness by the dastardly techniques he uses on his opponents. And tonight he faces that other killer, The Crimson Kid. I think that any of you who know the Crimson Kid, know how he got that appellation."

Emma was lost by then, totally absorbed in the changing kaleidoscope of ritualistic announcements and openings, to be followed by heaving and flying bodies, interspersed with close-ups of legs, necks, and arms being twisted, accompanied by groans, to be ended by switches to commercials, followed by further ritual. Periodically she took a swig of her Dr. Pepper.

Finally, they came to the last fight. Emma hardly heard the rustling of the mice in the kitchen or any other outside sound. The announcer came on again. "And finally we come to the fight that all of you have been waiting for, the fight of the century, the fight of two of the meanest, but at the same time most flamboyant, fighters that have been produced in this noble sport, the fight between the undefeated Fantastic Freddie and his arch opponent for a decade, Indian Joe. And let me tell you, folks, that when these two go for one another, it is pure mayhem. I wouldn't be an umpire in one of their fights for any money."

Emma, her hands on the sides of her face, watched with complete absorption as the first fighter, Indian Joe, appeared at the end of one aisle, a swarthy man in dark trunks with a blanket over his shoulders, clasped at the front. He wore an Indian headdress. He did few steps of an Indian dance periodically as he made his way toward the ring. He took off his war bonnet and ceremoniously handed it to an aide just before swinging into the ring. Once in the center, he did his final dance steps and raised his dark arms in a pre-victory sign. Without any awareness, Emma called out audibly, "Down with Indian Joe."

Then from the opposite aisle a flurry of activity as the opponent, Fantastic Freddie, appeared with flourish and aides. Emma had seen him before, almost since the time she discovered wrestling on television but each time she studied him anew as if there must have been something she always missed. There he was, even from the farthest distance, clearly a light skinned man with long golden hair. He wore a long sequinned golden robe which he swirled as he walked down the aisle, bowing and waving to greeters on both sides. Most whistled and cheered, though a few made catcalls or lauded Indian Joe.

Emma cried out, "Come on, Fantastic Freddie, you'll beat him. Come on, I'm rooting for you."

She waited in anticipation and a little fear as he got closer to the ring. She was wondering as she had the last couple of times whether it would happen again. But then it did, just when he took off his golden cloak in a grand flourish and turned completely around, waving to all quadrants. When he turned back in Emma's direction, his face was transformed as before. She couldn't help believing for that moment that the golden warrior was Rob, the young man who had held her in his arms in Sycamore Gullies. But soon afterward, as he mounted the ropes into the ring, she saw again the differences. Fantastic Freddie had a longer nose, a scar on his right cheek, and his hair was much longer. But as she settled back to watch the beginning of the fight, she thought, and perhaps even said aloud, "But he might have been his brother."

She said in a loud voice, "Get him, Freddie, Go get him, get him for Emma."

# CHAPTER 6

**M**artin was sitting at the coffee table in Oldenberg's office, the Transition Master facing him. Next to the plump man was the person Oldenberg had just introduced Martin to, Dr. Hanson. A tall, bearish-looking man with a full beard, he was saying, "I appreciate the opportunity to hear some of your ideas, Dr. Neumann. The topic you are concerned with is of considerable interest to me. You see, my job is to provide supervision in the psychiatric section of the Transition Office, and sometimes there are Transitionees who are so nonplused or shocked by the idea of changing into another being that they develop deviancy symptoms."

"I could visualize that," Martin said. "As Mr. Oldenberg will tell you, I was somewhat nonplused myself. I mean, let's face it, it's pretty much of a shock to find oneself in a totally different place, without knowing why and after a few preliminaries to be told that one has died and is now about to embark on a new life."

For once Oldenberg was not smoking his pipe. Instead he was doodling on a note pad; Martin wondered what. Martin could see that the Transition Master was listening, however, his head cocked toward them. Hanson continued, "Anyway, what we do is try to get the Transitionees stabilized enough that they can go off to their new lives with relative normalcy. But much of my interest in your project derives from the fact that, believe it or not, since I came to Earth, I have become a romance freak. You see, this kind of an emotion as a basis for mating or reproduction is a very strange concept in the universe generally. In fact, in all my travels to other living zones, I never heard of the idea of 'falling in love,' or phrases such as 'being in love,' or 'I love you.' But when the idea kept cropping up over and over in the conditions of the patients I had to deal with, I decided I had to learn more about it. So I did a little exploration and found that there was a vast outpouring of stories of people 'in love,' in novels, films, television, in short, in all the popular media of your people. It seems to be a primary theme of your popular songs also. But anyway, as I became more aware of this theme, I got hooked, as you say nowadays. I do understand it is more usual for your males to use crime and western fiction as your palliative reading matter and for your females to be concerned with romance. But I must admit that in that respect, I am more like your females. Tales of derring-do in the far west or of super sleuths solving impossible crimes do very little for me. But I am now an addict to the tale of supreme romantic ecstasy, love betrayed, disillusionment, and love again. I find it to be a good way to pass the leisure hours while here on Earth, that is, reading tales of romance or watching your soap operas, which seem to be mostly concerned with that topic." He paused. "Now, mind you, this is not to say that I accept this particular basis for mating as very sound. In fact, I feel, much as Harold here does, that it seems to be a bizarre, transitory phenomenon on a universal scale. But I do find it interesting in its current manifestation."

"Well," Martin said, "join the crowd. I'm coming more and more to that opinion myself, even though I seem to have had an infection of the love disease of particular intensity." Pause. "I suppose Mr. Oldenberg has told you that I am currently trying to research the topic, to a large extent for my own personal needs."

"Yes, he has, and he has told me of some of your findings, which I find quite interesting. That is why, of course, I asked to sit in on some of your sessions, if you don't mind."

"Oh no, the more the merrier. I have no great expectations that this is going to lead to anything profound, but I do find it interesting. And besides, whether something was interesting has long been a reason for participation by me, even when I was alive."

Oldenberg entered the conversation then for the first time. "Shall I call the girl and order us some coffee?"

"I'd like that very much," Martin said. "Another cup of that Nilgiri, if possible."

"I'm not fond of your coffee," Hanson said. "The taste is good but it gives me stomach burn, or what you Earthlings call heartburn. However, I do find your tea a pleasant drink, particularly your aged Shillong."

Oldenberg gave the order, then turned to Martin. "So, you seem to have gone through the last life somewhat faster than the earlier ones. This one was the mother of your first wife, correct?"

"Yes, Emma Fields. And it's true that I spent only about half the amount of time that I did with the father of my second wife, and less than with my own parents."

Oldenberg chuckled. "I suppose you are starting to get repetitious patterns, even with an N of no more than four." He turned to Hanson, "That's a little jargon derived from the Earthlings' methodology called statistics. In case you haven't encountered it before, it's basically a way of manipulating data to have them predict what you wish. This practice is particularly popular with what Earthlings call their dismal science, economics, and the one they use to sell their goods and to manipulate their elections, survey research."

"Interesting, and though I had come across the idea in my readings and in discussions with a few Transitionees, I had the idea that it was a means of analyzing data in a numerical way. I had not heard it referred to as a way of trying to control outcome."

"There is that other point of view," Oldenberg said without amplification.

Martin suddenly realized that with two Transitioners, he could learn even more and would find the talks even more stimulating. But he was proud of himself that he didn't get sidetracked. He had learned that kind of concentration in dealing with two generations of crafty students, intent on converting lectures to professorial war stories, material that rarely appeared on exams.

Martin brought the conversation back to where it had left off, saying, "Perhaps it's because I have come to recognize certain patterns in my parents' generation, but then also I suspect the relative shortness of my viewing and report may have something to do with the fact that a satisfying relationship is relatively uneventful. Nothing out of the ordinary really happened to the Fieldses. They were high school sweethearts, they got married as soon as they matured, and they raised a family in the town where they grew up, then they died, first husband, then wife, the usual order. Their sex life was about like everything else. They followed the standard moral code of the time, holding off until they were married. But after that they seemed to have been relatively well satisfied sexually and in other ways for the rest of their lives. Nothing extraordinary, mind you, no kinkiness or experimentation, mostly the missionary position. But that was standard for that age, it seems."

Oldenberg leaned back, smiling. "Well, it seems that you at last found a couple who filled each other's needs. The ideal pattern, as I believe you told me you anthropologists called it." He turned to the celestial shrink, "I must inform you that Martin here has been considerably disturbed by what he sees as a lack of personal satisfaction in the human mating relationship. It's a condition he seems to have brought with him from his living existence. This last life, that of his first mother-in-law, was therefore particularly significant."

"Ah yes," Hanson said. "I can see how that would arise when I consider the romance myth they promulgate, you know, like in the phrases 'until death do us part' and 'undying love.' And despite all evidence to the contrary, they particularly like to associate the word *love* with 'forever.' So Dr. Neumann here really saw one that worked that way. Interesting." Pause. "Was there anything in particular about this pair that was different from the others?"

Martin answered. "They were an amiable couple to start with. They got along well with other people generally, including their own children. Then too, perhaps it was significant that they stayed their whole lives in one place, achieving nothing of any great importance. They just lived together, working at making a living and raising children. And I would guess from what I saw, though there was nothing terribly exciting about it from my point of view, that they both enjoyed sex."

The tea and coffee were brought in then by one of the receptionists, the cups placed symmetrically on a tray, along with little silver containers of sugar and cream. A small dish of cookies shared the tray with the hot drinks. The men occupied themselves with fixing their own cups for a few minutes.

Hanson spoke first. "So, you feel you found what the magic formula was, that people who were relatively amiable, enjoyed sex, raised children and stayed put all their lives could have a lifetime of happiness."

"Yes, but I think there's at least one other component that promoted lifetime mating among humans then, one shared by the other couples I viewed, my parents and my second wife's parents. And that was that people in that generation just didn't consider breaking up very often. They began with the idea that they would stay married, and if things were very good, as with Emma and Rob, they stayed together naturally, but even if things were not so great, as with Josh and Alma, or my own parents, they still stayed married. This is not to say that people never divorced or left one another, but it was a very serious step then, one that most people wouldn't consider. It was nothing like the situation became during my lifetime, and particularly in California, where divorce and remarriage became a kind of game. We evolved a kind of multi-spouse mating pattern which we named serial polygamy. You know, in contrast to the old fashioned kind when a man would have several wives at the same time which we called synchronic polygamy."

Hanson said between sips of tea, "I never quite imagined all the complexities you humans got involved in because of your commitment to learned behavior, what you anthropologists called culture. Certainly the other animals, including your closest evolutionary relatives, the monkeys and apes, did not get into such complex and rapidly changing ways of dealing with life problems. It seems that this difference lends weight to the instinctive way of solving life problems."

That was hard to refute, Martin thought. The commitment to learned behavior did sometimes seem to cause more problems than solutions. But his thoughts were broken up by Oldenberg who said, "I must say, Jerry, that though your argument seems at first to be persuasive, that you seem to be falling into the same old goal trap, one that I've already discussed several times with Martin. We have to be clear on what we consider the goal of existence. You know that we in the System consider group survival as the baseline for success. And that means reproduction and population maintenance at least. And by all unbiased evaluations, Martin's species, *Homo sapiens,* has been most successful in that regard, certainly in comparison with the closest relatives, the monkeys and apes. Humans have reproduced in increasing numbers for five million years, until they are now found everywhere except in the lowest depths of the seas and on the tops of the highest mountains. In fact, their success in that regard is their greatest danger. They are so good at reproduction that they have the capacity of filling their planet beyond its carrying capacity. On the other hand, the monkeys and apes, with their instincts, have been driven to the wall so to speak, and by who else but their closest relative, the primate with culture, Martin and his kind. So I guess we can't really put down learned behavior as a survival mechanism."

With a napkin Hanson wiped his beard where some drops of tea had made it moist. Then he scratched his hairy cheek. He really had a luxurious beard, one that only a person of European ancestry or a Hairy Ainu could have grown. Then he answered, "I see what you're saying, Harold, that though the complexities and rapid change in human behavior may not promote happiness particularly, they have up to now promoted reproduction and child rearing, thus maintaining the species quite well."

"That's about it."

Martin found the interchange between the Transitioners very inter-

esting, far more than the simple exchange he had with Oldenberg alone
even though he respected the latter highly. But still he felt the discussion was getting away from the central issue, the life of Emma Fields. So
he said, "I guess I have only two other comments about her life, the
first of which simply emphasizes what I said before about lifetime com-
mitments. There was one incident in her early married life that probably would have produced a breakup if it had happened in later years,
notably the fact that her husband was probably going out on her. All
kinds of people have divorced on that issue in the latter half of the
twentieth century, even though it probably occurs fairly often in many
cultures. If a young man is handsome and in contact with females, it is
perhaps inevitable that he will be the subject of flirtations. I know I was
during most of my married years, even though I too was careful not to
encourage any of the females. And of course there are also delivery
and service people who see wives during the day.

In any event, opportunities are greater for a male. And it came to
the point during my lifetime that when such a person had an affair and
the spouse found out about it, the injured party usually sought a divorce. That wasn't always the case, and evidently it was not in my parents' generation. So when Emma found out about her husband's probable affair with an old girlfriend, she let it pass. And the best I could
make out, it did end shortly. If it had been in the latter part of my lifetime, it probably would have ended in a divorce."

"I had the impression from talking to other Transitionees that you
humans were supposed recently to have developed more open attitudes
toward sexual experiences. I am a little surprised that a simple affair
with someone of the opposite sex became enough for the injured party
to seek a separation."

"It's complicated, like other aspects of our mating pattern. We became more open in some ways, but we seem to have remained as jealous as any of our ancestors had been. I think it had something to do
with our concept of love. We treated it as a totally encompassing passion. If it was really true love, we kept telling one another, it should
have driven out all thoughts of other persons. And since there was so
little stigma to divorce by then, we took that route to solve the issue."
Pause. "Emma and her generation generally didn't do that. They sweated
their marriages out even if the spouse did play around once in a while,
or if there were other disappointments. Remember both Bruno and
Josh were generally disappointed in sex but neither considered a
breakup."

"Yes, so it seems," Oldenberg said and finally brought out his tobacco pouch and pipe and began filling it immediately. "And the other thing?"

"Oh, it was simply a repeat of the pattern of my own parents, though for a slightly different reason. Emma outlived her husband by more than twenty years, as my own mother did. Emma seemed to have managed by developing a secret fantasy life in which she kept his memory alive. She also had her children around until the end, but she spent a long period alone." Thoughtful pause. "I guess in terms of lifetime satisfaction, women nowadays in the favored societies have to take it for granted that they will probably have a lonely period at the end, sometimes quite a long one. You know, it wasn't always that way. In the primitive cultures and even in our own early history, women died in childbirth and from overwork early so often that it was usually the men who survived longest. But of course they usually married again, a pattern not duplicated by the older surviving woman nowadays." Pause, sigh. "Another of the unexpected consequences of technical advances. If female mortality had not been so drastically reduced, there wouldn't be so many lonely ones in their old age."

"Ah yes, nothing simple about that method of adaptation you people call culture," Hanson said.

By this time, Oldenberg was smoking his pipe again. In his relaxed manner he said, "Anyway, you seem to have been mainly correct in your assessment of your mother-in-law's life. And I imagine that should about wind you up with that generation, don't you think?"

"Yes, I guess so, at least for the time being. I'm sure there are other patterns of mating among our people of that period. But I do have to keep in mind the length of the report. These are not exactly whole life histories, but even the occurrences in regard to mating use up a substantial amount of paper. It's a little like the works produced by some of our anthropologists who relied on personal accounts. I am thinking particularly of the late Oscar Lewis, who made himself famous by producing book after book of the detailed lives of Latino families." Martin paused. "But besides, when I was living, I was frequently involved in studies of other peoples' way of life. And now that I have access to this totally unexpected resource, the Life Tapes, I am dying to exploit it for other cultures. So my feeling is that I should take a look at mating patterns elsewhere. Does that sound reasonable?"

Hanson was listening closely. He said, "I understand that you people consider other cultures as groups of your own species, but who have some significant differences in their learned behavior, is that correct?"

Martin grinned with pleasure. He could hardly believe that basic anthropological concepts would have spread so far as to become part of
the intellectual baggage of his mentor from the other world. But then
he checked himself with the repeated realization that, despite their appearances, these men were not human, and he had no idea how great
their intellectual capacities were. He said, "Yes, that's right; we consider
culture to be the total body of learned behavior of a people which certainly included their mating customs."

Oldenberg said with a twinkle in his eyes, "And I suppose, Martin,
that as before, you already have someone in mind." He added, "And of
course, his or her culture."

"Yes, as a matter of fact, I do. As before, I would like to call on my
memory of a living person, someone whose culture I had known to a
certain extent, but the details of whose life I was of course not privy to.
The culture is East Indian, specifically Hindu, and the person is Ashoka
Harinarayan, my field assistant on my first major anthropological field
trip. I got to know Ashoka pretty well and we used to talk about our
respective lives quite a lot. And though he told me some things about
his own life, and I observed a little, there was of course a vast amount of
detail that I never knew. Now if I could see his Video!"

"That sounds feasible," Oldenberg said. "Certainly I should think that
Hindu culture would present considerable differences from that found
in your country. And that should include the mating pattern." He turned
to Hanson, "How do you feel about that, Jerry?"

"Well, Harold, thanks for asking me. But you are Dr. Neumann's
project monitor, and you have followed him up to now. All I can say is
that it sounds good to me. And I certainly would like to be in on the
debriefing, if that's what you call these sessions."

Oldenberg had smoked his pipe down again. He rapped the bowl
into the ceramic ashtray. "As I mentioned before, I thought you should
move on after the last one, Martin, and I guess that would be a good
direction. Why don't you go ahead? There should be some new insights."

# ASHOKA

The small boy, perhaps seven years old, sat on the veranda behind iron
bars, watching the constantly changing scene on the street. He was slender, with dark wavy hair and tan skin, much lighter than many of the
men who passed on the street, but darker than most Europeans. He

had bright, expressive eyes. He was munching on a rolled-up *chapatty* (unleavened bread) as he watched. First there was a cart, loaded so high with wood boxes it seemed it would have to fall from top-heaviness. It was being pulled by a water buffalo, a man guiding in the traces behind the animal. The buffalo weaved slowly from side to side, taking cautious steps. Ashoka knew why the animal was so careful. He had seen buffalo lose their footing, then be pinned to the pavement by the weight of the cart.

Next came a dark-skinned man wearing a loin cloth, carrying a bundle of grass on his head. He moved rapidly with an exaggerated hip movement that took all the unevenness from his load. It was the earth-eating gait of a peasant carrier. Ashoka knew that none of the men in his family ever carried anything on their heads. The man was carrying the grass he had cut outside of town to feed his goats or sheep.

Several dogs came trotting from the opposite direction, all emaciated and with various patches of skin gone from mange. The front dog had a distended vulva, the others trying to get close enough to sniff while keeping a wary eye that the others would not attack, a female in heat followed by a lustful male host. There was a betel vendor across the street under a large neem tree. The man sat cross-legged on the serving space of a little roofed stand, waiting for customers. In front of his crossed legs were several German silver pots filled with the various ingredients that went into the chews he sold, moistened pan leaves, chopped betel nuts, areca, lime, spices, and tissue-thin hammered silver. The stand was on stilts just over the open drainage ditch into which he threw the leftovers and into which his customers spit the red juice from the chew. Big red splotches marked the cement of the ditch and adjacent wall.

The female dog kept just along the ditch, heading for the shaded area under the betel stand. A male got too close and started licking her distended vulva. She turned around and snapped at his nose. He yelped and pulled back. The female hurried quickly to the place under the stand and stopped, putting her rear against the wall. The vendor hissed and waved at the dog pack. Keeping their eyes on the vendor, the males backed off, though only a short distance, unwilling to abandon the female. She cowered, frightened to be where she was, but unwilling to deal with the males again. The vendor waved and hissed a few more times, then picked up a stout cane. It was not as heavy as a villager's fighting stick, a *lathi*, but it was a substantial piece of hard wood. The vendor leaned to one side and came down with the stick on the female's head, which was projecting just beyond the edge of the stand. The dog's legs folded and it collapsed into a heap, twitching. After a little she lifted her head and looked around with glazed eyes. Then she pulled herself onto her front legs and slithered off, hugging the wall of the ditch. The pack of males sprang into action, hurrying to catch up with the female but keeping well clear of the vendor's stand.

Ashoka took another bite from the *chapatty* and chewed it slowly. The scene continued. The next passersby were a pair of women dressed from head to foot in white garments, their faces covered by veils. He had asked his sister, Lila, what kind of people they were just a week before, and she had told him they were Muslim women. They weren't allowed to go on the streets with any part of their body showing.

Ashoka didn't have to wait long until the string of household cows started coming up the street. They were kept by individual families, usually only one or so, in little cowsheds at the backs of the houses. Men of the herdsmen caste took them out to graze on the flats along the river in the day and brought them to their homes each night. The herdsmen would even milk the cows when they brought them home, but Ashoka's mother, who had been raised in a village, insisted on milking the cows herself. Ashoka liked to watch her.

Their two cows were brought to the front doorway and the latch lifted. The herdsman poked them with a stick, and they ambled into the dark passageway, heading for their stalls at the back. Ashoka said to the herdsman, "Don't poke our cows. They are precious gifts from God."

He had heard his mother say that, and besides, he knew he could tell the herdsman whatever he wanted. The herdsman wasn't one of the twice-born like he was. The herdsman just slammed the door and went up the street with the rest of his charges. The cows continued inside to their dark stalls and up to the basket where the ground-up rice chaff and straw, mixed with a little molasses, was waiting. They both began eating, nuzzling each other in turn, each to get its share. Ashoka patted Milkmaid's Happiness and put his hand on Gentlelady's nose to feel the soft wetness. He closed the halfdoor and left the stalls.

In the kitchen, his mother was working on making *chapatty* dough while Lila was cutting up vegetables for the night's curry, both squatting over their work in the smoky kitchen. Ashoka's eyes watered a little when he first walked into the room. He said, "Mama, the cows are here, eating their food. I told the herdsman not to poke them. I also closed the door."

His mother wiped the hair from her eyes with the back of her hand,

"That's a good boy. Cows should be loved."

Ashoka edged closer to the cutting board where Lila was working. She kept her eyes on her task. He grabbed a piece of cauliflower and popped it into his mouth. She reached for him but he stepped back just as quickly and she missed. "Ashoka, you stop that!" she said in irritation. "That's for tonight's curry."

He screwed up his face, "I can do whatever I want because I'm a boy and you're just a girl."

He had learned increasingly the last few years that he could get by with much more than his sister could. But Lila said with a slight whine in her voice, "I don't care. If you do that again, I'm going to slap you. I'm a lot bigger, you know."

"That doesn't make any difference. A sister is not supposed to slap her brother. Mama wouldn't let you." He turned toward his mother. "Would you, Mama?"

*Mata* was pounding rhythmically and kneading the dough on a cleaned place of the clay stove. Without looking around, she said, "Now, you children stop that quarreling. Brothers and sisters are supposed to love one another and help one another."

Ashoka insisted. "But she couldn't slap me, could she?"

"Neither brother nor sister is supposed to slap the other."

"But what if she did?" He kept on. "What would you do to her, Mama?"

His mother sighed and put down the mass of dough. "Now Ashoka, sometimes you worry a mother. Just be quiet a minute and I'll let you go with me to milk Milkmaid's Happiness." Then without letting him have a chance to say anything else, his mother said to Lila, "You can start the curry as soon as you're finished cutting up the vegetables. It needs to simmer a long time. And don't forget to put in the spices I ground."

"Yes, Mama. What about the *chapattys?*"

"I'll take care of them later. It's best to make them just before you put them on the griddle." She lifted an aluminum bucket from a hook on the wall and said to Ashoka, "Come on, my precious. We'll go milk the cow."

They walked down the corridor, Ashoka in front, turning around periodically to speak to his mother. In the last few years she had gradually let him go in front, and now he always did. It was the way men walked with women all the time, he knew. He was beginning to take his place in the man's world.

The calf of Milkmaid's Happiness had pushed its head through the bars of its little cubicle next to the cows' room. Ashoka put his hand on its moist nose, and the calf rasped it with its long wet tongue. "Oh look, Mama, Blackcalf wants to get out. He wants his dinner."

"Yes, but he's getting big enough that he won't need milk much longer. Then we'll send him out in the field with the herdsmen."

"Are we going to keep Blackcalf when he gets big? Then we'd have more milk."

"Oh no, we can't do that. Blackcalf is a bull; he can't give milk."

"Oh yes, now I remember," the boy replied. Ashoka had noticed the penis and little testicles on Blackcalf some weeks before when the calf had been peeing. He remembered then that Marigold, the last calf they had, which had been a cow calf, had been sold. Marigold didn't have anything where Blackcalf had his penis. And she urinated through her back hole, just like the cows, with her back legs spread apart. He had tried to find out the details from Lila, but she had said, "Little boys don't ask their big sisters about things like that."

So he taunted, "Okay, I'll go ask Mama. She'll tell me; she'll tell me anything."

But Lila replied, "Oh no, she won't. Boys don't ask women things like that. I don't think Mama would like it."

He had thought about that a while and decided Lila was right. But still he couldn't get it out of his mind. He used to stand for a long time in front of the cubicle, waiting for Blackcalf to urinate. Once his father had come by and said, "What are you doing, standing here so much?"

For a moment Ashoka had thought of asking his father, but he had seen how stern his father could quickly become, so he just said, "Nothing, just watching Blackcalf."

But after his father passed, he thought of his Grandfather Govind. Ashoka decided to go to the old man's room, where he would be reading one of his holy books, his little glasses perched on the end of his nose. His grandfather liked to have him visit and liked to tell him things, and he never got stern. And that was the way he had learned that only cows give milk but that they had to have the seed from bulls, and the seed was in the testicles and came out the penis and went into the cow.

By this time his mother had put the milk bucket under Milkmaid's Happiness and was squatting next to her hind legs. She took two of the udders and began squeezing. Long, thin streams of milk squirted into the container. Ashoka was surprised at how strong his mother's hands were, she was such a little, thin person. The cow looked back a couple of times with its large brown eyes. Ashoka squatted beside his mother.

"Can I do that sometime?" he asked.

"Maybe, when you get bigger. Your hands are too small now. But by then you'll probably be too busy with your studies. So one of your sisters or sisters-in-law can do it."

"Will you give some to Blackcalf?"

"Yes, a little, But he's getting so big now that he doesn't need it much longer. He can eat grass and chaff from now on."

Ashoka remembered that at first his father used to let Blackcalf nurse a little, just to get Milkmaid's Happiness started, but as soon as the milk would start to flow, he would pull the calf back by a rope. His father did that because the calf was too strong for his mother, even when it was young. Only when they started keeping it in its separate pen all the time did his mother do all the milking.

His mother kept the milk flowing steadily, a tiny squatting figure with brown, muscular hands. Ashoka couldn't even see her face, the *sari* was so far down the sides. He said, "Mamaji, what will we do with Blackcalf since we can't use him for milk? Will we sell him like we did Marigold?"

A Sikh cattle buyer had put Marigold in a truck with some other calves. Ashoka had asked what they were going to do with her and had been told that she would be taken away and sold to some villagers who didn't have enough cows.

His mother said, "I think your Papa wants to let Blackcalf free when he's big enough."

"You mean he wouldn't belong to anyone?"

"Only to God."

"But what would he eat and where would he live? Wouldn't he have a cow shed?"

"No, he'd be free. You see that's a good thing to do because it makes Lord Shiva happy to know that a relative of his celestial mount, Nandi, can go and come whenever and wherever he wants. You know, you saw some of those bulls down by the temple and in the market. They are ones who have been released by Hindu families. They do it because it makes the gods happy."

"But what do they eat?"

"People in the market give them things, and there are food offerings in the temples they can eat."

Ashoka remembered watching some bulls rooting around in piles of trash in the market, pulling out leaves and peelings and rotten vegetables. He remembered seeing one bull peeling posters from poles and munching them up. He said, "I guess the bulls like it when they're free, don't they, Mamaji?"

"Yes, and they never have to work like the oxen in the villages."

His mother stood up with the container about two-thirds full. "Let's give Blackcalf a little, and then I must go back to the kitchen and get dinner finished. Your father and the other men will be hungry soon. Your brother's wife will be there, and I'll have to show her what to do."

Ashoka took one side of the handle and they walked toward the calf's cubicle.

\* \* \* \* \*

Ashoka grew up in the kaleidoscope of life of the Indian city of Uttarbad. He was constantly surrounded by family members in that extensive house of corridors and cubicle rooms. Except for his grandfather, the men went forth to their jobs as teachers or civil servants and the boys went to school. Women went to the bazaars with great circumspection and almost always in pairs. Otherwise, they stayed at home, cooking and taking care of children. Ashoka did well in primary and secondary school and went to Christchurch College afterward. Though his father was an orthodox Hindu, he wanted his son to have the best education available, and the Anglican College had such a reputation in Uttarbad.

\* \* \* \* \*

Ashoka was of medium height and slender. His black hair was slightly wavy and his skin the color of coffee with cream. He was eighteen years old.

He rode the Raleigh easily on Cantonment Road, heading toward the college. His books and tiffin tin were in the basket above the front wheel.

The street was crowded as it always was during the day and deep into the night with herds of water buffalo, cows, cars, trucks, bicycle rickshas, and endless streams of pedestrians. Ashoka hardly noticed them as he weaved in and out. The density of bodies and incessant movement seemed perfectly normal to him since he had known nothing else. He passed one place where there was an open urinal, a wall facing the street where men would stand and, without any exposure, urinate, the urine running down the wall and around their feet. The smell was high since men had been doing that throughout the day at that place as long as Ashoka could remember. At another place there was a body on the sidewalk against the wall. Passersby paid it little attention. It was not yet mid-morning, and there was frequently a body or so along that stretch. The city ambulance would pick it up by mid-morning at least.

He reached the intersection that led to Rambagh, where he stopped for a minute, his feet on the curb. There was plenty of time yet before his first class, probably enough for a cup of tea with Shyam or Prem. He decided to go through the Muslim neighborhood where she lived.

As he pedaled up the street, considerably broken up with chugholes, he went over how he had first noticed her. She was one of the few girls on the campus, wearing the long blouse and pajama-slacks of North India, a long thin scarf invariably thrown around her neck. She carried her books and other personal things in a plastic net bag. She was always with at least one other girl. She was very pretty, with light skin and long, shiny black hair in a plait down her back. There weren't many girls at that school, and most were Christians or Parsis or Hindus from the most progressive families. Muslim girls were few because orthodox Muslim families felt girls shouldn't be in public by themselves, or even with others their age. Also, the Muslims wanted their women covered when in public, and that wasn't permitted on the college grounds.

Ashoka had followed her at a distance and had gotten to know some of the classes she was in so he could be across from the doorway. And though he never approached her, he felt sure she noticed him. And then after several weeks, he had followed her when she left the campus. Waiting on the corner from where almost all the students left, he had figured she would come out with one of her friends to get a ricksha. She had, but wearing a black *burqa,* the head-to-toe dress of Muslims, as was her friend, though both had the veil thrown back. They had stopped a *purdah* (seclusion) ricksha and got in, letting the curtains drop. She had lifted the curtain on her side slightly as the ricksha pulled into the street. Ashoka wondered whether she saw him, standing against a wall, his bicycle at his side. In a way he had wanted her to, but he felt embarrassed at the same time. Prem Shankar had come by on his bicycle. "Hey Ashoka, come on, I'll ride with you."

Ashoka had stayed where he was. "I can't right now. I've got something to do before I go home."

"Okay, I'll see you tomorrow."

Ashoka had hurriedly left then because the ricksha had been swallowed up by the milling crowd on the street. It had taken three blocks before he felt sure he had it in sight again. Then he had tried to keep about one block behind. As he had watched the curtained vehicle, he felt that he saw the back curtain open a crack several times. He would slow down and let the distance increase. The ricksha had turned off on the road to Rambagh, and he was sure then that it was going to the Muslim district. It had stopped alongside one of the walled-in brick buildings. The two girls had gotten out, fully covered and veiled by then. The girl he was following, whose name he did not know, had paid the *rickshawalla* and the two separated, the other girl going across the street and disappearing in a doorway. The remaining girl had turned for just a moment and glanced toward where Ashoka was waiting at the corner, under a shrine tree. Then she too had hurried into the house.

As he approached her house this time, he recalled that since the time he had followed her, he had come by several times, usually when she had not come to school or during afternoons when she did not have classes. Nothing had happened except a couple of times he had seen a face in an upstairs window that remained for a moment then disappeared into the shadow. He had always kept moving though, slowing as he passed the house.

This time as he approached, he felt that something extraordinary was going to happen. The doorways along both sides of the street were well closed, and except for a lone ricksha pedaling down the street and a couple of carriers with baskets full of coal on their heads, there was no movement. From the side of his eye, Ashoka saw a mongoose running up the drainage ditch. Then just as he approached the house, the shutter of the upstairs window opened a crack and a small tan envelope fluttered down. The shutter closed immediately. Ashoka looked around hurriedly and then hurried to pick up the piece of paper, dismounting from his bicycle for a moment. He remounted quickly, put the envelope in his shirt pocket, and hurriedly pedaled away.

He didn't slow down until he reached Nehru Park, where there were benches and shade from a big banyan tree. Sitting down on the nearest bench, he was hardly aware of the incessant movement above him from the flying foxes, which were fanning themselves and bickering for space. He opened the envelope and took out the folded sheet of stationery. In neat cursive writing, it said in English, "Hello sir, my name is Umana. I am an English major at Christchurch College, which I like very much. I am in my second year. What is your name? Do you like Christchurch College? Sincerely, Umana."

Ashoka read it several times, turning the page over to be sure there was nothing on the other side. Then he smelled it and thought he could detect an odor of sweet spice. Finally he folded it again and put it back into the envelope and into his pocket. He leaned back and gazed at the monkeys eating zinnia seeds in the flower bed across the way. This was the first note he had ever received from a girl, and it was so extraordinary, he could think of nothing else. He had heard some of the other male students talk about notes from girls, but he had never known anyone who actually got one.

Ashoka finally stood and mounted his bicycle. He wheeled out of the park and into the busy street, heading for Christchurch. He met Shyam just under the overhang of the main building. Shyam was locking his bicycle onto one of the iron posts.

Ashoka approached his friend. "Hi Shyam, when's your next class?"

"English Lit, about twenty five minutes."

"I have a class then too. How'd you like to get a tea and some *channa* snack before? We could go over to *punditji's* stand."

The main eating place on the college grounds was run by a Brahmin and various members of his family. And though the students there were not all orthodox, there were many Hindus who would not eat prepared food unless it was done by a Brahmin.

Without their bicycles, they walked toward the stand. Ashoka took Shyam's hand in his own, holding his books with the other. Shyam said, "You act like something happened, and I'll bet you're going to tell me about it."

"It did. But let's get our tea and *channa* first. Then we can sit down on the steps in the shade. I want to show you something."

The food stand had snacks, both sweet and salty-hot, as well as some simple meal foods, unleavened breads and hot, spicy vegetarian curries, potato cakes, and milk curd. Mostly though the students got tea and snacks. Ashoka and Shyam both got a paper cone of *channa*, a hot spicy mixture of roasted gram, peanuts, noodles, and other crunchables, plus a cup of tea each. *Punditji* gave them their tea in crude pottery cups. Such handleless containers were discarded after one use. It was a simple way to solve the problem of pollution. *Punditji* had hard-fired pottery cups and saucers too, but they were only for people who drank their tea at the stand and who didn't worry too much about pollution.

Ashoka took a sip of the sweet, milky tea, then a large pinchful of the spicy hot munchie, enjoying the pleasant sensations both gave his mouth. Shyam turned toward him. "So, what is the big news. You're so mysterious."

With much flourish, Ashoka got out the envelope and carefully took the note out, handing it to his friend. "Take a look at that."

Shyam put his tea and snack down on the step where they were sitting and carefully read the note, then, "Where did you get it?"

"A girl dropped it for me." Ashoka couldn't hold himself back any longer, blurting, "I saw her in school here. She's a Muslim. She's beautiful and she noticed me too. I know it."

Shyam handed the note back to Ashoka and put his arm around his friend's shoulders. "So how did she give it to you?"

"I went by her house and she dropped it. Oh Shyam, you know what they keep talking about in the English poems and stories, about 'falling in love'? I know what that means now; it has happened to me."

Shyam pulled his hand away. "But Ashoka, that's for Englishmen, not Indians. You know as well as I that nothing can happen from this. Why, friend, she's a Muslim and you're a Hindu. And not only that, you're a Brahmin."

"What difference does that make if we're in love?" He quickly added, "I have a feeling she is too." He said it mostly in Hindi but the expression, "in love" was in English. Finally, as though he already realized the impossibility of what he was suggesting, "You know, as they say in the stories, 'love will find a way.'"

For the first time Shyam laughed. "Ashoka, you can't even say it in your own language. Those are foreign ideas, not Indian. We don't get married for love; we do it because our parents arrange it. It is impossible for respectable Hindu parents to arrange a marriage with a Muslim. Even the Muslims wouldn't permit it." He added, "Why, they even eat cows."

Ashoka kept turning the note over and over in his hand, but his expression had changed from exhilaration to somberness. Finally he said, "Shyam, don't you think we Indians are too backward? Look at the Englishmen, they 'date' girls and drink whiskey, and curse, and laugh at our superstitions, and they are a rich nation. And look at us: we can never be out alone with a girl, our parents don't want us to drink or curse, we have many customs and beliefs that the English find peculiar, and we're a poor and miserable people. There must be something wrong with our way of life, don't you think?"

Shyam kept his arm around his friend. "I don't know, Ashoka. I think there's something to what you say, but you wouldn't want to be like one of them, would you? You wouldn't want to get drunk and go staggering down the street, would you?"

"No, I don't think so. But I would like to try some whiskey, wouldn't you? Just to taste it. I can't understand how a liquid that is not heated could be hot like they say it is." He paused. "But what about this, what about never being able to go out with a girl? I don't think that's right; do you?"

"I don't know exactly, but that's the way it is. And you know as well as I do that even if someone were to tell his father that he liked a girl he knew from a distance, and that he wanted him to check her out as a possible wife, that she couldn't be a Muslim, or even someone from another caste. That kind of thing just doesn't happen. So what would be the sense of 'falling in love'? You couldn't do anything about it anyway." Shyam squeezed his friend's hand, then, "Anyway, you're not ready to get married yet, are you?"

Ashoka looked down sadly. "No, I wasn't thinking about that. It's just that I can't help thinking about girls sometimes." Pause. "And she's so beautiful, and her name is Umana."

Shyam looked at his watch. "Just don't think about it any more now. There's lots of other things to do and so many books to read." Pause. "It's time to go to class." He got up, followed by Ashoka.

\* \* \* \* \*

Ashoka finished at Christchurch with honors and then entered as a graduate student in sociology at Uttarbad University. He did well there also and learned much about class and caste and other social groups. He also took several courses in anthropology. He wrote his Master's thesis on laborers' settlements under Dr. Harilal, an anthropologist widely known in India and abroad, who was an undisputed master at the university. When Ashoka graduated, he took the civil service examination and did very well on that also. Not too much later he was given a job as a social specialist in the Labor Department.

\* \* \* \* \*

It was very hot in the small room. Ashoka could hear the voices of the crowd out under the tent. He reached up and straightened the headpiece, still feeling uncomfortable. He had been to the weddings of others and knew that he had to be dressed as the god Ram on that night, as his wife had to be dressed as Ram's consort, Sita. But it seemed so childish in a way compared with the way they did it in the European countries. Ah well, he thought, it would be over soon and then he could get on with his own family.

His uncle, Sukdeo, entered the room. "It's a good crowd, Ashoka. I think almost everyone's here. The musicians have come."

Ashoka nodded.

"How are you feeling? Are you alright?"

"I think so. I wish it was over, though."

Sukdeo handed him the glass of water he had brought.

"Here, this will make you feel better." Pause. "The pundit is getting ready. I'll come to get you soon."

Where was she, Ashoka wondered. Was she in another tiny room like he was? And were some of her sisters and aunts fixing her up and taking care of her like his uncle was for him? Were they painting the soles of her feet with red dye and plaiting her hair and putting scent on her? He was lucky, he thought, that his family was progressive. He had seen her before the final arrangements had been made. She had brought in a tray of tea and biscuits where he was sitting with his and her fathers. She had not even turned her head sideways or tried to cover her face with the *sari*, glancing at him quickly with big brown eyes. She was very tiny, but pretty.

Ashoka itched under the long satin robe. He unbuttoned the front and put his hand inside to scratch under his arm. Then he picked up the cloth that was lying in his lap and wiped away the sweat on his forehead.

He was lucky enough, he figured, to have a pretty young wife from a good family. The dowry had been the best that had been offered and would help his father pay off some of the debt he still owed from paying the dowry of Lila. If only Ashoka's wife-to-be had had a little more education. She was a village girl who had gone to classes only six years. She knew no English. He had talked that over with his father, complaining that he would never be able to discuss anything with her. But his father had been insistent that Ashoka's mother had had little education also but that she had been a good wife and mother. He insisted that a good Hindu wife did not need to go out in the world, that in fact it was disgraceful if she did. How could he, Ashoka, argue with that; or even more importantly, how could a son argue with a father? Ashoka leaned forward and pulled aside the curtain. He could see the long opening of the marriage tent and part of the crowd that had spilled out. Some, particularly the older men, were dressed in Indian garments, *dhoti* or *pajama* and *kurta*. Many others wore Western pants and shirts. All the women he could see were dressed in Indian garments. Most held glasses and sweets in their hands. His father had allowed them to have alcoholic as well as nonalcoholic punch for the wedding, mostly at Ashoka's older brother's insistence. There was smoke in the air from cigarettes. His father had arranged for packets of Players, as well as Indian cigarettes, *bidi*, to be laying around on tables. Ashoka could hear the Indian drums and sitar playing a marriage piece at the other end of the tent. He let the curtain fall back.

This was the beginning of the third stage of his life, householder. He had already passed through the stages of childhood and studentship, and now he would take up the responsibilities of raising a family. He hadn't exactly been ready, and it had taken several talks by his father before he had agreed. But as his father had said, he was twenty-three years old, and others would think it strange if he didn't get married soon. And then when the offer for Lakshmi had come, he had agreed. After all, that was the only way he would ever get to sleep with a woman. And his father had been insistent because he wanted to retire and begin his own final life stage, meditation and studies of the holy scriptures. As he had told Ashoka several times, he had fulfilled his own life responsibilities, including that of householder, and it would soon be time for Ashoka and his brother to take his place, releasing the elder to his time of meditation. That seemed reasonable, even though it pretty much ended the possibilities of Ashoka's other dreams, particularly going off to a foreign university for his Ph.D., as Professor Harilal had. Ashoka had thought many times of blond girls with exposed arms, necks, and even legs in England and America, but now he would see them only in magazines, Hollywood movies, or as distant tourists.

Ashoka's brother and uncle arrived then to help him to the ritual place. They stationed themselves alongside and supported him when he stumbled. The long robe made it difficult to walk. He was used to wearing his loincloth (*dhoti*) at home and *pajamas* or Western clothes at work. As they moved toward the central area where the pundit had prepared the holy place with rice powder, pieces of coconut, leaves, and candles, Ashoka was just vaguely aware of the other people standing at one side and watching. He did see Professor Harilal, Shyam, and many relatives on his father's side. Most of the strangers must be relatives on her side. She was crouched next to the altar, dressed in yellow, almost shapeless in the voluminous *sari* of the wedding ritual. She made a cloth blob, with no part of her body or face visible. Two other women, presumably her relatives, were crouched at each side of her. Ashoka hardly wondered about her body then, the tension was so great.

His escorts guided him to a place in front of the altar and next to her, and the ritual began. The pundit burned incense, lit candles, made offerings of flower petals and pieces of coconut, and kept up a steady recitation of word offerings in Sanscrit. Several times he put his hand to the back of his neck, presumably to brush away mosquitoes. Ashoka settled down to a kind of weary numbness, aware in only a general way of the small movements and sounds of the ritual. When the pundit blew his conch shell, Ashoka stirred. The pundit tied Ashoka's robe to the bride's *sari,* and the assistants helped the two of them to stand and circle the altar seven times. Afterwards, they were directed and pushed gently back down and covered with the marriage cloth. In the darkness under the cloth, Ashoka was aware of her trembling body.

He was alone with her in the bridal room. She sat on the bed, her legs pulled up, still wearing all of her clothing. She did not have her face covered but let her head hang down. The front part of the red line in the part of her hair, the mark of a married woman, was clearly visible. Ashoka reached over and pulled the top of the *sari* all the way back, exposing her face. He said, "You look nice."

She lifted her eyes for a brief moment but said nothing. He studied her nose ring, pure gold filigree with a dangling pendant. She was also wearing earrings. He was pleased that she had a good skin color, not the creamy white of foreigners, but not a dark brown either. He remembered that was one of the first things his father had told him, that she had a light skin color. Her father had insisted that her skin color be light enough to reduce the dowry by at least one thousand rupees.

Ashoka ran his fingers across her ear and the straight black hair that was pulled to the back into the plait that hung down her back. He said, "Are you alright?"

Without lifting her eyes, she nodded her head in a sideways rocking motion, the Indian gesture of agreement.

"Do you want to get ready to go to bed?"

She paused a moment but then without a word reached to her braid and began unplaiting it. Ashoka waited and watched. When she was finished, she let her hands fall to her lap and sat again. Ashoka got up and went into the tiny cubicle next to the bedroom where he took off his clothes, except for the *dhoti* and undershirt.

She was in the same position when he returned, though the light bedcover had been pulled back. He sat next to her on the edge of the bed and put his hand on her cheek. She remained motionless. He said, "Don't you want to take off your clothes?"

She looked up momentarily, her eyes liquid with tension. She nodded her head. Her body was tense when he gently pushed her down to a prone position on her back. She lay there quietly as he reached down and began pulling up her *sari.*

* * * * *

Life went on as before except that Lakshmi helped Ashoka's mother and his brother's wife in the house and kitchen during the day and kept all his clothing and other things neat and clean. She didn't talk much, but she was always ready when he wanted to sleep with her. The only thing he couldn't get her to do was to take off all her clothes in bed. But he got used to pulling up her *sari* and having her put her clothes back on afterward. He would go to his own bed afterward anyway. She didn't get pregnant right away and he knew that bothered her. She went often to the temple of Shiva and made offerings to the *lingam* stone.

Probably the most unusual thing that happened in that period was Ashoka's work and friendship with the American Fulbright scholar, Martin Neumann. Dr. Harilal had made the arrangements for Ashoka to be the anthropologist's field assistant. Ashoka had known foreigners only at a distance before, but the tall American became his almost daily companion for a year. On weekdays Ashoka would meet Martin after work, and they would pedal out to the compounds to interview factory workers. Also if there was some special ritual or other occurrence, they would usually go together. On the days that Ashoka didn't work in the Labor Office, the two of them had an irregular schedule, usually doing the interviews in the morning and visiting different places in the city during the afternoon. Martin always had many questions about what they saw.

Unlike the foreigners that Ashoka had seen at a distance, Martin hadn't been snobbish and was always willing to try something new. The anthropologist called that *participant observation.* When it wasn't too different, anthropologists would take active part in what they were studying. Ashoka quickly learned he could introduce the American to any kind of new food or take him to any kind of ritual.

* * * * *

It was the time of *Holi,* the Hindu festival of color. In previous years, like a good Hindu son, Ashoka had celebrated it at home quietly. Relatives would come by and sprinkle a little powder or colored water on one another. It was a tame affair. And there would be festive sweets and other foods. But that was about it.

Even so, when Martin had suggested they visit some of the laborers' compounds during the festival, Ashoka had not been against the idea. After all, he was working for the Labor Office and was supposed to be a specialist in their way of life, which had to include celebrations. So he agreed and they went to several compounds. The workers mostly seemed surprised. However, they seemed to take a genuine pleasure in squirting him and Martin. In no time, Ashoka's shirt and *pajama* had been turned into a fiery red, and Martin's clothes had become a strong shade of blue.

All that would have been unusual enough for Ashoka, a well-educated Brahmin, consorting with factory workers, mostly of low caste, but what had happened in Imliganj was far more than he would have expected. Unlike most of the compounds, this one was made up mostly of high-caste workers, Rajputs and Brahmins. And they had felt much more at ease with Ashoka, and even with Martin. So before they got well into squirting colored water, they brought out trays of sweets. "These are special for *Holi*," one of them said in Hindi.

"What's special about them?" Ashoka had asked, though he had an idea. However, he waited for an explanation.

"They're made with *bhang*. We take them on special holidays." Ashoka had heard about *bhang* as well as *ganja*. The working classes used them on festive holidays, besides drinking toddy and other alcoholic drinks.

The man said, "I don't know if the *Amrikan sahib* would take it. It might be too strong for him."

Ashoka turned to Martin. "Did you understand what he was saying?"

"I got a general idea but not everything. What is it?"

"Well, the sweets are made with *bhang*. You know what that is?"

"I've heard of it. It's some kind of Indian drug. In fact, I tried it in my pipe a couple of times when I was in a village. I got no effect at all."

Ashoka laughed. "Anyway, they're offering some to us. But they're afraid it will be too strong for you. What do you think?"

"Have you ever taken it?"

"No, it's mostly the lower classes who use it." Pause. "But I have no objections."

Martin said, "Okay, let's do it."

They brought out a tray with a pile of Indian sweets, milk boiled until it had become semi-hard, mixed with honey and spices and the slightly odd taste that must have been the *bhang*. They passed it first to Ashoka, who popped one in his mouth. Martin did the same, and the other men followed. The sweet was tasty, and one could just barely notice the extra ingredient. "What do you think?" Ashoka asked Martin.

"It seems okay, pretty much like ordinary Indian sweets, though I do detect a slightly different flavor."

"I think they must have been taking it before we came," Ashoka said. Several of the men were laughing or gesturing in unusual ways.

The workers passed the tray around again a couple of times, and Ashoka and Martin took one more each time. Ashoka grinned at Martin. "You're not worried, are you?"

"No, I told you I already smoked some in my pipe and it had no effect at all."

After that they squatted around, talking to the workers while some of the younger men continued in the courtyard, squirting one another with a kind of giant squirt-gun that ordinarily was used for greasing parts in the factories. It served well for the *Holi* dowsing. Martin went outside and took some pictures. Everyone settled down to talk in low voices. Martin came back and sat on the rope bed to change a roll of film.

"How are you feeling?" Ashoka asked.

"Fine, very relaxed. And you?"

"I'm alright too." Pause. "I was thinking that maybe soon we ought to be going back. You know I get to play around with my brother's wife today."

"Oh, that's right. I had forgotten about that. You have a joking relationship with her, don't you?"

"I don't know. Is that what you call it in anthropology? All I know is that I get to play around with her because she's the wife of my older brother." Pause. "Too bad you can't go to the women's quarters. You'd get some good pictures. But you know how it is with us Indians," he laughed. "We don't let outsiders where our women are."

"Yeah, I know. You Hindus can hardly be considered libertines, despite the phallic stones you worship and all that old erotic temple sculpture."

Ashoka stood up and walked outside, Martin following.

The streets were hot since it was late afternoon. Traffic was light. The shops and factories were almost all closed for the holiday.

Ashoka felt very relaxed, turning the pedals with hardly any conscious thought. After all, he had been on a bicycle since he was ten years old. He knew the streets so well that he hardly needed to think about directions. He turned the corners automatically. Once in a while he looked around to see if the American was following. He was keeping up pretty well.

Ashoka took Martin to the small room that was kept for guests. It had a rope bed with a mattress, plus a few other pieces of furniture. Outsiders were allowed to wait there. Ashoka's mother wouldn't allow them into the rest of the house because they could pollute the family's possessions. Ashoka said, "You look kind of tired. Why don't you take a nap?"

"Sounds like a good idea." Martin sat down on the bed. "I am feeling so-o-o-o relaxed."

"I won't be gone long. And I told you that afterward Lakshmi will serve us a meal. You know it's a big deal to her, the first time the *Amrikan sahib* is given food in the Brahmin's house." He grinned again.

Martin leaned back to a prone position and Ashoka left, heading upstairs to the walled roof area where the women would be. As soon as he entered the doorway, he was greeted with a dollop of colored powder and the giggling laughter of the three wives. Ashoka's mother was not there, which did not surprise him. She would be doing something in the cooking room or tending his father, he figured, even though she was getting pretty old. Her hands had become arthritic.

Ashoka rushed the girls then and grabbed the package of red powder his oldest brother's wife was holding. She feigned to keep it by pushing him but very shortly let go, laughing. Ashoka sprinkled powder on her and his other sister-in-law, even a little on Lakshmi. His wife laughed timidly but made no effort to sprinkle powder on him. And so it went until the four of them were leaning against the wall in exhaustion, colored from head to foot. Ashoka laughed until he thought he would collapse. Finally, he had no further energy so just leaned there until his breath returned.

"I think I ought to go down and get the *Amrikan sahib,* he'd like to have a picture of this. *Mamaji* is in the kitchen, isn't she? So she wouldn't know he was in the women's quarters. But anyway, he'll only have to come in for a minute."

When Ashoka went downstairs, his legs felt wobbly. It was almost as though he was walking on rubber. He went into the room where Martin was sitting on the bed, rubbing his eyes slowly with one hand. He looked at Ashoka as if he wasn't sure where he was.

"What's the matter?" Ashoka asked. "You look funny."

"I been lying here," the American said groggily. "I think it was the *bhang.*"

"What do you mean? Are you alright?"

"Better," Martin answered cryptically.

"Can you get up?"

Martin grinned, "Sure, but slowly." He let his legs fall to the side of the bed then, and started to get off.

"Here, I'll help." Ashoka said and took Martin by the arm. "We want you to take some pictures. Think you can make it upstairs?."

Martin grinned again in a foolish way. "Sure, but slowly." He picked up his camera, and they worked their way up the stairs, Ashoka holding him by the arm. The girls were watching wonderingly when the two entered the room. None spoke. Ashoka volunteered, "He's okay, it's just the *bhang*."

The girls continued to stare without comprehension. Ashoka steered the anthropologist to a wall. Martin leaned against it, his arms hanging loosely. Ashoka put the camera into the American's hands. "Just set it. We'll go on the other side so you can take our picture."

Fumbling with the snaps on the camera case, Martin answered groggily, "It's alright."

Ashoka went to the other side to join his sisters-in-law and Lakshmi. The four moved around for the best position, practicing camera smiles. Ashoka said, "Okay Martin, are you ready?"

"Ready. Just slowly," came the reply.

The American took several photos. Ashoka joined him then, taking the groggy man's arm again. "Come on, I'll take yours. It'll make a good memento. Then we'll get cleaned up. Lakshmi has our food ready. It's a big deal for her, you know," he said very seriously. "A big deal, a big deal."

He positioned the American against the wall and took a couple of pictures, laughing all the time.

"What's so funny?" Martin asked in slow speak.

"You look so groggy."

They went downstairs to the bathing tap on one side of the courtyard. Ashoka said, "You want to go first?"

"No, it's alright. Still tired."

"Okay, I'll show you how we Hindus do it. We're very clean, you know, always bathing or washing." He laughed at himself and wondered why he was laughing so much. It was just that things seemed to be extraordinarily funny, he thought, even things that were not really very different.

Ashoka squatted under the tap and began sloshing water on his face, arms and hands. "We Indians are very cleanly people," he said. "Very cleanly, very cleanly." He giggled while he put his fingers in his ears, blew his nose into the drain, and spit out a mouthful of gargled water. "Very cleanly."

He was aware that the girls and Martin were watching him with great interest. "Yes, very cleanly," he repeated for the third or fourth time. "We Hindus are very cleanly. But even the Muslims bathe before they do their prayers. You might say we Indians are some of the bathingest people on Earth." He looked up then with a wondering expression on his face, as if he had come up with an original idea. "You could tell me, Martin Neumann, because you are an anthropologist." He giggled. "You know about all kinds of cultures. Are we one of the bathingest peoples?"

Martin answered slowly, "Yes, I think so."

Then Ashoka's giggle became prolonged as he said between sloshings, "But in general, we're not such a clean people, are we? Those factory workers we visit don't have clean clothes very often, do they?"

He wasn't sure of Martin's answer but he knew next that he said, "That's very funny. One of the funniest things I've heard for a long time. Ha ha ha ha ha ha ha ha."

And the water sloshed and he was aware of throwing it back over his face and arms, and of being very wet and laughing endlessly. Then he became aware that the gazes of Martin and the wives had become fixed on him. He said, "Martin, my American friend, why is everybody staring at me?"

And Martin answered. "Ashoka, don't you know? You've been sloshing water and laughing for ten minutes without stopping."

Then he stopped sloshing, though the water continued to flow from the tap. He said, "How funny, sloshing and laughing, eh? Sloshing and laughing, eh? Ha ha ha ha ha ha ha." And he slowly keeled over until he was lying on his side directly under the tap, which continued to flow over his face and chest.

From then on, Ashoka was aware of being helped, though he felt very comfortable the whole time. Every once in a while he would giggle, though less and less. He was feeling so-o-o sleepy. They turned off the water tap, got him to his feet, and helped him to the guest room. He could hear Martin talking to Lakshmi in Hindi and he thought how strange it was that Martin could converse with his village wife, even more strange that she would talk to the American. A good upper-caste Hindu wife wasn't supposed to mix with strangers. But Ashoka felt so comfortable that he didn't pay much attention to what they were saying.

They had put him on the bed. He was sitting there cross-legged. But a couple of times his body turned to rubber and he let it fall down. Each time Martin and Lakshmi pulled him up. "Now just sit up a while, Ashoka," Martin said. "Lakshmi is going to get you something to eat.

That'll make you feel better."

Ashoka remembered saying, "But I feel fine."

His wife brought two brass trays, each of which was a heaping pile of rice, surrounded by several brass containers of curries, cooked vegetables, hot pickles, sauces, and curdled milk. Martin started on his, taking a small handful with his right hand and mixing it into the rice before putting it into his mouth. Ashoka watched in interest that Martin could eat Indian fashion, using no utensils and relying wholly on his right hand. Ashoka was aware that Lakshmi was standing just behind and to one side of him, holding his glass of water.

"Why don't you eat something?" Martin said. "It'll be good for you. And it's very good and spicy."

Ashoka watched dreamily. "Feel so sleepy."

"I know. I felt the same way while you were upstairs with the women. In fact, for a while I couldn't work up enough energy to get up. But that feeling went away. You'll be alright in a while. See, I'm okay now." Martin put a large piece of mango pickle in his mouth, followed by rice to take away some of the hot pepper burning. Then he took a swig of water, still using his right hand.

Lakshmi held out the other water glass for Ashoka. He took it wearily and drank some, saying, "Indian wives take care of their men, don't they, Martin? Bet American wives don't stand by husband with glass of water, do they, Martin?"

Ashoka was surprised at how much he had said. He handed the glass back to Lakshmi. She set it down and took some of the spiced potatoes in her fingers for Ashoka.

He said, "Look what I said, Martin. Indian wife even feed husband after he takes *bhang*, just like baby." He giggled.

"Go ahead, eat something, Ashoka. It'll do you good." The Indian husband took the potatoes and then some rice from his wife, chewing slowly and seemingly interminably. Finally, Martin said, "Swallow it, Ashoka, you've chewed it enough."

Ashoka giggled, thinking how funny it was that someone had to feed him like a baby and someone else had to tell him when to swallow his food. He felt his head nodding and looked down to see his hand in the pile of rice. Lakshmi lifted it and brushed away the rice grains. Then she carefully poured the contents of several brass containers on the edge of the rice pile and took his hand, to direct it in stirring the curries into the rice. After a bit she withdrew her hand and he let his stop again. "Come on, put some in your mouth," Martin said. "You can see that your wife is concerned."

"Can see it." And he lifted several fingersful of the rice and curry mixture toward his mouth. But each time he got ready to put it inside, he got very tired and let it fall back again. Lakshmi took the hand and directed it upward again. This went on three or four times. The last time, when his hand was just ready to put some food into his mouth, he said, "So sleepy." And letting the hand fall, he followed with his head and body. He remembered his face going into the mushy pile of rice and curry, and then he was asleep.

Ashoka was riding ahead, Martin following. He came to a street crossing, a roundabout in the middle of which was a traffic center on which a policemen would usually stand, giving directions. And though there was a good flow of traffic, it was not the busiest time. Instead of a policeman, a cow stood in the traffic center, placidly chewing while watching the passing cars, trucks, rickshaws, buffalo carts, cattle, and people. None of the Indian passersby paid any attention to the contemplative animal.

Ashoka pulled to one side and waited until Martin caught up. Martin stopped too and gazed at the cow.

"What's so interesting?" Ashoka asked.

Martin pointed at the animal in the center. "How Indian," he said. "Where else could you see a cow standing in the middle of an intersection, as if directing traffic?"

"I suppose they don't allow anything like that in your cities, eh? I never saw anything like it in the movies. The only time one sees cows there is when cowboys are herding them."

"That's right. Cows are kept in the country, and they're fenced up nowadays. Nothing like those free-roaming herds of the open range period. Nowadays there's even a law against allowing them to wander around in the city, or even to be there." Martin was careful not to mention that cows were in the city, on their way to the slaughterhouses.

A ricksha, loaded with a fat woman and numerous bundles, careened by, narrowly missing Ashoka's bicycle. He raised his arm in a warning gesture, crying out at the same time, "Watch it, you country bumpkin."

The ricksha driver paid no attention, grinding as hard as he could with his spindly legs.

Ashoka grinned at Martin. "You have to watch these ricksha fellows or they'll take the whole street. You don't know how lucky you are not to have any in your country."

Martin nodded and started off again. At first they got separated by the traffic but then Ashoka hurried to catch up with the American. The traffic had thinned by that time. They rode side by side the rest of the way. Ashoka broke the silence, "You know, Martin, I've had some very interesting experiences since you've been here. I never really knew an American before, and an anthropologist at that."

Martin answered, "Well, as you can imagine, it's been quite interesting to me too. I still can't quite believe that affair last week with the *bhang*."

"You know that was the first time I took any," Ashoka said. "The people in my caste don't take drugs, or even alcohol."

"Yeah, you told me that. I suppose we shouldn't have taken so much. But it tasted so sweet, and I had tried smoking it before with no effect at all. Anyway, no harm done. The amazing part of the stuff is that when its effects wear off, there's nothing that lingers on. It's nothing like a hangover."

They turned into the driveway to Christchurch College where Martin had his room. Ashoka always felt comfortable coming there because of the reminders of his student days. As they passed the food stand at the entrance, Ashoka said, "Would you like to get some tea before going in?"

"I don't think so. I think I'll have a beer when we get inside." Pause. "You can have one too if you want."

Ashoka hesitated but then quickly added. "I don't think so. Not if I'm going to have the egg." He still felt nervous about the forthcoming event, eating a boiled egg. He had known that Martin bought and cooked eggs on a hot plate and had thought about asking him for one for several weeks. He had never had an egg, or any meat, before. His caste was strictly vegetarian, and neither his mother nor his wife would have permitted meat or eggs in the house. Finally, when he knew that Martin was leaving, Ashoka had made up his mind and asked. And this afternoon was to be the time. But he figured it would be better to have plain water with it, not mix two forbidden substances.

Martin unlocked the door of the high-ceilinged tile and stucco room that he used as his office, bedroom, and eating room. Ashoka knew that Martin usually had the people at the food stand bring his meals to his room. He also knew that Martin kept a small supply of other foods there, some eggs, white bread, peanut butter, jam, and usually some beer.

Ashoka leaned his bicycle against one wall and Martin did the same.

"Sit down," Martin waved toward the small bed. Ashoka sat and reached for his cigarettes. "Is it okay if I smoke ?"

"Sure, I think I'll light up my pipe."

After both had taken a couple of good draws, Martin said, "You know, your wife was really worried about you the day we took the *bhang*. I really had a lot of trouble calming her down. And my Hindi is not all that good." Pause. "I kept telling her that the effects had hit me first, you know, when I was on the bed and you were in the women's quarters. But she just couldn't relax. It was as if nothing in the world mattered except your welfare."

Ashoka laughed. "Well, as a student of Indian culture, you know that nothing really does matter to the Hindu wife except her husband and her family, especially in the high castes. I'm sure you know that there is no widow remarriage allowed in our caste. So when something happens to the husband, the wife just turns into a family worker. I've seen some widows in the lineage, and believe me, it's not a great life."

"Ah yes," Martin who was opening a beer bottle, said. "I suppose next you're going to tell me that your caste used to practice widow burning on the husband's cremation fire."

"I never heard anything about that, though as you know it's been against the law for more than a hundred years now. It was one of the first Hindu practices the English outlawed." Ashoka leaned back and watched the American drink the beer directly from the bottle. "But you know, there's another thing that has Lakshmi worried, the fact that she hasn't given birth yet. As soon as that happens, my mother and the other women will be much nicer to her. She's really concerned about that."

"Ah yes, the traditional patrifocal family. I suppose we were like that in the nineteenth century, but it's all changed now."

Ashoka got up and tipped his cigarette ash into the tin ashtray on Martin's desk. "You know, Martin, she can't really understand why you only have one child. Like everyone else here, she knows some women can't have children. But once a woman has one, they think she can have others, and they wonder why your wife doesn't have more."

"I'm not surprised," Martin said. "We've already been through that several times since being in India." He mimicked, "You know, it's so sad that you have such a small family." Pause. "But you also know things are changing in the West. The families, particularly of the middle class, are getting smaller and smaller."

"But you're not saying that most families have only one child, are you?"

"No. The average is between two and three now, I think. But more than that is rare."

Ashoka got up then, not quite sure how to begin. But he knew it would soon be too late because Martin would be gone. He said, "I suppose everyone uses contraceptives, right?"

Martin had put the beer down and was filling the small saucepan with water. He plugged in the hotplate that was sitting on the edge of the large desk. Without looking around, he said, "Well, not everyone, but quite a few, I'm sure."

"I don't want as many children as they had in the old days, but I'm sure I'd like to have at least three. But you know many Hindus are against using contraceptives even if it is government policy." Ashoka was very curious to know what Martin used and though he phrased several questions in his mind, he never got up enough courage to ask them.

"Yeah, I know," Martin said. "That has come out in many interviews. It's continually surprising to me how little the factory workers seem to know about it, despite the government programs. He turned to Ashoka. "How many will it be?"

"What?" Ashoka had almost forgotten what they had come for.

"Eggs."

"Oh, just one will be enough."

Martin lowered three eggs into the water. The hotplate was cherry red by then and soon began to push up small bubbles, rolling the eggs around gently. Ashoka watched the movement in fascination. He was crossing another barrier. He remembered Gandhi's confessions in his autobiography when he had eaten meat and afterward had gone outside and vomited. Would eggs be as bad, Ashoka wondered. But then his thoughts changed again. He said to Martin, "Will you be coming back to India?"

"I don't know. Probably. Why?"

"I was thinking that by then I'll have a family of my own." And in a worried tone he said, "I do hope she can conceive. You know an Indian couple just has to have children. Sometimes it happens that they don't, but then there's much unhappiness."

"Yes, I know."

Martin took the pan off the hotplate and poured the water into the drainhole under the water tap. He ran cold water on the shells then put the eggs in saucers on the edge of the desk. Ashoka looked at his suspiciously. Martin laughed. "Go ahead. It won't bite. Try it."

"How do you take the shell off?"

Martin took one of his. "Simple, watch." He rapped the shell against the edge of the desk. Then holding the egg over the saucer, he peeled it, holding the glistening white oval in his hand for inspection. "There. Now you do it."

Ashoka followed the same procedure but let the peeled globe lie in the saucer. It looked faintly unpleasant as the rubbery surface of it had felt. But before he could ask again, Martin brought out a little folded paper and opened it up to expose a small pile of salt granules. "Most people eat them with salt, like this." And he demonstrated by taking a pinch in his fingers and sprinkling it on one end. The granules stuck easily to the sticky surface. Martin put the salted end in his mouth and bit it off. He grinned as he chewed. "See, it doesn't even move when you eat it."

Ashoka felt uncomfortable and a little embarrassed, but he had gone too far by that time to back out. "Okay, I'll do it too."

The first bite was not at all pleasant, especially the slick, rubbery feeling. He was glad of the salt granules. They were easy enough to accept. But it did eventually go down with the help of a drink of water, as did the rest of the egg.

Martin ate his second one, washing it down with beer. He laughed again. "We're going to have to watch you, Ashoka, or you'll become debauched like all us Westerners."

* * * * *

Two months after Martin's departure, Lakshmi was pregnant. A healthy boy was born, followed by another and two girls. Life settled into a regular pattern, Ashoka going off to work on his bicycle each morning early, eating his lunch from the tiffin container that Lakshmi had filled. Then in mid-afternoon he would return to the house, where he would read and visit with friends or the men in his family. The children also would visit him in his room. He would bathe late, put on a fresh loin cloth and *kurta,* to be served his evening meal of unleavened bread or rice and vegetarian curries and milk, followed by a sweet and a betel nut. He gave up smoking cigarettes. Sometimes before he went to sleep in his own bed, he would get in Lakshmi's to make love, she fully clothed. After the fourth child, he used condoms, which he could get at the Labor Office without cost. The government also had them available in the health centers, though very few workers bothered to get them.

Ashoka got promoted several times and finally was offered a job in the personnel section of the local power company. The distance to work was great, though the pay was higher, so he bought a motor scooter. He was doing well. He had good health also, though he was getting a little plump and beginning to lose his hair. Lakshmi's hair began to turn gray. The children grew and did well in school. Ashoka even let the girls continue through high school.

His mother died first, then his father at the venerable age of seventy-nine. Ashoka helped in the cremation rite for both, though it was his older brother who broke open the skulls to release the spirits.

\* \* \* \* \*

Ashoka was driving the Garuda 90 down Cantonment Road, weaving in and out of the crowds of people and animals with great ease. He had to take greater care than had been necessary on the bicycle because of the greater speed. He had kept his old bicycle, though he rarely used it any more. The scooter was so much faster and carried much more. This time he had Lakshmi on the rear seat, her arms around his waist. She said nothing because of the noise of the machine, though he suspected she was dying of curiosity. As a matter of fact, so was he. It had been almost thirty years since the time he had done field work with Martin Neumann. And except for a couple of letters in the first couple of years, there had been no further contact. Who could have expected when picking up the phone in the personnel office that the voice at the other end would be that of Martin Neumann? But even after all that time, Ashoka quickly recognized the voice, though the strangeness would not quickly fade. How could someone who had literally disappeared into a world that he, Ashoka, had never seen, and one that he knew only through books, magazines, and Hollywood films, appear again after so much elapsed time and say, "Do you remember me? We used to do field work together"?

Ashoka had stood with the phone held out for a moment, transfixed with a certain disbelief and then suddenly the memories began flooding in. He recalled the glistening peeled egg, and considered at the same time that it had not been the beginning of a new lifestyle or even new habits. After the American left, Ashoka had never eaten another egg, nor did he ever try a piece of meat. He had not told Lakshmi or any of the women in the family. He wasn't sorry he had done it and it didn't seem interesting once Martin left. Ashoka had returned to the totally vegetarian food of his caste.

He turned the scooter into the drive of National Hotel. It was the newest in the city and the highest building, primarily for foreigners and wealthy industrialists. There weren't many tourists who came to Uttarbad. It had been built as a factory town by the British and had remained such ever since. Few people came there who weren't involved in the leather or textile industries. These days there were more and more Japanese, men that Ashoka didn't remember seeing in the days when he had worked with Martin.

There were several Hindustans and British cars in the lot. Ashoka put his scooter in a place to one side where there was another, plus a couple of bicycles. Lakshmi got off and stood to one side while he locked the vehicle. When Ashoka started for the doorway, she automatically took a place behind him. After a few steps, he turned and waved her forward. "Come up and walk beside me. When you go into a fancy hotel, you're not supposed to walk behind your husband. Besides, Sahib Neumann would think it strange, that we are very traditional."

In a way, he thought, you couldn't blame Lakshmi. That had been the way she had been taught, and he had not tried to change her. Of course, she had never been to any social gathering given by a European or American before. But even so, Ashoka knew he would feel uncomfortable meeting Martin with his wife standing behind him. Anyway, it wouldn't hurt her to do something different, and they went into the hotel door side by side, she looking at the ground.

"If you'll just wait over there," the desk clerk said in English. "I'll give him a ring."

Ashoka directed Lakshmi to a waiting area across the lobby where there were a number of rattan chairs and couches, plus some side and end tables. "You sit there," he said. "He'll be here soon."

Ashoka sat down too. It wasn't the fanciest hotel he had been in but it was better than anything Uttarbad had ever had before. It was said that they served Australian beef and pork in the dining room and, for foreigners, whiskey. The prohibition laws prevented citizens from getting any. Everything looked new, much of it of synthetic material. A man was sweeping the floor, and a woman was dusting. Both wore clean clothes even though Ashoka guessed they were of the Sweeper caste. Few from other castes would do that kind of work, even Christians. Ashoka noticed that Lakshmi was nervously fingering the edge of her *sari* and peeking at him periodically. He figured that she felt uncomfortable being there in a strange place, and among strangers, with her face fully exposed. He had told her when offering to bring her that she wouldn't be able to cover her face. He still wondered whether it had been a good idea.

Several people got on or off the elevator across the lobby. Finally it opened and Martin stepped out, accompanied by a tall redheaded woman who was much younger. Ashoka would have recognized Martin on the street, despite the difference in his age. He really did look the same, only older. He seemed to be the same weight though his face was more wrinkled and his hair had turned white. The American waved in recognition and walked toward Ashoka, his wife staying at his side. Holding out his hand, he said, "Hello Ashoka, it's been a long time. I'd recognize you anywhere though."

They shook hands. "This is my wife, Constance. Constance, meet my old friend, Ashoka Harinarayan."

She put her hand out just like a man, and Ashoka shook it. "Glad to know you."

Then Martin turned toward Lakshmi, who was at Ashoka's side, but back a little, looking undecided. She was fidgeting with her hands, evidently unsure what to do with them. Martin turned his palms inward and pressed them together in the Hindu gesture of greeting and religious salutation, saying, "Namaskar."

The small graying woman smiled widely then and returned the gesture. She exchanged greetings with Martin's wife and they sat down. "It's been a long time, hasn't it?" Martin began. "And you seem to have prospered. I suppose your children are almost grown now, aren't they?"

"Yes, the oldest boy is nineteen and going to the university. And the oldest girl will be getting married soon. We don't marry them off as young as we used to though," he laughed. "But we Hindus still get uncomfortable when they get to be sixteen or seventeen and are not married yet."

Martin grinned, "Ah yes, some things change slowly."

Martin's wife said, "Are the marriages still entirely arranged by the parents? I'm interested because I took a course on the culture of India in college recently and we had a long part on marriage, the family and caste."

This time the comment struck Ashoka as humorous. "Well, that's another thing that doesn't change much. Whenever Westerners study India, they seem to spend more than half their time on those two topics. Sometimes you'd think Westerners never had marriages or families, much less caste groups in their society."

Martin shifted the topic, addressing Ashoka. "I assume that Lakshmi still doesn't speak English, right?"

"That's right, but she really never had any need for it. She stays home most of the time and when she does go out shopping, she always goes to places where they speak Hindi. This is a real event for her, to come into a European-style hotel."

Martin said, "I'm afraid that I have forgotten most of what I used to know. Apart from some greetings and buying things on the street, I don't seem to know very much any more."

Martin's wife spoke. "He's just being modest. I've seen him carry on real conversations with some of the ricksha drivers and market vendors." She added, "But I would imagine it's pretty frustrating for your wife, Lakshmi. That's her name, isn't it?"

"She's alright." Ashoka turned and spoke to the small, quiet woman.

She began twisting the end of her *sari* in her nervousness and turned her head ever so slightly. Ashoka knew she was embarrassed and wanted to turn her head away. But she answered him in Hindi, "I'm alright, husband. Just tell them that I'm happy to be listening to you all talk."

He turned back to Martin and his wife. "You know, even when they know the language, it's not the traditional Hindu custom for the wife to take part in a conversation among men. Even when they are present, they prefer to stay in the background. He smiled at Martin's wife. "And they know that European women are very different in that regard."

Martin's wife said, "I can see how it is and I'm sure it makes sense in other cultures, but it is difficult for me to accept."

"I'm sure it is. Westerners have always found a lot of our customs difficult to understand or accept."

Martin's wife immediately defended herself in the manner of Western women, saying, "I mean, I do accept the customs of other cultures. But I was just raised differently."

Ashoka was immediately struck with the necessity for the woman to insist on her individuality. It was so typical of Westerners, he thought. In fact, Martin had been the only Westerner that Ashoka had known who could accept the idea of the needs of a group without discomfort.

A waiter, dressed in an elaborate costume of tunic and pants with a flaming red sash around the waist and a turban of the same color, approached the group. "Would you like to have something to drink or a snack?" Martin asked. "He'll bring it here."

"I don't know," Ashoka answered. "We already had tea before we left. And you know we don't eat until late when it cools off."

"We could have a cold drink," Martin said. "Nonalcoholic, of course. But I guess that wouldn't bother you and Lakshmi, would it? Why don't you ask Lakshmi?"

Ashoka turned and spoke to his wife. Her response was almost inaudible. He spoke to her again and she made another just barely audible sound.

"She said she would take a Sher-kola. I guess I'll take the same."

Martin and his wife ordered soft drinks too, and the three of them went back to the conversation. Lakshmi again took her listening pose, squeezed into the corner of the couch on the outside of Ashoka, seeming childishly small. She looked at Constance shyly at frequent intervals but each time turned her gaze away quickly. Martin's wife often looked at the small woman also but kept her gaze longer. How open Western women are, Ashoka thought. They could stare at anyone, male or female, without embarrassment.

He spoke to Martin's wife. "'How do you find India, Mrs. Neumann?"

She had a most serious expression on her face, as if she had practiced it for making just the statement: "Oh, it's a very interesting country. Probably the most complex on our entire trip."

Martin had told Ashoka on the telephone that he and his wife were going around the world and that they were about two-thirds of the way.

"A lot of Westerners notice all our poverty and low standard of living. Hasn't that impressed you?" Ashoka asked.

"Well, you can't fail to notice it." And with her continued serious expression. "But it's all so interesting. And it's so much like I studied. I find it very fascinating."

The drinks were brought out, along with a bowl of ice and separate glasses for each. The *chaprassi* (waiter) started to put ice into all the glasses. Martin's wife said to her husband, "Do you think it's a good idea to use the ice?"

Ashoka spoke, "Oh, it's very clean. They make it here at the hotel. I'm sure you don't have to worry about it."

"But it's the water that's usually contaminated. Freezing it won't make it safe." She added, "I'm a medical technologist." At the same time she put her fingers over the top of her glass.

Martin looked uncomfortable, saying, "I think it's alright here, Constance."

She did not waver, however. "I don't think I want to take a chance. I'll drink mine without ice."

Everyone else took ice in theirs, including Martin. The group sipped their drinks, and the conversation waned. Then Lakshmi spoke to Ashoka in a low tone, saying more than she had all the time before, and looking up shyly every once in a while. He questioned her a couple

of times and she answered, then turned to Martin. "You didn't understand all that, did you, Martin?"

"No, I wasn't exaggerating when I said I've forgotten most of what I
knew, and I especially can't understand Lakshmi; she speaks so low."

"I hope it won't bother your wife because it's about your first wife."
He looked at Constance to see whether she would react. He really had
no idea how to deal with remarried women, since it never occurred
among the women in his caste or women with whom he was free to talk
to about such matters. Her face seemed to be a little tense, but she smiled
in the same practiced way that she had before, saying, "Oh no, I understand. It wouldn't bother me."

"Well, Lakshmi wanted to know how she is now and what she's doing."

"Tell Lakshmi she's fine and now works in an office. She has a very
good job."

Ashoka translated this to his wife, who listened very seriously and
then spoke again. She was showing more animation than at any time
since the group had gotten together.

Ashoka turned to Martin again. "She wants to know how many other
children you had and what happened to them and to your boy. You
know, the one you had here. His name was Daniel."

Martin grinned. "Ah yes, the affairs of the family. I'm only surprised
it didn't come out before. I suppose that's only because Lakshmi is so
shy. Well, anyway, just tell her that there weren't any other children. I
know it'll be hard for her to believe but you'll have to explain it all to
her later, how we in the so-called advanced countries are having fewer
and fewer children. She probably won't believe it, but you can try to
explain to her that there are industrial countries now, such as France
and Germany, which actually have negative birth rates. That is, they are
not having enough children to make up for the death rate."

"Is that so?" Ashoka asked. "I knew that family size was getting smaller
but I didn't know it had gone that far." He laughed. "We ought to send
them some Indians; they'd raise the family size."

Martin said, "You'll have to explain that to her some other time, if at
all. I rather doubt she'll believe it. But to get back to the topic at hand,
we did not have any other children. And the boy, Dan, is fine. He's a
big fellow now, married and off on his own. Tell Lakshmi he has a child
of his own. That should make her happy, to know that some Westerners
are still raising babies."

Ashoka translated this to his little wife and her face frowned and shone in turn, presumably shining when she got the news of the grandchild. She spoke to her husband again. While he was listening, his eyes were on the face of Martin's wife. She was very quiet, almost sombre. How strange, Ashoka thought, to have one wife listening to recollections about another. Impossible to imagine in his social circle. He said then to Martin, "I hope you don't mind, but Lakshmi is very curious. She has mentioned your wife many times in the past years. You know, she still tells the other women of the strange visit she had when your wife came here the week before you left. Do you remember when we all went on a picnic together, you and your wife and me and Lakshmi?"

"Sure, we went out to Hansen Forest, didn't we? As I recall, we went out to see the langur monkeys, and in two rickshas."

"That's right. But she just can't get tired of telling everyone about when you decided to drive one ricksha, taking her and your wife. And you went down a hill and couldn't hold the ricksha back, and it fell over and Lakshmi and your wife fell off into the leaves."

Martin laughed then. "That's true. I still remember the incident. And I can see how it would have impressed Lakshmi. Had she ever gone on a picnic before?"

"No, she didn't even know the word. It's one of the few English words she knows now. And she always uses it when she tells the story. She pronounces it "pheek neek.""

Lakshmi was smiling in her withdrawn way as if she understood what they were saying. When Ashoka stopped speaking, she touched his sleeve. When he turned toward her, she spoke in her near whisper. He turned back to Martin. "She says, 'Could I ask you who your first wife lives with now?'"

Martin answered quickly. "She lives alone. She has her own house, the one where we used to live together."

Ashoka translated this to the small graying woman, who fell immediately silent. She asked no more questions. Ashoka fell silent too, thinking how hard this must strike Lakshmi, she who had never in her life lived alone, nor in all probability ever would.

The conversation lapsed, no one seeming to want to take the initiative. Finally Martin said, "Ashoka, it seems to bother Lakshmi quite a bit what happened to my wife and me. Would you mind telling her that many people in the United States get divorced nowadays? And tell her that Amelia is in good health and has a good job and likes her house."

Ashoka translated that and his wife answered briefly. He didn't at first translate it back into English, so Martin asked, "What did she say?"

"She said she couldn't imagine a woman living all alone."

\* \* \* \* \*

Ashoka got all the children married, the dowries of the girls pretty well balancing those received for the boys so no real indebtedness was incurred. The girls went off to live in their husbands' houses, and the boys stayed home. Soon there were grandchildren.

Ashoka retired at sixty and after that spent most of his time visiting friends, playing cards, and reading. He had a shrine to Shiva built in the back of the courtyard where he spent more and more of his time, also arranging for an old priest to tend it. More and more persons that he knew died, but otherwise time passed uneventfully enough.

\* \* \* \* \*

He was sitting cross-legged on a mat in the courtyard, counting his beads with his right hand, reciting the prayers. His memorization ability had improved much the last few years, as he had concentrated more and more on the sacred literature. Also, his Sanscrit had greatly improved. He felt that he had almost become good enough to actually do some whole rituals, even though such had not been done in his lineage as long as he could remember. But still it was a good feeling to be able to recite so much of the Vedas and other sacred literature. It was proper, he thought, at his stage of life. In fact, he had been at the end of the householder stage for several years. He felt it was time to devote himself solely to religious affairs, as his father had at the end. It was comforting to be able to fulfill the Hindu stages of life so completely. And he knew that the only thing that yet kept him even slightly in the world of the householder was Lakshmi.

He heard the grandchildren, Mina and Narayanji, racing down the corridor, the same one he remembered having run down so often as a child to visit his grandfather. The voices were animated at first but lowered as the children approached. Narayanji appeared first, followed by his little sister. The two children stood in front of Ashoka until he had put the beads down and held out his hands, saying, "And what do grandfather's little birds find so important to twitter about?"

Narayanji spoke first. "Oh, we were talking about fixing food. I said that men couldn't learn how to make bread (roti) and Mina said they could if they wanted to. But I never did see any men making it. Can they, Grandfather?"

Ashoka smiled. "I guess they can. And some men do sometimes, some poor men in the city who don't have their wives with them. But they can't do it as well as women. Why are you children interested in that?"

Mina answered, "Oh, Narayanji said that when I get big I'd have to make *roti* for him and I said he could make it for me. And he said he didn't have to, that he couldn't, that that was women's work."

Ashoka put one arm around Mina's shoulder and the other around Narayanji. "You know, little Mina, there are some things women do and some things men do. And each is better at some things. And fixing food is one thing women do better. But why should little children think about such things? Now is the time to play."

Mina had withdrawn slightly, leaning away from her grandfather's arm. He pulled her toward him. "What's wrong, little Mina? You should be happy when you have your brother to play with and your grandfather to visit."

The little girl let herself be pulled toward the aging man who had lost almost all his hair. She turned her face toward him and it was sombre. He thought he could see tiny tears in the corners. "What's wrong, little girl? Tell your grandfather."

Then she blurted it out, though just barely audibly. "Oh, Grandfather. I miss Grandmother Lakshmi so much. She was teaching me how to make so many things. And she used to save special sweets for me to eat. And now she just lies so quietly in her room, holding her prayer beads. She hardly seems to know when I'm there. When will she get better, Grandfather?"

He pulled the girl closer, conscious of her delicate thinness. She seemed to be quivering slightly, perhaps beginning to cry in earnest. He said, "You mustn't worry, little Mina. We don't know about Grandmother. She's very ill and now it's in the hands of the gods. But she's an old lady and she's had a good life, raising sons and daughters who also had sons and daughters. A grandmother who has had all that is happy, even when she leaves this existence." Ashoka reached across to open the lid of the box in which he kept his books and other personal things. He brought out a small, elongated wooden owl, painted bright pink, and a yellow lion that sat upright. "Look, I've got toys for you and Narayanji. They come from Benares, the holy city. I got them when I went there on pilgrimage. You can add them to your collection of animals." He handed the owl to Mina and the lion to Narayanji.

The two children took the brightly colored animals and studied them. "The owl has such long legs," Mina said. "The owls in the picture books have short legs."

"It's a different kind of owl," Ashoka said. "The kind that they have at Benares, I guess."

"I like the lion," said Narayanji. "Though it looks kind of different too."

"Maybe all the animals from Benares are different," Ashoka said, pleased that the two children had shifted their attention away from the sickness of Lakshmi. To take their minds even further away, he said, "Isn't it about time to eat, children?"

"I guess so," Narayanji answered. "We were on our way to the kitchen when we decided to come visit you, Grandfather."

"And I think you two children are hungry, aren't you?"

Mina said then, "I just wish Grandmother Lakshmi were there. She'd have something special for me."

Ashoka patted the little girl. "Well, you should go because I'm sure your mother or one of your aunts will have something nice. And besides, it's time for Grandfather to eat too. I want you to tell your mother or one of your aunts to bring Grandfather's food. Can you do that?"

As soon as the children ran down the corridor, Ashoka got up to wash his hands and face at the tap. He dried himself with a towel and returned to the mat, taking off his wooden sandals and sitting cross-legged again. Then he picked up the prayer beads and began to recite in Sanscrit, his eyes partially closed. Soon the soft whispering of bare feet entered his consciousness. Lalimli appeared, carrying a tray with Ashoka's food. Since Lakshmi's illness, as the wife of the oldest son, she was expected to serve him and usually did. She was a good, traditional girl and kept her eyes downcast in his presence, rarely speaking except in response to something he said. She squatted, putting the tray down in front of him. It had the usual large brass plate with several *roti* in a pile in the center, surrounded by brass bowls containing the vegetables, legumes and cooked or curdled milk dishes. Also there was a glass-shaped brass container of drinking water. Lalimli moved backward a couple of feet in the waddling movement that was necessary from the squatting position. She turned her head slightly to one side and waited.

Ashoka studied the tray for a moment. It looked good, the usual dishes. He wondered for a moment how it would differ from one prepared by Lakshmi, she who had brought his food for more than forty years. Not very much, he knew, because she had trained the girls who came into the kitchen when they had married her sons. But there would still be some detectable differences in the spices. No two women could spice a curry or other dish exactly alike. Before beginning to eat, he turned to Lalimli. "How is Mother Lakshmi this evening?"

In a quiet voice, and without looking at him directly, she said, "She seems to be sleeping, though she's very quiet. She sleeps most of the time."

"Did she eat today?"

"A little lentil soup."

Ashoka could visualize the tiny body, lying under the single cover. Lakshmi had been a small person her whole life, but without eating what she ordinarily had, the body had become like that of a small girl. And since the sickness had come, she had eaten only a small portion of what she had before. No wonder that she was getting thinner and thinner.

He waved Lalimli away. "Thanks, Daughter-in-law, for the food. I'll eat now."

She pulled the side of her *sari* in front of her face, turned, and stood up. As she whispered away on her supple bare feet, he reached down and broke off a piece of the bread with his right hand, and using it as a pincer, grasped a mouthful of the spiced potatoes. Putting it in his mouth, he chewed it slowly with his premolars. He had lost all but one of his molars.

When he was finished eating, Ashoka pushed the tray back and went to the tap to wash his hands and mouth again. He sloshed water around in his mouth and spit into the drain several times. Standing, he could hear the far noises of low voices where the others had gathered. He stood up slowly because his bones ached. Readjusting his loin cloth, he made his way toward her room. His wood sandals made a muffled clack against the brick floor. He walked slowly because there was nowhere he had to be at any specific time. He had almost become timeless, he thought, a state most appropriate for one his age. It was the prelude to the timelessness of eternity.

The room was dark except for a small lamp on the table across from the narrow bed. The small image of the goddess Saraswati in the wall niche had a candle burning in front of it. There were orange flower petals and a few pieces of coconut scattered around its base. A brass vessel containing Ganges water was setting to one side. The tiny body of Lakshmi barely made a ridge in the middle of the bed. Her eyes were closed and for a moment Ashoka could detect no movement. He concentrated and finally saw the slow rise and fall of her breathing. He bent over to study her face and hands, which were outside the cover. The face was that of an old, old woman, deeply creased from a lifetime

of concerns. Her cheeks were sunken from the loss of her teeth. They
had wanted her to get false teeth for several years but she had resisted,
insisting she could eat rice and curries without teeth. Her small hands
and arms had lost much of their flesh. Under the cover, there was no
longer the shape of a woman, no rising mounds where breasts had once
been or the spreading rise of child-bearing loins.

Ashoka put his hand on the edge of the bed and said, "Lakshmi, do
you hear me? It's your husband, Ashoka."

There was no response. He stood quietly for a while, then put his
hand on her thin arm, saying again, "Lakshmi, do you hear me?"

The body remained motionless. He stood for long, looking in the
gloom at the small face and hands. He reached down to pull the
bedcloth over her face. Then he turned and left the room, shuffling
slowly. He stood for a moment in the corridor, listening to the low noises
from the kitchen. Then he turned back toward the courtyard. But instead of taking up his position on the mat, he went to the shrine. The
old pundit was squatting next to the lingam stone, murmuring prayers.
Without speaking, Ashoka squatted next to the other old man and took
out his prayer beads. The pundit did not raise his eyes. Soon the two of
them were murmuring.

# CHAPTER 7

Oldenberg stood to face Martin. He said, "Come on, we can go to the bar for a drink. I must say that I could use one after doing eight transitions and attending two committee meetings. We could talk there just as well as here. And I would imagine you would appreciate something also, no?"

Martin was holding his plastic briefcase which he had just brought from his room to make his appointment at six. It was later than an ordinary office appointment, but since he had become adjusted to life in the Transition Bureau, he had become progressively more unaware of the passage of time. In a way, he thought, it was already becoming like the timelessness of *nirvana*. Martin was beginning to see that if one was not connected with other peoples' schedules, one had no particular need for linear time. And if one were cut off from circadian time by being in a totally artificial environment, then even night and day became meaningless. He had noticed very early in his stay in the Transition Bureau that, apart from the main office, activities seemed to be going on all the time at about the same rate. There did not seem to be the waxing and waning of activity that he had known as a living person. The idea intrigued him at that moment, and Oldenberg, patient otherworldling that he was, waited. Martin said, "Sure, I guess so."

"Fine then. Dr. Hanson will be there too, and I presume he wants to hear your impressions of the mating life of your long-lost relations, the East Indians."

Again Martin was pleased and impressed that Oldenberg knew that those Aryans, the ancestors of Ashoka and his people, had split off from their European brothers, the ancestors of Martin, some mere 5,000 years before.

Oldenberg came from behind the desk and joined Martin. They

walked through the empty reception room and out into the corridor. Oldenberg said, "That is the lifeway you've just seen, isn't it, the Indians or Hindus, as you sometimes call them, the people you studied when you first became an anthropologist?"

Martin matched the stride of Oldenberg as they started down the long corridor toward the elevator. He was continually surprised at the length of the corridors in the Transition Bureau. But he put the idea away before getting too curious about it. So many things were slightly different, no matter how much the Transitioners tried to take on the customs of Earth, and no matter how effective the Illusion Department was in making things seem similar. "Yes," he said. "I just did the life of my old field assistant, who was certainly a Hindu."

Oldenberg spoke. "By the way, Martin, though I seem to have gotten a fairly good grasp of Earth geography, places, and people by now, there are still some things that puzzle me, and particularly the nomenclature. I just don't understand how you use the term *Indian*. Don't you have two widely separated people, the so-called 'red men' of the Americas and the people of the Asian subcontinent that they used to call Hindustan, who are both referred to by the same name, 'Indian?' It's very confusing."

They had reached the elevator and stood waiting, along with a man and woman, probably another Transitioner and a secretary, Martin figured. He answered Oldenberg's question. "I understand your confusion. It was often confusing on Earth too. But there's a fairly simple explanation. Our famous explorer, Christopher Columbus, was looking for the Indies, or farther India, and never found it. However, like many others with fixed ideas, he was convinced that he had when he found the Americas. The man was a great sailor but his geography was strictly limited, and when his mind was made up, that was it. The consequence, however, is that he didn't know where he was going when he started, and he didn't know where he'd been when he got back. So we got a major naming mix-up that has been troubling us ever since."

"Ah yes, that must explain why the Spanish king treated Columbus so unkindly in his old age."

"Not exactly. He was a person with some rather fixed ideas also. He was probably not easy to get along with. I think there were other problems also. But this could get pretty complicated."

The elevator stopped and the two men got on. The other couple waited to go down.

Oldenberg said, "Yes, I can see that it might. I suppose I need to absorb more Word Origin Tapes of your language. There must be a kind of history to the origin of every word."

"I'm sure there is," Martin said. "And I have been interested in such for a long time, probably ever since my days of studying linguistics. But when I found out about the Word Origin Tapes, I had almost the same reaction as I had when I first heard of Life Videos. Furthermore, the idea that one could absorb information totally by taking absorption tablets, attaching electrodes, and turning on the absorption player was mind boggling. Why, one could have the origin of a language's entire vocabulary in one's mind in just a little longer than it takes to say doodley squat, an expression made famous by one of our popular novelists."

By this time they were moving down one hallway after another, Martin keeping at Oldenberg's pace. They passed other persons occasionally. Oldenberg said, "We'll be there shortly, just two more turns."

The Transition Master said nothing more about word origins, so Martin said, "You know there are things that are difficult for me to understand in your system also. For instance, just before we started walking from your office, I was puzzling about the relative timelessness of this place. I am rarely aware even whether it is night or day. I know there are windows in certain places, but there doesn't seem to be much point in knowing since almost everything here in the Bureau goes on regardless of the time. The restaurants, snack bars, library, recreation rooms, all seem to be operating all the time, and since everything is lit artificially, one soon loses the feeling of time. The only place on Living Earth I can remember that was like it to a certain extent were the big city hospitals. They tended to take away the patient's sense of time. They were like this place in a number of respects, particularly in that they ran day and night and depended totally on artificial light."

"I see what you mean," Oldenberg answered, rather absently, Martin thought.

Martin continued, "Well, anyway, I sometimes get the feeling here that this is a little like what our religious writers used to describe as "eternity," or "nirvana," or simply, timelessness. And I was wondering whether there is some particular reason for it."

Oldenberg was carrying his unlit pipe in his hand, methodically rubbing the bowl with his thumb and forefinger. He said, "Only that, as I told you before, very few of the Transitioners and other workers here are originally from this planet, despite their illusionary forms, and on other astral bodies linear time is not usual. And as you can well imagine, the circadian time periods are wildly variable on different planetary and astral bodies. Periods of lightness and darkness can range from a mere flicker, which can pass in the blink of an eye, to what would be the equivalent of years on Earth. And of course there are planets whose rotation rate is the same as their revolution rate, which makes them have the same intensity of light all the time. Anyway, though I wasn't here when the System was set up, from my experience on other planets, I would guess that the Transition Bureau was set up with nonlinear, or what I suppose you earthlings would call perpetual time, simply because it would be less disruptive. The Transitionees need to adjust, of course, but because they are in the process of adjusting to almost everything else anyway, adjustment to a new form of time should be of little consequence."

By then they had reached a corridor where Martin had never been before and stopped in front of a solid wood doorway of a heavy, medieval style. Oldenberg turned to Martin, saying, "Do you understand what I mean?"

A couple of other men, garbed in tweed jackets and complimentary slacks, accompanied by a girl who was modishly dressed, approached the doorway and went in. Oldenberg reached out to keep the door from swinging shut but held it for a moment. Martin said, "Yes, your explanation makes sense. And it is very interesting."

Oldenberg smiled. "So, shall we go in?"

It was a large room with subdued light, carpeted with oaken posts and paneling throughout. Upholstered chairs were scattered about with various small tables alongside and between. Men, mostly middle aged, were reading papers or magazines or sipping drinks while talking in low voices. At one end a couple of men sat at a bar with drinks. Against one wall were booths of polished wood where other small groups were sitting with drinks and smokes. A couple of waiters were holding trays of drinks, moving slowly and quietly. Martin said, "You know, this place looks very much like an Ivy League university club."

Oldenberg answered, "It very probably has been designed with such an establishment as a model, you know, to give the place an academic air. You earthlings regard your universities as most august, do you not?"

"I suppose so, especially the Ivy League schools."

"Anyway, there's Hanson." Oldenberg pointed at the astral shrink in the back of one of the booths, smoking a cigarillo. "Shall we join him?"

"Sure."

The two newcomers greeted the psyche adjuster and made themselves comfortable. A waiter arrived shortly and took their orders, while Oldenberg stoked his pipe.

Hanson began. "I've really been looking forward to getting together again with you, Dr. Neumann, and particularly now that you have some new data. I found the last discussion quite stimulating. I hope you feel free to share some of your new thoughts."

Martin replied, "Oh, certainly. As you may not know, I was a university teacher for many years on Living Earth, and a pretty good one at that, I think. And as you may know, earthlings in that occupation are some of the talkingist people we have. It makes sense, you know, since they get paid for talking. In any event, many of them can talk for hours at the drop of a word, and moreover, they are practically shameless in what they talk about, especially those in social science. And I am afraid that I fit the model fairly closely. Like many of my colleagues, I long ago learned how hard it is to get other people to listen to your ideas, brilliant or not. As a matter of fact, having a captive audience is certainly not the least attraction of being a teacher."

Hanson took a last drag on his cigarillo and stubbed out the rest. "Good, good," he said. "So what did you find out this time? As I recall, you were going on your first cross-cultural journey, to view the mating life of your former field assistant in India, is that correct?"

"That's it. I went back to find out what happened to Ashoka Harinarayan, the Brahmin fellow with whom I shared the trials and tribulations of my first field trip."

"So how was it; how did his life compare with that of someone in your own culture?"

"Well, as you may know, those high-caste Hindus, and a lot of other people in that part of the world, really treated mating as a lifetime commitment. They did not countenance divorce. People lived together once they went through the marriage vows. And that made them try very hard to get along. Even when everything wasn't perfect, they stayed together."

Oldenberg was puffing contentedly by this time. He said, "You mean they never divorced?"

"Very rarely. A man could take on another wife if his own couldn't bear him a child but even so, the first wife would stay as a part of his household. But for the woman, a second marriage was impossible, even if her first husband died."

The waiter returned with the drinks, plus a large bowl of mixed nuts. Martin sipped his martini. "Very good," he said. "You know, this is one drink that should be had at bars. It requires very careful attention to the details of proportion and mixing. I made approximations for years in my earthling homes, but frankly mine were never fantastic. I just never took enough care. Ultimately I decided to save my martini drinking for visits to bars or restaurants."

Oldenberg and Hanson took generous helpings of the nuts. Oldenberg pushed the bowl in Martin's direction, saying, "Help yourself, they're good."

Martin said, "But they look like they're heavily salted. I'm really not supposed to. You know, high blood pressure."

Oldenberg smiled. "Martin, you forget where you are. This isn't Living Earth, and you're not a live earthling anymore. In fact, you seem to have forgotten as well that you are in Transition. Anyway, high blood pressure is a problem you no longer have to worry about."

Martin laughed and reached for the nuts. "That's true. How strange. But it's hard to shake off life habits, even here."

Hanson brought them back. "So, what else was different, Martin?" He quickly added, "I hope you don't mind if I call you by your first name."

"No, that's fine. I've never been a stickler for protocol. You know, that old-time American formality. And to get to your question, the one other thing that was very different was that they did not have love matches. Spouses were selected by the parents."

"That's quite different from the way of your culture, isn't it?" Oldenberg queried. "Your people had to find their own, and as you described before, they had to be smitten by some kind of strong emotion they called love. I'm just wondering, did those high-caste Hindus simply ignore the emotional needs of the two people? How did that work?"

Martin, "It seems clear that they played down the emotional needs, nothing like what happened during my lifetime in my culture, when 'being in love' was the be-all and end-all for mating. Even when people started living together without being married, almost all felt that a relationship, some kind of deep feeling, was necessary. Even sexual encounters would be permitted by most people only if there were strong feelings. Except for prostitutes and a minority of males, most people never got comfortable in having sex relations for the simple physical pleasure of it.

"But to get back to the Hindus. All the arrangements mentioned above were completely outside their system. There was only one way that you could mate and that was by being married, and then it was automatic. When parents arranged marriages, they were almost exclusively concerned with the potentialities of the spouses to produce and raise children, as well as to fit into the rest of the family. Whether or not the couple was 'in love' was certainly a secondary consideration."

Hanson popped a large Brazil nut into his mouth and chewed thoughtfully for a minute, then spoke, "And so I take it the relationship between the husband and wife was mechanical and formal; is that correct?"

"Surprisingly enough, that's not exactly what happened, certainly not to Ashoka and Lakshmi. Though like other traditional Hindus, they were not given to open displays of affection, even in private, they still seemed to have developed a strong bond of attachment. I don't know if you'd call it love, but it was a strong feeling of some kind. Probably from sharing a lifetime of domestic affairs, and even mating of a subdued sort, as well as sharing a few outside experiences. But there was never the intensity of feeling we seem to expect in our modern 'love' relationships."

"You seem to have gotten a fairly positive feeling about the Hindu way," Oldenberg said. "Particularly compared with that in your culture."

Martin took another sip of his martini and swirled the rest in the bottom, watching the olive roll around. He reached in the glass and took out the smooth green fruit, popping it into his mouth. He had suddenly realized he could eat olives again, a delicacy he had given up when he had his first stroke on Earth. And now again he could eat all the other salty things he wanted. He chewed it slowly, savoring the salt, vinegar, and oil taste that can be found only in an olive. Then he answered, "Yes, in a way I think I do. I began to have some doubts about the love match in my early middle age, and I'm afraid the idea grew. I couldn't help feeling even then that the arranged marriage was much more stable. They did everything they could to keep couples together and they were largely successful, and though I can't say that the parents were unconcerned with love, or deep affection, or whatever you want to call it, they considered this secondary. A man needed to be a good provider and a responsible father, and to fulfill his caste and religious responsibilities. A woman had to be a good mother and housekeeper, and take her responsible part in the great family. Perhaps the elders felt that if such qualifications were met, that husband and wife would naturally develop a strong affection for each other."

"And did your couple, Ashoka and Lakshmi, come to have such a feeling?" Oldenberg asked.

"I think so," Martin said. "They seem to have gotten more attached to one another through the years their children were growing up. Only toward the end did Ashoka begin to turn more in to himself, though he stayed with her to the time of her death. But by then I could see that he was concentrating more and more on the religious quest. In any event, that was most appropriate according to their beliefs. He had finished the third period of his life, that of householder, and it was proper to begin the last, that of the religious seeker."

The drinks were empty by that time. Oldenberg asked, "How about one more round? Then I'm going to have to be off, and I suppose you two have other things also."

"Yes, I'll need to be going too," said Hanson, "though I certainly want to hear the rest of this."

Oldenberg held up a finger to summon the waiter while Hanson continued, "Very good, Dr. Neumann. Your input may even help me in my Transition counseling. As you may expect, many of the Transitionees bring along some of the psychic baggage from their earth lives that tends to interfere with the Transition process. Unsettled love affairs seem to be hard to get rid of. Many people, particularly women, come in who have spent as much as twenty or thirty years of the latter part of their lives alone. Most are widows or divorcees. They keep brooding about it when they ought to be thinking about their Transitions."

Martin laughed. "Ah yes, even though I'm the wrong sex, I know about that. I spent the last twenty-five years of my life basically alone also, as did my ex-wives. And as you may know, my own particular brand of brooding led up to this little project. As Mr. Oldenberg may have told you, I am using the results of this inquiry as a kind of therapy, to get the brooding out of my system, as well as to help decide what to request for my next life. But if what I'm seeing will help your therapy with Transitionees, so much the better. We academics, even the 'ex's,' can't get free from the desire to get our results to the maximum number of users. That is one of the reasons we pushed the 'publish or perish' philosophy so hard. It was almost impossible to get a high professorial rank without a respectable list of publications, no matter what kind of garbage. So though I'm well past the need for that kind of consideration, it's still a kind of reflex to urge people to use my ideas."

Martin hesitated, realizing that he had done what he had done so often in classroom lectures, wandered off on a tangent in fascination with the sound of his own voice. He had lost the point of the discussion. Fortunately, he thought, he had trained himself during his teaching years to not be afraid to admit this to the class at the time, then asking the students where they were. Someone always knew what point the professor was heading toward when he took off. This time Martin said to Hanson, "I don't remember exactly where we were in the discussion. Could you tell me?"

"Sure, you were emphasizing how deep feeling seemed to grow throughout the life of Ashoka and Lakshmi, despite their not being 'in love' at the beginning."

"Ah yes. Was there some detail you wanted to know about it?"

"Yes, and perhaps it comes from my current perspective. You know, though I came here to work in the Transition Bureau from a System that couldn't have been more remote from the one here, with its Love Syndrome, I seem to have been caught up by the idea, I suppose from listening to the life stories of earthlings in my therapy sessions. If I were working in India, the Middle East, or some other place where arrangement of marriages was the usual way of doing things, I wouldn't hear so much about disappointed love.

"But in any event, your account of the Hindu way has provoked a thought. The way you've explained it, the arranged, lifetime marriage of those people was almost perfect; and it certainly seemed to fulfill the needs of the System. Surely, there must have been some disappointments or frustrations. For instance, I hear so much from Earth Transitionees about spouses having affairs, or 'messing around,' as they put it. Didn't your Ashoka, at least in his young manhood, wander around sometime?"

The waiter arrived then with another tray of drinks and a small plate containing crackers with cheese and different spreads. Martin was impressed. The place had class. Oldenberg passed the plate around and the other two took a couple of crackers each. Martin answered, "No, as a matter of fact, he didn't. You know underneath it all, despite his M.A. in sociology, he was a pretty orthodox guy. Though he experimented with me in a small way in trying some new foods, he remained a vegetarian throughout his life. And that is perhaps one of the best quick and dirty ways of judging the orthodoxy of a Hindu. In other respects as well, he followed the traditional ways, including remaining strictly faithful to his wife. After all, she was bearing children for him, and she was very accommodating, and even attractive in her young womanhood."

"I understand," Hanson. "Except for the fact that many of the American Transitionees whom I deal with seem to have had those same qualities in their spouses, and still they have had affairs. Do you think perhaps it is that the Hindus are not as strongly sexed as your American males?"

"No, I don't see that. The Hindus have a long history of eroticism, embodied in their art and literature. And even though they seem to have gone off on a puritanical bent the last few hundred years, there is no good reason to believe that their gonads are less active. No, I suspect it's their cultural upbringing. It's a pretty tightly controlled system which leaves little to the individual, and certainly not the sexual practices."

Hanson leaned back and took out his pack of cigarillos. "Do you mind if I smoke one?"

"Certainly not, I used to do it myself early in my lifetime. I gave up all uses of the Red Man's Revenge, tobacco, in the early seventies, when the great cancer scare became full blown."

"Why do you call it that? I find the practice a rather pleasant earthling diversion."

"You may know that we whites took the land and most of the way of life from the American Indians when we settled the Americas. Besides the land, about the only other things of theirs we found to our satisfaction were their many cultivated plants, such as corn, beans, potatoes, tomatoes, peanuts, and even my all-time favorite, the avocado. There are many others, and it makes an impressive list. Naturally, we didn't give them anything for this great boon to our diet. After all, we were the conquerors. But they slipped one time bomb in, tobacco. Not only did we take it over, we got the whole rest of the world addicted. I can see why. It's a great pacifier. Unfortunately, it is also highly addictive. Once you get young persons hooked, they have great difficulty taking the weed in moderation. Anyway, evidence accumulated in the seventies that cigarettes in particular contributed significantly to the disease of cancer, probably our most fearsome killer. The Red Man had achieved his ultimate revenge."

Hanson had lit his cheroot. He took it from his mouth, saying, "I of course, knew of the cancer-producing characteristics of the plant. In fact, a significant number of Transitionees seem to have died of the disease. But we from other Systems are hardly subject to it. In any event, I smoke only a few each day, usually after work when I'm relaxing."

Martin felt a little bad because he hadn't wished to be accusatory. As a matter of fact, he had even toyed with the idea of trying a cheroot himself but so far had not been able to break the thirty-year resolution. He said, "Oh, I wasn't trying to get you to stop smoking. I don't think it's so bad so long as it's done in moderation. That's true of most drugs, I think. Unfortunately, for quite a few, it's hard to be moderate. So most people become addicts. But all this is probably not relevant for people from other Systems anyway."

Hanson smiled when he put the cheroot back between his lips. He took a slow draw, blew the smoke out, then said, "Anyway, shall we get back to our faithful Hindu? I take it you believe that the Indian people don't 'fall in love' because they are trained not to. Is that the idea?" Hanson mused, "A little digression is that I never could quite understand the logic of that expression. 'Falling' sounds like it is an unpleasant accident. People ordinarily don't like to fall, do they?"

Martin stopped to ponder that one, then said, "I agree; it is an unusual expression. About all I can come up with is that it is supposed to emphasize the force of the experience. According to romantic thought, one does not drift into love, one falls into it or is smitten. And the latter term means 'to be hit.' Hmmm."

They looked at each other in puzzlement for a moment, then Hanson said, "I suppose we ought to get back to the issue, the Hindus, no?"

"Yes. So far as I know the Hindus are not trained not to love someone, but the times and places they can do so are strictly controlled. None of the mad affairs that could go on in my culture, you know, 'nooners' with office girls or nurses, motel rendezvous with other men's wives, or even back seat lovemaking in autos, as we had in my youth. It isn't that Hindus were never smitten by love or lust or whatever, but it was almost impossible to carry off such things in their society."

"It was so difficult?"

"Yes, probably a combination of guilt from their upbringing and social pressure. In fact, Ashoka, like many other red-blooded young men, was smitten at least once. He got excited by an attractive Muslim girl during his college years, but before he could even speak to her, he came to realize it was impossible. Nothing could come from the attraction. To follow through across religious, much less caste, lines meant cutting yourself off from all family attachments, financial, emotional, and all other kinds. It was a price that very few were willing to pay, especially for something so doubtful as 'love.' As a good Hindu, he knew the family went on and on, and non-kin relationships were impermanent at best."

"It makes sense," said Hanson. "And I can see that so far as the System's needs are concerned, the strong commitment to family is salutary. Their family makes a strong unit for reproduction."

Martin sipped his second martini, by then very mellow. He felt he could go on for a long time. Ideas were coming so rapidly he couldn't express them fast enough. This was the kind of idea flipping that really stimulated him. These guys from other Systems were really alright, he thought. It had been a long time since he had had this kind of opportunity. First, with Oldenberg, it had been a satisfaction that made him look forward to each meeting. But now with another Systemicist, it was getting to be really exciting. A strange idea flashed briefly through his consciousness, that there might be some way he could join the fraternity himself, that he could go on flipping ideas like this for all eternity, or for as long as the Systemicists stayed around. He knew it was crazy; there were still so many things he didn't know about the System or the procedures, much less his probable complete lack of credentials. But at least, he thought, these guys were interested in exchanging ideas, which meant he couldn't be so terribly far out. Anyway, he came back to the issue at hand, saying, "You're certainly right that the patriarchal, extended family system is ideally suited for reproduction, which is ironic in a way. If there is a fundamental problem that threatens the future existence of *Homo sapiens,* it is his reproductive capacity. The species got so good at increasing its numbers that by the end of the last century, when my previous life ended, we were rapidly running out of food. And the reason was that there were so many of us. We had actually been getting better at producing and processing food, but we just couldn't keep up with the increase in numbers of bodies year after year. And what was the most efficient reproductive unit the world has ever known but the family? And what country had the most efficient families in the world and the most aggravated population problem but India?"

"Very interesting," Hanson. "In other words, you are saying that the very basis for System success, reproductive capacity, got out of control and potentially destructive on Earth."

"Yes, that's it. And it's not solved yet. The industrial countries are just barely keeping India, many parts of the Middle East, Africa, and Latin America going with surplus grain, but the population in most of those places still keeps going up." Pause. "But that is another issue, isn't it? So far as providing life satisfaction, the Hindu system seemed to offer much, even if people never got the chance to select their own mates."

Oldenberg had been sitting back during most of the previous interchange though listening all the while, occasionally blowing smoke from the side of his mouth, like the mentor/professor basking in the performance of his prize graduate student. But then he offered a comment. "The deep family structure as you describe it seems to offer much to the males, but in comparison with your ways in the Western world, the women seem to be largely neglected. With all this male authority and masculine control, aren't the females, the wives and mothers, often frustrated?"'

"I suppose so," Martin. "It's true that this and most other deeply familial cultures are oriented primarily toward males. And I suppose women must frequently get the short end of the stick, as we used to say in my youth. But as you know, I viewed the Life Video of Ashoka, not Lakshmi. From what I saw, she didn't seem to suffer enormously, but I admit there might have been much that I did not learn about her secret sorrows."

"Are you intending to take a look at her life, then?" Oldenberg.

"I could, I guess. But I wasn't exactly planning on it. You know, there are so many lives that I simply have to cut down. I could spend eons in that library, and I don't think I have that much time. Pause. "By the way, how much time have I spent so far, and how much do you figure I ought to still have—that is, in linear terms?"

Oldenberg began knocking his pipe out, evidently in preparation for departure. He hesitated for a moment, then, "I think you've been on it now eight or nine days, and I guess I thought a couple of weeks for viewing would be enough, then perhaps another for writing up the final report. Then, I think we ought to get on with your Transition." Pause. "I don't really want to push you, Dr. Neumann, but you do know that your position here is somewhat ambiguous. I get occasional calls from my supervisor, asking what the delay is in getting you on to your next life. He still can't quite accept the idea of a Transitionee doing a research project. Anyway, I hope you can see that I have certain pressures too."

Although this information was not wholly unexpected, it still came as a mini-shock to Martin. He hadn't realized up to that point how enamored he had become of the whole exercise. He knew that he could go on much longer than the time allotted, probably for ages, but still he knew that wasn't probable. And he also knew that almost all research studies were locked into some kind of time frame, usually according to the money available. Furthermore, he had learned to curtail his activities in the days of his field studies to such limitations, so he could do it with Project Heterop also. He answered, "Sure, I understand. And I'll act accordingly. I think I'll pass up Lakshmi's life, though I would like to do one more of a deeply familial culture, and the woman's side. Do you think that's alright?"

"Yes, in fact I think that would be appropriate. What did you have in mind?"

Martin hurried then because he recognized that Oldenberg was ready to go. And for that matter, Martin was getting a little tired of the talk himself. It would be pleasant to go to the Audio Library and check out a tape of Space Music. He had learned that a vast collection of harmonious sounds was available, both of music played on unknown instruments and with bizarre vocals from other Systems, as well as natural sounds of air, liquid, fire, and movement of all sorts that occurred in unknown worlds. The closest thing to it he could remember from Earth was the electronic music of the late twentieth century and perhaps some way-out classical composers such as Stravinsky. Anyway, to Martin's ear it was a logical extension of music from unknown cultures, which he had first experienced when he came into anthropology.

So he said, "I was thinking I would view the life of a woman from another culture that is deep into familism, though perhaps somewhat less than India. I would like to view a Latin female's life, and as before, I would take one of a culture about which I have some firsthand knowledge, namely, Costa Rica."

"That's one of the small countries in Central America, isn't it?" Hanson.

"Yes, one that at the time I knew it was considered the democratic bastion of Latin America, the Switzerland of the New World. It was unique in some respects, but it still maintained a Latin base, especially so far as the sexes were concerned.

"As you may have heard, the Latins have been well known for their double standard, males seeking conquests while females tried to keep their purity, at least so far as extramarital affairs were concerned. Anyway, the male role has been described often under the term, *machismo*. To be *macho* was to be tough and assertive, especially in making female conquests."

"I can see the similarity to Hindu culture in the different behavior of males and females," Hanson. "But there seem to be some significant differences also."

"All I can say is that no one thing can be exactly similar to any other. That is a logical impossibility. But similarities can be close enough to be of value for comparison. And it seems to me the role of females versus males in the two cultures share some interesting points of comparison. And I guess the other thing is the interest in family affairs. Among Europeans, Latins are probably the most strongly oriented toward family needs. Even with our intense urbanization in the United States in the late twentieth century, the Latins still depended on family relations more than almost any other people."

Oldenberg, "I think that culture would be appropriate, and you still have several days left."

"Okay then." Pause. "Perhaps in a way, that would be better than a still very traditional culture. When I knew them best, the Costa Ricans were in a stage of transition, I'd say, halfway between the old and the new, the way that had already evolved in the highly industrialized cultures. And I guess in the back of my mind I'm planning to devote a chapter to the way it became in my own culture. The Costa Rican way might serve as a bridge of understanding between the old and the new." Martin picked up his martini glass and drained it. The others did likewise with their drinks and Oldenberg waved for the waiter.

As they were standing to leave, Martin was smiling inwardly. Hanson noticed: "You seem to be having some amusing thoughts. Want to share them?"

"It's funny to me though I'm not sure it would be to someone from outside the field, much less from some other Systemic background."

"Try me. I catch on pretty fast."

"What I was thinking of was that with my current activity, I am fulfilling the anthropological role with a thoroughness that could not be imagined on Earth. The anthropologist was a professional voyeur. However, most direct voyeurism among earthlings was an aspect of sexuality. Of course, there were all kinds of indirect voyeurism, in porno publications and movies and even in other professions. Probably the best known was psychotherapy, when troubled souls were encouraged to pour out their sex lives to therapists in the hopes of some kind of solution to their problems. But the only people who actually got around to studying a wide variety of mating behaviors were anthropologists. Little of that was direct, because in most societies people were not prepared to have others stand around watching when they were being intimate sexually. I know I never even got close to observing mating behavior of others during my field studies. But now here I am with the marvellous resource of the Life Videos and I can do all the voyeuring I want. Of course, it's still indirect, but I'm sure it's the closest anyone will ever get to direct viewing of mating in a natural setting. What wouldn't anthropologists and other human scientists have given for this resource, eh?"

"It would seem so," Hanson.

Oldenberg signed the chit, and the three left.

# ANNA

She was a pretty thirteen-year-old. Her skin color, coffee with cream, was lighter than that of others standing on the corner. There was one

Negro girl who was conspicuously darker, as well as having kinky hair. Anna was content that she was of Spanish origin, rather than one of the Blacks from the east coast. They might speak English, their ancestors having come from Jamaica, but people said they didn't speak it very well. And besides, the boys didn't really respect them. It was hard for the Black girls to find good husbands in San José. The boys just liked to play around with them, not marry them. Anna fingered the plait of her long black hair.

She was wearing her blue skirt and white blouse, the girls' uniform at most schools. Her body was already beginning to take a woman's shape, wider at the hips, narrow at the waist, and the beginning of small breasts. Her mother had given her a white bra just a month before, which she had put on proudly.

Finally, she saw the bus coming. When it stopped, she climbed on with a half dozen others. It was about half full. Anna was last to put her two *colones* into the change box, heading toward Silvia in the back. When she got about one-third of the way, an arm reached out and grasped her. She looked and saw it was that of an old man, much older than her father. He was heavy and mostly bald, and he had food spots on the front of his shirt. Anna tugged her arm, but that just made him hold tighter. He pulled her toward the empty seat alongside, "Come on, little flower, sit down."

She pulled harder. "I want to go sit with my friend, Silvia."

"Come on, sit here," he said. "It's nice here in front where you can see."

The harder she pulled, the more insistently he pulled her toward the empty seat. She looked around to see if another passenger would help. Several were watching, but when her eyes met theirs pleadingly, they turned their glances away. Anna quit resisting since it was only about thirty minutes before she would get off. She decided she could sit by the old man that long. However, she leaned forward, sitting on the front edge of the seat.

He put his arm across her shoulders. "And how is my little *chiquita* today? Coming back from school?"

Without looking up, she answered, "Yes."

"She's a very pretty little *chiquita*. And very nice to sit by an old man. She's also very warm, a warm little girl." He squeezed her shoulder and pulled her toward him.

Anna became aware of his odor. He smelled very strongly of ciga-rettes. Also, she got a whiff of his breath when he leaned down, a combined odor of tobacco and rum. She leaned away.

"Can't the little girl talk more?" he said. "I'll bet she can."

Anna nodded. He put his hand on hers. "Now, little sweet, say something to the old man. Then maybe he'll give you a present."

Anna tried to pull her hand back but that just made him hold tighter. He continued, "Say something, little girl. Talk to the old man. What's your name, *chiquita*? I'll bet it's a pretty name."

She didn't really want to, but she thought he couldn't do any harm by knowing her name. And maybe he'd leave her alone then. In a very low voice, she murmured, "Anna."

"Ah, Anna. That's a very pretty name, for a very pretty little girl." He volunteered then, "My name is Pedro. The old man is Pedro, and the little girl is Anna." He squeezed her hand. "Pedro likes Anna. And maybe Anna likes Pedro."

Anna didn't answer, just sat as quietly as possible.

He said, "Anna doesn't like to talk much, does she? Not to Pedro, anyway. Maybe she's shy. But Pedro will help. He'll tell Anna things she can talk about. Maybe she can talk about school. Maybe she can tell Pedro some stories she heard. Little girls hear stories in school." He patted her hand again.

She shook her head, whereupon he took his hand away, the one holding hers, and reaching into his pants pocket, brought out a small plastic flower. She watched him from the corner of her eye, though carefully, so he wouldn't see her looking at him. He held the flower in front of her. "See, old Pedro has a little present for the little girl. She gets it if she tells him a little story. Now, won't she tell old Pedro a story?"

The flower wasn't at all pretty, Anna thought. It was purplish with bright green leaves attached to a short stem. It didn't look new. She wondered how long it had been in his pocket. She imagined that it smelled like the old man, like cigarettes and rum. She shook her head.

"That's too bad," he continued. "Old Pedro would be very happy if little Anna would tell him a story. But little Anna is shy and doesn't talk much. Maybe her mama told her not to talk to strangers. And that's good to tell little girls. But they can talk to nice old men like Pedro. It doesn't hurt to talk to Pedro."

Anna noticed through the opposite window that the bus was going around Palos Verde traffic circle, which made her feel a little better. It was almost halfway. In another fifteen minutes they would be at her stop and she could get off. Her thoughts were quickly interrupted, however, by the insistent pressure on her shoulders as he turned her toward him. "Anna is a very shy little girl even though Pedro is her friend and wouldn't hurt her. But Pedro likes her anyway and wants to give her a present even if she won't tell him a story."

Anna wanted to pull back but she couldn't, his hand held her so tightly. He stuck the plastic flower into her blouse pocket and patted it down. He kept patting a long time, and she knew what for. She was glad she had her bra on. He grinned at her with his cigarette–rum breath, "Little Anna is growing up to be a big girl already."

Finally he took his hand back, though he left the other arm on her shoulder. She sat as quietly as she could, literally trying to shrink. He kept pointing things out to her but she refused to look across him and out the window. The bus began to empty. Silvia and her friends came by. Silvia asked, "You want to get off and walk home with me?"

Anna started to jump up, but the old man held her down. Silvia looked at the arm across Anna's shoulders. Still sitting, Anna said, "Yes, I'll get off now."

The old man, "You stay with Pedro, Anna. Just ride a little farther. You can see your friends later or tomorrow."

With supreme effort Anna pulled away and got up. The old man held her by the arm for a bit, but when she was standing in the middle of the aisle, pulling, he let go. She almost fell backward from the release, but quickly recovered and hurried away before he could reach out again. She felt exultant with her freedom.

Then she was outside, walking up the street with Silvia and the two other girls. The bus pulled away from the curb, and the old man waved from the window. Anna refused to acknowledge his gesture, looking straight ahead.

"Who was he?" Silvia. "He was holding you all the time. Was he some relative or friend of the family?"

Anna almost felt like tears, from what exactly she didn't know, whether from embarrassment or just release at being free again. She answered, "Oh, no, he wasn't anything. I never saw him before. He was just a dirty old man who smelled of cigarettes and rum and he grabbed me and wouldn't let me go."

\* \* \* \* \*

Anna Velasquez matured into a full-bodied woman, much sought after in high school and later when she worked as an apprentice seamstress. She ordinarily went out with her sister, Lupe. Things had changed since the old days when any really respectable girl would not be allowed to go out without a chaperon. Even so, her mother always wanted the girls to go out together. Anna knew Lupe wasn't exactly wild about having her along all the time since she was much prettier, but her sister minded their mother. Anna also knew that Jaime, their older brother, kept an eye on both of them, taking on the role of their father, who had died when she was eight years old.

\* \* \* \* \*

It was Sunday night. Lupe and Anna were riding the bus toward Mediana. It was medium full though no one was standing. Both girls wore fancy dresses. Lupe's was yellow flowered and just reached her knees, and Anna's was a satiny blue sheath with four-inch slits at the bottom. Both wore high-heeled shoes and some makeup. Anna also had on nylons.

"Do you know those boys?" Anna spoke in a low voice, indicating the group of four young men across the aisle several seats forward.

"No, I never saw them before."

"I thought you did because they spoke to us."

Lupe giggled. "You know that doesn't mean anything. Boys in a group like that always do whatever they can to attract your attention."

Anna pulled her skirt down though it wouldn't go far, it was so tight. Then she carefully smoothed the edges of the slits so they were as closed as possible, saying, "I know these slit dresses are the fashion and if you've got a good figure, you ought to wear them. But I still feel like I'm showing too much when I wear one. Is that why you never wear them?"

"No, I just like other styles."

"How do you think Mama felt about us going to Mediana alone and to a *retreta* at that?"

"You know how mothers are. They don't change with the times very much. But even so, she should be pleased some since she did the same when she was young. In fact, she met Papa at the *retreta* walkaround, though I'm sure her mother or one of her other female relatives had gone along. You know they were stricter in those days, and Mama, coming from a small town, was raised even more strictly."

Anna fingered the curls of her permanent. She had just gotten it three days before, on her afternoon off. They had cut it shorter than she liked, but that was the fashion. She said, "I still feel a little funny about going to a *retreta*, don't you?"

"Well, it's different. We could go to a disco or the movies but we do that all the time. And besides, it's so Costa Rican. You know they say we're famous for our *retretas*."

Anna laughed. "That's about all we could be famous for, I guess. This is such a little country, I imagine most people outside don't even know where it is."

"What's happened between you and Arturo? He usually takes you out on weekends, doesn't he?" Pause. "For that matter, you don't seem to have been out with him for two or three weeks."

"We had a breakup. He drinks too much and I told him so and he didn't like it."

This time Lupe laughed. "How can you find a Costa Rican boyfriend who doesn't drink a lot? They have to, you know, to prove their manliness. She giggled again. "That and making it with every girl they meet. Sometimes I wonder if it's worthwhile to try to be popular. Guys just expect too much from a girl."

"I wonder how it was in the old days, whether maybe it wasn't better. At least then a girl knew what she was supposed to do. Nowadays there's no way of knowing. And the guys are trying to get you into bed the minute they meet you."

They got off the bus at the Central Park stop, where the group of boys got off also. The boys lit up cigarettes as they headed toward the sound of music from the park pavilion. They jostled one another and talked in loud voices, turning periodically to look at the two girls. "Just don't look at them," Anna. "They're nothing but working-class boys, out to drink and smoke and make smart remarks to girls. They don't even have enough nerve to go out alone. They need to be with their buddies to have enough courage."

Anna ignored the fact that she was out with her sister and that most other people they were beginning to pass were also in pairs or small groups, both the men and women. But just when she got finished describing the boys ahead, as if to prove her point, the group of boys moved off the path to a darkened bench where one produced a bottle of rum. He took a swig directly from the bottle, then passed it around, and each boy took a swig in turn. One of them noticed her watching and made a gesture for her to come and have a swig also. She turned her head away in pique at having been caught watching them. "Come on," she said abruptly. "Let's go where the crowd is. I don't like to be around those boys."

"Okay with me; you're the one who's been dawdling."

They speeded up as they approached the sound of the brass band, surrounded by a thickening crowd. The band was playing a North American piece, Anna thought, one by Cole Porter, though she didn't know the music of that era well enough to be sure. "They play all the old-fashioned pieces at the *retretas*," mused Anna, "though I guess that's alright since it's a kind of an old-fashioned custom. I still feel kind of funny about coming. We could have gone to Leonardo's and then at least we'd have had a few dances."

"Oh come on, we're here now. It won't hurt, at least once. And besides, it probably makes Mama happy to know that you've gone to a real old-fashioned Costa Rican event for a change. You know she still thinks dance halls are not real nice."

They had arrived at one edge of the promenade, an oval walk about a city block long beneath the park's tall trees. At the sides were old men and women with small children, sitting on benches. On the main walk there were two lines of movement, girls in their late teens and twenties strolling on the inside and clockwise while boys of the same ages walked in the opposite direction on the outside. Anna and Lupe stopped short of the line, watching. The girls were generally sedate, though once in a while some would giggle. The boys were more boisterous. Some lurched as if they had drunk too much. Some of the girls would smile and obviously hold their gaze on certain boys, and some boys would do the same. A few would turn their heads after they had passed to look at a boy they had exchanged glances with when they had approached one another.

"It is one way to let someone know you're interested," Anna said. "I guess some of the old customs were pretty well tested."

"Yeah, this way you can really give someone the look without any interruptions."

They stood a while, then Lupe asked, "You want to join in, or shall we sit for a while?"

"Let's sit. I'm not ready yet."

It took a little looking to find a bench with free spaces and still within eyesight of the promenade. The girls watched for a while, studying and commenting on the passing lines. They knew one group of girls slightly, having come from the same church. When they came around the second time, one of the girls waved at Anna and Lupe. Anna said tentatively, "We could join them."

"Are you ready?"

"Sure, we came all this way. We may as well go around a time or so."

The two sisters joined the neighborhood group. Anna felt she was one of the prettiest girls there and set her walk accordingly. She had learned just how much to make her hips swivel to attract male attention and still not look like a street woman. She also held her breasts out, knowing their firm fullness attracted attention, no little because of the tight dress she was wearing. She was sure many men would look at her. But she would be careful whom she would respond to.

And so it came to be. Many boys let their glances linger, but Anna had well learned by that time how to observe boys without letting them know you were doing it. There were two or three she found interesting and on whom she let her glance linger. One in particular attracted her attention, a tall man with a light skin and very curly hair. He was smooth shaven, unlike most of the men there, who had mustaches. Most Latin males need to have mustaches, she thought, to feel manly. But not the tall curly-haired guy. He was also well dressed, wearing well-tailored pants and a turtleneck sweater, a cigarette in hand. Anna was a little surprised he had come to a *retreta;* he seemed like he would be more in place at a club or dance hall.

The second time they passed, Anna allowed herself the tiniest of a smile and fluttered her eyelids ever so lightly. She had learned how much of that too would attract attention without seeming silly. He smiled back ever so slightly. They passed one another slowly, so close it seemed they would touch. When they had passed one another by fifteen or twenty feet, Anna looked back. He had turned too, and their eyes met. They exchanged a smile almost openly.

"You really seem interested in that guy," Lupe remarked. "He is good looking. And he seemed to be interested in you."

"He's so tall and well dressed, he almost seems foreign to me, like maybe Italian or French. What do you think?"

"I don't know. There are some tall Costa Rican men. And some Costa Ricans even dress well. But he does look like he's from the better class."

They continued the promenade. Lupe began again. "I can ask Magdalena. She's been here several times and knows a lot of people. Maybe she can tell us something about him. You want me to?"

"Sure, though it's a little early. I'm not even sure he's interested." Quickly adding, "He seemed to be, though."

After one more tour, the two girls sat down just back from the double line of promenaders.

"What did you find out?"

"Magdalena did know about him. He's been here before, and a lot of girls are after him. His name is Guillermo Manzanar, and his father owns a big coffee export business. He's been to college and works in his father's business."

"That sounds very interesting," Anna said. How much better than

Arturo, she thought, who was only a carpenter.

They listened to several pieces. "You want to get into the promenade again?" Lupe asked.

"No, I think I've had enough of that. I would like an ice, though. And maybe we ought to move out to where we could be seen. You know, if someone wants to find us."

Lupe giggled. "Oh, I know, you want him to come over. You sure make up your mind fast."

Anna said in a little pique, "Well, why come to a place like this if you don't want to meet someone?"

"I guess you're right, but you seem so direct about it."

Anna said shortly. "Well, let's get the ices."

They walked to a cart where a man was selling fruit juices and ice cones. Each girl got a cone. When they turned back, Anna saw him right away, coming toward them, accompanied by a companion. She was sure he was coming to talk to them.

Anna was painting her fingernails when her mother entered the room. The older woman looked tired. Her age was hard to assess accurately except that she lacked any sparkle of youthfulness, and her skin was wrinkled and heavy. She had worked hard all her life, Anna thought, and it made her look older. Anna didn't want to be like that when she got to be her mother's age. The only way out was to have money and servants, and the best way to get those was to marry someone with money. And that was where Guillermo came in, she thought. He was the best-off guy she had ever dated, and he seemed genuinely interested even if he still saw several other girls. But what else could you expect, she thought, he was a Latin.

Her mother asked, "Where are you going tonight, Anna?"

"I think we'll go to a dance hall. Guillermo likes to dance." Her mother sat on the edge of the bed and watched Anna intently. Anna was sure her mother had something she was nervous about saying, probably about Guillermo.

And so it was. After the two of them sat quietly for a bit, Anna finishing one hand and beginning on the other, she broke the silence. "Did you want to talk about something, Mama?"

That was enough to get the older woman to begin. "You know, Anna, I want the best for you and my other children, and since your father isn't here, I have to take his place in a lot of things. Of course, your brother does everything he can and he's a good boy, but there are some things only a parent can do."

Quite a beginning, Anna thought. But that was like her mother. Anyway, Anna would wait her out, though by then she could almost figure out what it was going to be about. Anna nodded and her mother continued. "I know you think I'm kind of old fashioned in things like going with boys. But a lot of girls feel that way about their mothers nowadays. And I know the world has changed a lot from what it was when I was young but I don't think it's all been for the good. There are a lot of old-fashioned ways that were better, I think."

Anna was getting a little impatient. She had to leave in another twenty or thirty minutes to meet Guillermo, and this might go on for an hour. Guillermo didn't like to be kept waiting. Anna said, "Sure, Mama, I know a lot of older ways are alright. I never said they weren't. But what's that got to do with me? I do whatever seems right, whether it's old or new. And a lot of things have changed. You can't expect a modern girl to do things the way they did when you were young. Like only going out with a chaperon."

Her mother sighed, which made her look older. "No, I know girls don't do things like that any more. And I don't know that it's an improvement. But that's the way it is now."

Anna was finished with her fingernails by then, so she began to paint her toenails, which she had already filed. That way she could keep busy and not look directly at her mother. She said, somewhat shortly, "But Mama, what is it you want to tell me? Is there something wrong with what I'm doing?"

Her mother, "Nothing exactly, though I wish you'd bring the young man here more often."

Anna knew her mother was referring to Guillermo because she had not been seeing anyone else for almost five months. She said, "I did bring him to be introduced once, you know that."

"Yes, but he didn't stay very long, and you've not even brought him once to have dinner with us. You know, even if things have changed some, the family ought to get to know the fiancé."

Anna spoke quickly, "I never said Guillermo was my fiancé."

"But Anna, you've been going with him for almost five months now, and when a girl goes that much with one young man, most people think they're engaged."

"That's just an old-fashioned idea. Nowadays a girl can go with a boy as long as she wants. Besides, whose business is it, anyway?" Anna didn't mention that she had been trying to figure out how she could get

Guillermo to propose, but so far without any luck. She had held off sleeping with him so far, but it seemed unlikely that she would be able to do so much longer.

Her mother answered, "One thing that doesn't change, Anna, is that people do talk, both neighbors and relatives. Because, you know, they think of a family as being together. And when a girl marries someone, she brings another family into the situation."

"Why, the girl has to live with the guy, not the guy's family." Anna knew that in the old days newly married couples used to stay with one of their families, at least for a while, but in modern times most couples went off to their own house right after getting married, if they could afford it.

She used the last of the polish and still had two nails unfinished. "Oh darn, I just knew that would happen. I tried to stretch it out too. I'd use some of Lupe's but she uses a different shade."

Her mother said tiredly, "Anna, it isn't that I don't like your young man. I know he comes from a very good family. But you know some young men nowadays aren't serious. They just want to have their way with young women, even without getting married. And I think that's wrong, even if times have changed."

Anna studied the two unpainted nails, then muttered, "Luckily, I'll be wearing hose tonight and my nails won't show. I can get more polish tomorrow." She turned to her mother and said somewhat shortly, "Oh Mama, I know all that. And I want to get married too. But it isn't so easy as it used to be. Guys expect a lot more. And they don't want to get married right away all the time."

She thought about it herself and decided she didn't blame them too much; they had it pretty good without being married. Unless they wanted to have children, and Guillermo had made no indications that he did.

Her mother started to get up. "I know it's near time for you to leave and I don't want to make you late. I have a lot of sewing to do also. But just remember that it isn't good to go too long with a young man, because there's a lot of pressure to give in. And no matter what you think, people will talk. And it hurts the family reputation."

"Okay, Mama." Anna watched her tired mother leave the room, knowing she would go downstairs to work at the sewing machine for two or three hours. The girl opened the wardrobe and took out her tan pantsuit and a frilly white blouse.

She and Guillermo were in the middle of the disco's dance floor dancing the hustle, surrounded by other dancers. The light was dim, with multicolored moving shafts from the central rotating lamp. The light beams would move across the floor and walls and moving bodies, creating a sensation of even more movement. The whole room was in motion to the rhythm of the music. Anna kept her body moving to the same rhythm, in and out, facing Guillermo mostly, but sometimes turning away and coming back, constantly keeping her feet and body in syncopation with the music. She knew she had a good sense of rhythm and was a good dancer. She also knew she had a good body that attracted men's eyes. She watched Guillermo at the same time and was impressed by his body and rhythm also. He was lean and wiry and a good-looking Latin. Any local girl would be proud to get him for a husband and certainly a working girl like her.

The music stopped. He said, "Let's go to the bar and have a drink."

She took his hand and followed. There were a few other couples sitting, drinks in front of them. Small dishes of peanuts were on the bar also. She and Guillermo sat down. He lit up a cigarette, the smoke drifting upward just below the ceiling. He ordered drinks for both. She spoke first. "It's a nice place, a good size. Leonardo's is okay but it's too big. This is just the right size. And I think the music is better."

Guillermo didn't answer, continuing to smoke while sipping and swirling his scotch and soda. She said, "I'm glad we came here for a change. It's nice to get outside of San José sometimes."

He looked at her but did not speak. She studied him. He had been getting into these moods lately, and she was a little worried. After a bit she asked, "Is anything wrong, Guillermo?"

Without turning toward her he said, "No, not particularly."

"You look moody. Are you having a good time?"

"Sure, you know I like to dance." He answered a little shortly, "I'm alright."

They finished their drinks mostly in silence. He tapped his glass on the bar top absently. She said, "You want to go dance again ?"

"No, I think I've had enough. And it's getting late. Don't you have to work tomorrow?"

The reminder wasn't pleasant. Anna could visualize the crowded space in the back room where she worked with two other girls, making dresses and suits from measurements taken by Mrs. Hernandez. It wasn't that she didn't like sewing, but the conditions and pay were so poor. If she could have a shop of her own with her own girls working, it would be better. She, "Yes, it seems she has work almost every Saturday now. She has a lot of people who keep coming back to her, but she could get another girl. I get tired of working six days, even if I do get a little more money."

The bartender approached, a wiping cloth in hand. "How about another?"

Guillermo turned toward Anna. "I don't think I want anymore. How about you?"

She knew he didn't want her to have any more either. And she was pleased that he didn't drink as much as most men. But she also knew that meant he was ready to leave. She could have stayed longer, particularly since she knew that once they got home, it would be to bed for a short sleep, then up early to get to Mrs. Hernandez's house for a day of constant sewing. "No, I've had enough also."

Guillermo told the bartender, and they stood up to leave. Outside, he opened the car door, which pleased her. Many guys didn't do that any more, at least after a couple of dates.

They drove away in silence. The Casbah was located on a back road in Monteverde, and there were a couple of lookout places on the way down. Guillermo pulled off at one that looked out at the lights of San José. The glittering points in the distant valley and the moving beams of car headlights on the mountain road below made a spectacular sight.

He put the lights of the car out and his arm around her. She turned toward him, and they kissed. They usually did this before he took her home. This time he quickly moved his hand to her breast, over her blouse. She let it there, even though she didn't like the idea of getting her blouse wrinkled and soiled. But he didn't stay there long. While kissing her hard, he began to unbutton the top. She put her hands up to cover his fingers, gently pushing them away. But he kept at it, pushing against her. Finally she pulled back from the kiss. He had gotten the first button free and started with more determination on the next. She said, "Guillermo, what are you doing?"

"What's it look like? I'm opening your blouse."

She felt a little better to be talking about it, rather than pushing his hands away. "I don't think you should, Guillermo. You know what that leads to."

Then in a colder tone than usual, "Sure I do. That's where I want it to lead." He stopped. "In fact, I think it's time for us to make it."

Although she knew what he meant, she acted as if she didn't, "Make what?"

"You know what I mean. It's time for us to sleep together. We've been going together now for five months and that's a long time for a guy."

She felt there was something almost inevitable about the conversation, and even the outcome, but even so she felt she ought to resist, and the best way to do that was to keep talking. Guillermo had stopped fumbling with her buttons. He looked at her with glittering eyes, a little angry. "Look Anna, I like you and we've had some good times, but you must know a guy can't keep going with a girl as sexy as you all this time without wanting to sleep with her. And I've been patient, but there's a limit. I think instead of this we ought to sleep together." Pause. "And we don't have to do it here. I know a very good hotel not too far from here."

Anna knew they would get to this, and she just hadn't known how to avoid it. But still she tried. "Guillermo, I just couldn't go to one of those places at Los Piños."

She had heard from other girls about the rooms built in rows of hundreds at Los Piños, a suburb where call girls, street walkers, and loose girls brought men, and where rooms could be rented by the hour. "Hot sheet palaces" they were called.

Guillermo very quickly corrected that idea. "I wasn't thinking of Los Piños. I don't go to places like that." He said it a little angrily, as if his reputation was at issue. "No, I know a good small hotel on the edge of San José. I know the proprietor, in fact."

All of a sudden she had pictures of him taking a steady procession of girls to the small hotel. But she couldn't deny the validity of the explanation. So she tried another tack. "I know it may sound a little old fashioned to you, Guillermo. But I think a girl's virginity is important. I think she should save it for her marriage."

He looked at her with an expression which seemed part unbelief and part disgust. She couldn't be sure if it was natural or simply part of his technique. He snorted, "Well, I don't. That's an idea that has certainly gone out of style." He seemed to lose interest or at least acted so. He got out a cigarette and lit up.

She thought of buttoning her blouse again but knew she was wavering. Then he said, "I never ruled out the idea of getting married."

She answered softly, "Alright, Guillermo, I'll go with you."

* * * * *

Anna and Guillermo had a church wedding, and both sets of relatives came in considerable numbers. Anna's mother was particularly happy. His father helped Guillermo get a new house in the suburbs, and Anna quit work to become a full-time housewife.

It was pleasant to have so much space and to be able to decorate without considering the cost of everything. A boy was born, which pleased both of them. Lupe got married also. Several years passed. Anna learned to drive, and Guillermo gave her his old car when he got a new one.

\* \* \* \* \*

Anna was walking down Avenida Central, observing the scene as though she had not seen it before. It seemed as though San José was growing much faster than before. When she had been little, the city had seemed the same every time her mother brought her downtown on the bus. Now there seemed to be new construction and buildings everywhere.

In the old days, she and her mother would meet people they knew on the main streets. Now, as she surveyed the crowds moving back and forth, she recognized no one. They had all become strangers.

She went into the lobby of the Hotel Europa. Lupe was nowhere in sight. Anna continued into the combination bar and tea room. The Hotel Europa was in the medium price range, certainly not as fancy as the tourist hotels out near the airport, but not as seedy as those down near the central market where Nicaraguans and Panamanians stayed.

It was mid-afternoon, so there were not many people in the tea room, a young couple at one table, an older couple who looked like tourists, and a middle-aged, good-looking man alone. The latter was well dressed, in full suit and tie, probably a businessman, she thought. He looked at her with more than casual interest, and, without thinking about it, she exaggerated the swing of her hips a little. But she sat down on the opposite side of the room.

She ordered tea and looked out the window. This was not in the busiest section, but even so, there were a considerable number of pedestrians. It wasn't too long before Lupe came up the street.

Her sister looked better than before she was married, Anna realized. She dressed more fashionably and kept her hair, nails, and skin in much better condition. Marriage had been good for her, Anna thought, despite the problems she had endured.

Lupe sat down and ordered tea and cakes herself. "So how is the Manzanar family, Sister? How's Marco?"

"He's fine. He's with Mama. I dropped him off on the way. She always likes to keep him."

"And Guillermo?"

"The same. He seems to be very busy now, so I don't see him so much.

I didn't really imagine him to be such a hard worker, but his father's business is doing so well, they seem to need Guillermo a lot."

"Better that than to have him home all the time and be without enough money."

"How's Jesús? He gone a lot too?"

The waiter brought the tea and a dish of cakes. Lupe waited until he was gone. "Well, you know how it is, there's no change. He started about a year after we were married, and he's never quit. We certainly don't talk about it, but I know what he does. He finds someone he likes and meets with her two or three days a week for a month or so. Then when the attraction wears off, he drops her. Then in another month or so, he meets someone else and goes through the same thing again. He's no different from most other Latin men, you know. They have to prove their *machismo*."

Anna, "But how can you stand it, knowing he's out with another woman?"

Lupe smiled, Anna thought condescendingly, as if she, her younger sister, just didn't understand things well. "What do you expect me to do? He's a good husband. He keeps the family going, and he's good to the kids. He really doesn't waste his money, even on the girls he sees. And he doesn't drink too much and never beats me. In fact, you know I couldn't have afforded the clothes I'm wearing now if I had been single. Why, he even does his husbandly duty with me fairly often, when he's not too tired. That's part of the *machismo* pattern too, to prove that he can take care of several women at once."

Anna stared at Lupe. She and the other girls had all talked about this problem when they were growing up, and most had decided they wouldn't stand for it if their husbands started going out. After all, they had learned that Robert Redford and Burt Reynolds didn't do that when they fell in love. Of course, they weren't Latins, Anna remembered the conversations going, and Latin men were more hot blooded. But the girls had decided they would just as soon have a North American, especially if he was like Robert Redford or Burt Reynolds.

Lupe interrupted Anna's thoughts, "You act like you wouldn't accept it. What if Guillermo went out with someone else; what would you do?"

Anna wasn't sure, even though she had thought about it a lot lately, especially since Guillermo seemed to be away from home a lot more than before. But the question sparked an immediate answer, so she solved her dilemma on the spot. She snapped, "I just wouldn't stand for it."

"But what could you do? There's no law against it."

"Oh yes there is—the marriage vow. That's a law, and it says, 'Thou shalt not commit adultery.'"

Lupe laughed out loud at that. "Anna, I just can't believe you. We've had that vow through the whole history of Spain and Costa Rica, ever since we've been Catholics. And as far as I know, it never kept any Spanish men or other Latins from going out on their wives. Why, even the priests have had their girlfriends in the past, and as far as I know, many of them still do."

Anna knew all that was true but she still couldn't bring herself to accept it. She just hoped she'd never have to face the need to make a decision on that issue.

"What are you going to do now?" Lupe asked, seemingly wanting to change the subject.

"I have some shopping to do, then I'll go home and supervise preparation of dinner. That girl we have now is alright for getting things ready, but she can't cook. You know, she's just a village girl. And Guillermo wants me to fix the meals. He's quite old fashioned that way." She laughed, "When I think back on it, I realize how wrong I was about him before we were married. I thought he was the most modern guy I had met, and it turns out he's really old fashioned in a lot of ways."

Lupe got up then. "I've got to go too, to be home before the kids get there. And I have to pick up a case of Coke from the bottling company on the way home. I've already been to the market."

Anna was sitting in the easy chair in the living room, her mother and brother on the couch across from her. Jaime was smoking a cigarette. Anna said, "I have to do it, Mama; I can't live with a man who is seeing another woman. How would you feel if Papa had done that?"

Her mother answered tiredly, "I wouldn't have liked it, but I don't think many women did. But still most of them wouldn't have gotten divorced. One didn't do that when I was young. That's just become popular since you've grown up. It's a foreign idea, from the American movies and magazines. Why, they say almost all Americans divorce three or four times. Now the Costa Ricans, in trying to copy everything Yankee, are even copying that. There was a time when the family and marriage were considered sacred. I just don't understand how you can think about doing that so fast."

Anna was holding one hand over the other, the thumb of the inner one tucked between the first and second finger. She often did that when she was nervous. She said, "I don't know if it's modern or not, but I do know that it's not just the man that can go out and see other women whenever he wants while the woman is supposed to stay home with the children."

Jaime stubbed out his cigarette and spoke a little angrily. He was darker-skinned than Anna and had a thick black mustache. He said tersely, "Anna, you know more is expected of women than of men. Women are supposed to uphold the honor and morality of the family. Whether it's good or bad, men are not expected to stay so steadfast. And as you also know, many of them don't."

As she spoke, the feeling of anger and resentment grew. She had heard all that before. But to think of it coming from her own brother. It was alright for him to talk to his friends that way, but he didn't need to tell her that. She answered softly, "I just can't believe that any more, Jaime. That may have been the way it was before, but women have rights now too. We have an equal vote, don't we? Why can't we have equal rights in marriage?"

Jaime's eyes flashed. "Don't ask me; I didn't make the customs. But you know as well as I do that men and women are not equal in all ways. It's only in the United States that women demand to be treated equally in everything. But they don't respect their women either. And you know we Latins treat our women differently, but we also respect them."

"Ha! You call that respect? Going out on your wife whenever you feel like it and never permitting her the same right?"

"Well, in a way even that's a kind of respect. You know that when Latin married men go out with someone else, they're quite secret about it. And they take care of the family whatever they do."

"I just don't care about the 'Latin way' any more. What's fair for one is fair for the other."

They sat silently for a while, seemingly having exhausted that general topic without any resolution. Then Anna's mother spoke: "Anna, you have to think of the good things. Guillermo has been a good husband, supporting you and Marco very well, and he doesn't drink too much and he doesn't beat you. I think you should be grateful for the good things. So what if he does have one weakness? As Jaime says, many Latin men have that. And you also have to think about the family. Even if times have changed, we Costa Ricans and other Latins do consider the family important. You have to think of Marco. He needs a home and family." Pause. "Perhaps that's one of the problems. Perhaps you should have more children."

"Oh no, I'm glad we didn't have more. And besides, I'm not thinking about the family all the time; I'm thinking about me. What about Anna? Doesn't anyone ever consider her?"

"Now, Anna, you're exaggerating. Sure we think about you. In fact, we're thinking about you now more than anyone else. Why would we get together here to help you? Even Lupe would have been here if she could. But she has problems of her own with Jesús. You know as well as I that Jesús has been going out also. But Lupe has decided that she will stay with the family. And we think that's good for everybody. Of course Lupe would like it better if Jesús came home to her all the time. But that doesn't always happen. But we Latins don't break up a family because of that. Even to the wife, the breakup is usually worse than staying together."

They just kept saying the same things, Anna thought, emphasizing that the worst thing that could happen would be the breakup of the family. That may have been true in the old days, but it was no longer. Times had changed. A woman had rights as well as a man.

Jaime lit up another cigarette, exhaled, and spoke: "Even if you decided to get a divorce, how could you? It takes some money, and do you have any? And what would you do afterward? Guillermo is supporting you now."

"I know what you're thinking. But I thought about that too. I have a friend who got a divorce, and she knows a very good lawyer. He went to the university in the United States, and he's very good. She says I can get Guillermo to pay me alimony and child support for a long time, and I can keep the house too."

Her brother stood up. "Sister, I just can't believe you. You seem bound and determined to do what they do in North America, and you just refuse to listen to your own family. I can't see why you don't do like your sister. Don't you want to be a Latin?"

\* \* \* \* \*

It didn't work out as smoothly as Anna had expected. She couldn't get enough cash to pay the lawyer she had counted on and had to get another who had no impressive bag of dirty tricks. Guillermo, on the other hand, had the full support of his father and was able to get a most adroit legal game player. The upshot was that Anna got one of the cars, use of the house until it was sold, a small amount of alimony for a year, and permanent custody of the boy. It was clear that she could not support herself on that income, so she went back to work. After the marriage house was sold, she rented a small house and worked in women's clothing. After several years she was able to set herself up independently, hiring two girls to work in the back room of the house.

It didn't make her rich, but she got by comfortably. Marco grew and continued his schooling.

\* \* \* \* \*

The telephone rang just as she was putting the finishing touches to her makeup. It was Lupe. "Hi, Sis, what are you doing?"

Lupe and her mother usually called at least once each day. Generally the conversations were about themselves, family members, or neighbors. Anna said, "I'm getting ready to go out, putting the final touches to my makeup."

"It's kind of early for a date, isn't it?"

"Yes, I guess so. But it's not exactly a date. I'm just going to meet a fellow." Pause. "He's a North American."

There was silence at the other end, then Lupe said, "Well, that's different. What's the matter, Costa Ricans not good enough for you any more?"

"Oh Lupe, we're not going through that again, are we? You know I've been getting more and more tired of all these macho guys who can think of only one thing. And it's much worse when they know you're divorced. They seem to figure that you'll give in to them right away. All they have to do is take you out to a dinner and dance."

Her sister sounded tired when she answered, reminding Anna of her mother. "I guessed as much. You only go out with each one a couple of times. So who's this North American?"

Anna hadn't really intended to tell anyone right away, but if there was anyone she could trust, it was her sister. She said, "I want you to promise you won't tell anyone, at least not now, and especially not Mama or Jaime. It's my business anyway, but they'd be telling me what to do the minute they heard about it."

"Whatever you say, Sis."

Anna could hear the interest in her sister's voice. Just then Marta came to the door and spoke through the drape that served as a doorway between Anna's room and the workshop. She spoke in a whiny voice, "Señora, I've finished the skirt and it's almost 6:30. There's no one else in the shop. Can I go home?"

Anna spoke to Lupe first, "Just a minute, Sis, can you hold a second while I close the shop?"

"Sure."

Anna went out and locked the door after the girl, saying, "Come in tomorrow at seven sharp. We've got a lot of sewing to do."

"Yes, Señora." She made a kind of curtsy like girls from the country to people of higher status. She was lucky to have the job, Anna thought, learning a skill that she could use all her life, and without even having finished high school.

Anna came back and picked up the phone again. Lupe said, "You're working late."

Anna laughed, "Sis, you don't know how it is with us working girls, always early and late. That's the way when you make your own living. And all you have to do is fix the meals and keep the house for Jesús and the kids."

Lupe didn't respond, and Anna was glad. She remembered that Lupe had tried hard to get her to stop divorce proceedings. Instead Lupe said, "Tell me all about this big meeting. I'm interested."

"Well, you know how we used to read the personal ads in the papers and especially those from North Americans. I finally answered one and he called me, and I'm going to the Hotel Central to meet him when I'm finished talking to you."

"You didn't!" Lupe. "How do you know anything about him? You haven't even seen him."

"I know some things. He did have a listing in *El Tiempo,* and he told me other things on the phone."

"In Spanish?"

"Yes, his Spanish isn't too bad. He said he studied it in college and has been to Mexico and other Latin American countries several times. He keeps saying, 'Do you understand? Do you understand?' Actually I understand most of what he says."

"Tell me about him. What did his listing say? I do remember the ones we used to read when we were schoolgirls, when we all thought we would marry a rich, handsome foreigner. Do you have his listing?"

"As a matter of fact I do. I saved it because I thought you might be interested. Wait a minute and I'll get it."

She put the phone down and went to the table she used for keeping accounts and writing letters. The ad from *El Tiempo* was at one side where she had used it for writing to him.

She took it back to the phone. "It says, 'North American professor/ writer, tall, thin, desires relationship with a Tica (Costa Rican female), 25–45 years, who is slim and attractive. Please write, including a photo, to Dr. Martin Neumann at P.O. Box 730, 5210 Volcan. All letters will be answered.' That's all. What do you think about that?"

There was a pause, evidently while Lupe considered the information. When she did not answer right away, Anna broke in, "Well, what do you think, Sis? Imagine a professor and writer."

That seemed to get Lupe going. "It does sound interesting, but there's a lot of things he doesn't tell you. Why, you don't even know that he's not married."

"He did tell me more. He's from Los Angeles, where he teaches at the state university, and now he's here writing a novel. He lives at the inn of his friend, another North American, at Volcan."

Lupe digested that and responded without need for further prodding. "But still you don't even know what he looks like." Pause. "Nor his age. I would guess he's not a real young guy, being a professor. But he might be a real old man."

Although she had thought of the same things, Anna got a little irritated hearing it from her sister. After all, her sister didn't have to worry about finding a man. Anna said somewhat shortly, "That's why I'm going to meet him at the hotel. If he's as bad as you paint him, I don't have to see him again."

Lupe answered defensively, "Don't get mad, Sis. I didn't mean anything. He might be a marvellous fellow. And then he is a foreigner. I hope he turns out fine."

Anna looked at her watch. She just had time to fix something for Marco and leave for the hotel. She said, "Okay, no harm done. But I've got to be going or I'll be late. And though I shouldn't think it would be hard to recognize him, I should be there on time."

"Let me know how it turns out."

"Okay, but one last time, do not tell Mama or Jaime yet. You know how they are. They'd be telling me exactly what to do."

"Okay."

Anna knew she still looked very good as she walked from the parking lot to the hotel. She was wearing very high-heeled shoes and a tight-fitting sheath that showed off her ample breasts, well-built hips, and narrow waist. Her smooth olive skin and long dark hair were good too, very Latin in a Spanish way. She was sure she could have fitted into the Spanish upper class if her ancestors had stayed in Spain. Men looked at her as she tapped along the sidewalk, and more than a few spoke. And even discounting the Costa Rican male's natural tendency to flirt with every passable female, she knew she was attractive. But she paid no heed, keeping her eyes straight ahead and her walk fast. She was already about ten minutes late.

There were quite a few people in the tea room as she passed, heading to the lobby where there were several couples as well as a single woman and a couple of single men. She looked the latter over carefully, but quickly decided they couldn't be the professor. They were too dark and not tall enough, undoubtedly Costa Ricans.

She stood for a moment, surveying all corners of the room when a bellboy approached. "Can I do anything for you, Señorita?"

That pleased her, to be referred to as "Miss" when she was thirty-two and had a ten-year-old son. She answered, "No, I'm meeting someone."

The bellboy started to go away when she asked, "You haven't by any chance seen a tall North American with gray hair, have you?"

That was one physical characteristic he had told her on the phone and that she had deliberately failed to mention to Lupe.

The bellboy, "What was he wearing?"

"A brown corduroy jacket and brown pants."

The bellboy, "There was a man who went through here looking like that a few minutes ago. I think he went toward the bar."

"Thanks." Anna walked down the stairs. There were only a few people in the bar. It was too early for it to be busy, she knew. She decided that none of them was the guy. And when the bartender came to her to take her order, she said, "No thanks," and went back upstairs.

Just as she got upstairs, he came through the lobby. She was sure as soon as she saw him. He was tall and wearing the clothes he had described on the phone. His hair was certainly gray, almost white, and though he looked at least as old as her uncle, Pablo, he walked in a youngish way. He looked at her and she looked at him. At almost the same time they seemed to recognize one another. He approached her, "Hello, my name is Martin Neumann. Are you Anna Velasquez?"

The Spanish wasn't bad. She smiled and fluttered her eyelids once. "Yes, I'm glad to know you, Professor."

He offered his hand. "You don't need to call me 'professor.' I'm just Martin or Martin Neumann, if that makes you more comfortable."

She shook his hand. "Alright, Martin." She laughed.

"I'm sorry I missed you when you came. I had gone back outside, looking. I thought you might have been waiting somewhere else."

"It's alright. I haven't been here long."

He had some signs of age, creases in his forehead and cheeks, wrinkles at the corners of his eyes, and some loose skin on his neck, but he certainly did not look ancient. It was hard for Anna to guess the age of North Americans, but she felt he was probably in his early or middle fifties. That was alright, she thought. She wasn't looking for a handsome youth. She had had that in Guillermo and in many other young Costa Ricans she had gone with since the divorce. And they just didn't add up in the end. You knew they were simply trying to sleep with you as soon as possible, but always with their eyes out for someone else, and particularly after you let them. No, she needed someone she could count on, someone constant, and someone who had something else on his mind besides sleeping with a woman.

He asked, "Would you like to sit down, perhaps in the bar for a drink or in the tea shop?"

"I think I'd rather go to the tea shop. You can get a beer there."

He let her go first, but he didn't pull her chair out. A Latin guy probably would have pulled it out, but that didn't matter to her then. She knew that foreign men, and particularly North-Americans, did not have such fancy manners.

He ordered beer, and she had a pot of tea. She let him do the talking. Most guys she had been with didn't really want to hear a woman talk much. He said the usual things to keep a conversation going. "You live far from here?"

"About five kilometers."

"Drive your own car?"

"Yes."

"Do you work?"

"Yes, I have a dressmaking shop." She figured she would add a little information, just to speed up the process.

She knew that men would most likely respond to questions if they were about themselves, so she said, "You said you were a professor of anthropology. That must be interesting. I suppose you go on excavations, don't you?"

"No, I'm not that kind of anthropologist. I'm in ethnology. That's the study of living peoples."

She couldn't be sure that wasn't a rebuke. But how could she have known that much about anthropology? She had always thought they were the people who excavated Indian villages and tombs.

She tried another tack. "You said you were a writer. You write books about anthropology?"

"No, as a matter of fact, I write novels. I used to write books and articles in anthropology, but lately I've switched to fiction."

She waited a moment for him to explain further, but he showed no such inclination. Instead he switched to more expectable grounds and where she was more comfortable, personal relations.

"I suppose you're divorced?" he asked.

"Yes, eight years ago."

"Me too, though more recently, just a year."

"Do you have children?"

"Yes, one. But he's grown up now. In fact, he has a wife of his own." Then, with evident pride, "He's an anthropologist too."

She nodded and smiled. While he took occasional swallows of his beer, she sipped her tea. They sat wordlessly for a while, then she asked, "And how do you like Costa Rica?"

"Very well. I've been here before, though. This country is neat and orderly compared with other Latin countries. I guess that's why they call it the Switzerland of Latin America, do you think?"

"Perhaps. I haven't traveled so much as you, only to Nicaragua, and I agree that Costa Rica is neater than there." Pause. "And how do you like the Ticas, the Costa Rican ladies? I've heard that foreigners think they are very attractive. Do you think so?"

"Yes, they're pretty. I don't know if their basic looks are any better, but I think they dress and fix themselves up better than other Latins."

He had another beer while she finished her tea. By then she was feeling comfortable enough. She had even learned to talk a little slower and to keep from using any slang. She had also decided he would be okay to go out with, at least once. She waited for him. Finally he made his opening. "I guess it's probably time to go. I suppose you have a lot to do at home. Maybe your son expects you?"

"No, but I do have a meeting with my sister. She and I help in altar preparations once a week. I'm Catholic, you know."

Without any evident pleasure, he said, "I would have guessed it. Most people here are."

She knew that many North Americans were atheists, and those that did go to church were mostly Protestants. "I suppose you don't go to church, do you?"

He chuckled. "No, I'm afraid not. As you may know, many North Americans, and particularly academic types, are not very religious. And I would suppose those in the social sciences, like anthropology and sociology, are least religious of all."

She nodded. "That's alright. We Costa Ricans have heard a lot about that."

As if to prove that they had something in common in that regard, he added, "I was raised a Catholic, though."

He called the waitress to pay the bill. While they were waiting for the change, he said, "So would you like to go out with me sometime?"

She had long learned that you had to answer that question quickly, whether in the affirmative or the negative. If you didn't want to see a guy again but weren't positive enough quickly enough, some would try to wheedle or pressure you. And if you did want to go out with a guy but were not positive enough quickly enough, some would get the idea you weren't sure, and if they were timid types, though that was rare enough among Costa Ricans, they might back out. So you learned to make up your mind well in advance. And though this guy had some limitations, particularly his age, there were good points too such as his position in the United States, both status and financial. He could make travel possible, both to the United States and elsewhere. She answered with a smile, "Yes, I'd like to."

She had thought of touching the top of his hand with hers or saying she'd "very much" like to go out with him, but decided that might be going too far. It might give him a wrong idea or even scare him off. After all, she had never gone out with a North American before.

They were driving the circuitous mountain road toward Puerto Pacifico. He handled the Datsun well enough. He asked, "You come to the beach often?"

"Fairly often, though now with the price of gasoline, I don't come as much as I'd like. Also, my work requires a lot of my time."

"How is the beach at Pacifico? Is it clear?"

"It's not the best. The best ones are up north, but they take too much time for one day from San José. But I know a good place where they have cabins about four kilometers from town."

He, "I like to swim in the ocean, and particularly in the tropics. It's too cold for me in California."

As they started the descent toward sea level, it began getting warmer and more humid. She looked at him in sideways glances, deciding he was really pretty good looking despite his age. He was not at all heavy and undoubtedly the tallest man she had ever gone out with. And he had done well enough at the disco, not with the steps and agility of Guillermo, but still he kept right with it. Another thought occurred to her, that he was probably the oldest dancer on the floor the night they had gone out. She didn't really get the idea of what his intentions were when he held her as close as he did in the slow dances. She was used to that, because most of the guys she had dated the last few years tried to fold your body into theirs in slow dancing. But she didn't mind too much to be pressed tight so long as they kept moving. After all, in that position it was pretty hard for them to feel you up.

She and the North American had stayed until nearly midnight, he seeming to enjoy the dancing. So she was a little surprised while they were sitting one out at a table and he had suggested they leave. Most guys she knew would have stayed until one or two, at least. Maybe it was his age, she had thought. Anyway, she had answered, "Sure, if you'd like to. I guess you're tired, eh?"

"No, it's not that. I've just had enough."

"We can just sit awhile if you like and listen to the music," she had said. "We could order another half pint." It was one of those places where you ordered scotch or rum by the bottle, along with the mixers. He had not known about that custom.

But he had said, "No, I don't think so. But I have another idea. Why don't we go to the inn where I'm staying? There's a small bar there. Probably no one is in there now. The bartender leaves at about eleven if there aren't any customers. But I could fix drinks for us. And there's a good stereo system."

She still hadn't figured what his intentions were. After all, he had been most polite all evening, and she didn't think the close dancing was that important. But she had a built-in feeling regarding what a guy was after usually. She said, "I don't know. Maybe I ought to be getting home."

Then she had realized she had made a tactical error. She hadn't been definite enough from the beginning. He said, "But tomorrow is Sunday. You don't work then, do you?"

He had heard enough about her schedule by then that she had to agree. But he also knew that she went to church on Sunday. So she said the obvious, "No, but I have to go to church."

He said, "Okay, but I remember enough from my churchgoing days to know that there are several masses each Sunday morning. You could go to a late one." Pause, and with forced normality, "What I'm saying is, why don't you stay with me at the inn tonight? You'd have plenty of time to get to the late Mass."

Then it was out; he wanted to sleep with her too, and on the first real date. She knew she had to quash that idea fast and positively. Her indefiniteness had been what had given him the encouragement. She said,

"No, I have to be at the early Mass, with my mother and sister. Tomorrow is a special feast day, and the early Mass is the most important." That was not true, but she figured he didn't know enough about Costa Rican customs to deny it, and besides it was no more than a white lie. Otherwise, she'd have to tell him she just wasn't ready to sleep with him, and that would probably bother him more.

He looked at her questioningly but let the matter drop, waiting a bit, then resigning, "Okay, I'll take you home."

She was pleased that he didn't wheedle or beg because she had made up her mind by then, and she wasn't ready to quit seeing him. And so on the way home they had arranged to go to the beach the following Sunday. When the day arrived, there they were, coming down out of the mountain coolness onto the sultry plain of the coast. She reached for her purse and took out a cigarette. Before she lit up, she said, "Don't you ever smoke?"

"No. I did for a long time, but I gave it up several years ago. Now I don't miss it at all."

"You don't mind if I smoke, do you?"

"No."

She opened the window wide to be sure the smoke would be carried out. She was not sure how he really felt about her smoking.

The countryside changed. Gone were the green hills of pasture, corn fields, and coffee plantations. Instead the land was flat, cultivated in rice and sugar cane, and with palms instead of leafy green trees marking roads and villages. She watched the change briefly, then turned toward him. "I would imagine you got a lot of replies to your newspaper ad, didn't you?"

Without turning, he answered, "Yeah, quite a few. Somewhere between eighty and a hundred."

She knocked the tip of her cigarette into the ashtray so the ashes wouldn't get into someone's eyes. "A lot of Ticas would like to meet a North American professor and writer, I'm sure. I'm even surprised there weren't more." Pause. "Whatever made you think of it? I've often wondered why foreign men do that. You know we Costa Rican girls learn about the advertisements when we're still in high school."

He looked at her then with a grin. "Well, it's a long story, like a lot of things when you've lived as long as I have. I think I told you my field of anthropology was the study of living peoples. I started in India many years ago. You know where that is, don't you?"

His pronunciation of the country was not very clear, and besides she hadn't been great in her geography studies. But she was not about to admit any deficiency then. It might be beneficial to admit ignorance of a lot of things to a Latin male, but she had the feeling it wouldn't work with a North American, and particularly a professor. She said, "Sure," though she was not quite sure whether he meant the islands or the place where they worshipped cows.

"While I was there doing another study, I read the local newspapers for general interest. And also there wasn't that much to read. I became fascinated with the marriage ads. It turned out that a lot of middle-class Indians used the personal classifieds for finding husbands and wives. The ads were quite fascinating, because they gave a lot of detail about what they wanted in a mate and what they had to offer. For instance, the families of the girls would state how much dowry they would pay, and the families of the boys would tell how much education they had and how good a position they had in government or business."

"You say 'the families.' Did the families do it all the time?"

"Oh sure, in India all marriages are arranged by the elders. They don't believe in letting the young people do something so important, or even in letting them go out together before marriage."

Anna, "Oh, it must have been a little like that in the old days in Costa Rica. I think they used to have go-betweens or people who would help to find a proper spouse for your son or daughter. And they never let young people go out together without chaperons. Even my mother remembers that. But everything has changed now."

He remarked, "I wouldn't say everything. Costa Rica, and Latins generally, still seem to be more concerned with family affairs than North Americans. Anyway, in regard to the marriage advertisements, I collected several hundred from the newspapers and brought them back to the U.S. And, to make a long story short, I analyzed them and wrote an article." Pause, chuckle. "We have a system in the U.S. for academics called 'publish or perish.' A young professor has to publish so many words or he or she doesn't get any promotions. It was at that stage of my life that I was working hard to get ahead in the profession."

"That's very interesting," she. "You seem to have gone to a lot of places and done a lot of interesting things. Much more than me."

He smiled but did not respond to her comparison, saying instead, "One of my peculiar habits that I have learned through long years of teaching is not to get sidetracked. Once I get started on a story, I finish it. So, to finish this one. I did okay with the article, adding it to my bibliography and even getting a dozen or so requests for reprints. Then, years later, after my first divorce, I decided to join a dating service. In the U.S. people date of course, and though some of them get married, they don't have that in mind exclusively. Also, it is difficult to meet a lot of people in the city. In a way some of the same problems exist as among traditional people, like the Indians, except for different reasons. But it isn't any easier for someone in a Western city to meet a compatible person than it is for an educated Hindu with a lot of caste and other marital restrictions. So my membership in the dating club worked out sufficiently that through it I got married again. But then I got divorced again." Pause. "But that's another story. But when I came to Costa Rica, I found that people used the personal classifieds in somewhat the same way that we used dating clubs. So I tried it." He looked at Anna with a wry expression and said, "And what do you think of that?"

A funny guy, she thought, though different. But then what did she expect? Anyone who would use the personal classifieds couldn't be absolutely normal. Though that would include her too, she thought. She said, "I think it's interesting." Pause. "And what have you thought of it so far. How about all the girls you've met? You must have met some real knockouts."

"Actually I haven't met all that many. And those that I have met have been one time only. I wasn't interested in seeing them again. All, that is, except one woman who just wanted to be a friend. I did see her several times, but she finally decided she had to call me too often and if I didn't want to call her, she would stop seeing me. And though I didn't mind meeting her for tea and coffee, usually at my place, I wasn't interested enough to call her, so we stopped getting together."

"But I bet you met a lot of attractive young Ticas, didn't you?"

"Most weren't that attractive. Almost all were younger than me, most no older than their thirties, divorced, and had children.

Anna put the cigarette out in the ash tray. "Like me, eh?"

"Yes, and though Costa Ricans seem to be concerned with family affairs more than we North Americans, they are beginning to be more like us in respect to divorce." He looked a little thoughtful and perhaps a little sad when he said, "I guess they're about where we were a generation or so ago."

They had arrived at the edge of Puerto Pacifico, passing along the peninsula, which ran for five or six miles before it broadened into the port town. She said, "It's here that we can get a cabana."

"Where's the beach?"

"It's just beyond the cabanas. And it's best to get one before we get too close to town. The water is cleaner a little way out."

There were signs after signs with arrows pointing in to little sandy roads toward the palm-fringed beach area, interspersed with ramshackle eating places, dance halls, and little stores. The locals sat on broken-down verandas or walked along the roadside, carrying bags or packages, most in slow motion.

"Where shall we stop?" he asked.

"You can try any of them. They're almost all the same." He went to talk to people in the office of a couple and came back complaining about the price. She was a little surprised, since she figured he could easily afford the cost of a cabana for a day. Of course, they would only stay a few hours and would still have to pay for the whole time. Cabanas were not rented for part days. She thought of going with him since she was used to the system and they would know she knew the prices, but she decided it was a man's responsibility to make financial arrangements. Furthermore, she figured his Spanish was good enough for that.

He came back to the car at the third stop and said, "Okay, we'll take this one. We have to drive back to the end there." He pointed toward the end cabin in the direction of the beach.

As they were driving back, he complained, "The price is pretty high for just a few hours, but they were all the same. These people must have an agreement among themselves."

She chuckled, "Oh, they have a price for foreigners and another for local people."

He glanced at her in what seemed like a flash of resentment but said nothing. They arrived, and he opened the door with the key the manager had given him. They set their bags down inside and looked around. It was a small room with a double iron bed in the center, plus a couple of chairs, a chest of drawers, and an end table, all having been used extensively and maintained minimally. The toilet and shower were separated by a thin partition.

He set his bag down and sat on the edge of the bed, looking at her questioningly. She said quickly, "I'll go in and change first, then you can. Okay?"

He delayed but said finally, "Sure. I'll wait here."

She took her bag into the shower room and changed into her red bikini and halter. Going back into the washroom, she faced the mirror. Turning slowly, she admired her body. It was indeed well shaped; the breasts full, the waist narrow, the hips well filled out, and the legs well shaped also. Her face too was pretty with full, sensuous lips, naturally dark, which was appropriate for her olive skin. Her black hair glistened when she combed it. She would put it into a bathing cap when they went to the beach. The last thing she did was to put on the gold chain with the tiny heart around her hips. She pulled it around until the heart was loosely draped from her waist just halfway between her hip and navel.

She walked into the main room with her clothes and shoes in hand. He was lying on the bed, his head propped on the pillow which he had pulled to the end. He remained in the same position while she put her slacks and blouse on the bent hangers. When she turned around, he was watching her intently. She smiled and turned around once in a slow pirouette. "Well, how do I look?"

"You know, you're a very good-looking woman," he replied.

She smiled. "Well thank you, señor. That's a compliment, especially coming from the wise professor."

He grinned. "Now, now, we don't know the professor is so wise. After all, there are a lot of stupid ones."

She grimaced playfully. He continued to stare at her. Finally she started to get uncomfortable. "Don't you want to change now? The bathroom is yours."

He put out his hand. "No, not yet. I don't feel like it right this moment. Why don't you come over here?"

She studied him for a moment, extended on the bed. She could even see the bulge of his stiff penis. Still and all, she took a chance and went to sit on the edge. He put his arm around her and pulled her down on top of him, with strength but not forcefully. He lifted his head to meet hers and kissed her. She didn't pull back but kept her body stiff, returning the kiss ever so lightly. She knew what would happen if she responded, even halfway, and she didn't feel like it. Fortunately, he quickly got the message and didn't try a second kiss. Instead he leaned back and looked at her quizzically. "What's wrong?" he said finally.

She sat up. "Nothing. I just feel like going to the beach. Whenever I come this far, I just can't wait to get into the water."

He continued to stare at her, so she said, "I hope you don't mind. But that's the way I am when I come to the beach."

He looked at her again as if he would say something else but instead got up and went into the bathroom with his bag.

They walked a short way up the beach. There was a fair amount of debris on the dark sand. It wasn't a very attractive beach. Only a few people were scattered along the sand and even fewer in the water. He said, "It's not the cleanest beach in the world, is it?"

"No, it's because we're too close to the port. A lot of ships dump their oil and sewage into the water. It's necessary to go fifty or sixty miles north or south before you get to the very good beaches." She stopped. "Would you like to lay down here on the sand? There's not any people right near here, and most of the beach is the same."

He replied, "I guess so. Aren't you going into the water?"

"Maybe later. Just now I want to lay on the sand and feel the sun on my skin." She spread her beach towel on the sand and sat down to put skin lotion all over her body. "I burn very easily."

He watched her for a bit, then said, "Well, since we came all this way, I'm going to take a dip in the ocean. Sure you don't want to come along?"

"No thanks, you just go ahead. I'll be alright here."

He turned and headed into the water, diving shallowly after walking out twenty or so feet.

She stretched and soaked in the haze-filtered sunlight, pleasantly aware of the constant movement of the water.

He returned after a bit, water still dripping from his body. Stepping just over her, he let a few drips fall on her skin. She laughed. "You like to play around, don't you?"

He smiled. "I guess so." Pause. "I usually want to do something when I go somewhere new. And I suppose I'm usually trying to stay in shape."

She studied him. "You are in pretty good shape for a man your age." The moment she said it she was sorry, because it might offend him. Besides, she didn't really know his age.

"Thanks, but you do have to keep moving when you get to middle age."

Whether what he said provoked the idea, or he had it before, she didn't know, but she was a little surprised when he said, "How'd you like to take a run down the beach? I think that's what I'm going to do. Then maybe take another dip."

She laughed lightly. "You are energetic, aren't you? When I come to the beach, I come to relax. Besides, I probably couldn't keep up with you."

"Oh, that's alright, I don't mind slowing down. Or we could walk when we get tired running."

She waved her hand. "No, you go ahead. I'm too lazy. Maybe I'll go into the water with you when you get back."

He turned and began running across the sand.

"**D**id the professor ever call back?" It was Lupe on the phone. Anna was sitting at her work table, just having come in from the sewing room to answer the ring.

"No, the last I heard from him was when he dropped me off at home. He didn't say he'd call back, so I figured he wouldn't. I kind of had that feeling when we were coming back."

"What happened? You never told me."

"Nothing special. The trip to the beach was okay. He didn't seem so happy about getting a cabana. And then he wanted to go running and swimming as soon as we got there, and as you know, when I get to the beach, I just like to lay around. He kept looking at me funny all the time." She was too embarrassed to discuss the incident when he pulled her down on the bed.

"Afterward, we went to eat at a restaurant in town. It wasn't so great, but you know there's no first-class restaurants anywhere but in San José."

"None of that sounds so bad. Did you get in an argument or anything? I should think an older man, even if he was a professor from North America, would be pleased to be out with a good-looking, younger woman like you."

"Maybe, but you know they have different views on a lot of things. He is so impressed by how much concern we have for our families. 'So different from the North Americans,' he kept saying." Pause. "But then there we were, from two different countries, but both divorced. He's been divorced twice, in fact."

There was a pause on Lupe's end, then, "Too bad, Sis, I had hoped you'd find someone nice, but perhaps it's for the best. Maybe we're too different from them."

\* \* \* \* \*

**A**s time passed, the business did well enough that Anna was able to buy a bigger house. Marco grew up and got married, bringing his wife to live in Anna's house. Both she and Marco worked. Anna kept her figure, though despite the turtle oil and other skin creams, the wrinkles kept increasing, especially under her neck. She kept her graying hair black with rinses. Besides taking one trip to the United States and one to Mexico, she stayed in San José.

\* \* \* \* \*

**S**he was sitting parked on Second Street and Independence Avenue, smoking a cigarette, when Alfonso walked up the sidewalk, carrying a grocery bag. He was neatly and formally dressed, a typical well-to-do Costa Rican businessman. He was in pretty good physical condition except for the small pot, which was also typical of an upper-class Costa Rican male. His hair was mostly gray, though he still had all of it.

She reached over and opened the door. He put the groceries on the back seat, then got in himself. Leaning over, he gave her a peck on the cheek. She asked, "Did you get everything?"

"Sure, a pint of vodka and two Kentucky Fried Chicken Dinners." Kentucky Fried had come to San José at about the same time as the Pizza Hut and McDonald's Hamburgers. Anna could still remember how time consuming it had formerly been to get something to eat at traditional restaurants. The idea of carry-out food had been nonexistent. This was really convenient. Every Tuesday they would get such a dinner to take to Carola's Coffee House. That and a pint of vodka to use with the mixes that Carola sold were enough for the four to six hours they ordinarily stayed.

"How was it at the business this morning?" she asked in the same manner she had been starting the talks on their midday trips for as long as they had been seeing one another. How long had it been—seven years, eight?

His response usually varied according to how busy they had been. "It was normal. As a matter of fact, it was a little boring; there was so little to do." Pause. "I was happy to get away, that it was our Tuesday."

Their Tuesday, she laughed inwardly, how bizarre and in a way how predictable it had all become. She had known he was married when he called her after her visit to a woman in his office. He hadn't even tried to hide it. It would have been difficult if he had wanted to. What well-to-do, middle-aged Costa Rican male was not married? She had not been going with anyone for several months; in fact the number of men who asked her for dates had been decreasing steadily once she had reached her late thirties. Anyway, when he offered to take her to lunch, she had accepted, and they had a good meal at the Hotel Amsterdam. After that, it was lunch a couple of other times, and then he proposed that they take a room in the hotel where they were eating. They tried three or four others, and then, during a drive in the mountains just outside town, found Carola's Coffee House. They quickly learned that though Carola sold coffee and cake, her real business was renting rooms to couples.

Anna maneuvered the Toyota quite comfortably out of the traffic of central San José, past the central market, the hospital, stadium, and toward the hills of Colinas, where Carola's place was located. He said,

"How was your business last week?"

That was the second topic they usually talked about, after talk of his business. "It was okay, enough to keep me busy. You know it won't make me rich, but it's enough to keep me going. One thing that's been a big help has been the Toyota. My old car was really in bad shape. I could never rely on it."

He had just given it to her the year before, when she had laid it down in no uncertain terms: either he helped her out financially or she was going to quit seeing him. She had accepted from the beginning that he would stay married no matter what and that he would only be able to see her during mid-days when he was reporting to be on business. That was okay; men in his position kept mistresses, which did not affect their family lives much. Most wives knew, and certainly his did, that their husbands were seeing others on the side, and they accepted it as inevitable. Anna thought then what a bizarre turn of fate it had become, that she in her early years had divorced Guillermo for the same reason, and now in her middle years, she was living the role of the mistress. One thing particularly bothered her, which was that a man would support his wife and children totally while making little effort to help his mistress. Alfonso didn't even keep a room for her except on the day they stayed together. So she had told him that she just wasn't going to continue unless he helped out in some meaningful way. That was when he got the Toyota for her. It was a demonstration model that he got at a very good price through a colleague.

As they started to climb the hill toward Carola's place, she said, "Alfonso, why don't we go out somewhere for a change, say for a weekend? We might go to the San Carlos Islands or up to Luis Rey Park. We could stay at the inn there."

He looked uncomfortable. "You know I can't do that, especially not now. My wife knows I see you, and as long as I don't embarrass her, I'm sure she won't do anything about it. But if it looks more serious, she might take action."

Anna knew that he meant his wife might seek a divorce. She remembered what she had done. But she had been an opinionated young woman then who felt men and women should be treated the same. However, Alfonso's wife was different, more typical. She was older too; both of them were, Anna thought wryly. And though she would like to spend more time with Alfonso, she didn't feel like throwing the arrangement away. She, "I just thought I'd check it out."

He patted her knee. They turned up the last hill and pulled into the driveway of Carola's place. Both got out and went in the main door, where they were met by the maid. "Carola's in the back room. Did you want to see her?"

"No, just tell her that we're here," he said.

"She knows that. It's Tuesday," the maid said matter-of-factly. "Do you want the usual mixers, a bottle of ginger ale and one plain soda?"

"Sure," he said. "Which room?"

"Your regular, two."

˙ That's what it had become, Anna thought, regular. They regularly met on the street on Tuesday, regularly picked up chicken or hamburger dinners and a bottle of vodka, and regularly drove out to Carola's place. Married people could hardly be more regular, she thought. The only difference was that married people were together more often.

"Shall we go?" Alfonso was holding the key. It wasn't really necessary since no people came except those Señora Carola knew. Most weren't quite as regular as she and Alfonso, Anna thought, but all were fairly constant.

"Sure." She followed him to the room.

He took off his coat and tie as soon as he set the package down. She took out the bottle of vodka and poured them each a drink. Words were hardly necessary; they had done the same thing so often. She poured the mixers, the ginger ale for her, the club soda for him. One cube of ice from the small dish provided by the maid. She handed him his.

"Good, just what I need," he said. "Then the chicken with a drink afterward."

She sat down on the chair next to the bedside table and began to unwrap the food packages. As soon as they were open, he began on a batter-fried drumstick and the french fries, interspersed with swallows of his vodka and soda. She watched him for a while, occasionally sipping her drink. She wasn't very hungry, and watching him eat made her less so. He kept at it steadily, finishing off his vodka and soda and the three pieces of chicken quickly. She filled his glass again and gave him a paper napkin from the package she carried in her bag. "Thanks." He wiped his mouth. "Aren't you going to eat yours? Aren't you hungry?"

"Maybe I'll try one piece. But you can have the rest. And all the potatoes. They're too fattening."

"I know, but I can hardly resist them. Especially the ones from Kentucky Fried Chicken. I think they're better than the ones from McDonald's Hamburgers." He began on the potatoes, smacking his lips appreciatively.

When he was finished with all the chicken and most of the potatoes, he lay back on the bed comfortably. He looked so comfortable that if she didn't know him better, Anna would have thought he was going to take a siesta. She got up and put most of the paper from the package, napkins, and the empty bottle into the trash container and went in to the bathroom to wash her hands and face. When she came back, he had taken off all his clothes except his shorts, still lying back on the bed. He gestured for her to come. "It's time, dear, isn't it?"

She looked at him for a moment with displeasure, for what exactly she wasn't sure. Perhaps part of it was the predictability of it all, and perhaps part was that she knew she was second best, and perhaps still a third part was that he wasn't a handsome young man, which was more apparent when his clothes were off. His flesh sagged in many places. But then he gestured again, a little impatiently, she thought, saying, "Come my sweet, come to Papa."

She sighed and began to unbutton her blouse as she walked toward the bed.

She dropped him two blocks from his office and headed toward Los Arboles Park. It was too early to go home yet, and she felt depressed. You'd think the one day a week they had together that he could get more than three hours off. And particularly since he said they weren't very busy. But just eating that greasy food, finishing off a bottle of vodka, sleeping together, and then leaving after a short nap was depressing. There ought to be more companionship than that, even for a mistress.

She parked the Toyota just a block away and went to one of the tree-shaded walks. Other people were walking about slowly, some singles, but mostly couples, hand in hand, or arms around each others' waists. She was aware that the young men she passed made no remarks to her or even held their glance on her.

It was too early to go back to the shop. She had told Elvira, the head seamstress, she would be back just before closing time as usual. To come back at three p.m. would be embarrassing. She had a feeling Elvira and the other girls knew where she went on Tuesday, even though she had not told them.

The wind was cool, a breeze coming through the shade. But it made her sad. It was the end of the rainy season and the right time for cool breezes, one of the best times of the year. And yet she felt low.

Damn him, why couldn't he be more like a real boyfriend?

And yet even as she thought of it, she realized how inappropriate the idea was. He was not a young man, and he was married with three children and a place in society. How could he ever treat her like a young girl? She reached up and felt the loose skin under her chin, which she knew was there even though she couldn't see it. She saw it in the mirror when she got up each morning.

Anna watched the couples pass a while longer, then lit up a cigarette, stood up, and began strolling down the walk toward the Toyota. The clicking of her spikes was irritating. She wished she was wearing flats.

# CHAPTER 8

Martin and Oldenberg were strolling down a curvilinear walk made of Spanish tiles, bordered on both sides by verdant growth. They stepped into a grove of tropical forest trees with trailing lianas. Little flocks of bright-colored parrots and small troops of monkeys enlivened the topmost branches, so high the creatures seemed minute versions of the real things. The tile changed color and pattern, and then they were walking through an austere desert environment where moving life forms were less apparent. The only plant growth were thick-limbed cacti and succulents, plus sparse thin-leafed shrubs, most protected by spines on their branches and trunks. The intensity and kind of light, as well as the humidity, changed from that of the rain forest.

"This is really hot," Martin said. "Though, surprisingly, one doesn't sweat nearly as much as in the rain forest section."

"It's the lower humidity," Oldenberg said.

"Yes, I know. I remember the moisture of some real tropical rain forests that I visited during my lifetime, in Trinidad and Malaya, to be specific. I think it's perfectly incredible that the gardeners here can maintain such natural conditions on such a large scale so effectively. There must be some extremely advanced cultivation techniques on some of the other worlds."

"Certainly," the plump man said. "As you can imagine, there are planets where conditions are extremely difficult, mainly because of light, temperature, or moisture extremes. And where the inhabitants have survived, they have evolved technologies that enabled them to exploit the local environments effectively, especially light and moisture control."

They kept strolling slowly, occasionally passing another individual, but generally being alone. Oldenberg continued, "I am no specialist in cultivation techniques, but like anyone else who has studied at higher levels and who continues to seek information, I have picked up a few bits of knowledge about different technologies. And I do understand that your species managed to get around to moving surface water for cultivation. It is written that your Imperial and San Juaquin Valleys in California had fairly well-developed systems."

"Yes, that's true. They called it *irrigation* in my language, and without it our species would have had vast famines." Martin added, "Of course, we had set ourselves up for famines by constantly increasing our population to the new support level whenever we developed a new technology."

"How's that?" Oldenberg asked.

"Well, you may know that for most of the history of our ancestry, of the type we called *talking bipeds,* we had no technology worth speaking of, just some simple tools that only permitted us to get our food the same way as the other animals, by hunting and gathering wild products. Of course, our ancestors were a little more efficient through the use of their tools and presumably had more effective communication. But, let's face it, we were no more or less than super-foragers, like all the grass eaters and carnivores."

"Yes, I have read something of that," Oldenberg said, "but what has such to do with the population of your species?"

"Well, according to the best we can estimate, the world had only about one or two million of these primitive types at one time. And we think the world population thus stayed stable for a few million years. But then our ancestors got the bright idea of taming some of the animals and plants to use them for food and other purposes. Anthropologists called it the Revolution of Domestication. Anyway, it provided those of our ancestors who adopted the idea—and all didn't—with a far more abundant source of food. But did they live much more easily with the same numbers of people? Oh no, they simply started reproducing more, and soon the one million was fifty million and then a hundred million. And then there were other 'revolutions' in knowledge, like the use of metal instead of stone, and the development of cities and states to replace simple bands, and the invention of mechanical and combustion power sources, each of which gave our ancestors better materials or ways of using existing materials. But with each development they upped the degree of reproduction and extended the life span of individuals until the added advantages were effectively eliminated by the increased numbers."

Oldenberg had taken his pipe out by then and lit up. "That is interesting," he said. "What you seem to be saying basically is that improvements in technology have not really added to improved life quality, is that it?"

"Absolutely. There's no evidence that our ancestors who were hunters and gatherers, or their few remaining contemporaries, got any less satisfaction out of life than did *Homo urbanus* in Tokyo or London. And so far as famines are concerned, yes, it is certainly true that hunters and gatherers ran out of food on occasion. And some of them undoubtedly starved. But it has taken agricultural man with populations of hundreds of millions in a single state the capacity to work up famines on a vast scale, killing off millions at a time. It's all a question of numbers of bodies, and our species has certainly become proficient in generating a maximum number."

The two men had passed through the desert zone by then and were moving into another wild region, the northern tundra. The temperature began to cool off rapidly. Martin said, "Although I find this very interesting and a place I would like to come back to again, I guess I'd like to sit down somewhere. After all, this is our discussion session, isn't it?"

"Yes, assuredly. I just thought you might like to visit the Astral Gardens. I knew the last time we were together you seemed to be a little depressed because you were living in the 'timeless' interior environment of the Transition Bureau. I just wanted to let you know there were places to go outside as well. After all, many of us Systemicists have come from environments where we spent fair amounts of time outside too, however different the outside may have been compared with an Earth scene."

Martin quickly assured his monitor, "I do appreciate it, very much, and as I said, I will come back in my leisure to see the other zones." In the back of his mind the idea again came up that perhaps he could stay there for a long period, not just the ten days or so that still remained. To be an astral researcher and peep into other lives forever, that might indeed be paradise, at least to an ex-social scientist. Martin continued, "One other query and then I'm ready to get down to business, as we used to say, that is, the life discussion. What in particular is the function of the Astral Gardens to the System?"

"Oh, it's partially for diversion. Quite a few individuals like to stroll around outside during their leisure hours. Then too, it is a kind of research, I suppose, that is, by recreating the different types of growth zones of Earth, some have thought that new life information might be obtained. And after all, it's not that costly. I believe they have brought in only a handful of Astral Gardeners, and the workers are Earth Transitionees, people who for one reason or another were not ready to assume their new Earth life immediately and are filling in the time working in the groves and gardens. In a way it is somewhat like what you are doing."

"So, it's only wild zones that they re-create?"

"Oh no, there are also many cultivated areas, gardens and fields of the different types humanity evolved." Pause. "Not that there is much likelihood of new useful information, from what I've heard. Earth cultivation practices are quite primitive compared with those on many other planets. But some, particularly the gardens, are pleasant."

By that time, they were getting deeper into the tundra, where a strong cool wind was blowing across the stunted grasses and shrubs. In the distance, waterfowl could be seen circling a marshy area. Mosquitoes were becoming more numerous and aggressive. Martin shivered and said, "I'm getting cold as well as bitten up. What aggressive creatures our northern mosquitoes are! In the short, cool summer, they have to get their entire life cycle finished, and they do it with a vengeance."

Oldenberg blew tobacco smoke into the cloud of mosquitoes hovering around his head. They dispersed temporarily but regrouped in no time.

Martin continued, "If you don't mind, and if it's not too far away, why don't we go to some garden where we can sit down?"

"Sounds like a capital idea," Oldenberg said with some enthusiasm. Then, chuckling, "Just practicing a dialectal variation. I understand that's what upper class Englishmen say, while you Americans preferred 'a great idea.'" He paused. "And to answer the other part of your suggestion, no, the gardens are not too far away. Besides, we could go by Tube Jet. You've probably seen the entrances to the underground. We could enter any one of them and jet at just under the speed of sound to our destination in Capsule Cars. What kind of garden would you like to go to?"

"Well, there were several types on Earth in my day. I suppose some of the best known were the Japanese stone and gravel gardens, the French plant and flower formal gardens, the Arab fountain and water gardens, and the English flower gardens. At this particular moment, I think I would like to be sitting in the loosely structured, colorful abundance of an English flower garden. They usually have benches or gazebos in them, if my memory is correct."

"Great. We'll enter the tube at the next entrance."

Martin and Oldenberg were seated in a wood-latticed gazebo, surrounded by flowers of wide variety. Instead of mosquitoes, honey bees
and bumblebees fed in the wisteria blossoms growing on the lattice sides
of the structure. In the distance, a couple could be seen strolling slowly,
hand in hand, in the hazy sunlight. The temperature was ideal for an
English summer, the mid-seventies, Martin judged.

"This is fine," Martin said. "Your Astral Gardens are something else.
I doubt that there are any real English gardens that are any better."

"I must say it is rather pleasant," Oldenberg said. They sat in silence
for a few minutes, presumably soaking up the beauty and comfort of
the place. Then Martin spoke. "Where's Dr. Hanson today? I had the
impression he rather enjoyed our last meeting."

"Oh, he did, and I'm sure he wanted to be here today too. But you
know he has important responsibilities as a Transition Therapist. I'm
sure he or I told you before that his prime job is to get people into a
calm state of mind for their Transitions. Otherwise, they can make ridiculous requests as well as do other undesirable things. And as I told
you before, not a few individuals are unable to accept the reality of Life
Transition, having been so thoroughly indoctrinated by their theological leaders to other views of the afterlife."

"Yes, you did. And I can understand." Pause. "Did anything in particular hold him up?"

"Yes, he had to deal with a hysterical woman. She refused to believe
she wasn't going straight to the Christian Heaven and that she had to
live some more lives."

"I understand," Martin said, "though I rather hoped he would come.
He was a pretty pleasant guy to have around, I thought, despite the fact
that he was a shrink. That's the jargon we earthlings evolved for psychotherapists in the middle of the twentieth century, though toward the
end of that period people had almost forgotten the original meaning."

"And what was that?"' Oldenberg asked in his Earth-learning tone.

Martin looked at the Transitioner in puzzlement for a moment, then,
chuckling, said, "You know, now that you ask, I suddenly realize I'm not
sure myself. Though as usual with we earthlings, I have a theory: that
the term is derived from the original head shrinker, which referred to
the idea that someone who was crazy, or abnormal, as they later changed
the usage, had an overexpanded brain; it was the role of the curer to
'shrink' the brain."

"Ah yes, another bit of earth science exotica. Interesting for understanding earthlings, whether true or not." Oldenberg said.

Birds sang and fought for their territories and caught insects. Old-enberg finally brought out his pipe again, saying, "Well, it has been an interesting interlude, but I suppose we should get on with Project Heterop, eh?"

"Yes, I guess so, though in an environment like this, one might spend hours simply lazing." He looked at Oldenberg and said, "That's a term that means using time unproductively though pleasantly. Some of us earthlings who got imbued by the Work Ethic got to feeling guilty about so using time."

Oldenberg smiled. "Ah yes, I think I read that one of your econo-mists, a German fellow, I believe, referred to it as the Christian Ethic and so explained the success of the Europeans in the sixteenth to nine-teenth centuries. But though they may have been responsible for the early development of the industrial revolution and opening up of the rest of the world, it was the orientals who became the production and economic masters in the end, no?"

"Yes, so it happened by the beginning of the twenty-first century."

"And the Chinese, Japanese, and Koreans were hardly Christians, were they?" Oldenberg seemed to mull over that idea for a moment but then pulled himself back. "But let us get on with the matter at hand, if you please. What new insights did you obtain from viewing the life of the Latin lady, Anna?"

It took Martin a moment to refocus his ideas after the various tan-gents of the stroll, but then images of verdant Costa Rica and its olive-skinned people began to flicker through his mind. He responded, "Well, I did see the experience of a woman in a familial culture, as I intended. And truly the Latins are still more oriented toward the needs of the family than we Northerners. But even so, they were in throes of change. Things were much less rigid than in Lakshmi's Hindu India. For in-stance, young people did go out together alone, they did date, an un-heard-of occurrence in orthodox India. There were still memories among the older people of the days when such dating could only be done under strict supervision, but in contemporary urban life young people were free to go to bars and discos, the same kinds of places the young went to in most of the rest of the northern countries."

"I'm not quite sure that I see the similarity then to family-oriented India."

Martin plucked a long-bladed plant stem and, stripping off the green-ery, put it in his mouth, pleasuring in the feel of the knobby surface. "I'll admit it's a little hard to explain, but there was a feeling there that family members should help one another and maintain working relations through the lifetime. They even considered marriage as a lifetime commitment, though they had gotten caught up in the divorce epidemic, but admittedly less so than in the northern countries. Our heroine was caught in the middle; she did divorce."

Oldenberg had his pipe in one hand. With the other he fished through the pockets on one side, then switched hands and searched through the other pockets. Finally, he brought out his match box. Pushing it open, he searched to no avail. "It seems," he said, "that I've run out of matches. This is one of the problems of your pipe smoking custom, you seem to burn matches almost as much as tobacco."

"Yes, I remember. There are lighters too, you know."

"Oh yes, but somehow I get a positive aesthetic feeling from using wood matches rather than those little metallic lighters. It's what I believe you people in the late twentieth century called 'campy,' isn't it?"

Martin chuckled. "Well, I'm familiar with the term, but I never thought of the use of matches as part of the idea." Pause. "I'd offer you some, but unfortunately I haven't carried any for many years, ever since I gave up the habit."

"I'm sure I'll get by," Oldenberg said. "And perhaps someone will come whom I can ask." Pause. "But to get back to your account, you seem to be particularly caught up with the process of divorce, isn't that so?"

"Yes and no. It is a fact that I started my life with the idea that marriage was a permanent relationship and ended it, after two divorces, with the idea that marriage had become as temporary as most of the rest of the relationships in society. You know we had as a part of the Christian marriage vow a caveat that stated 'What God has put together, let no man put asunder.'

"It got so that practically no one paid attention to that one by the end of the century. Men, judges in particular, were putting marriages 'asunder' right and left. Why, some spent almost their whole lives doing nothing else. Even the ministers, the people who usually performed the marriage ceremony, got to where they were helping parishioners divorce almost as much." Pause, pensiveness. "I guess I say 'no,' that I didn't particularly look up people with divorces, but as I told you in the beginning of this study, I sought out lives of persons I knew in real life. And it so happened that after my first divorce, when I was already in my late forties, the ladies I met were almost all divorced. It got so that if you met someone of the opposite sex who was alone and older than thirty, you didn't ask them whether they were divorced. If you asked at all, you asked how many times. And so it turned out in Costa Rica. Almost all of the women I met were divorcees. And Anna was one of them."

Oldenberg fingered his cold pipe like an earthling who was truly addicted. "By the way, how did you meet all these Latin ladies, you a Northerner?"

Martin was impressed by how much Oldenberg had picked up of Earth customs by then. Of course Oldenberg must have known that you could get prostitutes, ladies for hire, practically anywhere, but genuine respectable natives were not that easy. He answered, "Actually, it was not so hard in Costa Rica. To those people the term *gringo* was a good word. They actually liked Yankees. And then too the Costa Ricans were probably more liberal than most Latins. But so far as the particular technique was concerned, I used personals, advertisements in the newspaper. It was a procedure I had run across in several places and one that was favored by Costa Ricans." Pause. "I learned about it in India, but of course there it was the parents who did the advertising. They left nothing so important as an addition to the household to young people."

Oldenberg leaned back then, looking up at the soft indistinct clouds so typical of an English summer sky. He turned toward Martin. "So what you are saying is that their familism was different, and one might say, looser than that of India, no?"

"Yes, certainly. And in some respects it always has been. In a certain sense the Indians had carried their strictness to an extreme as they had with most aspects of their culture. There were probably no people in the world with so many restrictions on what they could eat or touch. On the other hand, the Latins had institutionalized one characteristic of the mating drive that is evidently biological and thus universal in the species. That is, while they permitted the male to have multiple consorts, the female was supposed to be content with one only. They called the male drive *machismo*. A real man was supposed to make many female conquests as well as be super-masculine in other ways. That was a real problem for Anna. She floated between two worlds. She got started by picking up ideas of female rights from the mass media when she was growing up."

Martin took on his professorial role then, figuring that Oldenberg might not know what happened in this regard in the twentieth century. He felt a little odd, but his habituation to professorialism made it impossible for him to resist. He explained, "You are probably aware that there was a steady expansion of rights to the individual in the Western world through the last century. First, such rights were given to males, and later females started to get more and more. Well, by the end of the century, the most liberal were of the belief that the two sexes should be treated equally in all respects. That also included sexual activities. We had an expression in the old days, to wit, 'What's good for the goose is good for the gander.'" Martin added parenthetically, "Those are the male and female in that species." Pause. "Anyway, it wasn't until the late nineteenth century that most liberal people in the West actually started following that practice. Gradually they incorporated provisions in the legal codes that gave women the same rights as men."

Oldenberg fanned gently at an inquisitive honey bee. The insect circled the Transitioner's head a couple of times and then, evidently satisfied that he wasn't a flower, flew away. Oldenberg said, "Yes, of course I am generally aware of that development. It came as a surprise in a way. You know in our study of the planet Earth, before coming here, we were given a few lectures on the various life forms. And naturally we got something on sexual differences. And, as I recall, there were practically no species that were equal in behavioral potentiality. Males and females were just different and had different capacities and functions. And basically that seemed to have been the case with your so-called ancestors, the talking bipeds, as well. Then there was this development of equal rights."

"Yes, it was most pronounced in the Protestant liberal world of northern Europe and the United States, though the idea filtered into other cultures. We used to call this *diffusion* in anthropology. And of course it was resisted where there were other customs in conflict. The custom of the double standard, particularly the one embodied in the Latin custom of *machismo,* of course, did not justify equal rights for females. And that was how Anna got into trouble. She picked up the idea of equal rights in her girlhood and believed it so much that she divorced her husband when he started seeing other women. But then Anna found herself not very desirable to other males as a marital partner. The Costa Ricans may have come along to a certain extent by accepting divorce more easily than in the last generation, but they still resisted remarriage. A true bride was still supposed to be a virgin. Again, to make a comparison with Lakshmi, the orthodox Hindus had gone all the way. Remarriage for a female was impossible, and divorce almost so. No one even thought about virginity. When a girl married, she had to be a virgin."

Oldenberg was watching a large bumblebee travel from blossom to blossom, bustling its way into the chamber of goodies on each, backing out with its hairy thighs heavily coated with the reproductive power of plant life, pollen. He said, "You know, the bisexuality of plants with their method of transmitting genes is so simple compared to that of your species, don't you think?"

"Absolutely," Martin said, looking at the bee. "No problems of personality and temperament or conflict of customs like *machismo* and equal rights. Sex is beautiful with them, nothing more than the mechanical transfer of the sexual component. We anthropologists teach the science of customs, of learned behavior, and it is a particularly interesting and specifically human adaptation to living; but if I would make any prediction it would be that the very complexity of the cultural way will probably destroy the species."

Oldenberg continued watching the bee as it methodically covered the vessels of nectar, saying, "Yes, we Transitioners have long noted that throughout the universe the types with the best chance of continuing are the simpler ones or their descendants. Complexity and specialization, no matter how successful they seem at first, tend to be dead ends. The specialized type loses the ability to adapt to changed circumstances, and the simple one can go in many directions." Pause. "But to finish the story of Anna. I take it she got moved out of the consorting game because she rejected this custom of *machismo* you claim is so typical of the Latins."

Martin smiled, "Well, yes and no, as usual. She did give up her spouse for that reason and was never again able to get anyone else to marry her, including foreigners like myself, at least no one she would have. But in one of those surprising twists that happen so often in the human life cycle, she got back into the customs of her people in her middle age. By that time her choices of dating partners was quite limited. At least men who were interested in marriage were hardly interested in her. So she became the mistress of a middle-aged businessman. She ended up fulfilling the female role of the *machismo* syndrome anyway. One of those ironic twists of life."

"So did you find her life particularly unsatisfactory?"

"Well, again, I see stability in a consortship as a very positive end in itself, in a way that I never saw during most of my life. Then the goal always seemed to be immediate satisfaction. And in that sense Anna was a failure. She gave up what stability she had in her early years because she couldn't stomach the double standard. And then she lived one-half of the double standard herself, and without the stability she would have had, had she remained married. It is significant, I think, that her sister, Lupe, took the traditional route from the beginning, accepting the double standard when her husband started going out with others. She remained married throughout her life, and though I didn't view it in totality, from what I observed in passing, she got more out of her existence than Anna did."

Oldenberg stood up and stretched, saying, "Ah yes, there it goes again. Martin, you know you are coming up with the same conclusion over and over again, that stability and continuance in a consortship is above all else the most desirable outcome. In a way, you seem to already have made up your mind as to your final conclusion. That's not very scientific, is it?"

Martin grinned then like a fellow conspirator. "No, according to the scientific method you are not to have your mind made up before you get your data, but I don't think I've done that exactly. Because of observations of whole lives, I began to change my mind in this direction in my middle age while I was still living. From what I began to see, the mad pursuit of the perfect love relationship, which I did also in my early manhood and middle age, tended to produce more negative consequences than the methodical arranged marriage—at least in terms of an entire life span. So you see, I am merely following that hypothesis in the afterworld by utilizing the Life Videos, a source of data I never visualized in my wildest dreams."

Martin played with the stripped twig as he continued, still smiling, "Then again, I'm undoubtedly not the greatest scientist in the world." He corrected himself, "In the afterworld.

"You know anthropology itself has been held in low esteem by many of the other life scientists because of its lack of rigorous scientific procedures." Continuation of smile and professoration. "Some of our statistically oriented colleagues identify us as being 'high in interest, low in vigor.'" Martin chuckled. "And in a sense they are right. We really don't demand ironclad proofs for our conclusions. In fact, some of our even less disciplined brothers regard us as fellow humanists."

Martin looked at the plump Transitioner with a self-satisfied expression, one he knew had come almost automatically while he was still an earthling professor and was about to deliver the punch line of a long involved explanation. "I'm sure you can guess that I fit quite well into this last category. I have little doubt that during my living days I would have lasted a very short time in one of the highly disciplined sciences. I probably would have been thrown out. But my literary cousins probably would have accepted me as one of them."

Oldenberg stood up then and was facing the ex-professor. "I don't know about you, Martin, but I'm getting a little stiff. How would you like to take a stroll through the garden? And maybe shortly we ought to be heading back. As usual, I have a meeting to attend. There's an intergalactic conference on what to do about the Transition Process."

Martin was really impressed by the idea of conference visitors from all different points of the universe. The one thing that intrigued him was their potential varying appearance. How would they all look? Undoubtedly there would be a tremendous variety. But then he remembered that the Department of Illusions would have transformed them all to look like earthlings. If only he could hang on, Martin thought, and become some kind of permanent adjunct Transitioner. To think that he might be able to attend such a conference was mind boggling. He said, "Sure, I understand." They started down the path bordered by tulips and daffodils, toward an arbor whose trellis was covered by climbing roses.

He didn't have the nerve to ask all the things that intrigued him about the conference, but he did say, "It's not secret, is it?"

"Oh no, nothing special, simply that the intergalactic council has been concerned for some time with the expense of maintaining all these offices and support facilities." He looked at Martin. "I hope you won't be offended, but you know that Earth is really quite an insignificant place in universal terms."

Martin laughed. "That doesn't bother me at all. I had long ago decided it wasn't much, when I was still alive. In fact, one of the problems I had in accepting one of the standard religions, particularly those of the Judeo-Christian-Islamic triad, was that they advanced an idea of a universal system in which human beings were of central importance. I just never could understand how any god, whether Yahweh, Christ, or Allah, who was supposedly responsible for the whole universe, could still treat my species and planet as the most important creatures and place."

"I'd have to agree with you generally, Martin. We Transitioners find the earth rather interesting, and particularly in the life forms that evolved here, but frankly, in significance it's well down on the list of places that support life. I think in your earth numerical system, out of $1.4 \times 10^{100}$ places that do support life, your earth would be $1.399 \times 10^{100}$ in significance."

"That doesn't surprise me at all," Martin answered. His imagination soared when he thought of all the possible places in the universe with different life forms and that he might, in the best of circumstances, get to see some of them. It was almost like the mind expansion he had gone through when he first discovered anthropology and learned of all the different lifeways on Earth and that he might even get to see some of them. He said, "Are the galactic conferees considering alternatives to the Transition Process; I mean, do they have any specific ideas?"

"Well, yes, since they have had similar problems on other planets in other stellar systems. One of the possibilities would be to eliminate the multiple-life process for individuals and simply transfer all creatures into the afterworld by taking away their identity. It would be much like the Hindu-Buddhist idea of Nirvana except that it would be automatic, happening to each creature on its death. Nobody would have to earn their way to a higher level after a long and arduous life to get to the afterworld."

They passed through the arbor, beyond which was an exquisite mini-garden of tea roses. These had been a favorite of Martin when he had been alive. He periodically touched one of the flowers, almost automatically snapping off the dry heads of flowers that had gone through the blossom cycle and were trying to establish seed pods. That way, he remembered, you got the plant to put out more flowers in its desperate attempt to leave some progeny. In a way, it was mean, he thought, since you made the plant work much harder and still never allowed it to fulfill its ultimate destiny, to leave young behind. You did not let it produce seeds, using the additional flowers for your own pleasure. But that was the way it was, Martin mused, domestication was a process evolved to convert living things into creatures that would benefit their domesticators. Individuals were always sacrificed, forced to overproduce, either to their exhaustion or death, or modified in their behavior or growth cycle until they became total slaves or monsters—seeing eye dogs or pit bulls. And the same with plants. The hybrid corn stalk with two or three fat ears was almost unrecognizable from the tiny ancestral pod corn of the Valley of Tehuacan. But so it was, he mused, knowing that he had fully accepted the benefits of the revolution of domestication in his own lifetime, and it was thus a little late to be critical of that development.

Oldenberg brought him back to the ongoing discussion as they continued their slow walk. "Well, Martin, is there anything more you wish to tell me about the lady in transition from the old family way toward the modern impermanent relationship pattern?"

"No, I guess that's about all. Anna perhaps in a way was a good representative of the way things were going in the modernizing world, at least in the West. Families were weakening there too, though not as fast as in the advanced urban cultures such as my own." Martin grinned and quickly explained. "When I say *advanced,* I do not mean in quality, simply in urbanization. And as you may have read or learned in some of your Transitions, many people felt that the quality of life had deteriorated with city living. One of the best-known anthropologists in the generation before mine, Robert Redfield, became famous for his advocacy of that idea."

He continued, "And I suppose on a scale of one to ten, ten being the best in life satisfaction, I would rate the transitional familial way such as that still functioning in Costa Rica as a six."

"That's an interesting way of putting it," Oldenberg said. "What do you call that procedure?"

"Oh, it's nothing special, merely what is referred to as scale evaluation, a procedure that was widely used in the life sciences, and, I suspect, in many others. You rank individuals of a common type according to some preselected qualities. A ranking of one to ten is the commonest. That's because we humans feel most comfortable with that number, I suppose because we have ten fingers. They say that's why we developed our decimal system of numeration, that if we had had eight fingers we would have developed an octagonal system."

Martin felt a little guilty even before Oldenberg interrupted his discourse. The recently deceased man knew he would just have to remember that Oldenberg was the mentor and he the student. Martin knew he took liberties by coming on with his professorial role so frequently, but he justified his actions on the ground that Oldenberg was not an earthling. But even when he waxed professorial, Martin was still aware that the Transitioner knew far more than any ordinary stranger. How much more Martin couldn't know, but in any event he resolved to try to subdue himself a little more in the future.

Oldenberg said musingly, "Yes, very interesting. And how would you rank some of the other consortships; for instance, the previous one, that of the Hindu gentleman?"

"Well, I suppose in terms of total life satisfaction, I would give him a nine, pretty high."

"You mean because the consortship lasted the entire lifetime?"

"Yes, but also I think I indicated there was a fair amount of affection in the long run. It was no love relationship in the beginning, but those people generated something that was very close to that emotion and without the crises that occurred in Anna's life, and what I think became endemic in my own culture. When the love pact became the predominant criterion for mating, almost everyone considered divorce, and one-half or more did it, many several times. There were a lot of highs in the 'love' societies, but there were some pretty terrible 'lows' also. Our song industry relied chiefly on this theme, the great elation of falling in love and the miserable depression of losing those loves."

By then they were approaching the end of the English garden, and Martin could already see the next facsimile, a formal French garden in which all plants were established in geometric lines. None of the randomness of the English plot. Oldenberg said, "Well, I guess we ought to wind it up, Martin. I can see a Tube Jet station just before the next plot. And I must be getting back. Probably you too, no?"

He stopped then and faced the ex-professor. "I think your time is running out. You've got three or four days left, I believe. Got any ideas where to next?"

Martin felt momentarily uneasy at the thought that he was getting close to the end of watching Life Videos. But then he brought himself back to reality because he had at least three kinds of lives he wanted to see yet, and he just couldn't think of wasting time with that rich data bank available. He said, "Yes, as usual, but most specifically so in these circumstances, I do have definite ideas. I think that was a characteristic that teaching inculcated into me, the capacity to come up with ideas quickly. You know, students can really throw some curve balls at you." Aside, "That's an expression we used to indicate the unexpected. It comes from one of our American spectator sports, baseball."

Oldenberg did not interrupt, evidently with the recognition that Martin was just about to come out with his suggestion and that an interjection would only slow it down. Martin said, "You may not believe it, but I want to see the life of a chimpanzee in the wild."

Oldenberg looked at the researcher slightly askance but quickly recovered, saying, "That's not your species . . ."

"No, but I want to see the life in reference to my species because that is the focus of this study, no?"

"Yes, but could you explain? I suppose it is something connected with the studies in your former discipline, anthropology."

"Yes. And as you can probably recognize by now, I have been reading and studying in that field for so many years in my lifetime that I find I cannot even get away from it in the afterworld."

"I understand. Continue about these animals. They are quite close to your species in ancestry, is that not so?"

"Yes, our paleontologists believe that our humanoid ancestors diverged from those of the great apes between ten and twenty million years ago."

"That's according to your theorist, Darwin, no?"

"He didn't figure the time it took to happen, but yes, the idea of one species evolving from another is thought to have been his, or at least the evidence to back up the idea."

And with persistence, a characteristic Martin also knew he had acquired from his teaching, he continued. "Anyway, though, scientists do not think humans descended from apes or monkeys, despite all the hullabaloo of the monkey trials."

"I found those events rather interesting," Oldenberg said, "the idea that certain groups could prevent by law certain ideas from being taught. Of course, it is well known that teaching is always controlled to some degree for your species. After all, teaching is only an advanced form of brainwashing, no matter what fancy names we give it. The masters or professors are invariably intent on implanting their ideas in the uninitiated, no matter what devious methods they use; is that not correct? And the masters are selected through the societal leadership ultimately, persons who would hardly permit conflicting ideas to be taught, at least those they deem very important. For instance, I understand that your society would permit any kind of cant, so long as it supported the rights of individuals. But ideas that advocated social reality were only barely tolerated. It is written that the word *communism,* one such conflicting philosophy, was practically forbidden for a long time. I read that in your society one could only use the word publicly without repercussion if he claimed to be against the philosophy. And of course the same was true of the other side, except that at that time their no-no word was *capitalism.*"

"Yes, as one who has taught enculturation for so many years, I couldn't disagree. I suppose in the broadest sense, though many of us scientists acted indignant at the action of the religious advocates, that we were just as intent on implanting our idea of descent as they were their idea of creation." Pause. "But anyway, I am stuck with the scientific view now and have been ever since I learned about it. And that view teaches that the African great apes, the gorilla and chimpanzee, are our closest living relatives."

"Okay, I can see how those of your people who were interested in the evolution of you communicating bipeds would be concerned with such relationships, but what have they got to do with understanding the mating behavior of contemporary man?"

The two conversationalists had arrived at the entrance of the Tube Jet, from which the aroma of cool earthen air emanated. Both stopped. Martin said, "I'll just finish quickly so we can be on our way. One of the problems we had in understanding human beings was how to know what was natural and what the product of this enculturation or brain:washing. It started right after birth when a baby was either tightly swaddled, as the Russians did it, or wrapped loosely in a soft blanket, as we Americans did it, and continued to our very death. Another proper name for our species could have been *Homo conditionatus*. We were conditioned like no other variety of mammal. And the conditioning began so early, and was so intense and constant, that we students of human behavior had practically thrown up our hands in despair of ever learning what was natural or biological. That is, what unconditioned humans would have been like. For that reason, we looked around for some creature that was similar to us but had not been conditioned with such intensity. And if you haven't already guessed, it was the great apes, and most particularly the chimpanzee."

"I did figure that out, Martin, even as long ago as the briefing sessions on Earth life forms. I recall one session when several of us Transitioners discussed the similarity between humans and these great apes. They seemed to have hands almost exactly the same and faces were quite similar, if one discounted the hairiness. And as I recall, their faces were quite full of expression, in contrast to many other types of mammals. The one thing that seemed particularly different was that they did not habitually walk upright; they were not bipeds."

"That's true," Martin said, "and we believe that is the primary reason these creatures did not evolve into humanoids. They never stood upright and thus did not free their hands for exclusive tool use or carrying things." Pause. "But to get on with it, however different they are from us, they are the closest we have found of creatures that have not been heavily conditioned. They may be programmed biologically, as presumably we are too, but they are not conditioned as much through learning. Oh, this isn't to say that they never learned anything, but they did not have the complex kind of learning we humans got through language."

Oldenberg started to look restless. But still his patience held. "So, I take it you want to see the life of one of these creatures to find out how your species would be if the individuals did not go through that intensive brainwashing you emphasize so much."

Martin grinned. "That's the idea. Oh, I have no illusions that I will find out everything. For one thing, the parallel between us and the great apes is only approximate. Obviously, they are not exactly like us in all ways. For instance, the mating behavior is different because of biological differences. The great apes come into heat only periodically, like most of the other mammals, whereas the females of my species are sexually available throughout the year. That undoubtedly has made a difference in other behaviors. But in any event, the apes are more like us than any other creature."

"It's alright with me for you to see the Video of a chimp. I still can't see exactly how much good will come of it, but it is getting near the end of this project and I should give you some leeway, I think." He mused. "Though of course, Martin, I'm sure you recognize that I've been lenient throughout the project."

"Oh yes, and believe me, I appreciate it, Transitioner Oldenberg."

"So, I guess you will view the next life of a creature in a laboratory, zoo, or circus, since I understand that is what your species has done to most of them, using them for exhibit or experimental purposes."

"Oh no," Martin quickly emphasized. "We anthropologists have long ago given up our study of the great apes in cages. About the only people who still study confined animals are psychologists, especially the ones called behaviorists. They have gone through a special conditioning of their own. Wanting complete control of their subjects, they can hardly think of studies outside laboratories. We anthropologists and zoologists, and especially a type called ethologists, go into the field to study the animals in their natural habitats."

"Why is that?"

"Well, we have found that once you confine a creature and change its living conditions in significant ways, you cause it to change its behavior. It develops peculiarities, just as confined human beings do, for that matter. So we go into the field to study them. And that's the kind of tape I'd like to see, though I suppose there are tapes of circus and laboratory chimpanzees in the file also."

"Yes, as I told you in the beginning, Martin, there's a tape for every creature that ever lived. Though you'll have to go to another desk for nonhumans. Where you've been getting your tapes is only for your species. It seems that the catalog people set up three separate divisions, depending on the amount of use by the Transition Offices. There has been least use of the Plant Division, simply because of the relative simplicity of plant lives, I understand. A plant has very little leeway in its behavior, so there is little choice in deciding what its next life will be. A nonhuman animal has somewhat more choice available so the Animal Division is used more and has a separate section. Humans, of course, have the most choice, so they have a separate division. That's where you have been getting your tapes so far, from Mrs. Morrison, no?"

"Yes, that's the place."

"Well, you'll have to get your chimpanzee tape in the Animal Division, no matter that the creature is closely related to humans." He turned to enter the Tube Jet. "And so, unless you've got anything else that's important, I think we should be off."

Martin took his place alongside the plump man as they both entered the tube entrance, saying, "No, that seems fine. I'll let you know after I've seen it."

# HUMUNGUS

A single file of creatures of varying size moved through the mixed forest. At the front, sometimes ranging a good way ahead, were the biggest males. After them, generally clustered together, were the smaller females, many with babies hanging to their breasts or being clasped by one arm. Two couples stayed together and somewhat apart from the others. Younger animals were mixed in between, or followed the females. All moved in a four-limbed gait, the long front arms resting on the knuckles at each step. Once in a while an animal would stop to pick up a part of a plant or an insect. Occasionally the animals made grunts or calls but nothing with the complexity of a sentence. Nor did the individuals focus their utterances on others. They merely uttered cries of surprise or interest, as if to themselves.

It wasn't that they did not react to sounds; once when they were crossing the side of a hill where mist still trailed, there was a sound of whoops from the other side of the valley. The whole troop became silent, and several males ran forward in complete silence. The females and young continued in the same direction but more slowly. After some minutes there was screaming in the distance, and not long after, the band of males came back. One of the largest was carrying a branch, periodically striking the ground with it.

Martin figured it had been chimpanzees from another band that the scouting group had encountered and driven off.

The troop continued until they came to a clear place in the forest where several termite mounds were located. The old males went to the mounds first, carrying twigs they had picked up and fashioned on the way. They placed themselves around the mounds in twos and threes. Methodically, they would probe their sticks down the tunnels, then withdraw them carefully. They would draw the sticks through their mouths, biting hard on the insects hanging on. One shook his head and grimaced in pain a couple of times, evidently having been bitten on the lip or tongue.

The males soon tired of the activity and began drifting off toward a group of colobus monkeys that had appeared at the end of the clearing.

Humungus's mother, Diane, along with other adult females, then proceeded to feed. Although there was no such identification on the Video, Martin decided to give the individual animals names, simply so they could be identified throughout the report. It was a technique he had learned from reading the field reports of ethologists. He followed their procedure too in naming creatures for some special characteristic or similarity to some human. The latter was anthropomorphizing, he knew, but naming was justified. Without individual identification it was impossible to follow an animal over time. He named Humungus's mother Diane because she was particularly sleek and supple.

Diane was patient and adept, much more so than most of the males that had been feeding before. She was not even slowed down by the weight of Humungus, who had moved to her nipple to nurse. Occasionally she shifted her grip with the one hand she used to support him. However, he did pretty well himself, gripping her long hair tightly with his small hands. Sometimes she fished for termites with one hand and sometimes let him hang on by himself.

After awhile she moved back and hunched down, Humungus still cradled on her stomach. Two young females came near her, and one began tentatively to separate tufts of her body hair, searching for parasites or little granules of salt.

Diane grunted and lolled back. The other female stretched out her hand to touch little Humungus. He opened his eyes wide and grimaced. Diane put her hand on that of the visitor, but not disapprovingly. The young female let Humungus wrap his hand around her finger. Then she very carefully put her other hand under the infant and lifted him. She held him cradled, and he tentatively reached for her breast. Nuzzling, and finding it dry, he lay back quietly. Another female came near and touched the infant softly, letting her fingers trail down his arm. Diane watched the two younger females carefully but made no effort to prevent them from holding or touching her infant.

The band of males came back into the clearing. Bighead, one of the largest, was holding most of the carcass of a colobus monkey. It had one arm torn off and a big rip in its stomach. Bighead was chewing a bit of bloody flesh. Another member of the hunting party was chewing on the end of an arm. The rest of the party kept close to Bighead, though without crowding him. He came near the group of females. Diane reached over and took Humungus back, then moved toward Bighead, eyeing the bloody carcass. When she put out her arm as if to touch it, Bighead stared hard at her, then turned his back without relinquishing the carcass. She pulled back into the group of females. Bighead chewed contentedly, tearing out pieces of flesh and fur with his big canines. He chewed slowly as if he was not terribly hungry. Two of the other males came near, watching him patiently. He stared at them as he had at Diane, and they sat down a few feet away, playing with pieces of grass or sticks, but without looking at him directly. Finally the largest reached over and carefully touched the back of Bighead's hand. Without looking at him, Bighead continued to eat, but very slowly. Finally, he tore out what remained of another arm and handed it to the other hunter. That one took his piece and ate what was left more rapidly. Bighead then handed a piece of the side meat to another beseecher. The four hunters all got some.

The group dozed then, males generally together while the females remained in another area. Half-grown animals played rough and tumble on and around a small tree.

\* \* \* \* \*

Humungus grew rapidly, and it was soon apparent that he was going to be a particularly large male. He joined the play groups, and his increasing muscularity quickly gave him an edge over any animal his age, and even those a little older. The entire group moved daily, going from one type of fruit or plant feeding area to another, periodically making a fishing trip to termite nests. Sometimes they would chance on a beehive and rob it, though getting badly stung in the process. There were always some insects or bird nests to rob, and along the way the males would sometimes catch small game, usually monkeys, young baboons, antelopes, or bush pigs. At night they would build individual nests in low trees, curling up within calling distance of one another.

\* \* \* \* \*

Humungus was feeding on wild figs, as were most of the others of the troop, moving slowly through the grove. He saw the strange female first when the group was about to move off to another feeding area. She peered through the branches, obviously with some fear. He stopped and stared at her, then grunted. After watching him for a while, she moved slowly forward in a sideways movement. By then one of the females near Humungus came next to him and stared also. The stranger continued to come forward, and when she got near enough, she put out her hand and touched the other female's hand. The troop female growled slightly but did not attack or scream. Humungus then touched the stranger. Several of the other animals came up, including one adult male. When he got near the small cluster, the stranger turned around and presented her swollen buttocks toward the group. The big male sniffed her genitals, then turned away. Slowly the others started drifting off. The stranger followed the big male.

When they got to the grove, the troop became very quiet. They approached the edge of the clearing and watched for a long time in silence. Off in the distance, Humungus could hear an occasional sound from the hairless bipeds, a whacking or voice cry. This was only the second time he had been there, and it made him nervous. The hairless creatures had surprised them the last time after the troop had just pulled down two of the stalks. The upright ones had come running, making much noise, and when they got close, a couple of them had held up their black sticks and a tremendous noise burst out, a tongue of fire spurting from the end. One female had got stung in the leg by the fire stick, and she had been limping ever since.

This time the sounds did not get closer, and after a while a couple of adult males moved forward, soon to be followed by most of the others. Only the limping female and Onearm hung back. He was a male a little older than Humungus who had one arm paralyzed. Humungus moved forward just behind the group of lead males. He pulled back a little when one of them turned and stared at him in intimidation. While watching in the direction of the bipeds, the males headed for a stalk with a large cluster of yellow fruit. Bighead, who was in the lead, jumped and grabbed the bunch of fruit. It hung lower. Then another male, Apollo, grabbed it, and the weight of the two was enough to pull it down far enough that the others could grab hold and pull the whole plant to the ground. Several animals started to grab and pull off fruit when Bighead screamed and stamped the ground. They backed off. He pulled off all he could and moved away, but when some others moved forward, he came back. They retreated again. But he couldn't hold any more in his hands or mouth and finally turned back toward the forest. The other males descended on the cluster then, each pulling off as much as he could carry and then moving out of the clearing. When they were finished, Humungus and several females closed in on the remains. Humungus swaggered, waved his arms, and tried to hoot as he had seen the older males do. The females held back. Humungus grabbed most of the rest of the fruit.

About then the screams of the bipeds could be heard, and all of the apes that remained ran for the edge of the forest. Just as Humungus ran into the leafy sanctuary, he heard the loud report of a fire stick. He ran faster and dropped several fruit. Then he became aware of apes crashing through the growth all around, and behind the loud voices of the hairless bipeds. He was aware of several other animals as he cleared the top of the hill, even though he couldn't see them. Then it became quiet again, and Humungus couldn't hear the sounds of the bipeds any longer. He stopped at a fallen tree and sat down to eat his remaining bananas. When he was barely finished with the first, he heard an animal coming through the brush. It was another chimpanzee, though he didn't identify it until the branches were separated a few yards away. It was Apollo. He stared at Humungus, who had stopped eating for a moment. Humungus stared back. Apollo was a medium-sized, slender animal who was quick, though without the strength to be Number One. That was clearly Bighead.

Humungus started to get nervous, though he didn't turn his eyes away. He could see that Apollo was empty handed. Apollo growled low and edged forward. Humungus decided to keep his fruit so began to back up. Apollo jumped forward and, while grimacing and hooting, waved his arms about. Humungus changed his mind and quickly dropped the bananas. The adult male jumped forward and grabbed them while Humungus moved back and watched the older animal peel and eat all his fruit.

\* \* \* \* \*

Humungus grew continually, his muscles soon giving him great strength. He also had particularly large canines. Like all of the other growing animals, he became involved in establishing dominance. Most of the time no fight was involved; rather, he would square off with another animal and stare or show his canines. If that didn't work, he might stamp his feet, swagger, or pick up a branch and, running forward, strike it on the ground. A couple of times he even threw rocks in the general direction of the other animal but not with enough aim to come anywhere near. There were a couple of fights also, once when he challenged the strongest male of his age-group and once when he had already moved into the adult group, against an older male that Martin named Baldy. He had a bare spot on top of his head. Humungus got bitten hard a couple of times in that fight but gave as much as he received. He finally wrestled the other one down and kicked him. When Baldy cowered, holding his arms over his head, Humungus stopped. After that it was clear that Humungus was in the adult group, with no other male clearly dominant over him except Bighead. He got accustomed to going on hunting and scouting trips at the edge of the troop's territory, screaming at or attacking individuals from neighboring troops when they got too far inside the home ground.

* * * * *

Humungus was resting with his back against a tree when Maryanne came ambling slowly across the clearing. He watched her lethargically, occasionally brushing insects away from his eyes. He had seen her as long as he could remember, once holding a baby, though that wasn't too clear in his memory. But then he was only vaguely aware of the individual females in the troop. All he was sure of was that they were not strangers. Strange females did appear on occasion, usually when the group was at the edge of the territory and usually when their genitals were swollen.

Maryanne had larger hips and breasts than most of the females. And as she was crossing the clearing, Humungus could see that her genitals were swollen. She walked over to a group of females with babies who watched her with low interest. Maryanne swiveled to present her buttocks to them. One sniffed, but the others paid no attention, continuing to nurse or groom their babies or one another. Maryanne squatted and groomed one of the females a while. But she was evidently restless, for she soon got up and moved off toward a nearby male. Swiveling her hips, she turned to present her buttocks to him. He was chewing on a twig, which he took from his mouth. Then he leaned over to sniff the swollen membranes. He put his hand on one of her hips, but unenthusiastically. She leaned over to a belly crouch, her arms down, her buttocks up. He turned away and put the stick back into his mouth. After a bit she got up and moved away, presenting to several males in turn. Not one paid any interest after the initial sniffing. The same thing happened when she got to Bighead.

The troop started to get restless. Bighead got up, yawned, and moved to the edge of the clearing to stare out across the valley. The others soon followed and slowly got into motion, moving through the brush loosely abreast. Humungus moved slowly also, swinging his long, powerful arms easily. After going a short distance, he found Maryanne in front of him. When she was right in front, he made a move to one side, to go around her. But she moved so that she was still in front. He didn't feel like growling at her even though he was a little annoyed. Her swollen genitals made her different somehow. Even so, he tried to keep going, but whatever he did she was in front of him. If he slowed down, so did she, if he sped up she did also, just barely enough to keep him from bumping into her. If he went very slowly, she would crouch on her arms, her buttocks in the air, the same as she had done toward the first male. Then she would look back over her shoulder at him. And he was constantly aware of her scent.

All of a sudden he couldn't hear any other animals moving in the brush and he realized he was alone with her. He stopped and listened. She turned around and began pulling the hair on his stomach apart, grooming. It felt very good, as it had from his earliest infancy when his mother or other females did it. She took hold of his balls and played with them. His small cock hardened and he sat very still. She put her lips over his cock and he could feel the suction. He waited.

She let go of his cock and assumed the crouching position again. This time he mounted as he had in play many times. He held her hips with both hands and began thrusting. Then he felt his cock go inside.

They stayed together several days, traveling to one side of the main group, though within earshot. Occasionally they would see another chimp but made no effort to join him nor did any of the others approach the pair. Two or three times a day, they would quickly fuck. Otherwise they browsed or rested.

Then one morning when they came down from their nests, Humungus approached Maryanne but failed to get her scent. She was sitting. He approached and sat beside her. She put her hand on his arm lightly. He turned toward her and reaching down, put one hand under her buttocks and lifted her. The swelling had gone down. He put the finger inside and poked around. It was almost dry. He pulled his finger out and smelled it. No scent. He put the finger in his mouth and tasted it; no scent. He tried it again with the same result. He let her sit again.

They browsed together for a couple of hours though coming steadily closer to the main group. When they were almost among them, Maryanne ambled toward a group of females. Humungus watched her go.

He heard several animals coming through the brush in his general direction, Three males appeared, Bighead in front. The troop leader stopped and grunted low when he saw Humungus. The younger male became quickly alert. He could tell by the quietness of the group that it was a hunting party. That would mean red meat, the best kind. He got in place behind the others. They turned their heads to recognize him, then continued.

Bighead led them down the hill to where Humungus knew was a water hole. All of the animals got quieter as they approached the pond. They spread out at the edge of the clearing. Peering through the brush, Humungus could see several waterbuck as well as a small troop of baboons. None of the animals had spotted the chimpanzees yet. At one end of the pond Humungus could see several bush pigs, apparently three adults and three or four young ones. They were rolling in the mud, also unaware of the hunters. Humungus moved in that direction, along with the other three. All kept within the fringe of trees. Without any voice signals, the hunters spread into a loose surround formation. They all moved with great caution, carefully putting branches to one side with their hands and setting their feet down softly enough that there was only a slight rustling sound.

All of a sudden, one of the baboons spotted a chimpanzee and barked excitedly, soon to be followed by the others. Then the clearing exploded into action. The baboons ran for the trees. One female dropped her young one, stopped, and turned back to grab it while a big male stood alongside her, baring his canines.

The waterbuck ran in the same direction. The bush pigs got up, momentarily confused, mud clinging to their bodies. Then two of the adults and two of the young animals turned, and with tails held high, ran off grunting. By that time the chimpanzees had raced forward and surrounded the third adult and the last young one. Bighead ran toward the adult female, but she lowered her head and counterattacked, slashing sideways with her tusks. Bighead jumped back. The young pig stayed just behind the slashing female. Bighead jumped forward and back again when she counterattacked. Though her tusks were not as large as those of a full-grown boar, they were formidable. The other two chimpanzees closed in then and all took turns jumping in and back when she slashed toward them. One even got a grasp of the young pig's tail and pulled. But when it squealed, she turned toward that chimp and drove him off. Humungus was still back from the rest of the group, though getting closer. Finally, he joined the circle and began jumping in too. She faced one after another but began to weary. Humungus grabbed a large rock, and holding it high in both hands, ran forward on his hind legs like one of the hairless bipeds. When he got close enough, he hurled it against the female, catching her on the side of the head. He was surprised because he had never hit anything with a rock before. She fell, but only momentarily. While the chimpanzee hunters stood for a moment in indecision, she arose and groggily turned again to the counterattack. But she was hurt, the blood running from the wound the rock had made. All of a sudden, she slashed her way through the cordon and trotted away, not fast, but enough to get away.

The half-grown piglet started after her, but Humungus was too fast. He grabbed it by the hind leg and jumped on top of it. It squealed but could not get away, being smothered by his weight and choking hands. He held on tight, the other apes crowding around. Its struggles slowed. Humungus raised himself without letting go of the prey, even though it was only quivering by then. And there was Bighead, staring at him unwaveringly. Bighead reached forward and grabbed one of the legs of the piglet. For a moment Humungus started to let go but then stiffened and instead stood up, growling, and without releasing the dead pig. Bighead stared at him for a moment as if undecided what to do. Then he jumped up a nearby tree, and, standing on its lower branch, jumped up and down, showering Humungus with leaves and bits of branches. He jumped down and ran around Humungus, hooting angrily. Apollo and another of the troop hooted also. Humungus lifted the piglet and slammed it down, screaming. Bighead ran up to the side of a tree trunk and drummed it with his feet then ran straight at Humungus, waving his arms and baring his canines. And although his fear was intense by that time, Humungus did not retreat, continuing to hold on to the piglet.

Bighead ran the other direction, to the edge of the clearing, followed by Apollo and his companion. All three picked up branches and, turning again toward Humungus, came running and hooting at the top of their voices, thrashing the ground with the branches. They came at full speed, not stopping until they were just in front of the challenger. Humungus stood up to his full height and screamed at the top of his voice. All four stood immobilized for a moment as if frozen. Then Bighead let his branch drop. Humungus turned and slowly climbed onto the low branch of the nearby tree, where he began to tear at the flesh of the piglet. The others hunched below him, every once in a while glancing up furtively. After a while, Humungus let some pieces drop.

When he had eaten almost half, Humungus came down. Bighead was the first to approach him, watching at first, but then putting out his hand, palm up. Humungus did not turn away and Bighead put his hand on one of the piglet's hind legs. Humungus reached over and touched Bighead's hand. The former alpha male took a firm grip and the two pulled the piglet apart.

\* \* \* \* \*

No one challenged Humungus for many years. He was by all odds the biggest animal in the group, and he used his body well. Like all of the other males, he fucked most of the females, though he got out of the habit of going on consort trips with them. He sired many young apes, though he did not know, nor did he care, which were his.

\* \* \* \* \*

Humungus woke at the sound of the guinea fowls' cackling. He opened his eyes and saw the sun on the eastern horizon. It was shining weakly through the last layers of pink clouds. A late mosquito whined over his head, and he waved it away. The branches of his nest creaked. He looked down and saw the ground some thirty feet below. No sign of life there. He heard the waking noise of another chimpanzee, farting and belching. Looking across, he saw another nest at about the same level. A hairy face peered over the top.

Humungus rolled over. There was pain in his joints. It had been increasing and was especially bad after a rainy night. There had been a thunderstorm in the middle of the night, and though the first coolness had been refreshing, after a little while the lightning and blowing rain had become unpleasant. For a moment he had thought of climbing down and running down the hill screaming, beating the ground with a branch, and dancing in a circle, as he had done in his youth. But then he realized how unwise that might be in the middle of the night. There were few animals he feared, though meeting a leopard on the ground could be uncomfortable. He had therefore curled up with his hands over his head and shivered. Finally, the rain had let up, but by that time his body was soaked. Fortunately, he was mostly dry again by morning, though the long wet period had made his bones ache.

He climbed down the tree slowly and carefully. He wasn't as agile as he had been, and falling thirty feet would not be pleasant. He had done that a couple of times and didn't want it to happen again.

Soon there were sounds of the others from different directions. They were moving off in the direction of the structures. The hairless bipeds that did not have fire sticks had moved into the edge of their territory about a year before. Some were not only hairless; they had light skins. And though they had no hair on their faces and arms, they had body covers in pieces that looked like solid hair. Humungus had watched the lone one who followed them at a distance for a long time. It carried something on its shoulder and was forever sitting on a rock or log to look through its before-eyes device in their direction. But it never carried a fire stick. It came closer and closer but never made a sound, unlike the hairless bipeds with the fire sticks who ran out when the troop pulled down the stalk fruit. Humungus and the others had become less and less nervous. Then one day there was another biped who carried a shiny-eyed device on spindly legs. Humungus heard it buzz when the creature pointed it in their direction. He didn't know what it was doing, but it wasn't a fire stick.

The troop would make their regular circuit then come back toward the place of structures, the place where the smoke rose. Sometimes the first lone one would be behind. Sometimes it would be accompanied by the other one with the shiny-eyed, three-legged device. For a long time, the chimpanzees would stand at the edge of the clearing, watching the activity around the structures from behind the bushes. But slowly they moved out a little further.

They found unusual things. One day a female came across a shiny thing that had another tiny chimpanzee inside it. She walked around it, and the little one disappeared. Then she touched it, but nothing happened except that her finger touched the finger of the image creature, though without feeling it. Then one day a chimp found some stalk fruit. After that, there were small piles here and there that the first animals would grab, often more than they could carry. Many quarrels occurred and some fights. But then one day there was a small structure. Different animals hit it or pulled at it or jumped on it. Then one day when Elliott was prying it with a stick, it opened, and inside was a pile of stalk fruit.

That had been the beginning. More boxes had appeared, and sometimes they wouldn't open the same way. But the chimps would push and pull and hammer and pry, eventually getting in.

Humungus had been afraid at first that the bipeds would come shouting with their fire sticks, but when the chimps took the stalk fruit and it didn't happen, he and the others began to feel more at ease. They let the bipeds get closer. Some of the young chimps even let the upright creatures touch them.

This particular morning Humungus looked forward to the stalk fruit boxes because he had no wish to go traveling a long distance for wild fruit. He stopped momentarily at the edge of the clearing, noticing a female baboon near one of the boxes, searching in the grass. On her back was a half-grown black, riding piggyback. She brought up a banana peel and brushed it on both sides before putting it in her mouth. She looked at Humungus sideways as he passed, a flicker of a grimace on her face. Humungus looked all around, and the nearest male baboon he could see was a long way off, being groomed by another. The thought flashed through his mind that with one quick jump, he might easily grab the black and run, as he had done several times when he was younger. But then he thought of her loud barking and the convergence of all the adult males in earshot. He would surely have to run hard, climb fast, or be mobbed. And what with his aching bones, the idea just didn't appeal to him. He continued on, visualizing the delectable pile of stalk fruit. But the boxes were closed. Evidently the bipeds hadn't put any fruit in them yet. They usually did that fairly early in the morning. Humungus looked across the clearing and saw several other disgruntled chimps, either looking dejectedly at the boxes or hammering on them. Humungus began to move from one to another, inspecting each. He noticed that the other males didn't back off quickly when he approached, as they had formerly. One, Long Jim, didn't even pull his hand back. Only when Humungus stood up and waved his arms about, "waaing," did the newly mature male pull back his hand. But with all the checking, Humungus did not find a single banana. He did pick up one skin and dejectedly put it in his mouth, chewing slowly. It wasn't very flavorful, but it would have to do until whole fruit was again brought out.

The alpha male stopped right at the fringe of the clearing when he saw a little cluster of animals moving his way. He watched them until he recognized Old Minnie. Although he couldn't see her rump, he could easily guess she was in heat. She moved in a slow zigzag, going directly in front of each male, and swivelling with her rump facing him, crouched on her forearms. More often than not the male would mount her and copulate. If he wasn't interested right away, she would change her position. Also, more often than not, Minnie's weaning daughter, Hanna, and frequently another young chimp, would try to interfere, pushing against the male. No other male made any effort to stop each copulation, short as it was. Each one mounted and ejaculated in less than a minute. Minnie would scream at the moment of ejaculation, and then after resting a bit, and reassuring Hanna with hand pats, move on to the next. And so she made her way to Humungus.

Instead of presenting her rump immediately, she started to groom him, separating the hairs on his stomach carefully. He relaxed, feeling better than at any time since the previous day. Even his joints felt better. But she finally stopped, turned, and crouched. Humungus studied her pink bottom, at first with little interest. But she got up and moved over to present from another angle. He still watched her lethargically, wishing she were still grooming him. But at her third shift, after she had turned to look at him over her shoulder several times, he got up and mounted her. His cock was hard by then and went in. But just when he was thrusting as hard as he could, Hanna and the other youngster came to push against his face and shoulders. He was tired of that, even though he had put up with it for all the years he had been copulating. He turned his face to one side and with an exasperated grimace, kept thrusting. Finally, the ejaculation came and Minnie screamed. Humungus pulled out and leaned back with relief.

Minnie drifted off, and the alpha male leaned back to rest. Copulating had become a lot of work. Humungus could pass up a lot of females, but Minnie, despite her age, was the most irresistible. He dozed, dreaming of eating the juicy red meat of a young baboon. He was awakened fully by the closing of a door when the bipeds came out with a new supply of stalk fruit. A wave of interest passed through the glade.

Humungus moved back toward the main forest when he had finished, still holding a banana in one hand. He had eaten sixteen or seventeen before quitting, then letting the females and younger males take their turn. He was preparing to move into the shade of a large fig tree when he heard the unusual sound. It was not what one ever heard in the forest, rather a hollow sound, but of the shiny material the bipeds used. He stopped and looked back. Long Jim was running upright with a shiny box in each hand that he periodically banged on the ground as he came through the glade. Humungus was sure Long Jim had gotten the boxes from the bipeds' structure. As the newly mature male came careening through the glade, all the others looked up and got out of the way.

"Whomp, whomp," the boxes resounded, periodically intermixed with Long Jim's hoots. It was clear that Long Jim was displaying and challenging. He came straight toward Humungus. At first the alpha male thought of standing straight up at his full height and refusing to move aside. But he was too full then, and besides the "whomping" Long Jim was impressive. When the younger male got almost to Humungus, the old male stepped aside.

\* \* \* \* \*

And so it happened that Long Jim gained the alpha position. Perhaps he would have managed anyway, but the "whomp"-cans were enough to intimidate all the males, including Humungus. The old male moved to one side and went out on his own more and more. He rarely joined in hunting trips any longer, contenting himself with stalk fruit and wild plant products if they were not too difficult to collect.

\* \* \* \* \*

Humungus felt tired as he moved down the mountain toward the main group, which was feeding in a palm nut grove. He wasn't hungry, had not been since his nose had got clogged with mucus. He had felt bad like that before, but recently it had become more frequent, and this was the worst so far.

He was thinner than at any time since his youth, his massive chest seeming too big as he made his way carefully down the slope. He stopped to sit on a log, and when a beetle started by, he reached over to pick it up lethargically. But he did not put it in his mouth, instead slowly fingering it. When he got up enough energy, he rose and wearily began again.

He had been alone for several days, feeding very little because nothing tasted good. Also, he hadn't been to the stalk fruit boxes because more and more adult males would refuse to back off, and he rarely felt good enough to oppose them directly.

The voices of the other chimpanzees were still dim when he heard some twigs snap and leaves rustle. He stopped, trying to decide what to do. It was not a very good place to be, just on the edge of the adjacent band's territory. Humungus had helped chase several other animals from that band back into their own territory when he was younger.

Before he could decide though, the leaves opened and there stood three males from his own band, Clark, Gary, and John. They were newly matured animals who had recently moved into roles just below that of

Long Jim. They stared at Humungus for a moment, then John stood up and hooted. The former alpha male squatted, waiting. Suddenly John lunged forward, hooting all the while, and hit Humungus so hard on the chest that the older male rolled over backward. He tried to scramble to his feet and hands but by then Gary was kicking him. Humungus tried to fend off the foot blows, but with difficulty. He didn't have either the strength or the quickness. He was aware only of thumping feet and hands and much hooting and screaming. When he got to his hands and feet, Clark hit him hard with both feet and he rolled over again. Then one of them took his left leg and twisted it. Humungus couldn't prevent that, so he cowered. John bit him in the forearm and shoulder, making it bleed. After that Humungus put his hands over his head while the three jumped on him, twisted, bit, and screamed.

Then it was still. The old male looked around and was aware that he was totally alone and that all parts of his body ached. He wiggled the fingers of his right hand and, realizing he could move again without interference, slowly got up. He rested a moment to regain his energy and then slowly turned around and headed the way he had come, limping and aching all the way. He got far enough in the brush that he could be found again only with difficulty. He felt dizzy and lay down under some thick brush. The last sound he heard was the whinny of a hyena.

# CHAPTER 9

Martin was pleased when he saw that the astral shrink was in Oldenberg's office. He was surprised in a way that he had missed the man, though he had to admit that his reactions toward others in the Transition Bureau had been generally quite positive. He knew that underneath he was continually excited by the fact that they were from distant worlds. He just could not stop wondering what they would look like if they were not done up by the Department of Illusions.

Hanson was smoking a cigarillo. He offered his pack to Martin. "How about it, are you ready to try one?"

Martin eyed the brown tube and for a moment hesitated. After all, everything had changed. Tobacco would not harm him at this stage of his being, or nonbeing, he thought. He started to put his hand forward but then stopped and pulled back. "No, I'm afraid of all the things I gave up on Earth, the conditioning for not taking tobacco was the strongest. I just cannot bring myself to put it in my mouth again."

"Evidently you earthlings really got hooked on that plant," Hanson said. "I keep cigarillos and cigarettes in my office and offer them to patients to calm them down. Since they have ceased their earthly lives, the tobacco doesn't have any negative effect—I mean, it cannot make them ill or kill them through cancer."

Martin sat down. "It is a bizarre turn of events, to be using the stuff in the afterworld. But I'm afraid I just cannot."

"That's alright. There are obviously a number of other ways to get a high, or "kicks," as you earthlings put it. And when you realize how much your species depends on drugs for all kinds of purposes, it is inevitable, I suppose, that you would use them to promote pleasure."

Martin took the cigarillo then and tapped it against the ashtray absently. "That's true. I once used a very good book in my introductory class called *Gluttons and Libertines*. It had a whole chapter on drugs for pleasure, which Professor Bates called 'Shortcuts to Happiness.' A very apt title, I always thought." Pause. "One of the most interesting facts, I suppose, is that drug use is strictly a human activity. None of the other animals have been known to take drugs deliberately. Even those interesting apes I just saw on video."

"Ah yes," Hanson said, "your latest voyage into past lives. Harold told me at lunch today what you were doing, and I was a little surprised. You see, we mentalists from other worlds, at least those I know about, very rarely resort to studies of low-level communicators, those who lack the facility to symbol. We do not feel that what nonsymboling animals do will shed much light on the ones who do symbol."

Martin was quite impressed that the therapist evidently understood so well the idea of symbol use, that one could arbitrarily give meaning to anything one could perceive and then use that meaning for complex communication. It was an idea that he had rarely heard on Earth from anyone except anthropologists or linguists. At the same time he felt compelled to defend his latest video viewing. He said, "You may be right in a way. But we anthropologists have long been worried about the problem of knowing what human behavior is natural and what is the product of conditioning, what we call enculturation. And we've ended up in some unusual research corners, I guess. Perhaps studying our closest animal relatives is one such. Anyway, the idea is that we can thus find out the natural component in our behavior. And so, I couldn't help thinking after awhile about our closest living relatives in the biological chain." Pause. "It might well be an anthropological hangup, but as we anthropologists are so frequently fond of saying as a reason for studying something, 'Anyway, it would be interesting.'"

"Ah yes, and I must say I agree to a considerable extent. One of the problems members of your species seem to be particularly prone to is boredom. If there are not different or interesting things to do, you seem to get into a 'funk,' as you put it in your argot." Pause. "And this is particularly interesting to me because the other earth species seem to have little of this characteristic. So, to study something just because it's 'interesting' seems to me to be fulfilling a real human need. And I suppose a lot of the discoveries of your people were the consequence of such boredom-driven activity, no?"

"Yes, I think so." Martin kept expecting Oldenberg to arrive, and he felt a little uncomfortable that the plump man didn't come through the door. Finally, he said, "Isn't Transitioner Oldenberg coming?" Pause. "I'm sure I had an appointment with him." But he added quickly, "Of course I'm very pleased you are here, Dr. Hanson. In fact, I missed you the last time. But since Transitioner Oldenberg is my monitor, I feel pretty much bound to keep him informed."

Hanson put out what was left of his cigarillo and smiled at Martin, saying, "I understand. And you're not hurting my feelings. I think he will be here soon. He asked me to come and meet you and get started. If he misses some part, he can check up on it in the written report." Pause. "I hope that's okay with you. The meeting he's at is rather important. Again it's about cutting costs in the Transition Bureau."

Martin was sorry to hear that they were continuing in that vein. Since he had been thinking more and more of trying to work out a place for himself in the Bureau, the idea of a cutback wasn't appealing at all. After all, even if he were to be so lucky, he would still be at the bottom of the totem pole, and if there was any reduction, he would mostly likely be the victim. He said, "I hope it turns out okay."

"Don't worry, Harold will work something out." Hanson leaned forward conspiratorially, "And frankly, you should know he thinks a lot of your project, even though both of us know pretty well that whatever you learn will hardly affect operations." Pause, switch. "But let's get back to your apes. What did you find that they did naturally?"

With relief, Martin reorganized his thoughts onto the matter at hand, the consort life of Humungus the chimpanzee. "Well, they lived in one big group, and except for some couples who went off for a few days together, they were generally promiscuous. Each male had contact, including copulating, with a wide variety of females, and vice versa. There just weren't any long-term relationships, much less families. Why, there was no evidence that males knew who their own children were, or cared."

"Hmm. That sounds like the primitive hordes your early anthropologists used to discuss among humans. And I take it you are therefore inferring that the long-term relationship, particularly what your species tries to establish through a civil contract, marriage, must be learned. Is that correct?"

Martin leaned back. "I would say so. Even though we have been teaching for years that marriage, a socially sanctified union between adults, is universal, it could be that it is a product of cultural learning. Another reason to doubt its naturalness is the fact that nowadays we seem to be abandoning it more than ever before. We seem to be headed back toward short-term relationships, and ones that are not ritually sanctioned."

Pause. "I want to get some of the details of that way of life in before we get finished with this series."

Hanson leaned forward. "So what else did you find out with your nonenculturated primates?"

"I didn't exactly say they didn't have any enculturation, but it seems they didn't get nearly as much as humans did. Most importantly of course is that they did not have language, and that seemed to have been the main medium for intensive brainwashing."

Hanson lifted his eyebrows. "Brainwashing? I thought that was a term you earthlings used for political indoctrination. Furthermore, I understand those of you who favored the rights of individuals considered it to be a most reprehensible kind of conditioning, which only people of other political persuasions would resort to."

Martin chuckled, then replied, "Yes, I'm afraid that is how the term was used most often. But some time ago I, and I suspect quite a number of my fellow anthropologists, came to the opinion that the leaders of political cadres in Marxist states were far from being the most efficient mind shapers. Rather, it was Mom."

"*Mom;* you mean the human mother?"

"I sure do. Though in all honesty I would have to broaden the group that has been instrumental in shaping the mind of the growing individual. But Mom was always first. Even before she taught the child its first words, she was beginning to shape its mind. Though I never saw it personally, I can literally see the first procedure of the Japanese mother in conditioning her infant to accept the hierarchy he would need to live in when he became an adult. Long before it could speak, she would hold the infant up to face its father and tip it forward in a simulated bow. It couldn't even stand up yet, and its mother was impressing on it the necessity of showing deference to older males, and particularly to the father."

"I see what you mean, but it seems to me you are deliberately picking a dramatic example."

Martin got up then because he was feeling so professorish. He could almost imagine heading for a lectern to lean on, to expound more forcefully. But then he suddenly remembered where he was. He wasn't facing a group of freshmen and sophomores in an introductory anthropology class, they sitting with pencils poised. No indeed, he was talking to an other-world therapist from God knows what bizarre place, and God knows of what outlandish appearance if his true image could be perceived. Martin sat down, slightly embarrassed.

Hanson seemed to notice his discomfort and to try to put the ex-professor at ease. "I mean," he said, "that perhaps mothers in other cultures didn't do anything so significant as the Japanese; that's all I'm saying."

"Well, I don't know," Martin resumed then. "After all, when you consider the Western mother who slaps her child's hands because it is trying to eat an earthworm, you are definitely seeing an instance of impressing special food requirements on the infant before it can talk. And there have been a lot of cultures in which people ate worms, grubs, and all kinds of insects. The mothers of such praised their children for eating worms. Furthermore, there is no doubt that such creatures are a good source of protein." Pause. "And to take another example from another major culture, the Russians: they swaddle their infants at birth, I understand, a procedure that restricts their movements. There was a time when our psychological anthropologists made a lot out of that as a cause for the structure of Russian personality. I didn't personally accept that particular theory, but it seems to me that whether a child is left free in a crib or whether it is wrapped tightly ought to affect it some way."

Martin was beginning to feel a little ill at ease, recognizing that he was drifting off on a tangent. He was happy, therefore, when Hanson brought him back by saying, "Well, I can see that you humans are subject to a lot more conditioning, or enculturation as you anthropologists put it, than the other animals; and so I guess I can accept the idea that two people living together for a lifetime, united by a civil contract, could well be a consequence of learning. Not natural, as you put it." Pause. "And how did your unenculturated primates, the chimps, make out with their temporary liaisons; I mean, did it seem to add to their well-being or contentment?"

"I'd say so. The males and females generally took care of themselves, but when the females came into heat, a pair sometimes went off together for a few days. Otherwise, anyone could mate with anyone else. Why, even the very young males were allowed to try their hand at mounting females in heat." Martin chuckled at his word choice and then corrected himself facetiously. "Or should I say 'try their penis'?"

"So everyone got to participate, eh?"

"Yes, and I think it is quite significant in comparison with humans. You may know that though our species has in general favored long-term or lifetime consortships, which we tried to validate through the institution of marriage, there have always been some people who didn't manage. I know that when I was growing up men and women who never managed to get married were pointed out as sort of freaks, the ladies the worst. They were called old maids, and others pitied them. I remember two of my paternal aunts who were normally attractive but never married or to my knowledge dated. My mother and father, as well as other relatives, would have them over for a meal once in a while as an act of kindness. But that they didn't have partners of the opposite sex made them too odd to have around very long."

Martin considered his description of the "old girls," which everyone called them during all their adult lives and compared those lives with those of the chimps. With sudden revelation, he said, "Now if Gertrude and Philomena had been chimpanzees, they wouldn't have had to live their lives of aloneness nor miss the other experiences of their sex. Some males would have copulated with them, and they would have become pregnant and had babies. Granted, they wouldn't have had a ring on their left hand, nor anyone to bring home food or provide housing. But at least they would have gone through maternity like all the other females." Pause. "And they supported themselves all their lives anyway. It doesn't sound so bad to me."

Hanson got up for a drink of water. Then, turning, he said, "It sounds like you find the human way less satisfactory than that of the chimpanzees."

"I'm not exactly saying that. Some things, perhaps yes; others, no. But as you may have guessed already, I got into this study in the first place largely because I failed to get much satisfaction from my own consort relationships in life; and when I looked around, I saw that there were a lot of others in the same boat. And it wasn't a 'love boat,' as one of our popular TV series portrayed it. And so when I see a creature that manages that aspect of its life quite well with very short-term contacts, I begin to feel that what was wrong with the human way was the length and intensity of the pairing. The chimps didn't seem to worry about having a deep feeling for a particular individual at all. When they felt like a screw, to put it in the vernacular, they just went at it with almost anyone around. There was this one older female, Minnie, who seemed to do it with anyone who was interested. No complications. Nothing like the elaborate procedures we humans got involved in during our consort relationships."

"You mean the ritualization of the pairing in your institution of marriage?" Hanson sat down and lit another cigarillo.

"Well yes, that. In our traditional societies, it frequently took years before a couple got to it. But even recently, in what we called modern times, when we felt we had liberated ourselves from the dead hand of custom, particularly in sexual affairs, we evolved a thorough substitute for the ritualized long-term pairing, what we called 'the relationship'."

Just then the door opened, and Oldenberg entered. He looked a little tired, with less than his usual jolly demeanor. He walked over to the liquor cabinet. "Gentlemen, I think I will have a glass of sherry. After the cost-effectiveness meeting I just attended, I need it. How about you two?"

Martin waited on the transition shrink. Hanson said, "I think I'd prefer a glass of Chablis."

Martin took sherry, one of his earth favorites. He was pleased to recognize the nutty flavor of *amontillado*, and Spanish at that. Although Martin felt that California wines were excellent, better in some respects than the European originals, and that some of the sherries were not bad, the Spanish ones were clearly the best.

Hanson sipped his, then said, "I suppose the fiscal men were really out with their hatchets, eh? That's the rumor that's going around. What happened?"

Oldenberg sat down then and sipped his sherry. "Well, they are certainly in a cutting mood. You know they come out with outlandish demands and then our side counters, and we end up with a compromise of sorts. Their initial ploy was that we drop the whole Transition System and close all the offices. Their argument was that there were a lot of other worlds being neglected because so much was being spent here and that it was hardly necessary. A permanent solution could be made for the end of each life by simply eliminating the individuality of the essence and merging it into the Super-essence. You know, a lot like the Hindu–Buddhist *nirvana*, though without the successive lives and the 'wheel of karma' and all the other complications of those religions. When a being died, it would just automatically be merged into the Super-essence." He paused and sipped at his sherry again. "There's no doubt that it would save a lot of money. There would be no necessity for any Transitioners to help individuals into their next lives, and these offices could be shut. Then all the backup and attached facilities also could be eliminated, you know, things like the Astral Gardens and the Cosmic Amusement Park."

Martin was sad to hear this because he was counting more and more on being a part of the ongoing system. He had not yet heard of the Cosmic Amusement Park but could imagine that it had fantastic rides and entertainment.

Hanson said, "You know, I can see their point of view. After all, this is certainly a minute speck in the universe, compared with all of the other places with Life Systems. And probably a lot is being spent in proportion to its size. On the other hand, the Transition System is rather unique on a universal scale. And though those fiscal types would be the last in the world to admit it, it is possible that we might learn something here that would be applicable to other Life Systems."

Oldenberg sighed. "Ah yes, but you know, Jerry, how difficult it is to convince those beady-eyed characters of the value of any research. But we did our best, and for the time being we are continuing, though with some reduction in facilities and no new projects. For instance, we Transition Masters are now supposed to cut the time down for sessions from an hour to one-half hour. It will be difficult to get enough of a grasp of a passage person's life but I suppose we can manage it. After all, most of us Transitioners have been here a while now, and we should have more of a grasp of the problems of earthlings. This should make a Transition session faster."

"Anything else?"

"Well, as I said before, no new projects. For instance, the plans to set up an in-house educational system, based on a U.S. university, have been shelved. Then too, what they call marginal research projects—though in hearing the fiscal boys talk, all research is marginal—have got to be cut back."

Martin forced himself to keep quiet. But Oldenberg seemed to sense his unease because he answered Martin's immediate worry, saying, "Fortunately, Martin, your project is nearing its termination. And though the budget committee at first suggested that all projects not being done by Transitioners be phased out immediately, they did finally agree to let those of short duration go to completion, though with no possibility of extension, I'm afraid."

"I'm glad of that," Martin said, not yet airing his worry that this development would of course have a lot of bearing on his long-range plans also.

Oldenberg said, "They were willing to give you three more days. Do you think you can wind up Project Heterop in that time?"

As a matter of fact, Martin had indeed worked out how much time he would need, though he had not yet talked about it. Even though he was getting close to the end, he had wanted to keep the final date open in case some other possibility came to mind. But evidently that was not possible any longer. He said, "Yes, there's only two more Life Videos I feel are necessary, which I feel sure I can do in a couple of days. The first should be fairly short, one that I might do in quite a bit less than a full day. But the second should be long and might well use up the time left over from the first, and even require another full day." Martin felt reluctant to specify which Videos he planned to see as yet since he had not finished with his analysis of the life of Humungus, the chimpanzee.

"You can certainly have the two days and perhaps even a few days more to write up your report. Then, Martin, we will have to get on with the Transition." Oldenberg almost sounded apologetic, as if he was reading Martin's mind and did not want his Transitioner/researcher to get up any false hopes.

Martin decided not to push his case any further then, even though he was becoming more and more convinced that his period of life among the Transitioners was rapidly coming to an end. But he decided to go on in a positive fashion. What else was there to do?

Hanson helped by bringing Oldenberg up to date on the briefing so far, finishing by saying, "And Martin had just described how easy and uncomplicated the sex was among the chimpanzees, compared with the complexities of the human relationship."

"Yes, that's it," Martin said. "We humans downplayed the necessity for marriage in the late twentieth century and told each other that we had liberated sex from the tyranny it had been under in the nineteenth century and before, when you had to be married to do it. But instead of really making people free to do it with whomever and as they wished, or for the sheer physical pleasure of it, we evolved the relationship. That was a form of consorting in which people were supposed to develop 'deep caring' for the other before sex would be permitted. In fact, among most it probably became almost as monogamous as marriage, even though no ritual was involved. People could get just as jealous of a partner in a 'relationship' as they could a spouse. Nothing at all like the chimps, where both males and females took their pleasure with one another openly and briefly and with no hard feelings toward others. For instance, we humans discovered in the twentieth century that when people broke up a 'relationship,' they could be almost as psychologically devastated as if they had been married. That just could not have happened with the chimps and most other primates. They just did not focus so much on one individual."

Oldenberg took his pipe out then. The procedure of it being filled and lit pleased Martin. He had become used to his monitor's habit and looked forward to the aroma of the tobacco smoke. After a good puff, Oldenberg said, "But of course, you must remember again that the basic reason for pairing in Life Systems is to produce and succor young. And it is apparent that you humans evolved a different way from that of the other primates like the chimpanzees. Your lifetime, ritualized relationship, your marriage, seemed to have evolved because the young could be raised and trained more efficiently that way. In fact, I seem to have read somewhere that the females of your species, alone among the primates, are continuously receptive sexually, and this may have been a means of keeping the male around and helping. That is, as a reward."

Martin responded to that quickly. "It is true that human females are the only ones in heat all the time, so to speak, that is, of the primates. But when you get to thinking about it, even if the chimpanzees are only in heat for about ten days between periods and when not nursing young, then offering it to most everybody, the continuous gift of a human female, when one is married or has a relationship, is not such a great sexual reward. You know that, in general, one wasn't supposed to 'make out' with other females once one was married or had a relationship. Certainly one wasn't free to do it with anyone who was interested. That was called 'open marriage,' but it was found it wouldn't work for long. Jealousy would invariably raise its ugly head."

Martin continued. "I admit there is the theory of sexual reward, developed by the sociobiologists, I believe, but it doesn't seem very sound to me. The human female's continuous sexuality doesn't sound like such a reward when you consider that she was supposed to have exclusive rights, not to mention all the times she might be indisposed. You may have heard about the 'I've Got a Headache Tonight Darling Syndrome.'"

Oldenberg answered. "Yes, I understand it is the situation when the female is indisposed for any one of a variety of reasons; and that in your culture being sick was the only unassailable excuse for not fulfilling social responsibilities." Pause and consideration. "But even if the male didn't get so much sex in the marriage or relationship, I fail to see how that eliminates the sociobiologists' argument. If the function of continuous sexuality was the promise that the male would get a lot of sex, and he believed it, then the fact that he got less than he would in an 'open relationship' is, as you people say, 'academic.' The males would stay around, and evidently they did, at least a lot more than your chimpanzees, and I presume the rest of the monkey family, no?"

"Yes, no one could deny that. After all, apart from the gibbon, and I believe one South American monkey, we humans are the only one of the primates who managed for a long while with the family. Basically, the male stayed around and helped. Why, he even brought food home for the female and young, something no chimpanzee or any other primate in their right mind would do. When it came to food, apart from mother's milk and a little meat on occasion, it was everyone for him or herself."

"So plenty of sharing of sex but no sharing of food, eh?"

"Basically that's the case. If there was anything those chimps were ready to fight for, it was food, or perhaps territory. But it was unheard of for them to fight over a female. None of that mad jealousy that evolved with humans."

Hanson entered the conversation again. "It seems to me, Martin, that another difference, which I presume you would attribute to lack of brainwashing, was that the female seemed to be the sexual initiator most of the time, in contrast to humans. Is that not the case?"

"By all means. Nothing happened until she came into heat, at which time she tried to stir up the boys, so to speak. And that wasn't always easy. They seemed to be able to take it or leave it generally, though there was always enough interest that she ultimately could get some to copulate with her. Quite different than with most human groups in which the male was generally the aggressor and the female frequently played hard to get. Again, in the late twentieth century, during our period of 'liberal' sex, females were supposed to start things up as much as males. It was respectable for them to call men up if they were so interested, and to ask for sex if they felt like it. But I think such forwardness was not common. As best I remember, there was one woman in my lifetime who asked me to stay overnight at her house, though I had already indicated pretty clearly that I would like to have sex with her. Otherwise, it was always me making the approach and more often than not being turned down, at least the first time."

"That does seem like a significant difference. And you think the human female's attitude is also a product of your complex conditioning, eh?" Hanson asked.

"I'm afraid I do, that little girls were taught very early that they shouldn't do it, and little boys were taught that they should try to get the girls to do it. I still remember an incident about how such conditioning happened in our own society.

"When she was perhaps ten years old, one of my sisters was caught in the garage, showing her genitals to a little boy in exchange for seeing his. And though I don't remember the details, I do remember there was a great hullabaloo by my parents. The very fact that I could remember the incident sixty or seventy years later, while most occurrences that long before had been forgotten, indicates that some strong action, probably a spanking, was taken by my father and mother. They were certainly brainwashing that child directly, and presumably most of the rest of us indirectly. I know that I grew up with a pronounced shyness toward females, presumably the consequence of many such incidents."

Hanson chuckled then. "That seems to be another in the category of what I am going to call the 'Mom Did It Syndrome'; you know, blaming one's problems on one's mother's early influence. It seems to be one of the favorite explanations of shook-up earthlings."

"That's true. I think a lot of therapists would go out of business if their patients couldn't go back and blame Mom. And although I think the old girl has been treated somewhat too badly, there is no doubt that she was the primary influence in the early years. Why, that is even true of the chimps and other primates. They don't know who their father is, but the one who is a fixture in their early years is Hairy Mom." Pause. "So Mom ought to be blamed for the early influence on all us beasts with opposable thumbs. But one of the surprising things with us upright primates is that we almost always blame Mom for the bad things in our lives and rarely give her credit for the good. I know it was quite late in my life that I gave my mother any credit for imparting any useful characteristics to me. And I'm not sure my sisters ever did so."

In his usual manner, Hanson paraphrased Martin's ramblings to come out with a more succinct conclusion: "And so you are saying that it has been the human mother who has impressed on the girl that she shouldn't pass out her sexual favors freely; is that it?"

"Yes and no. She probably has been more influential than the father, but I think he is a much stronger influence than the primate male. After all, he's around a lot of the time, even though our counselors and other specialists in behavior of the twentieth century berated him for not being around enough. You may have heard that when we got deepest into our era of human rights we decided to bestow the same rights on females as on males. And if the mother had to be around the child a lot, so also ought the father. It was only fair, the equal rights people claimed. And though that never exactly happened, there was more participation by fathers in their children's upbringing than in previous times. And many fathers were known to encourage their boys to cast around freely in sexual matters while protecting their daughters, that is, preventing them from freely giving sex. But still and all, I would guess the most influential one in this matter has been Mom."

Oldenberg entered the conversation then, saying, "Martin, you were discussing the theorizing of that new breed of explainer in your midst, the sociobiologist, a while ago in reference to the continuous sexuality of the human female, is that not correct?"

"Yes, they became quite vocal in the 70s and 80s. They tried to explain a lot of human behavior as being a consequence of our genes rather than our enculturation. Though interesting, most of their explanations were near unprovable. The reasons they gave were sort of like light bulbs going on and lo, the biologist (of insects and what we then called lower forms of life) would have a reason for some human behavior that had always been puzzling. Thus, they explained that the continuous sexuality of the human female was a means of keeping the male around. But I always wondered if that were the only reason he stayed, or why he developed a ritualized legal entanglement called marriage, or why the 'relationship' followed." Martin stood again and said, "You know, I would appreciate another glass of that Jerez."

"Fine, I think I will also. How about you, Jerry, another Chablis?"

"Sure, It's quite dry. California?"

"Yes, one of the old standard Sonoma varieties, you know, followed from grape to jug with scientific calibration. They didn't do badly, I think, with the mechanization and testing procedures that came out of U.C. Davis. I must admit that some of the French and German wines are extraordinarily mellow, but when you consider the hand labor that went into making them, and consequently their cost, you have to think twice. I understand that many of the California procedures have been adopted in Europe."

They all settled down once more with their refilled glasses. Oldenberg again lit his pipe. Hanson said to Oldenberg, "I'm sure you will want to look at it in the report, Harold, but basically, what Martin found is that this nonconditioned primate, the chimpanzee, in its consort life was relatively free with others of the opposite sex, from the earliest age on. There were some temporary liaisons, but generally the female distributed her favors widely. Sex was available to practically all, and jealousy hardly existed. Not only were there no long-term consort relations, the father didn't have any interest in paternity. Martin feels this is the natural behavior of primates, including men, and that the changes in the human way are the consequence of brainwashing or what he and his colleagues called enculturation." Pause. "The rest you have heard since you returned."

"Okay, it sounds interesting." Oldenberg turned toward Martin. "Was there anything else?"

"I don't think so," Martin responded, "at least, not about the consort life. I might mention the one other matter that seemed significant and about which the chimpanzees were far more interested than sex."

"What is that?"

"Food, pure and simple. To get it, everyone was for himself or herself. Males took what was available first, according to their place in the dominance order, and adult females came second, followed by the young. With one exception, they just didn't share food. Papa did not bring home edibles for mama or baby. And for that matter, except for letting the nursing infant have breast milk, mama didn't pass anything on to baby. The only exception was meat, and that was shared mostly among adult males. When one of them grabbed a young baboon or colobus monkey, he sometimes handed over some to his hunting partners or other males. On occasion a piece would be handed to a female, though generally the ladies didn't get much of that most desired food."

"Not even if they were sexual partners?" Oldenberg asked.

"The most then, though it was a far cry from human ways such as prostitution or lifetime support in a little white cottage with a marriage contract." Martin smiled, "In the olden days human males were supposed to be most happy if they could convince the lady of their choice to marry them and raise children while being supported." Pause. "No, it seems to me, at least based on the evidence of what the other primates do, that most aspects of human consort relations, and certainly marriage, were products of social conditioning and served vital functions for a long time in human history." Martin stood then and turned. "But that period seems to have ended, and a long-term consort tie seems to be on the way out." Martin laughed, "As you can see, that doesn't bother me."

"Yes, that is apparent," Oldenberg said wryly.

Hanson added, "I have noticed that there are a lot of people needing Transition therapy who have been married several times. Despite their several failures to have a lifetime consortship, they still seem to be in favor of it."

"I think I can explain that," Martin said. "You undoubtedly know of the technique of particularistic explanation, that every occurrence can be explained in its own terms. Well, though that procedure occurs in all cultures, it was particularly favored in the United States, what with their emphasis on individualism. From very early, most people were conditioned to explain things according to each unique pattern of events or personage. So, it became almost inevitable that people would explain difficulties or failure in marriage as being due to the characteristics of their partner. Of course, few individuals will take the blame themselves, so it was always the other person who was inadequate. If there were troubles in a marriage or relationship, it was because the other person had some serious defects. Our people were not at all accustomed to explaining problems in accordance with social necessities. So, few people questioned the institution of marriage itself. And by blaming difficulties on the marriage partner, one could justifiably go on to marry another person on the assumption that the new one could be Mr. or Ms. Right, as we used to put it. Neat, eh?"

"It has its own kind of logic," Oldenberg said. He walked to his desk. Martin read the movement as an indication that his mentor wanted to terminate the meeting. So, before they dispersed, he said, hoping this time to sum it up as well as Hanson usually did, "Anyway, food was the matter of most concern with the chimps, not sex. And primarily because of that, they evolved pronounced dominance relationships. No equal rights among those hairy knuckle walkers. Each guy and gal knew who he or she could push around and who could push him or her around. Of course, it was interesting that they could do most of this through gestures and bluff, but when that wasn't enough, they could get rough, too. I'm afraid the other males trashed our hero when he got old and gray."

Oldenberg leaned forward. "Okay, Martin. I'm sorry I missed the first of your briefing, but you can be assured I'll read the report. And now you go on to your second last. You said you already had that one in mind. Another nonhuman?"

"Yes, and I'm going all the way this time. I want to see the Video of a representative of what I call 'the inheritor' and what the taxonomists call *Blattidae*."

"That, if I'm not mistaken, is a form of insect, no? A member of the order Orthoptera, along with grasshoppers, crickets, and mantis?"

"That's right. You're quite up on your nomenclature. The popular name for this one is, of course, the cockroach."

Hanson and Oldenberg both perked up. Hanson spoke. "I must say, Martin, you are really drifting a long way now. You're not going to tell us that you might learn something about human consort relationships by viewing this denizen of cracks and crannies in the household kitchen, are you?"

"I'm afraid I've got to hedge again by saying yes and no. Our own species obviously doesn't have a lot in common with this creature, or the other insects, except the very basics. It does have to eat and get moisture, and it does have to manage reproduction through copulation. But there are perhaps more differences. However, if we want to observe pure instinct, pure genetic behavior, where could we go but to the simplest creatures? About the only kind of learning we give the insects credit for is through experience. If someone swats at one with a newspaper and misses, then that guy is more careful the next time it perceives a newspaper in the hands of a swatter. But they seem to learn little through imitation and of course nothing through demonstration or explanation, the two ways humans learn most." Pause. "Not being a biologist, I am not up on the absolute latest in insect behavior of course. But it might be worthy of mention that the newly notorious sociobiologists, about whom we were just speaking, have used insects almost exclusively as their models of instinctive behavior. They assume that ants and bees and ladybugs do what they do because of their genetic makeup, giving them practically no credit for learned behavior. So I guess I'm safe using a cockroach for having purely 'natural' behavior."

Oldenberg looked a little dubious, and Hanson didn't look any more convinced. Oldenberg said, "I don't know, Martin. It seems to me that you did the chimpanzees for genetic behavior, no? And they are at least very close to your species in anatomy."

Martin knew he was treading on soft ground, so he quickly tried to broaden his argument, knowing by experience that that was one of the best ways to lay a smoke screen. He had become so fixed on the idea he was not about to give it up without a struggle, including a little tactical deviousness if necessary. He said, "Both things you say are true. But it seems to me there are still valid reasons for viewing the 'black bug' or water beetle, which this tough little creature has been called by his unwilling hosts, my species. One is that presumably an individual could be transformed into a cockroach through the Transition Process. The idea has already been tried in literature a couple of times at least, by Kafka in *Metamorphosis,* which didn't particularly grab me, and in *Archie and Mehitabel* by Don Marquis, which I found much more amusing. So, I suppose I or anyone else on the verge of a Transition could come out as a cockroach, no?"

"Well yes," Oldenberg said. "It's possible, though I must say unlikely. If you remember from our first talk, the ground rules are about the same as those in Hindu–Buddhist reincarnation, that the individual is put into his or her next life in accordance to how well he or she fulfilled the previous life role. And a human would have to have missed the mark by a lot to be transformed into an insect." Pause. "Furthermore, so far as I know, that would be quite unlikely for you, Martin."

Martin refused to give up, however, saying, "In that case, I'll have to explain my particular fascination with this particular creature. I think it is far more than just another insect, though the whole group is very interesting in its own way. And I'll have to tell you how I got around to calling these creatures 'the inheritors.' You may know that they go back almost unchanged for close to 250,000,000 years. That means they have been successful for a long time and through a lot of climatic changes."

Martin paused, recognizing that he was about to launch into one of his favorite professorial declamations. But it was only for an instant, since the two Transitioners seemed interested. And he found it almost impossible to stop once he got started on this topic. He had done it so often in front of introductory classes that he could go through the whole routine with no notes at all. He also knew that enthusiasm was helpful for convincing people. So he continued, "You know, most of our students had the idea that the evolution of species implied progressive changes and that the supreme achievement was *Homo sapiens* or what I facetiously sometimes referred to in my lectures as Homo the Sap. It was very difficult, if not almost impossible, for us college professors to disabuse them of that idea after all the brainwashing of the previous years that their own species was so marvelous."

"Sounds reasonable," Hanson said. "Early brainwashing must have been more effective than later efforts to change it."

"Anyway, for better or worse, I used to go through a sort of routine, and I guess the cockroach emerged as my 'straight man,' uh, 'insect' should I say? I again apprised my students that if we use uprightness as the primary index of humanity, we can give our ancestors credit for about five million years. But if we insist on tool using as the index of humanness, then we get only two million. And since then there have been considerable changes in the biological makeup of the creature we call man. And how does he stack up against the cockroach, who has been around in almost unchanged form for about 250 million years?"

Martin was waving his arms about by this time in professorial histrionics. He felt embarrassed in a way to be addressing two individuals from outer space in this manner, but he was pleased to note they continued to seem interested. So he went on. "By this time I used to have most of my students hooked. Oh, there might have been a couple staring out the window and perhaps one or two asleep. But most would be paying attention, and a few would even be taking notes. So I would say, 'And do you know what marvelous attributes this insignificant creature has in place of your marvelous brain? It has several, the most important of which are its short breeding cycle, large number of young, and ability to eat practically anything.' Then I would throw at them that some cockroaches are quite happy eating book bindings, and there's one variety that gets all it needs by eating the glue on the inside of TV sets. With a grand flourish, I would then go to the blackboard and write in large letters that variety's name, *Supella supellectilium.*

"The class would be quiet for a bit, soaking all that in. I figured they were trying to understand how they got in a class they thought was 'the study of man' and in which a pestiferous insect was being praised. Finally a brave soul would put up his or her hand and say, 'But man is in control. We can kill cockroaches.' And then exultantly, 'And they can't kill us.'

"This was always one I was waiting for. I would say, 'And how effective do you think our methods of killing them are? Do you think we are cutting down their numbers?'

"The student would look unsure, but being brave for ever giving the contrary in the first place, would say, 'I guess so. I know we have a spray in our house and when we use it behind refrigerators and stoves and in cracks, there are always a lot of dead cockroaches afterward.'

"Then I would pounce. With a triumphant smile I would say, 'Ah yes, the chemical solution. There's no doubt that we humans have learned well how to use the chemicals of the earth and I'm willing to give our species credit for that. And there's no doubt that we can zap a few cockroaches and some other insects. We get the slow ones and those who come too far out into the open. But let's face it, there are probably hundreds if not thousands of times more cockroaches on the face of the earth now than there were when our own ancestors starting building civilizations.'" Pause. "'Do you believe that?'

"Most of the students would look mystified, but the brave one would continue, saying, 'Well, Professor Neumann, I don't know about that. How could that be?'

"And then I would give the clincher. 'The cockroach of the Carboniferous, back 250 million years ago, was restricted to the bottom of the tropical forest floor, where it was warm and moist. And evidently from then on it could always find some places that provided that kind of miniclimate. And our own ancestors were also restricted to the tropics at first. But they started discovering and inventing things, and three that affected the future of the cockroach a great deal were fire, closed shelters, and the sewer pipe. How?' I would ask rhetorically, and then answer my own question, as the students knew I would, which is an old professorial gambit, of course. 'First, fire and houses permitted humanity to move into the colder zones of the earth, carrying the tropics along. And who should decide to go along but the cockroach, who learned very quickly that dirty floors and cracks and crannies in the bottoms of houses were very much like the forest floor. But then Man the Wise, which is what the scientific name of our species means, decided to live in crowded settlements called cities. And to get all the garbage and filth out of the way, as well as bring in fresh water, he invented sewers. And who should discover that these were veritable highways, again much like the forest floor, but our friend, the cockroach? As the cities and modern plumbing expanded, our little flattened friend spread out, eating every kind of food, garbage, and a lot else, that he came across. That was where his omnivorousness came in handy. How could the creature ask for anything more?'"

Oldenberg said then, "I suppose by that time some of your students were partially convinced that their species was not the sole success story in evolution, no?"

"Perhaps, though the idea of absolute human superiority is so deeply impressed on most children that even some fairly clear evidence to the contrary will hardly shake their beliefs."

"One thing you never explained exactly," Hanson said. "Why do you call this creature 'the inheritor?'"

"Well, just on the basis of its survival record now, that it has already been on Earth some fifty times longer than humankind, would make it the most likely to continue. But there is an even more immediate reason. You undoubtedly know that we humans got around to inventing some very destructive weapons in the twentieth century, most specifically our nuclear bombs and rockets. We had the capability of destroying most of the habited places on the planet well before the end of the century. And one new kind of mental gyration we got involved in was to figure out how many survivors there would be after such an Armageddon. The various 'think tanks' where high-level mathematicians and political scientists were hired by governments spent a lot of their contract dollars on such computations. It seemed like a bleak activity, but necessary nevertheless because our different governments found it impossible to cooperate, even if the final holocaust would be the result. Anyway, it all seemed rather ludicrous to me with my eye cocked on the cockroach, so to speak. So, I used to ask my students, 'And when the great nuclear conflagration takes place and the cities of the world are flattened, who or what do you think will emerge after the earth has cooled off?'" Pause. "And I think even the most diehard humanists, whether traditional or newfangled, could hardly argue that one away. Our little flat friends in the sewers and crevasses of the cities would have had the best natural bomb shelters in the world. And even if some of them got killed, what difference would it make? With their short reproductive cycle, the survivors would very soon have the world repopulated with cockroaches, probably living very well on decaying human flesh in the meantime."

"I understand," said Hanson. "And it is a very interesting story of adaptation. I can see how you became so enamored with this creature. But one thing puzzles me. You seem to be taken up so much by these insects, almost committed to their future, not that of your own species. How is it that you could become so interested in them and still continue to teach about humankind and culture?"

"Ah yes, it is a difficult question and one others posed during my lifetime. My only reply is that I always found all forms of life interesting, but because of various personal needs, I got involved in studying humans and their culture primarily. And frankly, I'm not sorry. Apart from me having been one, I think humans are very interesting animals. And the fact that their experiment in adaptation is much shorter than that of some other creatures does not make them less interesting. And though the odds are that the cockroach and other simple creatures will be the ultimate inheritors of the earth, I cannot be sure. Besides, now that I am no longer among the living, it's really academic, isn't it?"

Hanson got up. "I suppose so. Though you should remember that it will only be a few more days before you will again be a life form, as soon as your Transition is accomplished. In any event, I agree that you should be given the go-ahead to see the Video of the typical cockroach." He turned toward Oldenberg. "You think so, Harold?"

"Sure. Martin only has a couple of days yet. And if he can fit this one in along with the long one, I have no objections."

# HERITOR

Though the Life Video viewer was turned to the normal intensity, the image was dark. There was a shape but only barely distinguishable. Martin turned the intensity control one way without any increase in brightness; the other way, the image disappeared. He turned it back and studied the other controls on the panel. He had noticed from the beginning quite a number of controls that he had never touched because the image had been quite satisfactory from the first tape. But obviously something was wrong then, with either the tape, the machine, or his handling of it. He had used the speed switch from the beginning, slowing and speeding up scenes in relation to their interest. But there were several other switches, such as for color, distance (to bring faraway scenes closer), and image separation (to isolate particular forms in mixed scenes). Then at the end of one row he saw a switch marked *Nocturnal–Diurnal,* and a light bulb went on. He flipped the switch to *Nocturnal,* and the screen came to life, showing a flattened creature, antennae waving, moving slowly through a tunnel. He knew immediately that he was gazing at a cockroach in the complete darkness of underground.

Martin remembered once when he had gone through a similar experience, an afternoon in his late middle years when he had crawled a mile or so into a cave in southern Indiana with Dan and Martin's nephews, Lance and Burt. That had been a lark, but had not Martin been intent on proving his capability to the youngsters, he would have given up early. It had been eerie and even frightening to inch oneself through apertures only inches larger than your worming body in the unsteady light of headlamps. But then they had come into a chamber where water flowed and dripped, forming a pool in the center. The pool had reflected black water when their lights were turned on it. They had sat down and Burt brought out a joint. Martin didn't really want to smoke, being deep enough by then in bizarre feelings, but just as he had continued in the beginning when he had begun to feel queasy from squirming through narrow passages, he took his turn again. At least, he had thought, marijuana did not usually affect him very much.

Then Lance had suggested they turn out all their lights. It was totally eerie then. Martin couldn't remember ever having been in total darkness before in full wakefulness. For a moment he had felt that was what death must be like, but he quickly banished that thought; though death would cause the total elimination of images, it would also eliminate the consciousness of being able to perceive them. Also it would eliminate all other sensations, and particularly the one that consoled him in the cave, sound. The water kept dripping and the others spoke, though in falsetto voices as if one couldn't speak normally if one couldn't see. Burt, "Weird, ain't it?"

Dan, "Yeah, gives you a creepy feeling."

That was the world of *Blattidae*, the cockroach. The flattened six-leggers raced from light with more real intensity than Dracula ever had. And somehow the designers of the Viewers had devised a way to transform the lightless world of subterranean creatures so creatures of the day world could see them. The insect was feeling its way along the tunnel, exploring each indentation with its antennae. Martin could see a slight protrusion from its thorax. As he watched in fascination, a related thought occurred. He had learned to fiddle with the sound control while watching humans and chimpanzees, turning the volume off whenever he speeded the images to avoid the quacking that conversations then became, but turning it up again when he slowed the story to normal speed to hear everything that occurred in the critical instances of each life. He turned the volume up, and the shock of silence was considerable, even though he had long known that cockroaches and other insects lacked auditory languages. When he turned the volume to maximum, he did hear sounds though, small clicks and rustlings as the creature explored the crevasses, dislodging particles and brushing against projections. It kept moving, but so slowly Martin figured he would have to speed the tape up, that the underground explorer would go on for hours. But then it stopped, and after checking out one side crack thoroughly, and waving its antennae up and back the main tunnel several times, moved into the crack. Its body pulsed and it made tiny movements with its stick feet until Martin saw what was happening—a birthing. The protrusion at the end of the roach's body got larger and was slowly pushed out. It was the *ootheca*, the egg case in which there would be ten to forty tiny cockroaches in two parallel rows.

When the roach mother was finished, she felt from end to end with her antennae her masterpiece to life continuity. Then, evidently satisfied that she had fulfilled her destiny, she crawled back into the main tunnel and continued in the direction she had been going.

Martin did not expect anything remarkable for a while, so he speeded up the tempo. According to the chronometer, after six hours and eighteen minutes, the egg case began to open, revealing the parallel heads of what he counted as twenty-four creatures. The egg case continued to widen, revealing more and more of the tiny white bodies. Then they began to wiggle and shoulder each other out. Only a little time elapsed before all were outside the egg case and beginning to change color, their whiteness giving way to a browning.

Wow, Martin thought, a cockroach birthing. It certainly differed from one of his species. Once Mom had dropped her eggs, the little devils were on their own. His thoughts were interrupted by a new rustling sound, and a new form came scuttling down the tunnel, a fully mature roach. It came faster than the mother had, though waving its antennae just as actively. All of a sudden one of the antennae touched one of the newborns. The adult acted quickly, grabbing the young one with its mandibles and crunching hard. The struggles of the brown young one soon ceased, and the adult began slowly to munch the body. The rest of the brood scuttled rapidly away, their reflexes already quickening. Most squeezed into cracks as fast as they could locate them. Three or four raced up the tunnel. The Video focused on one in front, and the others soon faded from view. That would be the one whose life Martin would henceforth view. He decided to give it a name, as he did with the chimpanzees. Henceforth this particular member of the order *Blattidae* would be known to Martin as Heritor, it to whom the future would belong.

\* \* \* \* \*

Heritor grew to adult size in less than a year, learning to scuttle with ever-increasing rapidity and learning to navigate through a network of tunnels and cracks. He generally did not emerge outside the underground passages during the day, spending most of that time dozing in a crack. On occasion he passed others in the tunnels and was wary in the beginning, ducking into cracks whenever a large form loomed, though getting more courage as he got nearer to adult size. He began then to touch antenna with those he would meet before passing by. No other roach attacked him, though he did pass scenes of cannibalism on occasion, usually an adult eating a smaller roach. That didn't bother Heritor, since he had found out early that most plant and animal substances, including other roaches, could be eaten. And Heritor had no more compunctions in that regard than any other roach. In fact, like the others, getting enough food was the constant problem he faced. Most of his waking time was spent searching for edibles.

\* \* \* \* \*

The full-grown insect was inching slowly in the angle of a sidewalk and wall. It stopped to explore any little lump in its pathway, feeling it with its antennae before deciding to pass on or to taste it. There was little enough, once the partly desiccated half thorax of an ant, once a couple of seeds, and one time a mini-pile of something, Heritor could hardly decide what. He finally sensed, even though he was quite hungry, that it wasn't edible and passed on. A little further he came to a slimy trail around which he stepped to continue until he encountered the creature itself, a slug, its horns extended as it moved forward oozily. Heritor touched it only lightly, immediately recognizing the creature and pulling its antennae back. He went around. Although Heritor was comfortable enough around wet places, he kept his own body dry, stepping carefully through damp places on his stick legs. He had been rained on a couple of times and had not cared for that at all, crawling as fast as he could into the nearest crack.

He got to the end of the walk and, feeling his way around the corner, stood waving his antennae probingly. He had not come this far before. He could only see a few inches away, though this didn't matter much because he depended primarily on touch and body sensations for knowing what was around him.

He felt a little cool from the breeze coming from the open space beyond. However, a flow of warmth came from a crack just next to him.

(Martin recognized it as the space at the bottom of the back door of the house he had shared with Constance.)

The cockroach felt toward the warming and almost automatically moved toward it. He inched his way through the crack with no trouble. Inside the whole place was warm, and Heritor got more active.

Next to having food in his belly he, like all of his breed, needed to be warm. Not being a time-extending creature, he knew nothing of his variety's origins on the floors of tropical rain forests, hundreds of millions of years before. All he knew was that he felt better when it was warm, and he always gravitated toward warmer places.

After standing just inside the door for a bit, he began moving around the baseboard of the room. It wasn't as dark as he would like, but when he literally bumped into a morsel of food, he forgot his anxiety and after a touch-feel, began to eat it.

(It was small, but so far as Martin could make out, it was a flake of breakfast cereal.)

Heritor didn't take long to finish it off, after which he continued with more excitement. One gobbet after another was gluttonously devoured. He couldn't believe the quantity.

(Martin figured that the floor hadn't been swept for several days, which was unlike Constance, but possibly she was preoccupied with something, as she had been frequently during the final year of their marriage.)

Heritor had become almost full when he felt vibrations coming in his direction. He was ordinarily quick when giant forms loomed, but the amount he had eaten had temporarily stupefied him. The steps came nearer, and a flood of light filled the room. Heritor hurriedly tried to get to the protection of the wall. He heard new sounds and scurried faster.

(The control was picking up sounds as perceived by the roach which precluded words. However, Martin could imagine Constance saying, "Ugh, a cockroach." Martin could hear her footsteps and had a good idea what she was doing—getting a broom.)

Heritor was scurrying faster by that time, though he didn't get back to the door before the thing started thump-swishing behind him. It even brushed him when he got caught in the crack. He had thickened a little from the number of food gobbets he had eaten. He scrambled as hard as he could without getting through but when the door opened, he unfolded his wings and flew, the thing swishing behind him. He flew straight out, then careened around the corner where the light and swishing thing did not follow.

He stopped to rest for a moment, then slowly moved off the way he had come. He got more comfortable as he got farther from the beam of light.

* * * * *

The days passed much the same, Heritor either dozing or exploring for food. He became a full-grown member of his species, quick enough to generally avoid predators. As his experience increased, he learned ever more where food could be had. He became increasingly aware too of the other kind of his species, the ones who emanated a different scent periodically and stimulated him in a different way.

* * * * *

Passing down a tunnel, Heritor caught a particularly strong whiff of the essence and turned in that direction. Just before he got into the expanded cavernous place where weak light was filtering in, he almost bumped into another male, also heading the same direction. He quickly crossed antennae with the stranger and felt some tension, though the other made no openly aggressive moves. Heritor pulled back and continued more slowly toward the female in the center. He saw another male on the far side of the cavern, also facing the female. Heritor continued almost as if in a trance toward her. He had seen at a distance other roaches coupling, though he had not paid close attention.

(Martin knew that whatever the insect would do from then on was already inscribed on its chromosomes.)

The female turned to face Heritor, opening her wings and clicking them in a dance-like step. And without consciously deciding to do it, Heritor also opened his wings and minced in her direction. They danced back and forth, facing one another, waving their antennae and clicking their wings periodically. Out of the side of his eyes Heritor could see that the other males were moving agitatedly, though they did not come straight up to the female. The dance went on for several minutes, Heritor and the female increasing their touches. Then almost as at a signal, she crouched. And almost just as automatically Heritor turned to attach his genitals to hers, their bodies extended away from one another, the only point of contact their genitals. Heritor pulsed and felt the flow-squirt go from his body. They remained attached for several minutes until Heritor began to feel himself shrink and was about to pull away.

He had stopped seeing the other males, almost forgetting their presence. Then the heavy weight of one dropped on him and he felt jaws crunch down on his leg. What was happening from then on, he wasn't exactly sure except that there was a scramble of legs and jaws and antennae and Heritor felt deep fear, desperately trying to pull himself free from the female. Finally, with enough force he did, but he realized at the same time that he had only five legs left. There were more snapping jaws, and he got a slash on one of his wings, but he did get free. Pulling away, he looked back and saw two of the other males crouched over the female, who though still waving her antennae and legs feebly, was obviously being devoured. One of the males began to slowly crunch into her thorax; the other was nibbling off one of her antennae. Heritor hobbled away on his remaining five legs.

\* \* \* \* \*

The survivor healed with no great disability. Even the loss of the leg was no great problem. After all, losing one of five is far less serious than one of two. Heritor was soon moving back and forth with practically the same rapidity as before. And he added the new activity, copulation, to his routine, turning off whenever he got a whiff of the sex scent if he wasn't too hungry. He also learned to be more careful in the location of the sex act, refusing to get involved if the place wasn't secluded enough or if there were other adults around. He copulated many times with many females. The hot season followed the cool season two more times.

\* \* \* \* \*

He was dozing under a piece of bark in the gutter along the sidewalk, a weak light filtering in. It was warm enough, both from the air and the decomposing plant material. He was awakened by the swishing sound before the first jet of water struck. Awakening instantaneously, he was just prepared to run when the jet of water struck. (Though the Video only showed a powerful gush of water hitting the cockroach, flipping the bark away and striking the insect at the same time, Martin could guess that it must be coming from a hose. He thought it bizarre that probably the hose wielder was himself, washing down the sidewalk.)

Heritor tried to run but when hit by the full force of the squirting water had all he could do to keep on his feet. Even this lasted only briefly, and he was flipped end over end by the gushing water. He tried to get on his feet again and again, but each time, hit by the jet, he was knocked loose. Finally he gave up, letting himself be driven by the jet. His last perception was being slammed against a hard wall and being held there by the pressure of the driving water.

# CHAPTER 10

Martin was in a booth that opened toward the lounge, absorbed in the savage rhythms of the *Rite of Spring*. Somehow it seemed appropriate for the short but productive life of Heritor. Martin mused that if any classical music were appropriate as background for nonhuman life, it must be that of Stravinsky.

Martin saw Oldenberg enter on the far side of the room and look around, presumably searching for him. Oldenberg looked tired. He was not smoking his pipe. The Transitioner did not spot him, so Martin stood up and waved. Oldenberg saw the movement and walked toward the Transitionee. Martin stood waiting outside the booth. The music was totally inaudible, though Martin had turned it up high. The listening booths were so constructed that none of the quadraphonic sound escaped them, no matter how high the volume. It was characteristically sophisticated, as was all of the engineering in the Transition Building.

Oldenberg walked up to the earthling and offered his hand. Martin shook it, noting that the Transition Master's grip had become notably weaker. "I hope everything's alright," he said, concerned.

Oldenberg nodded. "Oh yes, it's just that I'm tired. You probably remember that we have to conduct a Transition now in half the time we used to. That means we go through twice as many in a given amount of time. And they can be wearing, even for us Transitioners. You may remember your own initial difficulty in accepting the fact of your death. And you were quite calm compared with many.

"And also, the administration is calling endless meetings, mostly about what to do with the Bureau. It wears one down after a while."

Martin knew the discussions had been continuing from comments he had overheard from others. But he had tried not to think about it; it was too threatening. He said simply, "I hope they get it settled soon."

"Oh yes, like everything else, there will be an end to it one of these days. And not too distantly, I think." Then, in an obvious effort to change the subject, Oldenberg said, "Hearing some good music? I remember you said you enjoyed the Music of the Spheres, no?"

"Yes, I find those natural rhythms fascinating, though this time I was listening to an earth classic, probably my favorite, Stravinsky."

"Well, are you finished? Because I can wait a short while."

It was difficult enough for Martin to get appointments these days with Oldenberg, and he sensed the man's fatigue, so he shook his head. "Oh no, it's alright. I can rewind the tape and listen to it over again after we're finished."

They sat down on naugahyde chairs. Martin waited a moment, expecting Oldenberg to light up. The Transition Master made no such move, instead sighing, "Well, it's getting close to the end, isn't it, Martin? Only another couple of days and you should be able to wind up the project."

"Yes. And it makes me a little sad, like the end of any activity from which one got some pleasure, even excitement. This one is even harder to let go because of my knowledge that there are so many Life Videos that I will never see. In that sense it would be better if I had never seen one. You know, it's like what I said very early, no social scientist could have hoped for more, dead or alive."

"Ah yes," chuckled Oldenberg, "you humans get so attached to certain people, things, or activities. Then when you are separated from them, you develop these powerful feelings of loss. From what I've seen, most of the other animals do not get so attached and thus do not experience such feelings of loss. Perhaps it is a weakness of your species." He added quickly, "In terms of adjustment and adaptation, I mean."

Martin sat for a moment musing, then replied, "I suppose you are right. However, you must realize, sir, that the Life Video collection is truly in a class by itself to an ex–social scientist. I think I indicated quite a while ago some of the difficulties people of my former profession used to experience in trying to get data about peoples' lives."

"Yes, you did. I was a little surprised, but it seemed reasonable, particularly when you consider the potentiality for deception your main communication system, language, provides."

"I'm learning more and more of the vastness of the collection since I started helping Mrs. Morrison in my time off."

"You mentioned that the last time we met. I would have thought you'd get enough of Life Tapes viewing them day after day for your project.

But evidently not."

Martin studied Oldenberg for a moment, then said, "You just cannot imagine the fascination these things have for me. You see, we on Earth never really developed any full-blown telepathic communication system whereby we could read each others' minds, as you mentioned was true with many non-earthly life forms. We basically had to depend on what we could see and hear, which with humans mainly meant language."

"Yes, I realize that. It is, of course, the basic reason for having Life Videos. There's no need to have them on the other worlds." Pause. "Anyway, I'm pleased that you have something interesting to do in your spare time. And I suppose Mrs. Morrison can use some help since she lost several assistants from the recent budget cuts."

"I think so. And she's a very good teacher. I believe it won't be long before I'll be able to find any tape."

"Fine. May as well do what you can in the little time remaining."

Oldenberg must have become more relaxed then because he began his customary ritual, taking out his pipe paraphernalia and getting ready for a smoke. "So, what did you find out about the latest one, the cockroach?"

Martin switched his mental set quickly. "Well, to get back to your earlier comment regarding attachment. *Blattidae* doesn't attach itself to any creatures of the opposite sex, close relatives, friends, or any others. Talk about loners, they are really that."

"But I thought they were found in large numbers together, particularly in your kitchens and cupboards."

"Yes, they are found at the same places but not as parts of social groups in the sense that we find humans or other social animals acting together. The cockroaches are merely in the same places because those are where food and shelter can be found. And as I said before, they reproduce quite rapidly. But they don't cooperate on anything. You may remember that the chimpanzees do work together for some purposes, to hunt other animals or to defend their territory. No cockroach would do anything like that. In fact, other cockroaches are even risky companions. They will eat anything, as I mentioned before; and that includes one another. They are quite cannibalistic."

Martin could see that his mentor's interest was perking up, which pleased him, as it always had during his many years of teaching. Oldenberg said thoughtfully, "Very interesting. Though I wonder, if they eat one another, how they can increase in numbers so successfully."

"There are counterbalancing forces. The fact that they eat one another merely stems from their general omnivorousness. But that is a real plus. We used to classify my own species as omnivorous, but humans are quite limited compared with those flattened six leggers. Those little devils would eat about anything that was remotely edible. That means they were not munching each other all the time. But if the occasion came along, they would rip into a weaker one of their own species with no compunction. And the one occasion that still produced certain feelings of repulsion in me was the time of copulation. If the couple were discovered by other adults, they might well be attacked, evidently because they were so preoccupied in the sex act."

"That doesn't sound like it would help in reproduction, in increasing their numbers."

"I guess it doesn't. But I'm not saying *all* copulating cockroaches got eaten, only a few; most, including my hero, Heritor, learned to hide themselves when they got involved in sex."

"Of course, in a way that is what you humans did also, isn't it? You would turn off the lights and close the curtains so you could do it in isolation, as I understand. It has been written that some never copulated in the light. Were they afraid of being eaten also?"

Martin laughed, "No, sorry, sounds logical but I'm afraid it was for another reason with humans." He remembered his early married days and Amelia's insistence that the light be off each time. "They used to call it prudishness. And they blamed it on the earlier generation, Victorians, they were called. But the attitude was more widespread than among those Englishmen only, and it lingered on despite the fact that we were supposed to have become liberated from tradition in the twentieth century."

Oldenberg had leaned back by this time, puffing contentedly on his meerschaum. "Ah, you humans, *Homo sapiens*, the Wise Man; you really made existence complex."

Martin bridled slightly at that, a similar feeling to what he had experienced while overseas during his earthly life when his country was criticized. He would be amazed afterward how ardently he had defended his birthplace, even about policies that he didn't particularly support at home. But he knew that when outsiders criticized your ways, there was an almost automatic response to defend them. "Well, you know we anthropologists developed the idea that customs had functions, that they made sense in helping particular societies to survive. And though I'm not about to claim that all customs are perfectly logical, even such little things as turning off the light when you copulate, I do think that most such have some logic."

Oldenberg seemed to recognize Martin's negative reaction, so he turned back to the original topic. "Well, what did you find out regarding your insect hero that would shed any light on the mating drive?"

Martin accepted the switch as tactically desirable and continued in that direction. "It's a lot like I thought, which is that, apart from taking precautions against being devoured or other potential hazards, the biological imperative seems to make those invertebrates take the whole thing in stride. When the female is ready to mate, the males get worked up and the one who can put on the best display will get to breed. But all that takes only a little of their time. The real drive is to get food, and that's what they spend most of their time on. In that sense the cockroaches are quite similar to chimpanzees, and I suppose most other creatures. As you may remember, the one thing chimpanzees would fight about was food, not sex."

Oldenberg had the slightest indication of a smile when he said, "Well, I had understood that you humans didn't spend very much time copulating either."

The grin was contagious, Martin following suit. "Actually, you're right. It was amazing how important my students used to think sex was in their lives, as if that was the kind of activity they would be engaged in primarily for most of their lives. But it only took a little effort to show them that when one considered the period before sexual relationships usually started, the frequent and sometimes long periods of singleness during the potentially active years, and the long period after the sexually active years, not to mention the various forms of abstinence from mates during the pairing years, the total amount of time spent in sex was not very much. And throughout the sex-on, as well as the sex-off, years, people continued to eat, some, as in the era of obesity, almost continually."

"That is generally what I had come to understand from the Transition interviews. So then the puzzling thing is why humans thought so much about sex and took it so seriously. For instance, quite a few used to kill one another because of violations of sexual codes, isn't that so?"

"I should say so, and particularly in cultures such as mine that brainwashed people to believe in romantic love. We developed a particular passion, called jealousy, which could easily provoke us to acts of violence. I should know, having once been assaulted by a jealous separated husband who tried to bite my testicles off. This is a particularly human capability, hardly shared by my friends the cockroaches, and I suspect all the other insects, reptiles, amphibians, and many kinds of birds and mammals. There are, of course, some other mammals who do fight for mates, primarily the ones who establish harems; but I think most non-humans can take sex or leave it, and when they leave it, they get busy with the real problem of life, getting food."

Oldenberg stroked the balding spot on the back of his head, still seemingly puzzled. "Then, Martin, what kind of explanation can you give for all this concern with sex by your species? If they do it so little, why do they think about it so much? Why, I understand there are vast industries based on the human need to be titillated sexually, all the way from perfume and ladies' underclothes to pornographic film. You'd think more people would get on to other activities."

Martin smiled then. "Well, I'll give you my theory, though I want you to know that we humans are given to another kind of odd behavior, cultural rationalization. There are a lot of things that we do, the reasons for which we really do not understand. We anthropologists had learned in our studies of other peoples that the commonest type of explanation for customary behavior was, 'That's just the way we always did it.' This was, of course, never true because cultures are always changing. Or some people would say, 'It's just the custom.' Which is just making the question into the answer. Or they might say, 'The reason our ancestors taught us not to eat pork is because it will cause trichinosis.' Or 'The reason we eat so much beef is because we need protein.' This latter kind of reason we call cultural rationalization, or justifying the behavior that already exists, whatever it is. It's certainly obvious that the trichinosis problem can be taken care of easily simply by cooking the pork thoroughly, and all proteins come originally from plants. No, I'm afraid the real reason my own people were so fond of hamburgers and the Jews and Muslims wouldn't eat pork was that was how they were respectively brainwashed. The explanation was an after-the-fact justification."

"And you are saying the other creatures, including cockroaches, don't go through such a process?"

"Well, as far as we know they don't, and the reason is not far to seek, or perhaps I should say the reasons. For one thing, our different societies have quite different customs, and whenever people from one come into contact with people from another, they notice differences. And sooner or later, each side gets into the business of explaining how logical their own customs are. You may have heard that in the country I came from it was claimed that capitalistic democracy promoted individual freedom, and this in turn promoted happiness, and our opponents, the socialists, claimed that group cooperation toward Marxian goals was the source of happiness. An anthropologist would have said that either or neither would promote happiness, using that term in its broadest sense. But for that matter the antisocial behavior of cockroaches could have been seen to promote satisfaction just as easily, at least until the creatures reached their violent ends. Anyway, the other part of cultural rationalization stemmed from language, I think. That is, our complex communication system permitted us to say all kinds of things, from describing actual occurrences to those that were patently the products of our imaginations. This is not to say that you can't lie with gestures or behavior, but the development that enabled elaborate deception was human language. It was just made for lying. Some such was deliberate, others quite unconscious. And I suspect cultural rationalization fits pretty much in the latter category. People believed the elaborate explanations they offered as to the logic of their customs, whether they were why you should turn off the light when you copulate, or why you shouldn't sleep with your cross-cousin, but it was perfectly alright to sleep with your parallel cousin."

Oldenberg put his pipe down and scooped a handful of some of the dry munchies from the table between them, saying, "I really haven't had a meal all day."

"Those are good," said Martin, "very similar to those Japanese rice tidbits I always enjoyed in my earthly existence."

After satisfying himself, Oldenberg said, "Okay, so language and cultural differences promote cultural rationalization. Interesting enough, Martin, though unfortunately we must get through this little get-together fairly soon. I have a late meeting I must attend."

Martin knew he had launched off on another professorial declamation. That was one part of his personal behavior that was so deeply ingrained that even death had not eliminated it. But he also knew his time was limited, both for the continuation of the project and for Oldenberg's time that evening. Once he got started on a topic that genuinely interested him, he had a terrible need to get some kind of closure. Even so, he tried to wind up as fast as possible, saying, "I understand and I'll finish what I'm saying quickly. What I may be saying about the reason for the human interest in sexuality may just be another cultural rationalization. But anyway, here goes. Our species has been blessed, or cursed, with an enormous capacity for imagination. What possibilities we thought about were often, if not usually, more vivid than the actual experiences. Thus, we did something called fantasizing—that is, dreaming up vivid images of what we might have done or what might have been. And I'm afraid there was no human activity in which we did more fantasizing than actually doing than sex. Our imaginations ran riot when it came to sexuality. Which is why we could be titillated by all kinds of things. Thus, all the sexual productions, from Maggie and Jiggs Big-Little books to Swedish pornos, or from high-heeled shoes to bound feet. We were great at displacement. I should know, having gotten most of my sexual excitement in my lifetime from fantasizing."

"Hmm. Of course, though you have made reference here and there to your own experiences, we haven't really talked about them in detail. I suppose I do need to look at your Video before your Transition conference though."

Again that topic! Martin was getting sensitive to comments that clearly implied the end was near. Even so, he decided to take advantage of the opening. "It's true. You may remember though, Transitioner Oldenberg, that I requested Project Heterop originally because I couldn't make up my mind easily about what kind of form I would like for my next time around."

Martin knew that wasn't exactly true, that he had had other motivations for life scanning, but at the same time he knew he was using language for one of its most significant functions, to influence someone else. And that definitely included withholding or twisting information.

Oldenberg said, without contradicting the deceased earthling, "I remember. The real problem, though, is time. It just is not possible to keep the project going much longer. The people at Central keep insisting that I get everything finished at once. I've been successfully holding them off so far, but it won't last much longer. I'll just have to have you finish Project Heterop very soon."

Martin decided to make one last gambit. "I understand. I know that the continual meetings are about that, and I honestly do appreciate everything you've done so far. So I'm suggesting one last Video, that's all. I do still have a couple of days, don't I?"

Oldenberg sighed. "Yes, I promised two weeks, I believe. And I won't go back on my word. But there is absolutely no question that you will have to quit then. I presume it's something quite significant to you theoretically, eh?"

"It's my own life. I want to go through the Video of Martin Neumann. I have a feeling that my life is a pretty good portrayal of what was going on in the industrialized countries then, that it spanned a period from when almost all people were married and marriage was considered a lifetime commitment to when we evolved a new social class, the 'singles,' and divorce became almost as common as marriage. In fact, I lived through that transition."

Oldenberg leaned back. "Hmm. I suppose this has been in the back of your mind for quite a while, eh, Martin?"

"Actually I didn't start with this idea, though I suppose as the project progressed, it seemed more and more desirable. Of course, there may have been a little subconscious self-deception going on. That might really be what I was aiming toward without even knowing it. That also is a characteristic of we humans. We are really great at self-deceptions. Perhaps most of the theory of psychotherapy, our way of trying to cure mental illness, is based on the human penchant for self-deception."

"Yes, I know about that. Hanson has pretty much brought me up to date on that field. Your concept of phobias is based on the idea that humans can develop fears of possibilities that don't or hardly exist, is that not so?"

"Unh hunh. People have fear of flying even though it is one of the safest forms of transportation per mile we have. Also, they fear heights and closed places, but those are dangerous only when people throw themselves off roofs or lock themselves into tight places."

Oldenberg began the body shifting that indicated he needed to be off again. Martin noticed him glance at his watch. But he did say, "Alright, go ahead. But remember, it's got to be done in two days at the latest. Then we have to do the Transition."

Martin was satisfied. He had been worried that he wouldn't get finished, that he wouldn't manage closure, which had always bothered him. Though he knew inwardly that he would be happy looking at many more Life Videos, at least this way he would feel the project had some kind of closure.

Oldenberg knocked out his pipe in preparation for departure. He had shifted to the edge of his chair when he asked, "Was there anything more you wanted to report regarding *Blattidae*?"

"No, I suppose so far as mating is concerned, I've told you the main points, that is, that cockroaches seem to go at it directly and get it over with so they can get on to the real need of life, getting food. The only other facet of their life that impressed me, though I suppose I shouldn't have been too surprised, is how fast and furious their lives are. In no time at all the eggs hatch and the young grow to adulthood, then very quickly becoming reproducers themselves, all with no personal attachment to any other creature and always with the constant threat of violent death. In fact, they do die all along the line, their saving grace as members of the species being that most usually produce some young before being annihilated one way or another."

"Yes, I can see that from the human point of view the life of insects would seem quick and deadly. But of course it's all relative, you know."

"I understand, but I'm afraid I can't help making comparisons." Pause, smile. "I suppose the most bizarre occurrence in the life of this creature, whom I named Heritor, was that he lived just outside my own house when I was last married and my ex-wife almost killed him with a broom, and I finally did the poor devil in with a jet from the hose." Martin quickly added, "I didn't have quite the feeling of admiration toward cockroaches then that I developed later."

Oldenberg was standing by then, but smiled at Martin when he said, "Maybe that's where you want to go in your next existence, eh, Martin?"

Martin responded quickly, "Oh, I doubt that, primarily because it takes too great a shift of mentality for a human to imagine himself as an insect. You know, our cultural brainwashing was quite thorough."

"Okay. I'll be leaving you now. But do get on with your self Video as soon as possible."

# MARTIN I

It was a bizarre experience to start from the beginning in viewing your own life, Martin thought, as the images began to flicker; however, it was interesting. And as Martin had long admitted to himself, any experience that was interesting to him needed basically no other excuse for occurring. Other thoughts rapidly flashed through his mind, one being that this was the perfect way to analyze a series of events, to have been a direct participant in them and later to be able to view them almost as an outsider.

Like a number of his colleagues, Martin had considered the problem of the insider versus the outsider for many years. Which could best describe a way of life? He had known, of course, that the insider, the one who actually participated in a social group, necessarily was more familiar with the occurrences and relationships. On the other hand, it was generally recognized that the insider was often so close to most of what he or she did that she or he didn't recognize their significance. How many of a society's members would bother to describe in detail elaborate acts of deference, such as bowing, when everybody did it? And the fact that almost everyone ate meat would only be quickly apparent to someone from a society of vegetarians. Now, in viewing his own life, Martin, having lived it, would be both insider and, in viewing it in a Life Video Viewer in the Transition Bureau, an outsider.

Then too, it seemed most appropriate in becoming an other-worldly voyeur, who had peered into the secret lives of creatures ranging from a cockroach to his own mother, that the ultimate act of voyeurism would be to peek in on his own life. It was almost like psychotherapy, the unraveling of a life to rearrange it in the future. However, the difference was that instead of relying on memory while facing a therapist, Martin would actually be seeing a re-creation of what had happened. And though he could hardly use what he would learn for straightening out the crooks in his previous life, he could use what he saw in choosing the next one. He settled down to view the passing scenes.

* * * * *

A hefty towheaded baby grew rapidly and healthily in a brick house in a working class neighborhood. There were two girl children also, tended more or less continuously by Esther. The father, Bruno, was a steady worker too, though exclusively on the job. He spent almost all of his free time at home though, playing with the children once in a while, but doing practically nothing to help tend them. In the working class, that was the woman's job.

* * * * *

The baby, Martin Neumann, who was sitting in a high chair, ate until he was full. Esther was busy on the working area of the kitchen cabinet, rolling out pie crusts. Periodically, she would brush strands of hair back from her eyes and glance at her son. He threw his spoon down. She finished laying the rolled crust over the last pie pan and trimmed the excess off the edge. Then sighing, she came over, bent down, and picked up the spoon, which she wiped on her apron. "Oh Martin, why don't you eat like a good boy? You can see your mama is busy."

He wrapped his chubby fingers around the spoon handle, and she turned back to her work. She had taken only a few steps when he threw the spoon down again. She turned around and said a little tiredly, also with a little anger, "I am not going to pick that up again for you, Martin. You can just do without your mush."

She went back to put the filling in the pie and placed it in the oven along with the other two. Just then a cry came from the next room.

"Oh, that's Catherine," she said wearily and got up to go toward the sound. In a short while the baby's crying turned into whimpers and then ceased.

The boy infant put one finger in the mush, then the flat of his hand. Gurgling, he stirred the cream-colored mixture around in the bowl, which tipped perilously on the edge of the high chair tray a couple of times. Then, apparently dissatisfied with so little action, the child picked up the dish and placed it upside down on his head. The heavy granular liquid ran slowly down the sides of his head. He let the plastic dish drop to the floor.

Esther came running into the room, holding the now quiet girl baby. She stopped, stared, and said, "Oh Martin, how could you? The moment I leave the room you do something like that. Oh, you kids will be the death of me yet."

She stooped and picked up the mush bowl to put it in the sink. "Now I'll have to wash you. You'd think I'd have enough to do, what with fixing pies and keeping a croupy baby quiet. Then you do that." She stopped then, as if with the realization that, after all, the boy baby couldn't yet understand her.

She stood in the middle of the room, still cradling the girl infant. "Catherine, I'm going to have to put you back in your playpen for a little bit while I clean up this mess."

The girl looked up as if with comprehension, but still whimpered when Esther put her back in the playpen. The mother returned and got on her knees to wipe the mess from the floor. Martin watched her while making baby noises. Then she went into the utility room and filled the deep sink. He could see her through the doorway, knowing already that was the place she used to bathe him. The girl infant was whimpering again when Esther came to get Martin. She kept talking back at the other child as she rapidly undressed him and put him in the tepid water. He splashed with pleasure when he was sitting down. She began to wash his head.

"Mama, I couldn't sleep," came the voice of the other child, Rosalie. Martin looked and saw his older sister standing in the doorway, rubbing her eyes and whimpering.

Esther turned and said, "Just sit down and play. I'm busy right now." Pause. "Or better yet, go in the other room and amuse Catherine."

"Don't want to," she whimpered.

"Well, you'll just have to take care of yourself for a while. You can see I'm busy." Esther kept washing the boy infant with determination.

Another cry from the other room, louder than before. For a moment Esther ignored it, but then stopped washing Martin and focused on the youngest. "Is she hurt?" she said, almost as if to herself, but then got up and went into the other room. The girl baby, Catherine, slowly quieted.

Martin played with the rag for a bit and slapped the water. Then his hand fell on his penis and he fingered it lightly. It felt good as he squeezed it, and the tiny testicles at the bottom. He was aware that the child sounds had become muted, his mother's voice clucking and reassuring. The whimpers of his sister stopped.

"Martin, what are you doing?" the angry voice of his mother broke through his fantasy. And just as he looked up, she reached in the water and grabbed his hand, pulling it away from his penis. He looked at her in surprise, she holding his sister, Catherine, in her other arm. Behind her was Rosalie, watching from a distance.

Esther spanked his hand. "That's bad, bad. Martin is a bad boy. Little boys don't play with their wee-wee."

Since there was no place to go, Martin just hunched up. She spanked his hand another time, then emptied the tub and dried him off, talking all the time with her displeased voice.

\* \* \* \* \*

The boy grew, spending most of his time playing in the house with his sisters or in the back yard. There was a third sister, Flora, so there were always lots of kids to play with. Like Rosalie before him, he started school at St. Patrick's when he was six and soon began to meet other boys his own age. He also began playing with the boys in the alley. Most of the families across the alley and at the end of the block were Kentuckians. Their fathers worked at the iron works or bag factory across the track, and their children went to public school. There were also other kids on his street and the neighboring ones who went to public school and were not Catholics. In fact, Martin soon realized that his family was one of the few Catholic ones on that street. The other boys used to call them Catlickers, and when he was with some other Catholic boys, Martin would call them Potlickers. He didn't have the nerve to do it when he was alone.

\* \* \* \* \*

Martin was in the alley playing marbles. He was using his best agate, though some of the other guys had hard shooters too. It was his shot. He went back behind the line and leaned forward to aim.

"Hey, quit leaning," Billy whined. "Anyone can do good shooting that way."

"You're allowed to lean," Martin retorted. "Just so you don't step over the line."

"Yeah, that's okay," Osro Henry, Martin's best Kentuckian friend, said. "You can lean too."

Martin was glad for that support because Billy could get mean. Then he'd make a hickey on your arm or trip you. Martin aimed very carefully and arrowed the agate toward the home square. It ricochetted against two other marbles and finally knocked one just barely out. However, his agate stayed within the four incised lines that outlined home base in the cinder dust.

"Aah, aah, aah," Billy Hartmann laughed. "You can't play with that crummy agate, even if you lean."

Martin responded as he thought he should, though he didn't really feel like it. He didn't like to argue with Billy Hartmann. "That's nothing to stay in home base. Everybody does that sometime. You do too."

"Not as much as you. If I did, I'd quit playing marbles."

Osro said, "Aw, why don't you keep quiet and play. It's your turn."

Martin was glad Osro was his friend because the Kentuckian boy wasn't scared of Billy Hartmann or almost anyone else. The Kentuckians, Martin knew, were almost all tough. They weren't hardly scared of any others, Catholics or Protestants, Dagos, or even Niggers.

Billy walked forward, holding his ball bearing shooter where everyone could see it. He stopped in front of the line and held it up. "You see that. It's one of the steel ball bearings they use where my old man works. He brought it home for me. It can crack almost any marble it hits, no matter how hard it is."

The other boy, Kenny Adams, spoke, "I don't think that's fair. I played in a game over on Singleton Street the other day and some kid tried to use one of those but they wouldn't let him. It breaks too many good marbles, and even shooters."

"It don't look fair to me either," Osro said. "No one else even got a chance to get one cause they didn't know you was going to bring one. I think I could have got my brother to bring me some ball bearings from the iron works. But besides, who wants to pay good money for marbles and then crack them all up."

"Nobody said it was against the rules before," Billy pointed out. "So I can shoot. Somebody's got to tell you about rules beforehand." He started aiming as though it were all settled but held back from shooting a few moments.

Kenny Adams said, "He's right in a way. No one told him he couldn't. And I don't think you can just make up rules on the spot. I still think it's dumb to pay good money for marbles and shooters, and then break them up with ball bearings. But maybe we ought to let him shoot this time and make up a rule against it for the next time."

Billy leaned forward. "There ain't no rule so I'm going to shoot."

Martin figured that Billy had decided it was best to go ahead while the group was undecided, that once he shot, there was little the others could do about it.

Billy shot. The highly polished steel sphere made a slight arc, hitting the ground just in front of home square, rolling in and hitting a blue marble, cracking it into pieces. The ball bearing lost some of its speed but still had enough to roll into Martin's agate. The agate didn't shatter, but a small sliver fell off. Billy yelled, "Aah, there it goes. There goes Neumann-Pecker's fine agate. Busted, hah."

Martin hated that name. Most guys didn't use it, but Billy Hartmann did when he wanted to get you riled up. Martin said, "It ain't busted, just a little chip off. And don't call me that name."

Billy looked at Martin and grinned in his mean way. "What's the matter, you don't like that?"

Martin noticed right away that Billy didn't repeat the odious name. The other boy didn't want to start a fight. He probably knew that if Martin got very angry, he could put up a fight.

Martin picked up his agate. Billy protested, "I ain't finished yet. Hitting two marbles will give me two more shots at least. Besides, cracking one up completely and knocking a piece off an agate ought to give me at least one more."

Martin flared. "Well, I for one ain't going to let my agate lay there and have you bust it all up with an unfair shooter. We already decided we weren't going to let anyone use one of those ball bearings any more."

"That was next time. Kenny said I get to use it this time."

"You already did. I don't think Kenny meant you could go ahead this time and break up all the other marbles. He meant you got one shot and you already got that."

"Cripes, the way you twist things. Kenny didn't say anything about one shot. He said this time. And my time's not up. I get to shoot again."

Osro reached over and took his shooter and marbles out of the square. "I'm going to quit too. All we're doing now is arguing. That's no fun. I think we ought to all quit. We can play again tomorrow." He added, "With the new rules."

Everyone picked up his own marbles and then they stood in indecision. Billy Hartmann broke the silence: "What's the rest of you guys going to do?"

"I got to go home to eat pretty soon," Osro said. "We're having barbecued spare ribs tonight. And besides, my big brother will be there. He goes out to see his girl after eating. And if I sit down with him, he tells me some of the things he does with her."

"It must be good to have a big brother," said Kenny. "They can tell you lots of things. Sometimes they're mean to you too, though."

"Well, Artis ain't," Osro insisted. "He's tough, but he never does anything mean to me. But that's because he's a lot older, I think. It's big brothers that's just a few years older that are mean."

"I got to get back soon too," admitted Billy, "to go out and get some cigarettes for my old man. He usually wants me to when he comes home."

"They sell you cigarettes?" Kenny. "I thought you had to be eighteen."

"Yeah, that's the law," Billy. "But it's my uncle's store, and he knows it's for my old man."

Osro grinned. "Didn't you ever get an extra pack for yourself. Who would know?"

Billy grinned back. "What do you think?"

"I don't know, but you could make it up."

"Just think anything you want. It don't make no difference to me what you think."

By this time they were moving slowly up the alley toward their houses. Kenny Adams stepped into an empty space between two garages and took out his dick to piss. Before he could let go, Billy Hartmann said loudly, "Wait, let's have a contest. Let's see who can piss farthest."

"Aw, what for?" groaned Osro. "It's late, and besides, we did it before. Anyway, I think you just want to show off your dick again. You think you're something great because you got a bigger dick than us guys."

"Naw, that ain't it. I just want to have a contest. We quit marbles early, didn't we?"

Kenny Adams stood holding his dick in his hand. "Come on you guys, make up your mind. I got to take a leak."

"Come on out here and we'll stand with our backs to the garage and piss outward. See if anyone can piss across the alley."

Kenny Adams whined, "Aw, no one could do that. Not even you, Billy, with your big dick."

"Come on and see then. I'll show you." Billy Hartmann stepped over to the closed garage door and started to unzip his pants.

"What if somebody comes and sees us?" asked Martin nervously. "I mean, what if somebody comes down the alley?"

Billy answered, "Aw, there ain't many people use the alley this time, and besides, if it's a car, we'll hear it."

"I don't care, I'll do it," Osro said and stood next to Billy.

Martin said, "I don't know if I got any piss."

Billy slapped him on the shoulder. "Come on, Neumann. Everybody's got some piss all the time. All you got to have is a dribble."

"Yeah, come on," Osro urged. "It don't matter who wins anyway. Billy just wants everybody to see how big his dick is."

They all lined up and took out their dicks. Billy said, "Okay now. When I count to three, everybody piss. One, two . . ."

The sound of a car turning around the corner at the end of the alley broke up the procedure. Each boy stood frozen, holding his dick in his hand. The car stopped at the top of the hill, and a garage door opening could be heard.

"Wow, that was close," stammered Martin.

"Ah, don't be so scared. It wasn't nothing. Okay, let's go for sure this time. One, two, three, pi-i-i-i-iss." Slowly the urine dribbled in short arcs from each dick. Martin was surprised that he had some too, though not much. Surprisingly, it wasn't Billy Hartmann who pissed farthest, even though he did have the biggest dick. Rather it was Kenny Adams whose stream went just about to the middle of the alley. He yelled, "I win, I win, I get the prize!"

Billy, "There ain't no prize, you know that. You just win, that's all. Besides it wasn't so much fun anyway." He shook off his dick and put it back in his pants. "I got to go or my old man will be mad. I'll see you guys later."

\* \* \* \* \*

When Martin finished grade school, he changed to Holy Cross. He felt the juices of his body more and more, particularly when he was around the girls of his class. Their breasts were swelling in the white blouses of their uniforms, as were their hips and the calves of their legs. Martin could imagine the round fullness of their thighs. He approached none, however, fearing rejection. He would avert his eyes quickly if a girl turned to see him looking at her. Often he would put his hand up to feel one of the pimples on his face or neck. Sometimes when he felt he wasn't being watched, he would squeeze one.

Fortunately he discovered the library, and soon he was packing home veritable stacks of books, at first about animal life and natural history, but soon about people as well. At night, totally separated from the world of rejection and acceptance, he would hunch breathlessly over his books hour after hour until brought back to reality by Esther who would say, "Martin, sit up straight. You're not breathing."

* * * * *

"Are you ready?" Rosalie was at Martin's door.

He put his hand on his tie. "I don't think I'll go. I wasn't even invited."

His sister strode determinedly into the room. "Come on now, Martin. You look fine. You'll be alright." She tried to take his arm. He shook it off, getting up.

"What's wrong? Are you mad or something?"

"I'm alright." His tone of voice implied that he was not. "I just don't feel like going to a party."

She reached for his hand this time. "Come on, Martin. I know it's hard for you. You're afraid girls won't like you. But you shouldn't be that way. There are a lot of girls who would like to go out with you, but you don't give them a chance. You've got to go out though. That's the only way you'll get used to them. Betty knows. We talked about it before. She's seen shy boys before, and she likes you too. It'll be good for you."

Martin pulled his hand back, saying with less irritation, "Alright, I'll go. You don't have to pull me though."

Betty Henley's house was the second up the street from the Neumanns', and when Rosalie and Martin approached, other couples and groups were moving up the walk and into the house. The girls were brightly clad in the short dresses and skirts of the era, their hair frizzed or bobbed short; the boys wore jackets and ties, their hair mostly slicked down. Martin watched the party-goers to see how many he knew. He recognized most from the neighborhood, though there were boys and girls he had never seen. He figured they must have come from Kriese Manual Training High School, the public school where Betty Henley went. The boys learned shop there instead of the Latin and religious studies he got at Holy Cross.

Betty Henley met them at the door. "I'm glad you and your sister could come, Martin. It'll be fun. We're going to play games."

Martin mumbled "Hello" and kept walking toward the living room,

where balloons and crepe paper hung from the ceiling. Bowls of cookies and apples surrounded the punch bowl; glasses were on a table in
the middle of the room. A small cluster of girls stood at the center near
one boy Martin didn't recognize. Taller and looking older to Martin,
he was talking freely with the girls. Most of the other boys stood to one
side in a cluster. At the other side of the room were the rest of the girls,
also separate from the boys. Martin looked around quickly and was
pleased to note that Billy Hartmann wasn't there. The only one of his
close friends he saw was Kenny Adams and his brother, Charlie. Martin
waved at Kenny, who was talking to his brother. Martin was about to
head in their direction when Rosalie said, "Why don't we go out and
get some punch? I see Vera Robinson and Sally Penner there. I'll introduce you to them. You'll like Vera."

Martin knew what his sister was doing, trying to break the ice for
him, helping him to get to know some girl. But he had great difficulty
accepting her help, for what reason he didn't exactly know. He felt embarrassed to be at a party with his sister, and yet he knew he wouldn't be
there otherwise. He had walked by the lighted windows of parties many
times, wondering longingly how it would be. He had never been invited, even though he was a junior in high school and seventeen years
old. It was Rosalie's doings, he knew, that had gotten him there. However, was aware that he was reluctant to talk to girls because he was afraid
he wouldn't know what to say. If he did speak, he might say the wrong
thing. It would be so much easier to join the group of boys where the
Adamses were. He said to Rosalie, "No, I don't want any punch now.
I'm going over to see Kenny and his brother."

He wanted to tell his sister that she should go on her own, that it was
embarrassing to be around where there were other boys and girls and
to be taken around by one's sister.

Rosalie looked at him a little sadly. "Okay Martin, I don't want to
hurt your feelings. But if you decide you want to meet Vera or one of
the other nice girls I know, come on over." She walked away.

Martin headed toward the group of boys. Kenny punched his arm
lightly. "I didn't know you'd be here. I thought you said you didn't like
parties."

"I don't, but my sister wanted me to come and meet some of her
friends. You know how sisters are."

"No, afraid not since I don't have any. But how'd it go, did she introduce you to some?"

Martin couldn't help not showing he cared. "Naw, I told her I didn't want to. I'm okay without my sister."

Kenny's older brother asked, "So why come to the party?"

Martin knew he couldn't answer that honestly; it would show he really cared. "Aw, I just came 'cause I didn't have nothing else to do." He knew that wasn't true; he had a whole stack of books he had brought home that day, two of Jack London and one by a new author he had come across by accident, Herman Melville, a book about a great whale hunt.

He had come because he couldn't resist the attraction of swelling breasts and hips and the soprano of female voices. Lately, his cock and balls had been giving him more trouble, even when he wasn't looking at a girl. It had become embarrassing to ride on a trolley because the jiggling would push against his balls and make his cock hard. If the ride was too long, his balls would ache afterward. And the only way to get rid of that was to jack off. He had started some three years before, despite the talks in his health classes about not playing with yourself. They told the boys it would damage their mind. When he walked wherever there were young girls these days, Martin would very soon have his hand in his pocket, holding down his cock.

Kenny's brother turned back to another boy in the group, a fellow Martin just vaguely knew. "One of us should have brought a bottle. We could spike the punch then."

"I don't think Betty would let you."

Kenny's brother protested, "Aw, we wouldn't have to ask her. One of us could just slip it in when no one was looking."

Martin felt he should act knowledgeable even though he had only drank muscatel wine once, and it was sickly sweet. "Where do you get your wine, Charlie?"

"Aw, I don't get wine. That's just for young punks. I get bourbon." He looked knowing. "And I know plenty of places where they'll sell it to you."

Martin said, "I guess bourbon is stronger than wine, ain't it?"

"You're not kidding. Just a little in that punch would really liven this party up."

Kenny chimed in, "Well anyway, I heard they was going to have some kissing games tonight. That won't be too bad."

Martin spoke quickly then in the most assured tone he could muster. "Yeah, that would be alright."

But as usual the assured front, almost a bluff, did not work well for him. Charlie, with a slight smirk, chuckled, "I'll bet you know all about that, eh, Martin? A real all-around kisser. I'll bet you even know how to do a French kiss."

Martin recognized the baiting tone and was sorry he had started, but felt he couldn't back out then. However, he kept his remark general because he knew if he went into detail, he would surely be found out. For the truth was that he hadn't kissed a girl yet. "I know enough about it."

"Okay," Charlie. "How do you do a French kiss?"

Martin looked at him then with a combination of anger and embarrassment. "That's alright. I know. Maybe you don't know and want me to tell you."

Charlie chuckled. "You don't need to tell me that, Martin. I know that you're scared of girls. You've probably never even been out with one."

Martin knew he was blushing and wanted nothing more than to be somewhere else. He fingered his balls through his pants pocket, but when he realized what he was doing, quickly pulled out his hand. One of them might notice. Fortunately he saw Rosalie waving at him and was glad to have a reason for breaking away then. "My sister wants me. I promised I'd help her and Betty Henley move some of the furniture for the games."

Before any of them could reply, he hurried away.

Martin was in the corner of the living room with Harry Benson, a boy who had a slight harelip. Martin was studying the thickening fuzz above the boy's mouth, which had already softened the outlines of the scar. Martin knew that Harry was doing everything he could to get the moustache to grow, and fortunately it seemed to be growing faster than that of most other boys his age.

The party-goers were in chairs and standing around the edge of the living room. The small dining area beyond it had been curtained off for the party. The curtains opened and the older guy came out with Sally Penner. He had lipstick smears around his mouth, looking serious and confident to Martin. No one kidded him as he came across the room. Some girls in a group tittered, but that was all. He sat down with a group of guys, wiping the lipstick with a handkerchief while Sally went to a girls' group.

"What do you think they did in there?" whispered Harry.

"Just kissing. What else?"

"I don't know, but I thought maybe he was feeling her up. He's older."

Harry shrugged. "I never played post office before. It seems like kind of a dumb game to me. All you do is wait for your name to be called then go behind the curtain and kiss however many times your letter calls for. And what if it's someone you don't even want to kiss?"

Martin didn't disagree, but he figured it was the only way the girls could get all the boys to take part. He knew that no matter how much he wanted to kiss someone, he wouldn't be likely to do it on his own. He said to Harry, "Ain't there somebody here you'd like to kiss?"

"Aw, I guess so. But there's sure a lot I wouldn't."

They had already played Spin the Bottle, and Martin had stayed in the second row so if the bottle tipped his way, he could act like it was the guy in front of him. He didn't care too much because the kissing then was all out in front where everyone could see and he was afraid he would blush too much.

Betty Henley came out with a note then and said out loud, to Martin's great embarrassment, "Martin Neumann has a letter from Amie Melrose and it's for three kisses."

Martin knew her, though not real well. He used to pass her with some other girls when he was coming back from Holy Cross and she was coming from Kriese Manual Training. He had thought she had looked at him a couple of times, but he wasn't sure that meant anything. A lot of girls looked at a lot of boys. Martin saw her get up across the room and, with eyes downward, head toward the curtain. He stayed in his seat. Harry pushed him. "You got to go behind the curtain with her."

Martin knew he was blushing. Then the loud voice of Charlie Adams came across the room. "Come on Martin, show everybody how to kiss."

Martin looked with anger at Kenny's older brother.

In a soft voice, Betty Henley urged, "Come on, Martin. Just three kisses."

Martin looked around the room and saw a variety of faces blurred into a giggling, grinning, taunting composite. One face in the middle, which seemed to be encouraging and kindly, was that of Rosalie. Martin got up and stumbled, blushing, to the curtain, followed by tittering and laughing voices. At that moment he would cheerily have destroyed the human ability to laugh, the cruelest punishment he knew.

It was much darker behind the curtain. A few feet inside, he could make out the figure of Amie Melrose, her eyes generally cast down but glancing up at him enough to give encouragement. Martin walked up to her. She closed her eyes and offered her pursed lips. He tried to purse his as he had seen Clark Gable do with Carole Lombard and aimed toward hers though only squinting his eyes. He was afraid he would miss. He touched hers, feeling the muscularity of the lips and the greasiness of the lipstick. There was a vague fruity taste also. It was very quick. When he leaned forward for the second, she put her hand on his arm and he felt her tit against his chest. The third time she put her arms around his neck. He surprised himself by kissing her another time on the edge of her lips.

She said, "Thanks, Martin."

He mumbled something, and they both went back through the curtain. They were greeted by many cries and laughter. Martin could pick out the jeering voice of Charlie Adams. "Ah, the great kisser returns. Yeaah."

With much relief Martin walked away from Amie and rejoined Harry Benson on the couch.

It was a great relief when Betty Henley's mother appeared with sandwiches and cake. That was the signal that the kissing games were over. Martin walked up to the food table with Harry. Rosalie was there also. She seemed to be trying deliberately to be where he was as often as possible. He felt a comfort from that, though an anger too that he had to depend on his sister. Martin and Harry filled up plates with lunch meat and cheese sandwiches, plus chocolate cake, and stepped back to fill themselves. To Martin, eating was perhaps the greatest pleasure of life, if it wasn't sleeping. The difference, though, was that if the sleeping was very good, you didn't remember anything about it, and the taste of foods eaten could be remembered a long time afterward. Martin was lucky that he didn't get fat like Ronnie Silverberg or some of the fat, pimply girls.

"How do you like the cake?" Harry said. "I think the icing is great."

"It's pretty good for a party. My mom makes some about the same. But down in the country, at church socials and threshing dinners, is where they really have cake, and all kinds of other good food." Martin couldn't imagine that he would ever get such an abundance of delicious food again as he had during the summers when he had stayed at his grandmother's country house at Wertzberg.

"Pretty good, huh?"

"They fix everything there. They grow a lot of it, even stuff for cakes. Did you know they have their own wheat ground into flour? And they wouldn't think of buying eggs or milk, because they had their own chickens and cows."

Martin could see Amie Melrose across the table with some other girls.

He was sure she glanced at him a couple of times and perhaps even smiled. And though he didn't dislike her, he turned his eyes away. It was always like that, he thought, as if he couldn't take any chances with a girl, no matter how much he was attracted. They could make you feel so bitter and rejected by saying something nasty to you. If only he had the confidence of Bobby Hartmann or that older guy at the party.

Rosalie walked up to him. As soon as she was sure no one else was listening, she said, "I'm glad Amie Melrose asked you in, Martin. She's a nice girl, and I'm sure she likes you."

He threw his sister a smoldering glance, saying shortly, "It was okay."

Rosalie tried to placate him. "I don't want to make you mad, Martin. But in some things I could help you. I'm just telling you these things for your own good."

"I know that." He would like to have explained how difficult it was to take help from your sister if you were a guy, even if she was older; that the other guys would kid you a lot. She meant well, but she just didn't know how important it was to be accepted by the guys. So he stayed silent, offering no further explanation. She stood there quietly for a while, nibbling slowly on a sandwich. Martin didn't move away even though he wanted to. But he felt it might bother her if he went away too quickly. She finally said in a muted voice, "Martin, Vera Robinson said she didn't have anyone to go home with and she asked me who you came with. I told her you came with me and, though she didn't say it directly, I know she'd like you to take her home." Rosalie's eagerness got the best of her. "I'd be happy to ask her for you."

The usual wave of fear rose then, as it did whenever it seemed imminent that he would be alone with a girl. He hated himself for the dual forces of attraction and fear of rejection that always played on him at such times, answering quickly, "No, you don't have to. I'm going out with the guys."

That was untrue, and he figured Rosalie knew it, but he had to say something. She urged, "I don't mind, Martin. And you don't need to worry. She knows you're bashful, so she won't do anything to make you feel embarrassed. You won't even have to talk all the time. She likes to talk a lot, and I think she'll talk enough for both of you."

Martin drank some of the punch to get the dryness out of his throat. When he didn't answer right away, Rosalie added, "It's alright, Martin. A lot of guys are bashful when they're young. But you got to get started. And Vera is a nice girl."

He felt the fear spreading to his feet and hands and throughout his skin in a detectable blush. To end it as quickly as possible, he snapped, "No, I've already arranged to go out with the guys."

She looked at him reproachfully, and he felt guilty, though relieved.

\* \* \* \* \*

Then high school was over, and Martin walked the grimy streets of Indiantown, job hunting. Jobs were scarce at any salary, though what salaries there were, were low. He tried posting bills in the sales office of a packing plant for a while and found it deadly in its boredom. Also, it paid very little. He switched to an auto parts factory, grinding the burrs off the ends of mufflers in the middle of the night at piece rate. He still believed in Hell then, and that job seemed what he imagined Hell would be like. After that he went into a new kind of hell, a wet inferno. He took a job on the cleanup gang of the same packing house where he had formerly worked as a clerk. For six or seven hours each night, along with a half dozen other young men of the working class, he wielded a high-pressure steam hose, blasting off gobbets of meat and fat from cutting tables where a few hours before men had hacked, sawed, and sliced the bodies of pigs, cattle, and sheep into hams, steaks, chops, and roasts. To put excitement into those hissing, steamy midnight hours, Martin and the other young fellows would hunt rats with their hoses, blasting the creatures with the steam jets. That job paid more, and he soon felt desperately in need of an auto. There was no other way he could think of to impress girls, or to carry them around, if they ever accepted. He got a Ford V-8 coupe and, joy of joys to a young man in mid-America, he had his own wheels.

\* \* \* \* \*

The Oldsmobile coupe was cruising along River Park Drive. Kenny Adams shared the front seat with Martin and Bobby Hartmann. No one was in the small back seat. Martin took a swig from the bottle of muscatel. If it were any sweeter, he would have been unable to drink it. Even so, he swallowed it as fast as he could, feeling the bite in his throat. Then he passed the open bottle to Bobby Hartmann, who was driving. "That was my fourth drink. I don't know if one bottle is enough." Martin was aware that his speech was slightly slurred.

Bobby protested, "Aw, what's that? You're not even driving. I've had the same number, and it don't make no difference to me." He tipped the bottle with his free hand and took a generous swallow.

It irritated Martin that Bobby should forever be claiming to be more capable of anything, from drinking muscatel to going out with girls, even though he knew it was generally true.

Bobby handed the bottle back to Martin, who handed it to Kenny Adams, who took his swig in turn.

There were other cars on the boulevard, even though it was late. Most had couples or groups of young men. A car careened around the corner and weaved up the street in front of them. "Look at that dumb bastard," Bobby gestured toward the other car. "He's drunk. He can't even hold his liquor. But he better not touch Bobby Hartmann's Oldsmobile."

Martin knew that was true. There was nothing that Bobby would fight about quicker than his Oldsmobile. In fact, everyone had to be careful about leaning on it. Whenever someone did by accident, Bobby would take a rag out of the glove compartment and wipe the smudge off. He was forever boasting about the car also, citing its horsepower and how fast it could take off or turn a corner. Martin tried to do the same with his V-8, but the truth was that he didn't know many of its capabilities. He thought sadly then that about the only thing he could claim superiority in was the books he read, even though neither Bobby nor the other guys cared anything about that.

The car approached a stop sign behind another with a couple in the front and back. The girl's face appeared in the back window, she looking at their car. Bobby whistled and held up the bottle of wine. The girl grinned, but the boy she was with looked back in anger and spoke to her. Bobby said, "Look, he can't even keep his girl from flirting with other guys. Bet if she was with me she wouldn't do that."

The Chevy two-door took off fast, the driver letting his clutch out quickly. Bobby had no trouble keeping up with the other car, however. The two raced down the almost empty street.

Martin felt his pulse quicken. Bobby grimaced. "This ain't so exciting as 'chicken' but it'll do. And believe me, no Chevy is going to beat Bobby Hartmann's Oldsmobile."

It had the most horsepower of any of the young men's cars in that neighborhood, and Bobby had done something else to the motor to make it go even faster. Martin had already gotten tired of the game of cars, but all the boys played it, and he felt he had to act like it was important.

The Chevy with the couples came to a stop light. Bobby pulled up alongside, stopped, and revved his engine to show he would race. The driver of the other car revved his too, though with much less noise. Martin knew that Bobby had put a cutout in the Oldsmobile tail pipe so the engine would make more noise. He could do so many things with cars and other machinery. That was because he had gone to Kriese Manual and had taken every shop course he could get. Martin had taken none in the year he had gone to Kriese, the only boy he knew of who had gotten through high school without taking shop.

"Brrrm, Brrrm, Brrrm," the Oldsmobile roared to the weaker response of the Chevrolet: "Raaa, Raaa, Raaa."

Just then a car glided slowly down the cross street and stopped as the light changed. "Geez, watch it. It's the cops," Kenny cried.

The police in the patrol car watched the two cars. Kenny hissed, "Put the booze out of sight. And go easy."

Bobby had already stopped revving the engine, as had the next car. "I have. I can see. You think I'm nuts?"

The Chevrolet eased away from the street sedately, and Bobby put the Oldsmobile behind it. The Chevrolet turned away within a couple of blocks and the three boys kept going straight on.

Bobby moaned, "Geez, what we need is some girls. It's no good out drinking and driving without any girls. How about going to Herschel's Drive-in? Maybe we can pick some up."

"How could we do that?" asked Kenny. "They're all couples already. The girls wouldn't come out alone."

"That's alright," Bobby. "There's the carhops, ain't there? They wear those short skirts at Herschel's. We could pick one of them up."

"How could we do that, they're working," Martin. "They wouldn't leave until after work. And even then most of them probably have boyfriends who come to get them."

"Geez, you can think of more reasons why something wouldn't work," Bobby. "No wonder you can't get a girl."

Martin took another swig from the wine bottle and passed it on. He felt more confident when he said, "Well, you got to be realistic."

"Ha, ha, ha. Realistic. There you go again with those two bit words you're always throwing out from those crazy books you're always reading. Why can't you talk regular?"

This topic invariably came up, and it bothered Martin. He knew he used all the new words he could even when he didn't know how to pronounce them. But he figured he had a right to say what he wanted. Furthermore, the confidence of alcohol was bolstering his courage. "I can use any words I want. Anybody can. It's a right called 'free speech'."

"Well, maybe there's something like free speech, but it still sounds like you're trying to put on an act, to be better than others."

"I'm not trying to do anything. I just use words that are right, and *realistic* is alright. If you don't know anything, that's your fault."

Kenny interrupted, "I never saw any guys argue as much as you two. Why don't you try to get along for a change?"

"Aw, Martin always acts like he knows everything. And he really don't know much at all, just that stuff from those crazy books he reads. But he don't know how to act."

That was probably true, Martin thought, but he would be the last person to admit it. "That ain't true. I know how to act as good as anybody else. You're just saying that."

They passed the bottle around again. Martin was feeling woozy, but he was afraid to stop, afraid that the other guys would kid him and also that he would lose his courage again.

As soon as Bobby Hartmann finished his swig, he taunted, "Did he ever mess it up the other day when I fixed him up with Marsha Greer. You know he never can get a girl on his own, so I decided to help. And she's very loose; I told him that. But what does he do? He starts crawling all over her the minute we got to the park. Everybody knows you have to take it easy, even with a loose girl. You should've seen him, he looked like he was going to rape her and right there in front of my girl."

Martin felt terrible then. If there had been any way to stop the discussion, he would have. He still felt ashamed of what he had done. But he had always been so shy before, not even trying to kiss a girl, even when he wanted to. So he had decided that he was wrong being so careful; he would go all the way, even if she tried to slow him down.

Bobby continued, "You know what she said when I saw her the next day? She said, 'That guy's really got hot nuts.' And she didn't want to go out with him again." Pause. "And it's not that she never let any guys do it to her before. I know plenty. But a guy's got to have some technique."

Martin tried to put on a little bravado. "I didn't do anything so terrible. I was just trying to feel her up. Everybody does that."

That had not been true in his case, Martin knew clearly. He had always been very careful where he had put his hands. It was just that since Bobby had told him this girl was loose, he thought he wouldn't have any trouble. If only a guy knew, he thought, how far he should go or how far was too much.

Bobby Hartmann snorted, "But you got to do it gradually. You can't come on a girl like a house afire. It took me three whole weeks before I could put my hand on Evelyn's tits. And even now she won't always let me."

Fortunately they shortly arrived at the drive-in, which was doing a booming business. There were a variety of cars, many souped up or re-modeled, parked, or coming or going. Most carried couples or groups of boys. There were only a couple with girls. Carhops in short skirts and tight sweaters, each wearing a tam, took orders at parked cars, carrying empty trays back, or bringing full ones. Bobby pulled into an empty space. The sharp turn made Martin feel queasy. He hiccupped, and the sweet taste of the wine came back into his mouth.

A well-shaped carhop approached their car. Bobby crooned, "Hi honey, what's a pretty girl like you here working on Saturday night? Why ain't your boyfriend taking you out?"

"He's working too," she said immediately. "What'll you guys have?"

"Cheeseburger and fries and a cherry coke." Bobby added with a slight leer, "Think that'll be sweet enough, honey?"

She ignored the remark, saying, "What with it?"

"The works."

She turned to Martin, who was trying to erase from his mind's eye the image of a greasy dish of french fries and a dripping burger. At that moment, he just could not think of eating anything, and particularly not some greasy meat. His ears were buzzing, and he had trouble focusing on the carhop. She repeated, "What'll you have?"

He ordered the only thing he thought he could get down. "Milkshake, chocolate."

"Anything to eat?"

Weakly and just barely audibly, "No, zat's 'nough."

Kenny ordered a plain burger and a shake, then turned to Martin. "You okay?"

"Sure, just little woozy. Be awright." It was getting laborious to talk, but he added, "Need more air. Open window."

"Okay. Maybe you'd better get out and walk around a little."

Bobby said worriedly, "Yeah, you're not feeling sick, are you? Because if you feel like you're going to toss your cookies, I don't want it in here. I redid all the upholstery on the Oldsmobile."

It felt more stuffy since they had stopped. No wind was coming in the windows. Martin mumbled, "Think I will."

Kenny got out quickly and was followed immediately by Martin, who walked to the back of the car, keeping his hand on the roof for support. He giggled sickly as he thought of smudging Bobby Hartmann's car and he didn't even care. He took in big gulps of air to try to clear his head and get rid of the dizziness, feeling ashamed that couples in adjacent cars could see him in that state. He sat down on the rear bumper, which made him feel slightly better. His stomach churned, and for a moment he felt as if it might come up. But he remained very still, and after a bit the queasiness went away.

He was aware of the return and departure of the carhop. Then Kenny returned. "The food's here. You want to come for your shake?"

"Not hungry."

"Come on, Martin. You need to have something in your stomach.

Martin thought he should answer but instead remained there lumpishly, too concerned with his churning stomach and buzzing, reeling head.

Then Billy was there and spoke, using Martin's first name, "You'd better come on up and have some of your shake, Martin. It'll do you good. I know it always helps me to get something down when I'm drinking."

When Martin started to get up, Kenny reached to take his arm, but Martin shook it off. "I'm alright. Can get there by self."

Kenny got in first, and Martin sat by the window, still gulping deep breaths. He was handed his milkshake. He studied the granular brown surface for a long time, aware of the unpleasant odor of cooked meat as Kenny and Billy chewed their burgers. Kenny urged, "Go on, Martin, have some. You need any help?"

Martin wiped his brow and was surprised to realize there was sweat on it because at that moment he was getting cool. "No, can do it alone."

He took the straw between his lips and sucked, watching the concavity increase on the surface of the shake. In its coolness the liquid was a shock at first, but then it became soothing as the walls of his throat cooled. He could almost feel the shake going into his stomach as a coating over the wine.

"How's it feel?" asked Kenny.

"Okay. Better."

When they finished and drove off, Martin began to feel much better. He kept his head at the window, taking in air. After a bit he felt like speaking again. "Feeling okay. Was just temporary. Fact is, think could use another drink."

Billy, "You were looking pretty sick back there. You don't have to drink any more. Me and Kenny can finish it."

Martin could foresee what would be said later if he quit then. He would be accused of not being able to hold his liquor. He was sure Billy would go through that routine since he was always accusing Martin of not being able to do something. Anyway, it was important to all the guys that you could hold your liquor. Almost belligerently, Martin retorted, "No, I want my share. And I feel ready for a drink right now. Who's got the bottle?"

Kenny produced the almost half empty bottle, the second of the night. "I don't know, Martin. You don't have to, you know."

Martin didn't believe that. Of course a guy didn't *have* to do what the others were doing, but they would throw it in your face afterward if you didn't. "Here, gimme that bottle. Don't let it be said that Martin Neumann couldn't hold his liquor." He took a particularly long swallow even though the first sweet bite was hard to get down. He coughed. "There." He handed the bottle to Kenny. "How's that for a drink?"

"That's okay, though I think you may be overdoing it." Kenny. "A guy has to quit when he's had enough."

"Aw, he's alright now that he's got something in his stomach," chuckled Billy. "A lot of guys get a little sick when they first start drinking. But you can't let that keep you from doing it." He reached for the bottle. "Let me have my turn."

They drove and drank until the bottle was almost empty. Martin had mixed feelings. On the one hand, the buzzing dizziness had increased, and the light bulbs along the road were going in circles. On the other hand, he felt like he could do almost anything he wanted. He took the last swig of the bottle and hurled it out the window. It hit a concrete wall on the side of the road and shattered. "What we need is another one." He was aware that his voice was very loud, almost a shout. "How about it, guys, want another bottle of good old muscatel?"

"I don't know where we can get any now. It's late, almost two o'clock."

"No shit? I didn't know it was that late. Ha, ha, ha, that's funny, almost two o'clock and no muscatel. How's a real drinker going to tie one on if no muscatel?"

Kenny said, "Well, I don't mind having another bottle. Since there ain't no girls, might as well make it a drinking night. And tomorrow's Sunday. Sleep late."

Martin was vaguely aware that Kenny was cropping his sentences also. "That's funny. When a guy gets drunk, speaks cut off. Ha, ha, ha. Speaks short – mean. Ha, ha, ha."

"Aw, you guys are just drunk," protested Billy. "You ought to get home and go to bed. How you going to pick up any girls if you're drunk?"

"Girls, girls, who wants girls? What Martin wants is muscatel, bottle of muscatel."

Kenny urged: "How about it, get bottle at Hoffman's Liquor Store, okay?"

"Naw, they're closed. And anyway, they don't sell it if you're under age," said Billy, knowingly.

Martin said, "Look lights. Go in circle." The light bulbs were indeed spinning dizzily by this time. "Stop guys, Martin wants look at spinning lights."

"What're you talking about? You're drunker'n a skunk." Billy snorted.

"Not drunk. Just want to see spinning light bulbs. Never saw spinning lights before. Very funny, all bulbs spinning, ha, ha, ha."

Kenny said thoughtfully, "He's right in a way; the bulbs do seem to be moving."

"Stop, stop, over there," Martin shouted. "Big light! Let Martin see big spinning light!"

At an isolated intersection, a single street lamp hung from a pole, supported by a forty-five-degree guy wire. Billy wheeled off the road beside the pole, rattling the gravel as he skidded to a stop. "Jesus, I don't know about you, Neumann. One minute you're sick and the next you want to check out light bulbs. It's crazy." He switched off the motor. "I just hope no cops come along. They'd probably haul us all in."

With the motor off, the quietness of the night became very noticeable. All Martin could hear for the moment was the "zee-zeeing" of insects in a patch of weeds off the road. Also in stopping he was aware of the heat of the car, added to that of the night. He opened his door and stumbled out. Kenny followed on his side, and Billy got out on the other. Martin walked directly to the lamp, and looking directly up at it, called out almost in a shout, "Hi light. See you, see you spinning. Lights don't spin. You're acting funny, spinning. But Martin will find out secret."

Billy laughed, "Jesus Christ, that's crazy, talking to a light. It's a good thing there's nobody else around here. They'd haul you off for sure."

Kenny warned, "He's right, Martin. You ought to keep your voice down. If somebody else heard, they'd think you was crazy."

"Aw, ain't nothing. Just want to see." He waved his arm toward the lamp. "But too high. Can't get to it." He looked around and saw the guy wire. "That's it. Climb up to light. Martin climb up to light." He headed for the wire.

Kenny said gently, "Come on, Martin. You can't do nothing there. That wire wouldn't help you."

"Sure, climb it, can climb it." He grabbed the wire and pulled himself up enough that he could wrap his legs around it. The braided half-inch strand was cold and abrasive. He was surprised that his hands didn't hurt any more than they did. He started to shinny up.

"Ha, ha, ha," Billy laughed, pointing to Martin. "Look at that crazy guy, climbing up a guy wire. I never heard of anything like that. Drunker'n a skunk."

Kenny stood under Martin when he was halfway up the wire. "Come on, Martin. That's high enough. You could hurt yourself if you fall. Don't go any higher. Come on down, and I'll help you."

"No, want to see spinning light." He kept shinnying, amazed at his strength even though by then the palms of his hand were hurting. He was vaguely aware also that he was getting his clothes dirty, if not tearing holes in them. Then all of a sudden the dizziness became wild, and the sour-sweet taste of muscatel came back into his mouth. His stomach was trying to get rid of it again. He stopped climbing and hung on until the nausea receded a little, then began shinnying down, holding on very hard with his dampened hands, wondering vaguely whether the dampness was sweat or blood. He heard Kenny's voice as if from a long way off, "Just come a little farther, Martin. I'll catch you."

Then his grip broke and he dropped. He was vaguely aware of arms cushioning his fall, and when he hit the ground it didn't seem hard. The distant voice said, "That's alright, Martin. You didn't get hurt. Just lie there for a minute."

Then Billy's voice entered his consciousness, also faraway. "Good thing he's as drunk as he is. That's why he didn't hurt himself. Drunk guys just go limp. Leave him lay there awhile."

The coolness of the ground was soothing, though it didn't keep the nausea from rising again. Martin was just aware of mumbling, "Sick, very sick," when he turned his head to one side and the sour-sweet mixture of milk shake, muscatel, and sauer kraut with spare ribs gushed from his mouth. He was only vaguely aware of trying to keep it from running on his clothes.

\* \* \* \* \*

Martin was stretched on his bed with the Bible open near the beginning. Next to it was an open dictionary. "And Elijah begat Joshua and Joshua begat Eleazar," and so on. He looked up *begat* and was pleased to learn that it was close to what he had thought. Other words were not. But he looked up almost all and then tried to pronounce them.

What really bothered him, though, were the stories: that the world was created in six days and that on the seventh the Lord rested; or that Jonah could live in a whale; or that Christ could walk on water. The fact that the priest and nuns called them miracles didn't make them any more believable. Jeez, he thought, if there were just someone besides his sisters with whom he could talk about those things. He had tried to talk to Sister Pious once because she had seemed to want to encourage him in his reading. But it had soon become clear that discussing the Bible critically was not something he could do with a nun. She had said, "If you want to talk about that further, you should go see one of the Fathers. But Martin, you know you're not supposed to be reading the Bible by yourself anyway. And you must have faith."

He put the book to one side and lay thinking. Should he openly refuse to go to Mass any more or should he pretend he was going and spend the time in the park? He could visualize the trouble that would ensue if he refused openly. That was one thing that Bruno and Esther just could not accept.

A car horn honked. By the sound he knew it was Billy Hartmann's Oldsmobile. Billy had replaced the regular horn with an extra-loud blaster.

Catherine appeared at the doorway curtain. "Martin, it's Billy Hartmann. He wants you."

Martin got up with the usual feelings of need and repulsion that Billy provoked in him. He needed the other boy because he seemed so successful and confident in all the things that mattered to a boy turning into a man in working class America: cars, girls, drinking, body building. But Martin also was repelled by the constant strain of trying to prove he too was capable in those activities. Moreover, there were his books and all the ideas that emerged of a universe far vaster than any that they ever talked about on the south side of Indiantown. The only people who would consider that greater world were the priests and nuns, but they would only consider their own version.

Martin walked outside and saw Billy parked down front. He went to the car window. Billy asked, "What's going on?"

"Nothing. I was just reading."

Martin had long ago decided it was useless to tell Billy what he was reading. Billy would either kid him about reading too much or ignore the topic. This time the boy trying so hard to become a man chose the latter, saying, "You going out anywhere today?"

"I don't know. I think my mother wants me to take her to a store where they got a lot of stuff on sale." Since he had gotten his car, it had become a regular chore for Martin to take his mother to places with sales on Saturday.

"That don't sound like much fun. Ain't you going out with a girl tonight?"

"No, I don't have a date."

"What about that girl your sister fixed you up with you told me about? Didn't you go out with her?"

That was Doris Hancock, a girl from Catherine's class. His sister had told him often enough that her friend would like to be asked to go out, so he finally stopped in the restaurant where she worked as a waitress and asked her. It had taken three trips around the block in his V-8 before he had summoned enough courage, and even then it had been very difficult to actually ask her. She had agreed though, and they had gone to a drive-in movie. He was so shy that she had literally to stand in front of her door with her eyes closed before he would kiss her. Since then he had not seen her again. It was so much easier not to deal with girls, even if he did have to spend most of his evenings alone.

Martin answered Billy about the girl, "Yeah, I took her to a movie."

"Well, did you do any good?"

It irritated Martin that the other guys always asked something like that so quickly, not particularly because he was against it, but because he never did. But even if you didn't get to feel a girl up, you didn't dare admit it. "I did alright."

"You mean she let you feel her tits?"

Martin found it very difficult to lie specifically. The best he could do was leave false implications. "Well, I can tell you she is really well built."

Billy put a stick of chewing gum in his mouth before answering. "I don't know about all that. From what I've seen, except that one time when you tried to crawl all over Marsha, you seem to be scared of girls."

Martin just could not let out his true feelings, maintaining the bravado he felt he had to have in Billy's presence. "I can just take them or leave them, that's all. I'm not a cocksman like some guys I know."

Billy continued, "Well, I got a date with Evelyn tonight. She's my regular girl now. She asked me if I had a friend and I told her about you, but I'm not sure. It would be okay to go on a double date sometime, but a guy never knows about you, either going all the way or so scared you won't even put your arm around her."

Martin knew that was true, and he just could not figure out why he couldn't have the confidence of Billy Hartmann and most of the other guys. Unconsciously he started to rub the tip of his finger on the window moulding. Billy said quickly, "Don't do that. You might scratch it, and I just got a new paint job two weeks ago. Jeez, it ain't easy to keep a car looking good with you guys leaning on it or scratching it all the time."

Martin stepped back. "I didn't hurt it. Gosh, the way you act, a car is fragile."

Billy started up the motor again. "It don't make that much difference to you because you don't take care of yours like guys do who really know cars."

That was true, Martin knew. He didn't spend as much time working on his car as Billy and most of the other guys. But after all, he explained to himself, he had not taken a single shop course. And the other guys never read anything but manuals or magazines about mechanics or girls. He was a little angry when he said, "Just spend all your time on your car and girls if you want. It don't make any difference to me."

"Okay, I was going to fix you up, but if you don't care, I know lots of guys who'd like to go out with Evelyn's friend. She's got a great pair of boobs."

"Go on. I got plenty of other things to do."

Billy let out the clutch and the Oldsmobile's tires skidded with the surplus power of the oversized engine. He always started that way, Martin thought, as he watched the big car pick up speed fast. Martin's old V-8 could never do that.

He returned to the porch and sat on the swing to watch the occasional cars and pedestrians pass, feeling the sadness of Saturday. Would loneliness be his permanent condition even while he was surrounded by people? Then Catherine came by with a friend. "Did that mean Billy Hartmann leave? I don't know why you go around with him."

Martin answered with some irritation. After all, Catherine was his younger sister. And talking about him like that in front of her friend was the best way to spread it all over the neighborhood. He said shortly, "It's none of your business."

Catherine soothed, "I didn't want to make you mad. I just don't like him." Pause. "If you're not going anywhere, maybe you'd like to go to the Saturday matinee with me and Matilda. We're going in about an hour. They have a comedy special—Laurel and Hardy and Buster Keaton, besides a Fu Manchu show. And we could stop at Schmidt's for donuts."

For years he and Catherine and sometimes Rosalie would stop after

a show to buy a dozen big glazed yeast donuts at the bakery next to
Circle Theatre and eat them on the way home. But somehow it didn't
seem right any more. "No, I don't want to. The Saturday matinee is just
for kids. During intermission they're throwing paper wads and airplanes
and gum and everything else they can slip in the theatre."

Catherine answered quickly, "We don't have to sit downstairs. Then
nobody could hit us."

"Aw, that's crazy, to go to a show for kids. That was alright when I was
a kid, but I'm big now." Martin said the last almost belligerently and he
knew why. Though he wanted to be grown up and thought he ought to
be, he really didn't feel like he was. It was as if he would prove by the
forcefulness of his words that he was a man.

Catherine turned to her friend. "Alright. You're only two years older
than me, but if that's the way you feel, you don't have to go. We can go
alone."

Martin was well aware that he wasn't much older than them, which
was another thing he couldn't understand, why a couple of years mattered so much. But he knew they did, at least to him.

The girls left. After a little while Martin walked back in the house.
Esther was sitting at the dining room table, darning socks. She looked
up and studied his face a moment before saying, "Going out?"

"No."

"Wasn't that Billy Hartmann out front?"

It irritated Martin that Esther and the girls were always watching him
and trying to get information from him. He knew he was generally irri-
table these days, and that awareness irritated him also. But there didn't
seem any way out of the situation since he didn't seem to control his
own fate. He was sorry he had answered so shortly, but he didn't seem
to be able to control himself. "Of course. You saw his car." In his mind's
eye he could see his mother going to the front window and carefully
pulling back one side of the curtain. That image irritated him also.

She kept her eyes on her darning, waiting a bit before answering,
"I'm sorry you don't feel good these days, Martin. But you know we all
must carry our burdens."

He could just barely contain himself because he knew she meant the
so-called weight that Jesus or God, or whoever he was, was supposed to
have given each person. But he knew she was reluctant to use the
name in front of him. He answered sullenly, "I don't know about any
burden."

She started to reply, checked herself, then said very softly, "I know you are troubled, son, but it would be better if you prayed more often."

He felt the anger then, rising like a volcano, but just before it seemed ready to erupt, he bottled it with no more response than a dark look. He started toward his room again when she said, "Martin, I think your father wants to see you."

He grunted a response without turning back.

Bruno was in the kitchen, reading the sports page of the Indian City Courier. He looked over his half spectacles when Martin came in, a kindly face creased at the corners of the eyes and mouth with smile wrinkles. Martin remembered many of the generous and kindly intended things Bruno had done for him, how he had urged him to study arithmetic so that someday he might be an engineer or pilot, how he had taken the boy to visit the company biologist so he could look through the microscope, and how he had taught him to shoot, first the .22 and later the 12-gauge. And yet Martin had come to a point when he could not tell his father anything that was really important.

Bruno said warmly, "Hello son, how did you like what the Warriors did yesterday?"

Bruno was crazy about baseball, and he had tried to get Martin interested. When he was younger, Martin had gone with his father to the Sunday afternoon games, but the sight of those men with paunchy bellies, made more obvious by their tight uniforms, standing around the field, wiping their sweating foreheads periodically did nothing positive for Martin. And he so hated their tobacco spit. He had only gone a few times to please his father, but he no longer did. He answered, "I don't know, Dad. What did they do?"

"Why, those suckers won the game! That makes them six and five in the league. They might win yet."

Bruno would never change, Martin thought. Despite the fact that the Indian City Warriors had not won the championship for as long as Martin could remember, his dad still had hopes. Anyway, it was something all the Neumann males seemed to think was important. Martin sat down. Bruno looked at the paper again, saying, "Listen, it says here 'In the second half of the eighth, Jimmy Powers, some call him Spitball Powers, struck two out and got a pop fly out of the third batter, making the score three to two.'"

Bruno looked at Martin, his eyes twinkling and creased in pleasure, almost as if he had thrown those balls himself. Martin answered, "That's good, Dad. I hope they'll win." Deep inside he really didn't give a shit.

Bruno read some more, smiling and laughing. It took so little to please the man, Martin thought. He waited until Bruno turned the page. "Mom said you wanted to talk to me."

Bruno looked up with incomprehension momentarily, then his face became serious. "Oh yeah, now I remember. It's something I been wanting to talk to you about." He looked around as if to discover whether someone was listening, then turned back. "It's something that we shouldn't talk about here. One of the girls might come through."

Bruno acted so conspiratorial, Martin began to feel funny, but he remained silent. Bruno almost whispered, "Let's go in the bathroom."

Martin tried not to stare at his father despite his feeling about the oddness of the opening. "Alright."

They both stood, and Martin followed the older man upstairs to the bathroom. Bruno closed the door, still conspiratorially. "Sit down, son." He indicated the toilet seat. Bruno sat on the edge of the tub, which was about the only other place left for sitting. He took his pipe out, then decided against it and started to lay it on the sink top but decided against that too, ending up by putting it in his denim shirt pocket. Martin had never seen Bruno put his pipe there before. The man was obviously nervous. Martin waited quietly.

Without looking at him, Bruno spoke. "Martin, you're growing up now, getting to be a man. And there are things a man does that boys don't do."

Martin was starting to become more uncomfortable because of his father's discomfort. Also, he was getting an inkling of what this was about, even though Bruno had not yet mentioned the topic. He wished he were in some other place, but still he held his tongue. Bruno looked at him then as if for encouragement or approval, but without getting it, went on anyway. It was as though a pause might make him stop altogether. He said, "You're going out with girls now, Martin. And that's what I want to talk to you about."

The son laughed inwardly without mirth because the number of girls he had been with had been very few and continuance with them very brief. Bruno continued, "It's right that you should go with girls now because someday you will want to marry and have a family of your own."

Martin was getting more and more uneasy, and his irritation was coming back. It was obvious that Bruno was about to talk about sex without having indicated in the eighteen years before that it even existed. Martin had heard of other fathers doing the same, giving their grown sons a sex talk without any previous warning. Somehow Martin had never imagined it would happen to him. He just couldn't imagine Bruno talking about the subject, even though there was good indication that he needed more of the activity himself. Martin had seen Bruno often enough at the top of the stairs calling down, "Esther, are you coming to bed?"

Martin thought maybe he could shorten the unpleasant interchange by saying, "Dad, I know about it."

Bruno looked at him with some surprise, as if he couldn't imagine such a possibility, but then said, "I know they teach you some things in school, especially the public schools, but there's lots they don't teach. Those are things a parent has to tell their children." Then as if to relieve the tenseness a little, Bruno said, "It's not easy, Martin, but it's a parent's responsibility. You'll realize that better when you have your own children."

Martin sighed inwardly. It was apparent that Bruno was bound and determined to get this speech said, no matter what. It was as if it were a once-in-a-lifetime occurrence, and that, uncomfortable as it was, once done, it could be forgotten. "Okay, then, what do you want to tell me?"

Bruno began at the basics. "Well, you know there are men and women, and even other animals are separated into males and females. And you know that females have babies. And that to make the babies, the male and female have to get together."

Martin figured that Bruno had shifted back to *male-female* instead of sticking with *man-woman* when he got closer to the details. Somehow it would be less intimate, though still getting the mechanical details across. Or was it because of Bruno's farm upbringing? Martin had an almost irresistible urge to jump up, open the door, and rush out. But he kept his eyes on Bruno's creased face, so intent and serious that it was unlike him. For a moment Martin thought the man in front of him was not Bruno, his father, the farmer who had come to the city, the man who maintained a respectable Catholic home and was raising four children to be what he hoped would be better off versions of himself and his wife. No, the person before him was simply every American man, perhaps every American parent, anyway, very frequently occurring. And the thought helped him hear Bruno out even as he skirted what people actually did. Bruno was saying, "Well, when men get together with women, they frequently think mostly about their own pleasure. They don't always think about the responsibility that goes with it."

Martin wondered whether Bruno was thinking mainly about responsibility when he was trying to get Esther to come to bed. It didn't seem like that to Martin. Another thought occurred to the young man, which was that even if Bruno was forcing himself to tell his son about the sex act, he just couldn't force himself to talk about what men and women, or even other animals, actually did. Was it the church that had tied everyone's tongues about the most vital act for the continuation of the species? Martin wondered, relishing the idea of putting the phrase into a sentence even if it was only in his mind.

It was fortunate, Martin thought, that when the guys talked about sex, it was just the opposite of what fathers told their sons. Guys talked about the pleasure and what one did physically. And they didn't talk about men and women getting together, they talked about fucking and screwing and sucking and the parts of the body that were used, cocks and cunts and tits and balls and thighs and lips.

At this point, Bruno's continuation was almost an interruption of Martin's thoughts, and what he said was almost a world apart. Martin was imagining a perfectly fantastic female body when Bruno said, "I know the temptation is great, especially here in the city, where a young man can meet so many girls, but your mother and I hope you will always remember you are a Catholic boy. And the church teaches that a man doesn't sleep with a woman until he is married to her. The purpose of a man and woman getting together is to have babies, a religious duty. Otherwise, it's a sin."

Martin couldn't believe it. The world as Bruno saw it did not connect with the world that Martin was living, the world of young men trying to make places for themselves and get whatever pleasure was available along the way. Bruno's world was one of responsibilities and sin and duty. Pleasure was hardly a part of it.

Bruno looked at his son then, still with a serious expression on his face, but relaxing. Apparently he had said what he had had to say. There was even the beginning of a grin, so much more like Bruno than the seriousness required by a deeply emotional subject such as sex.

Martin's head was spinning. He couldn't think of anything but the vast gulf of misunderstanding that separated him from the kindly man he was facing, the man who wanted nothing more than to be liked, especially by his son. Martin tried to smile so he could please that well-intentioned man. But he couldn't think of anything to say that might help bridge the canyon separating them. As noncommittally as possible, he said, "I know."

Martin had a momentary yen to reach out and put his arm around his father's shoulders, but refrained because it would probably embarrass the older man, and Martin wasn't sure it wouldn't embarrass him also. The Neumann men didn't do that kind of thing. Until his generation they had all been farmers, and farmers didn't show their feelings often. He and his father stood facing each other, neither seeming to know what to do. Finally Bruno broke by going over and opening the door. That seemed to be a signal that the two of them would return to the nonfrightening world of the speakables—sports, school, health, sickness, food—but not how one person adjusted to another.

Bruno said, "Think I'll go down and work on the washing machine. Your mother says the drain pipe is leaking."

"Okay, Dad. I'm going to my room for a while." Drearily Martin returned to his sanctuary, which, though not inviolate, was the closest to privacy he had managed in his eighteen years. He closed the door and threw the books that were lying on the bed onto the old upholstered chair his mother had moved in for him a few weeks before. The shade was already drawn on the single window. The room was cool and dark. The incomprehensible world of the outside was shut out.

He lay prone on the bed, his head on one pillow, the other pulled over his head. In his mind's eye he gazed at all the nonattainables of existence, welcoming females who were invariably beautiful, young men admiring his athletic prowess or performance with machines, parents who approved what he wished to do, travels to distant places, and even possible public acceptance of him as a writer of stories. The last was a fantasy that had only started to grow. But the images faded and were replaced by the nonsympathetic females who were invariably unattainable or undesirable, young men who were far better than he in the abilities that brought acceptance, parents who were cut off by misunderstanding and who relied on one solution for all problems—to devote more energy in seeking assistance from the ancestral god, the day-to-day grimy dreariness of Indian City, and the near horror of the nightly work sessions on the cleanup gang at the slaughterhouse. Martin felt tears trickling from his eyes and soon dampness on the pillow case.

He reached back and, putting his hand under his thighs, began fondling his cock. It responded by beginning to harden. He rolled to one side, put his other hand down, and unbuttoned his fly. He began stroking his balls. The tears dried up, and his eyes became fixed and shiny as he grabbed his cock and began pushing and pulling.

\* \* \* \* \*

Martin's world changed again in the late thirties. Among the young men a new topic came up, one about which he had heard very little as he was growing up: the possibility of going to war. There hadn't been much talk in his group about the Germans marching into Poland and even less about the Japanese in China. Bruno and Esther had joined a group, the Saengerbund, and went off to drink beer and sing German songs every couple of weeks, but Martin had nothing to do with that. He couldn't even speak German. What the events overseas meant to Martin and his friends was that they might have to go into the service. They had all registered for the draft, and they talked about what numbers were being called and whether it was smartest to wait to be called or better to enlist in one of the voluntary services: the Coast Guard, Air Corps, Marines, or Navy. And then the Japanese bombed Pearl Harbor and everything went into high speed.

\* \* \* \* \*

Martin looked down the long bar where men sat behind drinks. There was a sprinkling of brightly dressed women, several with dark complexions and black hair. He turned back to look at the bottle in front of him. The label read Carta Blanca. He studied it carefully, wondering in an unconnected way why there wasn't a glass alongside. Finally he decided and laughed low but audibly. He was drinking from the bottle. He took a sip then swiveled sideways wonderingly. Where was he and why? He looked at his sleeve and recognized the khaki. This gave him a certain relief. He remembered then that he was in the Air Corps, training to fight the Nips and Krauts. He laughed to himself at the thought that they had become enemies, people from faraway places about whom he had thought nothing until the draft came up. He volunteered to avoid going into the infantry. No one wanted that.

He hiccupped. A man dressed in work pants and shirt, smoking a cigarette, spoke, "How you doing, buddy? Helping whip the Krauts, showing them they'd better not mess around with the Yanks?"

Martin wondered in an alcoholic vagueness why people talked like that. They hadn't before, he felt sure. No one he had known had been concerned about either the Germans or Japanese. Of course, since he had been in service there had been endless training films showing the evildoings of those strangers and how to kill them. And the newsreels had been just as bad. Anyway, it seemed to be a matter of little concern to Martin then. He nodded drunkenly only to be amiable, "Sure, we'll whip them."

"That's the boy. We all know you'll do it. We're for you guys. Even us guys who can't get in." Then the man added before the opening got away, "Couldn't get in myself. Got a bad liver. But still helping out. Driving a semi between here and the east coast."

That seemed a little more interesting, causing Martin to wonder again where "here" was. He wanted to ask but felt that would be silly. Instead he said as if he had actually committed himself to the cause of the war, but noticing that it came out in a mumble, "Need you guys too." He added, from a newsreel it seemed, "Got to keep them rolling."

The guy explained how he hauled mattresses and furniture across the country, and Martin wondered vaguely how that helped the war effort. But he held his peace, taking an occasional swallow of beer. The guy said, "You seem to really like that beer. They drink a lot here in San Antonio even if it is from Mexico. But whatever else you say about them, those Spics sure know how to make their brew."

Martin nodded woozily. "Yup, their beer." He chuckled at himself that he had not said anything more and that it really didn't make any difference. No one really wanted to listen to him anyway. He picked up his beer bottle and emptied it in a long swallow. The truck driver continued, "Yeah, sure would like to join you boys. We'd show those Krauts something."

The man said it almost as if the war effort depended on his participation. Martin hiccupped once then lifted the bottle and tipped it to see whether there was any left. He looked toward the bartender, thinking of asking for another. But the bartender seemed to be studiously looking the other direction. The driver called, "How about another Carta Blanca for this soldier?" He turned to Martin, "It's on me, buddy. Little bit for the war effort, you know." Pause. "You can take care of a Kraut for me. Just put the name Herb Dengel on one of your bullets."

Martin thought that was funny, since there wasn't any way you could put a name on a bullet, at least not that he knew. Also, he still had no desire to kill anyone. The enemy remained indistinct, unknown people who lived far away. The only real distinction between the two types in his mind was that somehow the Krauts might be like his own grandparents and perhaps, in a general way, like his mother and father and their sisters and brothers, and the Nips would have slanted eyes, straight black hair, and short legs. In the newsreels they frequently called them apemen. But he did realize in his maudlin state that he had been trained to kill those people. He could now shoot a carbine and a .45, as well as a Thompson submachine gun and a grease gun. Someone expected him to shoot something larger than rabbits with those devices. He laughed, saying loudly, "Can shoot many kinds of guns now." He finished by grinning as if the truck driver were a fellow conspirator. "And they're not for rabbits. Ha, ha. Could you imagine shooting a rabbit with a .45 automatic? Wouldn't be nothing left but a patch of fur."

The truck driver took a swallow of beer. When the bartender brought another bottle for Martin, the driver pushed it toward the soldier. "Go ahead, have a drink. Make you feel better, buddy. Drink up for old Herb Dengel."

Martin reached for the bottle, but his grasp came up short. The driver pushed it a little closer. Martin hiccupped again, saying, "Good beer. Had a lot." He eyed the other man, and his face was blurry.

The truck driver, "It's okay, buddy. You soldiers have a hard life. Had to give up a lot. Don't hurt to tie one on once in a while."

"Thanks, old pal." Martin laughed again because that wasn't his style. He didn't make up to strangers fast and didn't call people "old pal." He picked up the bottle, and, holding it to his lips, swallowed almost half. There was almost no bite.

The driver said with admiration, "That's the stuff, buddy. Looks like you're a real drinker."

Martin eyed him, consciously trying to get him into focus but with little success. The driver continued, "Air Corps, eh, out at Langness Field, I guess? Going to shoot the Krauts and Nips from the air, eh?"

Martin's bladder was getting tight. However, he dawdled; movement seemed to be particularly undesirable, because not only was the face of the nearby man out of focus, almost everything else was also. And the room didn't seem very steady. He sat as quietly as he could, his eyes turning toward the table where two Mexican girls sat with two white guys. The girls both had large breasts. Martin considered the fact that Mexican girls in general had large breasts. Some said it was because they came from a tropical country. Girls developed very full and fast in the tropics, he had heard. He would like to fondle those breasts. One of the girls looked up, and her eyes met Martin's. He held her gaze longer than he should have. The guy sitting next to her looked at Martin and scowled, then spoke to the girl. She turned back.

"Pretty good lookers, eh?" the driver's voice entered Martin's consciousness. "Some of these Mexican girls are really something when they're young. 'Course they get old fast."

Martin looked at the man without speaking for a minute, as if what he had said was of no concern. Then Martin got up. "Got to take a leak; pipe's busted."

The other man pointed. "It's in the back, down thataway. Not the classiest place in the world, but it'll do."

Martin staggered when he got up and almost lost his footing. The driver grabbed his arm. "Take it easy, buddy. Can you make it?"

Martin nodded gently because his stomach was getting upset. But he was determined not to throw up there.

"Go back there with you if you want, buddy," the driver said.

"Not necessary," Martin mumbled and lurched away, hoping the Mexican girls weren't watching.

The driver was standing in the doorway of the bar, saying, "I still don't think it's a good idea for you to go off on your own this way, buddy. You know there are guys out there who would just as soon roll a soldier as look at him. There's a lot of guys who are not very patriotic, you can trust old Herb Dengel on that. Particularly some of the Mexicans."

Martin could think of nothing by then but getting away. The smell of smoke and urine in the lavatory had been bad, but the smoke and body smells at the bar had gotten increasingly oppressive until all he could think of was fresh air. And the first breeze of night air, even if it was warm, had made him more anxious. He could just barely hold himself to answer while leaning against the post that supported the extended roof. He said with some feigned toughness, "Can take care of myself. No need to worry,"

You had to say things like that, he said to himself, to prove you were tough, even if you didn't feel that way. The driver said, "Okay buddy, it's your business. But I still think you'd be better off sleeping it off in a hotel room."

"Thanks," Martin said abruptly, "going now." He turned and walked away with as much steadiness as concentration could bring. Even so, he brushed against the wall of the next building, conscious that the driver was watching him, hoping he wouldn't call. He didn't, and Martin staggered down the street. He concentrated on straightening his walk, evening out the lurches, and felt after a bit that he had succeeded to a certain extent. At least he stopped bumping into buildings and poles and later trees as he moved from the section of streets and shops to the walkway along a canal.

Even though he was concentrating on walking, his mind kept itself busy with images of the recent past. He wondered foggily whether everyone's mind was such a busy place, rarely being content with a single matter. If so, it must be a marvellous place, he thought, far more complex than those infernal motors he used to talk about with Billy

Hartmann and Kenny Adams and the other guys when he was still living in Indian City.

He hiccupped and stopped to lean against a telephone pole, wondering then how many Carta Blancas he had drunk. He knew he had walked into that bar intent on forgetting the dreary train and bus ride that had brought him there from Indian City, which had been sad too. Even the fact that Billy Hartmann and all the other guys were gone had made him sad. Not that he had liked Billy that much. But it was almost as though he had served a positive function in making Martin irritated or angry. But now he and all the rest were gone, most at various military fields throughout the country, a few already overseas.

Martin remembered with what high hopes he had left Indian City to join the Air Corps. He had seen enough film shorts of Jimmie Stewart, tall and laconic in glorious pilot's uniform, that he too had fantasized about being such a proud and glorious fellow. Among other things, he had been sure that being an Air Corps pilot would make him utterly irresistible to girls. But, he rued sadly, so few of one's dreams ever actualized. Not only had he been far too busy and shy to make contact with girls, he hadn't even managed to become a pilot. The Stearman biplane had been no problem, but the basic trainer had been beyond him. Before he could believe it, he had been taken on his last test flight and then found himself wearing the uniform of an enlisted man and heading for radio school. And then the leave with a visit to Indian City, the long, grimy train trip to Austin, followed by a bus trip to San Antonio, and the bar, and how many Carta Blancas he would never know. None of it was what he had hoped for, as he realized sadly so few dreams were.

Ah well, he thought, lurching forward again, things could be worse. At least he hadn't ended up in gunnery school. That was the most common destination for washed-out pilots, and their life span, once they graduated, was short indeed. It was said that they usually hosed the remains of a gunner from the turret of a B-17 or B-24. And he didn't need that, though he wasn't at all sure what he did need or what he would do with the rest of his young manhood.

He soon became conscious that it must be very late. There were few people walking the streets of this unknown, unexpected place. He had never been in Texas before, much less San Antonio. And somehow in his Midwesterner's conception he thought there ought to be dusty towns where horsemen rode by and gunslingers stalked the streets. But there were none such, no one in fact except an occasional single or couple.

Martin didn't know how he got there, but somewhere in his interminable walking, he found himself at a doorway talking to a middle-aged woman in bright face paint, wearing a gaudy, low-cut dress that let her ample breasts almost hang out. She was saying, "It's too late. We're closed already."

He looked at her in boozy indecision, his hand supporting himself on the door jamb. Finally he got the words organized, "It's okay. Just want a girl."

Her voice became sharper. "No girls. They're all busy."

Again a drunken pause, then he laughed. "That's okay, I'll wait." Pause. "Maybe you got Carta Blanca."

She started to close the door. "No girls, I said. You better get going. You're drunk, soldier. Our girls don't take drunks."

Within his alcoholic haze, shame assailed him. He was so drunk they wouldn't even let him into a whorehouse. He stared at the painted lady sadly, then said, "It's true. I'm drunk." Pause. "Not pilot, just radio operator." And he turned and stumbled down the steps.

The next he was aware was that the streets had changed and he was lurching along walkways beside canals. It puzzled him that a place that was supposed to be made of dusty streets was intersected by canals with willow trees overhanging the banks. He careened along, feeling the heat and listening to the incessant rasping of katydids, crickets, or other insects. Who could know what strange creatures they might have in southern Texas? He was fairly sure he said aloud, "It sure ain't Indiana."

He still bumped into trees, though less often. It didn't do any good trying to walk straight, he had decided. Besides, he was getting more and more tired. It was a good thing the night was so warm. At least if a guy had to sleep he wouldn't get cold. Then he realized there were fewer lights along the canals. He must be getting out of the center of town, maybe out of town altogether, he thought. That would be funny, to walk right out into the country. And that wouldn't be like Indiana either, he laughed to himself. It would probably be full of cactus and rattlesnakes and coyotes, he thought, picturing a desert.

Then he bumped into a large boulder and careened away from it, almost losing his balance. But the correction was too much. He had to quickly turn the opposite direction to try to recover. He found himself in a zigzag that carried him into a patch of weeds. They seemed to enclose and support him at the same time, so he relaxed. He felt his legs go rubbery and branches scrape his face as he slid to the ground. Then he was on his back, looking up though branches at stars, wondering whether he was going to throw up. He turned over so his cheek was against the ground and fell into a sodden sleep.

Martin put his arm around her waist and explored the swelling of her breast as far as he dared. He could feel the tightness of the bra as it spread toward the front. And while her body did not stiffen, it did not invite further exploration.

He leaned forward and kissed her, noticing the pocks on her neck as he got closer, pressing her lips. She kissed him more ardently than any of the girls he had taken out for one or two nights in Indian City. His cock was hard as a post, love juice having oozed out for the last hour. He tried to keep the bump unnoticeable by pressing it down with one leg. She didn't seem to notice.

They kissed and pressed one another for another hour. Periodically he would push against the ground with his foot to get the swing going, partially for relief from the ache in his balls, partially to stir up some air because it was so hot.

All the nights in Austin seemed to be hot; the days too, he realized, though the nights were what he would remember, perhaps because that was the first time he truly began to get intimate with a girl.

He leaned back. "When will your parents come home?"

"Oh, probably in another hour or so. They usually get back around eleven on the nights they go out to play bridge."

"They don't mind if you're alone with me?"

"No, Papa and Mama think you're nice, even if you are a Yankee."

How could it be, he thought, sitting on a swing during a hot summer night in Texas, holding and kissing a southern girl, he the son of Indiana farmers, Catholic, God-fearing people who had brought up four children who were expected in their turn to raise further broods of Catholic, God-fearing children. Even though their world had changed greatly, his father having been through the Great War and they having abandoned the small town/country lifeway of their parents, his parents still saw the world as one of constancy. How could they visualize him, their only male child, trying to learn to love in such a far-off place as southern Texas and with a long-legged girl who said "you-all" and called her parents *papa* and *mama* and whose middle name was Lee.

Martin heard a car start at the end of the street and listened carefully to know whether it was coming toward them, his hands motionless on her back. The car turned in before coming up the hill. She said, "It's alright; they know we sit here when we come back. They like it better than for me to be out in a car. They'll come in the front door."

Her parents were always with them, he thought, even when they were alone kissing and feeling one another. He shifted to relieve the ache in his balls, remembering.

It had been almost three months since he had met her at the USO, she presiding over the ping pong table. It had been quickly obvious that she was good, dancing lightly on her long legs and returning the ball effortlessly until she decided to smash. Then the ball would arc downward in a white streak and ricochet furiously from the table, rarely being returned by the opposition player. Martin had been impressed by the suppleness of her body and particularly the quickness of her shapely legs. Her smallish breasts were less exciting. She had a weak chin also, and pocks on her neck, evidently from girlhood acne. But Eva Lee, as she shortly introduced herself, was vivacious, so he accepted her when her previous partner drifted away. And though he had played in a number of army recreation rooms and wasn't a bad player, he had no chance against her. She kept sending the ball back effortlessly and he soon became aware that she wasn't smashing. He kept at it, and before long she began helping him correct his strokes. He didn't mind getting her help, and his strokes did improve.

Before long, he was heading for the USO first thing in the evening after duty, and they played and had donuts and coffee, and next he was walking her home. She introduced him to her parents, and the two went out together to shows and Mexican restaurants and picnics and college functions. She was a sophomore at the university, studying history.

Martin had a girl, he realized one night as he was coming in on the truck from camp, his first real one. He wanted to tell her he loved her but he was afraid to go that far. But even so, it was good, it made him feel important. He had someone in town who wanted to see him, and he had somewhere to go most nights.

He squirmed from the pain in his balls, knowing that he would have to go soon, that that was the only way he could get relief. It had become a pattern: they would stay until closing time at the USO or go out somewhere and return late, walking or by bus, to sit without a word on the porch swing to kiss and fondle. She seemed almost to expect it even though she made it clear early on that her tits and legs above the knees were off limits.

So he stroked and kissed those parts that were permissible while the juice welled up in his bone-hard cock until the ache became almost unbearable.

He leaned back, and before she could lean forward to him again, said, "I think it's time for me to go. Your parents will be home any time now."

"It doesn't matter. They'll go in the front door."

Martin and Eva Lee were sitting on the small porch at the side, in the shadow of the great live oak. It blocked most of the light from the corner lamp, leaving only a few thin rays to filter through. The two were almost invisible from the sidewalk on Cottonwood Street.

Martin got up, standing sideways so she wouldn't see the moist stain on his khaki pants where the jism had spread. "I must go anyway, though. The last truck to camp leaves in a half hour."

She got up. "Alright, honey. You shouldn't miss that. It would be hard to get back at this time without the camp truck, wouldn't it?"

He reached up to brush his short hair back and straighten his disheveled tie. He was almost certain there were lipstick marks on his face and collar. It was a good thing it was dark so the other guys wouldn't easily notice it. Martin felt proud but uneasy also at the attention he got in camp from having a girlfriend in town, and a college student at that.

She leaned toward him and he kissed her one last time, but short and lightly. He was intent on one thing only then, to get away. She said softly, "I won't be at the USO until Friday. Will I see you there then?"

"Sure, soon as I get in." He gave her arm a pat and turned away. She waved at him as he turned down the sidewalk and out of sight behind the hedge. He walked stiff-legged to the end of the hedge row, the last darkened place. He knew exactly where to go. He had done it so many times before—in fact, every night the past few weeks after leaving her. He looked up and down the street and saw and heard nothing. He was relieved to hear the screen door slam when she went inside.

Unbuttoning his pants, he pulled his cock out. It was sticky from the jism that had been spreading on it for an hour. A drop of the translucent fluid still hung from the tip, reflecting the street lamp like a tiny eye. He grasped the hard tube, filled to bursting with blood and love juice and began pumping in short strokes, holding it as tight as he could while still permitting enough looseness for his hand to rub it. As he began slowly, he remembered when he had discovered how to pump Foxy, the terrier at the back of the garage. Foxy had learned to pleasure in those pumping strokes too and would stand immobile while Martin increased the tempo. The little dog showing his pleasure by pulling his lips back in a pant grin. A big lump would form in the middle of Foxy's cock before the juice squirted out. Martin had figured out later that that lump was what kept dogs stuck together when they fucked. People would run out on the street and throw water or rocks at the poor creatures, who didn't seem able to pull apart, no matter how much punishment they received.

And just as he used to speed up on Foxy, Martin, standing in the shadow of the live oak in Austin, Texas, began to pump faster. His cock stayed hard but it had been in a state of excitation for so long by that time that it required a major effort to get the juice to come squirting out. Martin leaned with one hand against a telephone pole and pumped harder. A dog barked not too far away, but he paid it no attention, concentrating all his thoughts on the ejaculation. He squinted, trying to evoke the image of Eva Lee, nude and with legs spread. He couldn't produce an actual image of fucking her because he had never done it to her—or anyone else. The only real images of fucking that he could conjure were those of Maggie and Jiggs from Big-Little books. The boys had passed those around until they literally came apart. There were still a few around in the barracks, though Martin no longer made any effort to look at them. The pictures of those homely comic strip characters, no matter that they were naked and fucking, were just too unattractive and remote from the live bodies of the females in clinging, short summer dresses on the streets of Austin. He couldn't fantasize about Maggie and Jiggs.

The tenderness on the tip of his cock became more acute as he pumped harder. That was because he had been doing it too often, he knew. Besides beating it after fondling Eva Lee on the porch swing the nights they were out, he frequently masturbated under the covers in his barracks bed. He had to be careful with that though so he wouldn't get caught by any of his buddies. Frequently he would wait until the middle of the night when he thought everyone else was asleep. Then he would beat it off and ejaculate into a sock or handkerchief. But it had been so much lately that a little ridge of scab had formed around the head of his dick. It was a problem because too much friction caused it to hurt, but not enough would never bring the ejaculation. So he concentrated on the beginning tingle in his balls, even though his arm was tiring. He pumped harder anyway and the tingling increased until he was no longer aware of the pain on the tip. He knew his eyes were staring unblinkingly as he beat to a climax. The tingling intensified and spread through his loins and down the inside of his thighs and the juice came squirting up through the hot tube and out whitely, like mucous, in thick droplets, arcing downward onto the leaves of the hedge and on the ground. He stopped pumping, holding his cock hard until the surges of squirting juice began to subside and finally stopped. A droplet of jism hung on the end. He wiped it off with his handkerchief, leaning tiredly against the telephone pole as his cock began to go limp. A car came up the hill and into the drive. He squeezed deeper into the shadow of the hedge and hurriedly buttoned up. Low southern voices, her parents, for a few seconds, then the front door closing and quietness again. He slowly became aware of the insect night sounds and began walking down the hill carefully, keeping in the shadow as long as he could. Turning the corner onto Crockett Street, he began to walk faster toward the corner where he would find the camp truck.

\* \* \* \* \*

Eva Lee sent him several flowery postcards after he was transferred to Arkansas, but he delayed answering. He didn't know what to write her, apart from the fact that he missed those sweaty nights of clutching arms, kisses, and aching balls, but that didn't seem right to put in a letter.

Then in only a few weeks he met Amelia Fields at a dance. He felt guilty about not telling Eva Lee, but couldn't bring himself to explain honestly what had happened. Eva Lee thus became the first in a long list of unfinished relationships, a circumstance Martin finally came to associate with love affairs. Most of them ended without any clear-cut resolution.

Amelia seemed as passionate as Eva Lee, though with the same limitations, that one could put one's hands and mouth almost anywhere except from a line where the tits began to swell down to the knees. Naturally, one's cock couldn't be put anywhere, but that was what he had always expected. Nice girls just did not fuck. So when he and Amelia got together, they walked and talked and went to restaurants and shows, and kissed and fondled. It was as exciting as anything else he had done with a girl before and by then he had come to expect frustrations in the pursuance of girls, or at least the kind of girl that seemed to attract him. Martin proposed to Amelia by phone before he went overseas and resolved to be faithful. Besides the fact that it was no great stress to him since he had never had any anyway, that was what you were supposed to do when you got engaged. She said she would wait for him, and he had little doubt about that. That was how nice girls, the kind you married, were.

\* \* \* \* \*

Martin was finishing the last of the T-bone. The salad was hardly touched but he had eaten most of the french fries, as well as the bread. Also there was only a little of the beer left in the bottle. Amelia watched him, occasionally sipping her coffee. "Was it good?"

"Yeah, not very tough and done just about right." There was a little pink in the bottom of his plate where blood had seeped. He leaned back. "Don't you eat steak?"

"Not often. It's too much for me. I can't eat a whole one." She had eaten most of a chicken salad and a bowl of asparagus soup. He wiped his mouth with the napkin. "I don't think I can ever get too much steak." Pause. "Perhaps it's because I never had any when I was a kid. My parents didn't buy steak. They couldn't afford it."

"Did you get any overseas?"

"Oh yeah, the Army ships American food everywhere. We didn't have it all the time, but once a week at least." That was only true because Martin was in the Air Corps, he knew. The infantry guys had gotten by mostly with C and K rations, stuff they could carry.

She looked at him tenderly and reached over to put her hand on top of his. "Well, that's all over now, Martin. And I'm so glad you're back. It was such a long time."

It had been for him too, longer than he would have believed, even though it had only been two years. It wouldn't have been quite so long if she had answered more of his letters, he thought. And it didn't help much that she said his letters had been so good she was sure hers would have been dull by comparison. He hadn't cared that her letters be so wonderful, only that he would get some occasionally with some expression of feeling for him. She didn't know how hard it had been to keep faithful, what with all the available girls in England and France. The worst had been the cemeteries and small lanes in England where girls would let you do it standing up. They didn't seem to mind so long as they didn't have to lay down. Leaning against a tombstone was okay, however.

Amelia interrupted his thoughts, which even then he was ashamed of. "I'll bet you had a lot of chances with those foreign girls, too."

He knew it was meant as a question, she hoping that he would agree or disagree. But he knew he couldn't. "Oh, they're not so wonderful. It was just such a long time to be apart."

"I know. But I'm so glad we got engaged. Otherwise you might not have come back."

He had indeed avoided anything with the foreign girls until almost the very end. It had been easier for him than she probably knew. She didn't realize how shy he was. He could never go up to a girl and start flirting like most of the other guys could. He had indeed gotten to go with Eva Lee and Amelia in quick succession, but they had been his first. And once he had gotten overseas, with all the new customs and ways of speaking, the old shyness came over him again.

He would probably have never done anything if it hadn't been for Buddy Stumpf. But he liked Buddy, no matter that he was almost completely different from the other guys Martin knew. Although most of them were interested in fucking, they also had other interests. Not Buddy. There were no thoughts in Buddy's mind except the pursuit of women. He was either doing it or thinking about it all the time. After doing just the minimum of work in camp, he spent almost every night in the town of Coudoux, going from cafe to cafe to meet girls. He also went to every dance that was arranged and even to church a few times, although he claimed that didn't pay off well. And despite the fact that Buddy spoke very little French, he picked up more girls than all the other guys put together. He would even slip a girl into camp late some nights so the other guys could fuck her also. Martin had never taken Buddy up on that offer, both because he felt he should be faithful and because he was afraid he would get clap or syphilis. Whenever it happened, and the girl was being taken from one bed to another in the darkened tent, Martin would have to get out. He couldn't stand listening to the heaving of bodies, panting, and sometimes whimpering that went with the lovemaking. But when Martin went off to another tent, he couldn't help wondering how Buddy or anyone else could talk a girl into fucking total strangers. And there was no doubt they did it willingly, at least in the beginning. On some nights Martin had heard a girl whimpering, "No, no." And Martin would wonder what sort of sex the guy was trying to get her to do. After the girl had screwed everyone who wanted to in the tent, Buddy would give her chocolate and cigarettes, then drive her back to town.

Amelia tried again. "Is it true what they say about French girls, that they're very sexy?"

Martin started, with the sudden fear that somehow she knew. But he quickly recovered because he knew it was impossible. There was no one who had been with him there who could have contacted her. He felt guilty about saying it but felt he had to. "They didn't seem much different to me." But then he took the plunge. "But I didn't have anything to do with them anyway."

He hated himself and his mother and the church and all that had made him tell such a barefaced lie and feel badly about it afterward. Because that was what had been eating him. He had screwed, only a few times, but still he had done it and even enjoyed it. And he couldn't really blame Buddy. Of course Buddy had made it easy for him, asking him to come along several times before he went. But still, Martin told himself, if he had only gotten a letter, he probably wouldn't have done it. He knew it was rationalization, whitewashing his own case, but it made him feel better.

Buddy had come to the final solution when he had discovered and gotten well established at the whorehouse. There were unlimited girls, among the best-looking in town and mostly young. Moreover, they were hungry. It didn't take Buddy long to figure out that he could get all he wanted by hauling in cigarettes, chocolates, and other foodstuffs. How he kept one jeep almost exclusively for his own use Martin never figured out, but he had learned very early in his acquaintance with that amiable, lustful squadron clerk that if some military supplies or equipment were to be gotten by devious means, he would get them.

Buddy used his new currency, girls willing to exchange their warm bodies for material comforts. In exchange for favors, he arranged for those who would not arrange for themselves. And perhaps the most important key in the exchange system was the supply sergeant. Once Buddy got him used to being fixed up with one of the girls, Buddy got free access to camp supplies.

From then on, the nights were almost the same. Buddy would load up sometime before the end of duty hours and depart past one of the guards who also had been fixed up several times, and up to the back entrance to unload, keeping a sharp eye out for the MPs who raided the place every two or three weeks. Sometimes Buddy had someone else along, though generally he liked to go in alone, letting the other guys find their own way in separately. It was too risky to travel with a group. Once unloaded, Buddy would drive the jeep two or three blocks away and park in a lane the madame had shown him, a place unlikely to be spotted by MPs.

Amelia interrupted Martin's remembrance. "I can't believe a handsome fellow like you wouldn't have met some of those foreign girls. Probably you don't want to tell me."

Martin felt he was blushing and put his hands on his cheeks in a covering gesture, wondering how she could have imagined what he was thinking. Was it so obvious? It was difficult for him to lie, but since he had started, it was easier to continue. "The French girls were not easy to meet."

Of course he knew he was deliberately withholding the information that it was only the nice girls with families who were hard to get near.

Amelia persisted, "That's different from what we hear. They even say some of the soldiers are getting married to French girls."

There were some, Martin knew. Even some of the prostitutes had gotten American guys to ask them. In fact, the thought had fleetingly passed through his own mind in regard to Giselle, though his guilt had built up too much by that time for him to do it. In fact, he even stopped seeing her before he left.

Buddy had asked Martin to go with him several times before Martin agreed. Later he couldn't quite figure out exactly why he had been so reluctant, but he knew he worried about getting a disease or getting caught by the MPs. But most of all, he knew, was the guilt feeling he had about Amelia. After all, he was engaged and had promised.

But with Buddy's encouragement, he had gone ahead.

Giselle had been his second. And though Buddy kept urging him to try different girls, that seemed even more reprehensible to Martin. It was not only that he was betraying Amelia, but that he was betraying her over and over again. It was almost as though by settling on one, he was betraying her trust only once. In his mind it was the closest to a monogamous union one could get with a prostitute.

Amelia continued, "You must have been able to meet them at dances or in cafés. We hear that everyone goes to cafés to drink wine in the evening."

That was easy; Martin didn't even have to lie then. "You know I don't dance very well, and besides, they have different styles. And I didn't meet any girls at cafés."

No, it had been much more direct than that. Buddy had described almost all who lived in the house beforehand and made his recommendations. Then madame called the girls into the waiting room in turn. Buddy was pretty accurate, though he didn't really describe in detail how well-formed Giselle was, despite her size. Perhaps it was because she really loomed up in comparison with most of the others. And Buddy, being short himself, always looked for small girls. Giselle had large breasts and hips, with just a suggestion of extra weight. But her waist and ankles were slim. To Martin she exuded voluptuous sexuality, which was borne out fully when she took him back to one of the rooms.

Sitting there with Amelia, he realized that it hadn't been so often, four times for an hour at first and then twice all night.

He still wondered whether he would have continued longer if the MPs had not raided the place the second night he stayed over. He hadn't been sleeping soundly anyway, so had heard Buddy's low knock almost immediately. There was the quick pulling on of wool pants and shirt and the hurried scurrying down darkened corridors, led by madame's assistant, hearing the clumping and raised male voices answered by the softer one of madame in the front of the cavernous building. Then it was out through the back garden and over the concrete wall to drop into the lane behind. Outside he had realized he did not have his shoes on. He hurriedly pulled them on and followed Buddy to the jeep, staying in shadows.

Amelia tried again, "Well you must have had some kind of adventures there. I think maybe you fellows don't want to tell us what happened." She smiled, "Maybe it's because you know what ordinary lives we were leading back home."

Martin reached over to put his hand on Amelia's arm, still wondering how this tall, dark-haired, southern girl could have guessed so much. And though the pangs of guilt would come again and again in the years to come, at that moment he successfully shifted his interest to the girl he was supposed to marry as soon as he got back from the Pacific.

They smiled at one another, holding hands. But then her face darkened to a more sombre expression.

"What's wrong?" Martin.

"Oh nothing, just thinking."

"But your expression changed so much. Is it something about us?"

"I don't want to worry you." She forced a smile and gave his hand a determined little squeeze.

"I'd rather know if there's something troubling you."

She sighed. "Oh, it's just that we have so little time together. You know we didn't see each other more than four or five weekends before you left the last time. And now we have so little time before you go off to the Pacific."

He almost wished she hadn't said it because the thought depressed him as much as it did her. He had just refused to bring it into the open because that would make it seem even worse. To him, things not said were less real. Saying all your depressing thoughts just depressed you more. And he had to make her feel better, perhaps in the process making himself feel a little better also, he thought. He said, with forced lightness, "I don't think it will last long at all. After all, the Krauts surrendered, and the Japs have been pushed all the way back to Okinawa."

He wondered what such an exotic-sounding place as Okinawa looked like. He imagined it being full of banana and coconut trees and rice fields and slant-eyed people. Somehow, he just couldn't conjure a population of soldiers marching around in orderly fashion to commands of an unknown language. In fact, he thought more of a population of busy farmers. And also he thought of slant-eyed girls with straight black hair. He was ashamed again that another thought about strange girls had intruded. Fortunately, Amelia interrupted, still pensively, "I know, Martin. But they're still fighting. And I heard that when the Allies invade the Japanese homeland, there will be hundreds of thousands of casualties."

How interesting, he thought, that since so many people were dying, they had invented a new word for it. In wartime people didn't die; they became casualties. It sounded less permanent. And yet the change wasn't bad, he thought. No one really wanted to die, but again if you could avoid using the word, somehow it seemed less likely or serious.

He continued his reassurance. "But there have been the A-bombs. They say that whole cities were destroyed. Surely the Japs will surrender after that. They must know they can't win."

Martin tried to imagine what it was like, an unbelievable flash of light and a great searing flame, engulfing everything for miles. He couldn't. All he could imagine were wooden houses burning and bodies crumpling from the heat. For a moment he thought it was a terrible thing to do, but then quickly rationalized that you were allowed to inflict violence on others in wartime. And besides, those yellow-skinned, slant-eyed, little people had asked for it; they had started it all.

He didn't want to go, that was for sure. Not that he had had any choice. But he hadn't been in Europe long enough to gain enough points to be discharged. And to be perfectly honest, he hadn't had a bad life there compared with what the infantry went through; and apart from that one airplane crash and a few close calls from some of the last Messerschmidts, he had been in little danger. But the real point was that the war was practically over and there would be little or nothing for him to gain personally by going on.

If only there was some way to get out or to get assigned to a stateside camp, as an instructor or something. Because lurking in the back of his mind was the fear, which hadn't existed when he had gone overseas the first time, that perhaps it was his fate to be one of the final casualties during the last day or week of the war. And no matter how dramatic it sounded, that wasn't what he wanted. He wanted to marry Amelia and get back to college. There were so many things he wanted to learn about. There was no way he would go back to Indian City.

He continued in the same mode, to reassure himself as much as her, "Maybe it'll be over before we know it. Let's try to think of all the good things that'll happen then."

She withdrew her hand and reached for her purse. "Okay. I need to go to the ladies room. I'll be right back."

"I'll pay the bill and we'll leave."

They walked on the streets of New Orleans afterward, holding hands and talking about all the things they would do when they got married. Martin's cock would get hard when he shifted his hand to her waist and inched it up to the beginning of the swelling of her breast, but then soften when he brought it back to clasp her hand. They found themselves at a park on the edge of a canal and sat on the grass to kiss and fondle. Her fruity lipstick began to spread. He was sure he got marks on his face and probably on his collar.

They were on their way back to the town's center when they heard horns and whistles.

"What do you think that is?" she said.

"I don't know. Must be something important. Listen, I think I hear a lower tone—voices, it sounds like."

They hurried. She said, "I don't hear sirens. Must not be a fire. Besides, with that much noise, any fire would have to be burning half the town. We'd see a red glow."

The noise increased as they got closer. They turned a corner and came out on Hancock Street where people were running down the sidewalks and into the street, hugging and kissing. To keep from hitting pedestrians, cars were barely creeping and honking their horns. Martin and Amelia came to the stream of people.

A long-haired blond girl ran up and threw her arms around Martin. "Congratulations, you did it, you GIs did it."

All of a sudden Martin understood, and a wave of pleasure went through his body. But he wanted to hear it from one of them. "What; did what?"

The girl kissed him full on the lips. "You won, you won the war, the Japs surrendered."

Martin kissed her back, and she broke away to run up to a sailor. Martin turned toward Amelia. They smiled at each other, a little shyly, as when they had first met. She spoke first. "You know what that means, Martin. You won't have to go to the Pacific. You can stay home and we can get married soon." She put her arms around his neck.

They held each other tightly for a long time, Martin pleasuring in the feel of her firm breasts. The thought passed fleetingly that they were a far cry from the voluptuous tits of Giselle, but they were tight and would give him pleasure once he could touch them.

There was a heady feeling in taking part in what seemed like a momentous happening. Everyone on the street was jubilant, almost as though they had all helped bring it about. Though pleased, Martin couldn't help feeling that he had done little, having contributed in a small way to the war in Europe by hauling wounded to hospitals in C-47s and gasoline to Patton's advancing tank columns. But it didn't seem to him that his own participation amounted to much. Everything would have gone on just as it had if he had never existed. But he still didn't rebuff the hugs and handshakes of the triumphantly joyous as he and Amelia made their way through the crowds.

And then the crowd began thinning out. He turned to her. "What time do you have to get back tonight?"

The Baptist Hospital where she was getting her training had strict rules for the student nurses. They had to sign in and out as in the Army, and penalties were almost as stiff. She squeezed his arm, "Oh, tonight I have a late pass, until one."

He looked at his watch—9:15. "We have a lot of time then. What would you like to do?"

They walked in silence a while as the crowd became thinner. "How about going to my hotel then?" he said without looking at her directly.

There was a long pause, and he felt almost sure he had gone too far, wanting to withdraw his question, but still wanting to be alone with her. It seemed an age before she answered but she finally did, speaking in a low voice, "It's not far from here. I guess we can."

They walked in silence awhile, then she said, "When do you think we'll get married now?"

"I guess as soon as you're finished with your training. That'll be in January, won't it?"

"Yes, though I won't be finished with the State Board Examinations then yet. I had planned to stay on at the hospital until I got them finished. Do you think you'll be out of the Air Corps by then?"

"I should be. I lacked about thirty points for a discharge, so I guess that should take me four or five months. I won't be doing anything in the meantime, but I'm sure they won't let everybody out at once."

They arrived at the hotel and both stopped talking about the future. The imminent present was enough to cope with, to get past the beady-eyed clerks and bellboys with some dignity. When they got to the middle of the lobby, Martin said in a low voice, "Just wait here while I get the key."

His voice was so low, she wouldn't have understood anything but an obvious explanation. She just nodded. Trying to be casual, Martin asked the bald clerk at the desk for the key, imagining the man would demand to know who his companion was.

And though the clerk glanced at Amelia, he said nothing, nor did he change his expression as he handed Martin the key.

"Thanks." Martin hurried back. He felt hot on the cheeks and neck as though dozens of people were watching with accusatory eyes. He hated himself for not having learned by then to ignore the curiosity of others. Fortunately, the elevator had no one else on it. When the doors closed and Martin could feel the pressure from the upward movement, he spoke. "I just hate it in these hotels when everyone is watching you."

She stood apart. "Well, I didn't see anyone do anything."

"Maybe not, but it seemed that clerk looked us over."

"We're not doing anything wrong. People in hotels can have visitors. Why, where else do you go if you don't have your own place?"

There were places to go, Martin knew, places he'd been with Amelia and Eva Lee, parks mostly, but also movie theaters and porches and a few other secluded places. But it certainly was a problem even if you did nothing more than kiss and fondle. Even if you went all the way, there were other places: spots in parks, pastures, cemeteries, and church-yards, as well as indoor places in whorehouses or borrowed rooms. But where to go if you didn't have a room of your own was indeed generally a problem. And it irritated him that he should feel as guilty as he did then since he had paid for the room. She patted his hand, "It's okay. It's not worth getting upset about."

The elevator stopped, and they walked down the corridor to his room, she holding his arm. He opened the door and stepped back to let her in first. He closed the door softly, hoping not to make her nervous, but not wishing to seem secretive either. She glanced back but smiled to show she felt okay. "It looks like a good room," she said as she walked around.

It wasn't cheap, he thought, probably the most expensive room he'd ever taken, fifteen dollars a night. Why he'd taken such an expensive room he wasn't quite sure except that the visit had seemed special. And perhaps he'd had this very possibility in mind from the first. He couldn't be sure.

He walked over and put his arms around Amelia. She responded, though by no means with the passion she usually had when they were on a park bench. He kissed her and again she responded with less ardor than usual. She was probably nervous, he figured. Holding her hand, he walked to the bed slowly. She came along and sat on the edge. He put his arms around her back and kissed her as fully as he could, opening his lips slightly. Someday, he thought, he would try putting his tongue inside as Giselle had taught him, but probably not yet. She returned the kiss but eased back before it became too long. He turned to face her and pushed back on the next kiss. Then she was lying on her back, he leaning over her. He put his hand on her leg and felt down to the hem of her skirt. Bringing his hand forward under the skirt edge, he started to push it up. He kissed her again. Then he felt her hand on his, at first just on top, then pushing it downward. At first her push was gentle but when he did not immediately stop, it became harder. His cock was as hard as a board. He crossed one leg over it to hold the bulge down and hide the wet spot.

The two lay motionless for a while, bodies close but in suspended animation. Martin kissed her again, and when she responded as before, he decided to try opening her blouse. Perhaps nice girls were less nervous about their tits than their pussy, he thought. But after undoing the first button and moving to the second, he was again stopped. Also her body stiffened for the first time. He quit and leaned back.

She didn't refasten the undid button immediately but did pull her skirt down. They sat up, watching one another without speaking for a while. He broke the silence. "I thought you wouldn't mind since we're engaged."

"I'm sorry Martin, but I think a girl ought to wait for that until she's married."

He tried to make his smile look genuine as his cock rapidly wilted.

# CHAPTER 11

Martin sat in the lounge, watching from a distance as two older men played chess. One was very quick but frequently had second thoughts about his moves. The other was slow and deliberate. Martin was too tired to get up and go closer to see the actual moves, but the differential pace of the two brought back memories of his frequent games with Constance. She had been crazy about the game and always had a strong wish to win, but as their years together went by, her wins became fewer and fewer. She wasn't a bad player, but she was not methodical. It was surprising in a way because she was very methodical in other affairs, particularly concerning money, but so it was. In chess too often she would make a move and change her mind almost immediately. He almost always let her do the move over, whether she had taken her hand off the piece or not. Even so, her wins became fewer and fewer until during their last year together she hardly won any. He had laughingly said that was why she divorced him, trying to put levity into the explanation of a bitter event. And he didn't really believe what he was saying, though in his mind it underscored the fact that by the time they divorced, people were not required to have reasons. General malaise or any kind of disappointment with the mate was enough.

"Hello, Martin." Oldenberg's amiable voice interrupted the thoughts of the Transitionee.

He looked up to see his Monitor, pipe in hand. "Hello, what brings you here?"

"I was on my way back from a late dinner to read some of the endless reports they are handing out nowadays, mostly about comparable operations on other worlds. It's only a day or two before we begin voting." He sat across from Martin. "And you, you look so down, or shall I say withdrawn. What's going on, anything special?"

"I guess I'm really tired."

"What happened? I thought you were doing your own Video today. That should have been interesting, no?"

Martin stretched his legs, beginning to get that satisfied feeling he got when he had a good conversationalist to interact with. He had rarely, if ever, in his earthly existence had the opportunity to bounce ideas off a more satisfying person than Oldenberg. Thoughts began to flow. "I am mentally tired, no doubt about that, and perhaps for a couple of reasons. One is that I didn't get a chance to view any other Videos this evening." That was a new form of recreation he had developed over the last week about which he had not yet hinted to his Monitor. He had planned to take a look at the life of *Ramapithecus* that evening to find out whether that Miocene ape really had stood upright as the latest evolutionists theorized. "I suppose I might have squeezed it in, but I was just too worn out mentally."

The Transitioner gazed at him with his knowing, beneficent look. "I take it that seeing your own past was that wearing, no?"

Martin sighed, "Yes, I'm afraid it was. Though I looked forward to the experience with considerable excitement and am still not sorry for having done it, I found it very hard to watch the occurrences in my own life all over again." Pause. "You know, there was a favorite question among us earthlings, or at least those of my culture, which was, 'If you had your life to do over, how would you do it differently?' I was asked that as often as most others, I suppose, but I just could not imagine living my life over. Like most others, I certainly had not enjoyed all phases of my life, and also like most others, I really did not look forward to the end. But the idea of doing it over again was at least distasteful enough that I never could work up any enthusiasm for that word game." Martin smiled. "Of course I had no inkling of the Transition Process and the idea that creatures really went on and on, even if in different forms."

The Transitioner brought out his tobacco tamper and began pressing the charred remains down into the bowl. He looked at Martin quizzically. "It's not getting you down too much, is it? That is, enough to keep you from going through your Transition?"

"No, I'm alright. Seeing what happened to me makes me more introspective than usual. And I suppose that's not bad. After all, I am supposed to be getting some insights from this study that will assist me in the Transition, correct?"

"Yes, that's right. And you should be getting almost done, no? After all, you spent the whole day, which is more than you did with any of the others."

"That's true. It is taking longer, but I believe I said I thought it would take a couple of days. And I think that will do it. I am viewing more scenes in normal speed than I did with others, I think because there were a lot I didn't really understand while I was alive. Furthermore, some scenes, as in this first part of my life, had become rather murky by the time I was an old man. I really couldn't remember the details of what had happened when I was a boy in Indiantown."

The Transitioner interrupted, "Have you eaten?"

Martin chuckled inwardly, thinking how motherish the question was. That got him going on another tangent, that evidently creatures from other worlds did have some of the same emotional baggage as earthlings; or was it merely a part of their deceptive makeup, from appearance to behavior? Would he ever know? "Yes, I had a salad and bowl of soup at the cafeteria, but I'm afraid I was so preoccupied, I can hardly remember anything about them."

"You need something to help you settle down. Since you were at the cafeteria, you didn't have any wine. Have you been to the bar?"

"No, I came here immediately after eating."

Oldenberg's eyes twinkled. "They don't have drinks here either, though fortunately I came prepared." Whereupon the plump man produced a silver flask and two small silver cuplets. "Let's have a touch of cognac. That should help your state of mind."

He poured the two vesselettes almost full and handed one to Martin. Then he lifted his own. "And have a toast to the successful conclusion of Project Heterop." The Transitioner took a good sip, as did Martin. "It has been a rather interesting little project. If the cosmos were a little better organized, we might extend it or even do others of a similar nature."

The cognac burned slightly as it slid down Martin's throat, though it left that old familiar aftertaste. It had taken the French to develop really tasty firewater, he thought. Out loud, he said, "Well thanks, we'll finish it for sure now, whatever the consequences."

Oldenberg set his cuplet down and prepared to relight his pipe. "Anyway, since it is taking you so long, and since I'm here now, do you feel like discussing anything from the part you viewed today?"

The warmth of the cognac had descended to Martin's stomach, making him feel more and more comfortable. "Sure, I feel okay now. And I think it would help to talk about it a little, if you have the time."

"I have no more meetings tonight. And the reading can be done late. Besides, I'm really not into linear time. I'd be interested in hearing some of your reactions. Where did you stop, by the way, at any significant transition?"

"I think so, at the end of my days of growing up, when I started taking on the responsibilities of being a head of the household. That was a phrase that was used by tax and other government people in those days that was supposed to indicate the husband and breadwinner, more or less. It was already changing, since neither I nor most of my contemporaries were heads or chiefs in any absolute sense. And women's rights were becoming more and more significant, long before the era of E.R.A. Well before that we were not heads in the sense of being in control, though, even if one were the sole breadwinner as I was. The status of the man and woman in marriage was changing rapidly, even if some of us were rather old-fashioned in being the sole wage earner. Many families were evolving into two-wage-earner units, the husband and wife both working. I suppose in that sense I was rather anachronistic." Pause. "Not that it was my choice anyway. But as you will see later, the man in the late twentieth century was no longer the sole authority in the household, whether he was the sole wage earner or not. We had gotten into the era of sharing and that meant everything, including responsibilities for almost all decisions."

"But the period you saw today was the one before this, no, the one during which you were more or less molded by your society?"

"That's right, it began when I was first punished for playing with my 'wee-wee,' which was a circumlocution ladies used then to avoid using four-letter words like *cock* or *dick*, the preferred expressions of males. And it ended when I took up the trials and tribulations of matrimony. I think that was a significant transition. There were, of course, continuities, such as masturbation, but marriage for me ended the rather focusless period of searching that I had gone through before. From then on, for better or worse, during the days of my early and middle maturity I focused on one person, my wife, for almost twenty-five years."

Oldenberg rubbed the bald spot on the back of his head. "Hmm, interesting, twenty-five years of searching—your childhood and youth—and then the same amount of time as a married man. You would have had just a little over twenty-five years left, since you died shortly after reaching eighty. If we could characterize the last period in some special way, it would be rather neat—life in three stages." Thoughtful pause. "That's the magical number of your culture, isn't it?"

Martin smiled, pleased at Oldenberg's ethnographic tidbit and capacity for lumping, for seeing events comparatively. The man might have made a good social scientist, he thought. "Yes it is and, as a matter of fact, I think I can. The last period was that of singleness, a status apart from any kind of social unit. You know, one of our social scientists came up with two kinds of families, the family of orientation, which was the one each person was born into, and the family of procreation, which was the one in which one produced new members of the species. Both were families of reproduction, the first in which one was produced, the second in which one was the producer. Anyway, in the old days, one usually finished the years after reproduction as a secondary member of the family of procreation. That is, the grandmother or grandfather, or both, stayed with son or daughter and their new family of reproduction. As I mentioned before, this became especially true for females because so many outlived their husbands. But the pattern largely went by the boards by the time I had finished with my little family of procreation. Because of divorce, few or no children, and general unwillingness of grown children to take in the elders, families tended to fly apart. This contributed to the rise of the singles generation. There were actually two parts to it, those who had never married and those who had already been through the mill and found themselves alone. I was in the second group, which I suspect was the larger. So my last twenty-plus years were spent in the nul-family or the singles."

Oldenberg rubbed his pipe with his thumb, looking thoughtful. "So you are saying there were three periods you went through, as a part of the family in which you were produced, as a part of the family you produced, and in the status of no family." Pause. "But you married again, didn't you, and in the third period, that of no family, correct?"

Martin answered that quickly, partly because he wasn't quite sure of his answer. "Yes, I did. But in retrospect, I regard that union as merely the longest of my temporary singles' unions. It is true that I was married, but not with any possibility, or even desire, for reproduction. As a matter of fact, I had already had my tubes cut and was not really planning on marriage again. My ex #2—divorce became so prevalent at that time that we developed a new term, *ex*, to refer to any of our former spouses—talked me into it. In a sense that was a family of relationship rather than reproduction, a fact my wife accepted as much as I did. That is, she married me not to have children but to be psychologically satisfied, to be made happy, as they said then, and divorced me when that didn't happen adequately to suit her. A "relationship family" was a type we evolved during this latter period. It was in very little sense like either of the former types, being strictly a product of the late twentieth century." With that declamation, Martin took his cuplet and drained the last of the cognac, feeling rather proud of himself to have conceptualized the new relationship as well as he had.

Oldenberg, "Can I give you a refill?"

"Sure, the second is always mellower, though I had no trouble getting the first down."

The Transitioner also filled his own cuplet. "Okay, Martin, this new classification of social positions is interesting. But what about the part you just saw in your role of childhood and young manhood? What did you learn about how you were being socialized or shaped for your adult role of householder?"

"A number of things, though most are hardly earth-shaking. I was raised in the era when sexuality was deliberately controlled by the family. If they could help it, you didn't mess around, as we got to calling sexual affairs in the late twentieth century. The control began when you were an infant and tried to play with your genitals and continued into your early adulthood. You weren't supposed to 'do it' until you were married."

"I take it from the way you say that, that some males did."

"There were undoubtedly always some, but it wasn't easy in those days. You see, by the time you got to being with girls, you were hit by a double whammy, as they used to say. In contrast to a book that came out during the time of my late middle age entitled *Nice Girls Do*, I found out in my youth that nice girls don't. We weren't like the Hindus or early Costa Ricans, we could date, and we were even permitted to fondle one another, but I'm afraid most of us learned that the zones for fondling did not include the breasts or crotch. Even the thighs were usually off limits, particularly on girls." Pause. "That is, if you suppressed your guilt and tried, you found that the girls had been socialized even more strongly."

"Sounds like it was really tough."

Martin laughed, "None of that free and easy stuff as with the chimpanzees. No, I'm afraid our culture exerted powerful pressures over our primate heritage. We were by no means permitted to do what came naturally."

Oldenberg stretched his legs, then crossed one over the other. "I understand your psychotherapists made a lot out of the frustration you people suffered as a consequence of not being able to act naturally, that is, according to your genetic makeup. If that is so, you must have been pretty frustrated. Were there no outlets?"

"There were, as there usually are. Continual frustration without any other recourses can be pretty deadly. I suppose it can ultimately drive you *crazy*. That was a term we used in my youth for mental deviancy, which became unpopular when we got into the age of psychotherapy. There is a tendency among humans to change the name of a troublesome condition or object in the belief that it will actually change the condition or nature of the object itself. Our usual procedure was to substitute a Latin- or Greek-derived word for an Anglo-Saxon one, as *penis* for *cock* and *vagina* for *cunt*. In this case, we substituted *psychotic* for *crazy*."

"So what were some of these alternatives to sexual activity in your case?"

There were probably a number of such displacements, though I think the main ones, for other Americans as well as for me, were fantasizing, masturbation, and drinking. I think I told you earlier that we humans seem to have been endowed with great imaginative capacities, and that things we found impossible or difficult to actually do, we dreamed into existence. Of course, this occurred in many cultures. In fact, I recall that the Australian aborigines, one of our last surviving primitive people, called the time of the past, when gods and spirits roamed the earth, 'the dreaming.' To an outsider, it was a supreme act of fantasizing." Pause. "For that matter, an unbeliever could regard all religion as a consequence of the human ability to fantasize. But to get back to the topic of discussion, we also dreamed or fantasized about many things, sexual accomplishments being one. Probably the most common fantasy of males, which was certainly true in my case, was a beautiful woman in a provocative position."

Oldenberg nodded. "And the next, masturbation, which is what I recall is your human way of sexual self-stimulation, no?"

"That's the fancy way of naming it, of course. There were a whole variety of slang expressions also, as there were with most sexual activities and parts in my culture. Some I remember are *jacking off, jerking off,* and *beating your meat*. Those were male-linked terms, which naturally were the ones I learned. Whether females had special terms for their form of self-stimulation I don't know, because of course, until quite late in the twentieth century males and females did not use sex-linked terms when they were together. But there is no doubt that females got heavily into masturbation also, particularly with the use of dildoes or artificial penises. In fact, I once thought that American society of the 1970s and 1980s might have aptly been called the *dildo generation.*"

Oldenberg remarked, "I'm a little surprised at how much you indicate humans went in for such self-stimulation. Since the organs were evolved for stimulating each other, how is it that people got so involved in doing it to themselves? Was that true of the other animals as well?"

Martin leaned back and grinned slightly, amused at the direction the talk had gone. He had to confess to himself that he had never really thought about the why of masturbation, no matter how much he had done it. But as usual, he set himself to come up with some kind of explanation. "Actually, apart from the primates, ourselves and the monkeys, I don't know of other animals that stimulated themselves sexually, at least not enough to come to orgasmic ecstasy." Pause. "That's the state of sexual release we used to try to achieve, whether to oneself or in conjunction with a partner."

Oldenberg said thoughtfully, "Too bad Jerry's not here now since this information would probably be of interest and value to him for his Transition therapy sessions. Presumably, some of the 'hang-ups,' as you earthlings came to call them, would have involved this self-stimulation."

"Little doubt about it. In fact, when I grew up there was the idea, promulgated by the elders, that a guy could lose some of his marbles, that is, become dim-witted, by 'beating off' too much." Break. "Yes, I'm sure Dr. Hanson would get something out of this, but after all this wasn't a regularly scheduled meeting. We didn't know we were going to get together before the end of the viewing. So I'm afraid he'll just have to get it from the report." Pause. "Of course, I'd be pleased to go over it with him separately if you think it would help." Martin interjected, rather slyly, he thought, "That is, if there were enough time."

If Oldenberg recognized Martin's gambit, he did not let on, refusing to take the bait. Instead, he asked, "So what do you think is so special about your species and your closest relatives, the monkeys, that encourages this activity?"

"I think there is absolutely no doubt that it is the development of the primate hand, the dexterous appendage with the opposable thumb. The primate hand is sensitive and agile, and the fact that it can grasp things very well makes it ideally suited for manipulating the sexual organs, particularly for males. Hoofs and clawed feet just won't serve.

"We anthropologists credit the development of the hand as one of the major bodily changes that brought the cultural way into being, especially for handling tools and carrying things." He smiled. "But it also contributed to the human way for some secondary reasons, of which masturbation was one." Martin grinned even more as his thoughts carried him to his last remark: "You might call us *Homo sapiens masturbatus.*

"Apart from that ability, there may be some other characteristics of the humans and other primates that may have encouraged the development of the practice. One such that I just got finished talking about is fantasizing. To be able to imagine occurrences vividly requires great imagination, and we humans are certainly blessed, or cursed, with that. It's a corollary of boredom. Creatures capable of great imagination are also capable of great boredom. And both those characteristics, as well as frustration, are good motivations for masturbation. In other words, when life was shitty, as we would say in my later years when there was more freedom in the use of Anglo-Saxon words, either boring or frustrating, one could 'beat one's meat.' It did give a brief period of sensory fulfillment."

"You make it all sound so logical, Martin. It's a little hard to believe, though, that you humans got so far away from the basic cause for sexuality, reproduction. Were there really no other reasons for what might be called a cosmic deviancy?"

"I'm sure there were. Those were merely the quickest ideas that came into my mind. The more we talk about it, the more I think of other reasons. One, of course, is culture itself, the human way of social behavior. We hedged the male–female relationship with so many no-nos that a lot of people of both sexes gave up with the opposite sex, and either became homosexuals or turned to *playing with their own meat,* you might say. Of course that idea is also tied in with the new concept of sexuality, that it existed primarily to give people pleasure rather than serving as a basis for reproduction."

Oldenberg picked up his cold pipe and knocked the ashes into his hand, then looked around for an ashtray.

"There's one, at the next table." Martin got up to pick up a thick ceramic bowl, so thick that it looked as though it could withstand the banging of a pipe smoker. He set it down in front of the Transition Master.

"You said a third alternative activity was drinking. How did that serve to alleviate the frustrations of inhibited sexual activity?"

"You know, of course, that alcohol was our number one drug and it was used for a lot of human needs. But the best way I can describe it is that it gave you a *buzz.* You felt mellow and more at ease with yourself and the world after a few swallows. So when people got to feeling shitty, which included sexual frustration, they had a drink or two. This is not to say they didn't take drinks at other times or for other purposes, including to promote sexuality. In my own case, however, I started drinking about six or seven years after I began masturbating, and from then on I stayed with both activities, occasionally interrupted by sexual intercourse with a female. Well before the end of my life I had decided that drinking and masturbation had given me a lot more pleasure overall than copulation had. If pleasure was the name of the game, I would have had to recommend booze and masturbation over copulation, not that any of the young people would have listened to me. They generally thought you could have it all."

Oldenberg had filled his pipe by that time and produced a box of wood matches to light up. Then, after several short draws, he took a long one. Putting the pipe back in the ashtray, he looked at Martin intently. "One thing intrigues me though, Martin. The kinds of things you tell me are not at all what I hear from other Transitionees. There are times when I get the feeling you are not at all typical. How do you feel about that?"

Martin chuckled. "Ah yes, the sampling problem. It's a good question, and I'll try to answer it honestly. I think that in terms of sexual behavior in my culture I would have been within the normal curve but on one end of it, as our graphologists used to put it. That is, although most of us red-blooded American males were generally frustrated sexually and relied on displacement activities such as fantasizing through reading sexy literature, masturbating, watching spectator sports, drinking beer, and other pleasure-giving activities, I did them perhaps somewhat more than most. Perhaps I was more highly sexed, and also being more shy than most of my buddies, I had to rely more on these alternative activities." Pause. "One of the reasons you may hear little about these activities in your Transition sessions is that, despite the greater freedom of expression possible in the late twentieth century, masturbation, fantasizing, and other secondary activities were still not highly acceptable topics for discussion. People were expected to discuss their copulatory successes, not their ability to *get their rocks off* with dildoes. I know my ex-wife, Constance, had discussed at considerable length her sexual affairs with other guys years before she got around to talking about and ultimately giving me a demonstration of the use of her dildo."

A uniformed page entered at the other end of the room and scanned the loungers. His eyes stopped at Oldenberg, and he headed directly toward them. Martin had been impressed before at the almost instant ability of these fellows to recognize the recipients of their messages without ever calling out. He wondered whether they were not some type of creature from another world with some sensory or mental ability unknown on Earth, but made up by the Department of Illusions to look like an earth page, of course.

The young fellow stopped in front of Oldenberg and handed him a note. The Transitioner scanned it quickly, then stood up. "Sorry, Martin, but I'm afraid I'm going to have to leave. The System Administrators are calling a late meeting." He sighed.

Martin stood too. "Too bad. I guess you were counting on some rest, huh?"

The Monitor knocked his pipe out again. "Well, it will be decided soon. Tomorrow I think. And however it goes, it will be pleasant to have some resolution." Before turning away, he added, "Anyway, I'm glad we had our little talk. As usual, it has been quite interesting." Pause. "So you will finish it up by tomorrow? It will be an eventful day, the resolution of the Transition Process and perhaps even your transition, eh?"

Without enthusiasm, Martin answered, "I guess so."

The Transition Master turned and strode off down the hall.

# MARTIN II

They married and after that were the years of college. Martin first discovered linguistics, then anthropology, to start a lifetime career as a purveyor of the concept of culture, learned group behavior. He first got a job as an instructor in a small college in Michigan. Soon, too, he began traveling to many of the exotic places he had read about in his youth and learned about since becoming an anthropologist. Amelia went along gladly to Allahabad, Guiana, Enugu, Savannakhet, and many places in between. And when their son was born as a consequence of their shifting from condoms to the rhythm method, they took him along. They could never come to an agreement about having more children, so went back to condoms. And although Martin became more and more displeased with that method, it became less and less important because their sex life became less and less.

\* \* \* \* \*

Martin could hardly keep his eyes off the crossed legs of Jane Kleinschmidt. They were athletic, slimming at the ankles and knees, made more visible by the fact that she let her skirt rest two or three inches above her knees. Periodically she recrossed her legs.

"Now, as I was saying, the human pelvis is an evolutionary compromise. On the one hand, the aperture has had to be increased, through mutation and natural selection, to accommodate the large head of the human baby; and on the other, the total width has become considerably smaller to be suitable for uprightness."

Martin knew his eyes shifted toward her pelvis, though there was little to see. It was at least apparent that she had narrow hips, appropriate for the athletic legs. He turned his eyes away almost immediately, having quickly perceived that she was watching him watch her. He turned to the blackboard and wrote in big, scrawly letters the word *biped*.

"I'm sure you know by this time that most of the physical changes that occurred to our ancestors were a consequence of the shift to bipedalism, or uprightness on two legs." He paused and surveyed the room, waiting for queries. When none came, he asked directly, "Any questions?"

He could see a light smile on the face of Jane Kleinschmidt, and for a moment thought he would ask her to share her thoughts with the class but decided against that, figuring that she probably would. Another student, Bob Graham, raised his hand.

"Yes."

"I don't understand why standing upright would cause the species to have a smaller pelvis. Could you explain that a little further, Dr. Neumann?"

That took Martin's attention away because all of a sudden he didn't understand it, either. He had cribbed that bit of information from another text and it had sounded catchy at the time, but on the spur of the moment he couldn't figure out why an upright creature should have a narrower pelvis either. He urgently tried to rally his wits so he could come up with an answer that was, if not complete, at least plausible.

As Martin opened the door to his office, a female voice asked, "Could I talk to you a moment, Dr. Neumann?"

He turned and saw Jane Kleinschmidt right behind him, and another student from the same class across the corridor, watching them. "Sure, come in."

He indicated the chair to one side of his desk. "Have a seat." She sat down and crossed her legs again, putting her books on the edge of his desk. His glance went to her tits this time; he was so close to her. Average size, he estimated, though very firm, which was as it should be since she was probably only nineteen or twenty years old. He thought that so were Amelia's, despite the fact that she was more than ten years older than this girl and had already nursed their baby. He ruminated to himself, was he a leg man or a tit man? He decided he was both, and the truth was that a well-formed female body really stirred him up.

He faced her on his swivel chair, "Now, what can I do for you?"

She smiled. "First I want to tell you how much I enjoy your lectures, Dr. Neumann."

"Thanks, it's always good to learn that students are getting something out of our presentations." He knew his response was a little pompous and was not direct to her remark, but he felt a sudden need to keep the discussion formal.

"You seem to be able to sum things up so well."

Martin began to get a little uncomfortable. Though he liked being "stroked" as much as the next guy, he got embarrassed when the "strokes" became too blatant. Besides, he had to watch it with female students. They were just too attractive, and he had taken the vow. Plenty of professors took what came along, or even put out signals of their own. And so long as it was done discreetly, there was little to worry about. A standard topic of discussion on campus was what constituted the "moral turpitude" that a faculty member was supposed to have committed and that brought disciplinary action. No one could decide. Martin said, "Thank you very much, though I don't feel that my summaries come out that well all the time."

He remembered the mushy ground he had gotten on with that remark about the narrow pelvis. And though he had done some pretty fancy sidestepping, enough to confuse the Graham kid, he was sure the guy hadn't been fooled. Martin felt a little guilty about that and resolved to look the matter up for the next lecture. Then he would clarify the point to the class in general. He always felt that such little acts of honesty created a good impression on students and perhaps even helped one's ratings at the end of the semester.

"You just seem to have such a way with words, it's a pleasure to listen to you, Professor Neumann." Then as if to reassure him that her last remark was indeed well founded, "I know because I've had a lot of very dull professors." Quickly she added, "It isn't that they don't know their subject, but they just don't know how to lecture well."

Martin was pleased to realize that he no longer blushed in embarrassment at a compliment, even though he did still get uncomfortable on occasion. But, one could get disciplined for going too far with students, he again reminded himself. There had been the professors in the foreign language department who had given out grades for sleeping privileges. But of course, he thought, they were professors of Italian and were following some of the customs of Latin cultures; it was appropriate in a way, though such consideration hardly swayed the college administrators. And then too, they were only part-timers. Even so, he concluded, it was best to keep relations with students on an academic basis. He said, "I thank you again but I'm wondering what I can do for you. Did you come in to see me about something special?"

She took out her syllabus, which had a number of penned-in marks, and glanced at it studiously, though leaning forward so Martin could just see down her cleavage. "I thought I'd like to do the special assignment."

He leaned back as far as he could without tipping the chair. "Well that's alright, though you don't really have to do it for your grade. I'm sure you'll do very well with just the regular studies. The special assignment was really meant for students who needed to improve their grade." He tried to remember why he had started that. It was really just a busy work assignment to make up for inability to cover the regular material. Probably, he thought, because everyone else was doing it.

Martin smiled. "I don't want to discourage anyone from learning something extra. If you want it, I'll give you credit for it. The first thing you'll have to do is work up a bibliography, then bring it to me and I'll help you choose the material you should read. Okay?"

He leaned back then and took out his pipe. "It doesn't bother you if I smoke, does it?"

"Oh no, I love the smell of pipe tobacco."

He filled, tamped, and struck a match to his bowl of Edgeworth, pleasuring most in the first draw. When he exhaled, she said, "Oh, it smells so good."

Her skirt was high again, which was certainly no accident. After a quick glance, he forced himself to look away. They sat in uncomfortable silence. Finally Martin said, "Is there anything else I can help you with?"

She smiled then, teasingly, it seemed to Martin. "Oh no." Pause. "But I was wondering if you might want to go out for a coffee or beer. You don't have any more classes, do you?" She added, laughing, "I'm old enough for a beer, you know."

Martin's wish then was to get away. He knew he wanted to go with this girl, but everything told him he shouldn't, the guilt as well as the worry that he might really get into trouble. He knew her father was a wealthy industrialist and they had a fancy home on the north side. "Thanks, but I need to get home. My wife is expecting me to take her to the grocery."

It was good to insert a reference to his wife, he thought. He couldn't believe the girl didn't know he was married, but at least this would make it clear.

But she didn't give up so quickly, saying, "Oh I wasn't planning to be out a long time, just for a drink."

Since he had started on the refusal, it was easier to continue. "No, I don't think I'd have time. I'm probably late now." Whether she thought he was making it up or not really didn't matter then; he was getting the message across.

"That's too bad." Then she added, again in a flirting way, "You needn't have worried because I was going to have my sister along."

He got up with a headache. It seemed that every Saturday these days he had a headache, which often lasted well into Sunday. He opened the bathroom medicine cabinet and took two aspirins. Amelia's robe was hanging on the hook. She had gotten up early, to make cookies, she had said. She always seemed to be making cookies or pies, he thought, usually for some function of the PTA or the Ladies Voluntary Art League or the Friends of the Museum. She seemed to be busy every day, though he had to admit that she still kept the house clean and prepared the meals.

He tightened the belt of his corduroy robe and walked down the stairs slowly, keeping one hand on the side of his head as if he might press the headache away. It didn't help much, though it wouldn't take too long before the aspirins would begin to take effect. He tried to remember how long he had been getting them. They had become so regular, every Saturday, and lingering on into Sunday evening. It seemed he could remember their coming for at least two years. Perhaps, he thought, he ought to see a doctor about them. If the aspirins didn't help, he would call for an appointment. Still . . .

Amelia was dressed by then, wearing an apron and meticulously cutting cookies from a floured, flattened piece of dough. She looked up, "How are you feeling?"

"Just a little headache."

"You seem to get them frequently. Do you think something's wrong?"

It irritated him to be queried on this point, perhaps because he was a little worried about it. He answered more sharply than he intended,

"It's nothing a couple of aspirins won't take care of."

"Probably a cup of coffee would help." She had the ever-present electric percolator on, probably had had several cups already. The amount Amelia could drink in a day was incredible to him, and it seemed to have no effect on her sleeping or anything else.

"How are you feeling?" he asked.

"A lot better. I don't know what it was last night, perhaps some of that flu that's going around. Anyway, I felt bad all over."

Bad enough, he thought, to keep from sleeping with him. He didn't ask very often any more, perhaps once or, on rare occasions, twice a week. But even so, there seemed to be something wrong as often as not, either a flu, cold, stomach upset, premenstrual cramps, or just plain tiredness. They were a couple of sickies, he thought.

She wiped her hands and got him a cup of coffee. He put sugar in the dark brown liquid and stirred it slowly, watching the steam rise. "Where's Dan?"

"He's over with Nancy and Ev Bingham. They're probably watching cartoons."

"He's okay, isn't he?"

"Sure, nothing wrong with him."

He sipped the coffee, pleasuring in the hot bitterness, imagining sitting cross-legged in an Arab tent, sipping dark, thick brew.

Turning back to another flat of cookie dough, she spoke slowly and deliberately, "There was one thing I didn't mention last night. While you were gone to pick up the car, there was a phone call." Pause. "From a girl."

His headache had been receding, but just then it got a little worse. "Why didn't you tell me last night?"

"It wouldn't make any difference because she didn't say who she was."

"Even so, I think a person is supposed to report phone calls that come in when they're not there, don't you?"

"Maybe, though I think it's funny that a girl would be calling here asking for you and then not even saying who she was."

It was probably the Kleinschmidt girl, he thought, though that was pretty dumb, calling him at home. He said, "I told you when the other call came who it probably was. She isn't supposed to call a faculty member at home but she's a very forward girl, it seems."

"Well, you ought to stop her." Was that a touch of anger?

"I'll try, but you know I'm not even sure it's her. But I'll talk to her." He got up, carrying his coffee mug along. "But it doesn't mean anything. You know how it is with girl students. They sometimes get crushes on their professors."

She came back a little more angrily that time. "Well, I never had a crush on any of my instructors, and I just can't help believing that it doesn't happen except when girls are given encouragement."

"That's not so. After all, the professor is the wise man for some of them and perhaps more interesting if he is teaching some exotic subject like anthropology."

She turned to face him directly. "Well, I don't care about that. If a person is married, I think they ought not go around flirting, even if they are a professor of some -ology or another. And I want to make it clear that if you want to go around flirting with every girl student who sits in the front row of your classroom with her knees and bosom exposed, then you can do it on your own. You can have your freedom. To me marriage is an all-or-nothing proposition."

His headache got worse again. He set the coffee down, feeling that he needed to make one final defense, even though it might make his head worse yet. "I don't know why you keep saying that. I've never played around the whole time we've been married, and I have no intention of doing so. I can't help it if some student gets a crush on me."

That was basically true, though he had often wondered whether he shouldn't have followed up on one or the other of the feelers, the airline stewardess who ostensibly came in to talk about ancient Egypt, the divorced colleague who looked him up at conventions, other female students who just happened to meet him when he was crossing the campus. But he hadn't because that was the way he had been brainwashed.

"Want some more coffee?" It seemed like a deliberate effort to lower the tension.

"Not now, I guess."

"How about some breakfast?"

"I want to take a bath first."

"We have biscuits and eggs and gravy. Will that be alright?"

The thought of food just then, especially the thickened brown fluid with oil streaks that was called gravy, was not interesting, but he supposed he'd have to go through the motions or she'd really be convinced he was ill. He said, "Sure, but no need to hurry. When I come back will be soon enough."

He went to the bathroom slowly, trying to think his headache into oblivion. By the time he got there, he was pleased to note that it had dropped to a lower key. He turned on the water in the shower and as soon as he got the temperature right, stepped inside. The almost hot water felt very pleasant and he stood in the outpouring for a while, savoring the flowing warmth. Then he shampooed, working up a thick lather. After rinsing his hair, he turned the volume down and soaped his body from the top down. By the time he rinsed, he was no longer aware of a headache.

He reached down and began to finger the head of his cock. It began to stiffen, even though it was a little tender from masturbating the night before. He reached over and got the soap, working up a thick cream which he stroked onto the by then hard member. Slowly but methodically he began to push and pull with half-clasped hand. The soapy lubricant made it easy. He could hardly feel the tenderness on the tip any longer. He turned to one side so the stream of water from the shower wouldn't wash off the sudsy cream. This was one of the closest things to pussy juice he had found. And the beauty of it was that when you ejaculated, you could wash yourself without moving.

He slowed down once to listen for approaching footsteps. It was unlikely that Amelia would come into the bathroom, even less the shower. But it was possible that she'd want to ask him something else about breakfast. He heard nothing and so speeded up. His arm began getting tense and a little sore. Once he had to re-soap. But though the cock remained hard, there came a point when it seemed it would go on forever. He was pumping as hard as he could without any further feeling buildup. He knew that to come he would have to fantasize. First he tried to think of Amelia lying prone, her spread-legged body in missionary position. But that was no help at all. Although there had been times with her when he had pumped into a hard squirting climax, most of the times he remembered she had remained relatively passive, accepting his thrusts so long as there were no unusual positions. He tried to think back to Giselle, a procedure that had worked before, when he could imagine different positions, but it was getting progressively harder to remember the French prostitute. Then almost without consciously choosing it, the image of Jane Kleinschmidt came to his mind. Since he had never fucked her, he could hardly imagine a variety of positions. It was enough to try to visualize her unclothed body, the tightness of it, the muscular calves with slim ankles and knees, and thighs that became larger upward in smooth tightness toward the dark triangle where, in his mind's eye, he would thrust his cock. She began moaning and turning her head from side to side as he drove harder.

Then he could feel the tingle begin in his balls and come up the length of his hard cock. He gave a last hard burst of pumping and the feeling spread inside his thighs. And as the stream began coursing through the straight-out rod, he stopped the pumping. The jism squirted out in a low parabola, falling on the shower wall in thick, silvery gray drops. He stood tense hard, eyes glazed, until it had emptied, watching the juice run down the wall toward the drain. Leaning against the wall then, he let the warm water course over his body until his cock started to soften.

\* \* \* \* \*

As the years passed, Martin shifted universities and kept getting promotions until he was a full professor. Daniel grew to be a young man and started college on his own. They changed houses, moving up, which was easy in the expanding '50s and '60s. Amelia kept house and went to faculty wives' meetings or voluntary associations. Every two or three years they would go off on a field trip to some exotic place. Then Martin started to go alone.

When they moved to California, Amelia and Martin were differing on almost everything. Few conversations did not end in arguments. Martin moved into a separate bedroom. Amelia started on her first job since Daniel had been born.

\* \* \* \* \*

Martin got another cup of coffee and paced back and forth in the large kitchen, again admiring its dimensions. It was so big a small family could hardly have utilized the space. But of course that had been the idea in buying it, that they could spread out and not be in each other's hair. It was a copy of a Green and Green construction, a true California product. A giant redwood bungalow, not quite like anything anywhere else. Martin liked that house for its expansiveness and solidity, so different from the tract and subdivision houses they had lived in before.

He paced the length of the kitchen, still impressed that there were two built-in ovens besides more work space than any single family could possibly use except for open storage. But then, he thought, the previous owners must have had servants. Imagine, he thought, to have a house large enough to need servants.

But it wasn't a happy place. Nothing seemed to make the situation between him and Amelia any better. And now on top of their differences, they were spoiling their relationship with Daniel. Just the night before, the boy, almost a man, had rushed out of the house crying after a particularly bitter fight between him and Amelia.

Martin, feeling more restless the more he thought about it, set his coffee cup down and walked out of the kitchen. Passing through the dining room and into the large living room, he felt somewhat better just to be surrounded by all that oak paneling. He went to the front window in one of the alcoves and looked out. The street couldn't be seen because of the thick growth of bamboo that flourished on the edge of the lot. Amazing, he thought, how well so many plants could do, breathing the heavy smog of Pasadena.

But his thoughts quickly returned to the issue at hand: he and Amelia. Then the idea flickered again, separation. He couldn't yet think the word *divorce*. It was difficult enough to think separation. He had not considered it in the twenty-plus years before, even though, in some of the most bitter arguments, she had tossed the word at him. But it had always been, "You can go your separate way if you want to do such and such."

He had figured she never intended to take any such steps herself, that the verbal push only came out in the desperation of their differences. She probably never would either, he thought.

All of a sudden he had to have more space, even in that big house. He opened the massive oak door and entered the still cool California morning. One could just barely smell the smog. Later in the morning it would get heavy enough to smell clearly, as well as make one's eyes water. Then he found himself pacing the length of the house walkway and finally the sidewalk, his eyes down, with little awareness of cars or pedestrians, few enough that there were.

He became aware of moistness in his eyes, amazingly enough, tears forming in the corners. He had thought he had shed the last years before, so long before that he couldn't remember the occasion. It wasn't that he had never cried. In fact, as a boy through his teens he had wept and sobbed a great deal, stretched out in the misery of frustration on his bed. But he had slowly dried up, primarily, he thought, because the crying never changed anything. After it was over, things were invariably the same.

Someone had to decide to take a step, he thought. Otherwise this bitterness would go on through their middle years. How hilarious, he thought, middle age; they were middle-aged when this had to happen. But then he thought of the abundance of books coming out on the crisis of middle age, the empty nest syndrome, the end of a life stage.

And people who had lived twenty to thirty years together split apart. Furthermore, it was in California where this seemed to happen most. Starting with the show business people, it had now spread to all sections of society. Everybody was getting divorced—there, he had thought the word—that was the California way. Maybe that was why they had come here, without even being aware of it.

It wasn't a totally novel idea, he knew. He had already walked the streets of Alhambra, looking for an apartment. But it had seemed so drastic then that he had not taken the next step, nor did he mention it to Amelia. But it had to happen. And the only way would be if he split. His vocabulary had changed too, he then noticed. They used to say "went." But in California they said "split."

He stopped dead in his tracks and lifted his eyes. There was nothing to see but trees and shrubbery and houses back from the street, but it was as if he was seeing them anew. He said aloud, "By god, I'll do it. She never will, and somebody's got to cut the mustard."

It amused him that, no matter how momentous the event seemed, he was still able to muse on the fact that he didn't have any idea where that expression came from. It seemed to signify the making of a decision, but what "cutting the mustard" had to do with it, he couldn't figure out. He turned back and headed up the steps. "I'll do it this time for sure." Aloud. "I'll go in and pack my suitcase." Pause. "And go."

He felt as if he had gotten the process going just by saying it, that he had already done part of it. He always had that feeling of satisfaction, even accomplishment, when he decided on something, even if the doing was not in itself something he looked forward to. But saying it made the reality come closer. The time of indecisiveness was over and he could again work out a plan of action. He walked straight back through the house into his bedroom and reached up for the big suitcase on the top shelf of his clothes closet. Opening it quickly, he started to put extra shoes, socks, shorts, shirts, and pants inside.

He wouldn't need to take everything, only enough for a week or ten days. He could come back for more, his departure by then presumably having become a reality. He stopped to gaze out into the back yard, which he had been working on the last few weeks. It looked better, but there was still a tremendous overgrowth of bamboo interlocked with olive trees. It was still incredible to him how wildly things grew in southern California if one gave them water. And so many transplanted Easterners and Midwesterners had put the subtropical plants too close to one another. Then by failing to trim sufficiently, while continuing to water, they ended up with impenetrable tangles.

Martin looked away a little sadly, but with determination resumed his packing.

As he drove toward the university, he felt that he should be noticed. After all, he had a suitcase in the back, he was leaving home, going through a life transition. He felt that if someone had waved or honked their horn it might make the occurrence more meaningful. It would mean that the world was aware of the fact that he, a middle-aged man who had begun a partnership for life, was on the verge of breaking it. Somehow that act still seemed to be drastic, even though Martin knew that it was becoming commonplace. No one paid the slightest attention. The only signal he got was one honk from a motorist behind him, irritated that he didn't start quickly enough when the light changed.

The room at the College Arms was very small, a standard motel room in a place you could find in any medium or large American city, a place you would forget an hour after you left. It was of lathe and plaster, painted in mauve, copies of landscapes on the walls. A double bed, two chairs, a bedside table, and a writing table and chair made up the furniture. There was, of course, the ubiquitous TV set. The bathroom was clean enough, the toilet seat encircled by a band of crinkled paper to indicate its sanitary condition. It was a dreary place, primarily because of its restricted size and the fact that cheap drapes covered the one large window completely, screening it from the patio. The outdoors were excluded. He had taken it because there was a weekly rate and it was close to the campus.

Martin reached for the glass of scotch and took a sip. It was his second, and he was beginning to feel better. He had stopped at a liquor store on his way to the university, feeling sure he would need some that night. Furthermore, Amelia wasn't there to look at him askance if he had a second one. He put his pants and jackets on hangers, but left the small stuff in the open suitcase on the stand. The TV was turned low, and he would periodically glance at the picture. He was aware of it as company only, hardly noticing the kaleidoscope of bright young ladies giving weather reports and light news items while impeccably dressed men in their thirties and forties gave selective details of various criminal occurrences and accidents in California, the U.S., and the world. They called it "news." What was happening out there seemed to have slight relevance to the world of transition that Martin was trying to cope with.

An ad man came on, a person with a positive, smiling face, display-ing an impressive set of teeth, almost beaver-like in their size and white-ness. He was wearing an apron and carrying a baked ham on a tray. He was the most interesting thing Martin had seen since the tube was on. He flashed his teeth in an unbelievably wide smile, saying, "For the holidays, you can't do better than at your favorite Bimbo. For instance, you can get a sugar-cured Farmer Jake's boneless ham for $1.69 per pound and a shank portion for $1.09. Bimbo defies you to find better prices anywhere."

The voice continued, but the words became practically meaningless. Only the brilliant smile was real. But the announcement made Martin aware of another reality, the soon-to-arrive holidays. Thanksgiving was just over, and nights were already cool as the world slid fast toward the winter solstice. It wasn't really a good time to be alone, he thought. People committed suicide then. But what else could you do, he contin-ued in his musings, you had to take a stand sometime.

He took another long swallow of the scotch and felt pleased about that. Whatever else happened, he could have his booze now. And it might not be perfect, but it mellowed you out at the end of a day or a dismal period, never sulking or accusing you of inadequacies.

His birthday would soon be upon him as well. Amelia would have made a cake for that and she and Daniel would have gotten him a present, probably something he didn't need or want. But still there would have been a little celebration.

Oh shit, he thought, what is this maudlin self-pity? If you do it, you take the consequences. Others had. No reason he couldn't. He had to settle the matter, he thought, or he might even go back. He swallowed the last of the scotch and pulled his jacket on. The air was cool as he walked to the pay phone in the patio. He dropped in his dime and di-aled his home number. On the first and second ring he toyed with the idea of cradling the device. On the third ring it was picked up. "Hello," she answered.

"This is Martin."

Rising tone with query. "Where are you? Are you alright?"

Without permitting any lapse, "Sure, I'm fine. I'm at a motel."

"Oh Martin, what's wrong? What are you doing there?"

Clearly and quickly. "I left home, Amelia. I'm beginning a period of separation."

Silence, then a tense voice. "Martin, you couldn't. Something must be bothering you. Are you alright? There's nothing wrong, is there?"

Wrong, wrong, of course there was something wrong! They had been married for about twenty-five years and they didn't get along. But that wasn't what she meant, he knew. Her idea was that there was something wrong with him. And perhaps more comforting, it was something totally apart from the issue at hand, perhaps something acceptable in their social system as a blameless cause, a serious disease perhaps. That kind of wrongness was okay. One could cope with it. But he couldn't go through any such charade. "I don't think it's anything like you're thinking. It's just us. We don't get along anymore. I don't know why except that we've talked and talked about it until we're just going over the same things again and again. And nothing gets settled."

She interrupted, a habit that wasn't typical of her. She was obviously very concerned. "Martin, maybe we could go to talk to someone else, like a counselor. But I think you should come home now."

Quickly, "I can't right now, perhaps later, but now I think we should be separated. I've already got a place. And I'll continue to keep up the payments on the house and the other bills."

Longer silence, so long he started to speak again. But her voice came back just in time, changed, subdued and low, accepting. "Martin, I just can't believe this is happening. And I have a feeling if you stay away now, it will be the beginning of the end for us." Pause, continuation. "And I want you to know, that however many differences we've had, I still love you."

That was hard because the moment she said it, he considered the possibility and decided he couldn't reciprocate. Whatever love meant, passion, deep affection, respect with emotion, he no longer felt any for Amelia. He said lamely, "Thanks."

Pause, then, "Do you have everything you need?"

"Sure, for a week or so. Then I can come back for whatever else I'm short of. I don't need much."

A still longer silence. There wasn't much more to be said since they were no longer working things out together. She spoke, "I guess I don't have anything else to say. But wait a minute. Dan will want to talk to you. He's studying in his room. Will you wait while I get him?"

"Sure." When the phone was put down, Martin realized he had become chilled. A California night in early December could be cool indeed, even if the days were warmed by brilliant sunshine. The phone buzzed and clicked and an impersonal voice at the other end, "That will be another twenty-five cents, sir."

Martin reached down and was fumbling the coin in when Dan's voice came through, "Hello, Mart."

"Just a minute while I put another coin in."

The quarter slid down into the slot, and the voice said brightly, "You may go on now, sir. I'll inform you when your time's up."

"Hi Dan, studying?"

"Yeah, there's a geology exam tomorrow. It's not particularly tough, but there's a lot to remember."

"I'm sure you'll do fine." Martin still couldn't get used to the fact that the kid never came home with anything but *A*'s. Martin certainly hadn't racked them up like that. In fact, his grade point average had always just been barely high enough to get him into the next stage. After all these years, he still couldn't quite believe he had gotten through to the Ph.D.

Dan spoke with his most serious tone, which could be serious indeed, "Amelia says you're not coming back for a while. That you're separating."

It sounded so drastic, coming from the boy's mouth. Martin answered, "Yeah, that's right. I'm in a motel near the university. I'll keep all the bills paid, and you can get to school on the bike, can't you?" Actually Dan had been going on the bike mostly anyway, so that would hardly be a problem. Besides, there was bus service.

"Sure." Pause. "You're alright, aren't you?"

"Sure Dan, I'm fine." He added, "I'm sorry, but I think it had to be done. Your mother and I haven't been hitting it off very well lately. You know that. So I'm just trying a separation, trying to sort things out."

"Is it okay if I come over to see you?"

"Sure, anytime. You can see me at the university, but you can come over here any time also. It's nothing fancy, but we can talk. We could even go out to eat together some evening if you'd like." That sounded so normal, though "normal" certainly wasn't the way Martin felt. But what the hell, it wasn't a funeral. Might as well make it as good as you could, he thought.

Wordlessness again. When the most serious events in life occurred, Martin thought, words wouldn't work. The feelings then couldn't be reduced to a series of sounds with meaning or their written facsimiles. Finally Dan spoke. "Okay, Mart. It's hard, but I'll try to understand. And take care of yourself."

"Thanks, Kid. Stop in and see me tomorrow if you'd like." Pause, reluctance to break, then, "Bye." "See you, Kid."

The phone disconnected, and Martin held it to his ear a bit longer, but finally hung it up. Wow, it was getting cold. He turned back to his room. Inside, he poured himself another drink. The TV set was still on, but it had changed to a police show. Joe Friday, a plainclothes cop on the L.A. force, was giving instructions and explanations in telegraphic, clipped phrases. It had been interesting how he talked at first, but the guy had been on so long that the novelty was gone. Martin settled deeper in the chair and sipped his drink. He could feel his cheeks hot from the alcohol. He reached over and turned off the volume. Lieutenant Friday became a marionette or pantomime artist, which was better because it let Martin's thoughts roam unhindered.

What to do? The night was still long and he certainly was not about to drink himself into oblivion. What he needed was something to eat. So far as he could remember, he hadn't had anything all day. Still he wasn't very hungry. But he needed to get something down. It was said that Russian diplomats drank their American counterparts under the table by keeping the walls of their stomachs coated with fat while they *hoisted their vodka neat.* But the idea of putting greasy meat down at that moment repelled Martin. He considered the possibility of taking a long walk. The brisk night air would have a sobering effect. When he stood up, he stumbled and put his hand on the wall for support. He took the rest of his drink and poured it into the sink. Then he stepped carefully so he wouldn't stumble again.

After several turns, he stopped in front of his open briefcase and rifled through the papers. A small three-by-five note card dropped out. He picked it up and studied the name and number: Elvira Ferguson, 827-3218. He figured Marybeth Hodgson, the department secretary, would have thought he wanted the number to arrange some course problem. After all, Elvira was a major working for her M.A. and he was graduate advisor. How could Marybeth have imagined that he wanted the number to call the girl for a date? After all, she didn't even know he was separated.

He held the paper in his hand as he continued his pacing, trying to focus on the image of Elvira. She was big, almost six feet, and with a pleasant face. She wasn't heavy, but her figure was not at all perfect. Her hips were a little too big and her tits a little too small, and she had a loose-jointed way of walking. Ah well, he thought, one had to trade off characteristics, and face it, the girl was fifteen to twenty years younger than he was. And besides, she was intelligent, one of the brightest females he had taught since Kleinschmidt.

He stopped and looked intently at the paper, thinking, a date, him calling for a date? Why he didn't even know how. He had never been outstanding in that area when he was young, and it was twenty-five years later. Furthermore, he had done nothing in that regard all that time. He wouldn't even know what to say; what after she said, "Hello."

Would he say, "This is your professor speaking, informing you that you are doing very well in your studies, but that isn't the purpose of this call"? Or, "What I am calling about is to find out if you would be interested in going out with me—on a date? Socially? To play hanky panky?" God no, he couldn't get cute. He would be lucky if he just got the message across. He began walking again.

But what was he going through this for? What was he thinking of? He had just taken the plunge in separating. Wasn't that enough for a while? He hadn't been any good at this kind of stuff before he got married. And now, when his hair had turned gray! He walked into the bathroom and studied it. There were only a few thin streaks of the dark blond it had been. At least, he thought, the change had not been so marked as it would have been if his hair had been black originally. And, thanks for the good things, he still had it all.

He opened the closet door and purposefully pulled on his jacket. By god, he would do it. No use thinking about it all night. You could always think of reasons for not doing something. What the hell, she couldn't do anything worse than say, "Sorry, but I'm busy then."

But when? Every night? She could hardly say that. And then the worst dread came, that she might say, "But you're so old."

Don't be silly, man, he thought, she's too bright to say something like that. But still, she might say something embarrassing. Maybe another scotch would help. The pacing had taken some of the buzz off. He turned back for the glass he had just emptied.

He carried the drink with him, the piece of paper in the other hand. In a way he wished someone had been using the phone because it would be an excuse to not call. Inside the booth, he took a sip from the scotch, then put it down, the paper alongside. He dropped a dime into the slot and listened to it rattle its way down the little chute. It clicked, and the dial tone came on.

He dialed, concentrating hard on the numbers because in the dim light and without his glasses he could make a mistake easily. It connected, rang once, and he pushed down the support arm, breaking the connection.

He leaned back, scotch in hand. Christ, it was hard. But how could a grown man, a professional, who had been used to public speaking for almost twenty years, be as frightened as a teenage kid? Impossible to believe and yet there it was. He, Professor Martin Neumann, was a total coward. Jesus, hadn't he gone over all the eventualities? Hadn't he decided the worst that could happen was a refusal, and probably a diplomatic one at that? He took a good drink and approached the phone again.

This time when the phone connected, he hung on. After four rings, her voice, which he recognized instantly, saying, "Hello."

"Hello, this is Professor Neumann."

# CHAPTER 12

Martin turned the switch to "Off," suddenly realizing he was very tired. The screen went blank. The unexpected voice of the Monitor broke the silence, "You certainly seem absorbed, Martin."

The earthling turned quickly and saw both Oldenberg and Hanson seated on the rear chairs. For a moment Martin couldn't shift his mental set, staring at them with eyes out of focus. Then he recovered and smiled. "Wow, I didn't know anyone else was here. How long have you been here?"

Oldenberg said, smiling, "Only a few minutes. The time since you moved away from your house of marriage in California and started your divorce. Interesting."

It was getting easier to talk, though Martin still felt drained. It was as though what he had just seen had transported him to another reality, the kind Casteñada had described in best seller after best seller. And when Hanson took out his packet of cigarillos, Martin made a quick decision—he would do it. After all, it no longer made any difference to his health, and so much had happened that it seemed logical to take an aberrant action. "Dr. Hanson, if the offer's still open, I think I'd like one of those now."

"Sure, why not? They do have a calming effect. And perhaps you need something after going over your own life again, and as a sort of disinterested observer, so to speak."

Martin reached over and took the cheroot. He couldn't remember exactly whether one licked the sides of cigarillos before lighting up, so decided not to. Hanson lit the end of the tube of tobacco with a lighter. Martin drew in, at first cautiously, and the acrid smoke bit a little. But nothing further happened, and Martin relaxed. The smoke went into his lungs as in the old days. It tickled slightly, and he coughed a couple of times, but then the experience was pleasant.

Oldenberg remarked, "I suppose watching your own life in review is somewhat of an unusual experience, eh?"

"Yes, it is. In a sense it's like reliving what happened before. And much, at least in my life, wasn't really worth repeating, I don't think."

Martin took another drag on the cigarillo and felt a tingling, followed by a slight feeling of dizziness. He remembered from the days of his living how after some weeks of abstinence the first cigarette would create such a feeling. Once, in fact, he had run out of cigarettes while on a fishing trip, and when he smoked the first after that, he had fainted. He found himself lying on the ground afterward. This time he was careful not to take in too much, even though he wasn't at all sure the same reaction would occur. After all, he was a part of the afterworld. He said, "I'm a little surprised to see you two. We didn't have an appointment, did we?"

"No, we had a couple of Transitionees to discuss, which we did while strolling, and our walk brought us this way. Also, I remembered our discussion yesterday about the probable value of Jerry sitting in on any further discussions of your life, so we stopped in. Do you mind?"

Martin couldn't help wondering at that moment if other-worlders were as much given to little deceptions as earthlings had been. He remembered clearly that earthlings would frequently claim to be encountering someone by accident even when it was clearly apparent that they had come to that place deliberately. Or were the Transitioners really curious about his life and reactions on seeing it again? Or were they there to keep the pressure up for him to finish? But he put those thoughts aside without discussion, pleased that he had someone with whom to share some of the ideas that were tumbling over and over in his mind. "I'm very glad you came. I'm really worn out and about to call it a day, but if I don't talk about some of my reactions, I'll not sleep a wink tonight."

"It seems apparent you didn't get finished," Oldenberg observed.

Martin leaned back, turning inward to his ideas, gazing vacantly at the darkened screen, exhausted and pleased that he didn't have to see any more. "No, I didn't. I guess I got through about half, not in an exact chronological split, but what seemed to be a logical breaking point. I stopped just when my twenty-five year marriage ended and I began divorce proceedings."

You looked like you were well into your middle years, perhaps in your late forties, no?" asked Hanson.

"Actually, I was fifty years old. Over the hill, as they used to say, though still not decrepit. You know, they managed to lengthen our lives quite a bit in my lifetime. So that left me thirty-four years to go. I died, you know, when I was eighty-four." It still seemed bizarre to Martin to be contemplating his own death and discussing it so dispassionately, but everything else about what he had been doing the last few weeks was so strange that this hardly nonplussed him.

The room was becoming a little smoky from the cigarillos. Martin turned on the exhaust fan, which he had discovered the first day when he had checked out all the switches in the viewing room. He had not used it until now. The whispering device quickly sucked the smoke out. He gazed at the final tendrils being sucked oozily into the screened exhaust. Oldenberg decided to join them, taking out his pipe and smoking paraphernalia.

Hanson continued, "What was so logical about stopping then?"

"Until that time I had acted as though marriage was a lifetime affair, which we were brought up to believe in my youth and as we claimed in our vow, to the very end. When I divorced at fifty, I was in a sense joining the next generation. Times had changed gradually in my lifetime, but by then divorce was common. I was joining a great throng. There was a talk show announcer who operated out of San Diego in my later years, a guy by the name of Sid Slanted, who used to routinely ask married ladies who called him up if they considered their current union as permanent or merely one of several to come. Anyway, it had progressed so far by then that if you met anyone over forty who was not married, you ordinarily assumed they were divorced, the only relevant question being how often."

Oldenberg joined in. "So that was a time of transition to you, so to speak, eh? A transition of life rather than of death, no?

"I think so. In fact, what I did was a variation of a life occurrence that had been given a name by then, something called 'a mid-life crisis.'"

"Hmm, a time for a change of direction, no?"

"Yes, that was the general idea. It was a new kind of transition, or at least recognized as such. When I was young, they talked about females having a crisis at menopause, when they stopped ovulating. But by the 60s they were claiming that males went through something similar, without the basic change in hormones. In fact, most males, including myself, got more active sexually after their crisis. If you discount my masturbation, during my married years I indulged in very little sex. But after my divorce, I branched out in both quantity and quality. I haven't viewed that part yet, though I remember it well enough. I suppose that I had better wait to see it before we have that discussion, right?"

"I think it would be a good idea." But before the topic was finished, Oldenberg added, "You know, Martin, you were supposed to be finished today. You must know the administrators are pressing me hard." The Transitioner looked a little vexed and weary.

Martin said quickly, "I'm sorry. I suppose I can just stop, because I do understand your problem."

Oldenberg, sighing, replied, "No, you're so close to the end that I'm going to give you one more extension. You can have tomorrow. But you will have to finish your own life and save enough time for your Transition session."

That was it. There was really to be no more. The thought was not at all pleasant, even though it was hardly a surprise. The Transition Master had been emphasizing the termination more and more, so Martin could hardly complain. And he had to admit that in a sense he was getting closer to a logical closure than he ever had on any real-life research projects. There was the wild and active period yet to view, the period when he had literally sowed his wild oats, and then the decline into the quiescence of his final years. He laughed inwardly at the thought that in his youth they had talked of the late teens and twenties as the time when men had sallied forth in sexual and pairing wildness. It wasn't that way at all, he reminisced.

Like many of his contemporaries, he had been too inexperienced and poorly situated in life to take advantage of his youth, no matter the flowing of the hormones. It was only in the advanced years that the possibilities really increased, no matter that the hormonal flow was less.

Martin said quietly, "Yes, I'll be done by then. If you want to set up an appointment for my Transition now, it's okay."

"We can do it after dinner, say, 7:30, if that's satisfactory." He turned to his colleague. "Perhaps Dr. Hanson would like to sit in on it."

"Yes, I would. I can always pick up some new insights on earthling reactions for use in my Transition Therapy Sessions. And I must confess, I've gotten more than my share from these discussions so far."

"Okay then, it's set."

# Martin III

And that was the beginning of the dating game, which was more active the next seven years than in all of his young manhood. The separation turned into a divorce, and Amelia, with her share of the community property, went her separate way. It wasn't a happy parting, but it was not vicious either. They managed to keep lawyers from stirring up the broth.

To his considerable amazement, Martin learned to talk to girls over the telephone as well as in person, even to flirt a little. He learned to get their phone numbers, then call them for dates. To his great surprise, his age appeared to be hardly an impediment. Perhaps with Elvira, because she only went with him a few times and never let him kiss her. But he couldn't be sure that it wasn't for some other reason. After Elvira followed a series of women, and through them Martin learned how much he and the world had changed. There had been Kathryn Wong, whom he remembered primarily because she arched her back so powerfully when fucking and always wanted him to stay all night. But he had not yet become relaxed enough to sleep with someone all night.

Then there was Babette, with whom he went the longest, off and on. Their times together would be wildly passionate and then bitterly argumentative. Their sex was good. He remembered vividly the evening they fucked four times in no more than four hours. Babette had introduced him to, no, not oral sex—to cocksucking and pussy eating. And no, it's not just for presidents. And yes, it is permitted. And no, we're not supposed to call it what it is.

Their affair was almost aborted early because her estranged husband tried to bite Martin's balls off. It happened at a friend's house.

The telephone jangled several times. Evidently Tim, who was upstairs, could not hear it. Martin walked over and picked up the receiver. "Hello."

Silence.

"Hello, hello? Who is this?"

The sound of heavy breathing.

"Hello? Speak, or I will hang up."

There was continued heavy breathing, and then, "You mother-fucking son-of-a-bitch."

"Come on, Phil, that doesn't make any sense. Almost everybody who is fucking anyone over twenty-five is fucking a mother."

Incoherent sounds intermixed with heavy breathing. Then, "You asshole, you cocksucker, you lousy pervert. I'm going to run you clear out of the state of California."

This was frustrating. After two weeks of calls, he was as vituperative as ever. It would go on forever if someone didn't take drastic action. Martin decided it would have to be him, no matter the danger. Babette did say that he never carried a gun. "Look, Phil, we've got to settle this. Let's talk it out and put an end to these phone calls."

"I told you I wanted to meet you already—at midnight at the warehouse."

He certainly had, among other impossible places. Martin wasn't crazy. But, he was afraid that Phil was. Jealousy did that to a person. But these telephone calls at any time of the day or night had to stop. Tim was getting tired of them. And who could blame him? After all, he had rented Martin the room out of the goodness of his heart. Martin answered Phil, "Let's just get it all out in the open, at my place."

"When?"

"As soon as you can get over here."

Martin certainly did not feel calm about making these arrangements. He had never dealt with anyone who had flipped as badly as Phil had. Martin was certainly no macho guy, ready to take on someone who was furiously jealous. But these wildly accusatory calls had to stop. Otherwise, Tim would kick him out. And Martin had enough other troubles.

Phil answered, "I'm ready right now. Where are you?"

Even as Martin said it, he could feel his blood pressure rising. Once Phil had this information, it would be impossible to retreat. But Martin had started, so he continued, "You got a piece of paper?"

"Wait a minute."

Martin waited nervously. Phil came back to the phone with a terse, "Go ahead."

"It's in Pasadena. Take the Pasadena Freeway and get off at the Fremont Avenue exit. Got that?"

"Yeah, keep going."

"Turn north on Fremont; go past three stop lights, then turn east. Got that?"

"Yeah, yeah."

"Go about eight blocks to Whitfield and take a right. When Whitfield angles into a heavily wooded area, you'll see a road marked Whitfield Lane. That's it. Go to the first house. No address, just Whitfield Lane. It's the only house. Got all that?"

"Yeah, I'll be there shortly." He hung up.

Martin sat there in a state of numbness. What had he done? He had given his address to a guy who, by all evidence, wished Martin were dead. Martin could hardly believe it and all that had led up to it. And here he was, inviting the man to come—to do him in, or what?

All that had happened went racing through his mind. It was not really believable, at least to Martin. Here he was, a college professor, inviting to his house a jealous husband, a guy who wanted to do him harm because he had made out with his wife. And not only that, he was just recently separated, but still really married. Was this the California way, or what?

How could he have imagined the events that led up to this when he had started the dating game forty years ago? Or even much more recently, four months ago, when he had separated from his wife of twenty-five years. He thought of the irony that, though hardly exciting, his first marriage was the one period of personal stability he had ever had.

He tried to arrange the images in some kind of chronological order while he sat in a memory daze. His marriage had been in trouble already when they had left Maryland. Amelia had not wanted to come, but Martin was still in the old frame of mind; marriage was a lifetime affair. He talked her into coming out, but he was wrong. They just could not get into a discussion without a fight. And so, things went from bad to worse, and he left the house. He stayed in a couple of cheap apartments before he asked Tim if he could rent a room in Tim's wooded hideaway. Tim wasn't wild about the idea, but went along with it. Martin was department chairman and could hire Tim for part-time teaching. Anyway, there he was in Tim's secluded house, and he had just invited a man, crazy with jealousy, to come over and talk things out.

The way Martin got involved with Phil is another story. Phil was a documentary movie producer and found out about some of the films Martin had taken in Laos and Cambodia. He, Martin, and another anthropologist, made a couple of commercial films together. Phil and Martin got chummy. Phil was heavily into sailing, so he couldn't wait to get Martin to come out on his boat. He especially wanted Martin to meet his wife, Babette.

The sailing trip was okay. Babette was friendly as she unpacked the picnic basket. She was also stacked. Both she and Phil had come from France, so they had a European-style picnic. There was plenty of French bread and wine. It was a pleasant afternoon.

A few nights later, Phil called Martin and asked him to go out with him. Babette had thrown Phil out of the house and he was on his own.

Martin said okay and they bummed around some bars in North Hollywood. Phil told Martin all about his marital troubles. He assured Martin that Babette was just the one for him, but they had been having one
squabble after another.

The two men drank quite a bit. Phil did most of the talking, and it
was mostly about his wife. Martin just kept agreeing with him. Phil was
going to get his own apartment. Finally, they called it quits and went
home. They never came close to making contact with any women, which
had been Phil's stated purpose for the evening.

A couple of weeks later, Phil got a bug up his ass about anthropology. He had recently read Malinowski's *Argonauts of the Western Pacific,*
and he could talk about nothing else. Martin had never found it that
exciting, though he had heard about it from his early student days.
Anyway, Phil thought the *kula ring* and those Melanesian natives exchanging shells ritually was a real gas. It wasn't long before he proposed making a documentary film about it. Martin was lukewarm about the idea,
but Phil's enthusiasm was so strong that he soon convinced Arnold, the
other anthropologist. Martin backpedaled. And to make a long story
short, they soon had a project going in which each would put one share
into the investment. Phil would go to the Trobriands as the photogra-
pher. He talked to airlines, equipment companies, and other provid-
ers, asking them to donate stuff. And he was good at it. He was fully
separated from Babette during this period, living alone in his apartment.

A few days before it was time to leave they got together and had a few
drinks. At first Phil talked about the great film they would make. Then
he got very serious. "Martin, I'm going to ask you to do me a favor."

"Okay, shoot."

"Well, you know that things haven't been so good between me and
Babette the last few months."

"Yes." Martin took a swallow of his Chianti.

"But also, you know that she is my woman. She's really my type."

Again, Martin agreed.

Phil took a slug of his brandy. "Well, she's a woman who is used to
going out, you know, to parties and social affairs. She's not the type to
stay home at night for several months, doing her knitting and watching
TV."

Martin really didn't know her that well, but Phil's assessment sounded
reasonable. Martin still wasn't sure what Phil was getting at, when he
said, "Well, Martin, I haven't known you very long, but I like what I've

seen. I'm going to ask you to do me a big favor, with Babette."

Then Martin got it, or at least the direction Phil was going.

Phil continued, "I want you to take her out for me sometimes while I'm gone. To parties and dances and restaurants. You know, so she won't turn into a wallflower."

Martin had never had *that* kind of request before, but he did not object. He agreed to take her out. She seemed like a lively, even an interesting, person. And let's face it, her looks weren't hard to take. Beyond that, Martin had no clear-cut intentions.

It didn't take long, however. Before you could say *Gigantopithecus horibilis,* they went to bed together. Martin felt guilty, but, as happens so often, the excitement overrode the guilt. Anyway, both she and Martin kept telling each other that each of their marriages had already broken up. She assured Martin that she was going to divorce Phil. Martin's own divorce proceedings were moving even more rapidly; Martin hadn't seen his wife for many weeks.

It was clear as soon as they started hearing from Phil in the Trobriand Islands that things were not going well there. He had never believed Martin when he said that conditions probably had changed a lot from the days of Malinowski, who had been interned on the island during World War I. Now it was sixty years later, after another World War. There was no way that things could be the same. Phil found that commercialism had taken over. The natives were a greedy lot, and the fact that they tried to bum cigarettes from him really got to him. He also was bothered by the fact that they wanted to be paid to be in his film. Then too, he was bothered by the tourists and that there was a Hilton Hotel on the beach. He was no anthropologist interested in culture change, that was for sure. And to make a long story short, in only three or four months, Phil was on his way back. By that time, Babette and Martin were going steady.

Martin remembered one scene before the great fight very vividly. It was after Babette had gone to San Francisco to meet Phil at his request. She had come over to report what had happened. When she walked into the room, she was pale and super-serious. Martin could almost guess what had happened.

When she sat down, he asked her, "You want anything to drink?"

She shook her head and reached into her purse for a cigarette. "No."

He waited while she lit up and took a long drag. He waited some more. She reached up and pushed a tendril of hair up under her brooch. He sat down across from her. "Well, what happened?"

"It was bad, real bad. I had a rough time."

She was getting to him. He had been stewing about this ever since she got the letter telling her Phil was coming back. How did he ever get into this mess? So they screwed well together, and they had had some good times. And so Phil and she were, for all intents and purposes, separated. But there were so many others out there. Why mess around with your business partner's wife, even if they were getting a divorce? Martin thought he should have had more sense. But anyway, here they were, and wishing otherwise wouldn't help. He said, "Go on, tell me what happened."

"He really must have had a rough time out there."

"Well, that's because he never went anywhere except to other European countries. What happened to him was no worse than what's happened to thousands of anthropology students out on their Ph.D. field research. It sounds so exotic, but it could be hard to take." He waved the smoke from in front of his face. Since he had quit himself, he had developed a real aversion to the weed. She was smoking more heavily than usual.

Her next statement was like a blow. Not even any preliminaries. "I told him."

For a moment, he thought he had heard wrong. "What? You told him what?"

"About us. I told him about us."

Martin felt for a moment that the ground was moving. Like one of the mini-quakes that happen so often in California. But he had to be sure. "You didn't! Everything? You told him everything?"

She ground her cigarette out in the ashtray Martin had retrieved for her. Tim kept them around for student parties. He had also quit smoking. She said, "Yes I did. Everything."

This was impossible. Was she crazy? To tell a guy who had been out on a frustrating trip that she was having an affair with his friend! Martin said, "Why'd you do that? You must have known it wouldn't make him happy."

"I had to. I couldn't keep it secret. It was too important."

After that the affair really heated up. When Phil came back to Los Angeles, the threatening phone calls began. Martin was never called so many names in his life. But Phil didn't always speak. Sometimes when Martin picked up the phone, there was just heavy breathing. Martin never saw Phil, but he found out from Babette that he had moved into a side room of his film studio. He slept there.

Martin talked a couple of times to Arnold who said he had seen some of the film that Phil had taken. Despite the fact that Phil had cut the trip short, what he had taken wasn't bad, but there was no way they could work together. Arnold really didn't want to talk about it, but he made it clear that Phil was furious.

Tim was getting tired of the calls. Martin couldn't blame him. After all, he had rented the room to Martin out of the goodness of his heart. Martin had the feeling that he was going to be kicked out any day.

Martin still had a book open on the chair arm where he had put it when the phone rang. He knew he was not about to read any more. He heard Tim moving about upstairs in his quarters. Martin had been given the room next to the kitchen. He was sitting in the large living room, the party room. Tim gave a lot of parties for students. He was quite popular on the campus.

Martin got up and paced, then pulled the window curtain aside and looked out at the driveway. Phil would arrive soon, but there was time enough for him to take a walk and still be back before he came. Martin still had on his jogging shorts, having felt no need to change them.

Returning from the walk, Martin turned into the lane, still unsettled. He decided he had time to shave before Phil came. He walked straight to the bathroom and got out his injector razor.

Coming out, he heard a sound from upstairs. Good thing Tim was there. For a moment Martin considered going upstairs and telling him. But what could he have said: "There's a guy, crazy with jealousy, coming over to see me"?

Instead Martin went back to the living room and sank into a chair facing the window. He picked up the book and tried to read, but he couldn't keep calm enough to concentrate. He noticed he was reading the same page over and over. He closed the book with his finger holding the place, waiting and watching out the window.

Tires on the gravel. Martin saw Phil's Volvo slowly come up the drive. Phil parked, got out and came to the door. Martin did not get up and open it until Phil rang the buzzer.

Phil was deadly serious. He stared unblinkingly. He was unshaven. Martin tried to keep the situation normal, even though he knew that was ridiculous. He said, "Come on in."

Martin stepped back, and Phil passed in front of him. He walked to the center of the room without saying a word.

Martin followed. He felt very tense, but still tried to keep it light. "How are you doing?"

Phil didn't answer. He just turned around and stared. Martin tried to break the impasse. "Okay, Phil, you want to begin?"

Phil tried, but no words came. He was very tense. Martin was tense too, as well as scared. Then, in a sepulchral tone, Phil said, "Okay, tell me everything."

Martin tried to act calm. "Come on now, Phil. I can't tell you everything. What do you want to know?"

Phil continued to stare unblinkingly. "Everything, tell me everything."

Martin said, "Let's be reasonable. Let's sit down, and if there's something in particular you want to know, just ask." Martin turned to sit on the chair.

A blow glanced off the side of the head. The next thing he knew, he was on the floor and Phil was on top of him. Martin realized that Phil was between his legs while trying to hold him down. In the confusion that followed, Martin was aware that Phil had his mouth open, his teeth exposed, and was trying to spread Martin's legs apart. How he was going to deal with his shorts, Martin didn't know, but he was fighting back in defensive fear. Grabbing a loose table top, he hammered the top of Phil's head. Then he grabbed Phil's few remaining hairs, trying to hold him back. Tufts of hair came free in Martin's hand, and he thought how sad that was, because he had so little.

Suddenly the almost silent scuffle was interrupted by Tim's booming voice, "What the hell is going on here?"

Martin looked up and saw Tim coming down the stairs. He was 6'3", and imposing.

Phil stopped, then leaned back and up. Martin scooted back toward the chair and stood up. Tim said, in his most authoritative voice, "What do you think you're doing here?"

Phil scrambled up and began smoothing what was left of his meager hair. All three stood immobile, staring at one another like in one of those movies when the action is stopped at a single frame. Tim said, "I think you had better get out of here."

Phil looked around for anything dropped, then headed for the door. Before going out, he turned and said, "You motherfucker, I'm going to run you clear out of the state of California."

The car door slammed, and he left.

Martin began to pick things up. The room looked like there had been a bar-room brawl. Tim helped straighten things too. He said, "Jesus, Martin. How the hell did this happen?"

They were still picking things up when Martin's son, Dan, came in.

He had been out jogging also. Since Martin had left the house, he had come over every day or so to visit. When he walked in the room, he stared in amazement at the torn-up confusion. "What the hell happened here?" he asked.

Martin tried to explain. Dan listened. When Martin was finished, Dan said, "I just can't believe it. At your age! And you being a respected college professor at that."

That was the last Martin ever saw or heard from Phil.

A succession of women followed. There was the neighborly divorcee who survived on government aid and what she could get from her ex when she could locate him. Martin remembered Lucy as the sloppiest woman he ever dated. Her house was never clean, and it was filled with cats and dishes of cat food. Nor was she neat personally. But what bothered him most was that she had holes in her housecoat. He always wondered why she didn't patch them, but felt embarrassed to ask her. Actually Martin mostly enjoyed the visits of her children, ten-year-old Billy and twelve-year-old Charlene, but Lucy seemed to feel that if they visited him, she had rights also. So she would come to visit after the kids were asleep, seeming to assume she had fucking rights but requiring such long foreplay that Martin would often find it hard to stay in the mood.

And there was Marsha—dark, bright-eyed, and sexy, with hair like a giant fluffed-out Brillo pad. She had been so happy, she had said, when the Afro had come into style and she no longer had to try to straighten her hair. Marsha had tits the size of prunes but enough gonadal juice for three women, twisting and gyrating in such violent ecstasy when making love that it was hard to stay with her.

And there was Anne Marie, a tall, full woman, her tits as well filled out as her hips and buns. Martin was intrigued that one tit hung lower than the other. Despite two unsuccessful marriages, she still loved men, with few reservations. Sex was good, though Martin didn't get along so well with her otherwise. They finally broke up because she was constantly correcting his speech.

And there was Mint, the big, blond Air Force major. Mint was a beauty queen as a teenager, and the adulation she had received then seemed to have made a permanent impression on her. In her forties, she still seemed to feel she was gorgeous. And though she seemed to like Martin, she was not available sexually, the only woman he met in this second time around in the dating game who followed the old ways.

Finally there was Constance, another big one who also had a Brillo pad for hair, though hers was red.

They were lying on the imitation Persian carpet in the living room of Martin's house in West Los Angeles. He had sold the Pasadena house several years before and came to the west side to get away from the smog. Also, the small house fit his needs better. Its Spanish stucco style usually made a good impression on the women he brought there. It had a coziness that the giant living room of the redwood house had lacked. That one had been great for parties, but not fantastic for seductions.

"I just love your fish tank. What did you say that small orange one with the black stripe was, the one that stays inside the anemone?"

"A tomato clown. It's the only fish the anemone will let near it. The tips of the anemone's tentacles are poisonous to other fish."

She sipped at her Madeira, one of Martin's favorites, and one that Constance had not had before. The only kind of sherry she had had before, she said, had been cream sherry, which was far too sweet for Martin's taste. "I like it," she said, smiling in that languorous way of hers, blinking her eyelashes several times.

Constance had characteristics that didn't seem quite real to Martin. She seemed to respond too strongly at times, and she always seemed so pleased. He had never been around anyone who smiled so much.

The fire popped and a large spark flew out, breaking against the screen. "I just love to be near a fireplace," she said.

He placed his hand on hers, and she interlaced her fingers, still smiling. God, he thought, you've really come a long way, old man, from the ineptness of that first date after the divorce, not to mention the shy days of your youth. Imagine to have literally arranged a seduction pad with fireplace, fish tank, exotic objects on the walls and shelves, and even a respectable stock of wine!

She said, "I've enjoyed the evening very much. The dinner at the Keg-o-Wine was very good, and the show at the Music Hall was very English."

The Keg-o-Wine was one of his favorite restaurants, very informal and with nontraditional dishes. He had not been to the Music Hall before, but it had seemed appropriate for making a good impression on an early date, and indeed it had been amusing—particularly the big, buxom female who sang in British barroom style. Martin had been to Constance's house once before when she had fixed dinner, nothing fantastic, though she had apparently spent a lot of time and effort preparing it.

She leaned toward him enough that he figured she wanted him to go farther. He leaned forward tentatively, and she half closed her eyes, smiling. He kissed her lightly. When he pulled his head back, she was still smiling. "That was nice," she said.

He was getting aroused, his cock rising. He put his arm around her back and pulled her closer. She responded by putting her hand on the back of his neck. They kissed again, longer.

When they broke apart this time, he said, "Why don't we lie on the floor in front of the fire. It isn't too comfortable this way."

"Okay," she said, still smiling in her slow, provocative fashion and leaning forward while getting up. He took her hand to let her ease herself down on the blue carpet though he noticed she didn't let him hold much weight. She was a good-sized woman, not fat, though tall and well padded on the hips. She kept his hand to pull him down. He lay alongside her and pulled a couple of pillows forward to put under her head, he supporting himself on one elbow. God, he thought, he was going through the classic maneuvers of a seduction as though he had been doing it all his life. It still amazed him that he had managed this kind of procedure only when in his fifties.

"What are you thinking, Martin?" she asked.

"Oh, not much. Only how much I've changed in my lifetime. You know, when I was young I was so shy I could never do anything like this."

She twinkled. "You like it?"

"Sure, it's very exciting. I just can't imagine why I passed it up all those years."

"But you were married, weren't you?"

"That's true, and I was a straight arrow. I never went out on my wife."

She grinned conspiratorially. "You're just thinking of all you missed, eh?"

"Yeah, in a way."

They both looked toward the fire as a particularly large explosion occurred. Both seemed to turn inward for a time, wrapped in their own thoughts. Then she broke the silence, "But at least now you are making up for lost time. Probably got a dozen girls."

"No, not really. I never did learn to go that far, to date several at the same time."

"I could never do that either. I tried it once, but it really got me mixed up to be dating more than one guy at a time." Pause, then slyly, "In that case, I'm your one right now, eh?"

Mint didn't count. He could see her again if he wanted, but three months of holding hands and light kisses once in a while were not enough. The world had changed since he was a kid. So for all practical purposes, this big redheaded mop-top was it. "Yeah, I'm really not seeing anyone else."

She smiled. "I'm glad. And you know, Martin Neumann, I'm glad I met you." She squeezed his hand.

He raised himself and rolled partways on her, she lying on her back, her head on the pillow, her lips slightly apart. He leaned down and kissed her, long and deep. She responded fully, wrapping her arms up around his neck. They kissed again, and he started to run one of his hands down her body, over one tit, in the narrowing of her waist, and over her hips and thighs. She was wearing an ankle-length wool skirt that was fastened with large decorative pins, depending on an overlap to keep from being seen through. The skirt was evidently supposed to open partially from time to time as a provocative device, however exposing nothing but the long slit slip underneath. Still it was an intriguing female garment to him, serving its function well. She did nothing to prevent his exploration. His hand went to one of the pins and began fumbling to open it. It wasn't easy, though she still didn't take any moves to prevent him. He sat up and said, "Let me use both hands."

She stayed motionless, smiling slightly. "You want to do that, to open Pandora's Box?"

He was hot by then in tense excitement, answering, "Sure."

She smiled again and said, "Okay, but let's go into the bedroom."

Martin was sitting at the main table, dressed in a cream-colored leisure suit, Dan at one side in a green one. Constance sat adjacent to him on the other side, dressed in an orange ankle-length gown and wearing a sprig of lilies of the valley in her hair. Even for Constance, she looked radiant. She was holding Martin's hand. Her friend, Evelyn Grantsburgh, who had served as maid of honor, sat next to Dan, who had acted as best man. Beyond were other tables and chairs, which were gradually filling up. Constance's mother and father sat at one in the front. Waiters marched from table to table with trays of champagne.

The Edgemont Country Club was a fancy place, one that they had gotten for the wedding reception only because most of the members were in Constance's church. She had done a lot of checking around before they decided on that. Once they had decided to get married, Martin had said they might as well make it a good one since neither had had much of a wedding the first time.

"How are you feeling?" Martin asked.

"Wonderful, Martin. For a while there I didn't know if I could face Daddy or Mommy, but those two martinis sure helped. There was no pain afterward."

When Dan and Martin had come to her house to go pick up her parents at the airport, she had been almost giddy. Martin had never seen her quite like that before. "What's wrong?" he had said. "You seem so nervous."

"Oh, you know how I am with my mommy and daddy. I want them to accept me so much, and I just don't care at the same time. But this means so much to them. You know, they never approved of my first marriage."

"Yeah, I know, but really, what difference does it make? We're all on our own now. They'll just go back to Emmetsville when it's over."

"You just can't understand, Martin. It's all a product of my childhood. I've always wanted them to approve of me whatever I did."

He had put his arm around her shoulder and said jokingly, "What you need is a drink."

And before he quite knew what happened, they had mixed up a pitcher of martinis. He thought back on it and realized once more how well Constance could hold her booze. It had been one o'clock, pretty early to start on martinis, but he figured they could take some liberties on the day before their wedding. Anyway, she was as calm as a cucumber after the second one, including when they had met her parents.

People were stopping to congratulate them, and Martin was making the proper sounds, though only barely keeping his attention on their passing. He was preoccupied with trying to put some reality into the situation. It was hard to believe he had just gotten married, the second time around. It hadn't been in his mind at all. After all, he had done well enough the last seven years without the ritual. There had been lonely periods, true, but in between there had been the excitement of dating new persons. And God knows, that had been better than the unexciting years with Amelia and beating his meat in the shower. Had it been because he was really getting up there now, fifty-five years old? He certainly wouldn't be attractive much longer. Desirable women would consider him old.

Then too there had been the combination of events that made it seem okay. His nephew, Bruce Ricotta, had been visiting and on one Saturday morning had fixed breakfast for Constance and Martin. He fancied himself a gourmet cook. It had already been late on a beautiful cloudless spring day. When they were seated in the sunny little breakfast nook, Bruce had made a big to-do in presenting an elaborately wrapped package to Martin and Constance. Martin had given it to her to open, playing the gentleman. Under two wrappings of tissue paper was an oil can, and a note attached that read, "To Martin and Constance, For keeping the bedsprings lubricated. The noise makes it hard to sleep."

For a moment Martin felt it would embarrass her, but no way. She had held it up, eyes sparkling, and laughing, reached over to give Bruce a hug and kiss. He had blushed. It was true they had been going at it hot and heavy, and the spare bedroom was just adjacent. Bruce could easily have heard the creaking bedsprings and even Martin's long, drawn grunt-squeals when he ejaculated, even though he had tried to mute them when guests were in the house. Martin had taken the oil can with his left hand and put out his right for a handshake. "Okay, Old Bean, glad to accommodate. And sorry we've broken up your snoozes."

After breakfast, Constance and Martin sat on the patio while Bruce stayed in to write postcards. Martin was full and very relaxed, with a wine buzz. Bruce had produced two bottles of champagnes to go with the breakfast. For sensory pleasure, it was the best combination—woman, wine, and sun. The last was a California contribution. How could Martin have been negative about anything at that point? They had already talked about their separate plans to go to Europe the next year, he on sabbatical, she on a tour. So it had seemed natural for him to suggest they go together. She had smiled and her eyes sparkled. He was beginning to wonder already if she used some special substance to get that lustrous effect. "Oh, it would be wonderful," she had said in that girlish way. But then her face took on an edge of seriousness. "But what about Larry?"

Although Martin had not become totally thick with her son, he had managed to work out a *modus vivendi*. After all, the kid had adapted to quite a number of her boyfriends before Martin came along. So Martin said, "Why, just bring him along. It would be good for him to travel while he's still young."

Martin had been a little surprised that she had not come out with her usual bubble-over when she said, "Oh, I would like that so much, but I think it wouldn't be too good if we'd travel with a child without being married."

Martin had been a little surprised, but hardly shocked. He had known by then that she had lived with some guy for a couple of years before she had met him, but perhaps traveling was different. Anyway, there in the warm California sun, relaxed by champagne after a thoroughly satisfying sexual night, the suggestion didn't sound so bad. He had thought about it only a short while before saying, "Okay, let's do it."

And that had begun the chain of events that made it more and more inevitable. There was the contact with her church, primarily through Burnside, her irritatingly self-righteous minister. By the time they had gotten in the church for the wedding, he had become almost impossible. Martin and Dan almost had a row with the man when he started acting like a drill sergeant in the back of the church. And there had been the letter Martin had composed to send to her bishop in which he had promised to succor her and her son to his limits. And there were efforts to get closer to Larry. Finally came the intermixing of relations, Martin getting to know her parents, she getting to know Dan.

Martin's thoughts were broken when Constance tapped him on the hand. The husband of one of her friends in the church, Bernard Caldwell, called for a toast to the bride and groom. There were a couple of other toasts by other persons. Then Dan got up, and, holding his glass in the air, spoke very seriously, "I want to add a special one. Those of you who know me know that I have been very close to my father. So I was pleased to come and act as his best man, even though I don't think it's exactly customary. However, those of you who know Martin, know that he has not often followed ordinary customs."

That was not exactly true, Martin thought. He had followed through in a very customary fashion throughout his first marriage, for twenty-five years. Dan was probably thinking of the time since, which had not been very long, actually.

Dan continued, "Anyway, since I came to take part in the rite, I have come to know Constance. And I am very pleased to announce that I have found her to be an uncustomary and very likeable person also. They go well together." He raised his glass. "And I wish them the very best. A toast."

All drank. To Martin it was impressive, since Dan did not speak out openly too often unless he knew well those he was speaking to.

Constance reached over and gave Martin a hug.

Champagne was served without letup, and the food provided by the caterers was good. All ate and drank. Martin soon lost count of how many champagnes he had.

A second reception for close friends was held at Constance's house. When Martin walked through the front door, there were already a lot of people in the house. The record player was on. Martin couldn't figure out what the music was at first, though it sounded generally medieval. It didn't make too much difference what it was at that moment since the champagne had mellowed everyone. People cheered and held up their glasses when Martin entered with Constance. "To the bride and groom, hooray, hooray!"

And someone handed him and Constance full glasses.

Ali Musafar, professor of French, called out, "Speech, speech, from Professor Neumann."

Just like that character, that wily Arab, Martin thought, always trying to stir things up. Martin tried to ignore his colleague. But Musafar wouldn't let up, speaking in his accent-free voice, "Come on, Martin, we know you can do it. Come on, tell us what's going to happen on the honeymoon."

Martin grinned and held his glass toward Musafar, "Not customary, old man, for groom to give speech. But . . . hic . . . tell you what will do. Will give dance exhibition, show some culture." He took Constance's hand then, and she was mellow-fuddled enough to go along without questioning. Martin raised her hand and began improvising what he felt was an old English dance, trying to keep step with the record. He was amazed that he could keep going and that Constance could keep roughly with him as he stepped in and out, joining hands, then breaking apart, twirling, dipping, and stepping in stately fashion around the small room, his arm around her waist sometimes, then holding her at arms length, then solo, facing her. They stopped when the record did.

"Yeaa, yeaa. More, more!"

George Nutley, the old timer in the department, called out, "Neumann, you ought to get married more often. Might keep the arthritis from getting you."

Musafar held his glass up, "Come on, Martin, another. You're just warmed up."

"No, want to get some of the shrimp before finished." Constance's friend, Ella Caldwell, had boiled a large bowl of shrimp for this second reception. Constance said, "Come on, Ali, I'll show you how to use the roller board. I'll even do it in this dress. Makes good muscle tone."

Martin headed for the serving table, and when he looked back, a saucer of shrimp in his hand, Constance was standing on the board, her dress up to her knees so she could spread her legs, and calmly rolling the board back and forth across the cylinder, her eyes on Musafar, sparkling with pride, her cheeks flushed from the wine.

She had practiced on that board for hours, she had told Martin, and she certainly had mastered it. Martin had never seen her tip down.

"Where are you going, Hon?"

Constance was leaving the room while two or three others were standing around the roller board. Nutley was trying it with little success. Constance took Martin's hand, "Into the bedroom to change. I need to get into some slacks. Then I'll be ready to leave when the party's over."

They were going to Martin's house that night as if for the first time. That was for her parents' benefit, though Martin couldn't believe they didn't know the two had been sleeping together. Constance had claimed it would be good for appearances anyway. The next day they were to board a plane to Miami to get a cruise boat to the Caribbean. It would be the first time out of the country for Constance, and Martin was looking forward to it. Traveling with a person to whom it was all new, especially if she was a sexy female, sounded exciting to him.

"Okay, I'll be here. I'll go over and talk to your dad."

She held his hand tighter. "Oh no you don't. I think it's your responsibility to undress the bride, you know, so you get some practice."

He laughed, always pleased by her provocations even though there were times when they didn't seem quite genuine. "Alright, but no seduction now. That comes later."

She held his hand, not exactly pulling, but making it clear he was to go. They came to Evelyn Grantsburgh, who was talking to Caldwell. "Get your camera, Evelyn, and come along. Martin's going to undress me and I want a record."

Evelyn snorted, "Big deal, as if that is something new."

Constance laughed. "It'll be official this time."

When Evelyn got them placed right to get photos, Constance turned around. "Okay, unbutton down the back first."

"Right." Martin unfastened the small hooks with little trouble.

"Now pull it up from the bottom."

"Hold it, wait, let me get the first photo," said Evelyn.

They waited. "Okay Martin, pull it up."

That wasn't quite as easy, it being so long, so Constance helped.

"Get in front of her and pull it over her head when I say 'ready,'" instructed Evelyn.

He did, and Evelyn took more photos. The peach-colored slit slip stressed Constance's femininity. Martin could visualize the smooth skin on the stomach, the broadening thighs, containing at the apex the curly-haired pink triangle, the focus of love. Constance murmured, "And it gets closer now, Martin, the slip."

He pulled the garment up this time without assistance, leaving her clad only in matching pink bra and panties. Constance, "Bravo, you're learning."

\* \* \* \* \*

Five years passed and they did much together, traveling on Martin's sabbatical and on a much longer trip, he taking her to the places he had been before and exploring new ones. In between, they went to school together, he as professor, she as a student again. Most of the time there was lovemaking, including more fucking than Martin ever had had in an equivalent time period. He used all the techniques he had learned from girlfriends since his first marriage besides the basic missionary position. Larry was a dilemma, mainly because, though Constance wanted Martin to take the role of father, she had already developed specific ways of dealing with the boy. Then the real father, who got Larry for visits as often as he could, used still different procedures. And the boy had been around conflicting parents and their surrogates enough to have learned how to use their differences for his own benefit. Ultimately then, Martin pretty much washed his hands of the boy, figuring two opposing parents were enough.

Despite his relatively youthful appearance and behavior, age was creeping up more rapidly on Martin. One evening while stretched out watching a late movie, he had a stroke. And though he seemed to recover extraordinarily well, afterward the relationship between him and Constance progressively deteriorated. She ultimately refused to help him recover. He later thought that because of their age difference of twenty years, she became depressed at the thought of having to take care of a decrepit old man the rest of his life. She couldn't have known that he would recover completely with no aftereffects, and live many, many years longer in good health.

\* \* \* \* \*

The engines of the 707 became muted as the pilot changed the throttle to climb to altitude. As the plane went out over the Pacific, it banked to the left, and below, as far as one could see, were beaches. Of course, if it had been very clear, one could have seen much farther, probably beyond the beaches. In any event, the plane was soon out of the smog haze and headed almost due south. It was the end of another era, he thought.

The *no smoking* sign blinked off, though the one for seatbelts remained on. Soon there was a stir in the serving section of the plane's midsection. The stewards and stewardesses were getting their booze carts ready to help sedate the passengers.

It was about three hours to Mexico City and then hour-long, or longer, hops from one steamy Central American capital to another, the final destination San Rafael, Costa Rica.

God, he thought, how many times? He had begun when the C-47 was master of passenger carriers, through the DC 3 and 4, then the Connie, the Electra, and a succession of jets. It was a long time, particularly in light of the fact that he still wasn't settled down. Once more he was heading off to try to get his act together. The old ties were not completely cut, but it was quite clear that they would be. The divorce had been just too nasty for any possibility of re-cementing what once was. Constance's self-righteousness and the dirty tricks of the lawyers had taken care of that. He had tried to talk to her, to write, to communicate through her shrink, but no way. She wouldn't, nor would anyone else.

The stewardess arrived at his seat and asked, "Sir, could I fix you a drink?"

"Sure, how much are they?"

"One dollar, sir."

Amazing how many people addressed you as "sir" when your hair had gone all white, he thought. You were finally placed in some kind of honorific category. Age usually didn't mean much in this culture of throwaways, but, after all, honorific addresses didn't require much effort either.

"Okay, give me a martini; no, a double." Even though it wasn't like the old days when all drinks on the international flights of Costa Rica Airlines had been free, it wasn't bad. The price was right, as they said these days.

She put two packages of dry-roasted peanuts on the seat-back table, followed by the little bottles and the plastic glass with ice cubes. "That'll be two dollars please," she said, as if he might have forgotten.

God, what did she think, that he was partially senile? No, it wasn't her fault, it was only his frame of mind. The divorce, the divorce, how long would it take his mind to get rid of that? If the books were correct, a long time. He had been amazed to learn how many books had been written about divorces recently, humorous ones, the legal ins and outs, how to recover, what to do next, how to get your act back together. Well, here he was on his way to Costa Rica to shake the remaining cobwebs out. Costa Rica, the exotic land of his early manhood when he was first becoming aware of that kaleidoscope of cultures that were beyond Indiantown and even the U.S. Perhaps it could restore some of the stability he had hoped to achieve in the marriage that was.

He sipped his drink and watched the increasing buildup of cottony cumulus clouds. To him they had always meant summer or the tropics.

The fat Latin lady at his side got up, and, figuring he wouldn't know Spanish, said in barely comprehensible English, "Going out." She wedged past him before he had time to get even partially out of the way. He thought of answering her in caustic Spanish, but did not. It didn't seem worth the trouble.

He could see the beach cities, one next to another, as the plane diagonaled inland across the coast line. The past six months seemed to have been interminably unpleasant, what with the garbled communication between lawyers who cared little about the feelings of passion, affection, and caring that had turned into bitterness and insecurity, to be exploited through intimidation and dirty tricks. Because she refused, Martin had never talked to Constance again. The divorce wasn't over, but at least the interlocutory had been signed.

The only good thing that had happened was that Martin had started to write it all down, working in angry desperation in his tiny apartment in the mornings. In the afternoons or evenings he taught his classes. At night he watched the tube and drank booze restlessly, trying unsuccessfully to sedate himself.

And now finally he was breaking away, fleeing the scene, hoping something drastic would happen to give him back some of his old spark. It was a solution other persons who had gone through the shipwreck of legalistic divorce had tried, he knew. At least he was in more favorable circumstances than most because he already knew most of the ins and outs of traveling.

The fat lady returned to her seat, but Martin saw her coming this time and got into the aisle so she could pass without stepping on his foot again. When he finished his martini, the stewardesses began gliding down the aisles, handing each person a tray of bland food.

When he reached San Rafael, he wandered around in the parks and went to Key Largo and a couple of other bars reputed to be good places for pickups. But the truth was that he did not have enough courage to approach those who seemed interesting. Besides, the Costa Rican women, reputedly so accessible, did not make any overtures that he saw.

Then he met a Cuban-American businessman who had heard the stories of the availability of Costa Rican women also and had set out immediately to get one. What was the point of being away from your wife and family if you didn't have a fling? he asked Martin. Before Martin knew what was happening, they were sitting with a pair of well-used females in their thirties. Martin would have had trouble distinguishing them from whores. Even so, he danced with his as she rubbed her body against him in obvious provocation. Between dances, the two women and Francisco talked animatedly, but the speed of their conversation was too fast for Martin to understand much. He simply nodded amiably when someone seemed to speak to him. And when the place was about to close and the alcoholic buzz level was high, Francisco spoke to him in English, "They want us to take them to Las Ramblas. Want to go?"

"What's that?"

"It's a place in San Idelfonso where there are a lot of rooms available, you know, by the hour."

Yes he knew, like practically all the other single male visitors to San Rafael. It sounded much like the hourly seduction pads he had blundered into with Dan some years back when they did a motorcycle trip in Japan, though it probably was not so classy. He thought for a moment about the possibility of picking up something from the girl, but in his current alcoholic state and rootlessness, dismissed the problem. What did he have to lose? "Sure, I'm game."

Francisco spoke to the women, and the one with Martin squeezed his arm and rubbed her knee against his leg.

The taxi seemed to take forever to get there, winding through potholed streets, which were unpaved in many sections. The girls sat on the men's laps. Martin's legs were sore from the body bounces of his girl. It was a big Toyota, but hardly big enough for four adults in the back seat. But then they were there.

The place was a veritable beehive of a motel, extending in two stories, seemingly for half a block in three or four rows. Martin found it impossible to make an accurate count of the number of doors, but he estimated there must be two or three hundred at least. The taxi driver drove slowly, weaving his way through other cars going both ways. Martin soon figured that the driver was looking for an empty. Between every pair of rooms was a covered parking area, enough for two small cars. All seemed to be filled or, if someone was driving out, someone else was waiting to drive in. Francisco turned to Martin and said in English, "They do seem to do a good business here."

My god, Martin thought, this is the ultimate, mass fucking, the maximum number of couples in the smallest space, doing it in the shortest time. "It's hard to believe."

Francisco spoke to the taxi driver, who answered briefly. "It's by the hour, twenty *platas* per half hour, but with a minimum of forty." He laughed. "I guess they figure some people would do it in a half hour or less to save money, but the driver says twenty silvers wouldn't even pay for cleaning the sheets."

So this was a "hot sheet palace"? The price meant you could get the physical setup for a screw for four bucks. "Is this all they do here? I mean, can't someone get a regular hotel room—for sleeping overnight?"

Francisco answered that without going back to the taxi driver. "Oh, I don't think they care how long you stay. But you have to pay by the hour. We used to have the same kind in Havana. And the people around here know about it. When they want a regular room, they go to one of the hotels in the center of the city."

The driver stopped and waited for another car to back out before driving in. He called up the steps to a woman who was coming out the door with an armful of bed linen. She called back to the driver, who then turned to Francisco to explain. The women listened, Martin's holding onto his arm.

"He says the place is very full, Saturday night, and that this is the only room available. He says we could both use it."

"You mean at the same time or together? There's just one bed, isn't there?"

Francisco laughed then, evidently sensing Martin's discomfiture. "I don't care. It might be different to all go in together." He patted his girl on the butt. "And I doubt seriously that it would bother these girls."

All of a sudden some of the old revulsion came on Martin. Was this what it was all about, a lustful ramming into a hot, wet hole, with little preceding or following the act, paying the money, and crawling off to sleep or going away? If that was all there was to it, he wasn't sure he wanted any. He said then in a tone that was obviously truculent. "Ask them how much they want."

Francisco answered him softly, "I can't do that, Martin. These girls aren't really whores. They have children at home. They just sleep with guys when they feel like it. Most guys give them something afterward, but it's not required."

Ah, a halfway stage, Martin thought, amateur or practicing whores. When they got really practiced, they would do it full-time with no mincing around, the price set in advance. Martin disliked himself for thinking like that, for the women probably couldn't do anything that would pay any better. But at the same time he knew he was finished. He said to Francisco, "I'm sorry, but I don't think I want to go ahead with it; I think I'd just as soon return to the hotel."

Francisco cajoled, "Nothing's wrong, Martin. We can take turns in the room if you'd rather." He spoke then to the two girls. They talked back and forth briefly, then Francisco said, "Cecilia is sorry. She doesn't like to see you unhappy. She says you shouldn't take it so seriously. This is just one of the customs of the country."

How strange, Martin thought, that he should be given an anthropological explanation by a good-time Latin divorcée, who was probably not even a high school graduate. It reminded him of that old Mexican jingle:

"Oye colega, no tu asombres cuando veas
Al alacran tumbando cana.
Es costumbre de mi pais, hermano.
Es costumbre de mi pais."
(Listen friend, don't get excited when you see
A scorpion cutting sugar cane.
It is a custom of my country, brother,
It is a custom of my country.)

And since anthropologists advocated participant observation as a learning technique, why shouldn't he go ahead. And yet, and yet, there was the weight of the past.

He shoved his hands into his pants pockets, knowing full well that even if he got into bed with the Latin lady, he would never be able to get a hard-on. "I just can't. Maybe some other time, but I want to go back. You can stay here with Lucia. I can get another taxi for me and Cecilia."

Francisco spoke then, without rancor, "No, it's not that important. If you're going back, I am too."

The taxi threaded its way back through the streets and the potholes until they were in front of their hotel. Martin and Francisco got out. Francisco spoke to the girls then turned to Martin, handing him a little crumpled piece of paper. "Cecilia said she'd like to have your phone number so she can call you."

"It's in the phone book, the Hotel Madrid, and tell her my room number is sixty-eight."

"One other thing, we ought to give them something. It's late, and the buses aren't running any more so they'll have to go home by taxi. We ought to pay their fare."

"Oh, I think if we give them forty platas, that should be enough."

"Shouldn't we give them something for their time?"

"No, that's not necessary. You know, they're not really whores."

Martin never saw Cecilia again, though she called a couple of times to ask him to take her dancing. He got an apartment just outside the center of town and turned to his writing with a vengeance, taking long walks and exploring the city in between. But the Costa Rican women with their big breasts and short tight skirts kept intruding on his thoughts.

He met several Costa Rican females through his American friend, Arnold Deutsch, usually through the referral of one of Arnold's girlfriends. Arnold was a lot more gutsy about picking girls up than Martin was. One of the girls was Elena Ramirez, a divorcée in her middle or late thirties. She was a short woman, like almost all Costa Rican females, but was darker than most, with only the slightest wave in her black hair. With her very high cheek bones she seemed to have many Indian genes in her ancestry, even though she claimed to be pure Spanish.

They went out together several evenings, and on the very first, after putting down six to eight scotches, she went to bed with Martin. He couldn't really remember asking her. She just went along when he said he was going to turn in. The screwing wasn't fantastic, though by dint of a lot of concentration and effort, he did finally come and they slept fitfully the rest of the night.

Martin would probably have kept going with Elena if it hadn't been for that wild weekend in the country. He rented a car for the occasion and they headed for the east coast to her mother's *finca*. The Datsun maneuvered well on those narrow, twisting roads, Elena giving occasional directions. He studied her through occasional glances as he drove. She was smoking a cigarette, apparently quite at ease. Despite her Indian appearance, she showed none of the subservience of that remnant people. The Costa Ricans had pretty much taken care of their Indian problem like the North Americans, engulfing the trlbals and pushing the few who remained into the wastelands. Martin knew Elena was well off by Costa Rica standards, having gotten a substantial settlement, including a good house, through her divorce of a few years before. Martin had been surprised how many divorced women there were in Costa Rica since that people emphasized family relations so strongly. However, they were also ultrademocratic, more so than any other Latin country he knew of. And their democracy included equal rights for women, at least legally. And equal rights almost invariably led to a lot of divorce, he figured.

Elena said in Spanish, since she hardly knew a word of English, "I just love the *campo*, it's so peaceful there."

"It should be fun," he said, imagining rolling hills of sugar cane or beaches bordered with coconut palms, the long feathery branches in constant movement.

Elena continued, "She has cows and chickens and dogs."

Martin couldn't exactly understand why she included dogs in the list. After all, cows and chickens sounded rural enough, but there were plenty of dogs in all the cities and towns of Costa Rica.

"We can stop at one of the beaches beforehand and sunbathe." Why exactly Elena would want to sunbathe Martin wasn't sure, since her skin color gave her a permanent tan. In fact, her midsection and the band around her tits were hardly any different from the other skin areas. He figured she probably did it simply because she knew North Americans did.

"We'll have to sleep in separate rooms while we're there. I don't think my mother will be there, but Alfonso, her hired hand, will and he'd tell her. You don't mind, do you, just for a couple of nights?" She added, "You know it hasn't been very long since Costa Rican girls have been allowed to go out on their own, and many parents still think they shouldn't sleep with men without being married."

"Yeah, I knew that. It's not been so terribly long with us either, though I suppose a little longer."

The land began to change as they gradually wound their way down the mesa toward the humid Atlantic Coast. The coffee farms gradually gave way to pasture land, sugar cane, and pineapple fields. In between were strips of forest, though most of the original had long been cut down. The Spaniards had gotten started early converting the tropical jungles of Costa Rica into the closest equivalent of Spanish farm country they could manage. There were only isolated pockets left of the original rainforest.

Elena and Martin cruised along the coast and stopped at a couple of beaches she had been to before, to lay around in the sun, drink beer, and eat the corn chips they had bought at a kiosk. Once a local farmer came by with a machete and obligingly opened a few coconuts so they could drink the milk.

Toward evening they drove to the farm. It was a couple of miles inland from the coastal road, just where the land began to climb toward the mesa. They turned off the paved road onto a well-used dirt road, bordered on one side by a strip of houses and odd buildings that, though they weren't exactly shacks, were the next thing. Decrepit fences more or less encircled most. Nothing was painted. Mongrel dogs and chickens wandered around, in and out of the fencing. Cars, some of them surprisingly new, were parked in front of several.

Elena, "Just keep going and I'll show you hers."

Martin couldn't help thinking it was hillbilly country, Latin style.

"Here we are. Just pull in the lane."

And there they were, in front of a structure much like the others except it was built off the ground. Chickens and dogs scratched and snuffled underneath. Elena handled the gate carefully so it wouldn't fall off. Like most everything else that Martin could see, the gate needed repair. A dog ran out but stopped barking as soon as she called to it. They climbed up the well-worn stairway on which one step was quite loose. A man who seemed to be in his forties or fifties was sitting on a broken rattan chair. He was wearing a straw hat, Costa Rica country style, with little tassels hanging from the rear, denim pants, and blue work shirt. When he stood up to shake hands, Martin felt the hands of a worker. They were thick and hard like those of Martin's long-gone farmer uncles.

Elena, in Spanish, introduced him. "This is a friend of mine. He's from California."

Like a true countryman of the poor lands, Alfonso was amiable but volunteered little.

Elena asked, "When will mama be back?"

"In a couple of days. She went to Casa Grande to visit her sister."

Elena took Martin to his bedroom, which was about the same inside as the house was on the outside, in a bad state of disrepair. The wood floor had gaps through which you could see the littered ground under the house. It appeared that they threw their garbage through such holes, reminding Martin of some of the houses where he had stayed in Laos. The bed was some kind of wood frame with a broken-down mattress and dirty blankets. The wallpaper had peeled in many places; otherwise it was discolored in such a variety of ways the discolorations seemed to be the pattern. There were also holes in the walls. A very holy house,

Martin thought.

It was dark because there was no electricity and the one window was shuttered.

Martin suggested, "Why don't we open the shutter? This room needs some light and air."

"Oh no, that'll let all the mosquitos in."

Martin noticed the cigarette butts in a tin can on the floor next to the bed frame. "This must be Alfonso's room, isn't it?"

"Yes, but he wants you to have it. He'll sleep on the porch."

"I wouldn't want him to do that. He's the working man, I'm not."

"No, he wouldn't consider letting you sleep any place else. You're the guest, a distinguished Yanqui."

It still surprised Martin to hear the term *Yanqui* used in a complimentary sense. Costa Rica was probably the only Latin American country where *Yanqui* wasn't a dirty word. He said, "And where will you sleep?"

"I'll be in the room just next to the kitchen. There's a cot there. Then I can be close to the kitchen so I can fix you some country food."

The kitchen was tiny and like the other rooms except it was covered with soot from the charcoal fires used for cooking and had a wide open window in back. Evidently most of the garbage was thrown out there.

One thing you had to say about the peasants of the world, Martin thought, they took care of their disposal problems directly, simply tossing the stuff out. Fortunately, most had chickens and dogs, those indefatigable scavengers, and many had pigs as well. Nothing remotely edible laid around long.

"I'll fix dinner for us. But we'll have to go to the store first."

"There's a store around here?"

"Oh sure, just a little farther up the road." She added. "They have a generator for electricity so they have a refrigerator."

Elena and Martin went to the store in the car to get eggs, canned fish, and bread. Elena said, "Alfonso's got cheese he made himself and bananas from the farm. I think he's got cooking oil and sugar and some other things that don't need refrigeration. You want anything else?"

"How about something to drink? Does Alfonso have anything at the place?"

"No, he doesn't drink."

"That would make him different from most Costa Rican men, wouldn't it?"

"They do drink quite a bit. But you Yanquis do also, at least the ones I've seen."

Martin didn't say so, but some of the Costa Rican women did as well, including Elena. Anyway, it seemed the night would be long and there would be little to do once it got dark, so Martin figured some booze would help.

At the store several young men were seated at the roughly-built counter, bottles of beer before them. On the shelf behind Martin could see several bottles of high-proof country rum. "I think I'll get some beer and a bottle of rum. The beer's cold, isn't it?"

"Sure, they have a fridge."

"Okay, then I can have 'boilermakers,' Costa Rica style. That's a workingman's drink in the States, though they usually take bourbon and wash it down with beer."

They put the stuff in the back of the car and headed back. Just as they started off, Martin said, "We could just as well have walked; it's no distance, and we didn't get so much that we couldn't carry it."

She lit a cigarette, saying, "Oh, it's not a good idea to walk when you've got a car in the *campo*. Other people think you're nobody then. Also, it's hard for me to walk on the ground with these high heels.

Elena fixed rice and fried plantains and also served some of the pressed country cheese that Alfonso had made that day. He sold most of the cheese right there in the country, she said, though saving some for himself each day. Martin and Elena had a beer with theirs, and Alfonso had water. It was dark by then so they sat on the porch, using candles for light.

Martin began the conversation. "Elena says you don't drink."

"No, Señor. I gave that up when I got married and started to raise my family. It costs a lot of money for us poor Costa Ricans."

"I suppose so, but so do a lot of other things that people have. A lot of people, many not so rich, seem to need cars."

"Yes Señor, but I do not have one."

The mosquitos soon appeared, not the worst Martin had experienced, but pesky enough. He could see it would be a lot worse if they were at ground level. He brushed them away while he finished his food. Elena brought him another beer. When they were finished, she took the dishes away, The men sat quietly, Alfonso smoking a cigarette, Martin sipping his drink. He wondered why Alfonso thought of booze as expensive but not tobacco.

But that was the first he had seen the man smoke, and he figured such light usage could hardly add up to much.

Elena came back, Martin wondering how she managed not tripping in her high heels on that holey floor in almost pitch darkness. She said, "Is there anything else you want?"

Martin still had difficulty getting used to the way Costa Rican women waited on men, even those who were fairly modern. He said, "Why don't you bring out the rum and another beer? Bring two if you want one."

"No, I've had enough. My mama doesn't like me to drink much, and Alfonso would tell her."

Martin turned to Alfonso before pouring himself a shot of the country rum. "Sure you wouldn't like to try one?"

"No Señor, *gracias*. I am content."

Martin took the burning alcohol in one fast swallow and mellowed it with a long draw from the beer bottle. "Aaagh!" in a mixture of appreciation and shock. "That'll make a man of you."

Alfonso spoke to him softly, so softly and so without preliminaries that Martin wasn't sure at first what he said. "You have a family, Señor?"

"No, not really. My parents are dead. I do have three sisters, though they live far away."

"Ah, it is sad not to have a family, no? You do not have a wife?"

"No, I'm divorced."

"Ah yes, we hear about you Yanquis. You all divorce, some many times." He seemed to think that over for a bit, then a little sadly, "We Costa Ricans like our families, but nowadays there are many among us who divorce also."

Martin had read the statistics and knew there was more divorce in Costa Rica than formerly, but it had not yet become an epidemic as in the States. The subject was getting a little tiresome to Martin, especially in Costa Rica, where, no matter how advanced they considered themselves, they were still a familial people. He decided to become the interrogator, saying, "Elena says you have many children. Is that true?"

"Oh yes, Señor, I have four boys and three girls." He added, "We lost two boys."

"That's a good-sized family. It must keep you busy taking care of them all."

"Oh yes, Señor. Two of the boys work, but they do not earn very much. And the others are in school, which is expensive."

"I suppose all the children have to go to school nowadays if they want to succeed."

"Oh yes, Señor. It's not like it was in the old days when it was enough to read and write. And many couldn't even do that."

Martin poured himself another shot of rum, feeling the heat course through his stomach when he swallowed it. He felt better talking about Alfonso's lifeway, still an ethnologist at heart, even though this was a far cry from the field studies he had done in the early days when he was trying to climb the professional ladder. He said, "Well, is this your main job?"

"I have several, Señor. I go to different *fincas* to milk the cows and trim and cut back the brush. It's a lot of work."

"Then you must be gone a lot. You must not be with your family very much."

"No, it is necessary to be gone most of the time. There isn't enough work for a farm worker near San Rafael."

Martin wasn't sure whether it was the alcohol or the circumstances, but he decided to play the devil's advocate. "It doesn't sound as if having such a big family is so much fun. Don't you sometimes wish you had less?"

Alfonso looked a little sad but answered in a matter-of-fact fashion. "Ah, Señor, you know we Costa Ricans are Catholics and we must accept what the Lord gives us."

"But it must be very difficult to feed so many."

"When the Lord gives, the Lord provides."

In a way it made sense, Martin thought; all eventualities were taken care of, at least in the minds of believers. All was explained, and nothing happened for unknown causes. And that way of thinking was certainly the best for the majority of humankind. If nature abhorred a vacuum of space, humans abhorred a vacuum of meaning. People did not like to have to deal with unexplained events, so if there were no obvious explanations, they invented some. Still Martin couldn't yet let up on his self appointed task of needling, saying, "But if you work so hard, don't you ever do anything for pleasure?"

The sun-darkened man with the deeply creased skin and thick-knuckled hands looked at Martin in some puzzlement. "I do not know, Señor, exactly what you mean. It is a man's destiny to work and especially when he has a family. I must work."

A particularly persistent mosquito kept whining around Martin's head, refusing to flee from the steady waving movements of his hand. Finally, the sound of its busy wings stopped and almost without thought Martin slapped at a spot on the back of his neck. The whine began again as the mosquito flew away. Martin persisted, "But surely you must do something for pleasure." Pause. "Let's see, you can't go down and drink with the other men because you don't drink. Do you play cards or go visiting?"

Martin wanted to ask the man if he had a hobby but couldn't think of the word in Spanish.

"Oh Señor, we have little fiestas sometimes, usually with the family. But mostly I just work."

By this time Elena had come back and was sitting across from the hired hand, smoking a cigarette. She said, "You know, Alfonso is a great dancer."

So there was something. Somehow that information seemed to justify Martin's questioning. Man just could not live by work alone. He said, "That's good. What kind?"

"Oh, every kind, the rhumba, tango, samba, and many others. Everybody used to stop dancing when Alfonso started, just to watch."

"You mean he doesn't dance any more?"

Alfonso had been listening to this quietly but then offered, "Ah no, Señor, it has been a long time since I danced. When I was a young man I used to go to dances. But when I got married and the first child came along, I couldn't spend my time going out at night. That's for young men."

"Did you drink in those days?"

"Yes Señor, and I gave up drinking then too."

Martin poured himself another shot of rum, even though he was already feeling a little woozy. He quickly washed it down with the last of the beer, as if that might cool him off. He knew that was illusion though, that it was the alcohol that was making him sweat.

The group sat in silence. Finally, Alfonso said, "I think I'll go to sleep." He chuckled. "You know we farmers go to bed early because we don't have electricity—and we get up early. Have to milk the cows first thing."

Martin sighed, "I guess I will too." The beer was gone, and he did not feel like going to the store for more. Drinking the warm rum with no chaser did not sound interesting. And he was tired of brushing mosquitos away.

Elena went off to her cot, and Martin turned into the pitch-dark room. He stumbled against the edge of the bed and hurt his shin. Taking off his shoes, he lay on the mattress with his clothes on, having the vague idea they might keep bedbugs or other vermin off. Not that he'd seen any, but the blanket and uncovered pillow didn't seem to have been washed in a long time.

He lay quietly then, listening, feeling that perhaps his eyes would adjust and he would be able to see something. But that didn't happen. The room remained in pitch darkness. It was almost like the deep interior of a cave. Martin heard Alfonso groan once as he turned. There was a rustling sound from Elena's direction.

Then came the first scutterings, scamperings of tiny clawed feet, soon followed by squeaking. Martin had lain in bed before listening to the scurrying of tiny feet, in the upstairs sleeping loft of his grandparents' farmhouse, in the high ceiling hostel room he had used in India while doing research for his dissertation, in Laotian houses on stilts. He had even been nipped once by a rat deep in the night. But in those other places there had always been some kind of light. Also, the number of scurrying feet seemed to have been fewer, at least in retrospect. Here in the blackness of the shack on a Latin mini-*finca*, the sounds of the rodents' activity increased in variety and number very rapidly. Soon there was not only the sound of running feet, but also the sound of tiny bodies bumping and high-pitched squeaking from different directions. He tried to visualize what was going on. He decided that, apart from running here and there, the rodents were fighting and fucking. Territorialism and reproduction, he mused. But he didn't think of it calmly. As the noise increased, he could imagine some of the fights spilling out of holes in the wall or ceiling, and tiny furry bodies, still locked in combat or intercourse, falling on him. He raised to a sitting position and stared as hard as he could in the hopes of seeing something. No form came into vision. He listened for movement by one of the other sleepers but heard nothing.

He sat. Nothing fell. The night scufflers continued. He dozed, but was later awakened by a new outbreak of rodent passion. It subsided, and he dozed again, and finally the outline of the door frame began to emerge. Dawn was coming. He listened, but the walls and ceiling had become quiet again. Then he heard Alfonso stir on the porch. Martin swung his legs off the bed.

Elena was speaking as Martin steered the Datsun around the turns, climbing back up toward the mesa. Although still in sunlight, one could see the clouds forming blackly far ahead. She said, "I never heard so many rats before. Sometimes one or so, but not with the walls and ceiling full of them. Alfonso said they came down to the coast from the mountains because it's too dry this year and their favorite food is scarce there."

Martin looked at the lowering clouds and couldn't imagine dryness in that country. He said, "Well, it was an experience. I was afraid I'd get bitten."

"Oh they don't bite. They're not city rats; they come from the forest."

"I take it you didn't get much sleep either."

"No, I'm not used to such commotion at night. We don't have rats in my house in San Rafael."

"What about Alfonso; how does he manage?"

"Oh, he said he's gotten used to them. And he's not scared of them because they don't bite."

Martin chuckled, "Ah, the bucolic pleasures."

She put her hand on his leg. "I'm sorry that it bothered you so much, that you didn't want to stay another night."

"That's okay, there didn't seem to be a lot to do there anyway. And whatever else, I didn't want to go through another night like that. Did you?"

The first drops of rain hit the windshield, and the road soon became greasy. Martin slowed down and concentrated more on his driving. She lit a cigarette and blew the smoke out the window. Martin decided to leave his open a little longer also, even though the first drops of rain were coming in.

Elena answered, "Well, not especially. I don't like rats much either, but I'm more used to country living than you, I think. I could have stayed on. Then I would have fixed you some more real country food."

Martin was pleased with the thought that at least he had escaped more fried bananas, rice, and black beans. Probably the best thing there, he thought, was Alfonso's pressed cheese. He said, "That's alright. I appreciated what you did fix. And don't worry about me. I'm alright. A sleepless night won't make that much difference."

Indeed it wouldn't, he thought. In fact, since the divorce he could hardly remember a night in which he hadn't spent most of his time tossing restlessly.

By then they had driven into the first dense black cloud. It was difficult to distinguish the ground, the rain sheet merging into the glistening leaves on the side of the road. Martin slowed to a creep. Both he and Elena closed their windows except for a crack at the top of each. With her tobacco smoke, it would have become insufferable otherwise. Even so, the air inside the car quickly became thick, and the moisture accumulated so much that the inside of the windshield kept fogging up. Martin reached up to wipe it with a rag he had brought. Elena quickly asked for it. "I can do that, you've got enough to do the driving."

Ah yes, he thought, the Latin helpmate again. The women in this country were molded differently. They would help their man whatever. He let her take over the job. After a pause, she said, "I don't think you liked the weekend very much. And I wanted you to have a good time."

He didn't feel very good about it, but since he hadn't made up his mind definitely anyway, he decided there was no point making her feel bad. He said, "Oh that's alright, Elena, some things work out and others don't. You just have to take the good with the bad." Even as he said it, Martin realized how mushy and devious his pronouncement was, that in truth it would be unlikely indeed that he would continue seeing this plump Latin divorcée any longer. Not specifically because of the weekend, but she wasn't so great anyway. He must have been looking for an excuse, he realized.

The rain became so intense he turned on his lights and for a bit thought of driving to the side of the road to wait it out. But the thought of getting back, of getting the weekend over, pushed him on. He slowed yet again, shifting down to second gear, and peering with utmost concentration into the sheet of water ahead.

\* \* \* \* \*

Martin returned to Los Angeles and rented an apartment in Las Colinas. The house in West Los Angeles was sold and he got his half, minus several legal and realtor's fees. There were a few more unpleasant incidents but he finally got rid of lawyers, and the memory of Constance began to fade. There were times indeed when he thought the time spent with her had been no more than a nightmare.

In her place, there came a series of ladies, all of whom also seemed chimerical in a way, drifting into his life for a brief time then drifting out, usually without his understanding why. He met most at singles parties, groups dedicated to providing circumstances for widowed or divorced people to meet. There were some widowed ladies, but they were rare compared with those who were spinning aimlessly after divorce actions. The idea of the singles groups was to get around the vulgarities of the bar scene, the "meat market."

Most groups met on Friday or Saturday nights from eight to eleven in the social halls of churches or in large private houses. After paying an entrance fee of $5 to $10, one moved in to the snack tables, where cheese, wine, beer, crackers, and veggie sticks were served. Individuals munched celery sticks and cheese chunks while trying to hold conversations with others nearby, constantly checking the surrounding group for eye contact or appearance. If it wasn't a meat market, it was a combination meat and eye market, Martin thought.

In any event, Martin did meet several ladies at such meetings. One of the first was Norma Guilford, a TV freak. He was at the Unitarian Church Hall early that night and met her before the crowd got dense. She was good looking with long black hair that seemed natural. Martin figured she must be in her early to mid forties. He was going to a party of the son of a long-time female friend later that night and asked Norma to go along. It seemed to him that they had a good time together. In any event, she called him that first night as soon as he got home after leaving her off. She told him how much she had enjoyed the evening. They went out together several times more, but it soon became clear that what she really liked to do was watch TV. Each time he came to pick her up, the set was on, and he presumed she had just gotten up from watching it to open the door. Whenever they returned from anywhere, she would immediately turn on the set. She would usually disappear briefly into the bathroom, returning shortly to seat herself in front of the flickering eye. Lacking anything else to do during her absence, he would more often than not be staring at the screen when she came back. She would sit close enough to convince him that she wanted to neck and he would put his arm around her. After some kisses and restricted feels, she would say she was tired and needed to go to bed. So far as he could make out, "going to bed" meant by herself.

Then a couple of weeks after they had started going together, she made a change in the routine. Instead of just cleaning herself and/or urinating, she also put on a robe before coming back. And instead of merely sitting close though side by side, she turned sideways and leaned her back against him. He noted that from that position she could still see the tube. "What's on?" she asked.

"Cops and robbers," he answered, aware in a general way that it was the usual supercilious police investigator browbeating citizens. He disliked this type of show so much that he never watched them at home.

She said, "Oh, that's Bill Brady of 'On the Streets.' Do you want to see it?"

"No, I don't care for it. It was just on."

"I'll try the other channels."

When she leaned forward, her robe opened enough that he could see her bra. She switched channels until she got "The Love Cruise." Modishly dressed people were weaving in and out of groups on a vacation liner, flirting, dancing, laughing, talking. Romance. It took a little mental adjusting to switch from the violence and abrasive interchanges of "Streets" to the constant, vacuous flirtation of "Cruise." Martin soon distanced himself from that image also. He turned his attention to Norma, who seemed to be leaning against him in complete relaxation even while keeping her eyes on the flicker. When he would kiss her, she would momentarily take her glance away from the electronic romancing.

He felt uneasy that she didn't turn away from the image completely, but his cock was so hard by that time that he kept on.

He was surprised that, even when she was on her back and he above her, she was still peeking at the set between kisses. He finally asked, "How about turning it off?"

"Let's just turn the sound off. I want to see the end." For a moment he considered quitting, enough that his cock started to soften. He leaned back so she could stretch to turn down the volume, but when she returned to the same position, he moved over her again and put one arm under her back. After all, it had been months since he had been with a woman, he thought, and it was getting harder and harder to work up enough fantasies to successfully get an ejaculation by masturbation. The soundless voyage continued, and she peeked periodically while he kissed and explored her with his hands. She even returned his kisses, though with no great passion. Even so, he thought, that was pretty good of her. He thought of the tales he had heard in his burgeoning manhood of prostitutes reading magazines while being screwed.

Then the electronic couple were reconciled, fellow passengers and elaborately costumed ships' officers raised champagne glasses, and the show was over. Martin thought that she would then turn the set off, though he did not suggest it out loud. He couldn't figure out whether she was trying to avoid going any further in lovemaking or whether she just did everything while watching TV. For a moment he thought that it might be interesting to actually do it while watching the tube, or at least while letting her do so. He knew if he didn't concentrate on the face and body of his partner that he couldn't come.

She did not turn off the set, though she made no effort to break away. Martin kissed her deep, extending his tongue as far as he could inside. Again, although she responded little, she did not resist. He leaned back, "Want to make love?"

He had learned quite a while back that you could only "fuck" women after you had done it several times, that in fact a lot of them liked the word, though they were usually reluctant to use it. Anyway, one started out by talking about "making love." She looked at him with slightly dis-engaged eyes and, after thinking about it a moment, said, "You really want to?"

That set him back. Though he had hardly expected a passionate re-sponse by that time, he certainly hadn't expected that remark. In fact, it left him speechless for a time. Finally, he said simply, "Sure."

She thought about it a little longer, then said, "I guess it's alright." Then she added, "If you really want to."

That was the least passionate acceptance he could remember. It wasn't a refusal, but Jesus Christ and Mary, no wonder guys sometimes had trouble getting it up. Anyway, he was not prepared at this stage to drop the process. He repeated, "Sure I do," and reached for the belt of her robe.

"Let's go in the bedroom," she said, to his great surprise. What would happen to the TV program, he wondered as he stood up. Would it con-tinue if they weren't there to watch it? It reminded him of that philo-sophical question that had intrigued Amelia, did the tree make a sound when it fell in the forest if no one was there to hear it?

In any event, they made it to the bedroom and did it. It wasn't fantas-tic, but what the hell, he thought, how often is it fantastic the first time? She wanted to be on top, which was alright with him, he figuring he hadn't had any for so long that he could have come suspended by his feet from the ceiling. And she had apologized about the size of her breasts when he reached up to cup them; they weren't minuscule, though, considerably larger than the prunes of Marsha or the apricots of Constance, but not, of course, like the canteloupes of Anne Marie. Surprisingly, despite the long period of celibacy, Martin had to work to come with Norma, but he did manage it. Her being on top, some of the jism ran down his leg.

That was the end with her. Martin had thought it would be pleasant to sleep over, but she made it very clear after their disentanglement that she didn't expect him to stay there through the night. And when he was in the doorway facing her in preparation to leave, she said, "I have to get back. I'm leaking. You men fill us women with your juice, then we have to clean up."

Martin gazed at her, considering the difference in perceptions be-tween the sexes. To him the juice that females received from males was the basis of new life, and the fact that females had to clean up some-times merely indicated they had gotten more than they needed. So any female who treasured her motherhood, as had this one and most other divorcees he had met, could hardly complain about male juice, messy though it might be.

Driving back, Martin was cold and disconsolate. It wasn't so much physical as a new wave of loneliness. It seemed so difficult to work things out with a woman, he thought. If there were some things that one got better at through life, interaction between the sexes wasn't one, he thought gloomily.

He waited a week before calling, subconsciously hoping she would call him but secretly believing she wouldn't. She hadn't indicated that he shouldn't call, so he would make one last effort. There must be some meaning to human interactions, he kept telling himself, even between male and female. She answered after two rings, probably just up from the tube, he thought. "Hello, this is Martin Neumann."

Pause, serious tone, merging on funereal: "Ye-es."

"Could I ask you something?"

Pause, cautiousness, electronic voices in the background. "That depends. What do you want?"

"Nothing heavy. And I don't want to lay a trip on you. I assume you don't want to see me again. Is that so?"

No pause, but slowly, "Ye-es."

"Well, of course what you do is your own affair. I don't have any rights over you. But you know it's difficult for guys sometimes when women drop them without any explanation. Men are usually in the position of trying to read the minds of their girlfriends, and it's not easy. So, I'm just calling to find out what happened. Did I do something you didn't like?"

The pause this time seemed endless. Martin could almost imagine he could hear her breathing. He added, to fill in the gap, "I remember you said when we first met that you didn't play games. I mean, all I want to know is whether I did anything that bothered you. And believe me, I do not intend to continue bothering you. If you don't want to see me again, I'll tear up the telephone number here and now, and that will be the end of it."

The more he entreated, the more Martin felt like a masochist, as if he were really guilty of something horrendous. Nevertheless, he said again, "Do you want to tell me what I did?"

Long silence, then, "No, I don't."

Another pause on her end, long, long, long. Finally he said, "Okay, good-bye."

Norma was only the first. They flitted in and out of his life like tropical butterflies in a forest clearing, why in and why out he practically never learned. There was Sharon MacDonald, a divorced schoolteacher. She had great voluptuous breasts, which were particularly impressive because she was comparatively short. And she liked to kiss, which she early demonstrated to him and discussed at considerable length, noting that he seemed to like kissing as well. They went together for a few weeks, and to Martin they seemed to get along well enough. At least, apart from the fact that she would sometimes start dozing when they were sitting late, they seemed to have good enough times. Once when their kissing got particularly passionate and she made no attempt to stop him from fondling her breasts, he asked if she would like to make love. There was a pause, and she told him it was her period. Ah well, he thought, he could wait that long. What else could he do? But they got no more intimate until he figured out what seemed would be a perfect solution, inviting her out to a lodge at Rocky Desert State Park. He was pleasantly surprised when she accepted almost immediately, reading in her agreement a willingness to be intimate. The trip there, and the daytime activities, seemed to go well. It happened when they returned to their room after eating. There were two beds. And even though they continued to kiss and fondle until they went to bed, she got in the other. He took the initiative by asking, "Wouldn't you like to come in to my bed?"

Pulling the covers around her neck, she said, "No, I don't think so. I'm tired."

Ah, shades of Amelia and all the wives with headaches and other discomforts. "Okay," he said and turned over.

It wasn't until they were alone on the lodge patio after breakfast the next morning that they discussed it. He figured that was a good time since they had just eaten, and people were supposed to be at their most amiable when their stomachs were full. He started again. "I don't want to give you a hard time, Sharon. I've had a good time with you but I don't quite understand what happened. Do you mind talking about it?"

And though she did not appear to be excited about the idea, she did not say no. "If you want."

"I heard you tossing a lot last night. Didn't you sleep well?"

"No, probably from being in a strange bed."

"I didn't either." He thought as he heard himself saying it that it sounded as if he usually slept well, which of course wasn't so, hadn't been ever since the divorce. Rolling and tossing had become a way of getting through the nights. But perhaps, in his defense he thought, he had rolled and tossed somewhat more the night just past. He studied the big-busted lady and decided to come on directly, no beating around the bush. "You know, Sharon, I think it's usual when a woman goes off to spend a weekend with a guy to sleep with him. Isn't that your understanding?"

She looked slightly unhappy, and he regretted having put her in that position. But what the hell, how would he ever learn what was going on if he never asked anyone? The women he met certainly didn't volunteer much.

She refused to answer his question directly, saying, "I'm just kind of old-fashioned. I don't go to bed with men right away. I have to know the guy first."

Was a month right away? he wondered. It all depended. There had been a time, in his young manhood, when a year, two years, any length of time before getting the union socially validated was not enough. But certainly that had changed. Most of the women he had gone to bed with since his first divorce had been willing after two, three times out. Anyway, he was not about to turn the talk into a confrontation. He said, "That seems reasonable, though I suppose what different individuals consider getting to know someone varies. We've been seeing each other for four or five weeks, haven't we? I had the idea we had gotten to know something about each other. Oh not everything, surely, but quite a bit."

What an understatement, he thought; anyone who figured he knew the breed after ten, twenty, thirty years would have to be out of his mind. And yet, one continued to try. Martin went on, "And I thought we got along pretty well, didn't you?"

"It's been alright. I've enjoyed your company. You're a very interesting man."

And it continued through three cups of coffee until it began to sound like a record, already played many times. But as though he couldn't help it, he had to ask the same fateful question: "I mean, has there been something about me that displeased you?"

She studied him long, and he said, "I mean anything physical, or what I did, or anything?"

Another long pause, and she said, "There is one thing. I don't really like the way you smack your lips together. It's like a very old person."

That was one of the last vestiges of the stroke, that when his throat had been paralyzed he had almost choked on saliva many times. He had developed a habit of sucking in the liquid and then consciously swallowing it, along with a smacking movement of his lips. The paralysis had long gone, but he hadn't kicked the smacking habit. In a way though, he rued, she was right, it was like an old person because that was what he was becoming. Sure, young people had strokes on occasion, but that eventuality was certainly correlated with age. He looked at her and smiled, "I'm sorry, but you know you're right."

Still he didn't quit. Perhaps he would have if he didn't invariably wake up with a hard-on. So the procession continued as if there were an endless supply of searching females after something he was incapable of providing. He put an ad in the local *Singles Register* that produced a stack of letters. He met eight or ten of the most promising, but there was no spark. He hadn't asked for photos because he had decided from experience that most such were unreliable. Respondents invariably put in the best they had from the past ten years or so, and the resemblance to the living person was usually remote. But by not asking for photos, he got a collection of ladies who were unattractive physically, not to mention sporting many unusual habits. Practically all were divorcées. The one who stood out most was a lady in her forties who he thought of afterward as the Snickers Freak. She met him outside her small apartment in Venice. That in itself was a little unusual, but not so much that he was concerned about it. Who could know why she didn't want him inside her little single's pad? Who could know what kind of unusual companion or strange sight might be waiting, or nothing but her mental irregularities?

She was trimmer than most he had met, in fact she had a relatively well-proportioned figure. Her face showed the creases of age and sad experiences, and her hair was taken care of in the usual manner of women in middling age in American culture, the gray tinted out. As he studied it, Martin thought that it was a little unusual in being black. Most graying women seemed to opt for blond or red; why he wasn't exactly sure. Anyway, the hair of the Snickers Freak made an interesting variation, and the dying job seemed to have been done professionally.

She suggested they go for a walk along the beach, that that was her chief pleasure in living on the edge of the Pacific in that offbeat corner of Los Angeles. It didn't sound like a bad idea, since Martin had always felt pleasurably conversational while walking. So they headed north toward Santa Monica, he keeping his pace to hers. They went through the usual list of topics for middle-aged singles in the '80s, their jobs, what they did for pleasure, where they came from, what they thought of California, their divorces. Time passed not unpleasantly as they continued for half an hour, an hour, an hour and a half. Then Martin said, "You know, I'm getting kind of hungry. How about you ?"

"I'm not, but if you are, we could stop somewhere to get something. I could sit with you."

Well, that was a little different, he thought. Very few women he met these days who were younger than fifty conceived of fixing food, but most were ready to eat most of the time, so long as it was served in a restaurant or you could buy it already prepared. He looked at his companion's trim body. "I suppose you're on a diet."

"No, I just don't eat much regular food during the week."

His curiosity was piqued. This was certainly a different style. "What *do* you eat?"

"Snickers."

He waited for her to continue, but when she didn't, he said, "You mean the candy bar?" He was trying to recall if he had eaten any and what they were like. He seemed to remember the name from his child-hood and that it was some kind of rectangular bar of peanuts, covered with caramel and chocolate. The name *Mars Bar* stuck in his memory as similar, but without the peanuts.

She answered, "Sure, Snickers Bars."

He tried to digest that. There were plenty of fast food freaks out there, but this seemed to be quite different. It was bad enough to eat burgers and fries and donuts and cokes all the time, but at least one did get some of the nutrition basics from them. But a single kind of candy bar all the time was difficult for him to conceive as providing even minimal nutrition.

He probed, "You mean every day, that you don't eat anything else?"

He knew he was overdoing the inquisitiveness so was pleased when she answered without seeming offended, though he thought he did no-tice a tone of caution in her voice.

"That's all I eat during the week, but I eat raw vegetables on the week-ends."

Wow, he thought, a real food freak! How many different kinds of freaks were there? But still he didn't want to make the lady feel bad, knowing already that this was the first and last time he would see her. He had an image of carrying cardboard boxes of Snickers to her door when he came to pick her up. But that was just too much. He had long given up the idea that perfect compatibility was likely, but he couldn't reconcile himself to such disparity of behavior. She broke into his thoughts. "I know what you're thinking. You think that's too much of one thing, eating nothing but Snickers. I know what other people think. And I try to eat other things. This morning, for instance, I ate a graham bun with a glass of milk, trying to satisfy my appetite so I wouldn't eat my mid-morning Snickers. But it didn't do any good. I ate the Snickers also."

Martin started to feel uncomfortable. The poor lady was trying, but what could she do? He had never believed in shaming addicts, and this one was certainly that. He had the sudden quick idea that it might be alright if she ate a variety of candy. He said, "Don't you ever eat any other kind? I mean, like Hershey's Chocolate or Milky Ways or even other sweets like sweet rolls?"

He couldn't imagine that as normalcy, but it sounded better than eating one brand of candy all the time. However, she answered, "No, I just like Snickers. They're so good."

Wow, how could one argue with that! An addiction was an addiction. He tried to say something reassuring. "Well I must say, it doesn't seem to hurt your figure. You seem quite trim."

"I keep up with my exercises. I take aerobic dance classes four times a week."

Suddenly Martin felt that he was in a swamp, that the ground he was walking on had no rigidity. And almost just as quickly he realized that the cause of his feeling, the conversation he was in, was not really unique. He had been in many such during the past three years, and they were invariably with dating partners. Someone had called it the "dating game." But games had rules. And if the interchanges that went on between dating partners, the complex pirouettes and sashays, had any rules, he had never discovered them.

Someone else had said that dating took place in a jungle. "It's a jungle out there, Tarzan," it was said. But a jungle had solidity and things you could touch and see, some kind of reality, even if a sombre green. Martin was aware that the phrase referred to dating as being comparable to dealing with savage beasts. Maybe that was true for females, but the men Martin knew hardly seemed beastly. They might be more anxious for sex than their partners, but very few forced themselves on females. Most, in fact, were not very aggressive, and many were even quite shy. Rather than being lions, most were pussycats. No, the dating game could more logically be compared to a swamp, to a place where there was no solid ground, where double-talk and deception were the rules that were broken almost as fast as they were made. And there were all sorts of bizarre animals in the marsh.

Martin looked at his companion and tried to think of something reassuring to say. Finally he offered, "Well, I must say your diet is unique."

They stopped at a little fish place, where Martin had clam chowder
and a glass of wine while the Snickers Freak had a glass of water. He
never saw her again.

There were several others, and the last was a lesbian with a southern
accent. She was a flight attendant from Memphis. Martin met her on a
flight while going to visit Dan. He didn't know, of course, that she had
a long history of homosexuality. In fact, he felt quite up when she gave
him her phone number. She particularly admired his long silver hair
and beard; the former he had let get longer as the long hair era deep-
ened, and the latter he had grown since his divorce with Constance as
an indication of status change.

In a way, he thought, the encounter with Mary Kimberly was a fulfillment of one of the standard fantasies of the American male, to go out
with an airline stewardess. The image of those ladies being attractive
sexually had been promoted for as long as Martin could remember flying commercial. The stereotype was that they were worldly and ready
for anything. There was an unending series of jokes about them. The
most recent Martin could remember was when a pilot got to cruising
altitude, and setting the winged monster on autopilot, leaned back and
said, "Boy, what I couldn't do with a scotch and a piece of ass." Unfortunately, he had just finished announcing the plane's position to the passengers on the intercom and had failed to turn the switch back to "crew."
His words came out loud and clear in the passenger compartment. A
stewardess in the rear of the plane, who was preparing the first mixed
drinks, started up the aisle rapidly, saying to her colleague, "Oh my god,
he forgot to turn the 'passenger' switch to off." When she was about
halfway up the aisle, an old lady she was passing said in a cracked voice,
"You forgot the scotch, honey."

Ah yes, they were supposed to be urbane and sexy. Moreover, Mary
Kimberly said "you-all" instead of simply "you," and Martin had long
had a weakness for Southern ladies.

They went out together a couple of times, and things seemed to be
going well until they returned from an evening of listening to Dixieland.
They had drunk steadily, and he had to admit that in that respect Mary
certainly had been initiated. If she couldn't drink him under the table,
she certainly had no trouble keeping up with him.

She asked him into her little house, her first as a divorced woman.
Martin had learned that most divorcées moved into apartments after

the community property was divided, or if they had enough, got a condo. Mary was one of the minority who had bought a small house for herself and her son.

Martin, sitting on her couch, was in a warm haze from the booze. She got brandies and sat next to him. One thing was clear, which was that she fulfilled one stereotype—there was nothing shy about her. This wasn't the kind of girl that married dear old dad. He put his arm around her. She seemed to respond. He kissed her. She said, "You know, you're the first man I've been out with for several years."

He didn't really see Mary Kimberly as a lady who stayed home nights, busy with needle-work. "I'm a little surprised. You didn't give me the idea of being a wallflower."

"You don't understand. I didn't say I haven't been out. I just said 'with men.'"

He perked up. Another difference, another kind of freakishness, one that had become acceptable in his lifetime. She was the first such he had become involved with. His curiosity was piqued. "Well, that's different for me in two ways. You're the first flight attendant I've dated, and now the first gay person."

He chuckled, "It's bizarre in a way; though perhaps it sums up my sex life. I began in an age when if you were gay (he figured it inadvisable to use the term *homosexual* with one), you couldn't admit it. And I was almost picked up several times by guys who were out after good-looking boys. But I remained steadfast to my traditional upbringing all these years with indifferent results. And now in my late middle age (Martin still couldn't bring himself to use the term *senior citizen* in reference to himself), I go with a lady gay. Very interesting."

She looked at him expectantly, as if unsure which direction to go. But Martin had gotten his tongue loose by then so it wasn't difficult for him to continue. "So that's the story, eh? One of the questions, of course, which comes up almost immediately is, 'Why me?'"

She reached for her lit cigarette and inhaled deeply. She was a heavy smoker and had laughingly told him early in their acquaintance that she would probably die of cancer. He had inwardly agreed, though he said nothing, having long decided that gratuitous advice was hardly worth the energy of giving it. It did make her kisses less than ideal, however.

Exhaling, she answered, "Oh, I don't know. You just seemed like a nice man, and I have dated a few the last ten years—in between my female lovers." She grinned impishly, "You know, to find out if I was missing anything."

Martin put his arms around her waist until his hands met in front, just below her breasts. She certainly did have a tight, slim figure. "And did you find out you were?"

She sipped from the brandy. "No, not really. A couple of the guys were interesting. But you know that whatever they say, men are just interested in one thing, their own pleasure. And most don't really concern themselves with the needs of their partners. That's one thing about female lovers. They are more considerate, and being female, they can understand their partners' needs better."

He was a little surprised at the direction the conversation was going; even more that, despite her negativism toward his sex, she didn't seem to mind him having his hands on her. He could detect no stiffening or withdrawal. Perhaps it was a part of her personality, that she had sadly or apologetically told him about before, that she was a "people pleaser." He knew this was the age of doing one's own thing, not spending one's energy trying to please others. Anyway, he followed her bent, though trying to bait her a little: "I can certainly agree that females ought to be able to understand females better than males can. After all, males and females are basically different. But what about 'Vive la difference'?" He thought he'd throw in some fancy words. "After all, heterosexual mating requires two sexes. The only way you could have total sexual similarity is with unisexual mating or hermaphroditism, you know, like amoebas and earthworms." He was a little proud of himself for that one, a product of all his years of fast thinking in classroom lectures. In particular, he felt vain about the use of the word *hermaphroditism,* one of those that you didn't often get the opportunity to throw around. He had a vision of two earthworms intertwined, they each fucking on one end and being fucked on the other.

She smiled at him, but she made no effort to respond. He had no illusions that she was interested in a broad discussion of sexuality. Like so many other ladies he had met in his latter-day dating life, she was interested in the here and now, to achieve some kind of state called individual happiness. And comparing oneself to amoebas or earthworms would hardly help for that end in this, the age of psyche stroking. She said, "Anyway, women are more sensitive to each others' needs than men are. And once I switched to women, it's been progressively more difficult to accept the pushiness of men looking for a piece of ass."

What should he do? This wasn't the kind of conversation that led to screwing. He knew that was in the back of his mind, though not in any absolute sense. But still he just couldn't imagine what else a man and a woman would do late at night, sitting on a couch sipping brandy after a good evening together. He was undecided, however, until she put her hand under his and pushed it up toward her breast. He pressed lightly. It wasn't humungus, but of a respectable size and firm like all the other parts of her body.

Their talk slowed, and their gropings and feelings became more active. He got her blouse unbuttoned and undid her bra. She leaned back, and he got on top of her. It all seemed so natural for heterosexual mating, he couldn't imagine her homosexual acts. What did lesbians do, stroke each others' pussies with their hands, rub their pussies against one another, go down on one another?

When he began to undo her skirt, she spoke, "Let's go in on the bed."

Wow, it might still take place. He said, "Sure," and got up.

Sitting on the edge of the bed, he took off his shoes and clothes and threw them on a pile in the corner while she did the same except for her panties. Maybe she wanted him to take them off, he thought. When she lay back, he put one hand on one breast while kissing her. While he was fumbling at her panties, she stiffened for the first time. He stopped. She said, "I'd rather leave them on. I shouldn't anyway. I just had some tests. I don't think it's cancer, but until I'm sure, I shouldn't have sex."

He pulled his hand back, propping his head with it. "Oh, I'm sorry; you must be worried."

"Not really. Like I said, I don't think it'll be positive. But I should wait. I hope it doesn't make you too uncomfortable."

He felt that old familiar softening of his cock. "Oh no, I understand. I just had no way of knowing."

"You couldn't. And I'm sorry if it bothers you."

He could readjust. After all, sexual encounters were always so iffy that anyone who couldn't turn it off and on at the drop of a hat would soon be in deep trouble, he thought. God, when he considered all the hard-ons he had had that had come to naught, what difference would another make?

She broke into his thoughts, "Do you mind if I try something? It's different."

What wouldn't be? he thought. This woman was perhaps the culmination of unpredictability in a long line of unpredictable females. Another direction would hardly be bothersome. He said, "No, I'm open to anything."

He had a vision of her going down on him. She said, "You're not really a judgmental guy, are you?"

"I guess not. I figure there are all kinds of ways to accomplish a goal, what we used to call in my youth 'to skin a cat,' and believe me, I'm not at all convinced that my way is right."

She reached over to the bedstand drawer and brought out a pink plastic tube about ten inches long, rounded on one end and with a screw cap and switch on the other.

Wow, a dildo, the first he had seen since Constance had shyly brought hers out and ultimately gave him a demonstration.

Mary turned on the switch, and the little tube began to buzz, making a low vibration, enough, it seemed, to satisfy female needs. They evidently did not need a big horse thrashing around on top of them to stimulate their tiny clit, he thought.

Martin expected her to take off her panties then and poke the battery-powered tube between the cleft. Instead, she reached over and began running it up and down his belly and thighs. The tiny vibrations were different, but hardly stimulating. He couldn't imagine fantasizing with the little machine, and it had always been impossible for him to ejaculate without some kind of thrusting. In fact, he had never been able to come by being gone down on. She worked her way down to his cock and balls and poked around tentatively. His penis was not totally limp, but it wouldn't harden either. She said, "How do you like it?"

"Well, it is different. And as I said before, I like new experiences. But there's nothing sexy about it for me."

She stopped then and, holding the little buzzing machine in front of her, said, "I don't really think you like it."

"To repeat, it doesn't do anything for me sexually."

"You probably don't like me to do it either."

He shrugged, thinking how bizarre the scene must appear. "What can I say? It evidently does something for you, so okay. I'll just lay here and watch." He leaned back and put his hands behind his head.

They got together three or four more times and, surprisingly enough, to both evidently, they did screw successfully. By the time they got to it, Martin had been impressed so thoroughly that men didn't try hard enough to satisfy women that he worked his ass off. In fact, when they had gotten her exercise leotards and his clothes off the first time, he had the very devil to come, pushing up into her straddled crotch and seemingly pumping forever. Before he came, she tensed up and broke into a series of quivers, then relaxed while he drove to his climax. It was certainly thorough for both, though Martin wondered afterward if sex ought to be that much work.

Then she stopped, for reasons that he never understood, indicating clearly the last time that she would sleep in the other bed.

He took her to the airport for her return home the last time (she could get all the free flights she wanted on her days off) in the usual state of incomprehension. When she had checked in at the crew gateway, she said, "Come on, I'll get you a drink."

They sat in the plastic airport lounge and soon were served Bloody Marys. It was only ten o'clock, but the occasion seemed to call for some kind of excess. They sat watching their drinks, sipping occasionally, and even more occasionally exchanging glances. As was not unusual, Martin broke the silence: "Well, Mary, I'm sorry to see you go under the circumstances."

She flashed her usual impish grin, though it was subdued.

"It was fun while it lasted. I shall remember you as my California horny toad."

And while Martin didn't feel devastated at this latest breakup, there was a slight feeling of sadness. People who have been intimate, even if for only a few months, and who part forever, probably always have some feeling of loss. He studied her as she took out another cigarette and lit up. That was one habit he would not miss. He spoke again, "You know Mary, one of the toughest things I have with breakups is that I very rarely understand why. Things seem to be going well between me and my partner and all of a sudden she decides that's the end. It's very puzzling. You know there is the widespread belief that men never understand women, and I must admit that it has come to that with me, more as I get older. And maybe it shouldn't bother me, but it does. I keep thinking there must be some logical way to analyze these affairs."

She appeared a little reluctant, but spoke anyway. "Well, that was what I was telling you last night. You remember, from the Jungian seminar I went to, that people have these two components, analytic and emotional, and that men tend to have more the first and women the second."

He did remember, even though it had been very late, and he had become quite tired after discussing their relationship for three or four hours. As best he could remember, they had reached no conclusion. He said, "Sure, I remember."

"Well, as I told you then, I'm very much an emotional person, very feminine, and you are very analytic, very masculine. In fact, just what you're saying now indicates that. You can't have a feeling about our relationship; you have to try to analyze it."

Martin became a little irritated. He knew little enough about Jung's particular belief, though he had the idea that Jung, like most other psychoanalysts, had pretty much made up things off the top of his head. Moreover, there was every kind of crazy guru and seminar up at Big Sur where she had gone. That section of the coast was devoted to offbeat ideologies to promote individual fulfillment.

He said, "I don't know what you mean by saying I'm all analytic and that I lack feeling. I think I have the complete range, from deep love to deep hate. Isn't that feeling?"

She looked uncomfortable, and he felt sorry, for he had known early in their acquaintance that she was really not comfortable arguing issues. She just said, "It's not the same thing."

Martin made a last stab to abstract meaning from their breakup, saying, "I mean, is there something I did or something about me that you don't like?"

She paused long, but then with a very serious expression, "No, you're a very interesting man. And I've enjoyed being with you, but you just don't fulfill all my needs."

The realtor, Helen Klausner, was driving up the sweeping freeway north of Escondido. The countryside was spectacular, even for California, steep hills almost the size of small mountains, mostly covered with green chaparral (the rainy season), marked periodically by lavender flowering bushes. Large boulders stuck out on some hillsides. Other hillsides, just as steep, were cultivated with avocado trees on the upper slopes and citrus on the lower ones.

Martin said, "It's incredible how steep the hillsides are that are used for cultivation. You never see the trees planted in the bottomland."

"It's because the frosts settle there. Also, I think the trees like good drainage, and it is best on the sides of hills."

Martin was still surprised how knowledgeable the woman was about avocado cultivation despite never having dealt with rural property before. She had done her homework, as she had said she would. No, he didn't have any worries about the professional competency of Helen Klausner, whom his colleague, Randy Cliff, had recommended. He said, "Do you know what those blue flowering shrubs are?"

"No, I've been noticing them also, but I'm not really a nature specialist. There is a book in our office though on the wildflowers of California, and I can look it up."

That was another thing about her; she never tried to bluff. If she didn't know something, she admitted it. It gave him a feeling of comfort to be dealing with someone so honest.

The Datsun came to the top of another long, sweeping hill with an even more spectacular panorama in all directions. She pointed to a particularly high group of mountains, perhaps twenty or thirty miles to the northeast. "That's Palomar, the mountain with the observatory. There's a large national park there."

"Wow, I do believe this is one of the most impressive corners of California I've seen, certainly for being agricultural country. It looks a lot like northern Italy or the cultivated mountain areas of Spain."

"It is very nice, still not completely built up."

Martin could see a wide-winged hawk wheeling along one scrub hillside in effortless sliding movements, looking for rodent motion. Handsome, free creature. No wonder men had looked at it enviously for so long. And though one couldn't deny the achievement of the flying machine, it had none of the smooth control of the coursing bird of prey.

"What did you think of that last place?" she asked.

"It was fine, in impeccable condition, but perhaps more elegant than I need. I'll be living in it alone, you know."

"I agree. I didn't think it was necessarily for you, but it was worth stopping to see, for comparison, don't you think?"

This was the third time they had gone out looking for a place. She had started just after the holiday season was over, and he had to admit that she had narrowed in on his needs fast. Each time they had gone out, the places were more to his liking. He said, "Sure, I didn't mind it. And I won't say it's completely out of the question, but I doubt that I'll want to make an offer. It was in first-class condition, but the price reflected that fact too. I don't think I want to go that high."

Martin did not want to build a dynasty, an avocado empire, and he didn't want to overextend himself financially. He was comfortable from the sale of his other real estate and the liquidation of the house of his marriage, but he intended to keep it that way. All he wanted was a comfortable place in a secluded area where he could write and grow things.

She said, "I think you're right. It was overpriced. But that was just the asking price, you know. I'm sure they would accept a counter offer."

He looked at her before he answered, noticing again the very full breasts, sagging slightly. She was certainly in her forties, having been married twice, but still fairly well preserved. Her hair was dyed, which was typical. She had on a fairly stylish dress and wore high-heeled boots. Arnold Deutsch had used such boots as a tip-off that a woman was advertising her sexual availability. Could be, Martin thought. He had a flicker of interest in the beginning, thinking of asking her out. But it had passed and a sense of comfort had taken over. He realized then that he had quit the search for the warm, curved body with the juicy cleft. His cock still stiffened most mornings when he awoke, and he would fantasize briefly. But since there was no nearby female, it happened less and less, and a sense of peace like nothing he could remember was settling over him.

Helen broke into his reverie. "Anyway, I think this place we are going to now will please you. It looked very good when I was there the other day."

She turned the Datsun in at an intersection where there was a cluster of indeterminate buildings. On the roadside was a row of rural mailboxes and a large sign advertising "Cold Beer." Martin could see no establishment open. Only one car was parked next to the cluster of buildings. She turned the car up the hill to the left and began winding her way in on a twisting, potted road. It's condition indicated low traffic. After several turns and a steady climb, they came over a rise and saw a small house, barely visible through the numerous trees, which Martin figured were citrus. "I think that's the place," she said and turned in.

It was a one-story stucco house, facing a large expanse of asphalt and the citrus grove in front. On one side were several eucalyptus trees, plus several Italian cypress trees. A large concrete pool that was mostly empty was on the other side. It had collected rainwater and junk and was filled with tadpoles and leafy mud in the bottom. On two sides of the house there were luxuriant avocado trees down the hillside as far as Martin could see. On three sides there was a continuous vista of green hills and valleys, pocked occasionally by clusters of residential buildings. She stopped the car and they got out.

"Wow," he said, "what a view."

She glanced at the fact sheet she was carrying. "It says a 260-degree view."

"I believe it. It's one of the greatest I've seen in inland California." He looked all around and saw that there was a house across the road, just barely visible through citrus and avocado trees. Even so, the sense of privacy was great. What a place to write, he thought. And from the looks of how everything was thriving, it wouldn't be bad for growing things either.

No car anywhere in sight. Martin asked, "Can we go inside?"

"The people who live here are tenants, and they were notified. They said someone would be here. But they're not real anxious to show it, I understand. They're afraid if someone buys it, they might have to move."

That was certainly true in his case. He might be interested in it as a tax shelter, but his primary concern was to get a place to live, a hideaway for his later years.

She knocked on the door and was greeted by the barking of feisty dogs. No footsteps materialized, nor was there any other indication of human presence. Just then Martin became aware from the corner of his eye of a large moving body. He turned and saw a big mixed-breed collie coming toward them. "We have a visitor," he said.

She turned and saw it too. "Probably the family dog. Most everyone up here seems to have one. Does it look friendly?"

"It seems undecided, but not particularly belligerent."

He called the dog, holding out his hand. "Here doggie, come on, doggie."

The dog gazed at him for a moment then came slowly and with dignity, though also with measured tail wagging.

"I don't think it's mean," Martin said, continuing to call the dog.

It came to him and smelled his hand delicately. Then it increased its tail wagging and he put his hand on its head. "I think it's a big pussy cat," Martin said, relieved that the encounter had come off so easily. Though he wasn't particularly afraid of dogs, he had a little of that generalized unease toward the descendent of the wolf.

She did not pet the dog, instead turning the door knob.

The door opened. The yapping of the feisty indoor dogs increased. Martin could see them on the couch, in almost uncontrollable agitation, diminutive pygmy Chihuahuas. What a difference domestication had made, he thought, the hundred-pound hairy sheep herder at their rear and the tiny five-pound hairless food dogs inside. The Aztecs had raised them to eat them.

Helen Klausner interrupted his anthropological musings,

"You want to go in? We had their permission."

"I don't know. What do you usually do in a case like this. From watching you, I figured you try doors all the time, no?"

"Usually. You have no idea how many people leave their doors unlocked. Anyway, I think it's okay in this case. At least for a quick lookaround. Probably the lady of the house is out on some errand."

"Alright with me. I'm definitely interested in the place. Obviously you know what can and can't be done. We can just do a quick lookaround."

The little dogs were all mouth, never getting off the couch though yapping ferociously the whole time Martin and the realtor walked around. The house was nothing spectacular, three bedrooms, a pleasant enough living–dining room combination, and an offset kitchen. It was basically clean though and had possibilities, Martin thought. The one thing to its credit was that there were large windows in all rooms but the bedrooms, which permitted views of the stupendous chaparral hillsides interspersed with avocado groves. Almost without conscious thought, Martin decided he would put picture windows in each of the bedrooms.

They went outside to walk around the house. Here and there were boards, posts, and concrete abutments lying helter-skelter, evidence of previous residents' efforts to create something, now in neglect. He would put it in order, he knew, disposing of what had become junk and bringing the overgrown plants under control. In one place behind the house he would put in a vegetable garden and in many corners, flowers. Martin could hardly control his growing excitement.

They came back to the front, facing the hillside grove.

"What do you think?" she asked.

"I'm very interested. It's very close to what I was looking for." Martin could see himself hammering away at the keyboard of the old Royal, stopping occasionally to glance off at the green hills to the north and east. Ah, words would flow. "Well, is there anything else you'd like to see?"

"Just the grove. I'd like to go down the hill a way. Would you?"

"No, I'll stay here. I really don't know anything about avocados anyway."

The boots certainly had nothing to do with willingness to go off in the country, Martin thought, as he headed for the hillside. He entered between the twisting, spreading trees, which were covered with waxy leaves. He immediately noticed the abundance of suspended fruit on almost every tree. Testicle fruit, *aguacatl*, he remembered from having once looked up the origin of the name for a lecture. The Aztecs had named it so because of its shape and the way it hung. Very appropriate, he thought, and so descriptive compared with the innocuous names of European fruit.

Another bizarre musing drifted into his consciousness. How appropriate for him to be literally surrounded in his declining years by the symbol of that organ that had driven him so relentlessly for forty-five-plus years. Now at last, surrounded by thousands of reminders, he would be able to contemplate it without passion as nothing more than symbol.

He wandered down the wet earth perhaps eight or ten rows until he was totally surrounded by the subtropical trees. There was the illusion then that avocado trees went on interminably in all directions, not the mere five acres specified on the real estate listing. Martin stepped over and fondled one of the nubby dark green fruits and the sensation was very pleasant. He had a deep feeling that he would take root on that hillside and the hilltop above where the house was located. He had come to the end of a driven life.

Hurrying back to the top, he literally ran to where the realtor was sitting on a concrete wall. She turned, "What did you think of the grove?"

He spoke with a surety that had not often occurred in his life, "I want the place."

# CHAPTER 13

There was no one in the waiting room when Martin entered. It must have been late, though with the constant illumination of the Transition Offices that was hard to tell. He sat down across from Oldenberg's office door, ruminating on the great expanse of experiential time that had passed since he had come there first, when he had cautiously walked up the black, velvety corridor toward the beckoning light. It hadn't been that long in linear time, about three weeks, but he had gone through the lives of several individuals and finally his own, not to mention flipping ideas with afterworld persons. Incredible, he thought, more incredible in realization than the first inkling had been.

He thought of going up to Oldenberg's door and knocking, when it opened and the Transitioner greeted him. "Have you been here long, Martin?"

"No, not in linear time, though in cerebral wanderings more than a lifetime. I was musing on the incredible sights and sounds I have seen and heard these last few weeks—you know, the experience of viewing Life Videos."

"I suppose much of it has been strange. I noticed in the last couple of get-togethers after you had viewed your own life that you were a little edgy." Oldenberg waved with the sheaf of papers he was holding, pointing toward his office. "Why don't you come in, and we can talk about it. You know we have to come to a decision tonight."

Martin got up. "Sure, we may as well get going. I'm sure you are tired already. Probably been at meetings all day."

He walked into the office as the Transition Master stood to one side.

Oldenberg went in the direction of his desk chair, indicating the visitor's chair at its side. Martin quickly got the picture. Despite the otherworld person's easygoing nature, this meeting was to be business-like. They were not to dally in comfort on the couch, to sip sherry or Nilgiri coffee. Martin also quickly noticed that Hanson was not there. This was to be a straight-out negotiation between him and the Transition Master.

"Sit down, please." Oldenberg pointed to the chair, still maintaining his good mannered calmness. The only distinct behavioral difference that Martin could notice was that the Transitioner seemed yet more weary.

Both seated themselves. With his hands flat on the dossier in front of him Oldenberg began. "You know the primary purpose of our meeting tonight, Martin. And we must get to it very shortly. However, I think we can take a few minutes to go over your final episode, if you wish. And apart from my personal interest, it will be of use in helping decide on your next stage, eh?"

Ah, time was indeed becoming brief, Martin rued. His mind couldn't help drifting forward, wondering how he would indeed feel in the new incarnation. The curse and blessing of humankind, he thought, the ability to project in time, both backward and forward. But no, he wasn't there yet. He must use what time remained in idea flipping. It might be the last time.

Oldenberg prodded, "So what did you find out in that last period, Martin?"

The earthling shook the cobwebs out, quickly organizing his thoughts. "As I told you and Dr. Hanson the last time, the final cycle of my life, approximately one fourth, I spent basically alone. I was one of the latter-life singles in an age when singlehood became as common as divorce and family splitting."

"Yes, I remember even that you considered your second marriage, brief as it was, as merely your longest dating relationship of that period, no?"

"It was certainly no family of reproduction, my wife and I joining to fulfill each other's psychological and physical needs. As I'm sure I told you, we got married to make ourselves happy and we divorced as soon as we became unhappy. Our marriage had practically no social significance, nor did we assume social responsibility."

"I understand all that," Oldenberg said, picking up a pencil and starting a doodle. "When you say alone, you don't mean in absolute solitude, do you? Surely you must have interacted with some others during those twenty-plus years. After all, your species is a social one."

Martin put his hands down below the desk level and cupped his balls and cock through his pants. It was an unconscious gesture that he had had ever since he had become aware of his genitals. Oldenberg couldn't have seen the movement from his position, and it helped Martin concentrate. He said, "Not totally alone. In fact, I put in a lot of effort the first half of the period working in the dating game, or 'digging in the swamp of love' as I came to call it. And I did manage a dozen or so brief relationships besides the one comparatively long one, my marriage to Constance. But it seemed impossible to establish anything of permanence. And don't ask me why, because I never found out. Almost all relationships with females, including that with Constance, disintegrated without me ever finding out why. I just couldn't find out what the rules of the game were."

"That's a little strange since you were trained as a social scientist. Surely there must have been some kinds of procedures and rules. A relationship just can't exist without some predictability, and rules provide that, don't you agree?"

"Yes, theoretically, but I just never learned them, however hard I tried. I had no such problems with other relationships, but the male–female pirouette simply escaped me." Pause. "I don't think I was totally alone though. There was a widespread saying by ladies in dating then, to wit, 'I don't play games.' What that indicated to me was that many people did play tricks and deceptions. Of course their saying that was no indication they didn't do it. My ex-wife, Constance, for instance, early assured me that she did not 'play games,' and after what I later decided was several years of falsehoods and deceptions, she opted for the biggest game of dirty tricks of all, a confrontational divorce."

Oldenberg finished his little design on paper and leaned back. "You're saying then that you didn't learn much during your life in this area, eh? If such is so, it means that your people's other saying, 'Experience is the best teacher,' is not very true, wouldn't you say?"

"I guess I'd have to. I know that despite the attractiveness of females throughout my life, I didn't manage much better with them in the end than I did at the beginning. Of course, I tell myself that it wasn't all my fault—you know, we humans rarely like to take the blame for our inadequacies—that society was changing so rapidly during my lifetime that it was almost impossible to keep up. And I also tell myself that by the end of the twentieth century we had evolved a situation in which not only was the family no longer viable, but males and females had no other good means to relate successfully to one another, that the singles generation was almost inevitable. Everybody was out stroking their own psyche and splitting with others because they did not assist adequately in that noble act. Our individualism became rampant. Freud had won the century. The burdens of social reality were being assumed by other peoples, the Marxists and Orientals mainly."

"Hmm, it's a bleak picture you paint of Western civilization. Don't you think in part it's a product of your own aging and decline? Older persons usually do see existence through darker lenses, you know."

Martin considered that one carefully because he knew in general it was true. He responded, "What can I say; it's true that I came up with these generalizations at the end of my life, not at the beginning. Then the world was an oyster that I was only eager to pluck. And yet, as I mentioned earlier, I am no different from other earthlings in respect to my opinions. I defend them and surely sometimes when they are wrong. But as I always said, 'Why have opinions if you are not convinced they are right?'"

Oldenberg grinned. "I can see the logic in that."

Martin continued, "So, I must defend my position about the rampant individualism of the West by the end of the twentieth century, and specifically how it affected the relationship between males and females. Most simply put, I consider the total concern with individual fulfillment and denial of social reality as the cause for the breakup of the family, the great prevalence of divorce, the inability of individuals to get along together, and the rise of the singles' generation. Psychotherapists, psychologists, counselors, lawyers, and other caterers to the psyche were the instruments. This process was only beginning when I started to grow up but had come to fruition by the time I dropped out."

"Dropped out?" The Transitioner looked at Martin quizzically. "I thought that was a term you earthlings used for persons who depart from the mainstream, no?"

"Yes it is, and that is what I did. I struggled valiantly for forty-five years, trying perpetually to understand and establish a relationship with one female after another, but then I moved out of the dating/relationship game. That was when I bought an avocado farm in southern California and devoted the rest of my life to the cultivation of the testicle fruit and other growing things, besides putting my ideas, for whatever they were worth, on paper." Grinning, "I didn't have much else to do."

"The testicle fruit?"

"You didn't see the last period of my life, so you don't know. I bought a small avocado farm, where I spent my last years without feminine or

much other companionship. You may remember from our first meeting that I died at the age of eighty-four of a stroke while walking in my
grove."

The Transitioner smiled in remembrance. "Ah yes, though at the time
I wasn't quite sure what that fruit was."

"*Avocado,* which comes from the Spanish *aguacuate,* which came from
*aguacatl* in Nahuatl, the language of the Aztecs. It means testicle fruit."
Martin grinned. "And though I did not get that place for that precise
reason, I later thought it was so appropriate for me to continue with
the symbol of that organ that had driven me so relentlessly, even during the final years when I no longer depended on it for its primary function." Pause. "When I got finished viewing this last part, I thought I
might very descriptively be called 'the *aguacatl* man.'"

Oldenberg grinned in response. "You seem to get a particular pleasure from that idea."

"I do. During many dreary periods of my life, especially toward the
end, I got the most satisfaction from what I called 'idea flipping,' playing with concepts and trying to put them into words. After all, that is
what is most distinct about our species, our capacity to conceptualize
symbolically and then to generalize. As much as my balls bothered me
throughout my life, I always knew that they were only *part* of my generalized animal nature, no more. Balling, as the younger generation got
to calling it, what we called *screwing* in my young years, was an ability we
shared with all the other bisexual animals. It was only 'idea flipping,'
playing with concepts, that made us distinct as a species."

"You're saying the truly human characteristic is mentalling, no?"
Pause, reconsideration. "I'm sorry but now that I think of it, the concept I just verbalized as 'mentalling' is not truly a word in your language; isn't that correct?"

Martin, smiling, slightly professorish again. "Yes, in an absolute sense
you are right but in the sense of meaning, I think 'mentalling' is fine,
that is, conceptualizing symbolically and generalizing." Pause, attempt
at closure. "Anyway, that is what I ended up being, a 'mentalist'—not,
as we used to say in my youth, a cocksman."

At that Oldenberg picked up the dossier. "I think that should pretty
much finish off your viewing, Martin. So shall we get on with our final
function?"

Then it was imminent. There was no way to hold back linear time
any further. Now it would run its course. Martin gripped his genitals a
little tighter and hunched down as if still by some miracle he could

hold off the inevitable. Body gestures and a little magic were all that was left.

Oldenberg, "Okay?'

"Sure. No use stalling any further."

Oldenberg picked up the pad on which he had been jotting notes. "So while you were talking, I was putting down some possibilities. Shall I go through them?"

"Sure," Martin answered mechanically.

"Okay. Now as you may remember, those who have fulfilled their life roles fairly completely are able to take on most any other form, even a higher one, which leaves it fairly open for you, Martin. You seem to have lived out your life pretty much as most American males during that period of considerable change, you changing with the times considerably." Pause. "About the only significant difference I could note was that you seemed to have been somewhat overendowed with male hormone. But even that you handled, if not always to your satisfaction, at least without any great behavioral excesses. About the only thing you seem to have done much more than others was masturbation."

So that was it, that was a succinct summary of Martin's sex life, he thought. He had been driven and primarily fulfilled his needs by beating off.

Oldenberg interrupted the Transitionee's musings, "Also you found some other outlets, like exercising, drinking, teaching, writing, and growing things. But the one that was the most significant was the last you described. You went through life 'noodling,' as I understand it is known in your slang, or what you call conceptualizing or 'idea flipping.' In a very broad sense you seem to have done that as a compensation for not succeeding often with the animal drive of screwing, as you put it in your early days. In that sense, I must give you a high mark for humanness. When you were frustrated sexually, and perhaps in other ways, you turned your energies into 'idea flipping' or 'noodling.' That made a true human of you." Pause. "So in short, I can give you several choices."

Martin was trying to keep himself alert while still digesting the words of his monitor. After all, the Transitioner was boiling down his life with a terseness and probable accuracy that had never been done before and probably would never be done again. At the same time, Martin knew that the choice coming up would be his life. He couldn't take a chance on a mistake. He said, "Thanks; that is good to know, especially about my humanness. I wasn't always that convinced during my lifetime. But go ahead."

"Number one would be for you to take on another male human role. We could up you in terms of your early social circumstances, say, put you into an upper-class family with intellectual parents, say, academics or creative people of some sort. Then you would not have to go through quite as much social adjustment in your lifetime, and presumably you would get started with less trauma in your sexual makeup. I would guess you would have a good opportunity to live a more complete sex life, as well as continue with your 'idea flipping.' How does that sound?"

It didn't take Martin long. "No, sorry, no repeats, even if the cards would be stacked in my favor. I thought about that in life many times, and I decided very early that I just wouldn't want to go through that life again, even if chances for success were better."

"Okay, I didn't necessarily think you'd go for that one, Martin. But there are other choices."

Martin's thoughts were taken then to what they were doing—measuring his previous life to decide what kind of supernatural payoff he would get. Wasn't that what the Christian God did with the Devil when they were deciding the fate of a soul? He remembered something like that vaguely from his Catholic boyhood. It was also a literary theme, he knew. But wasn't it St. Peter who presided at the gates of paradise? That would be better for Martin since he could perhaps expect some help from his patron—Martin had selected St. Pete as his Confirmation saint because he had heard the old boy controlled the gates of paradise. Was this person in front of him St. Pete in disguise? Martin peered at Oldenberg intently but quickly decided that whatever he was, the Transitioner was no one from Christian mythology.

Oldenberg interrupted again. "Another choice would be a woman. Although it seems you humans practically never considered the female a higher form, probably in the latter years of your life she achieved a higher status in the West than ever before. And I do remember you emphasized several times that you relished new experiences. Perhaps you would like to take on the feminine form—to be she who brings new life.

"I understand that in your early mythology your species gave the female a somewhat exalted role as Earth Mother." He cogitated. "I believe it goes all the way back into the Paleolithic with your stone Venus figures." Pause. "To be a female would certainly be an experience of note for a male social scientist, even an ex."

Martin thought about that one and, in the sense of its novelty, was intrigued. How would it feel, he thought, to have a lust-filled cock rammed into your juiced-up labia, to be the rammed instead of the rammer? Or how would it feel to have that growth steadily expanding within you, you watching the bulge become larger day by day until the pains began, pulsating to a grinding climax, and then the total physical release, along with the realization that you had produced a life? No man ever did anything close to that. It would certainly be different. But no, he couldn't, he knew, whether because of the deep brainwashing that he had received in his growing years or simply that he no longer wanted any of the physical sensations of humanity. He had had enough as a male. He would be satisfied to know woman secondhand. Let some woman Transitionee of the future present the feelings of her sex. He said, "No thanks, I think I'll pass; I've had enough of the coupling and its consequences to our species. What next?"

"This may be different enough for you and still within your own species. You might wish to take on a futuristic form, say in the middle of the twenty-first century when I think sex will have become almost exclusively a matter to bind individuals together. That is, reproduction would have become a matter of laboratory control, semen production, insemination, and individual development from fetus to adult. Individuals would still have intercourse, but only to make them get along together better, since chemicals would be used to totally inhibit natural insemination. That would be the stage when sex would be used totally for pleasure. Would that interest you?" He added, "We do have a futuristic time extension capacity in the System."

Martin cocked his head on that one, then grinned. "You know, Dr. Oldenberg, if someone had made me such an offer when I was a young man, I would have jumped at it. Because you know then that I thought sexual activity was the prime source for human pleasure. I'm afraid I don't any longer. I now see it as a cosmic means of ensuring reproduction and perhaps with our own species a means of keeping the male around to help raise the young. But by the end of my life both functions had largely gone by the board. I'm not at all sure in retrospect that the nuclear family was the only way to raise human young efficiently, anyway. But in any event, the family seemed to be becoming obsolete in my day, a process I feel sure would have accelerated in the twenty-first century. And it is my feeling that once sex was relegated to a purely pleasurable activity, like eating or sleeping, then there would be little need to use it to bind individuals together. Everyone could get what sex they wanted when they wanted it, as they were already doing with food. We could have evolved fast sex chains for both sexes, you know, like

McDonald's or Jack in the Box or Arby's. Everyone would make their choice, pay their money, do their thing, and go on to other activities. No complications like relationships or love would be involved." Martin sighed, "No, I'm afraid that idea is no longer interesting to me."

Oldenberg looked a little grumpy, taking out his pipe, though not yet preparing to light it. "You certainly are being difficult, Martin. No particular form seems to please you." He gazed seriously at the Transitioner. "You may not know it, Martin, but I am trying to help you. We did get a temporary decision today on what to do with the Transition System, which is to cut back on all but the essentials. But it's still not permanently settled, and individuals with indeterminate status such as yourself will be much better off for now as bona fide life forms.

"Let me take the last idea then, that of becoming a member of a nonhuman species like those chimpanzees or even the cockroach you viewed. You certainly do not have to take one of them because in evolutionary terms they are considered 'lower.' But as you indicated in your talk with me and Dr. Hanson, the idea of 'lower' is a homocentric notion, that the cockroach in terms of evolutionary potential is probably more likely to succeed than the 'higher' forms. Is that what you want?"

Martin thought then of the simplicity of the life of the noncultural creatures, but he couldn't keep out of his mind the insignificance of the individual, the endless quest for food they were engaged in, and the short and violent life they lived. He knew that he couldn't psyche himself up sufficiently to voluntarily accept the outlook of a nonhuman, his brainwashings and life history having inscribed on him too deeply the ideals of *Homo sapiens*. "I'm sorry, Dr. Oldenberg, and again I see such a tremendous shift of view as interesting, but I'm afraid I can't do it. You see, the one activity I value above all others now is the human capacity for conceptualizing, of thinking in symbolic terms, and I would have to give that up if I became one of those creatures, or any other nonhuman, so far as I know." He grinned. "It doesn't matter that this human ability, conceptualizing, probably won't help my species to survive in the long run; I'm still stuck with it."

Oldenberg's face became very serious then, but he did not immediately speak out. Martin began to feel nervous. After all, the bizarre thought went through his mind that a soul could not really be so cantankerous when dealing with St. Pete or the Transitioner. Those types had the power; he didn't. To keep the situation from getting too tense, Martin spoke again quickly, "Of course, I'm speaking of earth life forms. I presume that the rules of the game would be entirely changed if a

Transitionee were able to take on a life from another world. But I had gotten the idea that that was not permitted." Martin wanted to pose the last as a question, but refrained so as not to press the Transition Master too far. If Martin were wrong, Oldenberg could correct him on his own.

Oldenberg replied, a little shortly, "I don't think that question ever came up. But you know, Martin, you agreed. So I'm going to insist that you accept some new life form." He began shuffling through the dossier which Martin knew was his. Then with finality, "I'm going to give you one more option; I will let you suggest a form. But then if there's no agreement, I'm afraid I'm going to have to decide arbitrarily."

All of a sudden Martin knew this was his opportunity. "Alright. But let me ask you a question first. Isn't it true that Mrs. Morrison in the Life Video Library is being 'RIF'ed, 'reduced in force,' as they used to put it in the federal bureaucracies on Earth, along with quite a few other individuals?"

"Yes, the System Administrators have decided to cut way back on the operation, and they are eliminating most of the service people, sending them back to their own worlds or to other posts in the System."

"Well, who will you have to operate the Life Video Library?"

"Actually, that's a problem. As you may remember from your Earth experiences, when efficiency experts decide to cut back on an operation, they frequently overdo it; they come down with a meat-axe, as the saying goes. And there was nothing we could do to convince them that the Library would soon deteriorate if we didn't have an efficient librarian in charge."

Martin felt so tense he took his hands away from his genitals, and, extending them on his pants legs, gently pushed them back and forth to wipe off the sweat. He said, "Well, sir, as you know, I have been helping her for a couple of weeks now, and I think I have a good grasp of the system. I was thinking that perhaps as a temporary expedient, you might let me take over. Strictly temporary, you know. And I don't need a title or position or anything."

The Transitioner's face slowly changed from thoughtfulness to a grin of realization. "Why Martin, you renegade. You don't want to leave us. You were probably working this up for some time."

It was Martin's time to be innocent, to use language in the deceptive manner it was designed for when powerful individuals had to be convinced. "Oh no, sir, it just came to me. And I do want to assure you that I would accept any terms or any time period."

The Transitioner closed the dossier and, holding it up, tapped the bottom to even out the papers inside. He spoke, "As a temporary expedient, I think it might be done. But remember, I said *temporary*."

Martin quickly drove in another nail. "After all, sir, I would hardly be missed in the Transition System; say, the significance of one cockroach."

The Transition Master laughed out loud at that one and stood up. "Martin, I picked up another term in my study of Earth slang the other day that couldn't be more appropriate—you are a silver-tongued devil."

Martin smiled then and relaxed. He had won the skirmish.

Oldenberg continued, "I will, of course, have to check this out with the Administrators first thing in the morning."

"Of course."

# ORDER FORM

**TELEPHONE ORDERS:**
   1-800-616-7457 (Have your VISA or MasterCard ready)

**FAX ORDERS:**
   619-728-6002

**E-MAIL:**
   niehoff@access1.net

**POSTAL ORDERS:**
   The Hominid Press
   P.O. Box 1481-53
   Bonsall, CA 92003-1481, USA

Please send the following book(s). It is understood that I may return any for a full refund—no questions asked.

| # | TITLE | PRICE |
|---|-------|-------|
| ____ | An Anthropologist Under the Bed – $14.97 | _____ |
| ____ | On Becoming Human – $14.95 | _____ |
| ____ | Takeover – $13.95 | _____ |
| ____ | On Being a Conceptual Animal – $13.95 | _____ |
| | Shipping: | _____ |
| | Total: | _____ |

Company Name: _____

Personal Name: _____

Address: _____

City/State/Zip: _____

**SALES TAX:** Please add $1 per book sent to a California address.

**SHIPPING:** $2 for first book, $1 for each additional book. Air Mail: $4 per book.

**PAYMENT:** ❏ Check; ❏ Credit Card (VISA or MasterCard)
   Card number: _____
   Expiration Date: _____
   Name on Card: _____

   Signature _____